Edmund Persuader

Volume I

By the same author

Stories

Tales of Arcadia

A Novel

Summer Sure to Die

Edmund Persuader

A Romance

by Stuart Shotwell

In Two Volumes: This Being the First, Containing

Acts 1 & 2

As human Life turns upon the same Principles and Passions in all Ages, I thought it very proper to take Minutes of what passed in that Age, for the Instruction of this.

—*The Spectator*

Mermaid Press of Maine

This is volume 1 of 2.

ISBN-13	(set of two volumes)	978-0-9841032-1-8
	(volume 1)	978-0-9841032-2-5
	(volume 2)	978-0-9841032-3-2

Publication Data
Shotwell, Stuart (1953–).
Edmund Persuader: a romance/Stuart Shotwell
p. cm.
ISBN 978-0-9841032-1-8 (two-volume set : alk. paper) — ISBN (volume 1 : alk. paper) 978-0-9841032-2-5 — ISBN (volume 2 : alk. paper) — 978-0-9841032-3-2
1. England—History—19th century—Fiction. I. Shotwell, Stuart (1953–). II. Title. III. Hampshire Romances, the.

Printed in the United States of America on acid-free paper.

Conceived, written, edited, designed, typeset, and produced by Stuart Shotwell. Maps by Stuart Shotwell. The map of Antigua is based on a 1747 map by Emanuel Bowen (1714–1767), used by courtesy of David Rumsey Map Collection (www.davidrumsey.com). The front cover image was inspired by an engraving of 1812 by Henry Moses (1782?–1870). Woodcuts are those of Thomas Bewick (1753–1828) and his school. The windmill ornament in the Antigua map, the chessboard on page 769, and the chess ornament on page 1550 were drawn by Arlene Kelley. This is a corrected version of initial private printings, 2004–2008.

This book is distributed exclusively by and directly from the publisher at www.edmundpersuader.com.

Mermaid Press of Maine regrets that it is not able to respond to queries, comments, reviews, or marketing suggestions concerning this or any other publication, and that it is not able to acknowledge, consider, or return manuscripts submitted in any form.

For my companion
in the roads and fields of Hampshire

Preface

Being a Scattering of Notes and Caveats about the Book in the Reader's Hands

It is truly said that histories always lie, and so, in some respects, must this one. Readers who attempt to find Brackensom or Hartswound Park or the village of Broadbridge will look on the map of England in vain, I am sorry to say; but at least the use of such fictional places has saved me from violating realities of which I know nothing.

I have endeavored to reproduce the manner of speaking of the places and times the reader will visit only so far as modern taste could possibly bear; and I suspect most readers will think I have given them too much of a burden in that respect. There are some expressions, quite ordinary in Regency England, that have acquired other, completely different meanings today, and I have avoided such locutions wherever I could. One will not find here, for example, the word *intercourse* in the sense "oral conversation," or the word *conversation* in the sense "sexual intercourse," neither of which meanings would have surprised a Briton in 1814. I do not pretend that I have written a book that could have been set down by a speaker of proper British English of that (or any) period, and the many Americanisms and anachronisms of expression I have allowed to stand will testify to my liberality in that regard.

Those who follow the history of the liturgy of the Church of England, and who track the geography and chronology of certain English social customs, will likewise discover anachronisms of which they may want to complain. Perhaps

I may mollify them somewhat if I admit to being aware of having taken these liberties.

My obvious borrowings from the Muse behind this book, that Grand Master of the human chessboard herself, are too great to be further noticed. It would be a long labor as well to list the many other books from which I have drawn sustenance during the creation of this dream. I will mention only a few: Before all, the wonderful history *Antigua and the Antiguans* by Mrs. Lanaghan (or Flannigan, as some say), published anonymously in 1844. Next, *The Trade Winds: A Study of British Overseas Trade during the French Wars, 1793–1815*, a volume of essays edited by C. Northcote Parkinson, which appeared in 1948. On the subject of foxhunting in Hampshire, I went to the best source I could—*Recollections of the Early Days of the Vine Hunt*, by J. Edward Austen-Leigh, published anonymously in 1865. This lore was filled out by the highly amusing essay from the same year, "Hunting Sketches," by Anthony Trollope. Readers who examine these latter two sources will find that I have purloined not only many of the curious old terms of foxhunting, but some of the hunting epigrams, anecdotes, and characters recorded there. And while I am acknowledging debts, I should mention that the chess game described in Act 3 is based on a game of Gia Nadareishvili. Dare I admit that it was played as late as 1950? But chess is timeless.

Although in its current form this novel appears in two volumes, it is only one book. In former times, printers consulted the ease of their readers more than now, and it was not unusual for books such as publishers today cram into small type in a single volume to appear spaciously composed in several. I would have preferred, in fact, that this story be published in five volumes; but I must yield thus much to modern exigencies. Publication of so large a book would not have been possible at all without grants from several sources. The generosity of these individuals is exceeded only by their modesty, and they wish to remain anonymous here.

Finally, it may puzzle some readers that I have termed this book *a romance.* But I use the term playfully in one of its several older senses, particularly that of a story of action with a heroic, even chivalric, protagonist and a strong love interest, often set in a foreign land (which of course the settings of this book are to me). Those same puzzled readers may be surprised to learn that the authoress whom I have mentioned did not see herself as writing romances, but something much more refined. I might cite as a model for my own use of the word the haunting classic of a later period, R. D. Blackmore's *Lorna Doone,* which is in fact subtitled *A Romance of Exmoor.* The present book, then, could be called *A Romance of Hampshire*—yes, of little Hampshire, a place so unassuming that even *she,* who reveled in the homelike and unassuming, did not see fit to set a novel in it.

❁ ❁ ❁

This trifle has not been the work that the world has chosen for me, but the one I have chosen for myself, to fill my head with images and words that please me—an anodyne. Austen-Leigh said of his aunt, "She wrote for her own amusement." She was an admirer of Steele, who in turn observed: "It is an endless and frivolous Pursuit to act by any other Rule than the Care of satisfying our own Minds in what we do." I could almost say that whether any readers ever discover this novel, or like it, does not concern me in the least; except that if any should do so, I shall be glad to have been able to share it with them.

Act I

White Edmund

Must I not serve a long apprenticehood
To foreign passages, and in the end,
Having my freedom, boast of nothing else
But that I was a journeyman to grief?

—Shakespeare

Chapter 1

Such wind as scatters young men through the world
To seek their fortunes farther than at home,
Where small experience grows.

—Shakespeare

That Edmund Percy must someday have a wife was a fact that he himself had assumed from boyhood on; but when he imagined the future Mrs. Percy, he had only the vaguest picture of what she might be like. It would be unnecessary to say that he thought she might be like his mother; for though most boys at least think they desire women who are the very opposites of their mothers, Edmund knew so few women closely that his mother could be said to have virtually defined for him what a woman was. He had no sisters—a circumstance which, by the way, greatly simplifies (or, if you prefer, impoverishes) a man's relationships with women throughout his life—and the only other women he knew at all well were his aunts, a few neighbors, and the serving women in his father's house. It is true that one of his aunts, his mother's sister, by her example came to exercise a great influence over his appreciation of the opposite sex as time went on; but still it can be said that what he wanted in a marriage partner, and why he wanted those particular qualities, were lessons he must learn through hard experience and no little sorrow. And having learned to want something extraordinary, it became his great challenge to secure such a partner. For a brief time, in despair of accomplishing an end that was to all appearances so improbable of success, even infinitely improbable of success, he actually gave over all such expectation and resolved to settle on whatever pleasing being should first come into his path. But that transient complacency, and the reason he renounced it, will be told in its place.

When he looked back on how he had come to pursue such a difficult course, it seemed to him that it all began on that day in April 1810 when he arrived home at Brackensom upon summons from his father. Until the chain of events set in motion on that day, he had been too busy to do anything in regard to the matter but to want a wife in the most dim, inchoate, and ineffectual fashion. Till then, marriage was something prudently postponed, not actively pursued; and he had never for any considerable length of time fallen in with an intelligent young woman his age, or for that matter, a vivacious one, or a pretty one; any one of whom might perhaps have captured his heart by mere virtue of obtruding on his attention for long enough. And then he might have undergone a most ordinary fate: suffered a long engagement, begun married life on the first chance of a living, honored his wife, and perhaps have been as happy with her as he was capable of being, in that unenlightened state—for he would indeed have been unenlightened as to the possibilities of married life and married love, make no mistake about it. He would in that case have lived the life of the sleeper, as most men and women do, unaware of what it is to love and to be loved passionately, both heart and mind, within the shelter of a secure marriage.

So let the tale begin on that April day.

⌛⌛⌛⌛⌛

The horses took the bridge at the River Brake with a certain aplomb—their hooves ringing, their harness ajingle, communicating their high-stepping, oat-fed willfulness right through the poles and the frame to where Edmund Percy sat inside the carriage. At the high center of the arched stone span they seemed to pause for a second as if to boast of their contempt for the cool, dark waters flowing away quietly to the south; and then they plunged on, out of the shadow cast by a great fair-weather cloud, on, into the soft sunlight of the spring morning, onto the road that led to Brackensom.

Edmund had the glass down, and the scent of the journey surged through the windows of the carriage—the smell of horses and horse leather first; then of the river that lay here directly beside the way; of the hayfields that ran down to the river between hedges of yew here and hawthorn there; and the wildflowers, still heavy with dew, of the unmown river bank. As a boy he had fished there, had dived into the Brake and swum in its lazy, friendly stream; fished, caught frogs in the shallows; found shelter on its banks to lose himself in *Robinson Crusoe;* gone bird nesting and bird hunting; and he had paddled a punt there with his brothers.

At the thought of his brothers, he turned his eyes away from the stream.

Brotherhood is a mystery, he told himself; but he could not dismiss the memories with that feeble truism. Perhaps it was the very springness of the morning, of the clean, damp smell of the river that brought it all back, all of his memories of his brothers, but most of all those of Alex.

Alexander was the second of the sons of his family. He and Edmund were closer in age—only three years apart—than Alex was to the oldest, Christopher, who was by five years the first. To the two younger boys, Christopher had been a kind of god who strode into their lives at holidays, home from school and full of the higher wisdom that life at Eton taught—not only the time-honored traditions of the tack on the chair and the inkwell poised on the upper edge of a door, but confidences of the school yard about the heroes of the times, about the dark and repulsive life of the poor, about the ways of men and women, and all the other topics about which boys chafed one another when they gathered in twos and threes, in briefly isolated insect clusters drawn from the great hive that was the school.

Alex and Edmund, by contrast, had a humbler knowledge, won together on the grounds of Brackensom itself. They stayed at home longer than Christopher; and those years before Alex went up to school were a Golden Age in Edmund's memory, and the two years after Alex left, and before Edmund followed him to Harrow, were a Dark Age. It had been an unintended harm for the two younger sons to go to a different school than the eldest, because it confirmed the divide riven between them and Christopher. They had felt almost like a separate family, as if Christopher were half-brother to them, though such was not the case. Alex had been, in many ways, Edmund's true older brother, Christopher simply a more distant relative.

It was from Alex that Edmund had learned sports. Alex had excelled, but his excellence had only made Edmund the more competitive. He grew taller than Alex, better muscled, and the matching of hand and eye that was sometimes erratic in Alex was unerring in Edmund. He became notorious at school for his passion for sports, and no mayhem or injury of the playing field could dampen it. It was not until he was fourteen that he began to realize that there was another field in which he could distinguish himself, inside the halls of Harrow instead of outside. One day he realized, somewhat to his surprise, that he was nearly at the top of his class, and perhaps in the thought that a little more effort could propel him to it, he began to pay some belated attention to classics, English literature, and the challenges of mathematics. These new interests brought balance to his life, sobered him, and raised his vision from the muddy ball and the damp greens; and not a moment too soon, as he would have been resourceless during the hard days and months that were to come in his sixteenth year.

There were many other things that Alex taught Edmund in which Edmund could not exceed his master. Alex had been a friend to all, powerfully affable; and where their teammates might rejoice in having Edmund's prowess and single-minded zeal on the field, they would take equal pleasure in the mere presence of Alex beside them, cajoling and exhorting and never at a loss for a word of praise or a flight of humor. Wherever he went he lifted the boys above their petty spites and grievances; he walked without a tremor of doubt on the shifting seas of their dirty politics and rivalries; and all loved him. Many a tense moment between rivals that might have turned to physical battle was eased by some incongruous joke from Alex's lips; many a little boy slipped from the clutches of a bully under the distraction of some witful remark. "Percy . . ." the boys would say, grinning and looking at one another and shaking their heads.

To be so inherently good became one of Edmund's goals in life, but he did not offer love from the same secure store that Alex naturally possessed. He was more diffident, perhaps for the very reason that he saw the brother he emulated more readily accepted than he himself. He came to accept this difference between them. He believed he would never be loved as easily and as generally as Alex, but he kept the model of his brother's openness and steadfastness before him, and perhaps he became in that respect more like his brother than he knew.

After his last year at Harrow, Alex had gone to the Royal Military Academy at Woolwich; and from there into the commission his father had purchased for him. As Edmund thought on this now, riding in the sprung carriage on the road beside the river of boyhood, the wrongness of the arrangement tore at him. It was not that he begrudged Christopher his rights. Christopher was the oldest son, the heir; and at that point in his life Edmund would no more have questioned his heirship than he would have flung defiance at the ways of God. By the understood order, one of the younger sons was destined from birth to go soldiering. His father had laid money by for Alex's commission; and without question Alex went, and with a will, with complete acceptance of his lot in life. Perhaps he seemed a trifle lost in leaving Harrow; but if so, no one saw it or imagined it but Edmund; and Edmund hoped, as surely Alex hoped, that wearing regimentals would involve no more difficulty than donning the scholar's gown. In fact, the qualities that had brought him honor among scholars brought him honor among soldiers—his ready offer of friendship, his irrepressible humor, his loyalty, his ability to stand above faction and petty intrigue. What was more, he was a steady shot, a good fencer, and could sit a horse in the worst of hard riding. The ladies—nearly a new species to the sisterless Alex—the ladies found much to like in him. He was like a native of the Americas brought to the British Isles, the fête of many, and destined to decline and die abruptly in a world strange to him.

A fever took him. He perished in his quarters, on English soil, at the age of twenty-three. So it was not soldiering per se that had struck him down. Still, Edmund wished that he had gone into law—saw him, in mind's eye, become the favorite of judge and solicitor alike, finding ways to move within the structure of the rules, to make the great grist-wheels of law grind their human powder less finely, to leave a spark of humanity still in the flour cast forth from the courts. Saw him successful, and independent. That independence would have been important; because after Alex's death Edmund went through his brother's papers and learned that he had engaged himself to a young Welsh woman, daughter of the owner of a colliery. Alex had never dared tell Hereford Percy of his plans, however. To marry such an outsider he would have had to stand up to Father—perhaps be utterly disowned for forming so demeaning a connection; which, though only a slight monetary loss for Alex, would have been a tremendous shock to them all, brothers and father; nearly as great a shock as, in the event, his quiet, sudden death had proved to be.

When Edmund thought of it, he saw again the punt on the river, the boy Alex asleep in it; only in this vision, Alex was a young man; and the moorings silently slipped, and the punt on the stream drifted away.

Edmund wrote to Bronwyn Floyd, returning her letters. She had already heard the news. The letter she sent in response was inchoate with grief, a striking contrast to the clear, light, happy missives with which she had peppered

Alex, cross-written and effusive, the letters of a girl; for she had been only sixteen years of age when they first met.

And so Alex ended. Edmund had often voiced those very words in his mind—"And so Alex ended"—and they stood for the unutterability of the loss, though never the loss itself, that came with no longer having his brother by him in this world. He was suddenly alone in life.

He felt his loneliness most during holidays at home. Christopher came, but Christopher was just an acquaintance, a friend by birth with whom he was on terms of reserved, polite acceptance. They wanted to like one another; but perhaps Edmund was still too young. And in interests they had gone wide from one another.

In temperament, too, they varied. Christopher possessed that confidence and insouciance of the oldest son. Like his father before him he was destined to hold Brackensom; and he had taken on the ordinary obligations of a boy's life—school, friends, even play itself—with an air of noblesse oblige. He was not a snob—or at least, not entirely so; it was only that his sense of privilege had robbed him from birth of those urgencies of existence that give edge to the hungers and salt to the pleasures of others less certain of their futures. Where other boys might study history vaguely aware that in lives at the bar or soldiering or sailoring they might find such lessons useful, Christopher seemed to do so saying, "Well, I needn't—but to oblige you, I shall." He was a boy who could be gracious who grew into a man who could be gracious; but the grace was a trace too airily bestowed. One heard "though I needn't" in everything he so freely and generously did. The worst, nearly the only, falling out Edmund and Christopher had ever had was the result of Christopher's attempting to give his youngest brother some money when they were just boys. The gesture, if inappropriate, was not ill-intentioned; it was Christopher's ever so subtle supererogation that Edmund had found in that instance insufferable.

Christopher was also a merry boy; and why should he not be? And Edmund, as he grew toward manhood, grew more and more serious, his own merriment more restrained, until he reached the point where when other boys guffawed at some joke or prank, he only smiled. The future cast no shadow at all on Christopher, but a longer and longer shadow on Edmund as he saw the hour of his independence approaching, a shadow indeed possessing a muffling and stifling weight and a coarse texture woven of uncertainties. Christopher could throw off trouble as a traveler sets aside his pack as he enters the inn; Edmund could never quite get that strap loose.

The events of his sixteenth year had given a decisive push to his turn toward seriousness. In that year the influenza had taken hold of the members of his family in turn and tortured them, taken them to the brink of existence and held them there over the abyss; and the flu had dropped his mother, Anne Percy, down that well of night forever. He sometimes wondered if his brain had been changed by fever, but he was certain his heart had been changed when his mother died.

Strange how the men in such a family, who boldly play the masters, are bound to one another most closely through the love they bear the women who serve them. The boys might differ from one another, and differ mightily from their father; but they all loved Anne Percy; and their father proved but half a living thing without her, a mere bundle of competing fears and sorrows and, too often, a mere idle rage without her soft presence to direct him into better usefulness.

She had been a source of stability for them all. Even her physical appearance promoted the illusion that she would never change and that so too the family would remain unchanging. She was only forty-two when she died, and her face, when they laid her out on her deathbed, was that of a woman of twenty. She died before she could grow old. She left three men and a boy behind who had relied on her to regulate their interactions; and the father now found it difficult to communicate with his sons, and the sons with their father. It seemed to each member of the family that the others became obstinate and obtuse. Even Edmund and Alex irritated one another.

Into this vacuum Edmund was drawn without noticing it. He became the mediator. When their father was arranging a commission for Alex, a long series of disagreements ensued between them; and gradually, at great cost of time and effort, Edmund negotiated a plan acceptable to both. He was then very much still a boy himself. They had been grateful to him, and his father especially so, who missed the abilities of his wife more and more as time passed.

The new burden came at a cost; but Edmund was, after all, still very young. The man of twenty-three who leaned back in the cushioned seat within the carriage, looking intently out on the familiar fields and woods of Brackensom as they streamed past, not noticing how the breeze of passage played with his thick hair—he did not look merry, as Christopher still might in returning home, even after their losses; yet sorrow had not disfigured or defaced him. His brow was clear above the strong bones of nose and cheek and chin, the face of a man; and his eyes were bright, quietly penetrating, though softened by the instinctive wisdom of love that had been given him by his mother.

The greatest flaw in his character at this time of his life was perhaps his certainty that he was well-equipped for his chosen role in life. He was girt, as he thought, in the armor of righteousness; but in fact that armor had never been tried, explored at its joints; and unknown to him were the thousand weak points where the thin, scrutating blade of passion might probe and tear what he was. He believed that intention, good intention, was a shield that would cover any failing in his moral armor; and his intentions were indeed good. For the avoidance of sin, or sin such as he knew it from first-hand experience, only a modicum of will power was required. Perhaps at this time in his life he fussed too much, internally, over the few things within him he could identify as sins: an occasional unkind thought, half-formed wishes that things could have been other than they were, a longing after a woman's pretty figure glimpsed in passing. He did not yet realize that such minor sins are the ubiquitous substrate of human existence; he did not yet carry the weight of more difficult and dangerous errors in judgment and failures of will.

After his mother died, he had begun to reflect on what the shape of his life as third son was to be, and it seemed to him that he was in most points unfit to minister to others as his father had destined him to do. He began to pay attention to religious instruction, to read the Bible, to study the rites and sacraments of the Church of England, to ponder age-old questions of theology, to observe the functioning of his church in society, to form opinions on its successes and its failures; but most of all, he began to pray, certainly more earnestly than ever before, and to gain that sense of ongoing communication with God that sustains the person of faith and gives him or her the appearance of quiet, stable, serene strength—though it may well be only an illusion after all. In the nation and era in which he lived, such serious attention to his vocation was an unheard-of exception. The sons of gentlemen took a position in the church with no more questioning of their spiritual fitness for the task than a modern-day candidate for a position in a corporation. Presentations to a living—that is, to a permanent position as rector of a parish church, with its attendant rights to live on the income of the parish tithes and the attached glebe—were literally bought, sold, even auctioned off in the open market like any other commodity; and many a gentleman's son took one without scrupling to consider his spiritual aptitude and became an indifferent or even an evil minister to the spiritual needs of his parish. Edmund Percy was determined that nothing of the kind should be said of him. He did not know it, but he was part of a historical trend: the Evangelical movement, a pietistic call to faith issued most notably by the Christian writer Hannah More, was making an effective and earnest call to the seriously religious of the upper class; and this summons was bound to have an effect even on those who were not willing to leave the Church of England.

As Edmund grew into young manhood, it came about that both men and women liked him: he was tall, straight, broad-shouldered, and in fact of unusually great physical strength, and his mien was calm and promised fairness to all. His voice was in ordinary conversation unremarkable, being only adequate to disclose his thoughts, but he made up for that mediocrity by endeavoring to entertain ideas that were well-considered and kind; and when he did speak in public, his voice was transformed into an arresting tenor instrument. In very briefest: he was an Englishman, showing many of the better qualities of his race and few of the worse. If for no other reason, you would have liked him for his lack of pretension. He made no assumption about you, either good or ill; he was more interested in listening to you and learning who you were than in talking to you and telling you what you should be; and such people are rare, rare and well loved wherever they go. When he entered a room, people felt soothed. Irritations that had been building toward a breach were let go. In the exclusive company of men, a speaker might hesitate in uttering a swear before him, and if it slipped forth before it could be stopped, the utterer would be reassured, somehow, by the Edmund's steady, quiet gaze, that he was not condemned for having uttered it. In the exclusive company of women, a speaker might find herself, to her own surprise, struggling to give a charitable interpretation to some misguided action of her neighbor.

Two other notable qualities he had as well. First, he could be, when inspired by events, remarkably persuasive. He not only knew by a kind of inspiration with what words someone might be persuaded, but he understood what we might now call the psychology of persuasion. People are not always persuaded at once. Oftentimes they must be appealed to again and again, steadily, and in a quiet crescendo of offered incentives; and often times the persuader himself must seem to fail before the persuaded can adopt for themselves the course he has been urging. Other times people resist merely to necessitate persuasion, and yield for the sheer pleasure of being gracious. Some resist merely for the joy of the skirmish, and need only to be entertained by persuasion for a sufficient length of time before they accede. And there are dozens of other modes of persuasion as well, which, when multiplied out by the variety of human circumstances, make the art of persuasion an infinitely varied and rich one; and though Edmund did not always succeed in it, he had a certain intuitive ability in it that set him apart. He was not, however, a manipulator of others—that is, he never sought to persuade others for selfish ends; except, it might be argued, when a certain strong passion urged him.

Second, he was no Hamlet, no Fabian of indecision. When he made up his mind to act, which he did on the basis of a confirmed sense of what was right, his actions appeared to others so startlingly sudden and swift and decisive as to be almost awe-inspiring. And in a world where those who instantaneously react are nearly invariably wrong in their actions, and nearly invariably make a worse muddle of the situation, plunging themselves and others into a tar-pit of violence and social confusion, Edmund was fortunate in generally being proved correct rather than in error by the ultimate consequences of what he did. If he had been willing to stoop to politics or warfare, he would have been remarkable for his leadership. As it was, his leadership took place on a far smaller stage—except for one or two signal instances—and to his friends and family he became a resort in times of trouble, even at a young age, and whenever they were in difficulty they would think to themselves, "I must ask Edmund. Yes, Edmund will know what to do."

He had attained his bachelor's from Oxford in 1808, and stayed on there for nearly another full year, living in the house of his father's sister, further studying theology. There was no immediate haste for him to begin his career; in fact, by law he could not enter the church until he was twenty-three years of age. Now that age was upon him, however; and he was due to be ordained at the end of August. Beyond that his position was uncertain, but his father had been writing to all his acquaintance in search of a living for him, and Edmund suspected that this summons home was the result. In any event, he knew he had his father's support until some such maintenance could be found.

The carriage now left the riverside and the coarse paving, if it could be called that, of the outer drive; it passed through a set of gates some fifteen feet high and ran lightly onwards over the immaculately raked gravel of the immediate approach to Brackensom. The change in direction, in motion, and in sound drew Edmund out of a momentary reverie, and he looked with interest on the lawns and woods of Brackensom proper. The prospect soon opened out, and the hall itself came into view.

The house had a splendid position near the crest of a hill. It had been built some forty years ago, by Edmund's grandfather, to take advantage not only of the far southern view over the hills of Surrey, but the view of the River Brake; which, after passing the obstacle of the bridge and a weir above it, flowed slow and broad through the heart of the estate. From the wide terrace on the south side of the house a brace of swans could often be seen in their majestic course up the water. The rest of its near view was a pleasing patchwork of field and wood, hay meadow and garden; through which the drive ascended until it reached a spacious, level lawn immediately before the house.

The dwelling itself was built of pale, dressed stone; and the whole was designed with consummate cleverness to appear larger than it truly was. Every trick of perspective had been exploited—the half-balconies before the myriad windows of the upper stories diminished in size more rapidly than the eye would expect, lending the façade a loftiness belied by the contrasting view from above. Even the leaders that carried water away from the roofs and gutters had been artfully tapered to preserve this illusion. Yet Brackensom was, despite this *trompe-l'oeil,* still a very large, even a vast house; and Edmund always had a disconcerting feeling, as he looked on it, that it contained rooms he had never found and explored in his boyhood. Perhaps that was the architect's whimsy at work on him. Yet he thought, as he looked again at the deceptive windows and the other features of which his father loved to boast, and as he wondered again if he really knew the place as he thought, how like it was to the man who dwelt there: suggesting a stature grander than reality, and hinting at mysterious places no search could find out; having many windows that looked over the land, in which Edmund, on the outside, saw only a reflection of the external.

The carriage halted before the stairs. Edmund stirred himself and opened the door before Davy, the groom riding beside old Tom, the driver, could descend and open it for him. He jumped down to a little chorus of welcomes: four servants were here to greet him, but foremost of them the housekeeper, Mrs. Trees. She was small and gray-haired, well along in years, and had been in service with the Percies since she was a girl of ten; but as she looked at Edmund, who had grown more and more her favorite over the years, her dark eyes had a dancing sparkle caught from the morning sun.

"Welcome home, Master Edmund!" she cried.

"Thank you, Mrs. Trees!"

"Your journey was good, I hope?"

"Splendid—fine weather all the way, and nothing untoward in coach or horse."

"Very pleased to hear it, sir. We had a bit of a mist off the Brake this morning when Tom set out to Neighbury after you, but he was sure it would burn away, and so it did."

"So it did—a beautiful day, and the house and grounds look in fine condition."

"But of course, sir, but of course." She turned to walk with him back up the steps into the house; and knowing his thought, said, "Your father is in the library with Mr. Burton. I am to let you know when Mr. Burton leaves, and then he wants to talk to you directly."

Edmund did not even think to be surprised that his father had not greeted him; in former times his mother and Mrs. Trees had met him when he returned from school on holiday, and he might not see his father until dinner. Rather, his being summoned before that hour was unusual.

"Very good, Mrs. Trees. I shall not put you to the trouble of seeking me far; I shall go up to my room and then out on the terrace with a book."

"Very good, sir. Anything to refresh yourself?"

"I am quite all right until dinner, thank you."

She gave him a final smile and a nod before turning aside in the hallway; and he continued on across the broad Italian tiles and up the wide staircase.

The interior of Brackensom played none of the tricks of its façade. Its depths and inner views were real. As Edmund ascended the stair and reached the first turning, he could see through the front rooms on the west side—the great hall where in his childhood his mother had held a ball for the neighbors, and the wide parlor called the Blue Room beyond it, with a view over the terrace. To the east, by contrast, was the library, its doors now closed for the consultation between his father and Mr. Burton, the steward of the estate. He climbed higher and came out on a hall with wide windows looking south, matched by as many doors to bedchambers on the north. The stairs went on, in lesser form, to a third story; which in former times had been put to use only when his aunts visited, that is, on rare occasions; and beyond which was another story, for the servants, and garrets as well.

He lingered a moment in the hall. His room was somewhat dark, and he preferred to take the sun while he had it, looking out over the terrace and the grounds to the distant Brake.

None of this that he saw was his, or ever would be his; he had understood that from a very early age, and never wasted time by desiring it; but he loved it still, and he knew he would always love it in the days ahead when he was settled elsewhere and came back to visit his father and then Christopher, when as oldest son Christopher was master. He felt sometimes like a man who has fallen in love with the wife of another, but buries the love away where none can suspect it and where indeed it can seldom trouble him; but in her presence it rises in his heart and makes its existence known, perhaps outwardly only in a studied amiability, but inwardly in a kind of painful fire; which the quick-eyed around him, the Mrs. Trees of the world, or his mother's sister, could feel burning in him, and for which they pitied and honored him, that he tried to damp a love that had no hope. Or put it this way: The times he had thought of being master here himself were but three or four in his life; but when the thought had come, in some moment of weakness, he saw that possibility as one does who remembers a fragment of a dream, and realizes that it is much deeper than what is recalled. Some part of him dreamed of this, but his better part was not aware of the longing.

A quarter hour later a servant came to him in his room with word that his father was ready to see him. He descended the stairs and found Mrs. Trees waiting in the hall—the commission was not to be lightly trusted to anyone else; she must see that he had received word.

"In the library, sir," she said.

"Thank you, Mrs. Trees."

He knocked once at the doors at the end of the great hall. An indistinct summons was heard, and he entered.

The room was rich in volumes bound in browns and golds, words plundered from every age of human civilization; but Hereford Percy had not opened one of those books in at least thirty-five years and sat as if unknowing of their existence, at a bare table by the window. This was his haunt. When the paper came down from town, or the latest agricultural journal, he read it here, and when the hour came for his correspondence—eleven in the morning, quite punctually, six days a week—a servant brought his writing materials from a desk at the side of the room; in the afternoons he had his tea here, and the surface of the table might be impeded for as much as an hour with a tray bearing a teapot, a cup, and a plate of cakes, tempting though generally left untasted. It was almost as if the barrenness of the tabletop were a reassurance to Hereford Percy that all was well in his world; though in these six years past the death of wife and son had suggested otherwise. Those events had given him to understand that life and death could not be controlled; they had charged a susceptible personality with fear that he might not fulfill the mission that, for want of any other, he had taken on as his purpose for existing.

And that mission was to improve on the wealth of Brackensom and hand it on to his eldest son, as his father and grandfather and forefathers had handed on their mite of wealth and power even before Brackensom had come to exist, handed on through all the shifting royalties and loyalties and revolutions of an England too, too busy with her wars and religious strife and struggles for power. Death, in taking Alex, had fired a shot of warning across Hereford Percy's bow; but he had not hove to; he had hoisted more sail and, as he thought, opened the gap. Christopher would live, would marry advantageously, to good family, and he in turn would pass on Brackensom to his son.

Perhaps if the table had not been empty before him—if he had opened the volume of Epictetus or Aurelius or Horace or even the Preacher—Hereford Percy might have guessed at the fragility of the chain in which he was a link, and found himself a higher utility in life than the mere augmentation and bequeathing of wealth. But philosophers and teachers of religion had never caught his attention. He went to church on a Sunday, and sat stoically attentive to the sermon, but that stoicism was all the philosophy he ever showed. He did what was expected of him as master of Brackensom, heir of Percies; his life was unexceptionable in every respect. He was like a man on a desert island who boasts of his virtue: high and dry on the isolation of his only ambition, he was not tempted by other goals or pleasures, and did not understand those who were.

Strange to say, his very singlemindedness gave him a certain stature and power over others. Edmund, though he saw the shallowness of that fixity of purpose, yet admired it and emulated it; it had been a powerful force driving him to focus on the destiny set out for him. It has been said that those who are pure of heart are single of mind; and so it is no surprise that singleness of mind is often mistaken for purity of heart. Whenever Edmund entered this room and saw his father seated here by the table, he felt under judgment and, listening as a defendant in the dock, heard the ten thousand voices of conflicting interests and passions in him testifying against him—sports and the out-of-doors, biblical studies, Greek and Latin and Italian and mathematics, the hunger for fellowship, and more and more the yearning for the constant company of womankind; and all of the thousand other dreams and possibilities that crowd a young man's thoughts. He sensed the foolishness of his reaction to his father, of the instant assumption he himself made that his own capacity must be being squandered and mismanaged, by mere contrast with that of his father, so steady, so monotone; and yet he continued to admire the other's singleness; and indeed, in a dissipated and distracted world, it was, though not a passion so much as an exercise in mere default, a thing to be admired.

No human, however, is utterly simple; every world, however smooth from afar, has its mountains, valleys, oceans, and secret caverns hidden from light; and Hereford had qualities worth emulating. In fact, his very singleness rendered him free of certain ordinary jealousies that complicate the lives of others. He begrudged Edmund not in the least that he could ride, shoot, wrestle, swim, and run, better than any living heir of Brackensom, or that he had excelled at sacred theology. None of these excellences encroached upon his own; and so he could be openly delighted with his son for such proofs of his abilities. This warmth of his father's admiration had been at times a comforting sunlight to Edmund.

His zeal for improvement was also striking. He meant to learn anything that could improve the tending and thus the yield of his lands, which were by no means all in rents, but in profitable corn and barley as well. He experimented, and reported the results of his experiments to the Society; and his plantings thrived and drew many visitors to Brackensom.

Thus, though the table at which he sat was kept bare, it was often so because of his absence, in his fields or outbuildings, watching the work there, brooding on new ways to make it better.

The improvement of the estate was an interest he should have shared with Christopher; by rights it should have knit him and his older son more closely together; yet Christopher had often been absent since his majority. He traveled throughout the Isles, or stayed with friends for long intervals, and he had his own dwelling in London. The truth was—and it was a truth obvious to Edmund—that Hereford's unrelenting focus on the welfare of the estate was so specific and intense it would be difficult for anyone to bear or to share for long. He feared for his brother; feared he would be drawn into some dissipation in the simple search for variety and relief; but so far he had seen no evidence to fuel this worry.

His father rose and came around the end of the table as he entered; he met Edmund halfway into the room and held out his right hand; and when Edmund took it firmly in his own, he gripped Edmund's right arm with his left hand, looking steadily into his eyes, testing him. Edmund met his gaze.

"Welcome home, my boy," said Hereford. Perhaps there was a tremor of emotion in that voice. This act of rising and meeting his son, too, struck Edmund as somewhat unusual, and he guessed at once that something in his father's world was awry—if only slightly so, for now Hereford was smiling. He looked on his son with that grateful expression the lord of a castle might wear as he surveys his second line of defense against an approaching enemy. Death might make an assault—might take Christopher too, God forbid; but Edmund would be true as steel, Edmund would be ready. Third son he might be, or second son, now; but he would carry on. Edmund could read this calculation and approbation easily in his father's face, from long knowledge of the language of the man's character, in which it was written there; and it made him suddenly glad of his coming independence, and made him pity Christopher for standing next in line to the mastery of Brackensom.

"Sit, Edmund," said Hereford, waving him to a chair. Edmund's mother used to insist that Hereford give the boys a day at home, at least, before he talked business with them. That prohibition was forgotten now; but he did restrain himself long enough to make certain conventional inquiries when he and Edmund had sat, facing one another over the dark tabletop. "Your health is good, my boy?"

"Excellent, sir," said Edmund. "And yours, I trust?"

"A little rheumatism, I find; nothing of any account. It does not slow me down.—Your journey was good?"

"Yes; and well arranged, Father. I am always grateful to see old Tom's face. And I am very glad to be back at Brackensom."

His father's face fell somewhat at this, as if it provoked a troubling thought; and though Edmund, keenly watching and reading his father's expression, was as fully aware of the intrusion of that doubt as even Hereford must have been, both father and son set it aside for the time and continued the requisite small talk.

"Have you heard from Christopher?" his father asked.

"Not since Easter, no." Then, guessing the question had a further motive he did not understand, he probed. "Is he well?"

"Of course—no bad news there.—And your studies are concluded successfully?"

"Yes, sir."

"Your last letter said you were going to take orders in August."

"As you have always suggested, sir. It has all been arranged. I am looking forward to it; though I have no further word of a living."

"No, nor I," said Hereford. "Though I am sure we shall find you one. A curacy at first, most likely."

Edmund and his father had had this part of the conversation many times; only now Edmund was surprised at the vagueness of his father's response, as he had expected some definite news on this point. The summons home, then, had been for some other purpose.

And now, perhaps again in an effort at procrastination, Hereford stood; when Edmund began to rise as well, he motioned to his son to remain seated.

Any moment, Edmund thought, *He'll plunge into it, God bless him. Whatever it is.* He watched and waited.

"Edmund . . ."

"Sir?"

"You will have to postpone orders."

This was the last thing Edmund had expected. He had been only five when his father had first told him he would take orders in August of his twenty-third year. There was a long silence, while Hereford paced nervously about, and Edmund took stock.

"I shall write at once to Twickenham," Edmund said.

"Excellent, yes. Let them know at once."

Another silence.

"Perhaps," said Edmund, since no information seemed to be forthcoming, "it would be well if I could offer a reason for the postponement. And of course I am curious myself, sir; though as always I defer to your wishes in these matters."

His father paused and looked at him suddenly and gratefully. "Bless you, boy," he said. "Bless you for that."

Edmund felt further puzzled, but held his peace.

"Yes, I know I owe you an explanation. I am coming to that"—and here Hereford laughed awkwardly—"with a little difficulty. 'Tis painful. I feel I am imposing on you, unfairly using you, to be quite candid."

"I cannot imagine such a thing, Father," Edmund said; the truth rose to voice itself before he could check it. His remark only increased his father's uneasiness.

"Well, wait until I tell you what is afoot. Then tell me you do not feel put upon."

He struggled a few moments more and then, as Edmund had foreseen, plunged into the account.

"Damned awkward! But here it is, lad. We have got trouble in Antigua. The overseer there has run off with the ready monies. The work has come to a standstill. We have no reliable agent to look after what we own."

Edmund's puzzlement increased again; but again he held his peace.

"I do not want you to think it is the cornerstone of our wealth," said his father hastily, misreading Edmund's intent expression. "Not at all—thank God!—it is trifling compared to what we have here at home. Besides, all the transactions for sale of our produce there are carried on in London, not in the islands; so there was not much for the scoundrel to take. But the plantation does represent an investment of good money—good money now going quite unused. That plantation is a part of Brackensom, in its own small way. I can no more let it lie disused than I can let Thorpe over there"—Thorpe was an abutting neighbor, whom his father had long insisted was envious of certain acres of Brackensom—"take over the barley field without so much as a cease and desist from me."

"Absolutely not, Father," Edmund said, for want of anything else to say, in the ensuing awkward pause. His father seized on the remark, turning fully to Edmund now.

"I knew you would see it that way," he said. "The Antigua property is part of what we are as Percies."

"Of course," said Edmund, finding that this view seemed to soothe his father, for whatever reason. "I know nothing of these matters, but it does seem that we need a new agent over there."

"Yes," said Hereford. "We do. That is exactly what I intend to provide, and at once."

"Very good, sir.—And how can I assist? To be candid, I understand that my taking orders at this time is inconvenient, now that this Antigua trouble has arisen, but I do not understand why that should be so."

His father turned again, paced, and then looked directly back at him.

"I should like you to go to Antigua, my boy.—There, 'tis as simple as that." Hereford showed evident relief at having finally uttered what was on his mind; but Edmund was thunderstruck, and for a long interval sat in silence, staring at his father in wonder.

"I, sir? To Antigua?" he said finally.

"Yes," said Hereford, rushing into apologia. "I know it seems odd. Here you are, about to be cut off from all participation in the wealth of Brackensom, and I delay your ordination by asking you to make a difficult and dangerous journey to accomplish something for which you are quite untrained."

"Utterly, utterly untrained, sir," said Edmund, shaking his head at the thought of coping with agents and sugar cane, or any matters of business.

"Untrained, but not *unqualified!* Not at all. And that is where your training is the finest that could be had for the task at hand: you were trained up *honest,* Edmund. Your mother, God rest her soul, gave you the openness that she herself possessed in the highest degree; and I flatter myself that I cherished and fostered that honesty in you, though I would not dare to compare myself to *her* in any virtue, in any moral quality."

"Ah, but sir, an honest fool is still a fool; and I am very much a fool in such matters. Business! What do I know of business?"

"Enough of that—enough of that. My judgment is that you are not unfit, that you shall not be. My concern is more about the justice of sending you at all."

Edmund was only further puzzled. "The *justice,* sir? How could such a service be unjust? You have given me everything, Father; you have raised me and set me on a course that will provide for my living. It would be but a small compensation to you for your time and trouble and expense in my education, if I could only discharge the task properly. But—"

"Bless you, boy—but you know perfectly well, or perhaps you are too generous to think it, that Christopher should be the one to go. And damn it, I say!"

Now at last Edmund guessed what was tormenting his father. He felt it wrong to make his youngest son undertake this voyage, to protect interests that were going to devolve only on the eldest—to postpone his own progress and advancement for Christopher's sake. In *that* light, he could see why his father struggled against scruples; though as he looked within himself, he found no resentment on that score.

"Well," said Edmund after a minute. "Here is a question: Have you advised Christopher of this?"

Again his father turned away, pacing uneasily. *So,* thought Edmund. *There is more still.*

"I have," said Hereford.

"And . . . his response?"

Hereford struggled again, and again blurted out the harsh truth: "He *won't go.*"

Here were words even more dumbfounding to Edmund than the news that he himself had been chosen for this unlikely journey. He sat stunned, looking about the room in amazement, seeing nothing. His father finally paused in his pacing and looked sharply at him.

"I see you are shocked," he said.

Edmund did not know what to answer.

"So was I," Hereford said. "So I have been, since this whole business blew up in our faces. I have put it to him directly, despite the uneasiness I have that any—that either—of my sons should travel anywhere while that monster is loose on the Continent. He offers a thousand alternatives—sending *this man* that he knows, or *that;* or else *this acquaintance, this agent* whom so-and-so recommends. He even goes so far as to suggest I send Mr. Burton—as if the property at Antigua were more important than Brackensom itself, which I know perfectly well he does not believe."

"Very puzzling, sir," said Edmund in a low voice.

"He is no coward," said Hereford bluntly, "or I should think he was frightened to go. But I have seen him take a hedge that I myself would not even have looked at in my younger days. I have seen him fall, and grin, and get up, and *leap* back in the saddle. That time he was caught in the storm off Ireland, he laughed it all off. I am more concerned that he is reckless than fearful. And I am more concerned he thinks the Antigua property of such small consequence that it ought not interrupt his pleasures for so much as an hour.

"And what *does* he do with his time?" he went on. "He spends precious little of it here, I can tell you. He ought to be dogging Burton, learning how the property is run; but instead it is shooting here, and fishing there, off to Windsor for the races, such-and-such a party gathering for a month at Brighton or Bath, or the winter in town—anywhere but here."

Edmund thought how difficult it would be for Christopher to spend month after month, or even week after week, in the sole company of his father and Mr. Burton.

"He is not dissipated, thank God," Hereford went on. "He is a good boy—a good man. I would not tolerate him if he were not. But he has no use for this Antigua business.—Shame on him that he should refuse it, and that his younger brother should agree to it on an instant's notice—should swallow down his imminent plans and say, 'Of course I shall go, Father.'"

Despite his father's bluster, Edmund could hear the fear and, even louder, the relief from fear that cried in his words. Hereford had asked Christopher first, having no other recourse; and had been relieved when Christopher refused to go. He might complain against Christopher, but he would have been terrified had his eldest son gone on ship for the West Indies. Edmund felt a familiar twinge of hurt that by contrast his own sacrifice and danger should be sufferable in his father's eyes; but so it had always been.

Hereford had continued to speak in the same vein in which he had started, but Edmund, perhaps for the first time in his life, interrupted him.

"Father," he said, "do not trouble yourself a moment more about the rightness of sending me. I shall go with a will, and it will be a mere pittance against the balance that I owe you. We must only take thought that sending me will not be in vain. I shall need facts, accounts, information. I shall need this information in as orderly a fashion as possible. If some good agent can be found to accompany me, so much the better. If someone you know, or know of, has recently returned from the Indies, perhaps I could speak with him and form some idea of what will be necessary. There may be gear to be purchased—I do not know. Let that be our concern, not some scruple over what cannot be changed."

Hereford's smile was a beatitude. "That's my boy!" he cried. "We shall sit down this afternoon, the three of us—you, me, and Burton—and take council. There is also Beckwith—he knows something of the situation; we must go and talk to him.—We *will* get an agent; I do not want you to think I do not intend to get an agent. My idea is just that you will go over with him, see that all is done properly, see that he is a trustworthy fellow. We have lost thousands by this other one, this McGinley that was in charge over there. He sold the crop, stripped the property, converted it, and absconded who knows where. We cannot let that happen again."

Edmund rose to his feet, something he had never done before in a conversation with his father without first receiving some kind of explicit indication that the meeting was at an end, even if it was only a nod. "No, sir," he said, "We shall not let that happen again. If I can, I shall put business there on a good footing. At the moment I only ask an interval to set my thoughts in order—a good walk about Brackensom will do it. And I ought to write to Twickenham at once."

"The very thing!" exclaimed his father. "A good walk about Brackensom will cure any ill, set any thinking straight—I have often remarked it." He spoke from his own experience, Edmund knew. Getting up out of his chair when melancholy struck and walking it off was probably the only thing that had kept him sane after losing his wife and son.

"What time would be convenient to meet with Mr. Burton, then, sir?"

"Two, I think—we shall say two. I shall see to it that Burton is there."

"Very good, Father."

"Go, Edmund—enjoy your walk. I shall gather some papers you ought to see. All will be done in proper order."

"Thank you, sir."

He went to the door, but his father stopped him.

"Edmund," he said.

He turned. "Sir?"

"I am very grateful to you for this."

"It is nothing," he began.

"No, no—it is everything. To be able to count on you like this. It shall not be forgotten." His father's tone carried some special significance, but Edmund had no idea how to interpret it.

"I do not do it for any reward, sir. I do it because it is the right thing to do."

"Of course, lad. I understand. Now go, enjoy your walk."

And after a polite nod from each, Edmund took his leave.

⌛⌛⌛⌛⌛

When he walked down the steps to the drive, the world seemed to be trembling beneath his feet. All Brackensom, familiar Brackensom, seemed to be aquiver in his vision. He paused in the drive and looked irresolutely to left and right, unsure which way to walk; and chose to go right, at hazard, before he remembered that this way led to the allee and the labyrinth and the hermitage, all of them good places to sink out of observation for a time.

He racked his memory about the Antigua property. All he knew was the cane stalks that used to come in a box at about this time of the year when he was a boy, divided up among the three brothers, a treat too surpassingly sweet to chew for long; and some very fine white sugar for Christmas cakes, and a dark molasses he had never liked, though his mother had savored it passionately on oat porridge. He had heard McGinley's name several times over the past few years, but no more than a mere several. And the name Antigua itself, and the name of the property there, Canebrake, how many times had he heard that in his life? It seemed only a score.

He recalled it better from his schoolboy geography. The West Indies or Antilles; and of them, Antigua among the Lesser Antilles among a smattering of other dots and blotches. How far was it from England? Something between three and four thousand miles?

He paused and looked around him. He had come into the allee. On either side of him was a handsome wall of green yew stretching half a mile over the countryside, terminating at a quaint hermitage his mother had had built when he was a boy. There were no such green vistas to soothe the soul in Antigua, he guessed.

And who for company there? He himself preferred the company of country families; but on Antigua, would they not be past all rustification? And the daughters of those families—he shook his head.

In a moment, with a great, wrenching effort, he began to rearrange his views. After all, it made no difference if he postponed taking orders. He might use the time on ship to better prepare himself. With a good passage there and back, and a generous interval on the island itself to see the new agent established and all in order there, he could be back in a year—and much the better for it. He had never had the benefit of a tour of the Continent, and as the youngest son probably never would have had such an opportunity, even if Europe should emerge from the state of convulsion in which it had been for the past decade and more; this voyage, then, would be his grand tour, a chance to see something of the world, though hardly the civilized world, before he took orders and set his hand to his life's task.

There were many similar thoughts to be mined from this vein; and as he now walked on, he heaped up as many as he could. It was actually a blessing that he had this opportunity; that Christopher, for whatever mad reason, had declined to go. The vision of himself on shipboard, looking out on the endless vistas of the seas, sharing the uncertainties of a sailor's life, even if only for a brief time—this made his heart race a little with interest and excitement.

In short, Edmund was still very young. To be told, in his twenty-third year, on the eve of his accession to a very serious way of life, that his anticipated responsibilities were to be postponed for a year in deference to other tasks utterly beyond his expectation—this was something akin to an unexpected holiday. Antigua beckoned him precisely because he knew nothing of it.

And yet he was haunted, even as he made this shift in his thinking, by one powerful negative. The mere idea of his being able to be useful in this endeavor seemed absurd. He feared that he would simply fail. The only thing he knew of business was that he knew nothing of it, which was, true enough, a good place to start; many failed in business for want of reaching even that starting point.

He resolved, however, to attack this deficiency with the same weapons he had formerly used against his ignorance of his destined role in the church. He would read—he must go up to town as soon as possible, or perhaps send to the booksellers. Anything that could be found on the Indies would be useful to him; he must also learn about the cultivation of sugarcane, which he understood to be the primary business of the property there; he must learn some accounting; and he must study the present political situation more closely. Though Britain was now mistress of the seas, events on the larger theater might be brought to bear, in unexpected ways, on the Indies; he must be ready for eventualities. The relations with Britain's former colonies in North America was also critical, as he dimly remembered that there was a trade in rum and molasses between them and the West Indies. Foreign trade in general was also an appropriate subject for his study.

Even as his thoughts ran on these topics, however, he did not forget his true profession. It occurred to him that what he saw, what he felt, what he did and learned, what he suffered on this voyage, would make him a better man and thus better able to minister to others. He was highly conscious of his callowness, his rawness; and the only doubt he had ever had about his career was that he was too young and inexperienced as yet to undertake it. This interval between university and orders seemed providential to him.

In short, again—after twenty minutes of walking, and twenty minutes of thinking, he had seen the hand of providence at work in this shift in his course and reconciled himself to it. He came back to the house in a very different frame of mind than that in which he had left it.

Chapter 2

I do marry that I may repent.

—Shakespeare

The wheel of preparation, once set in motion, gradually increased in its speed of revolution. On that first day home, Edmund composed a long list of errands to be done, sources of information to be tapped, paperwork to be drawn up, even supplies to be bought; and he spent several weeks in working his way through it, striking off each item. One necessity he enumerated was to come to some kind of understanding with Christopher. He did not want Christopher thinking that he was attempting to come before him in their father's thoughts by taking up the task Christopher had so persistently refused. He was by now so certain of the providential nature of the voyage to the West Indies that he felt sure he could dispel any jealousy Christopher might have formed in regard to it.

He did not find an opportunity to address this particular item of necessity for some time. He finally did so by sending a letter to his brother, expressing the wish to speak with him; and received the following response:

My Dear Edmund,

I have returned to town for this week and am at your service there. It would be to the purpose if you could visit me privately. I look forward to seeing you.

Christopher

The letter seemed both unusually affectionate and unusually brief. But these innovations were not the least of

Christopher's puzzling behavior, so Edmund withheld further speculation on them; and saying nothing to his father, he awaited an opportunity to go up to town alone.

He and his father had already been to London to speak with the family solicitor, Beckwith, before he had even sent his letter to Christopher; and on the next occasion he was called there, his father, who disliked travel, saw no need to go; and so on this journey Edmund went by himself.

His business, which included an interview with a possible agent, was quite lengthy, and it was late in the day when he climbed the steps at Christopher's lodgings in St. James. His knock brought Aiken, Christopher's manservant, to the door.

"Welcome to town, Mr. Edmund," said Aiken.

"Very good to see you, Aiken," said Edmund as he entered. "I hope you are well."

"Very well, sir; and thank you."

"Off to the country soon? I know you prefer it to town."

"I do, sir; kind of you to notice, Mr. Edmund."

"Off to the Lakes, then? Or Scotland, perhaps?"

"Probably elsewhere, sir," said Aiken mysteriously. Edmund saw at once that he was concealing something, and did not press him. "I shall show you to Mr. Percy, sir," Aiken added; and he then led the way across a short hall into the parlor, where Christopher was found reading through some correspondence.

The furnishings of the parlor where Christopher sat were, like everything Christopher owned or used, of the very newest and finest quality. The chairs and settees were lightly built and elegant—a matched array of dark mahogany from East India covered in plush blue velvet. The curtains, too, were a rich blue cloth, and crowded close on the jambs of the windows, rendering, in fact, the richly papered interior walls nearly too dim to be seen. Certainly the paintings that decorated these surfaces—spectacular land- and seascapes for the most part—could never be fully appreciated here. Such a display of wealth always caused Edmund some uneasiness: he could not help wondering if the funds behind it all had been borrowed; though he knew that his father thought it part of his duty to support Christopher in good style.

He had a fraction of a second to observe his brother before Christopher was quite aware he had arrived; evidently his knocking and his conversation with Aiken had gone unnoticed. He had never seen such serious preoccupation in Christopher before; he seemed either distracted, unwell, or unhappy. However, when he saw Edmund, he came to himself and brightened. His affable greeting was very much that of the old Christopher, except that it seemed to lack somewhat of the muted hauteur natural to him as eldest brother.

"Edmund—very good of you to come," said Christopher, rising to shake his hand.

"Very good of you to stay in town and make it possible," said Edmund.

"I have just had tea," said Christopher, indicating a tea tray on the side table. "Would you like fresh?"

"It is so warm today I will take what you have left there," said Edmund. "But thank you, it will be refreshing." Then, as a nonsequitur, he observed: "The town already seems to be empty."

"Yes! It is utterly boring!" exclaimed Christopher. "Utterly wretched! One feels one's very soul stifling for want of company!"

"You ought to come up to Brackensom. The spring is hastening on apace, you know. And Father would be pleased to see you there."

"Yes, yes—we shall talk about that—we shall talk about all that. You have finished your studies?"

"Yes. All went well. I was quite ready to take orders when this business about Antigua came up." The mention of Antigua seemed to put a pause in the conversation.

Aiken poured him a cup of the now lukewarm tea and offered him a plate of cakes, from which he amply supplied himself.

"That will be all, Aiken," said Christopher. "Let Mrs. Partridge know that Edmund will be dining with me, and of course staying the night here."

"Thank you, Christopher," said Edmund.

"Oh, do not mention it. It would be tiresome for you to travel home today.—And oh, Aiken, wait one minute: I shall have a letter for you. I want you to deliver this personally."

"Yes, sir," said Aiken, pausing and turning at the door.

"Excuse me one moment," Christopher said to his brother. The apology was an uncharacteristically thoughtful gesture; in other times Christopher would have let his younger brother sit and wait for his attention with little or no excuse. Either he had learned new manners from someone, or he was feeling grateful to Edmund over this matter of Antigua.

Christopher sat on the edge of a chair at the writing desk and wrote a note hastily, no more than a few lines; then sealed it carefully, wrote two words of address on the outside, and handed it to Aiken. It was an odd little scene, and Edmund had a strong feeling that the note had to do with his own arrival; but he said nothing about it.

Christopher now sat opposite him. At first he leaned back in the sofa and gave Edmund an awkward smile; then he leaned forward, touching his fingertips together and frowning seriously.

"Yes, you are to go to Antigua," he said.

"I have come on purpose to discuss that with you," said Edmund.

"Discuss it? What did you mean to say?"

"Only that I wanted you to understand the spirit in which I undertake the journey."

Christopher was surprised. "Whatever do you mean?"

"Well, I know that you might very well see it as your place to go. Father mentioned that he had asked you. I did not want you to think that I was trying to displace you in any way."

Christopher laughed, in a startled but not disagreeable tone; then he said: "How good of you to worry about that, Edmund! Even to mention it—sounds so much like something Mother would have done. You are *too* thoughtful."

Edmund started to respond, but Christopher interrupted him—and this action was very much in accord with his old manner of behaving. "No, do not concern yourself that I am alarmed or jealous because you are doing this instead of me. I am well aware that it is my duty; and though, frankly, my entire being recoils at the mere thought of a long voyage and a sojourn on a desert island—for that is what Antigua is, you know, compared to the places that keep my soul nourished—I say, I would have done it, as I ought; or at least, I think I would have done it; or at the very least, I know I ought to have done it—but for something else that has occurred, which makes it all quite impossible for me, now or ever."

Edmund once more started to respond, but Christopher continued talking, completely unaware of Edmund's attempt to speak. Now Christopher began to work himself around to a quite different view of the journey, one that partly rationalized his refusal to go on it. This shift of position with a view to rationalizing what he wanted was very characteristic of him. He could find an infinite number of ways of rationalizing away anything that disturbed his status quo.

"No," he continued, "I am so far from being jealous that I am grateful to you instead. I do not know what success you can have—to be quite candid, it seems a fool's errand to send one of *us* to that God-forsaken part of the world. What do *we* know that can be of any use in righting the situation out there? Father might just as well have sent a boot-black. We have not the least idea how to undertake anything to do with business—nor ought we. It is not our place. Here you are, a gentleman, about to be established as one of the noblest clergymen of the Church of England—a Percy, by God, in the service of the church, and right lucky the church is to get a Percy, too; and suddenly Father asks you to run off to

Antigua to play the man of business. It makes no sense. Which makes it all the more good of you to consent to it, for Father's sake."

At this pause Edmund did not even attempt to speak; for sure enough, Christopher talked on.

"And this really *is* for Father's sake. He has been so fearful ever since Mother died; and it only got worse when Alex passed away. He seems to think of Brackensom as a slender reed, imperiled by the fate of a bit of sugarcane field four thousand miles away. It was very touching really, to see how fearful he was for *me.* He desperately wanted someone he could trust to go on this journey, but even while he was asking me to go, even blustering about it and insisting on it, it was quite clear that he was alarmed on my behalf. That is another reason it is so good of you to step in, Edmund; he is nowhere near so frightened for you.—Not that he does not love you; no, no, of course I did not mean that. It is just the heirship, you know; you know he has always been quite fixed on that."

"Indeed," said Edmund, finally wedging in a word.

"So you see," said Christopher, coming around to the point again, "I am not at all jealous. I am obliged to you, very obliged to you. And when you come home—and I certainly hope you will be home by Christmas—I shall quite go to work for you like a very slave myself, and see if I cannot beat the bushes for a very fine living for you. I have got a great many friends, as you know; and some of them are getting to that age where they have the gift of these things; and we shall have to see you established. I do not think you will be at all the worse for a bit of bronze in your face (though I do advise you to avoid taking the sun if at all possible). Who knows but this delay in your career may turn out to be providential? It may give me the opportunity of finding something much better for you than I can at present."

"It is very kind of you to even think of it," said Edmund, secretly bemused that Christopher had gone from the state of one obliged to that of benefactor in the course of a minute or two.

"Not at all," said Christopher. "We are brothers. We are Percies. You are looking out for me in this Antigua business; and I shall certainly look out for you here at home."

Edmund was to remember these particular words in years to come, and relish the irony that events brought to them. For the moment, however, he was touched at his brother's expression of care for him, marred though it was by his mild hauteur.

Christopher having now seemed to have come to a period in his disquisition, Edmund ventured a question; and almost managed to bring it forth without interruption. "You mentioned a change in your circumstances that particularly makes it impossible for you to even consider such a journey. Ought I know more of this? I do not mean to intrude—"

"This is why I most especially wanted you to come here," said Christopher. "Something has indeed occurred; and I wanted to tell you about it. But I must have it from you on your honor that you will not tell Father about it."

Edmund was disturbed at this; he put down his teacup and sat forward uncomfortably. "I do not think that would be right," he said. "I am against telling Father things that will needlessly worry him; but somehow to swear to silence on some point does not seem proper. I am too obligated to him. I am not independent yet; and even when I am, I shall always have a filial obligation to him."

Christopher scoffed and immediately began to work out his rationalization. "Oh, Edmund, you have really gone all too serious these last few years! Of course you are a good son. Of course we are obligated to Father. I *know* all that. I am not asking you to keep a secret to Father's detriment; only to prevent his needlessly worrying. He would be very upset if he knew what is afoot; but it will make no difference to his health or his welfare, ultimately."

Edmund understood Christopher to mean that their father would not care about this secret when he had died;

and though he did not challenge Christopher on this point, he was surprised that his brother should be so crass as even to intimate it; to say nothing of the fact that Hereford Percy was likely to live thirty more years.

"Yes, but as a matter of principle," Edmund said.

"Oh, confound principle! Look, Edmund, I *must* tell you. I *must* tell someone. I shall not make you swear; but you must be like a Quaker then, and *affirm* to me that you will use your discretion in this matter. The moment I tell you, you will understand that it would be unfortunate for Father to know. Unfortunate not only for me, but for Father; and unfortunate for you as well, as it would—well, it would cause a good deal of pain and trouble, which likely enough you would have to sort out for us all."

"Christopher, whatever have you got yourself entangled in? It is not gambling, is it? Is it debt?"

Christopher burst into laughter that was almost merry. "Good God, man!" he said. "What kind of a fool do you take me for? I have put a little on the horses now and then, and I daresay I have never done anything so plebian as to actually *win*, but my debts are all firmly under control."

Edmund stared at him; and suddenly the little scene of letter writing made sense to him. "It is a lady, is it not?"

The atmosphere in the room changed instantly. Christopher rose from the sofa and began to pace about; for a moment he looked very much his father's son.

"No," he said distractedly, "It is not 'a lady,' Edmund. That is, it *is* a lady; but it is not *just* a lady—not just any lady. But you must swear to me—very well, *affirm* to me—that you will not tell Father."

"The secret is out, Christopher. No need to make a Quaker of me. What manner of woman could this possibly be, that you will not tell Father of her?"

"The best of women!" cried Christopher, with an emotion Edmund had never seen in him before. "A very *good* woman, a woman much better than I am, who promises to make me a much better man than I am or have ever dreamed of being.

A very fine mistress for Brackensom; a woman who will do all that any Percy could ever ask of her as the lady of that hall."

"Then why not tell Father? He would be delighted to see you married."

Christopher did not answer. Instead he paced; he looked wretched; he twisted his features into a grimace.

"She is already engaged elsewhere?" Edmund guessed cautiously. He had it on his lips to hazard that she was already married, but he refrained.

"No, no!" cried Christopher in exasperation. "You must stop thinking the worst of me, Edmund! She is all of one-and-twenty, unengaged to anyone else—not now, at least—and a maiden as virtuous as, as—" His voice trailed off; he had never been apt with similes. "As those virgins in the Bible, you know," he finished lamely.

Edmund started to speak, but as usual Christopher ignored him.

"You must only meet her," he went on. "And I hope you will. Tomorrow morning, before you go. It was her to whom I wrote just now, begging her to visit here, which is something of course I have never done before."

"Here? You have asked her to St. James? That is hardly proper, I think."

"She has an aunt who is very much on our side, or I think we would never see each other. Her aunt will bring her, if all goes well. She is so eager to meet you, Edmund, you cannot imagine it."

This did not entirely appease Edmund's scruples; for it would be no less improper for the aunt to come to St. James Street than it would be for the niece; but he let that go, and instead looked at his brother and laughed. "My dear Christopher," he said, "it seems you have frightened me very unnecessarily. This terrible secret you want kept from Father turns out to be the very thing he most desires in the world—his eldest son has found an eligible young woman to marry.

Whatever can be the cause of your alarm on this point? You need only have told him this and he would have let all the West Indies sink into the sea without a second thought."

Christopher paused in his pacing about, in evident torment. Edmund saw that there was more to the story.

"I must tell you," Christopher said.

"If there is more than this, you must indeed."

"It would be so much easier for me to do so if only you did not already know her."

"Know her?" said Edmund. "I? Who is she?"

"Well, you have never *met* her; but you *know* her. You have looked into a very intimate aspect of her mind."

Edmund regarded his brother in silence for a moment, and then took another tone. "Christopher, I have never known you to so willfully toy with another's ignorance. Whomever and whatever are you talking about?"

Christopher paced about for a moment more, and then finally turned to Edmund.

"Miss Bronwyn Floyd," he said.

At first Edmund was puzzled; but then he remembered the letters he had found among Alex's papers. "The girl to whom Alex was engaged?" he asked.

"Yes," confessed Christopher. "The very same."

Edmund instantly saw the difficulty. It had nothing to do with Christopher's having somehow come to replace his own brother as a possible husband to this young woman; such things were common enough, and Edmund could readily have cited chapter and verse from the Bible in support of the practice. It was rather that the woman came from a background of which his father would not have approved, not in a thousand years. Hereford Percy would have raised difficulties enough had Alex revealed plans to marry her, though in all likelihood his objections could have been overcome provided she came with enough money; but for the heir of Brackensom to engage himself to the daughter of a Welsh coal dealer or mine owner or whatever he was—

Edmund could not remember exactly, even if he had ever quite known for certain—such a condescension would be absolutely insufferable in Hereford's eyes. Hereford had, in particular, a strong prejudice against the Welsh that was based on some obscure event in the history of the Surrey branch of the Percies; and he would probably imagine any proposed bride of that blood as a Pictish warrior-maid with a leek in her battle cap.

The complete silence that now met this revelation was evidently crushing to Christopher's spirits. He came back from his pacing and sat down on the edge of the sofa, staring intently at Edmund for some sign of hope; which Edmund made no attempt afford him.

"It cannot be utterly hopeless!" Christopher cried. "Her father is fabulously wealthy, Edmund—fabulously so. He is the veritable Croesus of the British Isles, I tell you. She is his *only child.* That has got to count for something with Father."

Edmund could find nothing to say, though Christopher gave him the opportunity, for once; and when he continued to hold his peace, Christopher filled in the silence.

"He is not a coarse fellow at all. He is quite modest—I mean, for a Welshman—though I must admit I have never met him. He is very God-fearing and quiet and never pushes himself on his betters. He understands perfectly that the higher-born have questions about his company. He quite stays in the background; he gave her up to her aunt—who married a very refined gentleman, you know, the Hanscom who is first cousin to Lord Hanscom—to raise from infancy; in fact, you would rather say Bronwyn was Mr. and Mrs. Hanscom's daughter than her blood father's. Teachers were brought over expressly from the Continent to give her the finest education, since she could not go there. She has hardly ever even *seen* her father." At Edmund's look he added: "Oh, yes, I suppose I exaggerate somewhat on *that* point; but only slightly. No coarseness whatever has ever rubbed off on her. She is the most genuinely genteel young woman you could ever hope to find.—Did you read her letters, Edmund? The letters she sent to Alex?"

"Only enough to see what they were. It seemed an intrusion on her confidence, and on his. I sent them back once I realized what they contained."

"Well, I *have* read them. She made me read them so that I should fully understand that I was not the first to touch her heart. She has always been utterly frank with me. And I tell you this: if you had read those letters, you would have fallen in love with her too."

"Just as well I did not, then!" said Edmund. "It would have altogether too much to have a *third* brother in love with her!"

"Edmund, this is quite serious!"

"My dear Christopher, I assure you that the seriousness of this situation is one thing you do not have to impress upon me. She may be the very queen of heaven, but if she is the daughter of a collier, Father will have nothing to do with her. He will never countenance her blood coming into the Percy line. And Welsh, too! You *know* how he feels about the Welsh. It is stupid—it is incomprehensible—but it is a quirk that can never be mended in him. You will break his heart if you even suggest such a thing. This is absolute madness, man. I could not imagine any plan that had less chance of success. Whatever were you *thinking* when you nourished this affection in yourself? And how did it ever come about?"

"Do you remember the trip that Alex and I took to Gloucestershire for some fishing? It was in July, about two years after Mother died. My friend Upton has a place there."

"Who?"

"Upton. Charles Upton. The half-brother of Lord Esterbroke. Do you recall?"

"Oh, yes; I do recall Upton. He has been to Brackensom. A gossiping sort of fellow. And I do recall that you went away then, though I do not connect the trip with Upton in particular."

"I do not remember why you did not come," said Christopher a little guiltily.

"I suppose we all thought someone ought to stay home with Father."

"Very likely.—Anyway, we met her there, at Upton's. Her uncle and aunt, Mr. and Mrs. Hanscom, came to dinner and brought Miss Floyd along. One cannot be so nice about one's company in the country sometimes; and her connections by marriage are quite good. Miss Floyd was just a girl then, you know; sixteen at the time. I was quite struck by her beauty, but I confess I never thought anything more of her."

"Why should you? She is a collier's daughter," said Edmund.

"Yes," said Christopher sheepishly. "I suppose that had something to do with it."

"Very sensible of you. What happened then?

"Apparently Alex had no such scruples. And why should he have?" And here Christopher's voice became almost bitter, as if he envied the second son of the family for *not* being appointed to inherit the wealth of Brackensom; and perhaps at that moment he did. "I had no idea he was contriving some way to visit her. They have a mutual friend—I have met him since—a cousin of Lord Esterbroke's, whom she had known for years, a rather good painter, actually; and this Esterbroke fellow used to shoot at her uncle's estate, and soon Alex was going with him. And after he and Miss Floyd had formed a connection, and pledged themselves to one another, they had no scruples about writing to one another as well. I know they met on occasion at her aunt's house here in town. Then Alex died, and that was that."

"Yes; that was that," added Edmund quietly. It struck him how Christopher's phrase echoed his own, oft-repeated laconic summary of all that grief. Christopher, not understanding the significance of the comment, continued with his story.

"It just happened that I met her at Upton's again last year when I was going down to Wales for some shooting; and if she was beautiful five years ago, she is *surpassingly* beautiful now. Her eyes—you cannot look into her eyes without being moved to the depths of your soul. Almost I think I would wager that her eyes could win over even Father.—And her character, Edmund, is even more beautiful than her person. She is kind, thoughtful, sweet to all, caring and true. It took a great deal to coax her to open her heart to me—to raise it from Alex's grave, where she thought she had laid it forever; and though God knows I am not worthy of her, God also knows I shall try my best to deserve her." And here again in Christopher's voice was that new tremor of humility that Edmund had never remarked in his brother before; and in his eyes was a curious kind of hurt self-awareness of his human smallness that made him seem an altered person. Edmund could not help reflecting that Bronwyn Floyd must possess a powerful character indeed if it could make even this small dent in Christopher's self-centeredness; though he doubted the ability of anyone short of a saint to permanently banish that defect.

"You must admit," said Edmund, trying a new tack, "that appearances are not in her favor."

"What do you mean?" said Christopher.

"Look at it in the harshest light imaginable for a moment; because you can be sure that is what Father will do. I do not mean simply that she comes from lowly circumstances. Forgive me for expressing it this way, Christopher—I only do it to show you what Father will think: He will see a beautiful young woman with means but no name, an aunt who is somewhat of a social climber herself, and a father who absents himself from the tableau in the hopes that his daughter will get ahead. And she does: first she latches onto the second son of a very old and respected family, and then, that match failing, wins over another—and a better match it is, too: the very heir of Brackensom."

"You can think that of her! After having read her letters to Alex!"

"No, no, I told you: I think nothing of the sort of her. I do not know her at all. I only tell you what Father will think; and he will not pause to read any letters she has written, least of all those she wrote to Alex, which would hardly soothe him in any case. You must admit the situation is open to such a construction, and if it *is* so open, Father will put that construction upon it."

Christopher sank back into the sofa, looking hurt and hopeless.

"And speaking for myself, Brother," Edmund continued, "I fear for you too. I hope that my fears will be assuaged tomorrow when I meet this—when I meet Miss Floyd. But until then, I can only hope that you have not been duped, that you have not been preyed upon."

And here Christopher did a curious thing: he smiled softly at Edmund; and then laughed, softly again. "I shall recall those words for you tomorrow, after you have met her," he said. "And then you will laugh with me."

Edmund was shaken by the absolute certainty of Christopher's belief in the lady. He still pressed his point, however.

"You must admit the case is liable to this view, misconstruction or not. You will never even get Miss Floyd into Father's presence. You may very well never get yourself into Father's presence, if he ever hears of this."

Christopher's spirits collapsed once more. "Till this moment," he said bitterly, "I have never wished Father dead—"

For once Edmund interrupted him. "And do not start now, Christopher! It is a wicked, wicked thought! It will only bring you hurt. We must follow the ways God has appointed and trust His purpose; we must not bargain with the Devil in our minds to effect our cherished ends in some godless way."

"Of course you are right," said Christopher. "But must I wait forever simply to marry the woman I love? Do I have no rights whatsoever?"

"Are you absolutely contracted to her?"

"Absolutely," said Christopher. "In every respect. We are agreed to marry as soon as it can be brought about. And I would no more give it over than I would slay myself."

Now it was Edmund's turn to rise and begin to pace about. "What a time for this to happen!" he said.

"Yes. Your voyage has made things much more difficult," said Christopher, as if the journey to Antigua were all Edmund's doing. "We must act before you go away—if we possibly can. Your departure has brought us to it."

"Impossible! You are asking for a miracle. What, overturn a way of thinking that is positively hereditary to Father—in a week or two, a month at most? Give me till the Judgment Day, Christopher, and I could not do it, if Miss Floyd were a veritable goddess Vesta!"

"Then you will not be gone long? A six-month?"

"There is no telling how long I shall be gone. Passage alone, there and back, might take a six-month. The plantation is said to have come to a complete standstill. I might be gone a year or more."

"A year!" groaned Christopher.

Another possible line of attack now occurred to Edmund, and he wheeled his arguments upon it briskly. "Have you thought of the detriment to this young lady?" he asked. "Have you fully represented to her the difficulties—the impossibilities—of the case?"

"Of course."

"Because if you have not, Christopher—if you have not, then you have abused her trust, and her youth, and her lack of judgment. It was wrong of you to undertake an engagement to her that could never be fulfilled. You must tell her, as well as this Mrs. Hanscom, that your father will never be brought to consent. You must tell her that you are willing to be released from the engagement—as it is an engagement you cannot perform."

"Even if I could ever do such a thing, she would not give up hope so easily. She would see through my speeches; she would know that I will not give her up, in my heart, until the day that I die."

"Yes," said Edmund somewhat bitterly. "What can *they* have to lose, she and her aunt? If they force you to marry without Father's consent, they will have married into better blood, which is what they want. Why should they care for his feelings?"

"Again," said Christopher, "I shall recall those words to you. You will regret them then; you will apologize for ever imputing such motives to her."

Edmund paid no attention to this asseveration; he voiced a new concern. "Is there any danger of this matter becoming public knowledge?"

"No. She is little known in town."

"But there are servants everywhere—you forget that, Christopher. You forget that they have eyes and ears—and tongues. If Aiken lets drop a hint to Mrs. Trees on some visit home—"

"Aiken would cut his own tongue out first."

"You deceive yourself."

"Aiken *idolizes* her. So does every man who meets her. We are quite safe there, I tell you."

"You have a rationalization for everything, Christopher. You are impenetrable!"

"'Determined'—I think that would be the word you want."

"'Obtuse!'"

"'Adamant,'" offered Christopher.

"'Possessed!'"

"'In love,'" murmured his brother.

"Christopher, the best for you and for the girl would be to give it over, now, before it becomes known."

"Never," said Christopher. "Call me what you will."

"Shall I call you mule? Fool? Blockhead? Will any of those do? Madman?"

"I see we are getting nowhere, Edmund. You have come down to merely abusing me."

"I am trying to shake you awake, Christopher! By whatever means I can."

Christopher smiled painfully. "Oh, I am awake," he said quietly. "I am more awake than ever I have been before. Sometimes when I look back, I think I have been asleep all my life. In her eyes I see a Christopher Percy that I could be—a husband, a father. I have never really amounted to much, you know. I have been a mere timeserver, waiting to be master of Brackensom."

Such self-criticism was so out of character that Edmund found himself profoundly moved. He went about the room, thinking; and there was silence but for his steps on the polished floor.

"Very well," he said. "I shall not abuse you. I apologize for that. I shall wait to meet the lady. I only pray she is all you believe her to be."

Christopher sighed; he seemed at least in part relieved. "Agreed," he said. "We will discuss this no more until that time."

He stood. "You *will* stay here tonight?" he asked again.

"Of course, unless it inconveniences you."

"Not at all. And we shall dine in. Your appetite is legendary with Cook; you will find she is ready for you."

"Thank you," said Edmund.

"Supper is at eight—you are in town now, remember."

"Very good. Perhaps we ought to part until then? I shall go for a walk in the park."

"It might be best. I think we should be tempted back onto the subject. I know I would be."

"And I," admitted Edmund.

"Till eight," said Christopher.

As Edmund went out, his last glimpse of Christopher showed his brother sitting dully on the sofa, his gaze abstracted and his brow creased in distress.

Chapter 3

I cannot help feeling for those who are cross'd in Love.

—Austen

It was promptly ten in the morning when the knocker sounded at the front door. Edmund was with Christopher in the parlor; neither of them had been speaking—Christopher because he was fretting and pacing about the room, Edmund because he was rooted to the settee, trying to suggest a pattern for calm; though he admitted to himself that he would have been pacing if Christopher had not.

When the knock sounded, Christopher turned toward the parlor door and Edmund lifted his head and listened intently. He was surprised to hear a slightly warmer tone in Aiken's voice than usual as the man welcomed the visitors. It did seem that Bronwyn Floyd had made a conquest of Aiken, too. Edmund hoped so: it might well give the man an incentive to hold his tongue.

In a moment the parlor door opened and Aiken entered. "Mrs. Hanscom and Miss Floyd," he announced. As Mrs. Hanscom entered the room Edmund rose from the sofa.

She was a tall, well-made woman, about forty years of age. Though she threw one glance of keen interest at Edmund before accepting Christopher's greeting, her expression was otherwise mild. Edmund had immediate hopes for her: he had feared she would be foolish and romantic, the very type to encourage recklessly the folly of younger people; but if first impressions counted for anything, she was instead steady and sensible. As she responded to Christopher, her speech was good, betraying not a hint of any region but London, and the London of the best society at that.

"Mrs. Hanscom," said Christopher, "allow me to introduce my dear brother, Mr. Edmund Percy."

Edmund stepped forward and made a slight bow; she returned the courtesy. "I am honored to meet you, sir," she said.

"The honor is mine, madam," he said.

Until that moment Edmund had not permitted himself to look beyond Mrs. Hanscom at the woman who followed her into the room. Now, the formalities of precedence having been observed, he turned his eyes to Bronwyn Floyd, whom Christopher was already approaching; or rather they were approaching one another, mutually, with a hint of a rush, a haste; and they seized one another's hands, and looked one another in the face, and smiled, and for a moment were not only content with that mutual gaze, but blissful in it.

"*Bronwyn,*" said Christopher in a pleased whisper. He turned to one side so that both he and the woman whose hands he held now faced Edmund. "This is my dear brother Edmund."

The pregnancy of this moment was felt by all in the room. Bronwyn Floyd now advanced toward Edmund, but he did not in his turn step forward to her. She halted before him, about to curtsy, but for some reason not doing so. He extended his hand stiffly; but then she reached out and laid both her hands on his.

It was a spontaneous gesture, he was sure of that. He was watching her with minute care for any sign of insincerity, and in this movement, at least, he saw none. He looked down into her eyes, so soft and dark, and she looked up into his; and for a moment they stood thus, she appealing silently to him, he coolly measuring her.

What he saw gave a preliminary rebuff to the plans he had formulated for dealing with this crisis; but he still clung to them. What he saw was a creature, in the archaic sense of that word—one felt, in looking on Bronwyn Floyd, that she was a being created immediately by God, not of ordinary human geniture; as if the Creator, in a fine mood one day, had tossed off a quick but flawless sketch of womanly goodness incarnate. She was lovely, which is to say that her beauty *made one love her* almost in the moment of beholding it. Her eyes were a rich dark brown, almost black, beneath finely arching brows; her skin an exquisitely healthy pearl mixed from a natural palette of translucent pinks and pales.

As a man, looking on that face, Edmund could not help feeling as a hungry traveler might in finding a perfect, ripe fruit just fallen into sweet grasses on the side of the road, without a blemish or bruise, the perfect anodyne for hunger and thirst and the monotony of journeying. The feelings he now felt surprised him: he wanted to taste that face, kiss those lips; but the fruit lay beyond another man's wrought-iron fence. He set his yearning aside at once; but even as he did so, he thought how pleasant it would be to have this woman always at one's side. He could understand how Aiken could instantly become her ally; and he thought that his father, too, might form the very same wish, if he could see her: to descend to the breakfast table every morning and find her there, to see her beauty change over the seasons of life, as change it must—though it was a beauty that would never depart, only re-form in myriad ways.

"Allow me, too, to call you 'dear Edmund,'" she said.

Her appeal was almost overwhelming. His heart almost surrendered at that moment, crushed by her loveliness and sweet-temperedness; but his will rallied.

"When you are my sister, madam," he answered.

She dropped her eyes beneath the rebuff, and her hands slipped off his wrist. But in a moment she too had rallied. "I forget myself," she said, raising her eyes to his again. "Forgive me."

He stood silent, not daring to speak, because he was suddenly afraid he would forgive her not only for this uncalled-for endearment, but for all possible future transgressions as well.

"Perhaps we should sit," said Mrs. Hanscom.

"Yes," exclaimed Christopher anxiously.

Mrs. Hanscom seated herself in a chair slightly apart, as if to give the young people room. Christopher went to a sofa and held out his hand to Bronwyn, to summon her to sit by him; but she, apparently flustered at Edmund's continued coolness, did not notice the gesture, and sank into a separate chair where she was. Edmund, too, took a chair, a light and uncomfortable one, whose position he changed to suit him, facing both Bronwyn Floyd and the sofa into which his brother now settled miserably.

There was a very painful silence. The conversation began only slowly; and a strange conversation it was to be, with many windings and returnings to the one theme of it all: how Christopher and Bronwyn Floyd might be married.

"Do you have a house in town, madam?" he asked Mrs. Hanscom.

"We do, sir; though I visit it rarely, and my husband almost never. His family has long been resident in Gloucestershire, and we live there."

"Have you been in town long, then?"

"A week, sir."

"And what brings you here now, when all are readying themselves to depart for the summer, if they have not long since gone?"

Mrs. Hanscom and Bronwyn Floyd both seemed somewhat surprised by the question; and it was Bronwyn that took the lead in answering it.

"We came here expressly to meet you, sir," she said.

It was his turn to be surprised; at her frankness, if nothing else; which allowed him to indulge in a certain frankness in response.

"Then I will not put you off with polite niceties," he said. "I am grateful to you for any alteration of plans you may have made to meet me here, or for any dullness you may have felt in waiting for my uncertain arrival. Had I known of your purpose—had I known of your significance in my brother's life—I would have been more specific about my plans, or rather set all aside to accommodate yours. But Christopher has been quite secretive, so you must rather fault him than me."

"We understood," said Bronwyn, "that secrecy was necessary. You would hearten us greatly if you could assure us that such is not the case."

He was silent a moment, and his silence spoke more loudly than the words he then uttered in explanation. "I am afraid I cannot assure you of that; though I do not think that secrecy is a proper policy in any event."

"What do you mean, sir?" asked Bronwyn.

"I mean that any engagement that proceeds in secrecy is not a proper one, and cannot ultimately succeed."

At this point Christopher surged to his feet. "Oh, come now, Edmund! You have not taken orders *yet!* Surely you do not mean to ascend the pulpit and preach to us."

"I mean to continue to maintain what I told you yesterday. I mean—"

"Bronwyn and I *will* marry! No matter what Father says, and no matter what *you* say."

He was blustering on when Edmund succeeded in arresting him. "My dear Christopher," he said, "be silent a moment and listen to me. Make no error on this point: I wish you every happiness, and I would not stand in the way of any choice you make. You asked me yesterday if I thought Father could ever be brought to assent to this marriage; and I honestly told you no. How can my interview with Miss Floyd change that? It was an opinion based on my understanding of Father's prejudices, not on my ignorance of Miss Floyd's virtues; which I could readily have acknowledged, on your recommendation, though she remained *in absentia.*"

"But can those prejudices of which you speak be brought to change, sir?" asked Mrs. Hanscom.

"Madam, we brothers had a joke among us, when we were young, about the laws of the Medes and the Percies," said Edmund in answer. "My father is a good man, but single-minded; and out of that single-mindedness come all of his virtues and all of his failings. I fear one of those failings is inflexibility. I have no doubt that Christopher would forfeit his rights as a son if he even approached my father with this plan."

"Then—then—*confound all my rights!*" exclaimed Christopher, clearly wanting to use stronger language, but unwilling to do so before Bronwyn.

"Christopher," said Edmund, "if it were only Brackensom, you might easily give it up for love. But it is Father's heart; it is all that is left of our family. You will shatter both."

Christopher felt the power of this appeal and was silent. He sank onto the sofa and put his head in his hands.

The visit had been in progress for only a few minutes, and already they had reached an impasse; but as Edmund understood the situation, at this point they must arrive inevitably. He was dimly proud of himself for having stuck to his purpose in spite of being shaken by Bronwyn Floyd; and he hoped he would be able to continue now and represent fully to her and to Mrs. Hanscom the futility of what they sought.

Mrs. Hanscom, however, spoke first. "I fear we have all rushed to the topic nearest to our hearts," she said. "Let it rest for a few minutes, at least. We would like to know you better, sir."

"And I you and Miss Floyd," replied Edmund, "though I despair of any purpose in doing so."

"Despair, sir, is the counsel of those who have not yet made their prayers."

"Wisely spoken, madam. Were I a clergyman I would do well to lead us in a prayer now; but as of yet I would not presume to do so. And we are not Quakers here, to pray together without leading, though I think my brother was trying to make me one yesterday." He smiled faintly at Christopher, but his brother could not join him in his attempt at better humor.

"You can be assured we are staunch Church of England, and Tories into the bargain," said Mrs. Hanscom, who understood that a private joke was involved, and smiled slightly as she spoke.

"I am glad to hear it," said Edmund, smiling slightly in return.

Bronwyn Floyd now rose to her feet and went to Christopher. He stood at her approach and took her hand; she pressed close to him and spoke in his ear. He looked dubious at first; but unable to refuse her, he bowed, and said to Edmund, "Bronwyn wishes to speak with you alone. Would you be so kind, Edmund? I suppose my feelings are too large for this room, and must be suffocating everyone; though I cannot help them." Then, not without some show of self-pity, he bowed to Bronwyn again, and left the room.

She sat down on the sofa he had left. "Will you please join me here, sir?" she asked Edmund.

He was minded to resist on principle; but there was such genuine innocence and goodness in her mien that he could not bring himself to deny her wish any more than Christopher could. Accordingly he rose and went to sit beside her.

He felt almost nervous and alarmed sitting so close to her—she was that beautiful. He could smell a sweet, soft effluence from her hair and her body and her clothing that reminded him of musk roses in the garden at Brackensom on a June evening.

These charms, however they might work on him, were nothing compared to the power of the loving goodness that shone out of her face as turned to him, opened her dark eyes on him, and merely held him in her gaze.

"May I call you 'Edmund,' at least?" she asked.

He felt his resistance on this point instantly crumble. "Of course," he said.

"And you, if you would, must call me Bronwyn. If you can bring yourself to think of me kindly."

"It would be harsh judge indeed who could think of you otherwise."

"But you know how much I loved Alex; and it must seem strange to you that of all men on earth, it is his brother that my love should come to fix upon."

"I *have* thought it strange."

"Of course; and I myself have worried about that ever since Christopher made a conquest of my feelings. How it must look to you! As if I had set my lance to tilt at marriage with the Percies at all costs, and callously resorted to another son when God took the first I loved out of this world." And here she looked away, and a faint line of pain creased her brow just over the bridge of her nose; and her gaze became sad and abstracted. "You wrote very kindly to me then," she said. "I have carried your letter with me—with one of Alex's, the first he ever wrote me—ever since. It still comforts me greatly." She must have noticed in him some almost invisible twinge of surprise, for she went on to explain: "Yes, I still mourn Alex. How could I not? What a good man he was! And he was so infinitely dear in his manner toward me—toward everyone. You know how he could make everyone laugh."

Mrs. Hanscom emitted a half-stifled chuckle; and Edmund, too, smiled, if sadly.

"I thought I would never love anyone again," Bronwyn went on. "I was determined not to; but I was so young then—you might well laugh: I know how young I am still: no one knows better than I how very young I am. But I am older and a little wiser now than I was when I—when we all—lost Alex. I know now that God intended me to love again, again with all my heart; to be a wife and a mother. When Christopher began courting me, I had no wish to receive him as a suitor, though of course I loved him at once as a brother of Alex's. But he was so winning."

"Miss Floyd—"

"Please," she said.

"Bronwyn, then, if you insist. I was going to say that you yourself are very winning, though you may not be aware of it. But my brother, as you may not have had the opportunity to observe, is by nature somewhat engrossed in himself. So you may doubly credit your virtues in captivating him."

She laughed very softly. "Yes," she said, "he is wondrously proud. It is one of his dearest qualities."

"Dearest? How can you say that? How can pride be anything but a failing—a sin, if we speak frankly?"

"Because it does not signify in him," she said. "He is a good, loving person beneath the pride. The pride is only a cloak; and you must make him warm, sit him down by the fire of your affections, and he will take off the cloak as something for which he has no use. It is not so with all proud people, but it is with him."

"I fear his pride is not so innocent," said Edmund. "I fear it has led him into idle company at times, and encouraged him to incur expenses that his income cannot defray. I hope he has spoken to you about these things."

"He has been quite frank about his debts. He has laid them all out before us.—Is this not so, Aunt?"

"It is, Mr. Edmund. He asked Mr. Hanscom to verify that what he showed us was the extent of them, which my husband did, as far as he was able; and we believe we have a complete accounting on that score. My husband would have insisted on this, but Christopher was quite forthcoming of his own accord. He did not want it to appear that he loved Bronwyn for her wealth."

Edmund was silent for a moment. He had not expected to hear this.

"Besides," said Bronwyn Floyd, "my uncle says he does not owe so very much."

"Yes," agreed Mrs. Hanscom. "Mr. Hanscom said that for a young man of his position, a debt of twenty thousand pounds is rather modest."

"Twenty thousand pounds!" Edmund exclaimed.

They looked uneasy suddenly as they realized they had revealed a secret.

"Indeed, sir, though at first I had the same response to the figure, I am told that by today's standards it is nothing," said Mrs. Hanscom.

"I beg to differ, Mrs. Hanscom! Twenty thousand pounds is a fabulous sum. I would be hard pressed to know how to spend a fraction of that total, with assiduous effort."

"Then you have not kept up a house in town, or a coach and four, I expect," said Mrs. Hanscom.

"*Keeping* horses is one thing; *losing on* them is another."

"There has been some of that, we understand; but it is at an end."

"He has said so?"

"We have his word."

Edmund thought for a moment. "And you truly consider twenty thousand pounds to be nothing? No obstacle to this match?"

Mrs. Hanscom looked intently at him. "Mr. Edmund, let me be frank with you. Your brother and my niece love each other deeply. I am fully convinced of it. That is reason enough for them to marry; but there is more. It will be the making of them both if they become man and wife. It will be the destruction of them both if they cannot. Bronwyn could not stand another such loss; and your brother, I think, might well resort to his former manner of spending his time. My niece will gain a field for the enlargement and practice of her goodness and affection, which I believe to be boundless; and your brother will find his affairs instantly set to rights and Bronwyn's gentle but very steady hand henceforth at the helm of his life."

She paused, as if not sure how far she should go; but after considering Edmund, she apparently determined to say more. "Let me add this, sir. I have known Bronwyn all her life. She is an extremely practical and sensible young person. Her only weakness, which is also her strength, is that where she loves, she loves completely. She will make a very fine companion to a man. She is not like one of these ninnies so common today, whose excellence consists in playing the pianoforte badly, warbling a few French songs, and sketching a sleeping lapdog; she has a head on her shoulders. She will be an asset to you, to your family. I believe it."

Another silence ensued, as Edmund and Mrs. Hanscom looked eye to eye over the intervening carpet. Then he made a made a move that he hoped would surprise and challenge her.

"I appreciate your frankness," he said. "I am moved deeply by all that I hear. And though I love my brother, I have to ask what he brings to this marriage that is comparable to what you say Bronwyn brings. I agree that he is at heart kind; but in my experience his proud manner is not quite so readily shed as a cloak. He is a Percy, and that is something—that is much; but if your niece is all you say she is—well, frankly, she is better than my brother."

Mrs. Hanscom made a faint, wry grimace, and he saw at once that she knew exactly what he meant. "Ah," she said, "but she has chosen him to love. He will rise to meet her example."

"I am very young myself," said Edmund. "But in my brief experience, I have never seen that happen. History, too, teaches us so. When Octavia married Antony, he could not live at her level."

"Well," said Mrs. Hanscom, "I have the advantage of a few years; I am forty. I have seen such a thing come to pass upon occasion, and I believe it shall here."

Edmund turned to Bronwyn Floyd. "And you are willing to stake your happiness on this assumption?" he asked.

"It is not a mere assumption, Edmund; it is a proven truth. Christopher and I are truly one in our thinking. He says what I would say, before I open my mouth; he thinks what I think, even as I am thinking it."

Edmund recalled how only a few minutes ago Christopher was poised to shout *Damn my rights;* and he smiled at the thought that this gentle being before him had ever entertained such a hasty and furious thought. But perhaps it was significant that Christopher had restrained himself; that he had to that extent molded himself to her milder way of being.

"This is not a love transposed," said Bronwyn Floyd, as she saw Edmund hesitating. "This is not a brother loving a woman because his brother once loved her, or a woman loving a man whose brother she once loved. You know yourself how very different Christopher is from Alex. For me, this is a new love altogether, and certainly the same can be said for Christopher. And as such it is a very strong love, Edmund. It is a united love. It is certainly not a love that has arisen out of convenience—the obstacle we seem to face in your father proves that."

"Nor is my niece desperate for suitors," said Mrs. Hanscom. "At the risk of being indelicate, let me say that she has received three offers of marriage already, not including those of the Percies. One of them was from my husband's second cousin, a knight; another was from no less than a baronet; and a third was from a member of a very fine old family in Sussex, the Fulinghams. All were very wealthy men."

"I can well believe that Miss Floyd has been quite beset with proposals," said Edmund.

"Forgive me, sir, but are you being ironic? I do not know you well enough to tell."

"No, madam. I am quite sincere. If I had any doubts about the account you give, even the acquaintance of these few minutes' duration with Miss Floyd would remove them. Unfortunately for your argument, however, such offers as you describe rather give me hope for Miss Floyd's success in life should she give up this engagement than persuade me she must continue in it."

"Edmund," said Bronwyn Floyd, appealing to him, and placing one hand ever so lightly on his wrist. He looked at it; it was small but exquisitely rounded and shaped—and truly, as Mrs. Hanscom had said, gentle but steady. Then he looked up into her eyes again.

"Will you believe in us?" she asked. "Will you help us? Will you stand beside us in attempting to sway your father?"

As he looked at her he felt a half-dozen different waves of feeling strike him from different directions at once. One was an overwhelming attraction to her—he felt he might easily fall deeply in love with her himself. Another was a pang of jealousy, condemned as soon as felt, that it should be Alex and then Christopher who had won her affection. He saw that she was the kind of woman who loved out of an abstract ideal of loving—that once she had fixed her thoughts on a man and come to admire him, she brought all the power of the principle of that abstract love to bear, and loved him utterly and completely. If he himself had gone to visit her in the aftermath of Alex's death, returned her letters in person, it might well have been him whom she came to love.

It was a curious thing, he reflected, that a woman who inspired such thoughts only won greater power over others for her own purposes. He was thoroughly ashamed of being jealous of Christopher, and to make amends for that petty envy, he felt all the more drawn to offer his help to his brother and this young woman whom his brother loved.

Yet there was more than that, and more powerful: for one of the waves of feeling that struck him in this moment was not mere jealousy, but covetousness. Her closeness, her touch on his arm, the scent of her that he still breathed like an aura or an atmosphere he did not want to leave, the shape of her cheek, the light and darkness of those lustrous eyes, her breasts rising and falling within her morning dress, the rest of her attractive figure—all did their work on him; and he was ashamed, too, of this desire for his brother's intended bride, even as he longed to make some impossible pursuit of her.

And yet still there was more than that.

For it seemed, as they looked at one another in that moment, that she sensed his attraction; and perhaps there flickered in her mind the thought that she had had the ill luck to have missed the brother who of all the three would have made the finest partner to her. Her hand gripped his arm momentarily, and her eyes dropped; and then her hand slid away, as she took it back into her own safe keeping. Edmund, too, looked away, and found Mrs. Hanscom watching them closely, with a startled air. He did not doubt that she had read their thoughts; her gaze was too keen, too intelligent.

But what might have been was over in a moment. The entire history of their life together as a married couple, flickering dream as it was, had burst into bloom and withered in the very same instant. It left Edmund pained and cautious, and yet even more willing to help Christopher, if only to secure himself against thinking those thoughts again.

Bronwyn Floyd, too, returned to herself. She sat up straight and looked at him again, repeating her question: "Will you help us?"

He remembered his resolve to dissuade them from marrying, and determined one more time to act upon it.

"No," he said. "I cannot counsel you to persevere in this match. There is only heartache in it for all of us. I do not doubt your virtues, Miss Floyd; I do not doubt your affection for my brother. But if you marry him, you will deliver the crushing blow to the heart of a man who has seen the loss of a son and a very dearly beloved wife. Better that I myself should die than that my father should lose Christopher, on whom all his hopes are set. He, too, is a proud man; a man proud of his ancestors, proud of his home, proud of his unborn future; proud of the destiny of the Percies, as he perceives it—as he anticipates it. He is a solid believer in class; and between his class and yours, as he sees it, is an impenetrable wall."

"Am I not a gentlewoman?" asked Bronwyn Floyd.

"In every sense, to my mind. But to him you will come with a mark emblazoned on your brow that sets you beneath the Percies. I regret to speak frankly, but this is what I believe to be the case."

"And can his pride never be won over?"

"You will have no access to it to win it over. You cannot parley with a fortress that slays your emissaries."

"Has he no friends," asked Mrs. Hanscom, "no respected advisers who could be brought to bear on him?"

"No. He is very much alone in his pride."

"Does he have brothers? Sisters? I believe Christopher said you had two aunts."

"Yes," said Bronwyn Floyd, eagerly seizing this fact.

"He has a sister and a sister-in-law. He loves them; but if they came to Brackensom to advocate for you, it would be as if ambassadors had arrived there from China. He would not understand a word they were saying. To counsel him to ally Brackensom with another class would be like speaking Chinese to him."

"And he is that rigid?" asked Mrs. Hanscom.

"He is," said Edmund. Further apology seemed pointless; his father was who he was.

"But you, Edmund," said Bronwyn Floyd. "He loves you—I know he does. It is you who are our hope. Will you speak to him for us?"

"How can I persuade him? Do you ask *me* to be the one who thrusts this dagger through his heart? I cannot. I *will* not."

They did not take their eyes from him, despite his refusal; their hopes remained fixed on him. He cast about mentally for any argument he could add to those he had already offered.

"Besides," he said, "I go to the West Indies in a few weeks."

"So Christopher told us," said Bronwyn Floyd.

"Even if you persuaded me to intervene on your behalf—which you have not done and shall not do—I certainly would not cast my family into jeopardy before I go."

"Must they wait, then?" said Mrs. Hanscom sadly. "It is so hard for young people to wait. It scars them, sir. They ought to be setting up house; they ought to be having children and raising them. When they wait, they repine and sicken, often enough; I have seen it. A long engagement is a slow suffocation of the soul."

"How long will you be gone?" asked Bronwyn Floyd, her voice low and strained.

"I cannot say. But I ought not even have mentioned my going. It makes no difference. I will not speak for you."

The silence that followed this statement, which had the ring of finality, was long and very painful. He felt he had made his point at last, and turned to Mrs. Hanscom again.

"It would be best for them to part," he said, "to break off this engagement by mutual consent. Miss Floyd deserves far better than the insult she will receive from my father if this match is pursued. And what remains of the Percy family will then not be utterly shattered."

Mrs. Hanscom shook her head sadly. "I am afraid you and I may see the wisdom of that course, Mr. Edmund. But they will not. Forgive what looks like condescension in me; but I must say that I think you are young, sir, too young indeed, if you can even propose it. It is an impossibility."

"Then we have an impossibility on both sides." He looked at Bronwyn Floyd again. "You refuse to desist, and my father will refuse to accept you. If you persevere in this marriage, Christopher shall most likely be disinherited. The entail allows my father that choice; my grandfather, in point of fact, was a second son; the eldest was a dissipated man, by all accounts, and fell out of favor with my great-grandfather."

Bronwyn Floyd seemed to be struggling to control her emotions; she could not answer. Mrs. Hanscom spoke up instead.

"You *do* fully understand, do you not, Mr. Edmund, that money is not at issue? That we are not 'after' your family's wealth, or even after your position in society? I have told you how Bronwyn has been offered higher, and refused it."

He gave one more glance at Bronwyn Floyd's dark eyes, brimming with tears; and he said in reply, "Whatever I may have misunderstood your motives to be when you entered this room, Mrs. Hanscom, at this point you may count me quite a believer in their purity.—But it boots nothing."

His pessimism was again crushing to them. Again a silence followed. Mrs. Hanscom seemed to have tried every avenue of approach she knew; Bronwyn Floyd sat with her gaze downcast, her lips closed in a perplexed little frown. Yet as the moments passed, Edmund gradually began to think that the latter was praying; and in fact when she looked up again, she was quite altered. She wore a humble smile; and brushing the tears from her eyes with a rapid, dismissive motion, she stood up. "I shall go find Christopher. He must be quite in a sulk by now at being so neglected." She went from the room with a quiet, assured step. Edmund, who had risen from the sofa with her, looked after her as she went, and noticed with another jealous pang how gracefully she moved.

He seated himself again in a different chair, anticipating that his brother would again want the sofa. He found Mrs. Hanscom's gaze, now grown quite sad, fixed on him as he faced her again.

"We share a curiously similar position, Mr. Edmund," she said. "If we could clap our hands and see this marriage disappear in a puff of smoke, we would be sorely tempted to let it vanish forever."

"I would do so with a will, madam."

"Ah, but there you would err, sir, if you will pardon me for saying so. That is your youth speaking. What do we know of what is best for others? It is surely God's ordainment that Bronwyn and Christopher suffer this disappointment on their path to happiness. It will in all likelihood only strengthen Bronwyn's virtues, though as her aunt I fear it will leave its mark in sorrow as well. As for your brother, I think you may already see the improvement it has made in him, if I may presume to take note of it."

"Perhaps you are right, Mrs. Hanscom; perhaps this is the school in which they will learn their happiness to come. I certainly do not presume to know God's will. But as mortals we have to work with what little human understanding and judgment we have; and it is on those grounds that I have tried to dissuade you."

"I appreciate your good intentions, sir. I have found you everything I expected from Christopher's description: a good young man, thoughtful, well-spoken, and full of loving-kindness. That is why we have all pinned our hopes on you to help us."

"So you have said you do, madam; but you do so all in vain, as you see."

"No, I think not in vain, sir. You are indeed young; but there is a wonderful goodness in you that is coming into its first season. You will make a very fine minister to others, I think."

"I can second *that* hope, at least. But I doubt I shall be able to help my brother and Miss Floyd solve this difficulty they have created for themselves—created for us all."

"It will be resolved, one way or another; perhaps not in the best way. That depends on Mr. Hereford Percy, and whether he is as impenetrable as you say. It may not be resolved now; it may not be unriddled until you get back from the West Indies. But I incline to think that you will play a part in our salvation."

Edmund was somewhat baffled at this persistent faith in him, but said nothing in reply.

In a moment the lovers returned. If Christopher had been miffed by his banishment, he had now utterly forgotten his pique: Bronwyn led him by the hand, and he seemed to have been soothed by her touch as a wild animal is soothed by the touch of a saint.

They sat again in the vacated sofa, and Christopher began by addressing Edmund. "Bronwyn tells me you remain convinced Father will not yield," he said.

"Mrs. Hanscom and Miss Floyd have been quite frank with me on every point," said Edmund; "and while I have come to understand your affection for Miss Floyd, I have not been brought to approve of it. I still believe that this match can only lead to sorrow for us all."

"We cannot agree with you in that regard. We are too happy together to agree with you there. And if you love us, if you approve of our love for one another, that is much, Edmund. At least I know I shall not lose another brother."

The nobility of this thought seemed uncharacteristic, and Edmund looked closely at his brother. "Are you truly willing to give up Brackensom, Christopher? It really may come to that, you know."

Christopher again showed evident pain at considering this possibility, but in answering he found a polite way to say *Damn my rights:* "If I must give up Brackensom, I shall."

"God forbid," said Edmund, impressed by the unusual strength of character Christopher was showing.

"If that happens, Brackensom will be yours, you know," said Christopher.

"God forbid," said Edmund again, more painfully this time.

"I only hope that after Father passes on you will allow us to visit—to bring our children there."

"Let us not even talk of such a dreadful outcome. Brackensom is yours; the imagination staggers at any other thought. It would be the world turned upside down if I, a youngest son, should inherit. I have my destiny marked out for me, and I am happy with it, more than happy with it—eager for it to begin; and that destiny is to be clergyman to some quiet country town or village, where I may do some good, God willing; it is not to be master of Brackensom and heir of the Percies."

"Well spoken, Edmund," said Christopher, reverting at once to his pride. "God bless you for that. Brackensom is indeed mine by right. It would be wrong of Father to take it from me." He was beginning to go on, but Bronwyn Floyd skillfully quieted him by placing one hand on his arm, and then spoke to Edmund.

"What do you counsel us to do, then?" she asked.

Edmund shook his head slowly. "I cannot offer you anything like wise counsel," he said at first; but then a thought occurred to him. "Except perhaps this," he said. They all looked intently at him. "You must go back to Brackensom, Christopher. You must follow Father about like a dog. You must forget about shooting and staying with your friends; you must forget about idling away the season in town. You must forget about horseflesh, and Brighton, and whatever the Prince will be doing. You must learn to manage Brackensom. You must learn to grow corn. You must come to know the tenants."

"What? Become a steward?" exclaimed Christopher.

"No—become your father's heir in practice as well as in name. This is what he longs for you to do: to show an interest in Brackensom. Make yourself indispensable to him, and you will fortify your position against the time when he discovers your engagement to Miss Floyd; as surely he shall, sooner or later."

For once Christopher was silent; he looked aghast. What Edmund proposed was the furthest thing from his mind.

"If I may say," interjected Mrs. Hanscom, "this is God-sent wisdom. This is our only and best hope."

"It is," agreed Bronwyn Floyd with a stirring of excitement in her voice.

"But *living* at Brackensom with Father . . . you cannot be serious, Edmund!"

"I am very serious. Perhaps every month or every fortnight you could return here, to your lodgings in town; and with Mrs. Hanscom's assistance, you and Miss Floyd could spend a day or two in each other's company. Father would not be too aggrieved at a regular holiday of that sort in which he missed you, not when he contrasts it with the current state of affairs, in which it is only on rare holidays that he sees you."

"But . . . farming? And reading agricultural journals? And listening to pious old Burton hold forth on whether it will rain, and how high the corn is, and whether the tenants on Lord Crichton's side have paid their rents on time?"

"Dear Christopher—what do you do now that is more important than that? Stay up till all hours, drink too much wine, play cards, go to the races? And will you do all those things when you are married?"

"I hope I shall not become a clod when I am married!"

"I have no fear of that. The point is that if you act like a true heir of Brackensom, Father will be more disposed to make allowance for you."

Bronwyn Floyd gripped Christopher's hand and drew it into her lap. "It will not be so very tiresome, Christopher. I shall be together with you in thought every instant. I shall write you every day, and we will determine some way to get the letters to you through your Aiken and our Mr. Carver. It will be a way forward into the future; we have been stuck so long in these circumstances, like a great coach that has gone off the high road into a bog—this will put us back on our way again. At least there will be hope. And then when Edmund returns, we can reveal our engagement to your father; and we shall have Edmund's support—I know we shall." She turned to Edmund now. "Tell us we shall, Edmund," she pleaded.

The power of those eyes was wonderful; one could not help feeling noble in obliging her; and Edmund, almost before he knew what he was saying, replied: "If Christopher does as I suggest, I shall do my best to help you when I return."

"Ah!" cried Mrs. Hanscom joyfully. "That is something! That is indeed something!"

"You will do that, Edmund?" asked Christopher.

Edmund was already regretting his words; but he held fast to them as a promise. "Yes, I shall," he said. "But you must do your best to save our family, Christopher. And that means going to Brackensom, living at Brackensom."

Christopher paused a moment, thinking; and he yielded either to the incentive of having Edmund's assistance, or to the pressure of the hand that held his; or perhaps to the wisdom he perceived in this course. "Very well," he said. "I shall do it."

"Bravo, Christopher!" cried Mrs. Hanscom with delight. Bronwyn Floyd kissed him immediately on the cheek, and he flushed ever so slightly—something Edmund could not remember ever having seen him do—and looked abstractly about the room, suddenly quite proud of himself.

"I warn you, though," said Edmund. "I do not know how I can help you with Father. I only promise to stand by you and to speak the truth about Miss Floyd."

"The truth will be quite enough," said Mrs. Hanscom. "If we can only get your father to see the truth about Bronwyn, that will be more than enough to convince him."

"Yes," said Edmund. "The truth is always the best way."

"More than that," said Mrs. Hanscom, "it is always the easiest way, though it may not always seem so. It is when we are weak that we avoid telling the truth."

"Yes," agreed Edmund. "And I continue to object to this engagement on those grounds: that it is a secret, that it is a truth not told. I shall be considerably easier in my mind when my father knows everything."

"The difficulty will be in telling him *everything*, truly everything, about Bronwyn, before he closes his mind to her," observed Mrs. Hanscom.

"I can agree with that," said Edmund. "Except that, as I have said, his mind is already closed. But let us go forward and see what has been ordained."

⌛⌛⌛⌛⌛

The matter had been brought to a conclusion as successful and mutually agreeable as seemed possible, and Bronwyn Floyd and Mrs. Hanscom left shortly thereafter. Christopher saw them to the door, and he returned to the room eager to confront Edmund.

"What do you think of her?" he demanded.

Edmund considered his answer carefully. "She is a very beautiful young lady. And to all appearances, her inward beauty matches her outward appearance: she seems abundantly gentle, kind, patient, and virtuous. She reminds me very much of Mother, to tell you the truth."

Christopher laughed, and at first Edmund was puzzled at the reason; but he soon perceived, to his surprise, that his brother was laughing at his own foibles, something he had never done before, to Edmund's knowledge. "Look at me," he said. "How unreasonable I have become! You have praised my future wife in the highest of terms either of us could choose, and yet I am hungry for more, and it seems to me you have scanted your compliments to her." He sank onto the sofa where he had been sitting with her, and put his hand absently on the seat, as though thinking how a moment ago she had been there beside him. It was remarkable to see how he had been forced out of himself by his love for this woman. He had grown up suddenly, at the age of thirty, from the self-preoccupation of the adolescent to the views of a young man finally realizing that there was a whole landscape full of humanity beyond the frame of the mirror that showed his own face.

"She has affected you wondrously," said Edmund. "But in spite of all my admiration for her, I cannot help thinking, Christopher, that it would have been better for her, better for you, better for us all, if you had chosen another woman to be your wife."

"But I did not choose her; and she did not choose me. We were chosen for each other."

"So it seems to you. But—"

"No," said Christopher forcefully, turning to him. "Wait until *you* fall in love, and then you will understand. Make no mistake, Brother: I never in all my life imagined myself in this situation. I always thought I would be marrying some plump little scion of a good old family, who would be as dull and useless as I was, but would bring a good name with her. She would become mistress of Brackensom and I would get heirs of the Percies on her; and life would go on as it always has, dull and unchanging. But times *are* changing; and I will bring something better to Brackensom—new blood, new ways of thinking. My children will be better than I am, thanks to Bronwyn. And that will be good."

Edmund attempted to reply, but Christopher continued speaking. "And yet I cannot take credit for any of this. It all happened quite without my understanding or agreement. One moment I was sitting down at Charles Upton's table, where I had sat a dozen times before; and the next I was certain that I must have that beautiful little Welsh angel for my wife, no matter what it cost me. But you will not understand until you fall in love yourself."

"If that was the way it happened, it was indeed too rash, Christopher, too reckless, and all the more likely to end in grief for all of us."

Christopher eyed him calmly. "I wish you smoother sailing in love than I shall have; but I cannot wish you a better wife, for you shall find none."

"Enough of this," said Edmund. "We shall not come to agreement on this point, I can see that much. When do you propose returning to Brackensom?"

"I shall come with you this afternoon."

Edmund was astonished. "Truly? Christopher, that is wonderful!"

"You will see me ensconced as the junior steward of Brackensom before you head off to the West Indies, Brother."

"I had expected some delay, some procrastination, to be honest with you. I am delighted that you are sallying out to meet your troubles head on, instead of waiting for them to lay siege to you."

"But before we go home, you must reassure me on one point, Edmund."

"And what is that?"

"You must promise me that you will never tell Father about Bronwyn."

"I shall never offer any information of my own accord; but I will not lie to him. If he should hear anything, get wind of anything, and ask me point-blank, I shall have to tell him the truth."

Christopher considered this answer for a minute.

"Very well," he said. "I trust you, Edmund. As you can see, I trust you with my life, or with the shape of it: you could ruin me, destroy my hopes as heir of Brackensom, pour poison into Father's ear, and take everything for yourself. And yet I am certain you will not do that, as certain as I am that I love Bronwyn Floyd."

"That is something I can swear most heartily to you, Brother. I will not betray you. It will be one of the great honors, one of the great joys, of my life that I stood by you. And I hope we will weather it out, and be the happier for it in a year or two."

He had been about to add that he only wished Alex were here, that the three brothers could have stood together; but he reflected, just in time, that the situation would indeed have been different had Alex lived.

On their return to Brackensom, Christopher went immediately from the carriage to the library. Edmund would have waited until he was summoned; but his elder brother was not accustomed to observe such niceties, even with regard to his father. Edmund had no choice but to follow behind him, a bit travel-weary, and somewhat apprehensive about the kind of greeting Christopher would receive.

Hereford Percy was at first simply surprised to see his eldest son. He stood up from the table and exclaimed, "Christopher!"

Christopher stopped before him and said, "Good evening, Father."

"Well, well, let us kill the fatted calf!" said Hereford sarcastically. "Back at Brackensom? I thought you would stay away for shame, sirrah, until your brother went off to do your business for you in the West Indies."

"I am much obliged to my brother for his service," said Christopher. "You should know, sir, that Edmund and I have discussed all that; and we feel it is all for the best that he go and I remain." Edmund could not recall that their conversation on this point quite fitted this description, but he it did not surprise him that his brother remembered it that way.

"Ah, he is to go, and you are to remain," repeated Hereford, with eyebrows raised. "And where exactly are you to remain? In town? Or shooting in Scotland—following the crowd at Brighton?"

"No, sir. At Brackensom. I have come home, if it pleases you. I mean to start learning the business of the estate."

Edmund found the expression on Hereford's face on his hearing this news worth all the inconvenience of attendance on his brother: a joyful smile broke across his father's features such as Edmund had not seen there since his mother was alive. He came slowly around the table, as if barely trusting the words he had heard; and, his arms gradually opening wide, came to Christopher and embraced him heartily. "My boy, my boy!" he said. Then he doubted; he held Christopher at arm's length and looked him searchingly in the face. "But whence this sudden resolution?" he asked.

"'Tis long past time, Father. I am thirty years old." Christopher knew well how to turn past reproaches against him into his own arguments.

"True, too true. But what precipitated this change of heart?"

"Better not to question, Father," Edmund interjected with a smile. Hereford now took notice of him.

"Edmund, you must have had something to do with this!" he said.

"It was Christopher's choice, sir."

"Ah, Edmund—Christopher—you do not fool me. It was ever this way: Christopher taking after that proud old fool, his father, and Edmund taking after that sweet wise soul, his mother. But so be it." He looked Christopher fiercely in the face now, even as he took his hand in a loving grip. "You must not disappoint me now, Christopher. You must stick to your last here, once you have started."

"I shall, Father, never fear. I ask only that you allow me my lodgings in town still. I should like to stay there one or two nights every fortnight. It is important to keep up one's connections, you know."

"Granted," said Hereford, who would obviously have been willing to concede more than this if pressed.

"Then we shall start first thing in the morning. Edmund will report on his business in town, and I shall be at your service, sir, as it pleases you to instruct me in the management of the property."

Hereford could not help grinning and shaking his head in wonder. "If I were a papist," he said, "I would think your mother had interceded for us in heaven."

"Do not even speak of it, Father," said Christopher, falling in with the jest. "Edmund would never forgive me if I were the means of making you a Roman." He went suddenly and somewhat ungraciously away from his father, toward the window that showed a sunset fire illumining all the treetops in the east, and stood with his back to the others, looking out. Hereford gazed fondly after him, never noticing his ill manners. "Brackensom!" exclaimed Christopher as he looked out on the grounds and the sky above. "How good it is to be back here! Back here—looking forward to a day of joy."

Edmund winced at his incautious speech; but his father only said, "Yes! The day of joy when you bring a *wife* home to Brackensom."

Edmund could see Christopher freeze at the window; but Hereford rattled on, not noticing.

Chapter 4

For Britons, chief,
It was reserv'd, with star-directed Prow,
To dare the middle Deep, and drive assur'd
To distant Nations thro' the pathless Main.

—Thomson

Christopher was as good as his word, arising early the next morning to make a third at the discussion of Edmund's findings in London. He seemed to understand the issues involved; spoke up, and not out of turn, to express his opinion, and treated Burton civilly—never his custom—when the steward of Brackensom joined them. Clearly, however, Christopher was not buying his new self without some effort. There were times when Edmund observed him pressing the fingers of one hand over a small pocket in his coat that Edmund knew to contain a miniature of Bronwyn Floyd. Later in the day he took some time apart to write a letter, which Aiken was then dispatched to post at a distance from Neighbury. All in all, however, Edmund continued to be impressed at the change that the love of a good woman had wrought in his brother, and had some hope that the Percies might survive the shock of a Welsh alliance after all.

At their conference, there was general agreement to summon for a further interview the potential agent with whom Edmund had met in London. It was agreed that if Hereford and Christopher concurred in the choice, Edmund should sail with this agent, Albert Merritt by name, as soon as passage could be arranged; particularly as the season for hurricanes was approaching, and travel to the islands would soon be all the more hazardous.

To Edmund Mr. Merritt seemed all they could wish for in an agent. He had lived much of his life in the West Indies, had acted as agent in Jamaica to a wealthy family for many years, and had been to Antigua in a business capacity several times. He came highly recommended by Beckwith for probity and for experience in the sugar trade. He was willing to take on the agency in the Antigua estate for an indefinite period; as he told Edmund, he preferred living in the West Indies, and needed only a suitable position to make him happy there for the rest of his life. He stated his age as fifty-two, though he looked both more vigorous than the average man of that age, and considerably more weather-beaten; still, neither of these extremes was anything to cause surprise, given his vocation. He was well-spoken and neat in his personal habits, and had impressed Edmund as someone with whom he might spend weeks at sea and months in Antigua without enormous social fatigue. When they had met, at Beckwith's offices near the Temple, he shook Edmund's hand heartily, smiled pleasantly, and exchanged appropriate small talk about the heat in town before they sat down to discuss the situation at the plantation in Antigua. He seemed nearly a gentleman. In short, Edmund could descry nothing amiss about him as a possible agent for the family's interest.

Edmund did, however, feel one hesitation, based on something he could not describe or even so much as mention to his father and Christopher. He felt that their finding the man was somehow too good to be true. After the interview, on his way over to Christopher's, he had caught himself already making assumptions about the brevity of his journey and the small role he would need to play in the reestablishment of the business of the plantation; and a still, small voice inside him whispered that it could not be so very simple as that.

But appearances, at least, were favorable: Merritt responded with eagerness to their interest, made the journey to Brackensom; toured the estate, dined with them; and impressed Hereford Percy as the very man they had wanted all along. He was hired that day, received a small advance, and went back to London. He had warned them that it would be difficult to find passage, as most of the commercial ships headed for the West Indies in that season had already left; but two days later he sent word that he had secured passage on a ship bound direct for Antigua, leaving about the eighteenth of May. Or at least he and Edmund were to be aboard the vessel by noon of that day, as the exact time and even the exact day of sailing would depend on the uncertainties of the loading of cargo, the restocking of the ship, and the assembly of the crew.

The date held fast, and Edmund went down to London on the seventeenth with Christopher. He did not see Bronwyn Floyd at this time, as she would not arrive until the eighteenth, a Friday. He was disappointed at missing her; and with some shame traced back to this cause an uncharacteristic irritability he felt toward Christopher during the journey to town. But all that fell away on the next morning, when he stood in the hallway of his brother's house, shaking Christopher's hand and saying his farewell. It was the greatest voyage he would ever take in his life, or so he had every reason to expect; and he felt homesickness and the pang of parting more keenly than Christopher, who was rather thinking of a fair face and form he himself would see that evening than of any loneliness his brother might soon suffer. He forgave Christopher that; indeed, inwardly he forgave his brother for every little sin he had ever committed against him, as anyone would at such a moment; and prayed that his own little trespasses would also be forgiven and forgotten. Then he went out the door and down the steps. His trunk had already been sent out to the quay, and he had only a handbag, which he swung into the cab before mounting up himself. He looked back, but the door was already closed. He was again alone in London; alone as well in the wider world.

He had arranged with Merritt, however, to meet the man at the inn where he was staying, from which they were to go to the quays together; so he was not alone for long. He did not have to send into the inn for him; Merritt was waiting outside it. From the moment Merritt greeted him and climbed into the cab, he talked cheerfully—more than cheerfully, excitedly—about the voyage; and if Edmund had been disposed to be apprehensive, Merritt's eagerness could not have failed to work against any dread he might be feeling. As it was, Edmund found that once his farewells were past, his spirits began to rise; and Merritt only infected them further with keen interest in all that was happening, all the sights around, all the experiences that were to come.

"You are going to see something today that few travelers to the West Indies ever see," said Merritt as they clattered down Shadwell Street. "Most passengers come aboard downriver; but our captain is in too much haste for that." He nodded knowingly at Edmund. "I suppose you have never seen the West India Docks?" he asked in an important tone.

"No," said Edmund.

"They are magnificent, Mr. Percy—especially compared to what was there before them: not much more than a bog, the old Isle of Dogs. I remember what it was like the last time I shipped out for the West Indies—that was in '94; sixteen years ago it is now, but it seems like nothing. And what a change! What a change to the river."

"How do you mean—how is it a change to the river?"

"In those days there was nary a wet dock on the whole Thames. Imagine how it was: some fourteen, fifteen thousand ships a year in the river, coming and going. Not just West Indiamen, but colliers and timber ships—thousands on thousands in the coasting trade alone—and below Deptford were the East Indiamen, the biggest ships you could ever see, twelve hundred tons some of them. And then imagine all this commerce, sir, without a single dock to speak of! Everything offloaded right in the river. Why, each of your colliers might have a dozen barges swarming round it. And how many colliers does London need in a year? Imagine that figure alone—why three thousand or more, it must be. Multiply it out, sir! The river was like to paved over with barges, lighters, hoys, and punts. When I went out to the *Corona* in '94, I was in a mere bit of a punt, no more; and if I had not jumped up a half-dozen times and fended 'em off, we'd have been crushed by other boats, or capsized and left to drown in the Pool. Why, you could hardly move about on the river; and that is no exaggeration, sir. And that was at high tide; when the tide went out, the ships would hunker down and sit on the mud, and you had to fight your way down on an even smaller stream."

"It sounds quite colorful, at least, the way you describe it."

"Oh, but it was not a pretty picture, sir. It was madness, is what it was. The finest and busiest port in all the world—chaos, chaos is what it was. And the worst part was the thieves."

"Yes; I recall that when I was a boy, my father used to complain about the losses to our cargo here in port."

"The West Indiamen was always the worst hit. In the summer there would be hundreds moored in the Pool, ripe for the picking. There was gangs that roamed the river, sir, organized better than His Majesty's army: there was the Scuffle-Hunters, the Night Plunderers, the Light Horsemen, and the Mudlarks. And who could tell them from the lumpers?"

"The lumpers? And who would they be?"

"The men who work the docks. Often as not, they helped the thieves at their work. Sugar, rum, coffee, tobacco, ginger—they took whatever they could get, because they could always find a good price for it."

"This sounds insufferable, Mr. Merritt. Why did the government not take steps?"

"The government!" exclaimed Mr. Merritt. "God bless you, Mr. Percy, but what good is the government? It was the merchants that took steps. They organized a company: the West India Dock company. It had a capital of *over a million pounds.*" He uttered this stupendous figure with a sidelong glance at Edmund, to see the reaction it would produce.

"You do not say," Edmund responded obligingly.

"Yes, sir. The company was started in '99, and they finished work in only *three years.*"

"Is that not a great length of time?"

"Not at all, Mr. Percy; not if you consider what they did. They dug out some three hundred acres of mud in the Isle of Dogs. There is dockage there for *six hundred* ships. Not East Indiamen, mind you; your West Indiaman is smaller, more like two hundred, three hundred, maybe five hundred ton; but still a goodly little ship. The docks got all them ships out of the river. And other docks are still being built; so the situation is improving every day."

"But how did the docks help with the thievery?

"Ah," said Merritt, with a grin and a nod, "You shall see, you shall see, sir. They have a system now; you shall see it. The West India goods are quite safe. If things keep up as they are, in a few more years the thieves will be quite swept off the river, what with the clever measures they have taken—as you shall see—and the constables patrolling right down to Deptford."

They had now entered a maze of muddy lanes, and it was clear that the cabby was navigating more by the occasional glimpse of the masts of the West Indiamen over the roofs of warehouses and sheds than by any precise knowledge of the roads. Eventually they came to the edge of this district; it was bounded by an artificial moat—one of the recent antitheft measures at which Merritt had hinted. Beyond it was a wall that would further deter any thieves trying to leave the dock compound with any object of weight; and to the gate in this the cab driver made his way amid a mass of wagons jostling for access at the bridge and gateway. The sentry on duty challenged them, apparently seeing the cab as a fit vehicle to carry off stolen goods; and after the cab driver and Merritt had spent a few minutes in argument with him, Edmund suggested that they make the rest of their way on foot.

Once they had entered the docks proper, Edmund found himself in another world, teeming with riverfolk and seamen. On all sides he heard slang incomprehensible to him, and accents so thick he could scarce make out the meaning: not only the grittiest of London, but Scots and Irish and Welsh as well. The two gentlemen, or perhaps more accurately, the gentleman and a half, walked as though invisible through this rough throng; and Edmund felt as though he had descended into a vast open-air inferno with Merritt as his unlikely Mantuan. On all sides rumbled creaking wagons laden with hogsheads of sugar and rum, bales of leaf tobacco, and assorted other products of the West Indies. The incredibly powerful stench of the Thames assailed him—for not only was the river part sewer, but with every ebb it dwindled to expose long reaches of reeking mud.

After many inquiries they found they found the *Winsome.* A more inapt name could hardly be imagined, and Edmund's expectations of a sleek schooner were utterly baffled: the *Winsome* was a odd tub of a boat, built strictly for cargo. He later learned that she was in fact named for the family of the chief owner, one George Winsome. She was ship-rigged, about a hundred feet in length, and the sides were painted an odd yellow color, as were those of several other ships they had seen in the docks; it was apparently a distinction of West Indiamen to be yellow or black in hue.

"Rather wide through the middle, isn't it?" asked Edmund, as they surveyed it from the quayside.

"Begging your pardon, sir, but that's *she.* Bad luck to call her *it.* She won't like that."

"I stand corrected. I knew that, of course; but I cannot pretend to be anything but a landlubber."

"You have no need to be anything else, Mr. Percy.—All these West Indias are broad in the beam, as you shall see.

Slow but steady, and big enough in the belly to cram plenty of cargo into." He looked at Edmund suddenly, and his eyes twinkled and his mouth opened; but then he apparently thought better of what he had been going to say, and closed his mouth rather abruptly. Edmund had no doubt that he had been about to hear a coarse comparison of the ship and a certainly category of woman; and he was not sure if he was disappointed at missing it, or pleased that his aspect of morality and sobriety had deterred its utterance.

The crew was at this moment still engaged in the very act of cramming the ship: they were hoisting aboard enormous bundles of barrel hoops and stowing them into the hold, under the supervision of two men on the deck. Merritt led Edmund aboard, and by good fortune they addressed the right man with an inquiry as to whether he was captain.

They were welcomed; and the captain, who proved the soul of taciturnity, vouchsafed them a good handshake each; then stood contemplating them for several minutes without speaking. Finally he seemed to reach a judgment of approval; for he said, "Good! I was afraid ye'd be prissies."

"Hardly, sir," said Merritt. "I have spent most of my life in the islands. And Mr. Edmund Percy, as you can see, is as able-bodied as a gentleman can be."

The captain eyed Edmund piercingly, but said nothing further on the subject. He called to a boy who was loitering about and told him to show the passengers to their quarters.

As they were about to follow, Edmund said to the captain, "Pardon me, sir, but when do we sail?"

"On the next tide."

"Which is at . . . ?"

"Three o'clock or thereabouts."

"And how long do you expect the passage to take?"

"Oh . . ." said the captain, his keen look relaxing into vagueness and uncertainty, "hard to say. Depends when the convoy leaves Spithead."

"Convoy? You mean we do not sail alone?"

"No, sir," said the captain, raising his eyes in mild surprise at Edmund's ignorance. "It's against act of Parleymint."

"We should have to have a special license from Parliament to run alone," explained Merritt.

"How kind of Parliament to take care of us," said Edmund.

Merritt laughed. "It is to prevent insurance losses," he explained.

"*We* are not such as the likes of Parleymint are to be worrited about," added the captain. "It's Lloyds as they are worrited about."

"And what is your best and worst expectation for the length of the voyage, then?" asked Edmund.

"Oh, six weeks if we get to Madeira quick; four months if we don't," said the captain.

"Ah," said Edmund. "So the usual roundtrip is, what, a year or so?"

"Between nine months and a year," said the captain. "We'll do some island trade, and pick up sugar next May."

He left off speaking to them to shout at the bosun, who shouted in turn at the crew and the lumpers. Edmund and Merritt left them to their business and went below decks to their cabin. It was a mere closet with two beds hung like hammocks on either side, separated from the main hold by a wall of thin deal planks. Edmund's trunk took up most of the floor space on his side; Merritt's luggage consisted entirely of the single bag he had carried in the cab. The odor of sugar was so concentrated that it was actually a numbing stench, and every surface seemed to be covered with a fine, gray grime, almost like soft lead, the residue of sugar dust.

"We shall be spending most of our time on deck," said Merritt somewhat apologetically.

"So I see," said Edmund. He smiled gamely, and Merritt brightened with relief.

"Most of these West Indiamen have very fine accommodations for passengers," he said. "We had to take what we could get. I am very glad you are a good sport, sir. It makes all the difference."

"I hope I am. I think we shall get along, Mr. Merritt; and you must tell me if I impede your work in any way."

"Kind of you to put it that way," said Merritt.

They stowed their belongings in some crude cabinets they found, and in a minute more were back on deck, breathing the tar-laden air.

They took up a position out of the business area of the ship and watched the proceedings. Edmund found it all fascinating in the highest degree; he had never been near a ship before, and every block and rope and spar, every dingy flaxen sail now tightly reefed in hemp, seemed to him an object worthy of the closest observation. The bustle of the quays about them was also remarkable, though as Merritt explained, most of the outbound ships had already departed, and any inbound ships would be waiting in the islands for the next sugar crop. Edmund and Merritt spent an hour watching the stages of arrival of a ship in the slip next to their own. Merritt speculated that it was a runner, that is, a very fast ship sailing without convoy, which had had a quick voyage and was arriving with sea cotton or tobacco.

It was in the midst of this interest and general excitement, as Edmund and Merritt were leaning over the rail discussing the rigging the runner carried, that Edmund heard his companion give a small cough. Mr. Merritt looked surprised at himself. "The odor of tar must be a little too tart for me," he said with a little laugh. "I'm turning landlubber, I suppose."

"A little sea air will cure you," said Edmund innocently.

⌛⌛⌛⌛⌛

When the ship left the docks and crept slowly forth into the main channel of the Thames, it seemed to Edmund that his life was just beginning. He had not expected to feel so excited about what he continued to tell himself would be an intermission of only a few months, or a year at most, in his

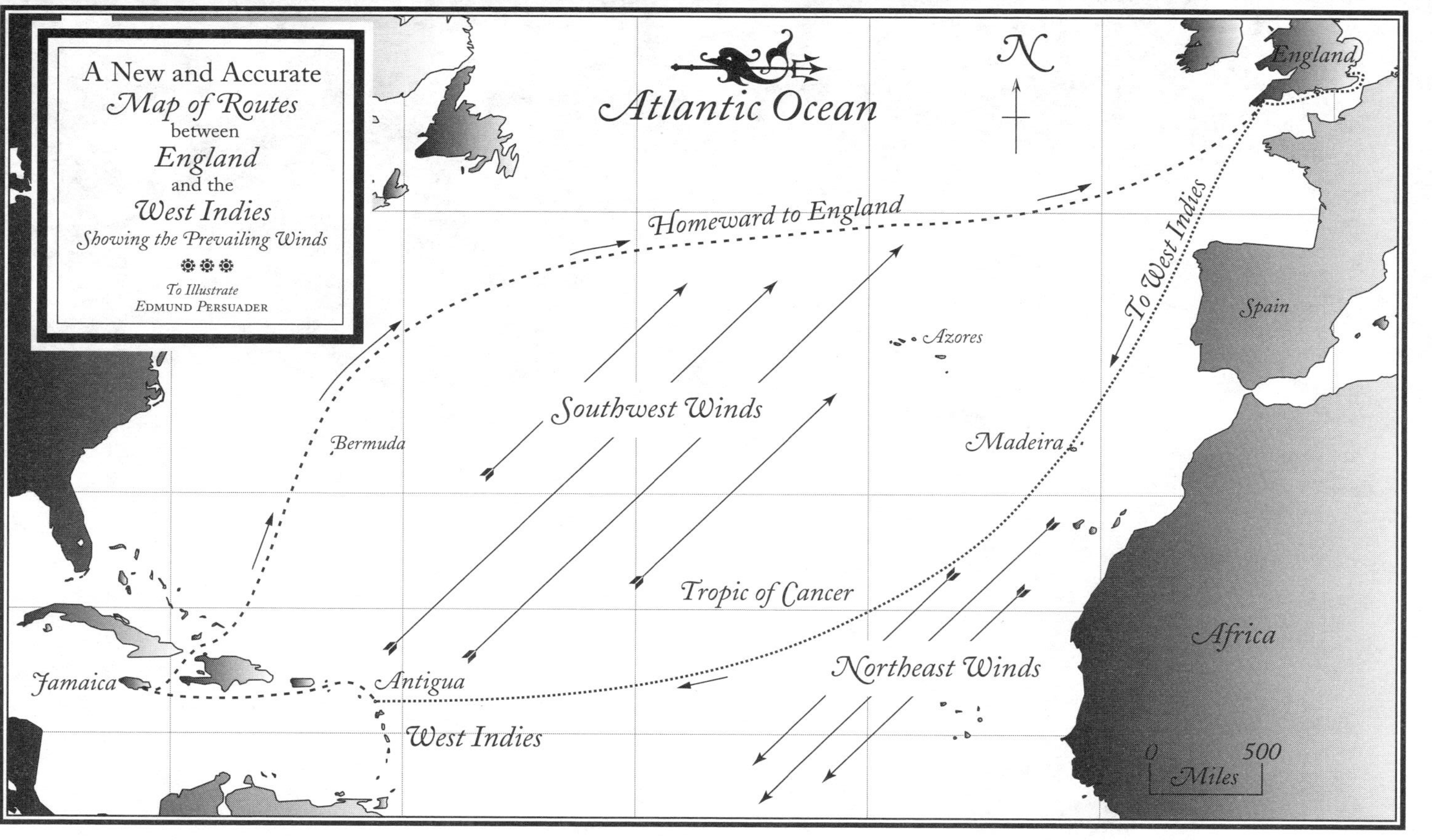
A New and Accurate
Map of Routes
between
England
and the
West Indies
Showing the Prevailing Winds
To Illustrate
Edmund Persuader
Atlantic Ocean
N
England
Homeward to England
To West Indies
Spain
Azores
Southwest Winds
Bermuda
Madeira
Tropic of Cancer
Africa
Northeast Winds
Jamaica
Antigua
West Indies
0
500
Miles

course toward ordination. But the scene poured its stimuli into every sense: the cry of the seabirds veering through the bright blue sky above, the shivering and rolling of the deck beneath his feet, the vast stench of the dirty Thames, the tang of salt and tar and aging sugar; and also perhaps some unknown influence streaming into a sense unknown to him, that told him he would change on this voyage, that never again would the same Edmund Percy look upon his homeland. He was nearly overwhelmed and dazed by this sensory flood. He stood by the rail, holding a ratline in one hand, looking all ways about him.

Slowly they worked their way down the river, which was busy not only with ships going out on the tide, but with those that had come in on it. Near collisions seemed the ordinary course of business; they tacked their lumbering vessel about within inches of ships moored or likewise inching seaward. As they passed Deptford, he marveled at the great ships of the East India Company, some of which displaced a thousand tons, per Merritt's estimate; and he heard from the agent horrific stories of the passage to India, with its grim mortalities and crippling fevers. Then they left the great city behind.

By dawn they were in the Channel. Then began a battle with contrary wind; they crept along the coast, turning southward with great difficulty at Margate, where, in company of two or three other ships, they picked up the protection of a navy vessel. Edmund naively assumed this was their convoy, a mistake he labored under until they had made their way, after nearly a week of hard sailing, to Spithead and the Isle of Wight. There he awoke one morning to the sight of some seventy merchant ships and three men-of-war assembled for the crossing. The *Winsome* and the ships that had accompanied it from Margate were the last to join—Merritt said something about how someone in the Admiralty had been paid to hold the convoy for them, and Edmund did not know whether he was jesting or merely talking; as the man did talk, very much, when his ever-more-frequent coughing allowed.

At Spithead they moored two days. A naval officer came to the *Winsome,* to give orders to the captain about staying with the convoy, about how to signal to friendly ships they met or to one another at night, about measures to take if the convoy should be separated, and other such matters; and then, on the morning of the twenty-eighth of May, their main escort fired a signal shot, and they hoisted anchor and set sail for Falmouth. At that port six more ships joined them, Scottish vessels that had come down the west coast from Glasgow; and then the convoy turned southward for Madeira.

Merritt had told Edmund that this first leg of the journey would be by far the worst, and he proved correct in the extreme. The convoy battled a contrary wind for the better part of a month. And this adversary, which rose to a gale at times, was not all that slowed their progress: no part of the convoy could travel faster than the slowest. The *Winsome* seemed to be always among the dawdlers, always in danger of losing sight of the others.

Edmund was pleased to find that he took to sea rather well. Despite week after week of pitching and rolling, he did not become physically ill, though he grew heartily weary of the endless motion of the ship beneath his feet. The food was very poor, enlivened only by the novelty of spruce beer, an antiscorbutic, which Edmund drank in preference to the exceedingly stale water. About a half-dozen of the sailors had severe dysentery, and several took fever as well; which seemed no surprise to Edmund, considering the foul air below decks, where their hammocks swung in close-packed rows.

As for Merritt, the poor weather and poor food did not affect him either; but only because he was beyond being affected by it. The cough of which he had given the first tentative sign in the docks at London quickly grew to a terrible, body-wracking, relentless spasm of the chest, accompanied by fever and chills, and leading eventually to a bloody expectoration. The ship's doctor, who seemed to be drunk most of the time, paid him infrequent visits, and evaded Edmund's keen questioning on the prospect of Merritt's recovery. Edmund himself cared for the man as well as he was able, but there was little he could do besides supplying him water and helping him from his bunk on those infrequent occasions when he left it.

It was impossible to sleep near him in the little cabin, and Edmund found a quieter berth on deck, where, with the permission of the captain, he slept in the hull of a cockboat. He bedded down on tar-scented hempen ropes beneath a sky of scudding clouds and wheeling stars, and on nights when showers blew in from the south, he pulled a heavy flaxen tarpaulin over his bed and slept within the soft, pulsing tattoo of the driven rain.

The contrary seas died away one night about forty-eight hours before they reached Madeira. Edmund woke to a brilliant dawn and a new wind, slightly off the port beam, that promised to allow much better progress southward. The sailors, and even the captain over the brief breakfast of biscuits and tea he took with Edmund, spoke of the final lifting of bad luck and the easing of some divine opposition to their progress. When, after the early meal, Edmund found Merritt dead in his berth, the captain and crew took the news with knowing nods and grim smiles of further relief. The man had evidently taken ill luck away with him, though they knew no reason why he had ever been such as to bring it in the first place.

And so, with a hasty ceremony, Mr. Albert Merritt was consigned to the waters, to rise no more till the sea should give up the dead that were in it.

Edmund's thoughts and emotions were all in conflict as he watched the body of the agent—sewn into the simplest of coffins, an old sailcloth, and weighted with a few odds and ends of old iron—slip from the end of a tilted board and splash like a shot into the sea. For one thing, he was struck by the ineffable and inexorable loneliness of the human individual. He barely knew this man; knew not if he had family or friends, or how Hereford Percy should contact them when he received the news. Merritt, with all his hopes and plans, his sins and triumphs over sin, had become mere clay in a dirty bag, to sink out of sight of all his kind and lie entombed at the bottom of an unthinkably vast and deep and heavy ocean. What afterlife awaited him, no one could know.

Edmund also felt his own loneliness. This man who would have taken the plantation in hand, with full knowledge of its operation from the beginning, was now of no more use to the Percies than the scoundrel who had lately abandoned it.

Again he felt insufferably callow. But it was his way, perhaps because he had grown up in observation of the stubbornness of his father, or perhaps because he was deeply imbued with the belief in British perseverance in the face of trouble, in the face even of impossibilities—it was Edmund Percy's way when struck with such a blow to grow more convinced that he would master the obstacles before him, and to grow more determined that he would enlarge and improve his faculties until he could wrestle and pin his destiny. There would come a time when his tenaciousness would be in vain, and he would have to learn a bitter lesson about setting himself up against the demands of providence; but for now he felt only a rebellion against uncertainty and inadequacy. If he did not have Mr. Merritt, he would succeed without him. He would fall back on his own values instead. He believed in deeply laid thought; in strength of body and willingness to use it; in prayer in the face of adversity; and in Christian loving-kindness. The first of these elements of his credo he now drew upon. He had become a player of chess in his days at Oxford, and the game suited his disposition: he enjoyed looking ahead, anticipating the consequences of each single move; and now that Merritt was gone, he felt as if the master hand had abdicated in his favor, that he himself must sit down at the board and play as best he could.

In this sense, Merritt's death was a relief to him. He had been awaiting Merritt's orders, wondering how he would be anything but a drag on the agent's actions, a family spy set to watch over him. Now he could act on his own; and though he would be bound to err, in his inexperience, at least he would have the satisfaction inherent in being a player rather than a mere spectator; and the thrill of *doing,* whether on the rugby field, or on the opposite side of a chessboard, or in this puzzling new field of running a plantation, was far more satisfying than only *watching another* do the acting.

Furthermore, he had secretly doubted that Merritt would ever be of assistance to his family. In some respects he had never really been relying on Merritt at all; he had assumed that he himself must eventually be the one to take over in Antigua, at least for some time; and some part of him felt reassured and vindicated by this outcome. Now that he saw his vague suspicions of such an outcome played out, on this fair, bright June morning at sea, he wondered at his prescience; and he prayed to the power that had perhaps given such foreknowledge to him, that he not be laboring under an equal doom of failure, an equal delusion of efficacy, and be as blind to his own fate as Merritt seemed to have been to his.

⌛⌛⌛⌛⌛

When they reached Madeira they halted for supplies. Many of the ships loaded wine for sale at their final destination; it seemed, from the great quantity they took aboard, that this powerful wine, heavily fortified with brandy, was the beverage of choice in the islands. Every inch of the *Winsome* was soon jammed with hogsheads, including the half of the passenger cabin vacated by Mr. Merritt. The captain told him that in the West Indies wine was drunk as *sangaree,* in combination with water and lime juice; he had the cabin boy mix some for Edmund, who found it better by far than the spruce beer.

Edmund took the opportunity to write to his father, leaving the letter in charge of the postal authority in the port for shipment out on the next packet or returning East Indiaman. The message ran as follows:

Mr. Hereford Percy
Brackensom, Neighbury, Surrey

The *Winsome,* Madeira, June 27, 1810

Dear Sir,

I write with regret to inform you that Mr. Merritt died of rapid consumption and was buried at sea on the morning of 25 instant. He had sickened immediately on our putting to sea and never improved. The surgeon aboard ship is quite useless, being constantly medicated with rum himself; but I doubt any particular care could have saved Mr. Merritt from his fate.

My plan remains firm: I shall see what repair of our circumstances I can effect in Antigua without Mr. Merritt's assistance. It would be best, of course, to continue to seek a competent and reliable agent, which I shall do in the island just as I expect you shall at home.

I am in good spirits despite the loss of the unfortunate Merritt, and I hope and pray that you and Christopher remain healthy. I sail in a convoy of some seventy-five ships, with the protection of men-of-war now increased in number to five, so you need have no anxiety on my score.

With respect and affection I sign myself

Your son,
Edmund

The convoy left Madeira on the thirtieth of June and slogged south again, though at a somewhat better pace than before. It was not until they had crossed the twenty-eighth parallel that they caught the trade winds; and then the release of tension in the ship was truly palpable. The fair wind came in at their backs; the sails were set to catch it, and would need little tending till the ship raised Antigua. The tar pot and the paint pot came forth; the ship was scrubbed, and as the ship swept effortlessly on its southwest course, it took on a fresh coat of yellow paint, picked out by gleaming black on the trim. The captain ordered a canvas stretched over a corner of the deck for the convenience of his passenger, and there Edmund sat, when he was not strolling about the deck; there he read through the favored books he had brought from home—the small Bible that was a gift of his Aunt Statira, a prayer book bound in purple velvet, a Greek New Testament, a much-thumbed copy of Horace, and the poems of Cowper. As the days passed, he felt a fool for having left his Dante behind, but he made do with the wealth he had.

Now Edmund first learned what heat was. He had never experienced anything hotter than a summer day in Surrey; and as they pressed south, the heat aboard ship, though relieved by a constant breeze, grew gradually to an intensity he had never even imagined. The old tars laughed at his discomfort and promised he would enjoy the summer sun in Antigua.

The sailors who had been ill recovered with the help of fresh provisions from Madeira and the fair, bright weather. When they crossed the Tropic of Cancer, two dressed up as Mr. and Mrs. Neptune, and the crew spent the evening dancing the hornpipe and singing ribald songs under the inspiration of a double dram of rum. Sounds of similar merriment drifted down the wind from the few ships that were actually slower than they were and so sailed to their stern.

Ten days after crossing into the Tropics, and some five hundred miles from Antigua, the convoy broke into three parts. A small part went south toward the Guianas; a larger part made straight on toward Barbados, from there to find their way along the island chain in company with ships from the Leeward Islands Station at Carlisle Bay; and the greatest part, bound for Jamaica and other islands, turned more northerly. The captain promised they would soon raise

Antigua; and on the morning of the second of August, the lookout gave a shout, and all crowded to the rails to watch a hazy, brown patch of land glide up over a clear blue horizon.

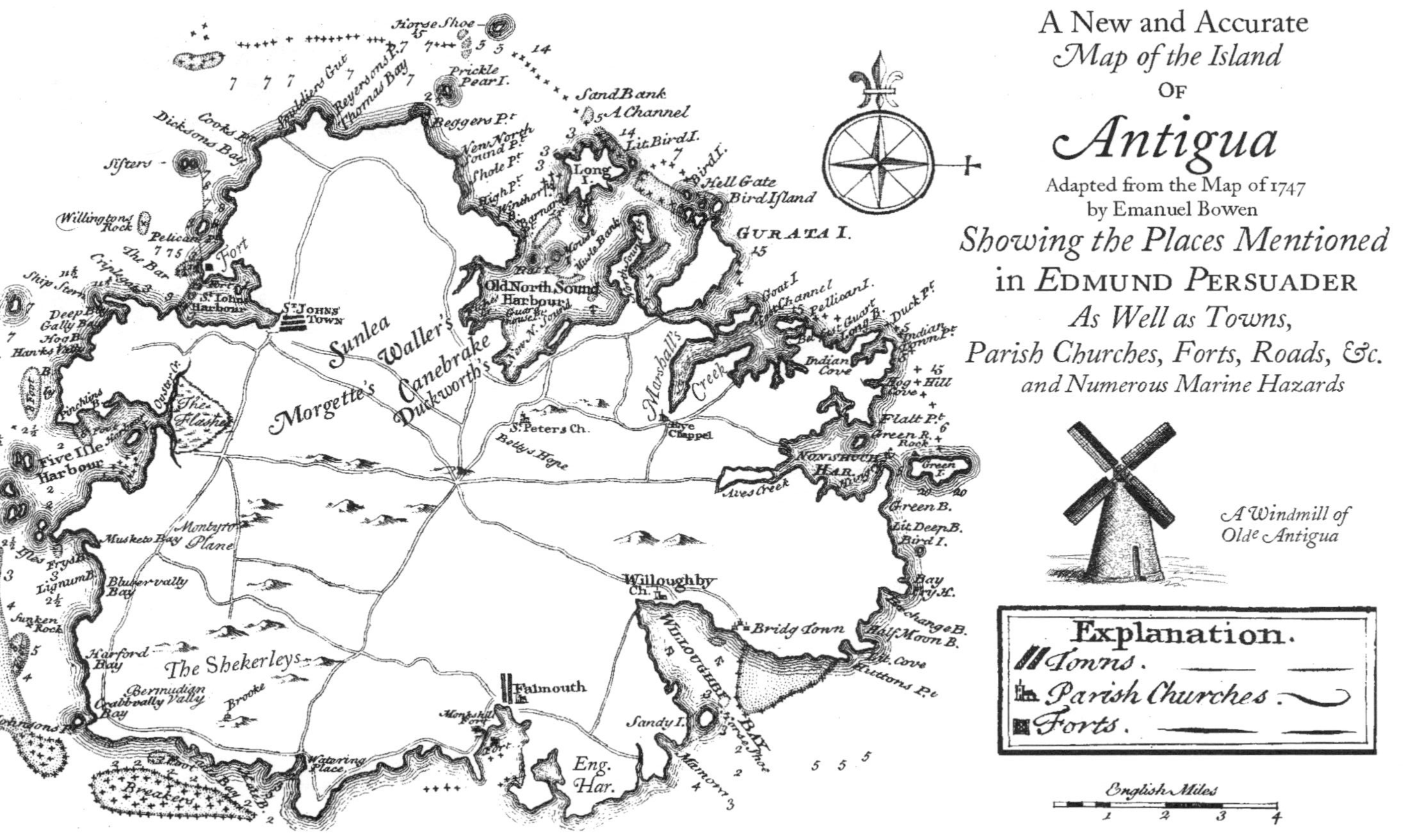

A New and Accurate
Map of the Island
Of
Antigua
Adapted from the Map of 1747
by Emanuel Bowen
Showing the Places Mentioned
in Edmund Persuader
As Well as Towns,
Parish Churches, Forts, Roads, &c.
and Numerous Marine Hazards
A Windmill of
Olde Antigua
Explanation.
Towns.
Parish Churches.
Forts.
English Miles
1
2
3
4
St. Johns Town
Sunlea
Waller's
Canebrake
Duckworth's
Morgette's
Old North Sound Harbour
Marshall's Creek
St. Peters Ch.
Betty's Hope
Nonsuch Har.
Willoughby Ch.
Willoughby Bay
Falmouth
Eng. Har.
The Shekerleys
Five Isle Harbour
The Flashes
Musketo Bay
Montyro Plane
Bluber vally Bay
Harford Bay
Bermudian Valley
Crabbvally Bay
Brooke
Watering Place
Breakers
Sandy I.
Bridg Town
Half Moon B.
Exchange B.
Green B.
Green I.
Indian Cove
Aves Creek
Gurata I.
Bird Island
Hell Gate
Long I.
Sand Bank
A Channel
Lit. Bird I.
Beggers Pt.
Prickle Pear I.
Horse Shoe
Reyersons P.
Thomas Bay
Souldiers Gut
Cooks Pt.
Dicksons Bay
Sisters
Willingtons Rock
Pelican
Fort
The Bar
Ship Stern
Deep Bay
Gally Bay
Hog B.
Sunken Rock
Johnsons Pt.
Flatt Pt.
Duck Pt.
Goat I.
Pellican I.
Lit. Deep B.
Bird I.
Huttons Pt.
Green R. Rock
Hog Hill Cove

Chapter 5

No! it is the whip, and the whip alone, which can give to England the cheap sugar she is promised.

—*Antigua and the Antiguans*

Antigua is a small island—about fifteen miles from north to south and eighteen miles from west to east, but so thoroughly pierced and indented with bays and creeks along the shore as to total only about a hundred square miles of land area. In the southwestern quadrant, which was the first Edmund saw from the ship, stand ancient eroded hills, the Shekerleys, the highest itself no more than about 1300 feet. From these one may easily see to several other islands that in Edmund's time were under British dominion. Diagonally across Antigua from the Shekerley Mountains is another upland, where the Percies' plantation was located; and between the two regions of higher ground is a broad plain, open to the sea at the west and east.

The coasts are ringed with miles of gleaming, friendly strand, but the rocks and shoals offshore are extensive and deadly. The *Winsome* skirted these to the west and made for St. John's, the main town and harbor on the island. It was then the summer rain season, and the hills and plain, as the ship grew closer to them, resolved from a vague brown mass into broad areas of darker vegetation interspersed with quilts of emerald cane fields.

Off St. John's the pilot came aboard. He was one of the few black men Edmund had ever seen, and Edmund watched him curiously as he went about his business. He spoke a dialect that at first hearing was almost incomprehensible—Edmund could not imagine how the captain and sailors understood the orders he gave, but evidently they did. It was also evident that neither the captain nor the men liked taking orders from a black; from something one of the seamen muttered, Edmund gathered that the pilot was actually a slave owned by a white on shore who would get the entirety of the fee the man collected. The sailors were so tardy in obeying him that at one point the ship grated lightly against a shoal just as it tacked. "War you go do?" observed the pilot calmly. "Run de ship on de rock? You listen me when I tell you put ovah de helm. I kin swim. Kin you?"

The ship crossed the bar, however, without further incident, and entered a fair little harbor, crowded with ships of several flags; though not, as Edmund gathered, as busy as it might have been without the trouble in Europe, or as it was in the time of the harvest, between January and June. Many of the ships were Yankee vessels, and many were coasters; and when the arrival of their own British ship became known, a gun was fired in salute from the fort overlooking the town to the north. The droughers were already launched, and swarmed around the ship as soon as soon as the anchor chain rattled over the side.

The town itself was not large, only somewhat over a hundred buildings, as Edmund guessed; almost all of which were painted white, giving the place—from a distance at least—a very pretty appearance. When his trunk was let down into a drougher, and he had bid the captain farewell and descended to it himself, and the black oarsmen began to pull for shore, then the town began to resolve into something not altogether so pleasing to view. It was not so clean as it had appeared; and that eager riot of humanity had commenced that is typical of island communities at the arrival of a ship. Swarms of black longshoremen stood ready on the docks and streets, and many more blacks going about their regular business had stopped to watch. Whites of rather unsavory appearance moved among them—idle seamen,

Edmund guessed, or the lees that seem to settle in every seaport town around the world.

Two black men were ready to be hired to carry his trunk when he reached the dock, and he succeeded in communicating with them that he wanted it brought to a place where he might hire a carriage to take him inland. They led the way with his luggage, and he followed behind, of little interest to the shouting and ebullient crowd, though that crowd was in turn quite shocking to him. The clothes worn by many of the blacks were so faded and threadbare as to be almost unrecognizable as textile material. But this was not all he found deplorable. Worse yet were the little black children who were running about absolutely naked; and perhaps worse still the black women who had tucked up their threadbare petticoats to expose their legs, from the knees down, to the cooling air off the water; and then, most incredible of all, on the fringe of the crowd as he was passing out of it, he saw two black women who for some reason had resolved to exchange the ragged jackets they wore, and casually stripped themselves bare-breasted in the process.

He began to feel he had not arrived on another island in another part of the world from England, but on another planet altogether, inhabited in the main by other beings than those he had previously known. Partly he felt disgusted by the place, partly intrigued, partly homesick, and partly simply disoriented. Events and impressions, which had come one after the other all too slowly for the past months at sea, now seemed to be accelerating out of control.

He hired a carriage for a very reasonable sum. The agent at the livery yard was white, and was able to assure him in terms he understood that the driver would know where the Percies' plantation was located. Before he departed the town he walked out again to find some provisions. He bought several loaves of bread and some bottles, which he had filled with water, as he had read that water was very difficult to obtain in the island, there being only a few springs, brackish at best.

He returned to the livery yard. His trunk and purchases were lashed on the back of a gig and he ascended to the seat beside the driver. They jolted forth out of the yard, turned onto one of the streets leading straight up out of the harbor, and in another minute were out of the town.

Here Edmund was struck by the sight of the many specimens of strange vegetation that grew on the outskirts of the place, the names of which he learned only later: palms, silk cotton trees, mangrove, manchineel, pine, oak, almond, mahogany, walnut, dagger log, black pineapple, and black Gregory or white-wood trees; and here and there, sea-grape, widdy-widdy, frangipani, cactus, and firecracker. Many of these trees and low bushes were in bloom. They soon passed into plantation country, however, where such vegetation had long since been cleared.

At that time in Antigua a very small variety of crops was grown; and though tobacco and ginger were cultivated, cane was king; or, it might well be said, Cain was king; for it was the worst instincts of humankind that were required to direct the production of sugar cane. England's thirst for sugar was unquenchable; and to grow rich by producing that commodity, a man must only lust after money so badly that he cared nothing for the abuse of his own kind as he pursued it.

Not only was humankind abused here, but the land as well; and to one who had grown up in the carefully sustained fields of a green Jerusalem, Antigua seemed not so much a land of agriculture but an industrial ground on which the earth was forced to manufacture sugar by the combined labors of multiple engines of human flesh. At first view, the various patches of cane spread over the gentle rolling central plain were attractive to the eye; but as Edmund drew closer he saw that the plantations were more like raw wounds in the earth from which sugar was being extracted, as blood is drawn out by a leech. Though he saw many fine houses belonging to owners and agents, his overwhelming impression was one of squalor and careless haste toward wealth.

Just out of the town the road ran along a field of cane that was being planted by a group of about sixty slaves. To his surprise, Edmund saw that perhaps a third of the laborers were women, though the work, under the merciless summer sun, was clearly of the hardest kind—digging broad trenches in the soil with wooden spades. None of the slaves wore shoes, and again their clothes were barely better than rags. They had all shed their shirts, even the women; and for the first time in his life, Edmund had a long view of breasts bare to the sunlight; living breasts that heaved with every breath, that shook as the women worked and moved about. He was so astonished and confused by this that he felt almost physically ill. He had heard rumors of the looseness and licentiousness of the planters and managers in the West Indies, but he had not believed them. Now he thought that those stories that had seemed so wild and incredible to him when he heard them in England might indeed have some basis in fact; for he knew that men who have power, opportunity, and impunity will not resist the provocations of lust for long.

As he stared at the women from the speeding gig, some of them paused for a moment from the monotony of their task and glared back at him sullenly. Immediately the black slavedriver near them cracked his whip in the air at their backs, and they lowered their heads and went back to work.

My God, thought Edmund, *they whip even women here.* The very idea of such a thing was almost unbearable to his sensibilities.

The gig jerked and rattled onward over the rough road. Now Edmund began to see gangs of slaves more and more frequently. The sheer number of blacks was amazing to him; soon he had seen hundreds, then easily thousands, at hard labor in the planting or in the cultivation of the burgeoning stands of cane.

The carriage now began to ascend into the higher ground. They passed along the frontage of an extensive plantation that seemed to Edmund to surpass in its slovenliness even those he had already seen, and he actually dreaded for a moment that it might be his own family's; but then he saw a huge workforce busy in it.

The gig went by the lane that led into this plantation, ascended a very slight rise, and then rolled down a very short slope. Edmund saw a man approaching on horseback, and studied him as the gig and horse drew near one another. If this stranger was to be the archetype of the planter or manager, Edmund guessed he would not find much compatible society in Antigua, for the fellow looked coarse and repulsive, and he eyed Edmund with a gaze both hostile and speculative. He was corpulent, and his inflamed nose suggested that drink was a major portion of his diet.

Just before they reached this rider, Edmund's driver turned sharply into a lane-end. Edmund caught a glimpse of a crookedly hung sign with the word CANEBRAKE on it. For better or worse, he had come home to Brackensom's outpost in the West Indies.

The lane, really no more than a track, ran up rising ground between fields of rust-colored sugar cane. The way was already partly overgrown, Edmund saw with dismay, and its condition made him wonder in what kind of state he might find the main quarters after it had been unoccupied for so long.

He had his answer shortly. The gig clattered up a long last stretch toward a cluster of low stone buildings—barns, storehouses, and sugar boileries, Edmund guessed. One of the buildings, which stood somewhat apart from the rest, was clearly the manager's dwelling, or as it was called in Antigua, the great house, though in this case the structure was modest. It boasted a small roofed verandah at the front and many windows, now tightly shuttered. About two hundred yards from it was a row of very ramshackle wooden structures, which Edmund at first thought to be large chicken coops; he only belatedly realized they were cabins for the slaves.

The driver pulled up in front of the great house. Edmund left the gig, climbed the low stone steps, and crossed the porch to the door. It was latched but not locked, and he thrust it open. Then he went about from room to room inside, opening windows and shutters and taking stock of the place.

There were only a half-dozen rooms—a larder, a parlor, a master bedroom, a smaller bedroom, another room utterly bare of furniture, and a kitchen somewhat separate from the house proper. So empty was the place that it seemed that the previous manager, or perhaps other thieves that had visited the house since, had made off with most of the furniture, for in all the place there were only a few items remaining—a chair, a table with a broken leg, two bedsteads without mattresses, and assorted and mostly useless odds and ends. The quarters were dusty but otherwise not unclean; and only in one spot, where some vines had made their way through a shutter and grown in a broken window pane, had nature made any serious inroad. He did see several large insects scuttling about, which he was later to learn were cockroaches; the equally ubiquitous lizards had invaded through the missing pane along the highway of the vine, and watched him from unlikely places with their bulging eyes; and he saw spiders larger than any he had ever observed in England. That was all that daylight disclosed, at least; the night might bring more noxious creatures with it. In general, however, he was relieved by the condition of the place.

In a minute more the driver had helped Edmund transfer his trunk and his provisions to the house. Then he went away down the drive, and Edmund was left alone.

He had absolutely no notion what to do. He walked about the part of the plantation in the immediate proximity of the house, finding every sign of the hasty departure and abruptly terminated production that had taken place months ago. The slaves had apparently long since fled, or at least they were not in evidence. The fields, so far as he could tell, were in part still ripening and in part completely gone by; and in any case, they would require a good labor force to tend. The idea of purchasing more slaves was utterly revolting to him, and he felt a twinge of frustration at having been sent on a mission for which he was so completely unfitted. For the first time he was even a little angry with his father for imposing this inevitably fruitless task upon him. No one likes to fail, and as he looked around himself, he could see no other outcome.

The strangeness of the land was almost suffocating. The heat was unbearable, unbelievable; the insane riot of weeds and vines and wildflowers pained his English sense of order, accustomed as he was to carefully tended field and hedge; the very angle of the sunlight was all wrong—direct and glaring, rather than athwart and mellow, as he was used to. He felt homesick and miserable; and worse than that, he felt trapped. He could not return home until he had his father's permission, and that would take months to secure, even in the best of circumstances.

Walking a little apart from the house, he looked helplessly about for human company. On each side of the land he assumed to be that of his family lay two apparently thriving plantations—one, that on the west, being the slatternly place he had passed, and the other, to the east, a very neat and orderly enterprise. On the latter could be seen a stone great house amidst a set of trim barns and slave dwellings—and from time to time as well, figures could be discerned moving about there, a reassuring evidence of human company at which he grasped eagerly. To the west, by contrast, the land bent around a broad upland slope, which concealed the neighbor's house.

Above the house on his own property, slightly to the east on a high point of the ground, was a stone windmill, complete with a vast framework of vanes, the cloth sails of which had been removed. He knew from his reading that such mills were used to crush and grind the cane stalks prior to extraction of the sugar; he had seen several others on his drive across the island from St. John's. The vanes of this particular mill were larger than the other examples he had seen, and it was proportionately taller; which height, coupled with its superior position on the ground, gave it more the look of a watchtower than an agricultural machine. So far as he could see from here, it was windowless.

He went through the slave cabins one by one. They were shocking to him. The worst hovel in England was superior to any of them—not only were they ill-roofed and vulnerable to the weather, they were full of a species of rats so bold that they did not condescend to flee at his approach.

Finally, in some perplexity, he went back to his belongings and retrieved his Bible. He was moved almost to tears as he held it, thinking of his Aunt Statira. It seemed strange to him that she had once held this book in her hands—she was so far away now that it was almost as if she, along with England itself, did not exist.

He felt the fabric of his reality begin to tear, and he shook off these thoughts. *God is everywhere,* he told himself. *That is what must be my support.*

He took a flask of water from his provisions, along with the sole chair that remained to the house, and went out on the verandah, where he seated himself in the shade. There for an hour he read very intently in the Bible, using its familiar words to beat back and quiet his apprehension, loneliness, and frustration.

At length he raised his head from the text. *I will find a way,* he told himself. *I must not be discouraged because I do not immediately see what that way is. I shall wait before I despair, if I find I must in the end despair. I will inquire of the other folk about and see if I can form some plan for returning this bit of Brackensom to production. It is the only part of the estate that will ever be in any sense my own. I shall make it a model of fruitfulness.*

And no sooner had he voiced these cheering thoughts in his heart than he saw a group of men approaching up the drive. Two of them were white; they rode on horseback. One of the white men Edmund soon recognized as the rider who had stared at him so angrily at the end of the lane. The others, some twenty in number, were black, and walked on foot. Their motion seemed awkward and constrained, and as they drew near to the house, Edmund realized they were hobbled and chained together. He rose from his chair and descended the steps, and in a minute more the slaves and their guardians drew up before the house.

The man whom Edmund had previously seen was dressed more or less as a gentleman; the other wore somewhat coarser clothing, and carried a long whip and a pistol. It was not difficult to guess that the first was a landowner or manager in the neighborhood, and the second his hired overseer.

"Good morning," said Edmund.

"Are you the new manager here?" asked the superior of the two whites.

"No, I am not. I am Edmund Percy, the youngest son of the owner. Our new manager perished en route from England."

The man looked at him with a mixture of contempt for his callowness and, unless Edmund imagined it, with grudging respect, apparently for his build. "Son of the owner, eh?" he repeated. "Come to make your fortune? I don't doubt but you will do what the rest of us have done."

"And what is that, sir?"

The man smiled—very grimly and unpleasantly, in Edmund's perception. "You will find that out soon enough," he said. "And we shall all find out about you, soon enough."

"And with whom do I have the honor of speaking?" asked Edmund.

"You have the honor of speaking to Joseph Waller."

"Waller? You are my neighbor then, if the information I have is correct—manager at Lord Vanstoke-Raynham's."

"That's right. To the west there. After your manager absconded, I came and rounded up your slaves. I have been keeping them for you these good six months." As he spoke he reached into a pouch at his saddle bow and drew forth a folded paper, which he thrust out toward Edmund. "I have been at some costs for this, and I expect to be repaid."

Edmund took the bill, and opening it at once, found it to be a trifling amount. "Very good, sir," he said. "I shall stand warrant to this payment, though you may have to wait a day or two.—I see here charges for feeding these men."

"Men?" said Waller in surprise.

"Yes; I presume these charges are for feeding the men who stand here."

"Ah, you mean the *negroes,*" said Waller. "Yes; they were not working their own gardens—I could not bring them back for that; I had to keep them chained the entire time to prevent their escape."

"Their *escape?* Where would they escape to, on such a minuscule island as this?"

"Oh, they find *someplace* to run to. Some run off and try to live like wild men in the Shekerleys. Most go into town and try to set up as tradesmen for themselves. They cause no end of trouble—have to be hunted down and brought back."

Edmund looked at the slaves. A more wretched crew of human beings he had never seen anywhere: they were half-starved, and many were shaking with the fatigue of merely walking up the hill. Most of them wore the remains of clothing so utterly past use as to have become one indistinct filthy gray in color; two had nothing on their bodies except some rags that girt their loins, and one was completely naked. This latter man seemed to have something seriously amiss with his leg, for he had lain down in his chains in the very dust, unable to stand, and groaned softly in agony from time to time. Clearly Waller had not taken charge of the slaves to assist a fellow landowner; rather he had seized the opportunity to add to his own labor force.

"It looks as if you put them to work," said Edmund.

"Of course I did," retorted the man. "Do I look like someone who would run an inn for abandoned slaves out of the kindness of his heart?"

Edmund stared at him now, irritated with his manner. "I assure you, sir, that you need have no fear that you present such an appearance," he said. "My point is that if they worked for you, it can be argued that you got value out of them, and your charges for their food ought to be reduced accordingly."

"Pay or don't pay, as you will," cried Waller, instantly glowering at him. "But I shall have you in court for it, you can be assured of that, if you attempt to cheat me!"

Edmund was disgusted. *To such a level sink common manners in the colonies,* he thought. "I do not dispute your bill," he said. "As I say, sir, you will have your money in the next day or two. I only point out that it could well be disputed."

Waller looked at him angrily; and in that moment, Edmund realized that he had come to the decision to dislike this man no matter what. Perhaps Waller disliked everyone instantly, but Edmund did not, and he found his own instantaneous and instinctive disapproval surprising.

"See to it," was all Waller would say; and then he turned his horse about. The overseer cast onto the ground at Edmund's feet a large metal ring with several keys on it, and then, with an expression between a leer and a scowl, he too jerked the reins and set his horse's head toward the road.

Edmund watched them go, expecting them to depart without further incident; but Waller had not ridden twenty feet beyond the coffle of slaves before he halted again. The overseer, curiously enough, did not stop, but rode on, scrupulously refusing to look at his master. Edmund had no such compunction, and looked on in continued surprise as Waller stared away up the hill toward the windmill with a kind of grimace of repressed rage. Suddenly Edmund had an odd sense that the windmill was looking back at Waller—that is, that there was someone in it who was watching, from the doorway or somewhere about it. But then, with a final scowl, Waller rode on and caught up to the overseer, who had stopped farther on to wait for him. The two then departed together.

When they were quite gone, the slaves visibly relaxed, if that could be the word for it. Their reaction was more like the collapse of men when some terrible tension has come to an end. Most sat down in the dust, and one began sobbing brokenly, as if he could not believe he had survived the ordeal of being in Waller's custody.

Edmund approached them now, and they looked at him dully. It was clear that they simply could not care what fate threw at them next; they had endured the worst already.

He picked up the ring of keys.

Dear God, he thought, *why did I never think of this? I would never have agreed to come here if I had known I would have to deal with men like this. What was I thinking? I knew we used slave labor, but I never thought what that meant—what kind of degradation and horror it involved.*

He looked the men over again. *Truly,* he thought, *I would not treat a dog this way, not the worst of all dogs. And these are beings with immortal souls! But for the agony that shows in their eyes, you might almost doubt it.*

And suddenly he did not care about anything else. Let the men flee if they would. He could not stand to see them chained. He went to the first one in the coffle and knelt beside him. It took him a minute to determine which key was required and how the lock worked, and the mechanism was so stiff with disuse that he thought the key might break off before he could turn it; but he did succeed in opening the hasp. When he had undone the heavy iron ankle cuff it secured, the man crawled away from the chain as though from a snake that had bit him and lay face down in the dirt with his hands over his head.

And so for the others. As Edmund undid the hobbles that bound the man with the leg injury, he saw that it had eroded the flesh and caused a severe infection.

When they were all free of their chains, Edmund stood again and surveyed them. They were all sitting up now, looking back at him with the eyes of hunted animals, awaiting his next move—all but the sick man, who only lay on his back and groaned.

"Come out of the sun," said Edmund. He went over to the edge of the verandah, where the house roof gave some relief from the furious sun, and motioned them to follow. It took a minute to persuade them to believe that he was serious and to obey him. They would have left their wounded fellow lying in the dust, but Edmund ordered two of them to bring him, communicating his intentions more with signs than words; or perhaps it was that they would not have trusted his words without the gestures he made.

He went into the house to fetch his loaves of bread and a large bottle of water. He wondered if they might not choose this opportunity to run away; but they were so weak and wretched that he thought they would not be able to go anywhere. Returning to the porch, he gave the bottle to the first of them in the ragged row they had made on the porch. They all sat up eagerly when they saw the water. The first man drank greedily, and Edmund had to stop him from consuming more than his share and make him pass the bottle along to the others. After that they shared it with some degree of equity. Meanwhile, he tore each loaf into seven equal pieces and gave one portion to each man. The sick man did not eat his share, but all the same he took it from Edmund and clutched it fiercely.

"We must get more food," Edmund told them. From what he had read of life in the islands, he understood that slaves grew their own food in something approximating kitchen gardens. "Is there any food in your gardens?" he asked them.

There was a long silence, broken only by the sounds of desperate chewing and swallowing. Twenty pairs of eyes watched him with dull suspicion. Finally, after he had repeated his question several times, one of the men spoke. Edmund had already noticed this fellow; he was in much better condition than the other slaves, and nearly the tallest of them all.

"Odda slaves come and take aw de food, Massa," he said.

"I see," said Edmund. "And you, what is your name?"

"Obah, Massa."

"Very well, Obah. I am Mr. Percy.—I say, Obah, are there any wildfowl in these cane fields?"

"Wi'fow'?"

"Wild birds; game birds."

"Oh, yes, Massa. Plenty. But you needs gun ifin you wan' catch 'em."

Edmund went into the house and fetched his fowling piece from his trunk. Returning to the slaves, he said, "I shall need two of you to go with me to find the birds I shoot down and carry them back. Which of you are the strongest?"

Obah got to his feet in answer; and in a minute another was persuaded to come too.

Edmund charged the gun and strode forth at once into the nearest field. Obah and the other slave followed at a distance. It did not take ten minutes before he had two brace of very plump wild game birds, of a type he had never seen before. He made his way back to the house and put his gun away. When he came outside on the verandah again, the men were all again sitting exhaustedly in the shade, looking hungrily at the fowl.

"Well, what is the difficulty?" he said. "Do you not know how to prepare a bird for cooking? These are for us all to eat; I have shot them—if you cook them, we shall make ourselves a better dinner than bread."

They stared at him in disbelief. They seemed to think it was some sort of a trick.

"You, Obah," he said, "do you not understand what I am saying?"

"Yes, Massa," said Obah. "You wan' us cook birds."

"Then what are you waiting for? Are you not hungry?"

"Oh, yass, Massa, sir, bery hungry."

"Then cook them."

"You gib slabes dese birds fo' eat, Massa?"

"Yes, yes, that is the idea. You do know how to cook them, do you not?"

"Oh, yass, Massa. We know!"

"Then go about it."

Obah rose abruptly and said something to the men that Edmund did not understand. For a moment they remained seated in astonishment, and then all but the injured man leapt to their feet and seized upon the birds with cries of relief and delight.

In yet another ten minutes the fowl were plucked bare, cleaned, and spitted. The men started a fire in an old cooking pit near the slave quarters and set the birds roasting. Meanwhile Edmund examined the leg of the sick man; he found the infection very severe. He gave the fellow more water to drink and cleansed the wound as best he could, applying what salve he had to it; but he doubted the man would survive without a doctor's care.

He called Obah to him and said, "Where is the nearest physician on the island?"

"Wassay, Massa?"

"Physician—doctor, apothecary."

"Ah, docta. Maybe St. John's, Massa." Then the man added, "You sick, Massa?"

"No, it is for this man here that I want a doctor."

Obah seemed not to understand, and expressed as much by gesturing and looking puzzled.

"Do you not see that his leg is badly infected? We shall be lucky if we can keep him alive by amputating it."

"Hard find docta help slabe, Massa," said Obah, still somewhat puzzled.

This was a possibility that had never occurred to Edmund. "But slaves must need medicine too. What do you do when you have an injury that needs healing, or suffer from some sickness?"

Obah looked somewhat frightened. "Don' know, Massa," he said; but Edmund had the impression that there was some option Obah was afraid to discuss.

He questioned the man at length without obtaining any more satisfactory answer. He gathered that the slaves treated themselves, and that a white physician would not take the trouble to travel to a plantation to attend a black man. Letting Obah go back to rejoin his fellows at the roasting pit, Edmund pondered this difficulty.

Can these slaves really be considered so expendable? he thought. In any case, his own should not be. He would set out to a neighbor's after they had eaten, to see if he could learn more about the customs in this place, and to try to obtain medical help. In the interim he did what he could to make the sick man comfortable on the verandah, and seeing he had drunk his water, brought him still more.

Over the next hour he spent watching and listening to the slaves, he realized that they could all speak and understand English without difficulty. In fact, they all communicated in that language; it was only because their accent and lilt were so heavy that Edmund had not immediately understood them, and in part because his own was so Oxonian that they had difficulty in apprehending his meaning. They were uncomfortable when he was near them, and would cease talking when he approached; but even when he was not standing by the fire pit, some of their conversation inevitably reached him.

If he had not been present and intervened, they would have consumed the fowl half-cooked; they were too hungry to care much for culinary niceties. He insisted the cooking proceed to its conclusion—he did not want them getting sick from eating undercooked flesh—and when it had, he undertook the equitable division of the meal, setting aside a portion for himself. They had no interest in plates, knives, or forks: each man received his steaming portion, which was really too hot to hold, and juggled it until he found a safe place in the shade to squat down on his haunches and tear into it. Edmund took his portion inside the house and found a knife, fork, and trencher with which to eat it. The meat was excellent in flavor, though a little tough; he thought his starving crew would especially appreciate it.

When he had finished he went back outside. The slaves were huddled in the shade again; most of them had already sunk into an exhausted sleep.

"'Scuse me, Massa," said Obah.

"Yes, Obah?"

"Massa want Obah get watah f'om cittern?"

"Ah, yes—show me where it is."

He followed the man around the house to a masonry structure, sunk into the ground, which he had seen before without comprehending its purpose. Obah threw back the cover on the top and they looked into it together. It was full nearly to the top. "Slabes too lazy steal watah," commented Obah. "Oddawise, he aw be gone. Bad heat come, he aw be gone."

"Well, that is one blessing," said Edmund.

"Yass, Massa. Mebbe dis a sign."

"A sign?"

"A sign dat tings change fo' us. Change f'om bad to good."

Edmund looked at him closely. "You suffered terribly at Waller's hands, did you not?" he said.

"Wallah bery bad man," said Obah. "Mistah Jones bery bad man."

"Mr. Jones is the overseer, I take it?"

"Yes, Mista Jones. He beat anyone he wan'. We stay in chains aw de time."

"You were in chains all this time? Since the manager here ran off?"

"Yass, Massa."

"And how soon after the manager left did Waller come and seize you?"

"A week, Massa."

Edmund, not knowing what to say, only shook his head.

He and Obah each carried a bucket of water back to the verandah and the men drank again eagerly; then Edmund sat on the steps while the slaves sank once more into an uneasy stupor.

He was even more baffled than he had been before the return of the slaves; for now he faced a moral question that seemed utterly intractable.

I should like to end this, he said to himself. *I should like to end this practice of slavery. I should like to see every slave in all the realms of Britain set free once and for all.*

It was a fine thought; but he realized that at the moment he could not even free the slaves under his control. They belonged to his father, not to him; and he had to make some account of the plantation, he had to try to make it work again—or so he had undertaken to do—and that would require slave labor.

He was deep in thought about his circumscribed options when he heard the rattle of a wagon coming up the lane to the house. It bore two men: a black who was driving, and a white man who sat beside him on the wide seat. The black, unlike Edmund's own slaves, was decently dressed in fairly new trousers and shirt; the white wore clothing—particularly his broad-brimmed hat—that suggested that he was one of the Quaker sect. They drew up immediately in front of the verandah, and the white man climbed down and approached Edmund.

"Greetings, friend," said the fellow.

Edmund rose to his feet. The slaves behind him had woken and now sat up in curiosity. "Good morning, sir," said Edmund.

"Morning?" said the man, with a little laugh. "I see you are fresh from England, where morning goes on all afternoon.—My name is Richard Duckworth. I am your neighbor to the east there."

"Yes—I have already admired your plantation from a distance. It looks very well ordered—in sad contrast to the current state of this. My name is Edmund Percy. I am the son of the owner, Mr. Hereford Percy."

"Ah!" said Mr. Duckworth, with great interest. "The son of the owner!"

"The youngest son," amended Edmund.

"Well, you will find we do not have such great prejudices against youngest sons out here in the islands, Mr. Percy. The islands are filled with youngest sons in the process of becoming richer than their elder brothers."

"That would indeed be a feat, if I should accomplish that," said Edmund grimly.

"Time will tell what you will accomplish," said Mr. Duckworth. "And where is your new manager?"

"He is wrapped in a piece of dirty sailcloth at the bottom of the ocean off Madeira," said Edmund.

"Ah!" said Mr. Duckworth. "I am sorry to hear that, now."

"Not as sorry as I am to have to say it. I would be obliged to you if you could recommend an honest manager who knows the business."

Mr. Duckworth laughed. "Now, *there* are two words one seldom hears in the same sentence—'honest' and 'manager.'"

"I am sorry to hear that," said Edmund.

"Not as sorry as I am to have to say it," said Mr. Duckworth.

They both smiled, and Edmund began to like the man.

"You are a Quaker, sir? If you do not mind my asking."

"I am a member of the Society of Friends, yes."

"Your sect is held to be one of great probity."

"Indeed, I hope so; and I do everything I can to further the world in that belief."

"Then what brings an *honest* man to earn his living in this God-forsaken place?"

Mr. Duckworth laughed. "It is not quite so God-forsaken as it may seem at first acquaintance. Indeed, I might even say that God brought me here—that is, I was inspired by the thought that I might do some good among the black population of this island, as well as earn a living for my family. You will find there are several like me here. We have a population of Moravians as well, who are very keen on improving the spiritual lot of our African fellows. But it is the

Methodists who have made a true inroad and done the greatest good."

"Is that so?" said Edmund curiously. "And what of the Church of England?"

Mr. Duckworth smiled and said, "The Church of England is asleep at present. You will find a parish church not far from here, and several others throughout the island, but there is little provision among their clergy for the care of souls, whether they are clothed in white skin or black."

"I am sorry to hear that," said Edmund. "Perhaps even sorrier to hear it than you are to say it."

"You are a Church of England man, then?"

"I should have been ordained this month, but this voyage intervened."

"Ah, I see. You were going into the church. But is that all forgotten now, and you are to make your fortune in sugar?"

"No. I am only to stay here until the plantation is productive again and under the care of a good manager. Then I shall return to England and become a clergyman."

"In some city parish, no doubt?"

"No, in the country. In some pleasant, rustic spot, I hope."

"I see."

Mr. Duckworth now looked Edmund's slaves over. "Our neighbor Mr. Waller has been here, I gather," he said.

"Yes."

Mr. Duckworth shook his head. "I hear two of your slaves died in his custody," he said.

"What!" cried Edmund.

"That is what I hear. After your manager absconded, we considered what to do about your slaves at our regular assembly. Waller offered to take them on. Some of us—some Friends and some Moravians—tried to stop him, but as he is neither a Friend nor a Moravian, he had his way, even though he is very little liked in the island. No one gave any thought to the length of time your slaves must necessarily be in Waller's hands. It proved too long for two of them:

one was beaten to death when he collapsed in the fields, and another died of sickness. There was of course a regular inquest into the death by beating; but this fellow Jones, Waller's overseer, claimed that the slave attacked him. As for the death by sickness, Waller was fined for it, for it is the law that an owner must obtain medical help promptly. But no fine could persuade him to mend his ways."

Edmund now said to Mr. Duckworth, "I am glad to hear that medical advice is available for slaves, then. I must seek some as soon as possible for one of my men."

Mr. Duckworth replied that he knew a surgeon who sometimes treated slaves, and more than that, he at once sent his own man in the wagon to inquire if the doctor would come in this case. When he heard how the injury had been occasioned, he told Edmund that there was a large penalty for chaining slaves except to prevent flight; though apparently it was never levied, as the owners always pleaded the necessity of the restriction.

"I say, Mr. Duckworth," said Edmund then, "will you come up on the porch here and give me some counsel as to how to proceed in the difficulties that face me? I am a stranger in a strange land, and there is much I need to know."

"I shall do so most gladly, Mr. Percy. I am very pleased to have a man such as yourself for a neighbor. I meant to invite you to dine at my house at your earliest convenience, if I liked the look of you; and I do."

"I am honored by your invitation," said Edmund politely, though to him somehow Mr. Duckworth's courtesy seemed all out of place in this wild part of the world. "Let me set affairs here in some kind of order before I avail myself of it."

"Of course," said Mr. Duckworth.

They then sat on the verandah for a half an hour—Mr. Duckworth on the lone chair, and Edmund leaning against the porch rail—talking over Edmund's immediate difficulties. They discussed the provenance of food and the other material Edmund would need, and how he could equip himself with horses or at least some mules and a wagon; and Mr. Duckworth offered Edmund the loan of his wagon to go to St. John's for provisions the next day. For the time being, he would send over some flour and other foodstuffs; he said the men would know how to make their own bread, which should keep them alive until some more varied food could be bought. They must begin to tend their gardens again as soon as they were able. Mr. Duckworth also promised to send over a couple of terriers for Edmund's use in ridding the cabins of rats.

In sum, Mr. Duckworth made every reasonable offer of advice and assistance. This in itself was greatly reassuring to Edmund—that he had not landed on some shore where even his own countrymen were hostile to him.

He was to find, however, that Mr. Duckworth was by no means typical of the West Indies planter. Edmund had little experience with Quakers in general, and so could not determine which of Mr. Duckworth's qualities were merely personal and which common to the adherents of his religion; but he found the man interested in the welfare of others not just as a Christian duty, but as a form of honest love in itself. He put himself in Edmund's place and considered not only the practical necessities of his situation, but also what his feelings must be; he spoke deliberately to cheer him, to suggest that what he had undertaken was not impossible, and that though it would take some time, he could yet put the plantation on a good footing. There was about this Quaker, as is often the case among deeply spiritual people, an air of almost childish innocence; which in most cases is so palpable that it allows them to recognize one another as such almost instantly, and by the same token to recognize those who are more worldly. A stronger contrast with Waller could hardly be imagined. Perhaps that was why Edmund recognized Mr. Duckworth as a good man so quickly, and why Mr. Duckworth seemed to take to him; for Edmund was then, and in some ways always would be, a man of a certain spiritual innocence. Edmund was to find, however, that Mr. Duckworth's innocent selflessness was combined with a very shrewd business sense.

At the conclusion of their conversation, Mr. Duckworth rose to return to his plantation on foot. "I know you will want those dogs at once," he said. "You will want your men to prepare their dwellings before the day goes on too much longer."

"I am very grateful to you," said Edmund. "Keep an account of what I owe you, and I shall settle up or repay you in kind."

"I shall do so," said Mr. Duckworth. He descended the steps; he turned and bade farewell; and then he hesitated. "Mr. Percy," he said, "would you walk a little apart with me here?"

"Of course, sir," said Edmund. He immediately went with Mr. Duckworth; and when they had gone out of earshot of verandah, the man turned to him.

"Tell me, Mr. Percy," he began; but some modesty forced him to stop.

"Yes?"

"Are you a married man? Have you a wife back in England? Or perhaps you are engaged?"

"No," said Edmund in surprise. "Why do you ask?"

"Well," said Mr. Duckworth slowly. "It is only that it seems you ought to be so. You are a good-looking fellow, certainly. And your manner is . . . it is such as would attract a kind-hearted woman, I think."

"I have been too much the scholar, I fear, to undergo that temptation," said Edmund.

"Temptation? Is it a matter of temptation, then, to do as God has appointed for us, and to marry?"

"Not at all, sir," said Edmund apologetically. "I spoke facetiously of my own preoccupation with scholarly matters."

"Ah—I see. I suppose that sort of thing might well remove one from opportunities to form a marriage connection." The man hesitated still, as if he meant to say something further on the topic; but then it seemed he decided against it. "Well, I shall not come back today," he said instead. "I shall send one of my men over with the dogs and the victuals; and when I hear from my man, I shall have him bring you word of what the doctor says. But I do hope you will come to dine with us at the earliest opportunity."

"I shall look forward to it, I assure you. The very prospect cheers me greatly."

"Good! That is good."

Still Mr. Duckworth hesitated. And now he looked up the hill behind the house toward the windmill, just as had Waller, though the expression he wore was not one of rage, but rather the pity of a righteous man for a hopelessly strayed and lost soul. Edmund was so struck that he himself turned and looked back up the slope, and again he had the feeling that the windmill was watching them. Then Mr. Duckworth spoke once more, in a low voice, as if he was afraid he would be overheard.

"And what are you going to do about *her?*" he asked.

Edmund looked at him closely. "Her?" he asked. "Whom do you mean, sir?"

Mr. Duckworth raised his eyebrows in surprise. "You do not know about *her?* Waller said nothing?"

"I have no idea what you are talking about, Mr. Duckworth."

"Ah—forgive me then. I did not mean to be mysterious. You did not know that there is someone living in your mill?"

"No—I absolutely did not. Who is it?"

"A young mulatto. People say she is Waller's daughter by one of his mistresses."

"One of his—mistresses! *One* of them! What, does this fellow openly keep mistresses?"

"Oh, yes. You have much to learn about our West Indian society, Mr. Percy. Many of the managers have at least one mistress, as do no few of the resident owners—even some who are married. They set themselves up sometimes with several, and live in the company of virtual harems—African harems."

"Do you mean their mistresses—are *black?*" said Edmund, still more shocked.

"Oh, indeed I do. Most of the slave women are only too glad not to have to work in the fields; sexual favors are a cheap price to pay to escape that."

"But that is—that is unbelievable, Mr. Duckworth! And what does society here have to say about it? Can these men be accepted into society here?"

"Perforce they are dealt with in business matters; but no, they are frowned upon by the better families." He smiled wryly and added, "Much the way we Quakers and Moravians are frowned upon."

"Well—I suppose it is obvious that I am shocked. And this woman who is living in my windmill is Waller's illegitimate daughter—by a black?"

"By another mulatto, yes. Technically speaking, she is his slave."

"Well," exclaimed Edmund in disgust, "why does she not live on *his* property? I shall turn her out at once!"

Mr. Duckworth regarded him gravely for a moment, and then said, "You might think twice about that, my friend."

"And why is that?"

Mr. Duckworth seemed reluctant to answer; but at length, lowering his voice still more, he said, "It is said that she is afraid to return to her father's house."

He uttered this one sentence in a tone of such significance that even Edmund, naive as he was in the ways of the world, could not doubt of his meaning. He was appalled once again.

"This is unbelievable!" he said again. "Still more unbelievable!"

"I do not tell you what to do," said Mr. Duckworth, "but I do mention it as a difficulty you must resolve. Waller will hate you for offering her shelter, if you choose to do so, and people—good people round about—will doubt your motives. If you drive her out, she will doubtless turn to prostitution in town to make her living. If you send her to some other island, Waller will accuse you of theft of his property, and he *could* make the charge stick. He is the most litigious man on all the island—always suing somebody for something, trying to make a little money. There is also some question about whether it is possible to legally export a slave, since Mr. Wilberforce and his friends ended the importation of them."

"Can her freedom not be bought? She could then be sent elsewhere without legal impediment and given some harmless and useful occupation—as a servant or seamstress, perhaps."

"Oh, Waller would never sell her. That is what I understand, at least. He wants her for his harem, but he is more than half-frightened of her, for some reason I do not know. He does not dare seize her and take her back—again, I do not know why, but my guess is that Waller, like many men of his ilk who have no God to rely on, is a very superstitious fellow; and I know that this mulatto girl is believed by the slaves to be a sorceress."

"A *sorceress!*" exclaimed Edmund, further amazed. "My dear sir! Do we not live in enlightened times?"

"Not all of us do, Mr. Percy," said Mr. Duckworth. "The slaves have a belief in what they call *Obeah.* It is some kind of black magic. It has led to all kinds of unrest and misdeeds among them. Last year the assembly made the practice of it a crime punishable by death.—Of course, some of us view that as a worse crime; but I shall not go into that question."

He looked up at the windmill again and shook his head. "I do not know what to tell you," he said in conclusion. "I only bring it to your attention."

"Well, I thank you very much for your information," said Edmund. "This is the last thing with which I ever expected to have to deal. I shall have difficulty reporting this to my father, indeed! 'Sir, the windmill is unusable because it is inhabited by a mulatto sorceress, the illegitimate daughter of our near neighbor to the west, an Englishman who keeps a black harem.' My poor father will send over to have me brought back to Bedlam in chains!"

Mr. Duckworth laughed softly. "Mr. Percy," he said, "if you keep your good humor about yourself like that, I have no fear for your wits. I commend you to prayer, sir; listen to the still small voice, follow the leading of the spirit, and you shall find your way."

"Thank you," said Edmund, in a tone not without some irony; for he recognized the jargon of the man's religion, and thought it amusing that a future clergyman of the Church of England should be admonished in those terms.

They said farewell, and Mr. Duckworth went on his way. Edmund remained standing before the house, looking up at the windmill, thinking over the difficulty its inhabitant presented; and now he was sure that he was in fact being watched in return, through some chink in the stone walls not visible at this distance.

In a short time two other blacks from Mr. Duckworth's plantation returned in the wagon. They brought the promised provisions and the couple of terriers, as well as some cast-off clothing for the three slaves who had none. Edmund roused his men, who, though still weak and exhausted, showed some animation at the thought of sport. Each equipped himself with a stout club, and the hunt began. The terriers were highly effective, and the men highly entertained by taking revenge on the rodents that had taken over their dwellings; and after an hour filled with the furious barking of the dogs, the squealing of rats, the gleeful shouting of the men, and the wild beating of clubs on the ground, a great slaughter had taken place, and the rats were banished.

When Mr. Duckworth's men had departed, Edmund gathered his slaves and spoke to them. He thought some general exhortation was necessary; the slaves, however, were amazed at being spoken to in this way. It seemed they were not used to being given the courtesy of having information about their future.

"I am Mr. Percy," he said. "I am the son of the Mr. Percy who is the owner. I am master here for the time being. I see you have been ill-used by Mr. Waller next door. I promise you that you will be well treated from now on. You will have food and clothing. You must work, but so shall I, each at our separate tasks. Let the remainder of this day be a day of rest. Recover your strength and health. Tomorrow you must get your gardens in order and start to grow food again. Thereafter we must work together to rebuild the plantation; we must make it productive—we must make the cane grow and gather the sugar. If we fail, my father will likely sell the place; and you will be sold with it, and there will be no guarantee of your fate then. For all I know, Waller will offer him the best price, and you will wind up Waller's slaves. But if we work together, we shall have some success, and we shall find a way to improve your lot. We shall repair your houses so the rats cannot get in—or the rain, for that matter. You will get some education. And most importantly, we shall worship together, and you will gain some understanding of the salvation offered by our Lord Jesus Christ."

They seemed to understand him; they certainly looked concerned at the mention of Waller. Edmund turned to Obah. "Do you understand what I have said?" he asked him.

"Oh, yass, Massa," said Obah.

"What was it, then?"

"Ifin we wo'k, you stay 'n' be good massa to us; but ifin we don' wo'k, you go 'way, and Wallah take us agin."

"That is about the sum of it, yes. Would you see to it that all the men understand in case I have not been clear?"

"Yes, Massa. But it be bery cleah, Massa. Either we wo'k fo' you, or we run 'way."

Edmund understood him to mean that if they faced the possibility of being enslaved to Waller, they would do anything they could to avoid it.

"Then let us help one another," said Edmund. He knew perfectly well that if these men chose to run away, he had not the heart to replace them; he would throw over the whole effort rather than go to a slave market and traffic in human beings. The mere thought made him disgusted with himself for ever accepting this task.

After promising them another meal at the end of the day, he gave them leave to go to their dwellings. Soon thereafter yet another slave from Mr. Duckworth's plantation walked up the lane; he gave Edmund the following note, written on an exiguous scrap of paper:

> Mr. Percy—
>
> My servant has returned from Dr. Mann, who says that he will not come, and in particular not today, as he has dinner guests. Perhaps you will have more luck if you see him tomorrow yourself. You must go southeast to the crossroads and then north about a half-mile to his house.
>
> The woman in your mill has some reputation with herbs; perhaps you might ask her in the meantime.
>
> Rich. Duckworth

Edmund was gravely disappointed by this. He went back to the verandah and examined the injured slave again. The fellow was panting with fever. He had not eaten any of his food—in fact, he had reduced the bread, which he still gripped in his hand, to a slimy ball of dough—but he was still drinking water at intervals. The infected leg was swelling dangerously, yet there seemed to be no recourse but to wait until the next day.

For the rest of the afternoon Edmund remained in some indecision about how to occupy his time. Sometimes he paced around the house and the outbuildings; sometimes he tried to read about the culture of the cane plant; and at length he took pen and paper and began to draw up a list of things that must be done, and to establish a plan of attack. Periodically he checked on the injured slave, only to become more and more convinced that the man was sinking.

When it was getting on time to think about feeding the men again, he went outside the house to find Obah. At that moment he happened to look across the fields and spied a small, red-colored deer on the edge of a stand of rusty cane. He at once fetched a heavier gun, loaded it, and set out across the field.

By then the deer had gone deeper into the old cane, but it was still readily visible from time to time above the stalks, many of which appeared to have been broken by some windstorm. If it had not been for that fact, he might never have found it, for it was much the same color as the cane. As it was, it was not overly shy of him, a failing for which it paid with its life when he closed in enough to get a good clear shot. The ball went directly through the creature's heart, and it sank to its knees without so much as a further breath.

He slung his rifle over his back, found where the deer had crumpled out of sight in the cane, and lifted it to his shoulders. It was diminutive, but heavy nonetheless; and he saw that when he came toiling up to the house out of the fields, the slaves were looking on in wonder at his strength. They had heard the shot and gathered to see what their new master was up to this time. They seemed barely to hope that he might share this meat with them as he had the fowl. Indeed, in Duckworth's discussion of customs in the island, his neighbor had told him that slaves generally received meat from their masters only on Christmas Day.

He slipped his burden to the ground and said, “There is supper for us, and breakfast as well. Which men among you knows how to butcher meat?”

They elected one who had apparently had some experience, and he was provided with a knife and set to work on the spot. The fire was rekindled, and the men went about in great excitement at the prospect of venison.

The sun was now declining and painting all the bowl of land within the island hills with a reddish-golden light. Night would come on quickly when it came, Edmund knew; in these latitudes the sunset was immediate and unforgiving. After examining the wounded man one more time, he guessed that he would probably lose him in the course of the night if something were not done. His thoughts turned to the chance Mr. Duckworth had offered—an appeal to the woman in the mill. It was a slim one—Edmund did not expect her to have expertise in anything more than a chamomile tincture—but it was all he had.

He went to where the men were gathered around the firepit, stoking the cooking fire and spitting the venison, and once again he singled out Obah. “What do you know about this woman in the windmill?” he asked him.

Suddenly the men, who had been chatting and laughing quietly, became completely silent. Obah looked frightened. “Hush, Massa,” he said in a whisper. “Don’ talk so loud. She heah you. She heah ebreyting; she see ebreyting.”

“I am not afraid if she does. What can you tell me about her? Does she have any skill in healing?”

“Ah, yass, Massa. She pow’ful! Pow’ful! Massa stay ’way from her. Build new windmill.”

Edmund laughed outright. “I shall hardly abandon the windmill to this woman because of your idle superstition,” he said. “We are not back in Africa, you know; we live in an age that does not believe in witchcraft; and moreover, a Christian age, one in which it is known as a scientific truth that the Lord guides and protects us if we rely on his goodness and power. What I want to know is whether she can help this fellow with the bad leg."

Obah looked exceedingly frightened now, as did the other men, and they all raised a soft chorus of no's to dissuade the master from availing himself of this recourse. They only provoked him the more.

"Silence!" he said. "I only asked for some information. I see that you are all too benighted and fearful to give me an intelligent answer. I shall go see this woman and judge for myself whether she can help."

They were stricken to silence. Edmund went back to the house and retrieved his gun, in the hope that he might see another deer while ascending to the mill; and then he started away around the house. Obah, however, intercepted him, running up from the firepit. Edmund had the impression that he had been deputized by the others to dissuade their master from his purpose.

"No, Massa," implored Obah, jogging along beside Edmund as he went. "Massa mus' not go to de mill."

"Why? Because a sorceress lives there?" scoffed Edmund, without breaking his stride.

"Not so loud!" begged Obah. "She heah you, Massa. She heah ebreyting.—She *be* a sorc'ress, Massa. She know de magic. She cast de spell. She ebil!" Having thus called a spade a spade, Obah looked frightened for himself, and darted a look towards the mill. "No, no," he corrected himself, "she not *ebil;* but she pow'ful, Massa."

"You will not frighten me, Obah, so do not try. A human life hangs in the balance; and what is more, a human life that so far as I know has tasted nothing of the consolation of Christian religion; and I shall not let that man go to meet his Maker without some knowledge of the salvation of Christ, if I can possibly help it. And in order to give him that knowledge, I must keep him alive."

"Mebbe Chris' pow'ful, too, Massa, I don' know; but Chris' not heah, and *she* heah."

"Christ is everywhere, Obah. I am not afraid."

Obah was awed, either by Edmund's courage or by his reliance on the unseen sorcerer Christ, and he fell away a few steps; but then he redoubled his effort—he was still quite feeble after his ordeal at Waller's—and caught up to Edmund. He laid a hand daringly on Edmund's arm and so brought him to a halt.

"Massa," he said, "please to listen to Obah jus' one moment. You good man, but you young. You come f'om England; mebbe you hab no witches in England. Listen: *Sometimes tings dat look weak be de mos' pow'ful of aw.* Massa understand?"

Edmund was struck by the oddity of his remark, and Obah capitalized on the attention he had gained by amplifying his message.

"Look," he said, "you big, strong man—taller dan Obah, and I taller dan almos' anyone. You carry deer 'cross de field on you' shoulders. You hab big pow'ful Chris' behin' you. But mebbe you make mistake, tink dis sorc'ress hab no pow'. Small tings sometimes mo' pow'ful than big tings."

"I will keep what you say in mind, Obah," said Edmund, deciding to humor the man. "Now, either come with me quietly, or go back and wait with the others."

At the mere suggestion that he might accompany Edmund to the mill, Obah turned on his heel and went away, though not without some backward glances that bespoke his apprehension for Edmund's safety.

Edmund laughed to himself and turned uphill once more, making his way through grasses now painted fiery by the rapidly lengthening light of the sun.

Chapter 6

These Obeah men and women are supposed to have entered into a league with the spirit of darkness, and by his aid are enabled to bring hidden things to light, and do many other marvellous actions; and to offend one of these persons was, they thought, to seal their doom.

—*Antigua and the Antiguans*

T*he mill* was a curious structure. He had already noticed that it was far taller than other such buildings he had seen on his journey across the island, some twenty-five or thirty feet in height. Though the tower itself was stone, the cap at the top, from which the axle of the sails protruded, was built of wood, and a very long beam or boom extended from it to the ground. At the lower end this boom was attached to a wagon wheel. He had guessed at once that by means of this boom the cap of the mill, and thus the sails as well, could be rotated to face into the wind; during this rotation, the wagon wheel that supported the boom would run in a rough track worn in the earth. He observed now that just below the cap a hatchway had been built into the stone; it led out onto a narrow platform, the function of which was perhaps to allow for inspection or repair of the machinery under the cap itself, or of the sails if they were swiveled about within reach.

As Edmund drew near this tower he saw that there were indeed gaps that had been left purposefully in the stonework, almost like arrow slits in a castle wall; perhaps these served the purpose of ventilation, but they would also let someone inside look out in any direction at will. The masonrywork itself was very crude; the pointing had been smeared over the stones almost like a stucco. By contrast, the door of the place seemed massively strong, and the great arms of the windmill were likewise formed of enormous timbers. They had been secured with a tether so that they would not move, but the slack in the rope allowed them to shift slightly in the land breeze that was now beginning to work its way up out of the center of the island with the coming of night, and with each capricious change of its direction the bare vanes creaked slightly.

The grasses around the mill were long, but a narrow footpath had been beaten through them to the entrance; he followed it directly and tried the latch. The door was bolted from within, so he knocked peremptorily.

He received no answer; and after waiting perhaps another full minute, he knocked once more and said, "Open up! I am the master here, and I wish to speak with you."

For another minute there was no response. The only sound was the breeze in the grasses and the occasional faint groan of the timberwork on its stout axle above him. He was about to repeat his demand when he heard the bolt scrape in its hasps. The latch lifted, and then the door swung inward.

The light of the sun shot into the opening of the door and fell over the female figure who stood there. She had turned half away from Edmund and had leaned back—almost, he might have said, had sunk back—against the doorjamb; and her head she had turned even farther away from him, as if frightened or ashamed; so that her face was in full profile.

He was startled in the extreme by what he saw, and for a moment stood speechless, staring at her. Her skin was of a warm hue, like very aged ivory. The sinking sun painted pink color into it, perhaps—he could not now be sure; but he would not for a minute have guessed she was not a white woman. Her features were not entirely those of a European, but they combined the best of the European and the African: her eyes were large, the dark pupil almost preternaturally so; her nostrils had a exquisitely slight natural flare, and her lips were full. Her hair, which seemed to have been recently brushed, was despite that attention wild in appearance; it was inordinately thick and black, with some individual strands and locks of reddish brown; and the whole mass of it had been pushed back over her shoulders carelessly, without a single ribbon or tie or any artifice of curls. At first he was not sure how old she was—for a moment he thought she was as much as forty, but then he quickly realized that she was young, very young: seventeen or eighteen; or then again, perhaps as old as he was himself—he could not tell. She was wearing a dress that was either a castoff or one that she herself had been given new at a much younger age, for it was far too small for her; it was faded, slightly dirty, and bore patches in a dozen places. The skirt reached only to her shins, leaving her ankles and bare feet exposed beneath the hem; and the upper part was stretched with an indecent tightness over her small breasts—in fact, the buttons over her chest were barely able to hold the seam closed, and the edges of the cloth gaped open to reveal the contours where her breasts touched one another.

No sooner had he taken in the sight of this extraordinary person than she confounded the picture he had begun to form of her by turning her head about suddenly, giving him a view of her entire face. For a moment he could not understand what he was seeing. The other half of her face—the side he had not been able to see before—was dark in color. He thought at first that it was dark with the pigment of the African; but then he realized that the coloration was rather a port-wine birthmark. By some cruel chance it lay across almost exactly one-half of her face, on her right side, so that in the profile she had first shown him—deliberately, he now suspected—it had been as invisible as the dark side of the moon; but in full view, as he saw her now, it became a glaringly obvious advertisement, however spurious, of her mulatto birth. The coloration did not, of course, affect the actual shape of her features, which were finely wrought throughout; but it produced an effect that was disconcerting at the least.

If her attitude had been frightened and shamed before, which he suddenly rather doubted, certainly now it was defiant and fearless. But as she looked full upon him, he saw in her eyes a mirror for the surprise she must have seen in his. She had the advantage, in all probability, of having seen him from a distance; but there was something in the near sight of him that surprised her.

"Who are you?" she said. Her voice was very soft and rich, and her accent was that of the island patois, a blend of African and British, but more refined that that of Obah.

"I am Edmund Percy," he said. Instantly he wondered why he did not repeat, "I am the master"; but now that he had seen her, there was something about her that discouraged him from defining their relationship in this way. Instead he added, "I am the son of the owner. I have come to see to the plantation until we can arrange for a manager."

She looked at him inscrutably. "Edmund," she repeated. In her dialect, the name sounded strange, two equally accented syllables: "*Edd-mond.*"

"That is *Mr. Percy* to you," he said.

"Ah," she said, raising her eyebrows ironically. "Of course. Mr. *Per-see.*"

"Who are you?" he demanded.

"But I shall not call you that," she said, as if she had not heard him. "No," she said. "You are so white—so white. You have come from England, yes? You are all so white in England. I shall call you *Ed-mund;* I shall call you *White Edmund.*"

"You shall do nothing of the kind," said Edmund in a short tone. "Who are you, and what are you doing on my property?"

"I am Janetta," she said.

"What is your surname?" he demanded.

"I am a slave," she said. "I have no surname. Unless it is my owner's name." He noticed she did not use the term *master*, which was to have been expected.

"And your *owner* is Waller?"

She set her head back and her eyes narrowed—narrowed almost to angry slits. Rage was eminently visible in her features; her mouth worked for a moment in a kind of angry sneer; and then she said simply, "Yes."

"And why are you living in my windmill?"

She gave a little defensive toss of her head that made her hair shake over her shoulders; and it was in that moment Edmund first thought to himself how beautiful she was.

"It is the only place I *can* live," she said.

"Why not live at Waller's, if you are his slave?"

"Because if I go back to Waller's," she said, "either he or I must die at once. And if he dies at once, then I die later."

He contemplated her for a minute. She tossed her head again nervously, staring back at him; and despite her anger and her threat of violence, he thought her very vulnerable and lonely and weak; and he pitied her.

"Well," he said, "I shall not make you go back to Waller's. Not if what I have been given to understand of the situation is true. But I imagine there will only be trouble if you stay here. We can discuss that tomorrow."

"You will let me stay?" she said in surprise.

"For the time being, yes," said Edmund. "Until I can talk to the proper authorities, have your case examined, and see if we can find a safe refuge for you somewhere—perhaps in some other island."

She smiled bitterly at him. "Authorities!" she said. "The authorities would be entertained by my shame. The authorities would be glad if I killed Waller; and after I had done it, they would be glad to watch me hang. It would entertain them. All you good, church-going Englishmen would be entertained to watch a half-naked mulatto girl swinging from a gibbet, kicking her pretty little dirty feet."

"If you kill Waller," said Edmund, mastering the extreme shock he felt at her speech, which was both bold and hopeless, "you will indeed doubtless be hanged. So do not kill him; and do not despair. There must be good people in this island somewhere to whom I can appeal on your behalf."

She leaned against the doorjamb again in a curious way. He had seen whores in London lounging in alleys and doorways like this, but had never stood so close to a woman as she did so. The posture she took seemed instinctively seductive, though he could not analyze why it seemed so to him. She drew her hair over the lower part of her face like a veil, so that only her dark eyes were exposed, for all the world like some denizen of a harem.

"White Edmund," she said, in a kind of dreamy whisper, as if speaking to herself. For a moment he wondered if she was insane. He gave up this speculation, however, and pressed on with his purpose.

"Look," he said. "I am told that you have some skill with herbs, with healing. I have a very sick slave down at the house. His leg is badly infected; I do not think he will survive the night unless he is treated. I have sent for the doctor, but the doctor will not come."

She laughed in surprise. "The doctor!" she exclaimed. "You sent for the doctor?"

"Yes, I did."

"What a little fool you are!" she said. "A big man like you—you could pick Waller up by the throat and break his neck with one good shake—and you think a doctor would come treat a slave!"

"I was told this doctor sometimes did so," said Edmund.

"There is a doctor who treats cattle and horses," said Janetta. "He sometimes comes to treat slaves. But it is too late in the day to fetch him now."

"Then that is not to the point. Can you do anything for this man?"

"You call him 'a man'?" she said curiously.

"Yes. That is what he is. He is a child of God, that is all that concerns me at present. He is suffering and like to die; and I should like to save his life if I can."

"Well said, White Edmund!"

"You *shall not* call me that," he said. "You shall call me Mr. Percy."

She laughed. "White Edmund!" she said tauntingly. "White Edmund! White Edmund!"

"You are very rude for someone in your position," he observed angrily.

"And what is my position?" she said. She pronounced the word "position" in a curious, lilting way that disturbed him for some reason. "My life will not be long," she went on. "I might die at any moment. Waller might come for me at any time with his men and his dogs and his guns. If he catches me, he will tie me with ropes and bind me with chains and do what he wants with me until I can find a way to kill him—until I can get to his neck with my teeth and tear open his veins and loose his foul blood from his foul body forever. He would just as soon shoot you or anyone who tried to stop him. So why should I care about anything? I do what I want, I say what I want. You would do the same, if you knew you did not have long to live—if you knew you would die at Waller's hands, or at your own, or on the gibbet."

"You are mad!" he said.

"Yes!" she cried. "I am mad! And you would be too, if you were the child of a man like Waller!"

He had evidently surprised her into uttering this; for no sooner had she said it than her face was contorted in disgust and she spat on the ground at her feet.

He said nothing for a minute, letting her calm down; and then he said, "Look, I have no intention of hurting you, or delivering you up to Waller. I do not know if I can protect you—you are right, I know nothing of the laws of this place.

But I do not mean to drive you away. I only ask if you can help this man who is suffering, perhaps dying, while we speak."

She was silent, looking first at him, and then away down the hill to the fire that now burned brightly in the pit.

"Yes," she said. "I can help him."

"Then will you come back with me straightway and do so?"

"Yes," she said.

She turned away from the door now and went back into the mill. He saw now that the mill machinery took up only a very small part of this lower chamber; of which she apparently did not make use, for she skirted the crushing rollers and slipped along the wall to a ladder that led to some upper room. She climbed it; and when she reappeared, she was carrying a basket with some herbs.

They started back down the hill together. He darted a glance at her as she walked beside him; and he saw with some ineffable and deeply troubling emotion how the tight dress clung to every curve of her body. She seemed to be literally in a state of starvation—she was indeed too thin to be attractive in the terms in which he understood feminine beauty; he was used to the sight of milk-fed English girls, and to thinking them what beauty should be; and the flat belly and pinched waist of this woman, or girl, or whatever she was, seemed unnatural to him; but at the same time that waist and belly exaggerated the flaring curve of her hips and the roundness of her buttocks. He looked away; and he told himself he must continue to look away.

The sun now set suddenly and utterly. It was astonishing to Edmund, even after having seen it on shipboard, how quickly the darkness supplanted the brief twilight in this latitude. They made for the fire, and as they approached, the savor of the roasting venison wafted up the hill toward them in the breeze.

"I will take payment for this," the woman said to Edmund suddenly.

"What kind of payment do you want?" he said skeptically, thinking his sufferance of her should be compensation enough.

"I want some of that meat," she said, unable to conceal her hunger.

"Very well," he said. "You will have some as soon as it is ready."

He saw now, somewhat to his surprise, that the men were not gathered about the fire chatting and laughing, as they had earlier when they were cooking the game birds. Instead they were squatting here and there about it, facing uphill towards the windmill; silently watching and waiting. When Edmund and Janetta appeared within the ring of firelight, they all immediately surged to their feet. For a moment he thought they were all about to succumb to panic and run away as fast as they could; but perhaps their fear rooted them to the ground instead.

"You, Obah!" the woman called peremptorily as she neared the fire.

"Yass, Miss Janetta!" said Obah.

"The master says I can have some of that meat."

"Yass, Miss Janetta!" said Obah again.

"See to it," she said. "Cook it well, but do not burn it!"

"As you say, Miss Janetta! We wait fo' you say, Miss Janetta!"

Edmund was utterly taken aback at the man's reverence for this mere half-starved girl.

"I go to heal this man with the bad leg," continued Janetta. "Do not eat until I return.—Who is he?"

"Johnny, Miss Janetta."

"Ah, I am glad it is Johnny. Johnny knows how to obey. Not like you, Obah!"

"Not so, Miss Janetta! I awus obey!"

"I am glad to hear it," she said wryly. "Otherwise—!"

Obah shook his head to emphatically to repel any implication that he did not do whatever Miss Janetta told him.

"Come," said Edmund. "I shall show you where this Johnny is." He picked up a burning brand from the fire to light the way.

She gave the men a long, penetrating stare, which they bore with considerable discomfort, before turning away to accompany Edmund to the verandah.

"How did you ever get such power over them?" Edmund asked her point-blank when they were out of earshot.

She shot him a bemused glance. "You would be frightened, too, if you knew what I could do to you," she said.

"Nonsense! I will have you know I do not believe in witchcraft."

"Ah! There are more kinds of witchcraft than you imagine. There is a kind for every task; and I think I know the very kind that would work on you."

"You would do better to think of the religion that will take you to heaven than to conjure the powers that will take you to hell," he retorted.

"Religion!" she scoffed. "What is religion but white magic? And a weak white magic at that."

"Nay," he said. "It is not magic; it is the truth. And the truth is more powerful than all of your superstitions. Those men are in your power because they do not understand the truth. And I am *not* in your power, because I *do* understand it."

"You *think* you know the truth," she said. "Someday you will find that the truth is not what you now think it is."

"It is not impossible that my understanding of the truth will grow," he said; "but it will never lead me into *your* power. Our Savior said that the truth shall set us free; and so it shall."

"Yes," she agreed, to his surprise. "The truth shall set you free, that is so; but perhaps it shall set you free into a freedom of which you never knew before."

They were now approaching the house, and he did not respond; instead he stopped and said, "You must wait here. He is naked; I must cover him up with something."

She laughed outright. "Do you think I have never seen a naked man?" she said. She continued on her way, and he had no choice but to continue with her. He rationalized this impropriety by telling himself that the Africans seemed, from what he had already seen of them, to have a different standard of modesty than the English.

He had set out a lantern so he would not have to fumble about in the dark for it; he lit it now and held it up over the prostrate figure of the sick man.

Janetta put down her basket and knelt beside Johnny. She took one look at his leg and said, "Oh, this is very bad! This is very bad!"

"I can see that much for myself," said Edmund. "The question is, can you do anything for him?"

Johnny, who had been in a stupor, now opened his eyes, and when he saw who knelt over him, he gave a cry of fear.

"Oh, shut your mouth, you fool!" she said to him. "Do you think Janetta is here to harm you? How could you be worse than you are? You will be dead by dawn if we do not do something."

Johnny was not capable of understanding much at this point, but at least he made no move to get away from his physician.

The woman took a cup that Edmund had provided for the sick man and filled it with water from a bucket. Then she took a handful of dried herbs from her basket, crushed them in her hands, and mixed them in the water. She forced Johnny to drink this, much against his will; she propped his head up on her lap and held the cup to his lips and poured it into his mouth, though he choked and gasped and made retching noises.

The effect was immediate. No sooner had he given a final swallow and a last belch than his body went limp. She gently lowered his head down to the floor again. "He will not fight the healing now," she said.

"By God, I think not," exclaimed Edmund. "It looks as if you have killed him."

"No, he is only asleep. But he will wake in an hour or so. He will be in much pain then; he will sweat and scream. That is good; that means his body is ridding the poison from his blood."

She also had some jars in the basket; she went through them and found one in particular, which contained a foul-smelling salve. She dug out a great gob of this material with her fingers and smeared it over Johnny's leg, from his toes to his crotch, where she matter-of-factly held his genitals aside with one hand so that she could apply it with the other.

The very strangeness of this situation now began to tell on Edmund. He had an alarming sensation of detachment and dissociation from reality. In the land where he had lived all of his life, he did not see such things.

"That is all we can do for now," she said. "Someone must stay with him tonight and force him to drink water, plenty of water. He must piss the poison out of his body—it is the only way to get rid of it. In the morning, if he is still alive, I will put more salve on him."

She washed the salve off her hands directly in the water bucket. "I presume he must not drink that," said Edmund.

"No," she corrected him, "it will be good for him to drink it. Let him drink this water I have washed in."

Edmund shook his head in amazement.

"What?" she said. "You would rather wait to get the horse-doctor? I tell you, this man will be dead by morning if you do that."

"That is what I have been telling you myself, if I recall," said Edmund. "So I will take whatever care you can offer. It is all I can do."

"You are a fool, White Edmund," she said, "but you are a sensible fool."

"That does not make sense," he pointed out.

"I mean that you are only a fool because of the things you do not yet know. When you learn them, you will be sensible and wise. Or at least I think you will. Sometimes you Englishmen are just unaccountably stupid."

"And sometimes you Antiguans are unaccountably incomprehensible," he countered. "Or so I am beginning to think."

She grimaced. "Good," she said. "That is as I want it to be.—Now, let us eat." She saw the portion of the game bird that Edmund had set out on a trencher for Johnny. "There is no point in wasting this," she said. "He will not eat for many days, if he ever eats again." She transferred the meat to her basket, and he realized suddenly that she was intending to go back to the mill.

"Will you not stay with him tonight and care for him?" he asked her.

"I?" she said in surprise. "Why should I stay with him? He is not *my* slave."

"No; but you are his healer."

She stood up. "I cannot stay," she said. "I cannot risk being taken by Waller or his men."

"But you have risked it all this time—however long it is that you have stayed in the mill," said Edmund.

"Yes, but if they attack the mill, I shall know it. The door is strong, and it will take them a minute or two to break it down. And I shall need a only few seconds to kill myself."

She had tilted back her head to look up at his face in the lamplight. Her dark eyes were arresting, but they did not stop his gaze from flickering down over her slender figure. One of the buttons of her dress had pulled open, exposing somewhat more of the roundness of her breasts, but either she had not noticed or she did not care, or she did not care enough to notice. But he himself hardly noticed either; there was something much more important about her that caught his attention; and that was the way her slight form seemed a veritable whip of energy and tense determination. He realized that she was perfectly capable of killing herself if need be.

"My God," he exclaimed, "you are serious!"

"I am indeed," she said. She set her mouth stubbornly, and her nostrils flared ever so slightly.

"And how will you commit this crime against God?" he said.

For answer she drew up her skirt and exposed one long ivory-colored leg as far as the thigh. There, in a leather sheath, bound to her leg with a leather strap, was a small knife with a bone handle. She plucked it out; and almost faster than the eye could see, she placed the tip below her breasts, pointing up under the ribcage toward her heart; the blade was wicked-looking, hollow-ground, double-edged like a dagger, and its razor edges glinted in the lamplight.

"One good thrust," she said. "Then I am beyond his reach forever. Sometimes I think I might as well get it over with at once. But other times I hope that he will die first—that one of his whores will kill him in some drunken rage, or that the English will shoot him down for the mad dog he is."

She put the knife away and dropped the hem of her skirt again. "So you see," she said, "I cannot take care of Johnny.—And I will not take him into the mill, if that is what you are thinking."

"Very well," he said.

"Now let us eat," she said hungrily.

He took up the lantern and they returned to the fireside. Part of the venison—a haunch of the deer—was well cooked, but the men had obeyed her and had not so much as drawn it off the spit. Obah divided the meat and gave the first portion to Edmund, who had a trencher ready for it. The second portion went to Janetta; she took it apart and squatted on the ground to eat it. She seized it in her hands and tore at it eagerly with her teeth, consuming it more in the manner of a wolf or a dog than any lady Edmund had ever seen. The sight of her ravening at that meat, her white teeth gleaming in the darkness, was one that he never forgot.

Again he took his food back into the house and ate with knife and fork by lamplight. The little ritual of the meal, which included the saying of grace, the familiar utensils, and a glass of Madeira, was soothing to him in the midst of this strange world into which he found himself fallen; and he did indeed feel that he had fallen here, as though from heaven into hell, or into middle earth. He thought with bitter homesickness of Brackensom. If all had gone as it should have, he would have been soon a clergyman, and no matter what his poverty then, it would have suited him more and pleased him more than this awful place in which he found himself. He thought, too, of Bronwyn Floyd, and with a similar kind of bitter homesickness. In contrast with this wild mulatto girl—but there was no contrasting them; it was like contrasting the members of completely different orders of beings—Bronwyn at the top of the order, and this mulatto at the bottom.

Still, he pitied this Janetta. He was shocked by her, for any number of reasons; but he pitied her desperation, and he saw her determination not to succumb to Waller as the proof of her innate nobility. He wondered what her story was, and especially who her mother was, and how that woman had come into Waller's hands. And not for the first time, or for the last, he felt a deep revulsion at the entire system of slavery; and his only solace in that respect was that he believed in his heart that God would not let something so very wrong continue for long. No; the good in the hearts of men and women would speak out against it. He himself would speak out against it, when he knew how. In the meantime he would try to be a master such as he imagined Christ would have been to these men.

When he returned to the fire, the men were lying about in a stupor of satiety. Janetta was nowhere to be seen; he presumed she had returned to the mill. Obah struggled to sit up when he approached, and then the other men, too, made an effort to be more alert.

"I shall need you to watch over Johnny," he told them. "You must take turns of a few hours each. You are to force him to drink as much water as you can, and help him up when he needs to pass it. Do you understand?"

The men were silent. There was something in their uneasiness that told him they would not obey him.

"What is the matter?" he demanded.

"Can't watch ovah Johnny," said Obah. "Wallah put de debil in Johnny. Go neah Johnny, debil take us, too."

"That is ridiculous," said Edmund.

He lectured them for a few minutes on the nature of God and evil; they listened stony-faced. Then he chose men to do the watching, and gave orders for the first to accompany him, and turned back to the house; but the man did not follow. Obah came after him instead, his head bowed apologetically.

"Sorry, Massa," he said. "Nobody help Johnny. Ebreybody 'fraid of de debil."

"That is utterly ridiculous!" cried Edmund. "I have never heard anything so ignorant and benighted in my life! Do you all care so little for this man that none of you will help him?"

"Oh, no, Massa—we aw lob Johnny. Johnny good man—sweet man, dat Johnny. But de Debil hab him. Nuffin' we can do now but wait till de Debil take 'im."

"Have you never seen a man get sick before? What are you telling me—that just because a man is sick with infection, the Devil is in him?"

"Yes, Massa. And dis be worse, Massa, 'cause Wallah *put* de debil in him."

"What *are* you talking about?"

"Johnny hab a wife. Wallah want her for cook in his house. Johnny 'fraid Wallah treat her bad; 'fraid Wallah . . . treat her bad. He try stop her f'om stayin' Wallah's house."

"By God," exclaimed Edmund, "this just gets worse and worse! I think it is Waller who is the Devil around here."

"Oh, yass, Massa," agreed Obah readily.

"But look, this wife of Johnny's—to whom does she belong? Waller, does she not?"

"Oh, no, Massa," said Obah. "She belong you. She be Canebreak slave."

"What! Then why did Waller not bring her back?"

"Wallah keep her cook in his house."

"Well, that is cool of him! And how many other slaves of my father's estate has he kept?"

"Dat be on'y one, Massa."

"And that is one too many," said Edmund.

He started off down the lane without wasting another moment, leaving Obah in perplexity behind him.

It took him no more than a quarter of an hour to find his way to Waller's. The moon was very nearly full, and lit the plantations laid out on the contours of the land like a great righteous lamp showing him his route.

The lane from the road in to the great house was not overgrown, like his own, but was yet in bad disrepair that did not augur well for Waller's management of the estate. The outbuildings as well, and the slave quarters—forebodingly silent, though he saw slaves sitting in several of the doorways—were nearly ruinous; but the great house itself was a handsome stone building, well kept up, and what was more, now well lit in every window of the ground floor. A half-dozen dogs heard his approach from far off and raised an alarm, but fortunately they were chained.

Even above the insensate barking of the dogs, he could hear voices within the house when he stood before it. These sounds from within ceased when he pounded on the door. A black boy answered his summons, and then stood staring at him in wonderment.

"Well, who the devil is it?" cried Waller from within.

Edmund walked into the house, heading in the direction of Waller's voice; it led him into a parlor off the main hall.

The sight that met him here was perhaps what he might have expected, if he had taken the time to imagine what he might see; but he had been so angry that he had not truly thought what he might encounter. Waller was seated at a card table with three black women, whose dress and general appearance suggested immediately to Edmund that they were the man's mistresses. Bottles of Madeira and brandy were on the table at Waller's elbow, but there were glasses all around the table, and the three women appeared very drunk.

Waller was thunderstruck at the sight of him; but when he had recovered, he did not seem completely displeased. "It is Mr. Percy!" he said. "Come, Mr. Percy, do you have need of a little refreshment? Would you like to play cards with us? It would be infinitely more entertaining to play against a gentleman for money than against a gaggle of black whores for nothing."

"You have one of my slaves," said Edmund.

Waller scowled. "And you have one of mine," he said.

"And who ever prevented you from retrieving her?" said Edmund. "I know not what you are going to do about your property, but I know what I am going to do about mine. I am here to take this woman back. Where is she?"

"Blast you, you will not have her till I have mine back!" said Waller.

"I think we both know why you will never have your daughter back," said Edmund, "and it has nothing to do with me."

"My *daughter!*" cried Waller, rising from his chair. "Do you dare to call that witch my daughter?"

"That is what she calls herself," said Edmund. "Now, where is my slave?"

From the man's posture and tone, Edmund had at first guessed that he would not get the slave out of Waller's control this night—that it would take some kind of legal proceeding. But such was not the case; and it appeared to Edmund later, when he knew something of Waller's standing, or lack of it, in the society of Antigua, that he did not dare hold another man's slave when that property was demanded of him—it would be an actionable offense, and the landowners who would have sat in judgment on him would have been glad of an excuse to fine him, if only to discourage him and make his life as miserable as they could.

"Very well," said Waller, "take her and be damned! But someday I shall come for that witch, and you will not stand in my way!"

"From what I have seen of her," said Edmund, "you will not take her alive. Now, where is my slave?"

Waller turned to one of his mistresses and bawled, "Get the creature!" She leapt up from the table and ran drunkenly into the back of the house.

"And as for you, Percy," said Waller, "I shall tell you this: I want your land. I shall give you a fair price for it. If you should ever sell it to anyone but me, you will regret it—I shall make you regret it."

"What do you want my land for?" said Percy. "You are only manager here."

Waller only scowled again. Edmund realized then that he wanted the Percies' land for the very reason that he *was* only manager. He wanted to be a landowner; to rise into the class above him, though Edmund did not see how that class could reciprocally accept him.

Now Waller's mistress reappeared with another black woman. Her clothing, like Janetta's, was barely enough to cover her nakedness, consisting of a coarse gray material that looked like nothing so much as a threadbare sailcloth, crudely cut and sewn to fit her body. In her person she was strikingly ugly, though she was not as thin as she might have been had she not worked in the kitchen. She shuffled along as best she could, hampered by a pair of leg cuffs connected by an iron bar.

"Take these shackles off," Edmund said to Waller.

"They are *your* shackles," said Waller.

"I do not care whose they are," said Edmund. "Take them off at once."

"I don't have the keys," said Waller. "You do, remember? My overseer gave them to you today."

The keys were of course back at the house. Edmund shook his head in disgust and turned to the woman. "I am

Mr. Percy," he said. "I am your new master. Come with me and I will take you back to your husband."

The sudden flood of bewildered hope in the woman's features was pitiful to see. She slunk as rapidly as she could down the side of the room and got behind Edmund, so that Waller could not reach her.

"Come along then," said Edmund. He went out of the house. The woman hurried along as best she could behind him.

Waller came to the door and said, "I shall give you five minutes to get off my property, Percy, and then I shall loose my dogs."

"Do so at your peril," retorted Edmund. Despite his bravado, he wished he had brought his gun.

He made his way down the lane again. The woman followed along behind him as rapidly as she could, staggering in the ruts. He could see that the shackles were quite painful to her, and he had to halt several times to help her up when she fell. The dogs barked continuously behind them, until they were about halfway down the lane, and then the yapping stopped abruptly. It was another ominous silence. Men's voices carried to Edmund on the light breeze, and he guessed that Waller and the overseer were loosing the dogs.

"Here," said Edmund. He turned to the woman and picked her up like a child, setting her on his shoulder. She gave a little cry and clung to his wrist and his shirt; but now they made much better progress. She smelled like old kitchen grease, but he might have expected worse, considering the conditions under which she had probably been living.

At the end of the lane the dogs caught up with them. Perhaps Edmund was now far enough from the house that the curs did not dare attack; or perhaps, like Waller, they were mere bullies without the courage to do so; or perhaps the sight of this strange double-headed giant frightened them; but in any case, they only tagged along behind Edmund for a few hundred yards, barking and snarling.

And so Edmund brought Johnny's wife, Betty by name, back to the Percies' plantation, riding on his shoulder. The slaves could not have been more utterly astonished. Edmund managed to get the shackles off, and the men summoned up the courage to carry Johnny into his own cabin, where Betty tended him.

The word went out that Edmund had faced down Waller in his own lair. His slaves told other slaves, and those slaves told their masters; and the tale doubtless grew in the telling. By the time Edmund went up to the nearest church, on the following Sunday, three days later, all of Antigua had heard of him.

Chapter 7

> As an episcopalian myself, I feel sorry that the Church of England should have been less forward some years ago in their labor of love. True it is there has been, from the time these missionaries first came to the island, up to the present, a great number of churches and parsons. But of these, few, I am sorry to say, practised the pure doctrine they pretended to preach; indeed, many openly denied by their lives what they taught with their lips: their motto was—"Do as I say, not as I act"; which conduct, although it ought not to make religion less respected, has in a great measure, a tendency to that effect among all classes.
>
> —*Antigua and the Antiguans*

Johnny survived the night, and even showed some improvement. The strange woman in the mill came down the hill first thing in the morning to examine him—and, as Edmund thought, to avail herself of the breakfast the slaves were cooking. The men showed the same fear of her by day, barely repressing the inclination to run from the sight of her as she approached their fire. When he took her into Johnny's cabin, Betty cowered in the corner, terrified.

She knelt by the man. He shied from her, trying to inch away across the floor, but his leg was too painful to move.

"It is better," she said.

"Do you think so?" said Edmund. He was not sure he saw a difference.

"Yes. He is still alive; that is one sign it is better."

"I suppose. Well, the credit must go to you, and to whatever medicine you gave him."

She looked up at him skeptically. "That is generous of you, White Edmund," she said.

"How so?"

"To give a slave the credit she deserves. What white man ever did that?"

"I am sorry that such a man as Waller has shaped your opinions of my kind."

"Oh, it is not just Waller. You are all like that."

"I hope to God I am not like Waller! And you are wrong; there are good and charitable people among my kind."

"Ah," she said, again skeptically.

She looked back at Johnny's leg. "I shall put more salve on it," she said. "Then we must wait and see.—Betty is taking care of him?"

"Yes."

She looked curiously at Betty. "Where was she last night when I came down here?" Then, before Edmund could answer, she spoke directly to Betty: "You were afraid, were you? You ran away when Janetta came?"

"No, no, Missy Janetta," said Betty fearfully. "I was at Waller's. Massa come, late at night, bring me home from Waller's."

Janetta looked sharply at Edmund. "You went to Waller's last night?" she said.

"Yes. I did not learn until late that he had neglected to turn Betty over to us; so I went and demanded her of him."

Her eyes were wide. "And he did not have his drivers beat you? He did not turn his dogs loose on you?"

"He turned his dogs loose only belatedly, as we were leaving. They did not attack us.—As for having me beaten, I should like to have seen him try it."

For a minute Janetta did not speak, contemplating him with a curious expression he could not read. Then she looked back at Betty and asked her something about Waller in terms that Edmund did not understand. Betty shook her head to indicate no.

"You were lucky, then," Janetta told her then. "I suppose it is lucky to be born ugly, if you are a slave."

"Yes, Missy Janetta," agreed Betty meekly. Then, for what reason Edmund did not know, or perhaps as a prideful boast to show that despite her ugliness, she was of some importance in the world, she said, "Massa carry me home on his shoulder."

When she heard this, Janetta stared at Edmund.

"She was shackled," said Edmund.

Janetta shook her head in grim wonder.

"Ah," said Edmund. "I am pleased I have surprised you."

"Surprise me all you like," she said. "You shall never break me; you shall never make me respect you—*white man.*" She took up the jar of salve and pulled off the stopper. Without another look at Edmund she began applying it, working again from the man's toes toward his groin. When she reached his genitals and pushed his testicles out of the way, Betty leapt up with an unreasoning cry of protest. Perhaps she thought this witch would make her husband sterile or impotent—that was all Edmund could guess. Janetta turned on her with something like a snarl.

"Shut your mouth!" she said. "If it were not for me, you would not have a husband now!"

Betty literally collapsed into the corner again, sitting on her heels and watching anxiously in silence.

Before Janetta returned to the windmill, Edmund gave her some provisions. She took them without a word of thanks—even, he thought, with some scorn—but she took them all the same.

⌛⌛⌛⌛⌛

The story of Betty's rescue reached Mr. Duckworth's plantation first of all, as Edmund discovered when he went to borrow his neighbor's wagon. It was his first experience with the grapevine that carried information on the little island, and it impressed him; for he knew it would carry ill news of him as readily as good. Mr. Duckworth was very curious about what had happened, but as they were both too busy to spend long in conversation, he made Edmund promise to come to dinner on the next afternoon and tell him the story then.

Edmund learned from him with what magistrate he should speak concerning his difficulty with his unwanted tenant, and on his way into town he stopped at the estate of this official, one Mr. Morgette, only to find he was not at home. The magistrate had a secretary, however, a mulatto freeman, who recorded Edmund's name and promised to send him a note when he had arranged an hour and day that would suit his employer.

Edmund had left the slaves hard at work on their personal gardens; he felt they could be trusted to employ themselves usefully on something of such great private interest to themselves. He took only Obah along with him, though he could see that the fellow was loathe to leave his garden. He understood it was the custom for slaves to grow their own food, and he was glad of it, for it would greatly reduce the charges on the plantation; but he did not see how they could be expected to work hard day after day without meat, which he assumed he would have to provide, at least until they could raise pigs and chickens of their own.

His initial purchases were extensive, as was to be expected. He had located a serviceable wagon in one of the barns, so he did not need to buy one; but he soon became the owner of two mules and a strong and rather ornery horse. Over the next few weeks he also acquired a few head of cattle, some goats, a litter of pigs, and some chickens, of which last he gave each of his slaves one hen. On this day, he bought more dry provisions and some household goods; he replaced the foodstuffs brought by Mr. Duckworth; and he put in an order for new cane stock to be delivered the first of the week.

He also bought new woolen jackets and new trousers of linen cloth for the men, and for Betty a woolen wrapper and linen petticoat—that is, per the use of the word in his time, not an undergarment, but a proper skirt. He had already been intending to buy them new clothing, but Mr. Duckworth had told him that the law not only required him to do so, but stated the precise garments that should be supplied; and he fulfilled the requirements of the law exactly. He thought about buying similar dress for Janetta, but his instinct told him it would not be wise to involve himself with her even to that extent. The jubilation of the slaves of Canebrake when he handed out these rough garments was truly pathetic to behold.

The following day was a Saturday. By long tradition the slaves of Antigua were allowed not only the Sabbath to rest, but a half-day off from field work on the Saturday before. It was not actually much of a holiday, since they must perforce use that time to cultivate the gardens that supported them. Edmund could have argued that his men had had time off already; but he felt it would be wrong to do so. Instead he put the men to work in the morning preparing the fields for the new stock, and in the afternoon, when they were at leisure, he went over to Mr. Duckworth's for dinner, as had been arranged earlier.

The estate of a prosperous Quaker suggests an inherent moral paradox. Mr. Duckworth's establishment was no exception. On his way to dinner, Edmund walked up a lane past acres of cane worth vast sums in sugar, a product in complete ignorance of which the people of Europe had lived for millennia without any detriment to themselves—in other words, past fields that fed an unnecessary, even a luxurious, taste. So much for the vaunted simplicity of the sect, he thought.

The Quaker's home, which was in absolutely perfect repair, was large, well-situated, and well-lit by dozens of windows let into the stone walls. The roof was made of imported clay tiles. The barns, sugar-boiling houses, and other outbuildings were likewise stone and likewise in immaculate condition, laid out with the view to efficiency, and thus adjoining the five squat mills that ground the cane—one wind powered and four animal powered. The slave quarters, which were extensive, were far better dwellings than most of the hovels of the poor Edmund had seen in England.

And yet Edmund could not help reflecting that all of this prosperity was created by the labor of men and women in bondage; and there was in that fact something vile and sinful that was all at odds with the profession of any Christian religion, particularly one so subtly righteous as he had always found the Society of Friends to be. He was troubled; and the sight of Mr. Duckworth's many slaves, though they were evidently well-fed and relatively cleanly dressed, did nothing to ease his concerns.

A black servant admitted him to the house and showed him into the parlor where Mr. Duckworth and his family were awaiting him. Mr. Duckworth greeted him with manifest pleasure and introduced him to his wife and two daughters. The wife was, like Mr. Duckworth, in her mid-forties; the daughters were close to Edmund's age. The names of the three women were Hannah, Ruth, and Miriam; but he could never thereafter remember which was which; though his failure to do so hardly mattered, as he called the lady of the house "Mrs. Duckworth," and never had occasion to speak to the daughters. After the briefest of introductions, they all sat to await the summons for the meal, the women taking up their work again.

In some respects, Edmund could have thought himself back at home in England. The sight of the three female heads bent over their needles and thread was soothing. But he soon saw that they were engaged in darning worn socks and mending undergarments, an occupation that at home would not have been considered seemly in company. Their dresses, too, were identically made of a plain gray stuff, and on that ground alone would have been repugnant to the average British female, even if they had not been made to an antiquated pattern. Every strand of hair on their heads was covered by a plain white cap—the frivolity of not even one curl had been allowed to slip into sight. The women themselves were utterly unlike the lively women of his own class—they said nothing, and though they listened to the speech of the men, they either were not interested in joining it, or considered it improper to do so. Mrs. Duckworth voiced an occasional opinion, when called upon by her husband, whom she thee'd in Quaker fashion; but from the two young women he heard nothing the entire afternoon, aside from a few words addressed to the household servants.

It is pleasing to feel one captures the attention of others, and irritating to find that others, particularly those of the opposite sex, take no interest in one; and Edmund felt that rather than being studied and appreciated by Mr. Duckworth's daughters for his personal qualities, he was written off as an infidel. They were not just indifferent to him; they both seemed resolutely determined to take absolutely no notice of him.

The very furnishings of the room were as sparse as the conversation. They consisted of a plain table and a half-dozen straight-backed chairs on a bare wooden floor. The only books in evidence were the Bible, a *Life of Fox*, some very well-worn tracts, and a few battered agricultural journals that looked as though they had been rescued from a rubbish heap.

For this drear sparseness of his surroundings, Edmund could console himself with the company of his host, who was a genuinely likeable man. The conversation started with Mr. Duckworth's request to hear of his nighttime visit to Waller's, a tale that Edmund told in a straightforward fashion.

"It was a bold thing to do," said Mr. Duckworth, when Edmund was finished. "But I think it was well to start off on that footing with the fellow. Let him know you will not suffer his encroachments.—How about that man of yours with the bad leg?"

"He continues to improve."

"Then you prevailed upon Dr. Mann to attend him?"

"No; I never sent to the doctor again. Waller's daughter seemed to have effected a commencement of a cure; and as I knew the doctor would want to do the exact reverse of her treatment, if only out of sheer pride in his profession, I thought it best to leave well enough alone."

"Very wise of you, Mr. Percy," said Mr. Duckworth with a smile. "And what do you think of Waller's daughter?"

"A remarkable creature!"

"Is she not? I wondered what you would think. As strange a being as ever God allowed to walk the earth."

"What is the hold she has over the men? It is striking to see them universally in awe of a mere half-fed slip of a girl."

"I do not know, though I have seen the effect of which you speak. It is a consequence of her reputation as a sorceress, clearly; though how she earned it, I could not say; and I think it is probably better not to ask. You will find, Mr. Percy, that these blacks have an entire culture that is invisible to us, with its own laws and principalities.—Did you have any success in your discussion about her with Mr. Morgette?"

"He was not at home. I expect I shall see him the first of the week."

"Well, I do not know what satisfaction you will get of him. It is not just that he is as arrant a Deist as you could find anywhere, despite his *pro forma* church-going. It is rather that he is a magistrate to the hilt; he will likely tell you that it is beholden upon you to seize the woman and deliver her up to Waller; and I would not be surprised if there were some antiquated law on the books that stipulates as much. There were many cruel laws regarding slaves here in Antigua, and not so very long ago. I am constantly afraid of running afoul of them, merely in trying to treat my slaves well and allow them as much dignity as I can."

"If it would not be impertinent, Mr. Duckworth," said Edmund, "perhaps you could explain to me your thoughts on reconciling the keeping of slaves with our Christian duty.

What of 'Thou shalt love thy neighbor as thy self'? How is that possible if we keep these people as our slaves?"

"Why," said Mr. Duckworth, "we can love them as our human brethren even if they are slaves. When you are in England, do you not keep servants?"

"Yes, but—"

"These are only servants to us. They have the name of slaves, but that is a legal fiction. I know that their souls belong to our Maker, not to me. My love for them is as Christ enjoined it: I see to the welfare of their bodies, I teach them to read so that they can study the truths of the Christian religion, and I lead them in worship on the Sabbath. And far better off they are for my love, I can tell you that—as a fact, and not as a boast. Compare them to the poor wretches Mr. Waller deposited on your doorstep the other day ."

"Mr. Duckworth, I honor and respect your intentions and your goodness. The material well-being of your slaves is evident. But it seems to me that your reasoning can be overturned by this one simple test: Would you trade places with them?"

Mr. Duckworth laughed heartily, though Edmund had spoken very much in earnest.

"I think I have made my point," said Edmund.

"Not at all," said Mr. Duckworth. "I would not willingly trade places with a slave, or with a servant of your father, either. How is that to the point? As I see it, I *am* a servant—a servant of Christ; and in caring for the slaves on my plantation, I serve my Master just as my slaves serve me."

"But with all due respect, sir, this is mere rhetoric, mere sophistry. The point I would make is that this system, slavery, denies to the children of God their freedom to live as they see fit—a freedom that is essential to the human being as created by God. You and I have that freedom, and we would not give it up, not even at the cost of our lives—or at least I can say as much for myself. How, then, can we cheerfully expect others to tolerate the same loss and lack? Does it not behoove us, if we are to love them as we love ourselves, to give them that freedom?"

Mr. Duckworth only laughed, shaking his head.

"Do you not find this system repugnant, sir?" said Edmund. "That is all that I ask; for I do myself, and am having trouble reconciling myself to the necessity of participating in it."

"Then you have even greater trouble ahead of you," said Mr. Duckworth, "for you cannot run the plantation you have with the small number of slaves remaining to you. You will have to purchase more; you will have to enter into the market. At the very least you will have to rent them; and it is not so easy to rent them now, since the law against importation was passed."

"But was it not run with this number before?"

Mr. Duckworth shook his head, smiling at Edmund's ignorance. "Not with twice as many. They have been running away, one after another, for several years now, and a great many left after your manager absconded."

"Where could they run to?"

"To St. John's, and sometimes to other islands."

"And they can do so with impunity?"

"Who can identify them? It is not so easy as you think. There are so many more blacks than whites here—some three thousand whites, and twelve times as many blacks. We can by no means keep track of them all."

"Well, how many field hands would I need, would you say, sir, to make the plantation produce a profit?"

"The rule of thumb is a slave for every two acres."

Edmund was aghast. "Dear God!" he exclaimed. "If that is so, I shall never succeed."

"Not unless you enter the slave market. Not unless you put your cash down on the barrelhead and purchase more human flesh; or, as I said, rent it. You had better reconcile yourself to that."

"But are you sure of this rule you mention? Is it borne out by your experience?"

"Indeed it is. Yours is not a large plantation, true. Yours is a one-mill, and mine is a five. Though I do not know your exact acreage offhand, the number of mills we each have is some measure of their respective sizes. I have two hundred slaves, and when we are cutting and boiling sugar, I could wish I had more. I do not see how you can get by with fewer than forty men, and all good workers."

"I shall have to plant less acreage," said Edmund.

"That will hardly do, I think. The place will consume your profits. You do not begin to make much money in this business until you begin to grow cane on a large scale. As cheap as slave labor is, it still costs something.—But do not mistake me, neighbor. I wish you the very best of success, and I shall help you in any way I can. I am very pleased to have such a neighbor as thee—as you. From what I have seen of you, I would just as soon you stayed in Antigua and never resorted to an agent. These managers are so often coarse fellows—you have seen Waller, and on his home ground. I think you know what I mean. You may take him as a fair specimen of the breed. Can you not convince your father to give or sell you the property here? You could make yourself a living. I myself was a younger son; I know how it is."

At the mere thought of remaining in this foreign land Edmund's heart sank within him, and his face must have showed it, for Mr. Duckworth immediately added, "Well, no need to think of that quite yet. See how you like living here. When you get used to it, I think you will like it. It is a beautiful place, and the living is not hard."

Unless you are a slave, thought Edmund; but he did not say anything.

"Of course," said Mr. Duckworth, "you may decide you do not like the place, or may find the plantation unwieldy to run within the limits you set yourself. In short, you may wish to sell. And if you do, I would be glad of the chance to make you the first offer."

"You are already too late for that," said Edmund. "Waller has already said the same."

"I am not surprised. He wants to set up as an owner here. I am sure he has skimmed enough money off the operation he manages to pay you something down. But I can pay you the whole amount in cash, or pay on your London banker, which would be safer. I would purchase the place lock, stock, and barrel, slaves and all."

"Well, I shall keep your offer in mind, Mr. Duckworth. You may be assured I shall broach the subject to you a lifetime before I ever do so to Waller."

Mr. Duckworth seemed satisfied with this. After a lull in the conversation he said, in what seemed to Edmund to be a nonsequitur, "I have a tract." For a moment Edmund did not know if the man was referring to a tract of land or one of the pamphlets on the table; but as he continued, it became clear he meant the latter. "Would you be willing to read it?" he said. "I would be pleased to discuss it with you. Your thoughts, as a student of Christian theology, would be very worthwhile."

"Ah, you mean to convert me," said Edmund, with an attempt at a smile.

"I would not mind doing so, true; but no—I mean what I say. A good discussion is one of the great joys of life; and you will not find me much of a student of your pagan philosophers, so if we are to discuss anything of weight, it must be our own Christian beliefs."

"Believe me, sir, I find myself so estranged here from everything I ever knew that I am clinging fast to my religion. I should not enjoy hearing it questioned at this time in my life."

"Well, I meant no offense."

"None taken, Mr. Duckworth."

Edmund wondered suddenly if his neighbor had a plan to make him a Quaker and marry one of his daughters off to him. The joining of their two estates, even in an informal way, would probably greatly increase the profit of both through the benefit of their shared labor. He looked again at the two candidates and felt a shudder of repulsion. It was not their appearance that deterred him. Though they looked very severe in their gray gowns and white caps, they were not by any means homely; rather, it was the apparent dullness of their spirits. They looked as if they had never felt a powerful emotion in their lives; and Edmund, as a child of his age, was a great respecter of passion, and guessed nothing could possibly be so insipid as to be married to such a partner.

To counteract this possible intention in his host, he turned the topic to his own future plans. He spoke, rather more expansively than he might otherwise, of his desire to become a clergyman in the countryside. Mr. Duckworth's interest in agriculture also led naturally into a discussion of Brackensom, and the improvements there, insofar as Edmund understood them. Mr. Duckworth drew him out to speak of his family, and he found himself talking of his father and Christopher; of his mother and Alex and how they had been lost; and even of his two aunts and their very different respective characters. Mr. Duckworth was curious about it all. He seemed the kind of person who would recall every detail he was hearing; and in fact on later occasions, he asked Edmund for news of his father and brother and aunts by name, and seemed to add whatever information Edmund offered to the store he had already laid up in his memory.

At length the black servant entered again and announced that dinner was ready. The remainder of the conversation that afternoon was exclusively about the planting and cultivation of sugar cane; and Mr. Duckworth and Edmund continued to be the sole participants in it.

⌛⌛⌛⌛⌛

The next day Edmund gathered the slaves in the sugar boiling shed and held a form of worship service. It was in every respect like a proper service, though without the sanction of the church. His discourse consisted of an explanation of

Christian beliefs and practices at a very basic level. For the most part his audience merely tolerated the ritual and the sermon; it was only when he was explaining the Christian principles of doing unto others as you would have them do unto you that they became interested, or rather, curious and puzzled. The news that there was life after death seemed very well known to them, and they actually looked as if they wanted to correct Edmund on certain points of information in that regard.

After an hour of this he felt like an idiot. He realized he had accomplished nothing, and yet he did not know how to do any of it differently. He could only hope that repeated encounters with religion would wake an interest in them; but he thought he should perhaps privately pray for some guidance toward a more effective way of getting the Gospel across.

Before the services, when the woman from the mill was in attendance on Johnny, Edmund had specifically invited her to attend. She had paused in her work and given him a stare of withering contempt, and the slaves who were standing nearby laughed—apparently at the idea that she would attend a Christian service. He spoke no further of the matter to her; he only paid her for her care of Johnny with some food, which she ate immediately, with wolfish hunger; and then he saw her slip off through the canefields on some errand of her own. He gathered from what the slaves said that she made a little money or payment in kind by casting spells and healing. He pitied her, both for her unsociability and her ignorance; and because he remembered what Mr. Duckworth had said about the seriousness with which witchcraft was viewed by the authorities.

A little before ten o'clock he rode his new horse up to the little parish church not far from Canebrake. The service was appalling—a perfunctory reading that consisted largely of incomprehensible mumbling. The rector was, if Edmund was not mistaken, somewhat inebriated, perhaps from his drinking on the previous evening. The congregation was merely doing its duty in attending and seemed to hope for nothing more; that obligation done, they stood outside the church for fully a half-hour, socializing in the blazing sun, though even the most demure of the womenfolk was soon damp with perspiration. This social time was clearly the reward that enabled them to endure the travesty of the service.

There was great curiosity about Edmund as a newcomer, though it was an awkward situation, as he had no one to introduce him. Fortunately, one gentleman singled him out immediately and introduced himself as the Mr. Morgette he had been seeking on Friday. He was a distinguished-looking man of about fifty, with a very beautiful wife and daughter in tow, and his manners were affable. "I went to school with your father," he told Edmund almost at once.

"Is that so, sir?"

"Yes; I have known for years that he owned Canebrake, though of course we never saw a member of the family here. I was the one who communicated with him when the manager eloped with the cash."

"Ah, it was to you that we owe that service. Then let me thank you very much for your care of an old connection."

"Of course, we did not know each other well at the time; but one remembers old schoolfellows better than the man one has met two days ago; and I have always kept an eye on Canebrake because of my acquaintance with Percy in the old days."

"You must introduce us, Papa," prompted his daughter, who was standing somewhat behind him with her mother.

Mr. Morgette proved himself eager to do so once he was reminded. His wife and daughter were respectively about thirty-five and eighteen years of age, and so alike in looks that Edmund had no doubt they were often mistaken for sisters—indeed, they were identical but for that certain *je ne sais quoi* that gives the beauty of an older woman an incontestable advantage over that of a girl.

"We must have Mr. Percy to dinner this week, Mr. Morgette," said the wife.

"Absolutely, Papa," said the daughter. "You must invite him; newcomers to our neighborhood are so rare; and Mr. Percy can tell us all the doings at home."

"Mr. Percy is coming to see me on business—I think it is tomorrow, is it not?" said Mr. Morgette.

"At two o'clock, sir," said Edmund.

"Well, can you not stay for dinner, then?" suggested Mr. Morgette.

"I would be delighted to do so, sir," said Edmund, though he wondered whether his slaves would do any work at all if he were not there to compel them.

Mr. Morgette soon introduced him to a half-dozen other gentlemen in the congregation, and these to their wives and sons and daughters. They took an enormous interest in him; he saw that to them he was redolent of England, and though from the way some of them spoke he could tell that they would never return there, or had never even been there, still it represented a sacred home to them, and a possible refuge should disaster strike them in this far outpost of civilization. He took the opportunity to inquire whether these planters might know of any competent manager for the estate, and though some gave it serious thought, others simply laughed. "I am sorry, Mr. Percy," said one. "If you want to make sure nothing goes awry here, you must stay. That is what we have found, and that is what we are all doing here. Many of us intend to retire to England when we have made our fortunes; but we have no illusion that we can do so before that: we know perfectly well that we might have the same problem you had at Canebrake."

This talk was very discouraging to him; it suggested that his exile here was to be extremely lengthy.

⌛⌛⌛⌛⌛

Mr. Morgette's estate was probably typical of the great Antiguan plantation at that time, certainly more so than Mr. Duckworth's. He possessed hundreds of slaves, five mills, an endless sugar-boiling house, and outbuildings of every description. The slave quarters were in disrepair, but the main house might well have graced a modest estate in England: it was stone-built, slate-roofed, and surrounded by handsome terraces accessed from within by Venetian windows and from without by elegant stonework steps. When Edmund entered, he heard the playing of a pianoforte in a distant room, a sound that brought him a pang of homesickness.

He conducted his business with Mr. Morgette before dinner. The magistrate saw him in a large office, shuttered against the afternoon sun, but still open to a fair breeze that was blowing from the northeast.

"Now, young man," said Mr. Morgette pleasantly, after he had greeted Edmund, shook his hand, and bid him seat himself, "what can I do for you?"

"You can bear with me, sir," said Edmund, "as I present to you a rather perplexing question."

"Ah," said Mr. Morgette.

"You are acquainted with this neighbor of mine, Mr. Waller."

Mr. Morgette looked irritated. "Not acquainted, no, sir; Mr. Waller is no acquaintance of mine."

"Forgive me—I phrased that inaptly. I ought to have said that you, as magistrate, must have the unfortunate duty to have taken notice of this fellow in your parish."

Mr. Morgette looked relieved. "That is a much better way of describing it," he said.

"Well, I understand this Waller fellow has a daughter."

Mr. Morgette now appeared agitated and uncomfortable. "Really, Mr. Percy," he said, "do we have to talk of such things? I always think that gentlemen ought to keep the tone of their conversation as high as possible."

"Forgive me, sir—I must beg your forgiveness; but I do not know how to explain my difficulty unless I lay out certain facts—facts as unpleasant, or I might even say, as *disgusting*, for me to utter as for you to hear."

"Oh! Very well, then," said Mr. Morgette, sitting back nervously in his chair. "Yes, we all know this fellow Waller had a mulatto mistress and got a child on her."

"A mulatto?" repeated Edmund. He recalled that Duckworth had told him this; but it struck him now that none of the women he had seen at Waller's house had been mulattos.

"Yes. He bought her in Jamaica, I believe. I never met her, of course; but I believe she had been given an education—had read literature, and could sing, as well as play the pianoforte. He has pretensions, you know, this Waller fellow. He thought he could *buy* himself a refined wife!"

"Did he marry her, then?"

Mr. Morgette was horrified. "Good God, no, Mr. Percy!"

Edmund had apparently committed a terrible faux pas even suggesting such a thing, and he spoke on to cover it. "She is no longer with him?" he asked.

"No. She died some years ago—I think it would be about ten years or so. There was some question at the time as to whether Waller had not killed her in a drunken rage; which is of course against the law here in Antigua—despite what people at home erroneously believe about the way we treat our slaves. I would have seen him punished for it, but we could not get a witness, or any proof, or even the most circumstantial of evidence. And it may in fact have been that she killed herself. She fell—or leapt—headfirst from one of the upper windows of his house—it was that kind of thing. One could not blame such a creature for taking her own life to escape such a man."

"No," agreed Edmund. "At any rate, this daughter is now I know not what age, perhaps two- or three-and-twenty, but certainly grown; and has fled from Waller and taken refuge in my sugar mill."

"Well, you must evict her," said Mr. Morgette immediately. "You must send her back to Waller. She is his chattel—his personal property."

This was not the answer Edmund had wanted to hear. "Well," he said, "is she in fact his? I believe Waller does not own the plantation—"

"No, of course he does not; Lord Vanstoke-Raynham does. But the mulatto is not his lordship's property; she is Waller's."

"Pardon me for asking, sir, but is that a certain fact?"

"Oh, yes; I have requested every owner or renter of slaves within my jurisdiction to report their chattel to me; and I have examined the register with great care. It has proven a very useful practice; I mean to recommend it to the assembly to be enacted as law."

This seemed conclusive; Edmund tried another tack. "Cannot his lordship be appealed to on the grounds that this fellow is a despicable scoundrel?"

"Oh, I hardly think so, Mr. Percy," said Mr. Morgette somewhat scornfully. "His lordship can hardly want to know what Waller does, as long as the man remits his profits. His lordship has better things to do. I suppose, yes—if he were to do something particularly heinous; but I would not think you could represent the current situation as extraordinary enough for Lord Vanstoke-Raynham's secretary to trouble him with it."

"Well, let us leave that possibility aside then," said Edmund.

"Let us leave the whole question aside, if you would."

"That I cannot yet do. I am afraid I must venture on a truly indelicate topic here, Mr. Morgette."

"Any topic that concerns Waller will revolt me. He is a disgrace to the parish. So you can hardly distress me more than you have already."

"The difficulty is that if I send this mulatto back to Waller—back to her father, sir—she will probably be incestuously violated by him."

Mr. Morgette was staggered. "Sir!" he exclaimed. "What are you saying? Think of what you are saying! Do not give Waller a means to accuse you of defamation!"

"I only report what the mulatto herself has expressed to me as her fear—and quite convincingly, I might add. The probability of what she says is supported by the testimony of my other abutting neighbor, Mr. Duckworth; who, though he is a dissenter, is nonetheless honest, so far as I can tell."

"Oh, well," said Mr. Morgette in relief, "if it is only what the mulatto tells you, it is nothing. She is widely known to be mad. As for this Mr. Duckworth fellow, he is pleasant enough for a *Quaker*—believe me, I do appreciate it that he does not pepper me with his thees the way others of his sect do—but he is known to be very soft on his negroes, ruinously soft; he sets a very bad example, and makes the slaves of others grumble and feel discontented."

"I have spoken with this mulatto myself," said Edmund, "and though I saw a very violent grief and despair, I did not see persuasive madness. And from my encounter with Waller, I would guess that what she says is possible."

"Oh, come, come, Mr. Percy! We live in an age where such things simply are not done! You have been reading your Bible too much—what is it, Lot or one of those old fellows who got involved in that kind of unspeakable thing? That is the trouble with revelation; it comes in the form of such nasty parables."

"But I suppose my question is, sir, is there no solution to this difficulty? Can you not, as magistrate, order Waller to sell the mulatto to the parish, and then can the parish not find a better master for her elsewhere, preferably in some other island?"

"Oh, Mr. Percy," cried Mr. Morgette, actually laughing at him now, "this is really too fanciful! I could find no grounds for doing anything of the kind. There is no recourse—you must evict her—in fact, you are required by law to seize her and turn her over to her legal owner; or if you are incapable of that, you are required to allow him free access to your property to seize her himself. There are in fact penalties incumbent on him if he does not do so, and of course on you if you do not allow it. This is a serious situation, Mr. Percy; I cannot emphasize that enough."

Edmund was utterly baffled; but he at least saw clearly that the law was not going to help this poor woman, and that he might very well run afoul of it if he himself assisted her.

"Well," he said, "I thank you for clarifying these matters for me."

"Yes," said Mr. Morgette, "and now that you know what your duty is under the law, I have no doubt you will do it.—Was there any other question you had for me?"

"No, sir."

"Then I propose we go join the ladies before dinner."

Having been, as he saw it, extremely useful in the matter, Mr. Morgette rose and led Edmund to the ladies' sitting room.

They spent the remaining time before dinner in this place, a very commodious parlor on the north side of the house, away from the sun and open to the breeze. When they entered, Mrs. Morgette was playing the pianoforte, and Miss Morgette was lolling on a sofa. The latter rose abruptly to her feet with undisguised interest when she saw Edmund, and immediately attached herself to him; so much so that at one point in the next half-hour Mr. Morgette actually attempted to intervene to allow Edmund an opportunity to talk with someone besides her. During this time Mrs. Morgette continued sitting at the pianoforte, though she did not go on playing; and, as it seemed to Edmund, regarded her daughter with a certain degree of jealousy, and a contemptuous look that said, "Be as flirtatious as you like; I could take him from you in an instant if I put my mind to it."

Edmund found the attentions of Miss Morgette even more unpleasant than the lack of interest he had met from Mr. Duckworth's daughters. It was clear that this young woman felt suffocated in the place she lived—stifled by her equally beautiful and more mature mother, by her overly attentive but dull father, and by the absence of society that might have offered distractions in England. She flirted at Edmund in the most ostentatious fashion—he had never before believed that women actually batted their eyelashes, and she literally squealed her approval of the opinions she requested of him—and she proved herself not only desperate for a change in her circumstances, but willing to do anything to effect it, even though, perhaps the saddest fact of all, she was too giddy to grasp what was required and to do it.

When he escaped from the place after dinner he found his spirits had descended another notch. The Morgettes were clearly among the best families in Antigua, and they had nothing to offer him in the way of society he might wish to seek out. As he walked home, he actually thought with some yearning of Canebrake and the business of planting, and resolved to immerse himself in it. At least the work on the land had a reality and authenticity of which the society of people like the Morgettes did not and never could partake.

Chapter 8

No! dear as freedom is, and in my heart's
Just estimation prized above all price,
I had much rather be myself the slave,
And wear the bonds, than fasten them on him.

—Cowper

When *Edmund* returned home from dinner that day, he found that no work had been done in his absence. He rounded up the men and reproached them, but in response received only sullen stares or undisguised indifference. He saw he would have to play overseer himself until he could find someone to act in that capacity, though he wondered whether he could find a man who would not prove too cruel in discharging his duties. He would have doubted it was possible to compel such men to work without cruelty, if he had not had Mr. Duckworth's example for it.

All in all, the situation was very puzzling to him. In England he had been a part of a very rigid system of masters and servants. He had occasionally seen recalcitrant underlings, though he had known of them only briefly, as they were always instantly let go. Employment was difficult to obtain, and, though Edmund was not fully aware of these economic realities, wages were barely enough to live on, so servants who found a position as good as Brackensom offered were slow to venture on open insubordination. The entire economy conduced to keep the poor in subordination to the rich; for the poor, in fact, life was a trap, a pit without exit, little better than the lot of these Antiguan slaves; though again, Edmund had never realized that it was so. There was also an elaborate hierarchy of which Edmund knew little, within the employment system itself, by which a housekeeper or head butler or shop owner or any master tyrannized over his or her immediate inferiors, and so on down the ranks.

That evening, sitting in the empty house by himself, he considered the slave system in its bare outlines and could not see why any of his men would work at all without the threat of starvation or beatings. As for himself, he knew one thing: it would be morally wrong for him to resort to such things. He was so brought up that he did not stint at browbeating them, or speaking to them sternly, for he did consider that he offered them some kind of employment and could expect some obedience on that score; but he would never order a man to be whipped. He would literally rather be whipped himself than do so. If his success depended on beating the men, he would declare himself a failure and report as much to his father.

As might have been expected, it did not take the slaves long to perceive this morality in him. His physical size and strength, as well as his natural traits of leadership, kept them obedient for a few days; but gradually they did less and less, wandering away in small groups to hide in the old cane when they could evade his notice, and taking advantage of even a momentary absence or distraction on his part to shirk their tasks. He turned away for a matter of seconds, and found some reclining full length on the ground when he turned back. The more they disobeyed, the more they saw he was not going to react with violence; and so the more they disobeyed.

Finally he went up to talk to Mr. Duckworth. His neighbor was more than happy to show him his own methods; they were, after all, intimately connected to his religious beliefs, and he openly suggested that they were successful because the underlying religion was successful. Mr. Duckworth's plantation was a kind of community of workers rather than a miniature slave state. The slaves knew exactly what they would receive—food, clothing, comfortable shelter, kindly treatment, regular leisure, respect for their marriages and families, even an opportunity to learn to read. For this they had to work; and they seemed to be to some extent resigned to that exchange. Edmund knew for a certainty that any of them would have preferred to be free, and still reproached Mr. Duckworth for participating in obstructing their freedom; but he had to admit that the evil was a lesser one than he understood was common elsewhere on the island. He took home this lesson, but he was not sure what to do with it.

On Friday, a little after he and the men had returned from the mid-day meal, discipline broke down altogether. He had sent two men to one of the sheds for some tools, and they did not come back; when he returned from summoning them, the rest of the men had sat down in the full sun in the field, laughing and chatting together, and did not rise when they saw him.

He called for silence, and they would not listen. He grew angry, and called for silence again; and this time there was something in his voice that made them attend him.

"What do you mean by this?" he said. "We must work; we must grow cane. I have explained this before. If this plantation fails, you will all be sold; and from what I have seen of this island, you will have a worse master."

They looked at him with complete indifference, and for the first time he realized in part what it must be like for them, to face only a life of slavery. How could they really care who beat them? Their true master was slavery, and what difference did it make what mask that monster wore? Why should they rise to their feet to work now to prevent their having a different overseer at some time in the unknown future?

"You, Obah," he said. "You know I have treated you well—as well as I can, considering the circumstances. Are you not ashamed to sit there without working?"

"Shamed, Massa? No, Massa. You good man, Massa. You no slabe ownah, you no oberseer. You nebber make us work. Bettah gib up, Massa. Go home."

"Go home? So that you can go work for Waller again?"

They looked uncomfortable at this thought, but they knew he was bluffing.

"You nebber sell us to Wallah," said Obah. "You Christian. Christians don' believe in dat."

"All I ask is that you think for yourselves. We must get on with this work if we are to make Canebrake productive again. Would you not rather live here than somewhere else?"

"I don' know, Massa," said Obah. "Obah gots hisse'f pretty li'l negro lady he like, ovah Bridgetown. Maybe he sees her agin ifin he gets a new Massa somewheah else."

The men laughed.

"But if we were successful here," said Edmund, "you could come to me and tell me about your lady friend, and I would see what I could do to buy her and make her your wife."

"Obah don' want no *wife,* Massa," said Obah, and the men laughed again.

Edmund would have tried to explain that he was talking about a general principle of cooperation and mutual respect; but he saw that they were determined not to understand the principle, and would have an answer for his every persuasion.

In desperation he said, "For the last time, I am telling you, I shall have to sell every last man jack of you if you do not work for me, and work as hard as you can. Are you with me, or are you against me? If you are with me, stand up and put your backs to the task; if you are against me, go back to your quarters and get out of my way."

To his complete astonishment a look of terror came over their faces and they instantly leapt bolt upright.

By God! he thought. *They are listening to reason after all! All it takes is a little desperation to convince them.*

"That is better," he said, surveying them with relief and satisfaction.

But as he did so, he realized they were not looking at him; they were still paying no attention to him. He turned about and found the woman from the mill standing about ten feet behind him.

She, too, paid no attention to him, or so it seemed. She came forward slowly and stopped beside him, looking at the men with an expression of pure contempt.

"*You stupid dogs,*" she said.

The effect of these three words on them was uncanny. Some raised their eyes to her, and even their hands, beseechingly; others looked away, and several actually shielded their faces with their hands as if her evil eye would blight them on the spot.

"*You stupid dogs,*" she said again.

One man actually began to whimper.

"Shut up!" she told him scornfully. She surveyed them now as Edmund had, but with ineffable loathing in her expression.

"Do you know why I hate you?" she said.

No one would dare attempt an answer.

"Because you are *stupid dogs!*" she cried furiously.

"Mis'ress—" Obah began.

"Shut up!" she cried again in a venomous tone. "You, Obah the fool—*you* should speak to me?"

He shook his head to indicate that he had no longer had any such aspiration.

She sneered at him. "And I thought you were the smart one here, Obah. I said to myself, if there is anyone who will see what is going on here, it is Obah! And now I see how wrong I was! Now I see that Obah is far, far stupider than I could have thought!"

"No, Mis'ress—"

"*Shut up!*" she shrieked.

Obah now joined most of the other men in hiding his face in his hands.

"I will say just this," she went on. "Just this—I will only say this, and I will only say it once. Where will you find a better master on this island?—Nowhere. Not even Mr. Duckworth would treat you so well. If you want to be one of Mr. Duckworth's little dogs, go—go live with Mr. Duckworth."

She suddenly punctuated her speech with a strange cry—whether a word or an inarticulate sound, Edmund did not know which—a kind of *aiee!* that made the men flinch in terror.

"I will tell you what you have here for a master," she said, pointing a finger at Edmund. "You have a *man*. Yes, a *man* for a master. I suppose I can hardly blame you for not recognizing him, for not knowing him when you see him; because you have never seen such a thing before. A man has a heart; a true man has a heart. And when he sees evil, his heart troubles his mind." She paused to spit furiously on the ground. "And I tell you stupid negroes," she continued, "I tell you—if you ever find such a master—*hold fast to him!* Once in a lifetime you will find a man—once in a lifetime. The rest are devils, all devils! We walk through hell, always we are walking through hell in this life, walking through the devils; so if you find one man, do not cast him aside!—You, Obah!"

"Yes, Miss Janetta?"

"Do you want to work for a devil?"

"No, Miss Janetta."

"Then don't be a fool."

"No, Miss Janetta."

She was silent for a minute, watching them tremble and cower before her. Edmund noticed how the sweat was standing out in beads along the edge of her brow, along her hairline, and how her dress was so damp that it clung to her slight figure.

"From now on," she said, "any man who disobeys the master *disobeys me.*"

Eager to show their compliance, they lowered their hands from their faces.

"Do you understand, Obah?" she said.

"Oh, yass, Miss Janetta!" said Obah. "I un'erstands!"

She picked out another slave, who had seemed to Edmund to be the least capable of the lot. "Azaz!" she said. "Do you understand what I say?"

"Obey de massa," said Azaz.

"And what happens if you don't?"

"Missy Janetta be angry," said Azaz.

Her eyes flickered over them coldly.

"Now," she said, "pick up your knives and get to work."

They obeyed her instantly, turning their energies on the stand of old dead cane that had to be cut down. In a few minutes they had made more progress against it than they had all the previous morning.

When they were hard at work, Janetta turned to Edmund. "What the hell are you doing?" she said to him.

He was taken aback, and though socially she was very much his subordinate, his natural politeness asserted itself in his surprised response. "Pardon me?" he said.

"I said, White Edmund, what the hell are you doing here? You must plant the cane stock in your barn before it dries out and dies. There is no point in cutting down this cane here until you have planted the new stock."

"But where can I plant it? There is no place but this old field."

"*That* was a canefield," she said, indicating a weedy expanse off to the west. "It would be simple to plow and harrow it. That is what you ought to be doing first."

He was taken aback. "Why did the men say nothing of this?" he protested. "I specifically asked Obah if he thought cutting this old cane was the next logical step."

"And he let you do it. Why should he care? Obah is stupid. He thinks it makes no difference if you succeed or fail. But maybe he will learn. I think he will learn, and the other men, too, when they have a chance to."

"Well, I had better take them off *this* field and put them to plowing that one."

"No," she said. "Let them work. Let them sweat. They deserve it, the stupid dogs. Let them cut out here for an hour. Then we will take three men off and we will get them plowing the other field."

She stepped forward and cried, "Faster! Faster, you dogs! Cut that cane!"

Incredibly, they seemed to redouble their efforts; the dead cane flew from their knives. Edmund had had no idea they could work so fast.

"Are you going to be my overseer?" he said to her then.

She looked at him sidelong at first from that darkened half of her face, and then turned her eyes toward him. Her features, with their peculiar marking, were all a puzzle to him.

"Yes," she said, as if she had not thought of it that way. "I will make these dogs work for you."

"I will not have any cruelty," he said. "I will not stand for it."

She smiled oddly. "What!" she said. "Ah, you mean no whips, no beatings, no chains. Very well. I have something they fear far more."

"What is that? Your *Obeah?* Your witchcraft?"

She looked at him coldly. "It is death to practice *Obeah,*" she said. "Or so your white brothers here have decreed. So do not speak of it."

"Very well," he said. "But it is not right to rely on superstition to frighten these men into doing what you want."

"Into doing what *you* want, you mean. And did you not try to rely on *your* superstitions to make them do what you want?—But do not worry, White Edmund. I will not interfere with the superstitions you are trying to teach them. Go ahead, make them all Christians. You will not lessen *my* power over them, not one little bit."

"Why are you doing this?" he asked. "I thought you were determined not to approve of me."

"I did not say that; I said you would never make me like you."

"Do you think I am trying to do so?"

She glared sourly at him. "Yes," she said. "I do think so. I think you want everyone to like you."

"I suppose I do, at least at first. Until I find they refuse to, for whatever reason. I think it is only natural to try to like others, and to prefer to be liked by them."

She shook her head. "You were not meant to own slaves then, White Edmund. Who would cut cane in the sun for ten hours a day out of anything but fear?"

"Love is stronger than fear," he said.

"Love!" she exclaimed. She spat on the ground. "Show me the slave who ever loved a master! That is a lie you whites make up to excuse your crimes against us."

"But why are you doing this?" he persisted. "You say you do not like me, and yet I am also certain that you are not afraid of me—or anyone else, for that matter."

"So long as you stay here," she said, "I have a place to live."

"Ah! Then this is to be a covenant between us, is that what you are thinking? You become indispensable to me, and I protect you?"

"You would protect me even if I did not help you," she said. "But you cannot protect me if you do not stay."

Now she gave him one last contemptuous look. "Go back to the house," she said in a tone of finality. "Do whatever you white men do when the slaves are busy working. I shall make sure the work gets done, and I shall do so better than any *man* you could hire."

⧗ ⧗ ⧗ ⧗ ⧗

He left her and went away, up on the hill where the windmill stood, which gave him a vantage over the plantation. He watched the men work from afar, and watched the little figure in the ragged dress that was in turn watching the men at work.

He was not sure what to think of this event. In one sense it was a godsend, an answer to many prayers—a way to make the plantation succeed without resorting to violence. But perhaps it was a worse form of coercion. If he asked Obah or Azaz whom they would rather obey, Janetta or that fellow Jones who worked for Waller, whom would they choose?

He hoped that this recourse would only be temporary—that as Janetta herself had said, the men would come to see some benefit for themselves in cooperating without the threat of *Obeah,* or whatever it was. But the larger question was not laid to rest; which was why they should want to cooperate within the slave system at all. Why should men, and women for that matter, want to work for the wealth and comfort of another, when all they got for it was a bare subsistence? How could that compensate them for the loss of dignity and freedom of will that slavery brought? The obvious answer was that they could not possibly want such a condition on such terms.

He had never confronted these issues before this past week in Antigua; and now he could see their application not only to the slave system, but also to the economic system of England. Men and women there were nominally free, but the vast mass of them essentially had no choice as to how to live their lives. They labored for him and his class. Indeed, if he and his class had not existed, the poor itself would not exist. With his wants and needs, and the servicing of them, he kept the poor in their poverty, just as the plantation owners kept the slaves in their slavery; at home the situation was only more entrenched, more cleverly disguised by tradition, by the lies that, as Janetta had said, the wealthy made up to excuse their crimes.

These thoughts did not come easily to him. Many emerged only as inarticulate feelings that later achieved their crystallization. But he knew his Bible well, and there was no question in his mind that Christ had enjoined an equality of wealth on his followers; and if Christians held fast to that truth, and did not shirk it, and applied it to the society they saw about them, the result must inevitably be that they wound up on this hill, looking down on the system from afar, and seeing its injustice.

And yet he, Christian though he wished to be, was caught in the meshes of his own life and family as well. He wanted to make this plantation work. How could he brutalize these men to fulfill that personal goal?

There was only one further answer to this further question. He must join them. He must make them his fellows, in both work and reward. He would labor as they labored; they would eat and rest as he ate and rested. He would make this plantation a miniature but mutual society that would set an example; an example that would be the first crack in the monolithic idol of slavery. Not even Mr. Duckworth condescended to get down off his horse and work beside his slaves—no, he had rationalized the need for his greater leisure and comfort as necessary to his leadership of the whole operation; and though Edmund did not doubt that there must be a leader, he far preferred the leadership of the captain who draws his sword and leads his men forward on foot to that of the general who stays behind the lines like a coward. He did not in that moment stop to think how the general who stays behind the lines is thus saved from being brought down by the enemy's bullet.

He went down the hill again to the place the men were working in the cane. Janetta saw him return with some surprise. He picked up one of the spare knives from the pile of tools. Then he waded into the cane alongside them and began to cut at the dry, coarse stalks, at first very clumsily and ineffectually.

After about ten minutes his heart was pounding and the sweat was pouring from every inch of his flesh. He paused for a moment to catch his breath, and it was then that he saw Janetta standing close by, watching him intently, with an unfathomable expression, partly puzzled, partly pleased.

As he looked at her, she turned and went to the pile of tools, where she picked up another knife; and then she, too, stepped up to the cane and began to cut. A shout went up from the men, and they grinned and laughed, though Edmund was not entirely sure why. He thought she might chastise them again, but she said nothing.

And so they all worked together in the blazing sun, master and slaves, alongside the strange woman who was herself, literally and figuratively, half master and half slave.

Chapter 9

horrendum et dictu video mirabile monstrum.
nam quae prima solo ruptis radicibus arbos
vellitur, huic atro liquuntur sanguine guttae
et terram tabo maculant.

I behold a ghastly omen, shocking even to tell: in the instant the bush is wrenched broken-rooted from the soil, gobs of black blood ooze from it and dabble the earth with gore.

—Vergil

E*dmund Percy,* youngest son of the Percies, of the estate of Brackensom in Surrey, now entered the time of his bondage in Egypt; or say, of the strange prologue to his life that would remake him.

It was not long before word of the odd doings at Canebrake were widely known; and he was not so effusively greeted by the parishioners after church on Sunday. People said he had become a slave to his slaves.

Mr. Morgette actually took him aside one day and said to him, "Mr. Percy, I really must speak with you. People are talking, you know, about how you work in the fields alongside your own negroes—work *like* one of your own negroes, in fact."

"I am short of hands, Mr. Morgette," said Edmund, having no illusion that he would ever be able to make Mr. Morgette understand the true reasons.

"How many negroes do you have?"

"Twenty, not counting the woman who keeps house for me."

"Ah, yes, I see the difficulty; Canebrake is far too large to run on twenty hands. But you must find another solution.

You must rent slaves elsewhere, if you cannot afford to purchase them."

Edmund had by this time learned that it was virtually impossible to rent slaves anymore, since the traffic in slaves had been quashed by Parliament, and Mr. Morgette knew that reality as well as he did.

"You must understand," continued Mr. Morgette, "that it demeans you as a gentleman to do this work. I cannot understand how you stoop to it."

"I have told my father that I shall repair the fortunes of Canebrake," said Edmund; "and I consider it a filial duty. I shall do so if I must effect it with the sweat of my own brow; and this seems to be the case."

"Yes, yes, I appreciate your fidelity to your family, and to your father especially. But in the long run, you know, it cannot help. It will harm the system we have here—it will make the blacks question the distinction between them and us, which is critical to maintaining our control over them. We do not want them thinking they are our equals, or we shall have another Haiti on our hands. You would not want to be responsible for any bloodshed, would you? Or, God forbid, for any successful insurrection? Think of me, in my position as father and husband, and as guardian of the law that protects other men's daughters and wives."

"Mr. Morgette, I cannot see how my resorting to the only option I have in order to accomplish the very necessary work of my plantation can lead to violence."

"But you do not know how our system works here," protested Mr. Morgette.

Oh yes I do, thought Edmund; but he said nothing.

"Now, look here," said Mr. Morgette, "does your father know what you are doing? I do not think he would approve."

"My father knows only that I am carrying out the commission he gave a grateful son, and he trusts me to do so to the best of my abilities."

"Really, Mr. Percy, there is such a thing as too much piety!"

"I am sorry that what I do offends you, Mr. Morgette, but I cannot see that I have any other choice."

"Now, look—look at it this way. How can you be invited into good company if you associate with slaves at their level? Why, I know men of our class who refuse to even touch a thing a slave has touched. We had a governor here who kept a pair of silver tongs with him at all times, in case he had to receive even so much as a letter from the hands of a black. Such gentlemen we have as do not deign to speak directly to a slave, but only to a white overseer. True, I am not so nice; I have very well-mannered black servants in my household, and as you know, I have a mulatto secretary, who does a splendid job. I do not look down on these creatures in the least. But others *are* fussy; and they will look down on you if you do not preserve a proper distinction between yourself and the blacks. You will not be invited to the balls in St. John, or to any of the good houses round about. Why, I fear that even Mrs. Morgette has begun to question whether you are good company for my daughter." Then he paused as another thought struck him. "I say, my daughter did not scare you off that time you had dinner with us, did she, Mr. Percy?"

"Of course not," Edmund lied boldly.

"Well, then, give over this silly business of acting like a black man, and come up to our house again for dinner."

"I am afraid that my duties are so compelling, sir, that I really cannot leave them. The business here in Antigua is poised on the brink of failure—I shall not disguise the seriousness of the situation."

"Are you thinking of selling out?" said Mr. Morgette with sudden and considerable interest.

"Not if I can possibly help it," said Edmund coldly. "And if it means I must work like a slave to prevent it, work like a slave I shall."

"I see you are a *very* stubborn man," said Mr. Morgette, who had great difficulty imagining how anyone could resist his logic. "But you know you cannot keep it up. It is brutal work. You are a white; you are a strong man, and a young man, but you are not fit for it. The heat is too much. These slaves—how long do they live at most? Thirty-five, forty years? The labor breaks them. You will be old before your time, or you will be weakened and succumb to fever."

"What you say is true," said Edmund. "But I hope someday to draw upon more labor, and divide the work among more hands, so that it will not be so punishing."

"Well," said Mr. Morgette, whose manner now also grew somewhat cold, "I am only telling you what people are saying. It is of course up to you to decide what to do. But if, in my capacity as magistrate, I think you are jeopardizing the safety of the whites in the island, I shall take further measures against you. I shall write to your father, at the very least."

Mr. Morgette was correct in his implicit suggestion that Edmund cared little for white society in the island. It was not that he was antisocial; certainly he was not used to holding society in contempt. In Antigua, just as at home, he made broad allowances for human peculiarity—even enjoyed oddity and idiosyncrasy. He would have found Mr. Morgette amusing had he himself been an idle traveler, visiting another clime. But he was not; he was a slaveholder and the manager of a plantation. When he was absent from the land, at church, or visiting Mr. Duckworth's, or buying supplies in town, he thought about Canebrake obsessively—wondered how the men were getting on in their work, whether there was some more efficient use of land or labor or time. In part his preoccupation was unconsciously modeled on that of his father, who had been obsessed with the improvement of the Brackensom estate almost to the point of neglecting the very family for whom he was supposed to be improving it. In part this fixation of his was, as he had explained to Mr. Morgette, the satisfying of a deep-held sense of filial obligation. His father had never failed him; he would not fail his father. But more than either of these, his preoccupation drew off his dream of starting a better way of life for the population of this place, a more Christian life.

He was not the first to have that dream. The Quakers and the Moravians had it as well, men and women who looked upon blacks as their equals in the eyes of God. But Edmund's dream was more radical, and as such, he kept it concealed as well as he could; it was more noble, and as such, less practical; and it had more of principle in it (for nothing is based absolutely on principle) and as such was disturbing even to those like Mr. Duckworth who were also trying to find a better way.

Not that he turned Canebrake into a commune. Neither he nor his slaves had ever seen anything but a hierarchical society. Betty was his cook and housemaid; the men called him master, and he called them by their first names, the only names they had; the men slept in their quarters, and he in the great house; he made the decisions and gave the orders, and they obeyed. True social equality was as unthinkable to him as anarchy, with which he would have equated it. Rather, he meant Canebrake to be more like Brackensom and less like the estate of men like Mr. Morgette—a place where men and women might choose to be subservient, but it would be a choice they made, for their own ultimate advantage.

It was significant that in his remonstrance Mr. Morgette had not mentioned Janetta. Certainly he knew of her working with the other slaves; but either he found the entire subject of her too disgusting to broach, or—what seemed most likely—he never for a minute assumed she was doing anything other than the work of an ordinary field hand.

And in fact, after that first day, Janetta had never needed to make a threat or assert her authority again. The men worked in absolute obedience to Edmund, never questioning him; though he did notice they were not as productive on those occasions when Janetta absented herself on one of her mysterious errands.

As it proved, he could never have accomplished anything without Janetta. She had witnessed the business of planting and harvesting sugar from an early age, and was both able and—more critically—willing to communicate it to him. Furthermore, from certain things she said, it seemed that she had worked as a very young woman, between the ages of twelve and fourteen, in the boiling house, and had acquired considerable skill in that operation.

The work of growing and harvesting sugar was brutal in the extreme. The plantation was portioned into areas called "pieces"; each of these pieces had to be cleared of the dead and dry standing cane that had gone to waste in the absence of the manager. Various planting holes were then dug by hand throughout this cleared piece, each a yard square and a foot deep, and cuttings from viable cane buried in the ground. Once a piece was planted in this way, the workers must go on to the next piece, the notion being that the cane would ripen in stages, facilitating an extended and thus more manageable harvest. As soon as a piece was planted, the weeds began sprouting in it, and they must all be eradicated, and constantly re-eradicated throughout the growing time. Vermin of all sorts attacked the cane, from insects to rodents to deer to birds, to say nothing of rusts and molds. The cane plant was a voracious feeder, requiring heavy mulching in old cane "trash," or leaves, and deep manuring, which the Percy plantation could not provide until Edmund was able to get a small herd of cattle, goats, and sheep grazing on some of the property. It was customary to require the slaves to carry on their heads, from pasture to canepiece, open-work baskets of manure weighing some eighty pounds—from which the liquor of the filth drizzled, and fragments fell, adding further insult to the noisome labor. Edmund instituted a more humane method using wagon and mules, but from the wagon the manure inevitably had to redistributed by hand down the rows of each piece.

The planting of the entire property had to be complete, in the ordinary year, between June and November; and having arrived in August in his first year, Edmund had even fewer months in which to work. These were the wet months on Antigua, and cane planted any later might not grow, or might not survive, or might not ripen properly. The cane plant itself required not just a few months to ripen, like the crops with which Edmund was familiar in the shorter growing season of England; no, it required a year or even more, during which time it must be coddled and cultivated and its relentless appetite fed.

Harvesting typically began in January and continued through May. The harvest time was a constant, grinding blur of mad labor. The cane was ripening apace in every part of the plantation, engorged with liquid sugar. First it had to be stripped of its trash and the trash borne away to be burned or to bed the animals or stored to mulch the next crop. Then the lofty standing cane had to be cut down with knives—actually heavy billhooks—and fastened into bundles; and again, these massively heavy bundles were by custom carried to the mill on the heads or backs of the slaves. Edmund again used the wagon and mules for this part of the task; but merely manhandling the bundles on and off the wagons was crushing work, and each acre might produce thirty wagonloads of cane. It was almost unbelievable to Edmund the first time he saw how much juice these loads contained. Janetta guessed that each had the equivalent of a hundred gallons of raw liquor; and of course, in constantly handling this material, the clothing of the slaves was saturated and their skin encrusted with sugar. And so it went for acre after acre.

At the mill, each stalk had to be fed through vertical rollers not once but twice. The juice was carefully caught and directed onward. Previous to Edmund's arrival, the slaves had had to transport the juice in enormous and heavy earthenware carboys downhill to the boiling room, but at

Janetta's advice Edmund installed a system of pipe to carry the cane liquor down the slope.

The boiling room, too, was a re-creation of one of the quadrants of hell. Vast copper kettles were kept fired to the very high boiling point of the sugary fluid, and the hot liquid was repeatedly skimmed. Each kettle represented a different stage of refinement, and the liquor had to be transferred from one to the next, until it reached the smallest, which was stoked to a searing heat. In this last distillation stage, the juice became a viscous sludge the color of excrement, but reeking searingly of sweetness. The master boiler then slaked or tempered the sludge with lime to make it crystallize into something at last a little resembling sugar. But this was the crisis of the operation: the liquor must then be watched every second, and the instant it was about to form into a semi-solid mass of granules, it must be instantly ladled off into a cistern, a process called "striking the sugar."

From the cistern the semi-molten sugar was packed into earthenware pots; these heavy pots were then transferred by more back-breaking labor to the drying shed, which must be kept constantly heated. Every few days the molasses that had accumulated in the pots was decanted, until finally, after about a month, the pots were empty of all but a block of golden muscovado sugar. The top and bottom of the block were cut off and reboiled; the remainder was spread in the sun for a time to dry. Then it must again be collected and packed into hogsheads, each of which weighed about a thousand pounds. The behemoth hogsheads were coaxed and manhandled one by one onto a heavy wagon and taken to the harbor for shipment to England.

The worst part of all the harvest, aside from the punishing physical labor, was that so many of these operations were ongoing simultaneously. Some men must be stripping the trash, some must be cutting cane; some must be lugging cane to the mill, and at least one man feeding the dangerous rollers; someone must constantly stoke the boilers, someone must skim the liquor, and Janetta must watch the stages of the distillation always; some must ladle to the cistern, and then to the pots; some must carry the pots; some must drain the molasses; some must break up the blocks of muscovado and spread it to dry; some must pack it in hogsheads. Edmund might have had the willpower of an ancient hero, and he still would not have had enough hands to do all that must be done.

⌛⌛⌛⌛⌛

One result of his efforts had never been looked for. He grew physically stronger. His daily labor was a form of enforced training. What little of the softness of the leisured class he had possessed burned away. When he sat up in bed in the morning, his belly looked to him as it had when he was a boy: he could see readily beneath the skin the valleys that separated the muscles of his abdomen; only now those valleys were deeper than they had been in his youth. From week to week and month to month a glance in the mirror might take him aback: his shoulders grew more thick and broad, his arms mightier, and on one occasion when he turned about in front of the mirror to inspect a minor cut he had received, he was startled to see that his back had become an altogether new landscape, with unfamiliar contours of muscles under the flesh.

This necessary growth must be fed. It was one of his first concerns to start a little herd of cattle on the property, and to gather a number of fowl. The latter flock grew so extensive that his neighbor Mr. Duckworth protested it to be excessive. In order to ensure the proper care of these birds, he gave many to the slaves to be their own property. All of Canebrake ate eggs, and ate them at morning, noon, and night; often he and the slaves ate from their abundant flock of chickens; and occasionally he ordered one of the cattle slaughtered, and then all would gorge themselves on steak and every form of other form of beef. He gave each of the men a goat for milk. He saw to it that they had not only the supplies of food that he was required by law to give them, but better still, and in greater quantity; and they augmented these foods with those of their own growing—potatoes, eddoes, plantain, yams, guinea corn, and the ubiquitous widdy-widdy weed that grew everywhere.

The increase in health and strength among them was striking to see. Like him, they grew broad of shoulder and thick of arm. The emaciated and broken beings Waller had deposited on his doorstep became powerful and handsome. One, in fact, whose name was Warner—apparently because he had been set, as a very little boy, to warn the others of the approach of the overseer on the plantation where he then lived—grew to surpass even Edmund in size and sinew. Great legs the man had, and arms like beams, a neck like a stone milepost. If ever Edmund needed two men for some particularly heavy task, he would call Warner to his side, and between the two of them they would see it done.

His practice in this regard caused trouble for him as well. Mr. Morgette openly reproached him for coddling his slaves and overfeeding them. "I was riding by Canebrake the other day, sir," he told Edmund once, "and I saw a dozen of your negroes working in the cane by the road. What great brutes you have made of them with this overfeeding! My wife was with me, and she was quite terrified by the sight of them. Imagine all the island's negroes become such prodigies! They would rise and strangle us in our beds before we knew what was toward. You set a very bad example, Mr. Percy: other slaves will be jealous of the rations yours receive. Slaves ought to be kept in a weakened state—you must always feed them just slightly less than their labors require. Why, I hear you feed them *beef* upon occasion. That is scandalous! Let them eat widdy-widdy. It is good enough for cattle; it should be good enough for them. Do not forget, Mr. Percy, they are *machines,* not *men.* You are not in England; you are in the West Indies. There is more than just an ocean of water between those two worlds; there is an ocean of custom as well." And he issued many more reproaches of the same kind as time went on. He would also periodically renew his threat to write and complain to Edmund's father; and indeed, Edmund thought that someday the magistrate would be goaded to it; but he did not let that deter him from doing what he believed was necessary.

Even Janetta put on strength. She remained too slender, to his mind; but her arms and shoulders, her legs and buttocks, filled out and became shapely with muscle. The chest visible over the décolletage of her childish dress was no longer hard sternum and lurking ribs, but showed a smooth underlayment of muscle. One day while they were working, Edmund heard one of the men laugh—a sound instantly stifled in fear. When he turned to see what was transpiring, he found Janetta stalking haughtily away from them, holding her dress closed with one hand. The buttons had finally given way. She did not reappear among them for another twenty-four hours; and then she was wearing another dress, equally ragged, but not quite as revealing.

The plantation, he was quick to learn, was an entire economy in and of itself. It was a constant effort to keep food of good quality coming in at the right time. He had to obtain fuel as well, for the boilers and for cooking, and Antigua itself had long ago been divested of its primeval forest, so firewood had to be brought, at no small expense, from the endless woodlands of America. So with many other articles the plantation required—building timber, barrel staves, even wheeled wooden vehicles from barrows to wagons. The running of the plantation required skills as well—of carpenters and masons and wheelwrights, to name only a few; and these must be hired and brought in as necessary from the freed population living in St. John's. Arranging for this took him away from the work cordon at times, and kept him up long after the men were asleep, as he drew up lists of requirements, balanced the books, and weighed how he would lay out his available funds. He kept a scrupulous ledger, taking the advice of a mulatto manager employed by Mr. Duckworth, who revealed to him some of the simpler mysteries of double-entry accounting.

He also gained a practical knowledge he had never had before. He saw how the gears and wheels of the windmill worked; he had to repair the wagon when it broke down, or at least oversee its repair; he had to direct the men in the refurbishing of their quarters; he watched at closer vantage than any gentleman in England as countless objects used about the place were constructed, from barrels to baskets to boxes. He saw how things went together, and how they would fall apart if measures were not taken against their disintegration. He learned how to tie a rope, lash down a wagonload of goods; how to saw a board straight and drive a nail; how to balance a load on his back; how to guide a barrow; how to build the hottest fire possible; and a thousand other such things.

Thus he acquired strength and skill he would never otherwise have had. This acquisition was a consolation to him in his exile; but still, it was only a scant consolation. If a man has never intended to become a joiner, or a brewer, say, he can only pride himself so far on the acquisition of that skill; for he knows that in acquiring it, he has only prorogued the accomplishing of the true skill that he longs to practice, whatever it may be.

⌛⌛⌛⌛⌛

These labors did not just continue for a season; they did not just continue for a year; they went on for two years, and then dragged into a third, with no end to be seen. Edmund had always been an active person, but he had always combined his physical activity in a healthy way with intellectual work—he had read widely from boyhood through university and beyond. Now his reading was restricted to an hour or so after dinner before exhaustion overcame him, and to a few hours on Sunday. He had very few books—only those he had brought; but they proved sadly sufficient to occupy the time he had. He had never before known what it was to work at hard labor day after day, to feel his intellect growing duller with disuse; and now at the very least he began to understand why the working classes in the land of his home could sometimes act like brutes: he saw that in fact they had been brutalized by the work required of them. His very understanding of who he was began to grow dim. That is, he began to forget the full range of his interests, and many of the beliefs that guided him began to fade like ghosts into the vivid and difficult immediacy of his surroundings.

He worked so closely with the slaves that he inevitably came to know them better. Camaraderie, however, was not possible. They wore masks, personas, presenting the fictive personalities they thought their oppressor wanted to see—that of silly and ineffectual children, requiring constant supervision to keep them from dawdling or from spoiling even the very tools with which they worked. They never relinquished the ploy of playing dumb. In order to survive as human spirits in bondage, they had to make a hidden world for themselves within the world of slavery, a private sphere that they certainly did not want or trust him to enter. He could not blame them for that, certainly; rather he blamed the system of slavery, and himself for being a part of it.

Unlike the men, Betty did become a little more familiar. She played the role of housekeeper, which she dispatched almost like a mother to him, though she was not much older than he was; or rather, more like an older sister. He would have recognized the hallmarks of such care if he had ever had such a sibling: her concern for him was zealous and authoritarian, distanced and ironical, and only yielding to his will—on those few occasions when it opposed hers—under a daringly dry protest, a kind of shadow version of

Janetta's open insolence. It was her job to care for him in basic ways—to cook his food and to clean his house and clothing; and she seemed to be able to compel herself to do so only by invoking her genuine human nurturing instincts. She survived her servitude, in other words, by attempting to nurture her master as she would have freely nurtured an individual of her own choosing. But he knew that her concern for him was only mandated by the relationship in which they each found themselves.

For his part, he treated these slaves as kindly as he knew how. But what is kindness worth, in the context of servitude? Nothing. It is a lie, and Edmund felt himself a liar and hypocrite every day. True, it was better that he speak softly to them and provide them as much food and leisure as was possible, given the fact that he must exploit them; but the kindness of a jailer is meaningless unless the prisoner comes to see the jailer, too, as a kind of prisoner in the system. Though Edmund felt himself just such a prisoner, he knew the slaves could never share that view.

On three days a week he took time in the morning to teach them to read. Some of them were eager to acquire this skill, and others were defiant and pretended to be unable; but as time passed, and those who had quickly learned were set to teach those who were dragging their feet, the hunger for the ability infected every last one of them. At the end of the first year he was able to obtain for each of them a personal copy of the Bible, though he was disgusted to find that it was only through the agency of the Moravians that this was possible, not through any resources of his own church. They were thrilled to actually own books; and he counted as one of the greatest pleasures of his life, both then and thereafter, the sight of them all as they sat about in the barn, on any barrel-end or box they could find, with their heads bent over the Scriptures, reading aloud in various passages, at various volumes and facilities, in a kind of holy cacophony.

Then the questions arose on all sides. He had never before seen the Bible through the eyes of someone not steeped in its traditional context, and he had to admit that to the newcomer, it was full of very strange things—things that not even he could explain to them, for all his years of reading and training. He continued his Sunday worship services with them, but they never seemed to be able to make the connection between what they read in the Bible and what happened at those services. The best he could do in that respect was to teach them the Lord's Prayer; and again, it was a moment the mere memory of which could, even in later years, bring tears to his eyes, when they first faltered their way through the recitation of the *Our Father who art . . .*

His best friend during all this time continued to be Mr. Duckworth. If he had any question about agriculture Janetta could not answer, or would not pretend to answer even if she did not in fact know about it, he would betake himself to his neighbor's house, and Mr. Duckworth always helped him. He dined with the Quaker at least once every fortnight. After the first few occasions, he gave up all expectation that the women of the family would join in the conversation, though they were always present, and seemed always to be listening intently to the men's talk. Sometimes he fancied they paid more attention when he talked of home—of Brackensom, of places he had been in England; but if they were in fact more interested, they did not give him any certain and objective evidences of the fact; it was only something that he guessed.

His efforts, earnest and assiduous though they were, did not bring much fruit. In the first year, some of his men were hunting for landcrabs at night with torches and set one of the canepieces on fire. Much of the crop in several pieces was consumed before they could get the blaze under control—which in fact was only possible because Mr. Duckworth mobilized nearly his entire workforce to help. Mr. Morgette pestered him about the incident, for fines were to be levied in such cases, and Edmund did wind up paying a small sum to assuage the law, over and above the losses he had already suffered. In any case, he had a small harvest in 1811; it consisted only of the cane planted by his predecessor that had somehow grown to maturity without care, and despite the weeds that choked it. When the first major harvest came, in the late winter and spring months of 1812, the island was in the grip of a terrible drought, and the cane ripened too rapidly, and then died and dried and was ruined before he could get it all cut and processed. Thus in the first two years all the work of the slaves barely paid the costs of running the plantation.

When he planted in the summer of 1812, however, he put in a new cane stock that originally came from Tahiti. It was said to be hardier and a third more productive, although there were also rumors that it exhausted the soil more rapidly. Mr. Duckworth was leery of it, and counseled Edmund against its purchase; but Edmund was by that time somewhat desperate to turn a profit, and figured he had little to lose. Many planters were interested in his experiment; they lingered in the road as they passed by Canebrake to survey its growth, and sought him out after church on Sundays to inquire about it; but he could not help feeling as if they were betting on him to fail once again.

⌛⌛⌛⌛⌛

In all this time no manager had ever arrived to take over his task. Towards the end of November of his first year in Antigua he had received the following letter from his father:

Mr. Edmund Percy
Canebrake, Antigua

Brackensom, Sept. 21, 1810

Dear Edmund,

I am in receipt of your letter from Antigua written Aug. 7. I assure you that since I received it I have been making continual efforts to find an agent. Both Beckwith and I have examined several candidates, and they have been found wanting in the extreme. I fear that the profession of being a manager in the West Indies tends to draw men whom one would not willingly trust. One of those with whom I met was drunken and dissipated, and our interview did not last five minutes. Furthermore, bad references seem to swarm over these men as flies over a freshly manured field—no sooner do I begin to think one a possibility than I learn of some unsavory or dishonest behavior in his past. I am sure you have the situation well in hand, however, and am pleased every time I think of your presence there.

Concerning the shortage of slaves, I of course authorize you to purchase more as necessary and as available. I regret that this unpleasant duty should fall to you, but such are the circumstances.

The good news from Brackensom is that your brother has taken an interest in the estate such as I have never before seen in him. I may fairly say that in the months since his return here he has become a true heir of the Percies. Every morning after breakfast we confer with Burton on what will be done on that day and in the near term, and like as not we walk or ride out to make sure that the work is being done properly. Then we return home, and spend the rest of the day until dinner in correspondence or reading. I have not been able to interest Christopher in the agricultural journals yet, but I have hopes that that may come. He seems to have a great deal of personal correspondence, which surprises me; but better that he is here, and writing to his acquaintances, than that he is with them at the races. He also has been to town several times since your absence, and I suspect will go more often when the season begins. He has spoken of going to acquaintances of his in Gloucestershire to shoot, but I hope he will instead be content to go out with me and partake of our own excellent sport at Brackensom.

I am also keeping my ears open for a suitable living for you in the neighborhood; but there are no new developments there.

Christopher and I are both well, and I have heard recently from both of your aunts that they, too, are in the best of health, though I do suspect your Aunt Andromeda is still depressed in spirits after the unexpected loss of your uncle; but it has been only a short time. Also, I regret to report that yesterday old Mr. Cathcomb died. You never met him, I suppose; he was butler here from the time I was a boy until a little before you were born. Who ever thought he should live so long in his dotage! His daughter has taken care of him all these years, and they say she is now quite aged and infirm herself.

I shall send, under this same cover, some observations Burton has concerning your accounts; he has some suggestions as to how they might be made more simply. It is to be regretted, indeed, that you do not have such a man as Burton by your side out there in the West Indies.

With all affection I sign myself

Your Father

This letter was to prove the pattern for those which arrived at regular intervals throughout Edmund's time in Antigua. Sometimes Edmund heard more details about dismissed candidates; sometimes there were no candidates at all. At length he came to the conclusion that his father would not be able to settle on anyone—that some inability to make a decision, perhaps attendant upon age, had begun to afflict him. No sooner had Edmund been forced to this conclusion than a letter arrived stating that Beckwith and Burton had found a manager, and, against his father's inclinations, had insisted that he be hired and dispatched at once to Antigua. This woke great hopes in Edmund. He toiled on with redoubled effort, thinking that he would be relieved on every day; but the weeks mounted to months, and the months went by, and the man never arrived. What happened to him between London and Antigua, the Percies never knew; but either he had collected his advance money and never even taken ship, or he had suffered the same fate as

Mr. Merritt, or he had found a better position at some point en route. There was an agonizing correspondence concerning him, in which Edmund wrote for particulars of his voyage—what ship he had taken, when he might be expected—and Hereford wrote back insisting he would must surely have arrived before Edmund could even receive the letter Hereford was sending; and then Edmund wrote further letters in an effort to persuade his father and Beckwith and Burton that in fact the man was not to be expected; and then, when they were persuaded, they must investigate from their end and report to Edmund before they could take new action.

Edmund himself scoured the island for someone suitable. This search gave him a far wider acquaintance than he would otherwise have had. But it was as fruitless as his father's. The only unemployed managers to be found were men such as Waller—indeed, many of them were cronies of Waller's, and tales were told of their gambling and debauches that made Edmund shake his head with disgust. For some time he had hopes that Mr. Duckworth would persuade a cousin of his to come from England and take up the task; but that possibility eventually evaporated like the others.

At length—sometime after the beginning of his third year in Antigua, that is, in the fall of 1812, he gave up hope. He realized he had locked himself in a strange prison indeed, one that was fashioned by his sense of filial duty; and it held him more securely than any prison of brick and stone. He saw now that no manager would come from England—he himself would work on until he broke. His father did not know what was at stake; he thought Edmund lived the same sort of life of leisurely supervision that Hereford and Christopher led at Brackensom. As Edmund saw it, he had only three choices: he could revolt—defy his father's wishes, throw off the yoke, return to England, and let Canebrake revert to weeds again; he could try to talk his father into selling the place; or he could cease to throw himself heart and soul into it, in which case he was certain that it would dwindle. The first of these possibilities was abhorrent to him. The second, selling the plantation, he felt he would not for some time be able to persuade his father to do, if at all. The third—simply to play the gentleman, and let Janetta lead the slaves in their work—he was sure would prove a failure. His certainty on this latter point arose out of a feeling he had about Janetta herself, an intimation that was growing more naggingly clear with every passing day.

And this suspicion was that the only reason she was in the fields at all was in order that she could be with him. She did not show any mildness to him—she was coarse, abusive, abrasive as ever; but when he went out to work, she soon appeared beside him; and when he had to stop, to attend to some other business, she rarely stayed in the field long without him. She then turned over nominal command to Obah. He could not help concluding that she felt no reason to endure the work unless she could be by his side.

He thought that perhaps his presence gave her a sense of safety. Or perhaps it was pride on her part, a thought that if he was too good to work on a given day at a given hour, so was she.

⌛⌛⌛⌛⌛

One Saturday afternoon during that fall of 1812, Edmund sat on the verandah to write another report to his father, thinking it would give him the opportunity to make another plea for relief. The men were working in their gardens, and Betty, too, had left her household chores to work beside Johnny. About mid-afternoon he looked up from his task to see Janetta approaching, her basket laden with what he now knew to be tobacco leaves, perhaps a payment in kind for healing or for a love charm or some other species of magic. She paused by the front steps.

"Is there fire in the hearth?" she asked. "I have none."

"Yes," he told her. "Or there ought to be at least an ember. Betty made me tea a while ago." Without a word she went up into the house. He went back to his writing. In a minute she came out and sat down on the steps.

It was uncharacteristic of her to stop in his company in this way. He saw she was now smoking a cigar she had apparently rolled from the tobacco leaves.

Before he had come to Antigua, he had never seen a woman smoke, and even now the sight remained both repulsive, surprising, and amusing. He sat for several minutes secretly watching her, highly intrigued and entertained. Eventually she turned to look at him. "And what is so amusing?" she asked.

"In England, women do not smoke."

"I do many things that women in England do not do," she said dryly.

He contented himself with affirming the truth of this, and went back to his writing. In a minute, however, she interrupted him.

"Do you smoke?" she said.

"No," he said.

"Why not?"

"I do not know. It is a habit I have never acquired."

"A habit? It is a pleasure you never tried, you mean."

"Well," he said indifferently, "perhaps some day I shall." And he went back to his writing.

She rose from the steps and came to him. "Perhaps today is the day," she said.

"I do not think so."

"Here—try it; go ahead."

She thrust the cigar toward him.

If she had not been so very beautiful, she would never have persuaded him; and in that moment there was a generous softness about her that was interesting. The sheer novelty of being offered a cigar by a woman was also very piquant. He took the cigar and put it to his mouth.

"Don't breathe too deeply," she said. "Just taste the smoke, as if you were rolling a mouthful of wine around on your tongue."

He followed her instructions.

"Ah, yes," he said, with great surprise and pleasure, "that is capital!" The flavor of the fresh tobacco was indeed wonderful. He tried a few more puffs and then offered the cigar back to her.

"No," she said. "You keep it. I shall roll another for myself."

She fetched her basket and sat down boldly at the table where he was writing. He watched in fascination as she swiftly and skillfully rolled herself a flawless little cigar. When she was done, he gave her back his cigar and she lit hers from it. Then they sat smoking together.

It was as odd a thing as he had ever done—share cigars with a mulatto, with a slave, and with a woman at that. But—and perhaps under the influence of the nicotine—he continued to find this oddness amusing.

She rolled several more cigars while they sat together. When she was done she pushed them across the table toward him.

"Why," he said, "thank you, Janetta. That is very kind of you. May I pay you for those?"

"No," she said. Her frown told him not to press the matter. "You are kind to me," she said. "I want to be kind to you."

"Well, if this is to be a change in your general policy, I am glad you warned me. If you were to suddenly stop calling me a stupid white man, my humility might be severely tested."

"Oh, I shall not stop doing *that,*" she said. "Not unless you stop being stupid, which I do not think will happen anytime soon."

"No, probably not."

She looked at him with a little smile. "It is good, is it not?" she said.

"The cigar? Yes, it is excellent. I never knew what I was missing."

She considered for a moment. "What about coffee, White Edmund? Have you ever had coffee?"

"Oh, of course. We have coffee at home."

"Do you like it?"

"Actually, I prefer tea."

"Then you have not had coffee."

"No, I *have* had coffee. I simply prefer tea, that is all."

"No—I tell you, if you prefer tea, it is only because you have not had good coffee."

"What a curst wench you are, Janetta! May a man not prefer something you do not prefer?"

She picked up a little sack that was in her basket. "Coffee," she said. "Coffee roasted this morning by Mama Jee at Shreveton's. No one roasts coffee like Mama Jee. I shall make you some."

"But I already have some tea. There is plenty in the pot still."

She picked up the teapot, took off the lid, and cast the contents over the rail.

"Can there *be* a more bold and obstinate being on this earth than you?" he exclaimed.

"I doubt it," she said. She went inside.

He shook his head in wonder; then he continued writing his letter.

In a quarter of an hour she returned with the same pot, now filled with coffee, which she set down next to him. Then she took her basket and went down the steps.

At the bottom she paused. "I assume you can pour for yourself, White Edmund?"

He was so amazed by her boldness that he did not reply. She started to leave, but then paused once more.

"Oh," she said. "I left the coffee beans in your larder. Let me know when you want more."

With that she finally left.

He sat for several minutes, scarcely knowing what to think. Then he poured himself a cup of coffee and tasted it.

It was wonderful. By the time he had finished his second cup, he was quite converted.

Not long afterward, Betty came in from the garden to make his dinner. She took the teapot and cup away while he continued to work. In a minute she came out on the verandah again, carrying the teapot.

"'Scuse me, Massa," she said.

"Yes, Betty? What is it?"

"Massa, when I left, I made you a pot o' tea. This yeah ain't no pot o' tea; this yeah's a pot o' coffee."

He smiled at her consternation. "Yes," he agreed. "It seems to have undergone some kind of transformation."

She looked at him suspiciously. "Who make you dis coffee, Massa, ifin you don' mind my axin'?"

"Janetta came by with some tobacco and coffee. She insisted on making me a pot; and I must say, it was quite good. I think I shall have coffee from now on, rather than tea. She said she left the bag in the larder somewhere."

"You gwine take dat fum her?"

"Why should I not? I thought it was uncharacteristically kind of her. It would be a shame to refuse her gift and discourage such kind acts in future."

"You innocent as a picnee, Massa, ifin you don' min' my sayin' so. Dat witch nevah do nuffin' for nobody lessen she gits somefin foah it."

"Well, she got nothing out of me, I can assure you. I offered to pay her, and she was quite scornful of my money."

"You watch out, Massa. She put a spell on you. She put a spell on odda mans before you."

"I am sure she has, Betty. But have no fear on my behalf. She is too rough for me, too wild by far. I shall marry a gentler creature than she is."

Betty looked skeptical and thought about this for a minute. "Dat be good, Massa," she admitted finally. "But you betta hurry up and marry right quick, or you miss you' chance."

"I tell you, I am not concerned."

"Well, you just don' take nuffin' from her mouf, Massa."

"What? From her mouth, did you say?"

"Never you touch nuffin' her mouf has touched. She git you dat way, Massa. She cast a spell on you dat can't be broke—until some *odda* witch do da same."

Edmund thought of the cigar and smiled condescendingly. "I shall be sure to watch out for that," he said.

Chapter 10

Among these young daughters of a glowing clime, many very beautiful girls are to be met with. . . . They possess a sylph-like movement and elastic step; while the large, black liquid eyes, the glossy jet hair, the long eye-lashes, and the soft olive tinge of their complexions, relieved by rosy lips and dazzling white teeth, would form no bad model for one of Mahomet's *houris*.

—*Antigua and the Antiguans*

In January 1813 the great harvest at Canebrake began. The Tahitian cane stock had thrived; the stalks of the first piece were engorged with juice, were veritably bursting, oozing, dripping juice. The madness began, the mad grind of labor day and night; and for nearly five months straight it continued unabated. Never had Canebrake raised such a crop, never produced so much sugar. The barrels with the Percy mark that were sitting on the quayside in St. John's grew week by week to an astonishing mountain; they were the talk of the town. The managers and owners of the larger estates eyed them in astonishment and envy, thinking how if the Percies could produce so much muscovado on their comparatively small strip of land, then they themselves could add at least a third to their own output.

By the last week in May the last sugar had been boiled and barreled and shipped. Yes, a new crop must be planted behind the old, and that work was waiting to be begun; but for a time, for a few days, there was blessed lull. When Edmund returned from town after seeing the final hogshead hoisted aboard a vessel bound for England, he gave orders to the slaves to butcher one of the beef cattle, and the men feasted and sang by the firepit; and after he had eaten a goodly steak and drunk some fine Madeira, he cast himself down on his bed in his room in the great house and lay partly awake and partly asleep, dozing and dreaming of Brackensom, and of how he and Alex used to punt on the Brake; until at length, a little before midnight, the sound of thunder rolling down the hill quite woke him up. He still lay on the bed, however, listening to the sound of the men laughing and shouting in the distance.

He was tired in every sinew, but he knew it was a weariness that would pass away on the morrow and leave him stronger than he had been before. He did not mind it; indeed, he minded nothing now, none of the brutal work he had done or had made the men do. They had succeeded. The profit would be enormous this season. But he did not know where that left him—except stuck here for another year. The enterprise had carried him along, his drive toward the goal, the harvest; now that he stopped climbing for a moment, he could see that the vista ahead was that of an infinite range of such mountains.

And his men, what had this work won for them? A beef dinner and a new suit of clothes.

As he thought of the clothes he groaned and sat up. He had forgotten to hand them out; they were still in hampers in the back of the wagon. If it rained, they would be soaked. Not that it mattered much, but he would distribute them now; he would not wait until morning.

He had never undressed, so he had merely to rise, dash some water in his face, light a lantern, and make his way outside. The stars in the sky to the northeast were blotted out by a single thunderhead, and as he looked in that direction, a sliver of lightning leapt down to the earth. It was not a large storm; it might or might not cross Canebrake, and at any rate, he guessed it would not reach this far for some time.

As he approached the firepit, he was surprised to see Janetta standing just outside the circle of the men. He had never known her to join in their festivities before; although it could hardly be said even now that she was doing so. She had taken up a position apart from them on purpose; she stood with one hand on her hip and the other playing with her hair, hypnotized by weariness or the fire or both. For once the men seemed at ease in her presence. He wondered if she had supplied them with a little alcohol, but if so, there was no sign of cup or bottle now.

"Hey!" shouted someone. "Heah de massa!"

The cry went up from all. "Hey! Heah de massa!"

"What you doin', Massa?" said Azaz. "Betty say you fast asleep. What you dream about, Massa?"

"I have been dreaming about cane a thousand feet high," said Edmund. His joke was greeted by a cheerful groan.

"Too high, too high, Massa!" said Azaz.

"Come with me a moment, Azaz," said Edmund. "I have new clothes for you all."

"Ah, bery good, bery good!" said Azaz. The other men expressed their pleasure as well, laughing and clapping and shouting.

He took Azaz to the wagon and between the two of them they brought back the hampers of clothing. He handed them out; there was little to distinguish one from another; the jackets were much the same size, as were the trousers. All the same, the men were pleased; and Betty even more so. She was now very pregnant, and he had bought her a very large new petticoat.

For quite some time there was chaotic hilarity as the men tried on the new jackets, swapped them about to obtain the best fit, and strutted about playfully. Edmund was looking on, laughing wearily, when suddenly all the men grew silent. They seemed frightened, and some looked toward Janetta, and some away from her, but in such a fashion that he knew her to be the cause of their change of mood. It was odd; he had not heard her say anything.

"Oh, now you gwine catch it, Massa!" one of the men near him whispered.

"Why?" he said. "What have I done?"

No one answered. The men stepped back out of the way, and Janetta approached him.

She stopped before him. Her eyes seemed to glitter in the firelight.

"What?" she said, in a cool, even tone. "No dress for Janetta?"

"Ah," said Edmund. "Of course." He reached into the bottom of one of the hampers and pulled out another petticoat. He held it out to her, smiling.

"Oh ho!" shouted the men. "New dress fo' Miss Janetta! New dress!"

"What you got to complain about now, Missy Janetta?" said Betty in a bold tone.

Janetta gave her a look that made Betty shrink back behind Johnny. Then, snatching the petticoat from Edmund, she shook it at him and cried, "A slave petticoat! A slave petticoat! Do you think I can be *bought* for a slave petticoat?"

"There is nothing on all the broad earth that can buy *you,* Janetta," said Edmund.

"That is right!" she cried. "And don't you forget it, White Edmund! Don't you go giving me a slave petticoat!"

He had in fact reserved it and not given it out with the rest because he had no idea how she would receive it. And now, to the horror of the watching slaves, she cast the petticoat into the fire.

"That's what I think of your petticoat!" she said to him furiously, stamping her bare foot.

"Ohwee!" mumbled Betty. "Ohwee, why he no give dat petticoat to me?"

"Shut your mouth, Betty!" said Janetta; and she was going on to heap still more insults on her when Edmund spoke.

"Janetta," he said. His tone got her attention.

"What?"

"I do not know if this will please you or make you more angry than ever—one never knows *that*—but I do have something else for you."

She regarded him in sullen silence. He reached into the hamper again and pulled out another gift he had bought in case the first did not please her. It was another dress—not luxurious by any means, and not much in the style of the times, but a green printed cotton, utterly different from the plain Osnaburg linen of the slave petticoats.

The silence, as he held the dress out to her, was complete, was loud in itself; the crackling of the fire and the rumble of the approaching thunder were faint by comparison.

For a long time Janetta only looked at the dress. She seemed almost to be studying it. Then she reached out and drew it slowly from Edmund's hand. She shook it open; she surveyed it; she held it against her body, with one hand at the collar, and the other across her waist; and she looked down at it, turning toward the firelight to see it. Without a word, of an instant, she ran away into the darkness.

No one moved. Someone muttered, "What she gwine do now?" but in the main, no one dared volunteer a comment.

What a strange creature! Edmund thought to himself yet again. *Woman, child, witch, mad woman, slave—and yet indomitable, ever indomitable.*

"Well," he said, after a minute, "I shall bid you all good night.—It looks as though that storm will come through here. It would be just as well if we all went to sleep."

Still no one spoke. And now, as suddenly as she had left, Janetta came back; only now she was wearing her new dress, and her old dress she cast into the fire.

She was transformed. It was only a cheap cotton dress, but it fit her well. The bosom was closely snugged to her small breasts and narrow waist, the sleeves reached to her wrists, and the skirts were long enough to conceal her bare legs and feet. For the first time in Edmund's acquaintance with her, she did not look like some castoff slave clad in castoff clothing.

She stared at him as if hungry for his reaction. If he had laughed or sneered, there was no telling what she might have done; but he was taken aback by her beauty, and she must have read that in his face. She looked down at herself, and then back at him.

Then she raised her head—tilted her head back, so that her long, slender throat was lit by the fire—and she laughed, as he had never heard her laugh before. He had heard her mocking laugh, short and caustic; but he had never heard this laugh before—this peal of wild glee, almost as if she had not a care in the world; though somewhere in it he heard trouble and pain, still, ineradicable. She ran lightly up to Edmund, holding up her skirts an inch, although in truth they were not so long that she needed to; and she gave him a playful little slap on the cheek.

He knew not what kind of custom this was, but evidently all the others did. Perhaps something must be given in return for a gift, or bad luck would ensue; and she chose to give a slap. Or perhaps it was some wild African coquetry; it had more of that air to it. But whatever it was, she approved; that was now evident to everyone; and the slaves laughed and clapped and shouted. She did a dreamy little dance around the fire, the bare white soles of her feet flashing, and her arms whirling at her sides like the vanes of the mill. The men provided accompaniment, falling into a rhythmic clapping.

A boom of thunder cut short the merrymaking. Immediately rain swept down upon them. The men scattered away from the fire, running for their quarters, still laughing and shouting. Edmund seized the lantern and ran back to the house.

In the shelter of the verandah he paused. He set down the lantern and looked out at the rain, which was illumined from moment to moment by flashes of lightning.

Mad creature! he thought again. *Who indeed could ever guess what should please her and what should make her angry? I pity the man who has such a capricious being to wife. No, give me a woman I can understand, if such there be.*

No sooner had he thought this than she appeared in the faint ring of rain lit by the lamplight.

She was completely drenched. The cotton clung to her figure and he saw it in outline, every curve and contour, every hollow and every projecting roundness—from the hollow of her neck, the graceful bow of her shoulders, her small breasts that shook as she moved, the standing nipples—to the hollow of waist and curving hip—to the valley of sodden cloth between her thighs. She swayed in the rain and laughed; she ran her hands over her breasts and belly; she shook her wild, dark, rain-soaked hair so that it lashed about her face.

He seized the lantern and went immediately inside. He closed the door firmly behind him and stood there for a moment, holding the latch down in case she should try it. He heard her feet on the verandah, a light patter within the heavy scudding of the rain; and then he heard her laughter—not cruel, not sarcastic—but in the same tone of briefly-lived joy he had heard in her voice before. Then the feet pattered on the verandah again, and she was gone, her laughter engulfed by the storm.

He reeled into the parlor and seized his Bible from the table. He sat down, clutching the book, but only as some primitive grips an apotropaic totem. He was sexually aroused, so much so that he was actually in pain.

Why did I not see this happening? he thought. He looked back over all the times he had seen her in the field—countless times—so damp with sweat her scanty dress had clung to her, and showed just as much as he had seen tonight; and he knew now that all along, moment by moment, this craving for her had been building in him. How could it not? It was as if they had been thrown together, man and woman, on the shore of an island with no other company; it was as if they were Adam and Eve, the sole representatives of their species here—caught between two societies to which neither belonged, the white gentlefolk on one hand and the Africans on the other.

Did she desire him, or was she only playing some mad game? He did not know; but he knew, now and certainly, that he craved her deeply.

"This *must not happen!*" he said to himself through clenched teeth. "This is a sin if ever there was one! I must get away—I must go home, before this world captures me forever, and I forget who I am!"

Yes, he thought. *If I lie with her, I shall forget who I am. This is like the Isle of the Lotus-Eaters.*

Then it seemed that Antigua burst upon his senses. The rain roaring on the roof and the windows, the crack of thunder—these were just immediate sensations. His memory now seemed to vomit into his brain all the sights and sounds and smells he had never dared to admit he had sensed: the grand color and light of dawn on the green fields, the crystal violet vault of the night sky with its infinite puncturing of stars; the reek of sugar, sugar, sugar, everywhere; the stench of the acrid sweat of toiling bodies; the feel of the cane in his roughened hand, the ache of weariness in his bones, endless heat; the mercy of a breeze, the sting of salt air; and on and on, all bursting in his brain like a fireworks of hungry thought. He was become one open nerve, a nerve on which all of this island impinged, prickling it, searing it with sensation; and all at the incantation of a slender, half-mad mulatto girl.

"Oh, my God!" he said then; "I must stay away from her, at all costs! I must not let this happen!"

He bent his head over his closed Bible; he put it to his brow; but it felt cool to him, deliciously cool, all too deliciously cool. The *sensation of the thing* had become more than the denotation of its word.

He set it aside, put out the lantern, and went to lie down on his bed. Not to sleep; he knew he would not sleep; but to lie there, waiting for sleep, though he was weary enough to sleep days on end; seeing her body again, clad in the green dress, swaying in the rain.

Janetta did not appear in the morning of the next day, a Saturday. "She be off dancin' in her new dress," observed Obah, a remark the other men greeted with a daring snicker. It was not unusual, however, for her to absent herself without notice at times; and one of the men observed that the upper hatch of the windmill was open, and a bit of the green dress could be seen in it; she must have hung it up to dry while she either slept off her exhaustion from the night before or went about the business of preparing herbs. Edmund tried not to imagine her without it.

When the mid-day meal was over, the men went to work on their gardens, and Edmund walked up to Mr. Duckworth's house. He found the family sitting together in the parlor—they, too, seemed a little dazed with the harvest effort just past. Mr. Duckworth greeted Edmund happily, though the women were as impassive as ever.

"Might we go out for a walk together, sir?" asked Edmund. "I have something I should like to discuss with you."

"Of course," said Mr. Duckworth. He exchanged a look with Mrs. Duckworth as he rose to his feet.

They walked out through the pasture where the cattle were kept, instinctively heading toward higher ground and one of the mills.

"What is it, my young friend?" asked Mr. Duckworth finally.

"I have resolved to urge my father to sell Canebrake," said Edmund.

"Ah!" said Mr. Duckworth. "To you, do you mean?" He seemed very pleased.

"To me? No, no—that is not what I mean. You once offered to give us a good price for the place. If you can make us that offer now, and I consider it fair, I shall urge him to take it outright and not put the place up to auction. I mean to sell the slaves as well, you see; I have not the money to buy them myself and set them free; and I know you will treat them well."

At this response Mr. Duckworth's attitude completely reversed itself. "I am sorry to hear this!" he exclaimed. "I am very sorry—and very surprised as well. What has made you decide to go away? Last year was difficult for you, I know—it was not a good year for anyone—but you have done splendidly this year, even when again others have not done so well. That new Tahitian cane! It was a gamble that paid off."

"I will tell you why I must go," said Edmund. "I am changing—I am forgetting who I am."

"Well, it is no wonder. You have had no company but that of slaves for almost three years. You have not been a part of your own society. We have been grieved not to see more of you; and I know you have seen very little of the families of the established church."

"It is not that," said Edmund, "though I admit that is part of it. It is Antigua itself."

"Oh?" said Mr. Duckworth, as if to say, "I do not understand."

"Yes, it is something about the place. I feel that it has filled up my senses, and now they have broken under the load. It is like water filling the pond behind a dam, drop by drop, and suddenly the dam gives way." They stopped now on a little rise and looked back down on their two plantations. "Look at it!" he said. "Look at this place! It is so very beautiful; and yet it is as though I never noticed it before, or never let myself notice it; and now, this morning, I feel as though I were drunk or drugged with it."

"What has happened that has made you feel that way all of a sudden?" asked Mr. Duckworth.

"I cannot say," said Edmund. "It is just the long accumulation; and now the harvest is past, and I have the leisure to perceive it."

"But what is wrong with finding beauty in this part of God's creation, just as you have before in England?"

"Because it is changing *me,*" said Edmund. "It is breaking down what I believe in. No—it is not so much *changing* my beliefs; it is making me forget them, overwhelming them in sense."

"My friend," said Mr. Duckworth, "you are too much alone! I know what you mean; but you need the company of a wife and family. It is not natural for a man such as you to be alone in this world, and you are paying the price. You need a helpmeet, that is all."

The thought of Janetta as a wife went through Edmund's mind, and he shook his head at the mere impossibility of it. It would be very difficult to effect legally, for one thing; for another, it would mean exiling himself forever from England and his family, and in disgrace; and for a third, he had been thinking only last night how a man who married her would be trying to marry the wind that blows up dust-devils on the sand of the shore. But he said nothing of this.

"You are right," he told Mr. Duckworth. "I know you are right. I must go back to England and find a wife."

There was a pause, the pregnancy of which Edmund did not notice, so sunken was he in his own thoughts.

"There are wives to be had in Antigua, you know," said Mr. Duckworth finally.

"What?" said Edmund skeptically. "Miss Morgette? Or some other young thing of the kind? I do not think so.—No, sir; I am quite determined that it is best for me to go. If I do not go soon, I shall sink—sink into I know not what." He turned now to Mr. Duckworth somewhat desperately. "Will you make an offer, sir? That is what I should like to know."

Mr. Duckworth was silent for a minute.

"What if I were to buy the place and make it over to you?" he said.

"Make it over to me?" said Edmund, not understanding.

"Yes—on terms, of course. You would have a mortgage. I would not charge you interest. You could not find better terms. If you keep on as you have begun, you will own the place in five years, and be a rich man in fifteen or twenty; and then may take your money and your family and go back to England if you like; or perhaps you will have grown to love this place so much that you will stay here."

"Rich!" exclaimed Edmund. "In fifteen or twenty years! Sir, I shall be an animal if I stay here that long. I shall be a Waller—worse than a Waller. I shall be a heathen who worships *Obeah.*"

Mr. Duckworth put his hand on Edmund's shoulder. "My boy, my boy," he said soothingly. "You are seeing this in altogether too desperate a light. I know what you are suffering; and it is nothing that a good wife will not cure in short order. I do not suggest you stay here without one. No, marriage is part of the cure—for you, at least, as it is for many good men. 'It is better to marry than to burn.' But marry, and I will give you good terms on the property, and you will have a life here such as you could never have in England, as a curate trying to live on fifty pounds a year, discoursing to a disaffected congregation in a mouldering country church. Do you think *we* are far removed from civilization? I tell you, I grew up for my first ten years in a little village in Lancashire, and never was there any place, not even in deepest Africa, that was so far off the beaten track! If you took that course, you would surely look back with longing on your lost chance to own Canebrake. Stay—stay and be your own man. With your intelligence and energy—why, if we join forces, someday you will return to England three times as rich as your older brother! You will buy an estate three times the size of this Brackensom you talk of, and right next to it! He will send over to you every day for advice on how to manage his affairs."

But Edmund did not think of the picture Mr. Duckworth was painting for him; he thought of the mad girl in the green dress dancing in the rain.

"I shall become a brute if I stay," he said. "I shall care nothing for morality or law or religion. I see now why my brethren in the church here are spiritually asleep. The place, the very air here, has lulled them, sapped them. It is as if the sugar is a drug."

"The gentlefolk are no different here than they are at home," said Mr. Duckworth gently.

"But *I* am different here, at any rate!" exclaimed Edmund.

Mr. Duckworth hesitated; and then he said, "Why do you say so? Have you done anything that makes you a changed man?"

Edmund darted him a pained look. "Engaged in any debauch, do you mean? No, *that* I have not done, thank God! Though I do not exaggerate if I tell you that I feel in imminent danger of it.—No, Mr. Duckworth, you will not persuade me. Even if I saw any candidate for a wife among my small acquaintance here, I do not believe that recourse would cure me, not so long as I remain here. If you would make us an offer, say so. I do not even need to know the exact amount; only tell me today that you do intend to do so, and I shall write my father. But do give me the amount as soon as you can, and I will follow up my letter with that addendum."

Mr. Duckworth thought for a minute. "Let me say this," he said finally. "I shall make you an offer. I should like some time to think what it would be. In the meantime, you think on what I have said."

"I shall only be deceiving you if I pretend to be considering it, sir. My mind is made up."

"Just promise me not to reject it outright."

"I cannot promise that."

"Then allow me to ask you about it again in a few days or a week."

"That I shall certainly do; but you shall find me adamant."

"If that is the best promise I can wring out of you, so be it."

They were silent a moment, looking down at Canebrake.

"To be honest with you," Mr. Duckworth said then, "the price I shall suggest would not be as much as you might get from one of the other planters—I do not make quite the profit they do, and we both know why. But if you do go home, I shall promise you to look after your men as I do my own; and you have seen what that means. That is the only addition I can make to the offer, though it is intangible, and perhaps of no interest to your father. Perhaps he will not like the idea of a private sale, and will want to auction the place. The slaves alone have become quite valuable since importation ended."

"I hope he will follow my recommendation," said Edmund. "I shall present it to him in the strongest terms I can. He is a good man—his only failing is pride; pride and a fear for his posterity that extends even a little to me. But pride will not enter into this decision, except on my side of the argument: it is certainly beneath the dignity of Brackensom to engage in this vile practice of slavery, that much I know. You may tell me that the men who work my father's land in Surrey are not much better, in actual fact, and I take your point; but they do possess a modicum of freedom—they can throw over everything and set sail for America if they so choose, they can become master of forty acres in the wilderness there; and that, by God! is freedom of a precious sort; freedom that the slaves here do not have."

"There, there," said Mr. Duckworth. "You are all worked up, Mr. Percy; you are badly out of sorts. This last effort to get the boiling done has strained your nerves—and no wonder. You have done the work of twenty men by yourself. You must get some rest."

"Well, that is good counsel, I do not deny it. But I mean to go home to England. I have decided."

"But keep my offer in mind, and think on it over the coming days, when you are not so overwrought. You will never get better terms on which to build a fortune."

"I thank you for your care of me, Mr. Duckworth," Edmund said. "I need only to know of your willingness; that is all I need. As for myself, I tell you again that I have decided to go home; and for the sake of my soul, the sooner I do so, the better.—If you will excuse me here, sir, I shall walk back to Canebrake through the fields."

"Will you not come to dinner, Mr. Percy? It would do you good to spend some time with us."

"It would—you are right," said Edmund; though as he thought of those expressionless women in Mr. Duckworth's house, he rather doubted the truth of what he was saying. "But I have a letter to write. Please excuse me. The sooner I begin to write it, the sooner I shall be settled in mind."

"Very well," said Mr. Duckworth, in a tone that suggested that he was unable or unwilling to conceal his disappointment.

"Good day, then, sir," said Edmund. He nodded politely and then turned away toward Canebrake.

"Do remember my suggestion," said Mr. Duckworth.

"I shall," said Edmund, pausing a moment. "And I do assure you that I am very grateful for it, and honor your kindness in making it; and am deeply pleased at this token of your esteem." These phrases were well meant, but too much an afterthought, and too hastily uttered.

Mr. Duckworth looked disappointed and grieved; but he did his best to rally, and added, "You will be all right, Mr. Percy. Take some rest, and we shall talk again."

Edmund nodded to him, as the only way he could think to respond without disappointing his friend yet again; and then he strode away to Canebrake.

⌛ ⌛ ⌛ ⌛ ⌛

That afternoon he wrote the following letter to his father.

> Mr. Hereford Percy
> Broadbridge, Neighbury, Surry
>
> Canebrake, May 26, 1813
>
> Dear Father,
>
> I pray that you and Christopher are in the best of health, and that the affairs of Brackensom continue in the ascendant.

In an earlier letter, which I hope you have received, I reported to you that the harvest was going well; it is now complete, and I append a separate accounting of the barrels of sugar we have now shipped. You will see that it exceeds our best effort of any year to date.

I write in this letter to report my thoughts concerning the plantation. I offer them with full respect for your wishes in this matter, thinking only that it would be improper of me to withhold my estimate of the situation. Your will shall be law to a grateful son in this matter as in all others.

I have been here going on three years now. Despite the gains we have made in the operation of the plantation, I have come to an unfavorable conclusion concerning the property: This is no business in which the estate of Brackensom should be concerned. I shall explain my reasons.

First cause: This enterprise depends on the perpetuation of the moral and spiritual degradation of those human beings who work the land. In the beginning I justified their enslavement by telling myself that they were being bettered through their association with civilized Christian folk; but I now see that the reverse is true: the Christian folk here are being morally compromised in their continued exploitation of other children of the Divine Father. I include myself in this: I feel the onset of a decline in my moral rectitude that is very alarming to me. It is no more right, in my humble opinion, to enslave and work these men than it would be to enslave and work my brother Christopher; and the Bible teaches us that God looks with disfavor on those who cast their brother into slavery. It also teaches us what must be the wages of those who do not treat their fellow men with the love our Savior has enjoined upon us. I know it will be utterly repugnant to you, sir, to think that this stain of evil, however distant from the banks of the Brake, could ever taint the arms of the Surrey Percies.

Item: The hiring of laborers is not feasible. The work of growing, but more particularly harvesting, sugarcane is so brutal than no one could be persuaded to do it at a wage sufficiently low to insure the profitability of the plantation. In short, if we hired labor instead of using slaves, we would not be able to offer our sugar at the price our neighbors set; and we would be quite "out of the market." It would, furthermore, be difficult if not impossible to put together a force of hired workers of sufficient size for any length of time: there would be no way of finding the men or of guaranteeing their continuance at their tasks for more than a few days.

Item: The moral dilemma in which we stand is exacerbated by the fact that we are desperately undermanned. The requisite ratio of labor to land for growing cane is one slave for every two acres. I fear that without reinforcement the men I have will soon break down under their labors; and yet to enter the slave market and purchase the flesh of men is utterly repugnant to me. The renting of other men's slaves is not practical here, and has not been since the overseas trade in these poor wretches was abolished.

Item: The planters live in perpetual fear that the government at home will outlaw slavery in its dominions altogether. If that happens, the planting class as we know it will be destroyed. The planters cannot thrive, they cannot even live, without brutalizing their fellow man in slavery.

Item: The land here is utterly hostile to a reliable return. In all of the year it receives a bare forty or forty-five inches of rain, and almost all of that in the rainy season. There is no river on the entire island from which to draw water, and precious few springs. Every drop that falls from the skies must be caught and husbanded in cisterns. The soil on our plantation—what there is of it—happens to be inherently good, but already shows signs of depletion through years of hard farming, which no manuring can mend. The seasonal drouth can either force the rapid and successful maturation of the crop, or devastate it—either at hazard. Occasional and unpredictable hurricanoes ravage the island, flattening, shredding, and uprooting crops; destroying buildings; terrifying the inhabitants and livestock; and sinking ships in the harbor laden with cargo. Imagine subjecting the fields of Brackensom to the caprices of the Devil and his crew on an irregular basis, and you will have the effect exactly. What is worse, the island is virtually indefensible. An enemy might put in to land at any of fifty places and march without impediment over most of the island, burning and looting and slaying at will. In the old days the French did this regularly, and they might do so again; and even more to be feared in this regard are the wily Americans, who, as history has repeatedly shown, have utterly abandoned the morals once nurtured in them by Mother England. I can only think that there may easily be found an investment less subject to the whims of nature and man for the funds that have been put into this West Indies enterprise.

Item: The modest size of our plantation, relative to those of others, will put us to a perpetual disadvantage as far as the price of sugar goes. The larger estates here produce more cheaply per pound, using land and labor more efficiently. They will set the price, and we will sell our crop at that price, or fail to sell it entirely. If we were larger, and had more hands, we might even be able to undersell them in the market; but there is no land to acquire here—all is as strictly rationed and apportioned as in the hedgerows of home.

Item: In comparison to the other resources of the estate, the plantation here in Antigua is minor; and yet I believe that given its uncertainties, it will ultimately deplete Brackensom of monies that might be better spent in securing our English home against future upheavals there.

Item: This war with America, whose causes I cannot pretend to understand, is causing costly difficulties for all the planters. The West Indies use a huge number of barrels for the shipment of sugar, rum, and other goods; and the United States possess the only forests that can be mined for such a quantity. This strife will wreak havoc here in the islands.

Item: Our neighbor here, one Richard Mr. Duckworth, will pay us a very handsome price for the place. I believe he has long viewed our Canebrake as the perfect extension to his own lands, if he can get it. With your permission, I shall enter into negotiations with him concerning the sale; he has in the past told me that he could pay us cash on our London banker. In the meantime, I have requested him to make an initial offer, which I shall forward to you in a later posting. Furthermore, this Mr. Duckworth is one of the better sort on the island. His slaves are decently fed, decently clothed, and decently housed; though I cannot say he provides for their spiritual welfare as I might wish, as he is a Quaker. Still, he does teach his slaves to read and supplies them with opportunity to worship; and I cannot help but think that a dissenting Christianity is better than none, as it may lead one on to the true religion.

Item: Parliament has discovered that the wealth of the West Indies is an excellent source of revenue, and it is likely that the taxes it levies on our produce will increase markedly in the coming years. This remains a speculative objection, but considering the ever-growing hunger of all governments for money to waste, it is an eminently plausible one.

Item: Parliament has made it as difficult as possible for the West Indies planters to sell their produce abroad. Even if this barrier were removed, our markets would not necessarily expand; for the prolonged war in Europe has driven the French and Germans to rely on grape and beet sugar, and they have quite learned to do without cane at all.

Item: There is some talk that the British colonies on the mainland of South America will be allowed to export directly to Britain, and that their produce will be admitted to English markets on an equal footing. The plantations there are vast, the Indian population large and readily put to work, and materials such as wood for barrels and for boiling fuel far cheaper to obtain. This development, though again speculative, would prove more destructive to the West Indies sugar trade than perhaps any other. We live on our monopoly; if that is broken, we are lost.

That, in sum, is my estimate of the pressures that bear upon the future of Canebrake as a productive resource for the Percy family. I await your decision in this matter. If you do choose to follow my advice, it would be useful to have a power of attorney to make the sale for the estate. Specific stipulations concerning the price you would like to receive would also be necessary.

I send my fondest regards to you and Christopher, and I make my prayers for your continued health.

Your obedient son,

Edmund

After he had delivered this letter to the post in St. John's on Monday, he realized that a burden had begun to lift from him. At last he had seen and proposed a way out, a way home, a way back into his life and into his familiar self, though not a moment too soon. As he started from St. John's, he looked at Antigua with a kinder eye—not as a prison to him, but as a place of sojourn.

This pleasure was short-lived, however. As he neared Canebrake and saw the men working to clear the fields for the next planting, he reproached himself for his momentary satisfaction. For the Africans who had been stolen from their land and compelled to come here, there was to be no going home. Antigua was their prison, and would be the prison of their children and grandchildren.

He went back to work beside them. He might have avoided it. The task was not so pressing. He might have looked on, or he might have found things to do indoors, working over the ledgers or drawing up plans and lists of requirements; he might simply have served out his time—perhaps as little as three months including the voyage of the packets to and fro, and his father's consideration of his advice—until his letter could be answered, and as he hoped, answered in the affirmative. He had little doubt that the sale could be executed in a matter of days thereafter. But he did not take this easy course; he went back to work.

"Massa happy," observed Elijah when he fell in beside them again. The men all laughed. "What you happy 'bout, Massa?"

He felt a pang; he could not tell them that he was happy at the idea of going away.

"The harvest is in," he said.

"Just mo' plantin', then anothah harvest," said Elijah. "Work jes' goes on 'n on."

"So it does," he agreed. "Well, we must work for our supper, I suppose."

"I s'pose."

He felt himself to be a hypocrite. He had never had to work for his own supper; but that thought only made him pitch in the more.

⌛⌛⌛⌛⌛

In the days that followed, he felt the force of Elijah's words. The harvest receded into the past, and the work seemed to stretch forward forever into the future. They planted a new field of cane and tended to those already growing and ripening. Janetta worked beside them as before, and her new dress soon began to look frayed and pale. Edmund did his utmost not to look at her, but he feared that she quickly noticed his uneasiness. He might have expected her, when she detected his discomfort at her physical presence, to mock it or be scornful of it. He thought it odd that she did not give him so much as an ironic glance, let alone sneer at him for his new fear of her sexuality. But at those moments when he did happen to glance her way, he almost always found she had anticipated him and was already looking at him; and her gaze mirrored his own. They must necessarily speak together, for he relied on her advice concerning the work of the plantation; but now he felt a new tension tugging at them, perhaps born of his changed attitude toward her. Then an event occurred that broke down yet another barrier between them.

One day not long after the harvest, he was working in the fields with the men when he began to feel strangely light-headed. At the end of one row he stopped to rest for a moment, and the earth seemed to shift beneath his feet. Janetta stopped beside him, breathing hard and wiping away the sweat that had gathered on her forehead. She saw something was wrong with him.

"What is it, White Edmund?" she asked.

He looked up the hill. The sunlight was playing tricks, splintering inexplicably into rainbows, as if the sky had become a convex prism.

"I think I am not well," he said. "I shall go back to the house. Will you keep the men working?"

"The men will work," she told him, as if there could not possibly be any question of that. "What is wrong with you?"

"I do not know," he said. "I shall sit down for a few minutes; I shall be all right."

He began to walk back to the house. The farther he walked, the farther away the house seemed; he walked and walked like a man in a mathematical paradox, and finally he won his way back to the verandah. He climbed onto it with shaking legs and made his way with difficulty inside.

He sat in the first chair that he saw. "Dat you, Massa?" said Betty. She came waddling in from the kitchen, one hand on her belly and one hand on the small of her back. She looked at him strangely. "Dat you, but I not sure it *really* you." She shook her head. "You don' feel good?"

"No, Betty," he said. "I do not feel well; but I shall in a minute. Bring me some water, please."

"Missy Janetta know you not feelin' good?"

He did not even have time to answer; Janetta herself opened the door of the house and entered the parlor where he sat. She, too, eyed him strangely.

He felt he must look like a sick dog as he raised his eyes to her. She herself seemed to him to grow more beautiful by the instant, as if she were shedding her mortal form and donning an ethereal one even as he watched.

"I never saw you before," he said to her, and then wondered what he meant.

"Oh, Missy Janetta, I t'ink this be bad," said Betty.

"Get him some water," said Janetta, although she could not have heard him request it himself. She came close to Edmund and peered into his eyes.

"You will wear the finest white," he said to her, though he immediately wondered what he meant.

She put her hand on his brow. Her touch felt like a blessing, and he groaned at it.

"You have a fever," she said. "How long have you had it? When did you start to feel sick?"

"Not sick," he said. "Now I can see. Couldn't see before."

"Get into the bedroom while you can still walk," she said. "I don't want to have to carry you. Up! Come, now—do as I say!"

She took one of his arms and drew it over her shoulders as if to support him. He laughed at her drunkenly.

"What? You skinny, slight little thing? *You* are going to carry me?"

"If I have to!" she affirmed. "Now, get up, you big stupid horse of an Englishman, and come with me."

"Oh, very well," he said. In his mind he stood up and began to walk with her; but then he found that he had done nothing of the kind. She made a chiding sound and tugged on his arm.

"You oaf!" she said. "Get up!"

"Oaf? That is word I have never heard you use before."

"I shall use worse if you do not move!"

Before he knew what he was doing, he lurched suddenly to his feet. She put one arm around his waist and used the other to hold his own arm across her shoulders. With this grip on him she managed to steer his unsteady steps out of the parlor and into the bedroom. There she maneuvered him beside the bed and made him sit on the edge of it. As she began unbuttoning his shirt she cried, "Betty!"

"I comin', Missy Janetta."

"Bring water to wash him with."

"Some in de pitcher dere, Missy Janetta. Pretty fresh—put it dere jes' now."

When Janetta had bared his torso, she poured some water into the washbasin and then washed his upper body. The water felt wondrously cool to him, and he momentarily revived.

"You say I have a fever?" he said, in something like his usual tone.

"Yes. You will be sick for several days at least. There is no stopping it now."

"Will you look after the men?"

"The men! The men! Don't you know yet—they are not *men*—they are just black slaves. How are you ever going to be a white man, White Edmund, if you don't learn that blacks are not men?"

"I do not know it yet," he said, "and I never shall. They are men, like you and me." He stopped and looked at her chest and the sweet hollows of her neck and throat. "Or like me, anyway," he amended.

She knelt and undid his boots. "You mustn't," he said.

"Shut your mouth," she answered tersely.

Betty now entered with the drinking water. When she saw that Janetta was undressing the master, her eyes grew wide. "You know what you doin', Missy Janetta?" she said tremulously.

"Of course I do, you stupid cow!" retorted Janetta. "Now put that glass down, and get out of here. I shall want some hot water for tea in a minute—make sure it is ready."

"Yes, Missy Janetta," said Betty, turning about with difficulty and making her way out of the room.

Janetta had his boots off. "Now," she said. "Lie down."

He refused to move. She put one hand on his chest and pushed him down onto the bed as though he were a child.

"How did you do that?" he asked. The brief lucidity he had experienced was already receding.

She undid his belt and unbuttoned his trousers.

"Oh, no!" he told her.

"Do not be an idiot."

He could not stop her. He could not focus his attention on what she was doing long enough; or else there was a lag in his comprehension, so that she had finished what she was doing before he even saw how she was going about it. In a moment she had stripped him naked and set his clothes aside; then she took up the wet cloth and sponge-bathed him without any concern for his modesty.

"You are getting the bed wet," he observed, in an ineffectual attempt to deter her.

"It doesn't matter. You are going to sweat as you have never sweated before. This bed will be drenched."

Only when she was finished this task did she cover him by drawing the sheet over him to the waist. Then she came to stand by his head. She rinsed the cloth and wiped his brow with it.

"Listen to me," she said. When he made no response, she said, "White Edmund! Listen to me!"

He managed a yes.

"I am going up to get my herbs. You are going to lie here and wait for me to get back. You are not going to get any mad ideas about going any place."

"Never fear," he said, shaking off his confusion for another brief moment. "I could not move."

She wiped his brow gently again. He had never known her to be gentle in this way, and he put his hand up, almost involuntarily, as it seemed to him, and laid it on hers as she wiped his cheek.

She looked on him grimly. Then she whispered, as if he could not hear her, or as if she was sure he would not remember what she said when he was well again: "Now you are mine. For these few days, you are all mine."

Then she went away and left him for a few minutes, alone in the grip of the increasing confusion of the fever.

⌛⌛⌛⌛⌛

The course of the illness was as violent as its onset. The delirium was extreme; the passage of time was marked only by inexplicably rapid alternations of day and night and the gathering and dispersing of figures around him. He saw Alex again, and spoke with him at length, though neither of them could say anything but nonsense. His father came, too, and frowned over him, seeming partly angry at him for something, and partly terrified that he would die. Christopher and Bronwyn were there, and sometimes Bronwyn stayed, and became that strange woman with the face that was half-white. At one point three gray shadows filed into the room and exclaimed over him; and then Janetta entered, and an altercation ensued, as Janetta shrieked and raged at the gray beings. Then the gray beings went away, and he was convinced they had been the three Fates, come to cut the thread of his life, and Janetta had driven them off. At another time he conceived an overwhelming urge to take his horse and ride across the island to the sea, to get some relief from the terrible fever that racked him. Janetta could not hold him back, and he got as far as the stable before Janetta's cries brought the men at a run, and Warner and a half-dozen others overpowered him and carried him back to his bed.

He experienced moments of relative lucidity as well. By comparison with the delirium, these were almost blissful. He lay quietly on the bed, and Janetta sponged the sweat from him. She seemed almost tender in her care. Sometimes he would catch her hand clumsily as she wiped his chest or brow, and she would smile ever so slightly, a faint smile that revealed a deep pleasure; and then she would tug her hand free and continue bathing him. She constantly forced him to drink, cradling his head in the crook of her arm and holding the cup to his mouth; and at those moments, her face would be very close to his, and she would stare at him hungrily. Sometimes she seemed overcome by some emotion, and went away in silence for a few minutes, though if he called her, she came rushing back.

Sometimes she spoke to him in a kind of fond, abusive style. "You stupid Englishman," she would taunt him. "Why did you go and get sick? What was the point of it? So that Janetta would take care of you?—What, do you think this is easy for Janetta? If you only knew, this is the hardest thing Janetta has ever done." If he tried to thank her, she would grow angry and hold his mouth shut with one hand, insulting him until he held his peace. At times she was sullen; but then her irritation would give over to some act or word of extreme kindness.

She forbade Betty the house. She did everything indoors that needed to be done. She prepared amazing little delicacies from fresh fruit to tempt him to eat. She not only emptied the chamber pot, but when he could not go to it, she brought it to him. When the bed was utterly drenched, she would force him to get out of it, and then would turn the mattress and put on fresh sheets.

Modesty was out of the question. In his fever he ceased to care about it. And one night he woke out of a wild dream to see her naked as well, standing in the lamplight, sponging herself clean. The sight was more than he could endure; he closed his eyes, and underneath his eyelids the glimpse he had had of her seemed to fragment into a blur of whirling, kaleidoscopic images.

And as suddenly as the sickness had come, it went away. He awoke one morning weak and exhausted, but fully lucid. Janetta was not there. He rose and dressed himself, and then went out on the verandah and sat in a chair. In a few minutes she came around the house with a basket. She did not seem surprised to see him up; doubtless she had perceived last night that his fever had broken. Though she was, of course, her usual sullen self, she also seemed a little sad.

"So, White Edmund, you are better."

"Yes," he said.

"What a god you are!" she said. "That fever would have killed anyone lesser."

"I am no god," he said. "But I do have a God, one and only one, who has helped me get through this."

"Oh, is that so?" she said mockingly. "How odd that I did not see *Him* beside me when I was staying awake all those nights, caring for you as if I were *your* slave, and not someone else's."

"Thank you, Janetta," he said.

"For what?" she said, suddenly angry.

"For taking care of me."

"You fool! I only did that so you would not die. If you die, the next Englishman who comes here will drive me out."

A pang of guilt and grief went through Edmund as he remembered his conversation with Mr. Duckworth and the letter he had sent his father. What would happen to Janetta when he left? He must strike some bargain with Mr. Duckworth to let her stay in the mill.

He leaned his head wearily on the back of the chair. "Say what you will," he said. "You are a strange, mad creature. It is as if you do not want anyone to know how kind you are, inside, under the anger and the sullenness. But I know, Janetta. I have seen how kind you are, and I shall not forget it; not for as long as I live."

"Oh, shut your mouth!" she said abruptly; but she seemed confused, and he thought she might almost be about to cry. "Now I suppose I ought to send Betty back to fuss over you and annoy you," she said.

He looked at her slender body, and the craving for her that his fever had kept in abeyance came back instantly.

"You had better do that," he said.

A pang seemed to go through her, too; and she turned without another word and went away.

⌛⌛⌛⌛⌛

Within a week he had fully recovered and returned to working in the fields. Neither he nor Janetta ever referred to the time of his fever, except on one occasion. The crew had stopped at the end of a row of cane to sit down for a spell and drink water. They happened to be near the boundary with Mr. Duckworth's land, and some of Mr. Duckworth's men were working not far off. The two groups called back and forth, bantering with each other. Just then Mrs. Duckworth and her daughters came through the field, carrying home some baskets laden with produce from one of their gardens.

The sight of the three figures in gray triggered a memory from Edmund's fever. He was staring at them in puzzlement when Janetta noticed. She laughed harshly. "They won't ever come here again," she said to him.

"Who? Mrs. Duckworth and her daughters?"

"Don't you remember?"

"No—was it when I was sick?"

"They heard you had a fever and came over to care for you." She laughed. "Stupid cows! And I drove them away like cows, too."

"What!"

She laughed.

"Why did you not tell me this?" he said.

"I thought you knew. I had left you for a minute to go up to the mill; you were lying on your bed, without a stitch on, when they went into the house."

"Oh, my God!"

"I suppose they were shocked. They had covered you with blankets by the time I got back. I was furious. What a stupid thing! Cover a sick man with blankets! I told them to go to hell."

"Janetta!" he said in horror. "You did not do anything of the kind!"

"I did too. I pushed one of the little baby ones, and I tore the stupid basket out of the big one's hands and threw it out the door; and I told them to get out and never come back. When they ran out of the house I ran after them, and flung the basket at them."

He put his head in his hands in disbelief.

"And I used words they probably don't even know," she said, laughing at the recollection.

"I hate to think," he said. He got to his feet and went immediately after the three Quaker women.

After a minute, when they noticed him purposely following them, they halted and turned to await him.

"Mrs. Duckworth," he said as he came up to them, "I have just been informed of an incident that occurred when I was recently ill. I have no recollection of it myself—my fever was very high, I am afraid—but from what I have just heard, you and your daughters were gravely insulted."

"Think nothing of it, Mr. Percy," said Mrs. Duckworth.

"How can I think nothing of it? It grieves me terribly to think that my good friends and neighbors were so abused."

"What matters, Mr. Percy, is that thee are well. Our almighty Father has looked after thee. The care thee received may have been a little coarse, but it seems to have been effective."

"It is very kind of you to look at it that way, ma'am—very generous. But it grieves me still that you and your daughters should be exposed to such abuse."

"She is very possessive of thee," observed Mrs. Duckworth. He took this as a reproach.

"She was indeed so on that occasion," he said, "but that was most unusual. I think it was the thought that she would not be in command of the battlefield that drove her wild."

"Ah," said Mrs. Duckworth. "Well, Mr. Percy, do not be concerned on our behalf. We are still loyal friends and neighbors to thee."

"But I should like to apologize to Mr. Duckworth as well. Would you tell me where I can find him?"

"He has gone to St. John's. He will be back before dinner. Will thee join us, Mr. Percy?"

He balked at this. "Perhaps some other time, Mrs. Duckworth. Or perhaps I shall walk up after dinner to talk to Mr. Duckworth."

"Very well. It will be pleasant to see thee at any time."

"You are very generous, ma'am—very kind and forgiving."

"What else should we be, Mr. Percy?"

"Indeed, ma'am; indeed.—Good day, until later, then."

"Good day, Mr. Percy."

As he walked away he realized he had neglected to so much as nod in greeting to the two daughters or address them in any way; but he thought it unlikely that they would care.

Janetta had already set the men working again when he went back. She looked at up him with a grin from where she crouched, tying a bundle of cane gleanings. "Did you *soothe their injured feelings?*" she asked ironically.

"Where did you ever get that phrase?" he said in frustration. "I swear, Janetta—sometimes you talk the King's English as well as if you had been brought up in a girl's school in London; and sometimes you are as foul-mouthed as a Billingsgate fishwife. Not that you ever lose your accent, mind you."

"My mother taught me," she said. "She read to me by the hour.—You are surprised? You did not know that." Then she added: "How could you? I never told you."

"Well, however you talk, it makes no difference to your manners! Crude, most of the time; and every once in a while, kind; but only in such a way as to make one wonder why you cannot make the effort more often. I cannot understand you."

As usual when he was reproaching her, she paid no attention, but continued to think her own thoughts. "Yes," she said, "my mother was Waller's bought whore; but she had an education, and she tried to give me one. Someday I shall take vengeance for what he did to her."

"Vengeance belongs to God," said Edmund.

"Good! He will be pleased, then, when I become—what would your holy men say?—His instrument in the matter." And so saying, she brandished the knife she had been using.

He said nothing further, and she went back to her task. Then she said, "I wish you had seen those gray cows running away, clutching their baskets in one hand and holding their bonnets on with the other. You would have laughed too, White Edmund!"

And now, to his own surprise, a laugh did escape him, very much against his will, as he thought of the three bland Quaker Fates driven away by this lithe, hot-tempered little Antiguan Fury.

She stood up and grinned at him, delighted that she had surprised some laughter out of him. "Ah, White Edmund! You are not so cold and stupid after all!"

He laughed outright. "If my manners were as bad as yours, Janetta, I would tell you to shut your mouth."

She grinned still more broadly. "That's better!" she said. "Tell me to shut my mouth. Go ahead—it will be good for your soul."

"Although I doubt that, I shall indulge your wish, and say: *Shut your mouth,* Janetta."

She emitted a hoot of pleasure, and the men looked around at her from their work. "Did you hear that?" she said to them. "The master told me to shut my mouth!"

They did not know how to safely react to this news. She ignored them and turned back to Edmund. "Antigua will make a real man out of you yet, White Edmund," she said.

They looked at one another, and he saw the same hunger in her eyes that he felt in his own heart. He turned away and went elsewhere to work.

⌛⌛⌛⌛⌛

Later that day he visited Mr. Duckworth. He had another reason for speaking with his neighbor: the Quaker had been slow in making the offer Edmund had asked him for. Mr. Duckworth received him in his usual kindly way, in his parlor, with his womenfolk silently knitting and sewing about him. "I have offered my apologies to the ladies earlier, sir," said Edmund. "But I am come on purpose now to offer them particularly to you. I understand your wife and daughters visited me when I was ill. I have no recollection of it, I am sorry to say, or I would have known to apologize sooner. I was very delirious—I dare say I have never in my life been so ill. I just learned this morning of their visit."

"First, sit down, Mr. Percy," said Mr. Duckworth.

Edmund did so, hat in hand, though the Quaker, true to his kind, was still wearing his own.

"And now," said Mr. Duckworth, "What is there to apologize for?" He obviously had heard the whole story, but was being polite by pretending it was of no importance.

"Apparently your wife and daughters, sir, were badly used by the woman who was taking care of me at the time."

"Janetta Waller, do you mean?" said Mr. Duckworth.

"Yes, sir."

"Perhaps it was not such a wise choice, Mr. Percy—if you will permit me to say so—to let that woman take care of you."

"It was not a choice at all. I was overcome by fever and absolutely delirious. I was quite as helpless as an infant. I could no more have stopped her than I could have stopped the fever in its tracks."

Mr. Duckworth looked at him keenly. "An apt metaphor, Mr. Percy," he said. "I fear this Janetta woman is very much like a kind of fever for some men."

Edmund was shocked that Mr. Duckworth was speaking in this way in the presence of his family.

"Well, I can assure you, sir," he said, "she is not so with me. I am grateful to her for her care for me; but she is a wild creature, very coarse, as might be expected, considering her upbringing. She has been a great help to me in keeping the men working—I really do not know how I should have done without her. They are all very much in awe of her, and they do as she says. As you doubtless have observed, she has become a kind of overseer, strange as it may seem; and I am glad of it, for how they could be brought to work without the whip I scarcely know, and I certainly am not such a one as to ply it on them."

"And what do you give her in return?"

He was surprised at the question. "Why, nothing. That is, I give her a place to dwell that is safe from Waller, up in the mill."

"Is that all?"

He could not understand this line of questioning. "Well, food—I give her food as well. She was half-starved when I came to Antigua, and I am pleased to say she is not quite so bony now as she was then."

"And you are sure that is all?"

"Really, Mr. Duckworth, I do not understand your questions. That is all I have ever given her."

"Not long ago she acquired a new dress."

"Oh, yes—I gave her that as well, when I gave the slaves their six-month allowance of clothing, after the harvest."

"But this dress, Mr. Percy, was not such as you gave the other slaves."

"Why, no—it was not. She is such a strange, curst creature that I had an inkling that she would not like what they wear. I really had to buy her something—what she had been wearing was most indecent. I attempted to give her the usual garment, but she flung it immediately into the fire. So then I gave her the other garment I had brought, which is the dress you have seen."

"That was perhaps not wisely done, Mr. Percy."

Edmund was perplexed. "And why is that, sir?"

"Are you really so innocent? But I suppose you are not familiar with the ways of men and women on our island. It is very common for a white man who wants to make a black woman his mistress to give her a dress—an uncommon dress."

"Oh, my God!" cried Edmund.

"There is no need to blaspheme, Mr. Percy."

"But I had no idea! It was done quite innocently, sir, I assure you."

Mr. Duckworth smiled softly. "Yes," he said. "I am sure it was." He stood up and came to sit closer to Edmund—he sat on the edge of the seat, leaning forward, and looking earnestly into Edmund's eyes. "I fear for you sometimes, Mr. Percy. You are too innocent. It is an admirable quality in you; but I fear it will not do in Antigua."

"And you, sir—are you not innocent as well? Innocent and good? I think you are."

"I hope I am—indeed I hope I am, as you say. But as innocent as you may think me, and as I may be, still I have seen much evil, much more than you have. I can see the world through the eyes of the evil, whereas you cannot. You can only see through the eyes of the good. I hope you never lose that quality, Mr. Percy; but if you are not careful, Antigua will break it in you."

"Well, I shall take your words to heart, sir. But I am not sure how I ought to amend my behavior, or how I am to foresee these errors if I do not even know they exist."

"Do you not see an obvious correction you must make?"

"And what is that? I am afraid I do not."

"You must send this Janetta away."

"Send her away!" he cried in dismay.

"Ah," said Mr. Duckworth. "Are you attached to her, then?"

"No—no, it is not that. But I have considered this before, when I first came to Antigua. I spoke to Mr. Morgette concerning it. At the time he told me that my only recourse was to turn her over to Waller; and that I could not do—I believe you yourself would not do such a thing either, Mr. Duckworth."

"No, I would not. But there are other places she might live."

"Where? Instruct me, sir; you will find me glad to listen."

"Indeed, I cannot tell you; but I am sure that if she is cast out on her own resources, she will find a place. She will land on her feet, believe me."

"What? I am simply to drive her out and trust her to find shelter somewhere?"

"Exactly."

"Why, I could not do that, whatever the cost to my reputation. She requires protection from Waller. She has some measure of it where she is; I doubt she would have any such protection elsewhere."

"Do not delude yourself. It is impossible she would not find another protector, Mr. Percy."

Edmund took his drift and was still more amazed. "Are you telling me I ought to drive this poor woman into the arms of sin?" he said.

"I am warning you that you are in danger yourself," said Mr. Duckworth. "You cannot protect her without destroying yourself. You must let her go elsewhere. She has her wits about her; she will survive—nay, she will prosper, mark my words."

"Prosper in the works of the Devil, Mr. Duckworth!" And now Edmund looked around at the women in the room, who were impassively and silently working, as if they were paying no attention to this very interesting conversation. "Really, sir, I am amazed that you discuss this in present company."

"We are all deeply interested in your welfare, Mr. Percy," said Mr. Duckworth.

"That is very kind of you—very kind. But as I see it, I have a Christian duty to protect this woman from sin, if it lies within my power to do so; and God has, for reasons unknown to me, put it within my power. I must protect her; and so I do. I hope neither you nor anyone will teach me not to protect the weak and vulnerable, or not to care for those who would fall directly into sin without my support."

"Have you ever tried to save a drowning man, Mr. Percy?"

"No, sir."

"The greatest danger lies in not being pulled down yourself."

"What are you saying?"

"I am saying that you cannot save the whole world. It will pull you down. And this daughter of Waller's is one part of that world in particular that you cannot save."

"Well, there is this difference between us, sir: that you, in my opinion, are content with half-way measures against sin; and I am not."

"Yes, I know; you would abolish slavery."

"Indeed I would, sir—as quickly as I can snap my fingers. And I bitterly regret that I have been caught in this trap at Canebrake."

"And you fault me for seemingly perpetuating slavery?"

"With all humility, sir, I own I have reproached you with that in my mind. It seems to me that for all your thoughtfulness toward your workers, you still think of them as *slaves,* as people whose destiny it is to be enslaved, people whose very definition as living beings is that of creatures who ought to be compelled to labor for others; whereas they are, rather, free human beings struggling in an unjust condition of enslavement that you perpetuate—a condition that is contrary to the order and will of almighty God and his loving Son."

"I understand what you say, Mr. Percy, and I respect the feelings that compel you to say it. But your Christianity is idealistic, and mine is practical. Look at what I have accomplished here. I have two hundred men and women under me, who are well-housed, well-fed, well-clothed; taught to read and write; and given some understanding of the Bible truths and of God's salvation. Compare your own situation: you have twenty men whom you work so hard they are too exhausted to educate. You palliate your use of them by working alongside them—that is how you make excuses to your conscience. I submit, Mr. Percy, that you are squandering the excellence that God gave you—the brains and the goodness that were his gifts to you. He did not make you to be a field hand; he made you to be a leader of men."

Edmund started to respond, but Mr. Duckworth held up a hand to ask for his further attention.

"This is what I propose to you," he said. "I shall buy your estate from your father. Stay here; join forces with me. You shall be part owner with me of our combined estate, in proportion to the land that was your father's; and you shall over time pay to me a purchase price for that share, equal to what I paid your father. It will not take you more than a few years to pay me back."

"Mr. Duckworth," Edmund said, "This is an offer much like the one you mentioned before."

"Better than that offer, Mr. Percy."

"Aye, sir, I own it is a better one. I am most touched by your generosity. I am deeply moved by it—by your generosity and your belief in me, your confidence in me. But I have never planned to stay in Antigua. I always meant to go home to England. I shall become a clergyman; I shall find a living; and I shall marry. That was once the sum total of my ambition—to be a clergyman and to help those in my parish in what small way I can. It is true that shortly after I came to Antigua I developed an ambition to prove that there was a better system for these islands than slavery; but in spite of my—well, I suppose I should say, in spite of my rather blockheaded delusions, I see that I am not persuading anyone. I must go back to England. Your offer of a partnership is most kind, but I must very respectfully decline it."

"It is your loyalty to your church," said Mr. Duckworth, as if suddenly understanding the reason for Edmund's refusal.

"It is that and my loyalty to everything, sir. To England, to life there as I have always known it; to my family; to my hopes and dreams.—And by God, Mr. Duckworth, what I would not give for the sight of a good English girl! I think I would marry the first woman I met after I stepped off the ship, if she should only be possessed of half the grace and charm that I remember in the females of my own kind!"

"Mr. Percy, Mr. Percy—will you not once come to service at our meeting house?"

Edmund stared at him in amazement. "What!" he said. "Mr. Duckworth, what kind of a nonsequitur is this? I tell you how much I love and long for my home, and you bid me to your meeting house?"

"But you have told me how poor the services are in the parish church here. Can you not try ours just once?"

"I would sooner set foot in a mosque!" cried Edmund, exasperation overwhelming his good manners.

"Oh, come, come, Mr. Percy. We are your countrymen, after all; we are Christians, not Mahometans."

"My country, sir, has a state church; and that church is the Church of England. God forbid that I—"

"Do not exercise yourself, my friend. Only take it in thought, and let it be as God directs you."

"Yes—in that I can agree with you, sir. May it be as God directs."

Mr. Duckworth turned to his wife now and said, "Mr. Percy and I have some particular business to discuss."

She rose at once, and her daughters with her, and they went out without another word. Edmund thought it altogether too late for Mr. Duckworth to be scrupulous about what they overheard; but he did not guess what his friend still had left to say.

"Have you determined on a figure that I can relay to my father?" he asked Mr. Duckworth when the women had left.

"I have," said Mr. Duckworth. He took a minute scrap of worn paper from his pocket and handed it to Edmund. It showed, in a very fine hand, a computation of the value of Canebrake. Edmund studied it and readily saw that it was both just and generous, even if it did not reflect the exorbitant value that other planters might set on the plantation.

"Very fine, sir," he said. "I thank you. If this is a definite offer, I can write to my father at once, and perhaps get my letter on an early packet.—Thank you, sir. This will be my deliverance."

"I hope it will be your deliverance indeed—and the foundation of your fortune."

"Ah—you mean still to persuade me to stay."

"I do."

"Well, you are too kind. But please do give up that thought.—I shall go back to Canebrake and write to my father at once."

He began to rise, but Mr. Duckworth stopped him by saying, "Stay, stay a moment, Mr. Percy."

Edmund could not but accede to this wish. Mr. Duckworth kept him waiting impatiently for several minutes as he apparently tried to find a way to frame what he had to say.

"I have suggested a partnership," he said finally. "Perhaps you think that a business engagement alone would not offer sufficient surety of my intentions."

"That is no obstacle, I assure you. You are the plainest, most honest man I ever knew, Mr. Duckworth."

"But it may seem inexplicable to you that I should decide to make you my partner."

Edmund had never gone so far in his thinking on this matter as to have such a difficulty, and it took him a moment to put himself into the hypothetical point of view Mr. Duckworth described. Then he said, "I suppose that if I were to consider your offer, I would not find it inexplicable at all; I would flatter myself that I should be as honest and hardworking a partner as one could wish for."

Mr. Duckworth smiled. "You must let me get to my point, Mr. Percy."

"Forgive me, sir."

"You spoke of a wife. What if I were to tell you that I mean to find you a wife into the bargain; a wife you will very much approve, when you know her better. I should like you to marry my daughter Hannah."

Edmund was dumbfounded. It required all the polite breeding he could command not to exclaim with disgust at the thought. To be married to such a cold, unfeeling woman would be a kind of hell he had never imagined. To compound his consternation, he did not even know which of the daughters Hannah was. Neither had shown the slightest inclination for him. He assumed it was the older one; but he was not even really sure which was the older.

Now he understood the full import of Mr. Duckworth's plan; but he did not see it as his friend did. He saw that not only would Mr. Duckworth keep him in Antigua, enmeshed in the business of running a plantation, with all its attendant evils—he would saddle him with a woman who cared nothing for him. He did not think to ask Mr. Duckworth how his daughter felt; he assumed she did not care one way or the other.

"Of course," continued Mr. Duckworth, "she should be married within your church. She would find that well within the scope of our beliefs. And your children could be baptized and raised in the Church of England. She would still attend our meeting, however; and I hope you would find yourself amenable to that. I hope that someday you will join us there; but that shall be as God wills."

"Mr. Duckworth," said Edmund, "I do not know what to say."

"Say nothing, if you do not know what to say. Take my offer away with you and think on it. I believe that it is the need of a wife that is driving you to England, just as much as it is your loyalty to your church; and I offer you compensation for both, if you will only avail yourself of them."

"Sir, I understand that there is no way in which a father can assert greater confidence in a man than to make him an offer of his own daughter in marriage. This cannot help but make me feel that I have won your esteem—esteem far greater than I can deserve. No one—no one but our Lord—is more aware than I am of my own failings and sins—"

"Mr. Percy," said Mr. Duckworth, interrupting him, "go home now. Write your letter to your father. But think about what I have said. She is a very fine young woman, Mr. Percy. She will be a great help to you. She will ease the ache in you. She will reconcile you to life here. You will make your fortune, and go home in good time to England, where you may do more good than you could ever do as a poor clergyman. You shall see."

Edmund could not refuse an offer to be released from this conversation. He stood up at once; but then he hesitated a moment.

"Let me clarify one point," he said.

"Yes?"

He indicated the slip of paper in his hand. "Is the offer you have set out for Canebrake contingent on my marrying your daughter—on my becoming a partner with you?"

"No, Mr. Percy. Even if I should lose you as my son, I would like to have Canebrake."

"Good. Then I shall have no qualms of conscience in conveying this offer to my father."

"Do go ahead, Mr. Percy. But think on the advantages to you if you stay. I make you an offer at which many a young man would jump indeed. Do not miss it. Do not wind up back in England, living in a cramped, cold, run-down rectory, wishing you had taken me up on this offer. And like as not, though it may seem uncharitable to say it, you may find yourself with a cold, ungrateful woman who cares nothing for you. That happens all too readily these days in England. I have seen it."

"God forbid," said Edmund. "God forbid that I should marry an unfeeling woman! I shall say amen to that with a will, Mr. Duckworth."

Chapter II

καί τὸ τὴν ὥραν διασῶσαι. καὶ τὸ μὴ πρὸ ὥρας ἀνδρωθῆναι, αλλ΄ ἐτι καὶ ἐπιλαβεῖν τοῦ χρόνου.

And [I give thanks] that I preserved the flower of my youth; and that I did not become a man before the proper hour, but even postponed that hour.

—Aurelius

H*e wrote* the addendum to his father that very evening, and the next morning he was at the post office in St. John's. He was fortunate; the mail was to go downwind to Jamaica the next day, and from there soon after to England by mail packet. All he could do now was wait.

Wait; wait and work; and he told himself he would not slacken his efforts on the plantation. But despite this resolution, his zeal began to ebb the instant he had hope that he would soon return to England, though he did not notice the falling of its tide. The slaves, by contrast, saw the falling off, and took what surcease from labor they could get from it.

None of them had an inkling of what was afoot. Mr. Duckworth understood the value of silence in this matter, and though clearly his wife and daughters were apprised of his offer, they were nothing if not discreet. At times Edmund's conscience smote him, for he had no idea what provision to make for Janetta. He only hoped that Mr. Duckworth, when the matter was finally in his own hands, would not be able to bring himself to dislodge her from the mill any more than Edmund had.

At first the rising hope that he would soon be leaving made it easier for Edmund to disregard her. But as the weeks passed and no answer arrived from England, the immediacy of her presence overcame that temporary infusion of strength. Mr. Duckworth's warnings in themselves seemed to turn Edmund's thoughts where they should not go. He could not look at Janetta without thinking why he should not be looking at her, and then inevitably his mind must stray into the very thoughts he was trying to avoid.

Forbidden physical desire is built of a thousand such nested paradoxes. When Edmund was not within sight of Janetta, the thought of her was in some ways repugnant to him. He knew perfectly well that she was filled with rage and despair; that what tenderness she was capable of was rare and fleeting; that her character had been formed in Waller's house under the most violent and sensual of impressions. She was not only not of his race—an obstacle that counted for much in his day—she was also not of his class, which was an obstacle almost equally insurmountable. They had little common experience and little to say to one another. He found her bitterness and her insulting and impertinent attitude coarse and tedious despite the pity it awoke in him. When he thought of the typical well-bred Englishwoman in contrast to her, his heart seemed to melt with yearning—for the gentleness and kindness of his mother, or the gracious wit of his Aunt Andromeda. As he had told Mr. Duckworth, a little gracefulness would have gone a long way with him, especially after his immersion in the crude and brutal world of forced labor. For superficial reasons as well, Janetta was not to his taste. She was beautiful, incontestably—he had never really been able to deceive himself about that; but it was a lithe, feline, slender kind of beauty that he had never grown to like. At home he had been taught to like the statuesque; and certainly she was too thin, however much better fed she was now than when he had first met her.

And yet—and herein was the paradox—when he saw her, when he actually held her in his physical vision, those considerations became as nothing. The stark curves of her body were so shapely that they woke in him not only the coarsest of lusts, but a transcendent longing after beauty in the abstract. He wanted to draw and paint and sculpt her curves, describe them in verse. As she worked beside him in the field, he saw her from every side, every angle. He knew from observation how firm her buttocks and breasts were—he could not help it, for half the time her dress clung to her, and for the rest, she might be leaning over facing him and he might glimpse her breasts within the slack bodice of her dress, or leaning away, in which case he could not help but notice the shape of her lower body.

His lust for her was so visual that at times all his self-persuasion to rout her from his mind was for naught, and the vision of her body pursued his consciousness, keeping his attention even when he was not with her; and then he cared nothing for English women, and he yearned on, yearned still for the body of that one wild mulatto.

As for her, he now had no doubt she felt the same. As often as she caught him eyeing her wantingly, he caught her looking at him the same way. Sometimes their eyes would dwell upon one another defiantly; but most often he would turn away, often even walk a distance away, to be apart from her. She had a countervailing instinct to gravitate toward him—he really did not think it was conscious; but often, after several hours of labor in the fields, he would look about and realize that he and she were close together, and fifty yards distant from the others.

When he was apart from her, particularly in the house at night, he prayed constantly for some relief from this lust. But no relief was given to him. He ascribed this withholding of solace to the insincerity of his repentance; for the moment he saw her, he desired her again. What was worse, he began to enjoy his desire, even though it was unfulfilled.

He fought his impulse not only with prayer but in other ways as well. He took Mr. Duckworth's former advice to heart—paid a call on the Morgettes, and after he was again disgusted by Miss Morgette, on other families he knew in the neighborhood. They were all surprised and, though not openly hostile to him, clearly wary of his attention. He could see that they now valued him more as an object of negative gossip than as an addition to their society.

In consequence of this belated visiting, however, he did receive an invitation to a ball. He determined to go. The appointed evening came; he dressed himself in his evening clothes, which had not been on his back in years now; and he got as far as the front steps of the verandah before it occurred to him that he had no gloves—that he had sacrificed them in some task in his first year in Antigua before his hands had hardened to their unaccustomed labor. He inspected the palms of his hands. They were roughened, chapped, even lined faintly with an embedded dirt that no washing could remove. What woman would want him to take her hand, even her gloved hand, in such a hand as this? He had the hands of a yeoman now, not a gentleman. A few months of leisure would repair them; but no instant healing was to be had.

He went into the house again and changed back into his ordinary clothes. Then he sat by himself on the verandah as the evening came on, smoking a cigar. The very tobacco seemed an aphrodisiac.

⌛⌛⌛⌛⌛

Betty's pregnancy came to its term and she went into labor one Wednesday evening. Johnny immediately went over to Mr. Duckworth's plantation, and several of Mr. Duckworth's women slaves returned with him to assist with the birth.

The labor was difficult and prolonged, however, and when Edmund went over to the couples' cabin on Thursday morning, Johnny was looking frightened. Apparently the report of the midwives was not good. Edmund had Johnny summon the head midwife to him; and this woman, a very large and competent-looking woman by the name of Sarah, only enlarged on the bad news.

"Dat picnee in dere de wrong way, Massa Percy," she said. "I don' know if it *evah* come out."

"I shall call a doctor at once," he said.

"Go 'head if you wants; but I don' know what *he* kin do."

Edmund rode at once to Dr. Mann's house, and somewhat unexpectedly found the physician at home; but Dr. Mann was at first unwilling to return with Edmund to Canebrake, and it took Edmund some twenty minutes to persuade him to do so.

They were at the door of Betty's cabin about two hours after Edmund's first inquiry. At the threshold, however, Dr. Mann balked and would not go in. "You must get all those negroes out first," he said.

"They are just the midwives," said Edmund, a little puzzled.

"I shall not go into such a confined space with that many negroes."

Edmund looked at him in incomprehension.

"I am not jesting," said Dr. Mann.

"As you wish," said Edmund. He told the women to step outside the cabin, and then he and the doctor entered.

He himself had never seen a woman in labor, and the sight shocked him. Betty was completely naked, propped on heaps of rags and even some old lumber. Her knees were drawn up, and her sex was completely exposed. She was covered with sweat, and her eyes rolled drunkenly in the delirium of her exhaustion. He had been hearing her cries all night long, but now she had not the strength to make them.

He looked away while the doctor examined her, but then Mann called for his attention. "Look here," he said. Edmund did as he was bid. "Do you see this bulge here?"

said the doctor, pointing to a distinctive smaller dome at the base of Betty's enormous belly. "That is the infant's head, pushing up against the inside of the womb. I don't know what these negro women may have done in an effort to get it out; they may well have already broken its neck."

Edmund shook his head in frustration. "What is to be done?" he asked.

"There is only one thing that can be done. I must cut her open and extract the infant."

"But what is the risk to her?"

"She is only a slave, Percy."

"What are you saying?"

"I am saying she is only a slave. Rumor has it that you seem to have forgotten the distinction between us and the negroes, so I am reminding you that she is not one of us. What happens to her is of little consequence other than economic. The point is that if we do not extract the infant, she will die. If we do extract it, and if it is still alive, you will have a slave with which to replace her—and in fact a more valuable slave, if the infant turns out to be male."

Edmund stood in silent horror, which the doctor took for indecision.

"Mr. Percy," said Dr. Mann, "I know many planters here on Antigua who care more for their dogs than they do for their slaves. And though I do not go so far, that attitude does not surprise me. A slave is merely an economic asset. She will die soon anyway; all slaves die young here; they are simply worked to death. That is why I am reluctant to take them in my care—it is largely a pointless exercise, unless I can prolong their economic use without an injurious cost to the owner."

The doctor took Edmund's continued stunned silence as a kind of affirmative. "I shall go ahead, then," he said.

"What is the risk to her?" Edmund demanded again.

"To be perfectly frank with you—I should expect she will be dead from puerperal fever within a day or two if I operate. It will occasion some further inconvenience—you will have to find a wet nurse for the infant."

Johnny, who had been listening to this conversation in terror at the doorway, now burst into the cabin and flung himself on his knees at Edmund's feet. "No, no, Massa!" he cried. "Don' let 'im cut Betty! Don' let 'im kill my Betty!"

It was a dilemma requiring the wisdom of a Solomon, and Edmund felt himself utterly unfit for it. The mere sight of the naked woman had so shocked him that he could hardly think, and now he was being called upon to solve a problem in the most advanced calculus of human life.

"Johnny," he said, looking down into that man's wide and terrified eyes, "do you understand what the doctor is saying? It is a choice between saving the baby and nothing. Betty is likely to die one way or another—we have got to get that baby out of there."

"No, no, Massa!" begged Johnny. "De picnee come out, you see! Leave de picnee dere, Massa, leave de picnee!"

"Is there absolutely no chance that the mother will survive?" Edmund asked Dr. Mann.

"In cases like this, I sometimes think I ought not even bother to sew up the womb again," said the doctor. "It has never proved worth my trouble."

Some instinct told Edmund what to do. It was certainly not a rational decision, because reason would not have led him to it, even if he had been capable at that moment of rational thought.

"No, Dr. Mann," he said. "I thank you for your trouble. I shall pay you for the inconvenience I have caused to you, and for your visit. But I shall not require your services any further."

It was the doctor's turn to be stunned. "What!" he cried. "Mr. Percy, what are you saying?"

A long and bitter argument then ensued. The doctor felt that his professional reputation had somehow been challenged or set at stake, and when he found that Edmund had no rational objections to offer, he was only the more incensed. Finally he left the cabin in disgust.

Edmund followed him out to his gig. "Allow me to compensate you for your inconvenience, Dr. Mann," he said.

The doctor, in a voice choked with fury, specified an exorbitant sum. Edmund paid it without question. As Dr. Mann pocketed it, he stared with contempt at Edmund and said, "You are out of your depth in Antigua, Mr. Percy; you have only proved now what I and the other gentlemen of the island have long suspected of you. If I were you, I would go home as soon as possible."

He climbed up into the gig, laid his whip to the back of his horse, and drove off at a smart pace.

The midwives had swarmed back into the cabin as soon as the doctor had left. Edmund went boldly into the place now; his instinct was beginning to form into a resolution.

"Do you see any course of action?" he said to Sarah. He had to repeat his question in simpler terms before she understood him.

"No, Massa," she said. "We done tried ebreyting. We done pushed down de picnee's head from de outside, but it don' stay down. She ain't open enough to put a hand up in dere and move dat picnee from de inside. Picnee's s'posed to push 'er open, push its way outta dere. It jes' can't do dat."

"I shall go get Janetta," he announced.

On hearing this, Betty seemed to come to herself; she cried, "No! No! Not dat witch!"

Johnny, too, who had slunk back to the doorway and had been listening from outside, now cried, "No! No, Massa!"

"It is our only chance," said Edmund. He left the cabin; but Johnny ran after him and again flung himself on his knees, catching Edmund by the leg.

"No, no, Massa! Please don' let dat witch touch my pic'nee!"

"What possible objection can you have?" said Edmund. "Johnny, that woman you call a witch saved your life. Have you already forgotten?"

"Dat witch touch my picnee, she mark him for de Debil! He be de Debil's slave all his life!"

"Don't be absurd, man! She will save Betty *and* your baby, if anyone can! And if you would pray to the Lord instead of to your Devil, you would not fear your Devil half so much."

He was facing back toward the cabin as he said these words; and now he saw the midwives flee, one after the other, out the open door, and head through the cane fields toward Mr. Duckworth's. The sight made him angry. He realized that he was going to be truly alone in this decision, and he could not even reasonably justify it to himself.

He shook off Johnny's grip and once again climbed to the windmill. At his knock Janetta opened the door instantly. She did not even attempt to disguise the fact that she had been waiting behind it, expecting his appeal.

"It is Betty," he said.

"I know it is Betty," she retorted. "The whole island must have heard her screaming last night."

"Well, will you come?"

Her expression was dull and resentful. "I see you called the doctor first," she said.

"I am required by law to do so," he said.

"Then let the doctor help you," she said scornfully. She made as if to close the door in his face, but he thrust out one hand and held it open.

"All right," he said, "scorn and fleer all you like—and when you are done with your petulance and your insults, and when you are done making sure all around you know how wise you are and how stupid they are—for God's sake come down and help this poor woman."

A little shudder or tremble went through her. For once she had no caustic retort to make. She looked down and aside—for the first time in his acquaintance with her, she actually lowered her eyes as if in shame. Then she raised them to him again.

"Not for God's sake," she said. "But for your sake, White Edmund, if you ask me."

"I ask you please to help me," he said.

"Very well," she said. "That is all I need to hear."

She picked up her basket of medicines, which was in readiness beside her on the floor, and together they returned to the cabin. On the way he told her what the midwives and the doctor had told him. She listened in silence and made no comment. As they approached, Johnny loped in a circle about them, crying out in anguish and begging Janetta to spare his baby from the Devil. She paid no attention to him.

Edmund halted at the door and drew aside for her to enter. She went inside; but when she realized he was not following, she set her basket down and came back out. "What?" she said. "Do you think you are going to stay out here?"

"I know nothing of women and childbirthing."

"Well, you will know everything about them before we are through."

"But I am a *man*, Janetta. It is hardly proper. I am a gentleman—or at least I was before I came to this forsaken place."

"No," she said, with a return to her usual bitterness, "you are no gentleman. You stopped being a gentleman when you became a master of slaves; and before we are done, you will be covered in the blood of a slave. And as for knowing nothing of women, like as not you will have put your arms to the shoulder up into the very bowels of one; so you will no longer be able to plead innocent."

"I tell you, I know nothing of these matters!" he said determinedly.

She put her hands on her hips now and stood with arms akimbo, regarding him with sudden suspicion.

"How old are you, White Edmund?" she said.

"I am six-and-twenty."

She eyed him narrowly. "You . . . you are *a virgin,*" she said in slow realization.

If she was trying to shame him somehow, he was not going to let her. "I have never had carnal knowledge of a woman, if that is what you mean," he said defiantly.

"'Carnal knowledge of a woman'! You talk like a book."

"It is just that I have never heard the term *virgin* applied to a man, that is all."

"What difference does it make? The fact is that you have never lain with a woman."

"What should you expect?" he said, irritated with her for reasons he did not stop to analyze. "How could I be anything else *but* without such experience? My religion forbids sexual knowledge outside marriage."

"What? Did Jesus say anything about that? I never heard it before if he did."

Now they forgot the groaning and suffering woman in the cabin, gripped by the topic that was at the forefront of both of their minds.

"Christ most certainly taught us not to commit adultery," said Edmund, "which includes any sexual knowledge not sanctioned by marriage. Besides, such chastity is the accepted practice even under a natural moral code."

"Accepted! Accepted by whom, White Edmund?"

"By civilized people—by decent people."

She laughed. "Oh," she said, "by *fools,* you mean. All the *rest* of the world is getting itself as much 'carnal knowledge' as it can, and as fast as it can."

She had succeeded in annoying him on this topic as she never had before. "It is hardly foolish to avoid sexual experience before one is married," he protested hotly. "The evils attendant on such premature indulgence are very well known: pregnancy out of wedlock, disease, profligacy, heartbreak, prostitution, the rejection of society—"

"And after you have observed this idiotic chastity—what if the woman you do marry turns out to be a cold bedfellow? What if you find yourself shackled for life to a *lump, a dead fish,* who is frightened when you get into bed with her?"

He stared at her perplexedly, and she laughed. "Ah," she said, "I see that is something that never occurred to you! You hardly even know what I am saying! You would have no 'carnal knowledge' yourself—you would marry a woman who had none either—and the two of you would never know what you were missing! You would wallow about in bed like a couple of half-wits, without the faintest idea what you were about. It would be a miracle if you got her with child at all! I cannot believe that any nation is so stupid as to endure such a practice. But you English are *beyond* strange." She shook her head in expression of her amazement.

"Say what you like," he retorted. "I can see no error in my beliefs."

She sneered and laughed.

A louder groan from the cabin caught their attention and returned it to the pressing issue.

"I shall not come into cabin again," he said.

She was standing on the step of the place, and her face was almost level with his. She reached out and seized his shirt in her fist. "By your God," she hissed, "or by the Devil if you prefer, you *shall* come with me, and you *shall* help me, and be damned to your propriety! I shall need you; do you think I can do this alone? *You* sent the doctor away, *you* sent the women away, *you* chose to rely on me. You have no choice. Now *get in here!*"

There was no denying what she said. He had taken on the responsibility by summoning her. With considerable reluctance he let himself be drawn up the steps and into the cabin.

She knelt by Betty and examined her. He came and stood close by. He found, to his further alarm, that he was already becoming inured to this sight.

"Please, Missy Janetta," Betty gasped in a hoarse voice, "please don' give my picnee to de Debil!"

Edmund expected Janetta to snap at her and tell her to shut up; but instead she took a damp cloth and wiped the poor woman's brow.

"Do not worry," she told Betty. "I shall protect your baby from the Devil."

"Oh, t'ank you, Missy Janetta!" gasped Betty.

"Now, what did that doctor say, again?" Janetta asked Edmund. Her tone was incredulous.

"He said that this bump here—do you see?—was the protrusion of the infant's head against the inside of the womb."

Janetta rolled her eyes in disgust. "Stupid white doctor!" she exclaimed. Then to Edmund she said, "Pick her up—come, there is no time to be lost. You have carried her before, carry her again."

Nothing Edmund had ever done before in his life had ever cost him so much sheer willpower—to pick up a naked and over-pregnant woman, and a woman of another race, no less, writhing and gasping in pain, and oozing vital fluids.

"Bring her outside," said Janetta. She led the way, and when they had descended from the cabin, she found a half-barrel and set it upright so that Betty could be seated on the flat end. She stood at Betty's back to support her, and gripped her by the shoulders.

"Listen to me, Betty!" she said.

Betty groaned to show that she was listening.

"You must piss! Do you understand me?"

"Can't! Can't!" groaned Betty.

"You must! You must try! Go on, now."

For perhaps a minute they waited; and then a stream of urine began to run out over Betty's engorged genitals and drip to the ground. It increased in volume by the second until it was very strong. The stream continued to flow for an inordinate length of time.

Edmund was by now too shocked to be further shocked. He looked on in numb amazement. Janetta glanced at him and laughed, though not cruelly this time.

"You are surprised," she said. "You have never seen anyone make so much water. That is not the baby's head the doctor saw—that is her bladder. Her bladder is so full the baby can't get past it. Those black cows from Mr. Duckworth's should have known better, even if the doctor did not."

It took many minutes for Betty's bladder to empty. Edmund later thought that it must have held at least a gallon of urine; it was miraculous her bladder had not simply burst.

The sounds Betty now made indicated some relief. Edmund carried her back into the cabin.

"Is that it?" he said to Janetta. "Is everything going to go all right now?"

"Oh, no," said Janetta, shaking her head. "This is not going to be easy. But it is not as bad as the doctor thought."

⌛⌛⌛⌛⌛

Janetta's prediction of further difficult labor proved to be correct. It was two more days before the baby finally was born. Edmund and Janetta were awake throughout that time, except for intervals when one of them might nap dazedly while the other watched the slow progress of the labor. The moment when the baby boy finally slid from the birth canal into Janetta's waiting hands, the three of them felt such relief and triumph—the four of them, in fact, for Johnny was still waiting by the door—that Edmund found himself laughing and weeping at the same time. Janetta, too, was laughing. She handed the baby off to Edmund so that she could bind the cord and cut it with the knife she kept at her thigh. Betty immediately passed into a profound sleep.

Janetta washed the little boy and wrapped him in a piece of linen. Johnny was too skittish to hold him for long, so Edmund did the honors, sitting on the floor in the cabin, leaning his back against the wall, while Janetta cleaned Betty and set the simple place to rights as well as she could.

This was the first baby Edmund had ever held. The little mewling thing in his arms woke a deep and ineffable yearning in him for children of his own. He looked at Janetta as she crawled about by the mat where Betty lay, and though he still felt his lust for her dimly even in his exhaustion, he knew she could not be the mother of his children. He closed his eyes and took himself back to England in thought; imagined himself in a snug rectory there, and the midwife bringing a baby boy or girl to him to hold like this.

I must go home, he thought desperately.

He sensed Janetta before him. When he opened his eyes, she was watching him sorrowfully.

"Why that look?" he asked.

She instantly grew defensive and bitter. "No matter," she said. "Give me the baby. You go back to your house and get some sleep. Johnny can help me now."

"But you are exhausted, too," he said.

"And I shall sleep, as soon as I have the chance. In a while I shall have to wake Betty to nurse him; and then I think it will be up to the two of them. Or perhaps I can send Johnny to see if one of Mr. Duckworth's women will come over for a little while, until Betty is rested.—Here, give me the baby."

She took the baby from his arms, and he rose to his feet stiffly. He went slowly to the door and descended to the ground. Johnny was sitting on the steps, looking as weary as it he had given birth himself. "No more shirking," Edmund told him. "You must help Janetta, and then you must help Betty take care of that baby."

"I don' know nothin' 'bout pic'nees, Massa," protested Johnny. The remark reminded him of his own protest to Janetta two days ago. He looked back at her and she smiled at him; and he smiled too.

"Believe me," he told Johnny, "I have found that ignorance will not protect you."

He looked back again just once as he walked away. Janetta was still standing in the doorway, watching him, and dandling the baby with great tenderness.

⌛⌛⌛⌛⌛

After church on Sunday Mr. Morgette sought him out directly. Dr. Mann was with him.

"A word with you, Mr. Percy," said Mr. Morgette in a challenging tone.

"Sir," said Edmund civilly, pausing in his departure.

"Dr. Mann says that you refused to let him treat one of your slaves the other day."

"That is true."

"This is a serious matter, Mr. Percy," said Mr. Morgette. "There is a law against this."

"I should imagine that the law only applies if the slave in question is injured as a result."

"Dr. Mann tells me that the deaths of a mother and child must have been the inevitable consequence of your action."

"To the contrary, sir, both mother and child are doing well. It was an exhausting labor, but not otherwise untoward."

Mr. Morgette looked at Dr. Mann.

"Impossible!" said Dr. Mann.

Edmund was all mildness. "You gentlemen are welcome to come to Canebrake to assure yourself of these facts," he said. "A healthy baby boy was born yesterday, and when I left to come to the service this morning, he was alternately feeding and bawling lustily. It was very kind of Dr. Mann to attend us the other day—and I compensated him handsomely, if I may say so, for his inconvenience—but all has turned out for the best."

Dr. Mann was deeply and painfully chagrined. "It is not possible!" he protested again, though more feebly this time.

"Perhaps not," said Edmund. "But it is divine providence; so let us question the event no further.—I trust you and your family are well, Mr. Morgette?"

"Yes, thank you," said Mr. Morgette, very much off balance.

"And I hope the same is true of you and your family, Dr. Mann," said Edmund. With a slight but courteous bow he left them to their conclusions.

Chapter 12

"For how," would many exclaim, "could they enforce the seventh commandment when they wilfully broke it?"

—*Antigua and the Antiguans*

N*ot long* after these latter events, it happened that a small cane piece belatedly ripened. It was located in what was the wettest part of the plantation, if any quarter could truly be called such, and Edmund had noticed in other years that it was slow to come to maturity. He had been watching its slow ripening with a very farmerly disgust. It would not be efficient to give over the new planting for the two weeks required to cut and process the cane; but when he calculated the value of the muscovado the cane would yield, he determined that it could not be squandered.

Accordingly the men were set to cutting, and carrying, and stoking the boilers, and Janetta presided at the boiling vats again. The recent harvest was reenacted, though on a far smaller scale; for the cane piece in question was indeed very limited.

The linen sails of the mill were brought out and reinstalled, and for a time the great vanes swung lazily but inexorably in the early summer sun. So far as Edmund knew, his mill was during that time the only one active on the whole of the island. The shafts of the machine ran all day, day after day, giving forth a dull rumble that could be heard for a mile or more in all directions.

Edmund had hoped that the intensity of this labor might provide some relief to him in his ongoing struggle. He stayed away from the boiling house, either working in the field or feeding the cane stalks through the crushing rollers in the mill. He avoided Janetta in every other manner possible as well. But his care was to no avail, in particular because for the first time he noticed a phenomenon Mr. Duckworth had warned him about: during sugar harvest, the slave population grew much more promiscuous. Edmund had no doubt that it was the availability of sugar that caused this increased sexual activity: generally the slaves of Antigua and the other sugar islands were kept on very short rations; but during the harvest they ate sugar copiously—there was no stopping them. The harvests at Canebrake itself had been so brutal and wearying, shorthanded as the plantation was, that his men, no matter how well fed they were, had neither time for nor interest in such activity. But this harvest was not quite as hectic as the full harvest in the late winter months. The men stole over to Mr. Duckworth's plantation after dark and found welcome partners there, and on any given evening the border between the two properties was the scene of sometimes noisy liaisons between a dozen of Canebrake's slaves and as many of Mr. Duckworth's. Mr. Duckworth complained, and he and Edmund discussed the matter; but short of locking up their slaves, which neither of them wished to do, they could see no way to stop this illicit communication.

This sexual activity, or rather Edmund's full awareness of it, made his own woes worse. It seemed, in fact, as if the entire universe was urging his surrender. The sultry air by day, the cool breezes by night, worked each of them to sensitize and sensualize him. He lay in bed, awake in the darkness, like a man with a wound, feeling a pain that the laudanum of sleep would only worsen with its disordered sexual dreams.

⌛ ⌛ ⌛ ⌛ ⌛

One evening the field work was done. The last of the cane had been milled; there remained only further boiling and decanting and drying and packing. He went from the field directly to the great house for dinner; and when he had washed himself and eaten he went outdoors to watch the sunset from the verandah.

He was so preoccupied with his thoughts that it was not until darkness had almost fallen that he noticed that the mill was still running. The breeze had fallen to a mere whisper, so the rumble of the wheels was sporadic and slow; but it would be best to disengage the mechanism. He debated whether he should just leave this task for Janetta to do; but for all he knew, she had gone away on one of her healing errands.

He did not bother to light lantern. He climbed the hill at once. As he reached the boiling house, he heard a clatter of implements there, and he guessed Janetta was still at work; so he continued onward to the mill, avoiding her.

The vanes of the mill were drifting through their rotation so slowly that it was a simple matter to catch one and secure it. Then he went up in the loft to throw the mill mechanism out of gear. The upper room was too dark for him to see what he was doing, so he groped his way to the hatch that opened through the roof and flung it wide; it let the last remaining hint of soft twilight into the room. He went to the mechanism, inserted the long iron bar that was used to shift the critical cogs out of contact, and disengaged them. Then he turned for the ladder again.

He halted for a moment, however, as he saw Janetta's very few possessions spread out on the floor of the platform. He surveyed them curiously: a coarse cotton mat and pillow on which she slept; a cast-off china cup, cracked and chipped; a basket containing neatly-wrapped foodstuffs; a basket with some toilet articles, including a brush and comb and a small silver mirror—doubtless a gift of her mother; her basket of herbs; some stoppered jars full of salves; and a bag made of knotted string, full of clean rags for use during her monthlies. It struck him that, despite the fact that they served her feminine purposes, these possessions were like the belongings of some soldier who was always ready to move on at an instant's notice.

He heard the rungs of the ladder creak slightly. That could only mean that she had returned to the mill and was just ascending to the loft.

He felt a kind of panic; he wished he had not lingered to look at her things. This meeting would be so much easier if it had taken place in the doorway or on the path; but now she would be between him and his exit.

She emerged through the hatchway. She showed considerable surprise as she saw him.

"I was just disengaging the gears," he said.

She did not answer. She climbed off the ladder and stood on the platform.

He looked at her, and she at him. Then, slowly, he went to walk past her to the ladder, averting his eyes. She came a few steps toward him, however, and he stopped abruptly.

Suddenly she seized him and clung to him.

If she had said anything, even so much as his name, he might have resisted her; but she said nothing, she only clung, first to his shirt, and then to his chest, throwing her arms around him. Her breath was a raw, gasping sound.

He pulled her arms from him and pushed them down and away from him, but the instant he loosed her she threw them around him again, seizing him by the shoulders this time and holding her face up to his, and making a sound of pure, desperate longing, utterly hopeless longing; longing and long desire.

"No, no," he said gently. "No, no, Janetta, you mustn't." He tried again and again to disengage her hands, but each time she only seized him again, making that incoherent longing sound, that desperate moaning of want, of craving. He felt her breasts against his chest; and suddenly he had taken her in his arms and leaned over her and she was kissing his face with long, hopeless kisses, as if each one would be her last and in a moment he would vanish and she would never see him again.

"No, no," he said, "you mustn't—mustn't—Janetta—no."

But then she held his head in her hands and set her lips on his lips, and he felt her tongue slip between them and play over the tip of his tongue; and a fire seemed to run through his frame that melted everything in him. He caught her closer to him. One of her hands went down and undid the button at his waist, tugging his trousers open; then her arms went around his neck; then she was climbing on him—she had wrapped her legs around his waist.

It was only a few seconds, it seemed, from the time she had stepped onto the boards of the platform to the time they were making love. Never in his life had he wanted anything so much, and the wild longing cries she now made only made him want her more, even as he had her; as they swayed and clung to one another, surging against one another; and then as he reeled, and lowered her to the floor, and they continued into climax, now both making that inarticulate cry of desperate want.

No sooner had she ceased writhing and crying in ecstasy under him than she sobbed and burst into weeping. He raised himself off her in fear that he was hurting her, but she jerked open the front of her dress, exposing her breasts, and pulled his head back down to rest against them; and then she held him, sobbing and stroking his head with her quick, strong hands, over and over again.

He found that despite his orgasm his body was not sated: he had yearned for her so long that even now it was as if they had not yet made love at all. He sat back on his heels, seized her dress, and tugged it off her; the knife she wore strapped on her thigh came off in the bundle, which he cast aside. The sight of her nakedness made him feel dizzy and drunk, as if the blood had fled from his brain. He pulled off his shirt, stood and took off his shoes and trousers, and then lay down between her legs again. She was looking at him with amazement; but when he entered her again she clung to him fiercely and cried his name joyfully in her strange patois.

⌛⌛⌛⌛⌛

He was awakened perhaps an hour later by the intensity of the moonlight, which had shifted until it fell directly into the little room in the top of the windmill.

His limbs were heavy and stiff from the day's labor and from the suddenness and deepness of the sleep that had engulfed him after lovemaking. He pulled himself gently from Janetta's arms, and dimly noticed how the leg she had put over his in their final instants of consciousness now could not be loosed without a slight tug of the mingled fluids that had dried on their flesh. In that novel sensation there was something wonderfully intimate, as if their very flesh had bonded and clung longingly together.

She lay back on the floor, moving without fully waking; her head found its pillow again, and she was at once deeply asleep.

The moon lit her body with a pale but brilliant splendor. He sat and looked with awe at the beauty of her face, throat, breasts, belly, and private parts; he thought he had never seen any sight more beautiful in all his life. He was in a new kind of shock. He had feared that if he made love to her, he would forget who he was; but now he felt he had instead discovered who he was.

Out of some instinct he did not analyze, he rose unsteadily and went to the short flight of steps that led to the opening in the upper wall. It brought him up into the moonlight, where there was a ledge on which he could sit, leaning against the framework of the window behind him, and look over all below.

The night was calm; the land was drenched in a faery dimness. He could see all the plantation, the house and the cabins of the men, see the cane piece they had just finished cutting and the acres waiting still to be planted. In this direction he could see over Mr. Duckworth's land, and see where that man's distant house was dark; and see beyond the rolling curves of the island, to the sea in the farther distance, vast and dimly aglitter.

Though the moon was full in the violet sky, it had not blotted out all the stars, especially in the west, toward which he turned his eyes now. It seemed to him that he was looking deep into heaven, a heaven spangled with an infinite number of constant lights, variously bright, hung by God in arrays and patterns that held meaning only for the angels.

And in that moment Edmund Percy had an awakening such as few are allowed. He felt, as it is commonly expressed, at one with everything—with the sleeping land, with the earth, with the great seas, the immeasurable reach of sky and space, with moon and stars; and he felt, felt rather than consciously knew, the Presence that dwelt in or somehow informed or flowed into all—all that It had created; all that It was, in being everything.

How little his understanding of God had been to this moment! Something built out of book reading and words repeated by rote, a mere habit of thought formed of vague impressions taken in during hours spent in church from boyhood on. Here was God in person, richer in love and vaster in wisdom than he had ever begun to guess.

He looked back down through the hatchway at Janetta. She too was a part of God—her delicious beauty also part of God—their lovemaking part of God. He *understood* suddenly that God had intended the act of love between man and woman to be as theirs had been—free of shame, passionate and kindly and overwhelming, utterly overwhelming.

He looked back at his thoughts and actions in respect to women and saw only a confused hunger that was half-ashamed of itself. The feelings that a fair face or figure awoke in him, the beautiful curve of breasts, the roundness and shapeliness of bare arms or of thighs delineated by a mischievous wind that pressed full skirts tightly against the flesh beneath—the softness of hair, the warmth of lively fingers grasping his own in a handshake—the feelings such things had from time to time awakened were but dim primordial inklings of this greater truth: that God was *in* the love between man and woman—that God was in the act of love, as God was in everything good and loving.

Dear God, he thought, *what a prig I have been! What a stupid, narrow-minded, ignorant prig!*

He thought at once of Bronwyn Floyd and his yearnings for her, which he had been barely able to admit to himself.

If I *felt such feelings toward her,* he scolded himself, *just imagine what Christopher felt! And I would have denied Christopher this! I would have counseled Christopher to give over his dreams of loving Bronwyn as I have loved Janetta—no, his dreams of something greater than I can ever have with Janetta. His love for Bronwyn could be sanctioned and fostered and nurtured by the bonds of marriage and the hopes of society. He would be well expected to retire to bed each night with her; and all would be delighted at the fruit of their lovemaking. And this, this I would deny my brother! In my infinite wisdom of twenty-three years I advised him to give over his aspirations for such a love!*

He realized in an instant now how much wiser Mrs. Hanscom had been. She had understood the immense power at work between Christopher and Bronwyn, the longing that was driving them together at all costs, because she, Mrs. Hanscom, had herself lain beneath a man in lovemaking. Christopher, too, had been wiser than he; and had he not said, "Wait until you love; then you will know"?

He groaned; and then he prayed to be forgiven.

⧗⧗⧗⧗⧗

For some time he sat there in the glory of the night, penitent and silent. Over and over he vowed to mend his ways and never to slight or underestimate the power of love. But for all his vows, he feared greatly he would forget what this moment had revealed to him, and lapse back into his old habits of thought. He prayed that God would not let him forget; he prayed that this knowledge would let him have mercy on others; he prayed that his insight this night would make him a better man than he had ever been or ever could have been without it.

At last sleep began to urge its demands on him again, and he went back down the steps to where Janetta lay. He arranged some clothing to make a pillow, and then settled himself beside her. As he drew her close, she moaned in her sleep and clung to him.

And so he slept again, as if drugged, hoping he would not forget, would never forget.

⌛⌛⌛⌛⌛

Before dawn she shook him awake. They looked at one another, and he knew she was thinking the same thing: this must be kept a secret if they could possibly manage it. He rose and dressed without a word, and then he went to descend the ladder; but before he could do so, she scrambled after him, still naked, and caught at his shirt and kissed him impetuously several times. He almost cast aside his better judgment and stayed to make love with her one more time; but then she released him. She had only been saying farewell.

He stole back to the house in the twilight. There he washed himself and dressed again before Betty came in to make his breakfast. By seven he was back at work.

So was she. But all was changed. The anger and sullenness, the long, hungry glances, these were gone; instead she seemed quiet and at peace. Occasionally in their work their eyes would meet, and hers held no mocking bitterness. He sometimes caught her looking on him with a faint smile.

To him this change in her was thunderous. It seemed to him that the men, too, immediately noticed it; he saw significant glances among them, and he heard from time to time a buzz of voices where a knot of them had gathered that sounded like speculation. Some seemed to look at him with something like envy, others with pity, and still others with a dispassionate curiosity—the kind of scientific interest a naturalist might show for a bird dying in a vacuum jar.

Unfortunately the work, brutal though it was, gave him too much time to think. And thought was now his enemy; for it brought back the memory of all the values to which he had once adhered. As the day wore on, the wonderful vision of the night became more dim, and his sense of sinfulness grew greater. Here were the facts: He had gone against his own best judgment—he had lain with this woman. He had committed fornication. On the very verge of returning to England, or at least so he had hoped, he had made this irretrievable error. The only thing he could think to do to set it right was to make Janetta his wife. He had known, at one time, that marriage with her was impossible. He did not know it anymore. The only way he could excuse or rationalize what he knew to be a sin was to tell himself that he would marry her; and if there is any extenuation for him, it is that he was far from the first to resort to this delusory penitence.

This device, this plan, however, was sheer desperation, not reason. He did not know how he could marry her. He had heard from Duckworth, in some passing conversation, of the case of one Gilbert, who had married a mulatto woman in Antigua. He had been refused a civil license to do so by the authorities, and could only marry her by publishing the banns in the Methodist chapel. To Edmund, the thought of turning apostate from his beloved ancestral church was utterly repugnant; he could no more contemplate it than he could think of bearing arms against king and country. No; as well as he could eke out any course, it would be to purchase Janetta from Waller, set her free, and then find some place where the law allowed a white to marry a mulatto—or some place where he might trick the authorities into thinking she was white; though the more he looked at her wild beauty, the more African and exotic she seemed to him. Failing that, he would live with her; for he had no doubt that the sin of living with her would be less than the sin of lying with her once and then abandoning her merely because no law would sanction their marriage.

Sometime in the course of the day Mr. Duckworth's proposal occurred to him again; and even if now it was impossible that he might take it up, elements of it began to appeal to him. What if he proposed to his father to buy this plantation from him, making payments over several years? He might well persuade him to do so, for the plantation was separable from the entail, a mere investment that could be traded at will, and his father might be willing to resign it to be the foundation of the livelihood of his youngest son, especially if he were well compensated for its loss. Then Edmund might live on here, bringing Janetta into his house as his wife in his own eyes, if not in the eyes of the law. How was that any worse than what Waller did, or any number of other white men, both managers and owners, throughout the West Indies?

There were, however, countless objections that could be marshaled against this plan. Sooner or later word would get back to his father concerning what he was doing; and even if Edmund could have borne that shame, certainly his father could not, and would doubtless break off the connection and end whatever purchase arrangement they had. He must go to some other island, then, where he was not known. He would set up as a manager—he had already seen the scarcity of honest men of that profession; and Janetta must be his mistress until such time as he could contrive to obtain for their union the blessing of the church.

It was indeed a plan, but it made him sick at heart. It was wrong, but only a lesser wrong. But it seemed that he had put himself in such a position that a wrong of some kind was the only possible course. He came to this unthought-of, this previously unthinkable situation, with all the assumptions about morality and matrimony that had been the basis of his existence heretofore, which he could not force to dovetail with the reality of what he had done. It was as if, thinking murder the most heinous of all sins, he had come to himself to find a dead man at his feet and a bloody knife in his hand; or knowing arson to be wrong, to find another man's barn blazing before him, and the incendiary torch alight in his fist; or any of a thousand other paradoxes. And yet knowing full well that there was no way to right what he had done, he persisted in vainly trying to make it good, desperately trying to give it a context that could square it with his morality.

He tried not to think about how this decision meant the utter shattering of his life. Gone was the career he had planned—gone was England, gone was Brackensom—gone the company of his father and brother—gone his dreams of life in a country parsonage with a mild-tempered woman. Everything he had ever been or hoped to be was now gone. His long training was negated. And the irony was that it was his old moral training that was ensuring the destruction of the self that he had built. He had set his foot in a trap, and he was compelled to chew off his own limb, though it meant the certain death of his self.

These finalities were truly unthinkable; so he tried his best not to think them.

At the end of the day, after the men had already dispersed to their dwellings, and he was turning for home himself, he met Janetta ascending the path to the mill. She stopped when she met him.

"You will come tonight?" she asked in a terse whisper.

He had anticipated this moment in the course of the day, and resolved that it would be wiser if they refrained from seeing one another; but at her question, his resolution instantly vacated all hold on his mind.

"Of course," he said.

For a moment her face bore an expression of grateful and painful relief. Then she smiled at him in a way that made his blood race. Still smiling, and looking at him hungrily as she went, she slipped past him and continued on to the mill.

He bathed and then ate his dinner, both weary and stimulated beyond measure. Betty seemed to take ages scouring the pots and dishes, for she stopped periodically to fuss with the baby; and it was fully dark before she went away to her cabin. Then he put out the lamp and went up the hill.

Janetta was waiting for him when he climbed the ladder—she pounced on him with a little laugh. She was already naked; she had bathed, and she smelled faintly of some scent, perhaps wild lavender, that was barely redolent above the cloying sweetness of the air in the mill. "We must talk," he said.

"We will talk," she said, "but later, later, White Edmund. Make love first and talk later, that is a good rule. That way you will make sure you do the loving—otherwise it may be lost in the talking."

In an instant she had persuaded him. They made love until the moon rose. This time was different from the last: though hungry for each other, they were not desperate; and their passion took its leisure, and found new paths, new ways to achieve its end, ways he had never dreamed existed.

When they were done, she cradled his head against her breasts and said, "Now talk to me."

He laughed a little at the humorous abruptness of her command, and then grew serious. "We must marry," he said.

She laughed lightly. "How is that possible? The world says I am colored; and there is no denying that you are white."

"We must find a place where it is possible," he said.

"Ah, my White Edmund," she said sadly. "Never shall it be possible."

"Then we must live together as if we were, until the day comes that God makes it possible."

"I will live with you as long as I can," she said. "But think what you are saying. Waller has long since suspected you have made me your mistress. Soon your slaves here will know it, and then the slaves at Waller's will know it, and then he will know it for certain. We are watched by a thousand spies. The best we can hope for is to keep our secret for a few days or weeks. And when Waller knows for certain, he will come after me. The idea of my pleasuring anyone but him will drive him to distraction. If you try to stop him, he will shoot you dead. Or perhaps he will simply shoot me himself, some day when I am walking down the road."

"We must go away," he said.

"How? I am Waller's property. Are you going to steal his property?"

"I will go to him and make him an offer. I will buy your freedom. You will be a free woman, Janetta!"

She laughed bitterly. "He will not sell me," she said. "Owning me is worth more than any money to him. Why should he make you happy in the possession of me, when he can thwart you by not selling me? Making others suffer is the highest pleasure he knows."

"I shall try, in any case. If I do not succeed, you and I shall steal away together. We can be onboard ship, bound elsewhere, before he knows it."

"And what then? He will pursue you. He will have you hung for a thief."

"If he attempts it, we shall expose him."

"Expose him? What would you expose?"

"Expose him as a man who keeps a harem of mistresses."

She laughed, bitter still. "And who will care? The West Indies is as full of black harems as Araby itself."

"But it is fornication!"

"So *you* say. But most of the planters do not think intercourse with a black or colored woman can possibly be fornication. They think no more of it than pissing in a field. I have heard Waller describe it as a mere function of nature, an act of discharging a bodily excretion into an appropriate vessel; that is all."

"Well, then, we shall tell the world that Waller has made unspeakable advances to his own child. The crime with which he has threatened you will win us a sympathetic hearing."

"White Edmund, sweet White Edmund, my poor little innocent . . . the world is full of fathers who have lusted after their daughters. They will only pity Waller for not succeeding. They will not side with you."

"Oh, Janetta—now you go too far indeed! I cannot believe such a thing for a moment."

"It is true. I could name you a dozen white men on Antigua who have had what you call 'knowledge' of their daughters. Some of them are men I know are known to you."

"Nonsense!"

"You are too good a man yourself to believe it," she said. "But it is true all the same."

She was silent a moment before she spoke again. "No," she said, "This plan of yours is a pleasant dream, Edmund, but it is only a dream. We are in prison here. Or I am, at least. You will go back to England someday and leave me here. You will marry a silly little English girl. Sometimes you will think of me, but not often. I shall not live to trouble you long."

"No," he said flatly. "I shall marry you and no other."

"Oh, shut your mouth," she said, both fondly and sadly, caressing his head and kissing his brow.

"I shall not shut my mouth! I shall determine how it shall be done, and I shall do it."

She grew serious. "Listen to me!" she said severely. "If you make *one move,* White Edmund, even *one move,* you will bring the whole world down upon us."

"Well, what shall we do, then? If the world is as dark as you paint it, what can we do?"

"We must only keep on as best we can."

"What kind of answer is that?"

"It is no answer at all. There is no answer. Do you not see? There are some things for which there is no answer. My life has always been that way, so I am used to it. You are not; but now you are in my world, Edmund. You have tasted my mouth, and all the tastes of the world will be bitter in yours, as they are bitter in mine."

He did not in the least accept her pessimistic view; but he saw that there was no persuading her at this moment, in any case. He did as she said—he ceased to plan, for this night. He took her in his arms and held her close, and they were silent.

Chapter 13

Never Mark Antony
Dallied more wantonly
With the fair Egyptian Queen.

—Cleveland

This was the time of heat. When he looked back later, he felt it again: the heat by day as they worked in the fields, the heat of their lovemaking by night. Usually he went up to the mill after dark, but sometimes she joined him in the house. Often they were too exhausted to make love more than once a day; but on alternate Saturdays, when the slaves all went to town to sell the surplus from their gardens, they spent the long afternoon and evening making love again and again in the narrow bed in his bedchamber there, and she did not leave until a little before dawn.

He felt drenched in love, drenched in beauty, as if his heart had been, all his life, a desiccated sponge waiting to soak up the waters of a woman's tenderness. He awoke in the morning with her by his side, and the sound of birdsong and breeze seemed a rich language of joy. The lush beauty of the island by day and the sky of stars by night now were like a fortified wine to his senses. Her beauty woke in him an appreciation for all beauty, a wonder for all wonders, and an awe for all things. It seemed that in that ubiquitous beauty he saw God almost in veritable presence—coaxing the songbirds into the sky, drawing from them their music, or cajoling the wild colors forth from the buds of the flowers, scattering the winking of the stars across the heavens of an evening.

He was one of those simple-hearted among us, who, when they are given cause, however slight, love abruptly and wholly. And Janetta did give him cause. She could be moody, sullen, curst; but when she loved him, she lavished tenderness on him. On awakening she would cover his face with dozens of kisses, while he laughed and tried to reciprocate. She would gaze upon him and smile, longingly and lovingly and mysteriously and shyly. She would caress him as if she were touching something infinitely soft and fragile. She grew playful, in a manner he had never seen in her before.

Yet in all of this tenderness, she never opened her mind to him. She said little; she told him nothing of her past and let him see nothing of who she was. The little exercise in history building that lovers so relish, when they tell each other tales from their childhood or their later past—that was all out of the question for her. She made it clear that she had no past, only this present, or rather that she had a past such as she would not inflict on anyone she loved. When he spoke of the future she grew at first silent and sad, and finally irritable and caustic. This was a warning to him, but he refused to listen; he refused to listen because if he had desisted from making his fruitless plans, he would not have been able to go on living in that limbo of lost lovers, flying in the whirlwind, bound nowhere.

⌛⌛⌛⌛⌛

There was one form of knowledge she was not shy about disclosing to him. She knew much about making love. How she had learned it, he never asked. He was an innocent when she found him; she taught him what she knew, and together they discovered things neither of them had ever even suspected.

One evening after lovemaking she said to him, "You will know well how to please your prim little English wife,

White Edmund. She will not be so prim when she has lived with *you* for a month."

"*You* will be my wife," he said to her.

She ignored him and laughed softly, lewdly.

"Oh, I wish I could be a fly on the wall, watching you," she said. "I would like to see what you do to your prim little English wife. I would like to see how surprised she is; I would like to see her overwhelmed by pleasure—new pleasure, night after night; greater and greater pleasure, night after night—I would like to see all her silly ideas about what a man and a woman do in bed turned inside out. I would like to see her look at you as you follow her to bed—frightened of what you will do to her, but hungry for you, starved for you, ravenous for the pleasure she will have. I would like to see you teach some prim little English girl to lust after you as I have lusted after you. I would like to see her find you in some dark corner of the house in the middle of the day when you two are all alone there and catch you by your coat and draw your face down so that she can kiss you and kiss you; I would like to see her slip her prim little white hand down—thus. Some prim little clergyman's wife!"

"I shall marry you and no one else," he said stoutly.

She paid no attention to him, still occupied by her libidinous fantasy. "Oh, how I should like to see that," she said.

He was irritated with her. "You do not take me seriously," he said.

Finally she heard him. "About what?" she asked. "About this marriage with me you talk of?"

"Yes."

"That is because you are dreaming, White Edmund. You are dreaming of something that can never happen. Do not even talk of it.—Now, listen to me—no, no, hush, listen to me. I shall hear no more of your foolish talk about marriage. I shall give you some advice.—Are you listening? Hear me—no, hear me, Edmund. To all appearances this

English girl may be prim. But you must look for some sign that she is *willing* in bed. All the world thinks that every man craves a woman who is meek and submissive, but that is not so; she need merely be *willing*. Such a woman will keep a man's interest forever. But you must not rely on the opinion of the woman in question; for almost every woman will tell you that she is willing. But most of them do not even know what willingness is; for they do not know what loving is."

"I will hear no more of this talk," he said, turning on his back and looking up into the ceiling of the mill. "Before all other things," he said, "a woman must be kind, in my opinion."

"And am I so very kind? No. I am a shrew; I am curst—you have called me that yourself. But I am willing in bed—I am *very* willing in bed—and so you have not yet cast me out."

"Ah," he said, "you act curst; but that is only playacting. Your heart is kind, and that is what matters to me."

"Now," she said, ignoring his comment, and continuing with her lesson, "here is something else you must learn. When you want a woman, White Edmund, you must press close to her. You must bring your face close to hers—like this—and you must touch her. Even if all you can do is seize her hand, you must touch her. Touch will do everything."

"Ah," he said, "were you so deliberate when you broke down my resistance? Was that all planned?"

"It was not deliberate. I could not help myself; I could not keep my hands off you, that evening when I found you here, and we were alone together. But it would have worked just as well if it had been deliberate."

"I doubt that!" he said.

⌛⌛⌛⌛⌛

As the days passed, however, she grew more desperately attached to him, and less willing to contemplate any future rival. Once when she was lying in his arms after lovemaking, with her back against his chest, she demanded to read his palm. She pried open his teasing fingers and studied his hand for a minute while he laughed at her foolishness. "Ah!" she said, "you will live long, White Edmund! Very long indeed. You will grow to be a very old and fond and foolish old man. I need not fear that Waller will shoot you."

"And you?" he asked. "Surely you have looked at your own hand."

"My life will be short," she said. "But it does not matter, as long as yours is long. Before I met you, I never cared for anyone or anything—certainly nothing for myself. But now that I love you, I can be glad; for I know that you will be happy.—No, no, do not close your hand yet; I must see how many children you will have."

She examined his hand again. "I cannot give an exact number," she said. "But I can see that it is about a half-dozen."

"Only a half-dozen? Why not make it twenty, you little liar?"

"Let me see . . . let me look at whom you will marry."

She studied his hand again, while he stifled a chuckle.

"She will be dark," she said.

"I know that!" he said, whispering with fierce affection in her ear. "I know that, my dark Janetta!" And he closed his hand into a fist so that she could not read anymore.

"No, no, let me see! I am not finished!" she cried.

There ensued a playful tussle in which, after they had rolled about on the thin mat that was their pallet, she managed to catch hold of his hand again, and he allowed her to pry open his fingers. Then he tried to withdraw it, and she slapped his chest warningly; he relented with a laugh.

"Yes," she said, with great conviction in her voice, as she looked at his palm, "she will be dark, and her skin will be very fair."

He laughed and stroked her hair and her birthmarked cheek.

"She will be a queen," she added suddenly now, in a surprised tone.

He laughed again. "A queen of what?" he asked. "Queen of witches?"

"No, no—I do not understand. She will be some kind of a queen, a ruler.—Does England have a queen?"

"Yes, of sorts. And much though I honor her, I can only say, God forbid I should marry her!"

"She is old, then, this queen?"

"Well, she is into her seventh decade; and I can promise you, that is old to me."

"Then it is some other queen."

"Ah, yes, perhaps. The Queen of Sheba, or maybe Queen Mab, the queen of the faeries."

"You mock me," she said; and her tone was bitter.

"Indeed I do," he admitted. "You only torment yourself with a figment of your imagination."

"No," she said bitterly. "I see this woman—I see this dark queen; and you will love her more than you ever loved me."

He laughed and tried to take her in his arms, but she would not let him; she evaded his embrace and slipped away from him.

"You will love her more than me!" she said angrily. "Who is this woman?"

"Janetta!" he said soothingly. "Do not be silly. I know no queen; nor is it likely I ever shall. You are the one I love."

"White Edmund!" she demanded in an accusatory tone, "Who is this dark queen?"

"My love, do not be foolish! I know no such woman."

Then she seemed to go mad. She stood up and seized the iron bar that was used to pry the cogs of the mill out of enmeshment, and slashed at the machinery—at the wall—at the embrasure of the window, crying the while, "She shall have you—and I shall not!" and the like, punctuated by that peculiar cry he had heard before, the *aiee* that had woken such terror in the slaves, but now uttered in a tone of enraged despair. He scrambled to his feet and caught her and wrested the bar out of her hands. Her eyes had become slits of rage, and it was only when he gripped her tightly that he was able to bring her back to herself.

They made love again, and she was particularly wild—kissing him and weeping and moving eagerly with him. Afterward she sank into an exhausted sleep; he lay quietly holding her slight figure in his great arms.

The Dark Queen! he thought to himself wonderingly. *How can she have so frightened herself with a figment of her own fancy?*

⧗⧗⧗⧗⧗

One day he had occasion to go up to Mr. Duckworth's to return a plow he had borrowed from him. He drove the wagon up to his neighbor's plantation, and as some of Mr. Duckworth's men lifted the plow down from the back, Mr. Duckworth came out of the great house.

"I return your plow in better shape than I found it, sir," said Edmund. "The rivets that held the right mouldboard were cracked and about to give way, and I had the smith repair it."

"It does not surprise me to hear of your scrupulousness, Mr. Percy," said Mr. Duckworth, "though it was not necessary for you to take the trouble and expense."

"You are all too kind to lend it to me."

He went to Mr. Duckworth and shook his hand; and though the fellow was as kindly as ever, Edmund detected something sad in him.

He knows, Edmund thought.

They stood for several minutes in silence that was otherwise unaccountable.

"I have not heard from my father yet," said Edmund finally.

"Well, sometimes the mails take far longer than we can believe they should, especially when we are impatient for a response. And your father has his decision to consider, and doubtless must consult with your brother, as well as with his advisers."

"And your offer still holds?" asked Edmund.

Mr. Duckworth, who had been evading his gaze, now looked directly into his eyes; and he saw that Edmund knew he knew.

"Oh, yes," said Mr. Duckworth. "Though it does not seem now that it will work out as I had hoped it would."

Edmund was stricken with shame, though he had never intended to fulfill his friend's wishes in any case.

"I am sorry for that," he said sadly. "Believe me, I am sorry for that."

"You were right," said Mr. Duckworth. "You would have been better to flee Antigua when you felt yourself in danger. I am sorry I encouraged you to stay."

"But sir, it was hardly your doing! I stayed because I had to stay."

Mr. Duckworth shook his head. "But what will be the end of it?" he wondered. "I fear it will be evil—evil for you, my young friend. I fear it will shatter you."

"Perhaps it will," said Edmund. "But I mean to go away; to become a manager on some other estate."

"Ah," said Mr. Duckworth uncomfortably. "You have learned to live as most do in the West Indies, then?"

"Until I can do right, I must continue to do wrong, trying to do the least wrong I can."

"I see what your thinking is," said Mr. Duckworth.

Now he patted Edmund in a sad and fatherly way on the shoulder. "God be with you," he said. Then, without another word, as if he were too overcome with grief to trust himself to speak, he turned and went back in the house, leaving Edmund standing alone in surprise by the wagon.

As he drove home he thought of his friend's failed hopes. He consoled himself somewhat with the thought that they had always been preposterous. The idea of Edmund's marrying one of those passionless gray Quakeresses was inconceivable. But now a new thought struck him: Janetta had made all other women seem as passionless as those bland gray beings under Mr. Duckworth's roof. After the kind of love he had tasted, he could never be content with a well-bred English woman, raised, as she would certainly have been, to think that sexual intercourse should serve only the purpose of getting a family—as an evil to be endured, something *done to her* by a man, and hopefully as rapidly ended as possible on each of those rare occasions on which it must be submitted to. He knew not all the women of his nation viewed the act in such a light, but there was no question in his mind that the majority of women in his social class would be gravely shocked and disgusted if they were asked to participate in lovemaking of the sort in which he and Janetta indulged every day, of their own free choice. He might, it was true, find an affectionate and innocent woman, and gradually seduce her into these fuller pleasures; but his very soul revolted at the thought of such a deliberate alteration of another's inclinations.

No; Janetta had spoiled him for any happy marriage with his own kind. He might, if he were not determined to marry her, resign himself to marrying some pleasant Englishwoman, knowing that he must carry his greater knowledge of the possibilities of married love as a secret that could not be communicated to her—a secret she would be constitutionally incapable of comprehending, a secret she would find revolting and horrifying if she so much as glimpsed it in him. But such a marriage now seemed to him a pale excuse for life.

He had no idea, in his innocence, how many people live out such shadow marriages, matched, or rather, mismatched with a spouse unequal in sexual knowledge and desire. It is the way of the world; and the hours of one's life spent in the company of a partner truly attuned to one in such pleasures—those times, if they ever occur at all, are too soon ended, and become a standard in the memory that secretly makes a sham and a mockery of the married love that follows.

Chapter 14

It was not only the soreness of spirit which this state of affairs inflicted upon the coloured man, but as Prejudice was the offspring of Slavery, it was consequently the groundwork of that horrible system of licentiousness which rendered Antigua among the other West India Islands famous, or rather *infamous,* for so many years. The coloured women participated in the *prejudice* of their masters, and as they became the mothers of female children, they reared them up in the same spirit, and inculcated into their minds that it was more honourable and praiseworthy to inhabit the harem of a white man, than to be the lawful wife of a man of colour. This conduct was, of course, the grave of all domestic peace, the destroyer of connubial love; and by its dire, its *demoniacal* influences, caused the fairest island in the world to become, in a moral point of view, a dreary marsh, exhaling the poisonous miasma.

—*Antigua and the Antiguans*

N*ot until* September did the answer come from his father.

Mr. Edmund Percy
Canebrake, Antigua

Brackensom, Aug. 12, 1813

Dearest Edmund,

I have been for some time in receipt of your letters of May and June concerning the sale of Canebrake. I have discussed the matter with Christopher and with Mr. Beckwith, and we are unified in our belief that the course you propose is the best. Mr. Beckwith thinks that we might get a somewhat better price if we sold the estate at auction; but Christopher and I are keen to spare you and Brackensom the disgrace of such an undertaking. Mr. Beckwith has also inquired into this Quaker of whom you write, Mr. Duckworth, and finds that he has a solid connection with our banking house here. In a time of war such as this is, the certainty that we shall indeed receive our funds after the sale is a powerful inducement not to deal with some unknown, as we should necessarily have to do in the case of an open auction.

All the same, we do not wish to constrain you in this matter. You are our general in the field, as it were, and must ascertain the most favorable conditions and act upon them. If the sale to some other individual should prove more advantageous, we empower you to make the sale to him. We urge you only to be sure of the collection of the monies he exchanges for the plantation.

I enclose with this letter a power of attorney to make the sale, as well as some other papers to the purpose drawn up by Beckwith. You will see that these papers empower you to take a portion of the sale in cash, should it be required to pay your personal expenses in returning to us.

Your brother joins me in hoping you can make a speedy end to your absence from Brackensom. Christopher, indeed, shows such impatience to have you at home that he has been almost importunate in urging the sale of Canebrake. Though I do not indulge my feelings as openly as he, I too, have yearned to see your face again, dear Edmund, and to see you embarked on that career in the church for which you were bred up.

In this regard, forgive me if I mention that I have received a communication from one Mr. Alphonse Morgette, who claims to have been a classmate of mine at school. He is apparently magistrate of the parish there in Antigua; doubtless you will know of him. He complains that you are undermining the social order on the island by working alongside our slaves in the field, and begs me to order you to abstain from such behavior. This preposterous charge is utterly beneath our notice, and I would never dream of condescending to reply to his wild exaggerations. I know that you would never do anything that did not befit a gentleman and a scion of the Percies. Mr. Morgette's letter, however, does suggest that I have forced you into a position truly untenable for a gentleman. You have had to become involved in the day-to-day operation of Canebrake in a fashion that is not proper. I blame my own continued failure to find a suitable manager. The rest of the fault lies with your extreme piety, my dear son, and your zeal to carry out the commands of your father; and I would be the last to fault them. In any case, Mr. Morgette's letter has only confirmed me in my decision that Canebrake has become an encumbrance and must be disposed of.

We hope you will conclude the sale as soon as possible and sail on the first ship home, preferably a packet—the expense is no object. If I could have both my sons safe with me at Christmas, my mind would be greatly eased.

Your affectionate father,

Hereford Percy

This letter, which Edmund had been eagerly awaiting for months, was, in the event, nearly enough to overturn his reason. When he had first written to his father he was looking for this response to save him from temptation. After he had fallen into his sin, he had longed for this letter to provide him a way to set his sin right. But the letter confronted him with the terrible cost of what he had done. His father yearned for him and feared for his safety; his brother needed his help in the difficult battle that lay ahead over his engagement to Bronwyn Floyd. Both his father and his brother must now and forevermore be as if dead to him. He would not be in England this Christmas, or indeed, for any Christmas.

Whatever the force of the emotions he felt reading the letter, he did not show their effects outside the privacy of his parlor where he read it. When he emerged, he was determined. His father had empowered him to sell the place to whomever he thought best. He knew who that would be.

He took his bird gun, charged both barrels with heavy shot, and went out and saddled his horse. Then, without saying a word to Janetta, or even signaling his departure by waving to her across the fields, he rode down the lane and turned—not east, not toward Mr. Duckworth's—but west, toward Waller's. He retraced the way he had last walked with the emaciated Betty on his shoulder, years ago. On his route down the lane to the house, he passed a huge cordon of slaves working in the fields under the supervision of Jones and several black slavedrivers. Jones stared at him in undisguised astonishment.

When he reached the great house, word had gone ahead of him somehow; even as he rode up, Waller strode out on the porch, amazement and outrage vying in him.

"What the hell do you do on my plantation, Percy?" he cried.

"I come at your own invitation, Waller," said Edmund.

"What the—!"

"Did you not tell me once that if I ever wished to sell Canebrake, I should let you know?"

These words staggered the man. He came to the railing of the porch and gripped it. His black mistresses filled the doorway behind him, gawking at Edmund.

"What?" said Waller. "Are you going to sell?"

"Here are my terms," said Edmund. He named the price Mr. Duckworth had offered, and then he said: "That does not include the slaves. I mean to sell them to Mr. Duckworth. And the livestock as well—I would not consign even so much as the life of a chicken to your care."

Waller started to speak, but Edmund silenced him by holding up his hand.

"There will be one more cost to you," he said. "You must set Janetta free."

"Be damned to you!" cried Waller. "Be damned to you! I know what you do! You have made her your mistress, Mr. High-and-Mighty Percy, candidate for ordination in the Church of England! Do you think I do not know?"

"I ask only that you set her free, in proper irrevocable and legal form; I do not want to make her my slave. When she is free, she shall choose what she wants to do. Doubtless she will go away from this island as soon as she can. What she will do, neither you nor I can say. But whatever it is, it will be her own free choice."

"She will go with you!" cried Waller. "That is what you want! That is what you have agreed with her!"

"I have agreed nothing with her. She does not even know I am proposing this to you."

"You lie! You lie, Percy! Your very speech is a vomit of lies!"

"Think on my offer, Waller," said Edmund. "I shall give you until noon tomorrow. You know that in any case you shall never have her; she will kill herself before she can fall into your hands again, or kill you if she can manage it. She is already lost to you; why not profit by that loss? Why not become master of your own plantation?"

Waller seemed to be struck by what Edmund said; but still he refused to concede. "Be off!" he cried. "I shall turn the dogs loose on you!"

"I am ready for them this time," said Edmund, laying his hand on the stock of his gun.

He turned his horse about slowly. "Think about what I have said, Waller," he added. "You have until noon tomorrow."

⧗ ⧗ ⧗ ⧗ ⧗

He waited to tell Janetta what he had done until they were alone in the mill that evening. He thought that she would fly into a fury, but she did not; she only fell silent and turned away from him; and when he took her in his arms she was limp and unresisting. As he turned her to face him, he saw she was weeping. This abject despair was the last thing he knew how to address.

For a long time she would not speak to him, no matter that he coaxed and cajoled and begged her; but finally she put her arms around his neck and held him tightly; and he heard her say, in a barely audible voice, "It is the end."

"It is *not* the end!" he protested. "It is the beginning, Janetta! You will be free, and you shall come away with me to Jamaica. The sugar business is still booming there. I shall take a post as a manager, or more likely as a schoolmaster, and you shall live with me until we can find a way to marry. Once we have done that, I care not what happens."

"Oh, Edmund," she wept, "you are only doing this because your morality tells you that you ought to."

"Yes, my morals do say I must do this; but it is not the only reason. I love you, Janetta."

"Yes," she said, "you do; you do love me." She released her grip on him and looked him in the face, caressing his cheek lovingly, while the tears still ran down her face. "But it is only because of your goodness that you love me. I am a bad woman; I have nothing to offer you but what little broken affection is left to me. You were not made to be with such a woman as me, and you will not be happy with me."

"I could not now be happy with anyone but you," he said.

"Ah," she said, smiling sadly. "You think I have corrupted you with my love. Now that you have the 'carnal knowledge' I have given you, you do not think any English girl could make you happy. But you will find one who will. You will find one who knows the secret you know. You may have to teach her still, but she will be a willing pupil, because she will love you, and better than I could."

"My love," he protested, so grieved that he was barely able to speak, "do not talk this way."

"My love," she said sadly in answer, "it is over. I do not know how it will end, but end it now shall. It was not you who put this all in motion—you must remember that, when

I am no longer here to remind you. It was I, that evening when I seized you and could not let you go; when I put my life in the balance against this love I have had with you, and I chose to love you and die."

"This is utter madness! Janetta, we shall escape. Even if Waller does not agree, I shall make the sale to Mr. Duckworth, and you and I shall flee together. Waller cannot stop us!"

"Edmund, Edmund," she said, in a voice more soft and sweet than she had ever used, "you are not in your world—you are in mine. Do you not understand that? Sensible plans—forethought—sound reasoning—persuasion—none of them work here. Here there is only madness and violence and death. I saw my own father hurl my own mother to her death, because she would no longer submit to him. She chose to die rather than love him; and I chose to die rather than *not* love you. Are those the kinds of choices you and those you love are forced to make in the world you come from? I do not think so. *Persuasion only works when it has something to work on.* You must have a society; you must have morals and rules and laws to work within if you would persuade people. Here there is nothing to hold us all together. You think Antigua is a mirror of England; but it is only a broken mirror, and we are only its pieces. Here the only thing that matters is money. The minute you Englishmen come here and resign yourselves to using slaves, you give up everything that makes you English. You become lower and more broken than the men you enslave. You may strut about and shake your fist and make us more miserable at your will, but you are only fooling yourselves into thinking that you have power over anything significant. What is power over slaves? Nothing; worse than nothing. To be openly trusted and given power freely by another—that is something. But your lust for money has made you all powerless. It has robbed you of your morals; it has robbed you of what could make you great, the teachings of your Master. It has driven you out of your best selves and forced you to descend into filth—to *become* infinitely worse filth than your victims could ever be."

Suddenly a pang of fear went through him—a fear that she was right, and that he would not be able to control the outcome of the events he had set in motion.

She saw that he was frightened. "It is all right," she said soothingly, caressing his cheek. "I knew all along that this had to happen. And for you there is still a chance to be happy. That means everything to me."

She paused now, looking at him earnestly. "Whatever happens, my love," she said, "you must promise me one thing."

"What is that?"

"You must not take vengeance on Waller."

"Indeed I shall," said Edmund, "if he touches one hair on your head—if he or any of his minions lays one finger on you—I shall throttle him."

"No, no," she said, shaking her head. "Then he will pull you down with him. Do not let him do that. You will not fix one sin, as you call it, by piling another on top of it. And they will hang you for it—the men here will cheerfully hang you for it, just as they would hang me."

He did not answer.

Then she smiled, though still with great sadness. "There," she said, "Do you see? We ought to have made love before we talked, as I have always said we should. Now we shall never make love the same way again; because we shall always be thinking it is to be the last time."

Then they did make love; but it was as she had said, bitterly sad, and for the first time he wished they had not. He lay awake for a long time afterward, insisting in his own mind that she could not possibly be right—that this world, too, would yield to the demands of persuasion and reason, and that they would somehow escape it.

Chapter 15

The root of all West Indian misery—*illicit love.*

—*Antigua and the Antiguans*

At about eleven o'clock the next day, Waller sent over one of his lesser drivers with a message for Edmund. It read:

> I agree to your terms. Meet me at the office of Gascomb in St. John's tomorrow at eleven o'clock to draw up the papers.

It was unsigned, and the crabbed hand was barely legible; but Edmund was not expecting anything handsome.

With joyful vindication he told Janetta about it. She looked away and would not speak to him.

"You shall see," he said. "Tomorrow, by noon, you shall be a free woman."

"Free of the earth, perhaps," she said.

After the noonday meal they both went back to work with the men as usual. Edmund did not want to alarm them with any indication of change until the deal was settled. They had worked for about an hour when suddenly Edmund noticed Janetta stop what she was doing. She straightened and turned her face into the breeze, and she sniffed the wind for all the world like a hound scenting a deer over hill and hedgerow.

Without a word she left the field and went up to the windmill. The men noticed her strange behavior and stopped working to watch her. In a minute the hatch at the top of the mill opened and she climbed out. She stood now on the window ledge, facing into the wind again; she was clearly smelling something on the breeze.

Baffled, Edmund searched the faces of the men for some clue as to what she was doing. To the last man they showed terror and uncertainty, but they said nothing. They stood in a silent knot while she disappeared into the mill again, and then emerged and returned down the path.

She walked up to Edmund and looked gravely into his face.

"Hurricano," she said.

The men began to jabber wildly. He silenced them with a word, and then said to her, "How do you know?"

"I can smell it," she said.

"But look, there is not a cloud in the sky."

"This is the way it always is," she said. "The hurricano feeds off that warm air. Somewhere over the horizon, there, to the northeast, it is bearing down on us. If I am right, within the hour you will see the clouds appear in the east and north. By night it will be raining; it will rain all day tomorrow. Then, tomorrow night or the next day, the winds will come; bad winds."

"What must we do?" he asked.

"By the end of today we ought to have the livestock under cover, and put away all the tools and equipment. That is all we *can* do."

⌛⌛⌛⌛⌛

Within the hour the clouds she had foretold did appear in the northeast—great long, striated things, gently bending across the roof of the sky on the horizon—the edge, as she described it, of a great, whirling storm. The wind shifted to the northwest. By nightfall the rain had begun, at first as a soft and gentle shower, and then, after a lull, continuing in a downpour of greater intensity; and so on through the night, as bands of heavier and heaver rain alternated with dry or nearly dry lulls.

This was not a new phenomenon—Edmund had been three years in Antigua, and tropical storms of varying intensity had swept over the island from time to time. But even he had a sense of a larger, more powerful storm presence behind this rain. He and Janetta lay together in his bed in the great house; they made love almost as a kind of habit, and then stayed awake for a long time, holding one another, listening to the rain, and saying nothing.

Before he left for St. John's the next morning, he took Janetta up to the windmill. There was no need to tell her to lock herself in. He offered her the use of his guns, but she wanted none of them. She had her knife, she said, and it was the only weapon with which she was familiar.

After he had heard her bolt and bar the stout door from inside, he went to where Obah and the others were gathered in one of the barns. They were supposed to be doing indoor chores—assembling barrels, cleaning the boiling pans, and the like; but the work so far was clearly little more than pretense, and the men were milling about, or sitting idly by, nervously awaiting the storm.

"Obah," he said. "I am going to town on business. If anything happens while I am gone, I want you to take the wagon and come after me directly. I shall be at Mr. Gascomb's, on Popeshead Street; it is above the tobacco shop there. Do you know where it is?"

"I seen dat tobacco sign, Massa," said Obah.

"Good. If they will not let you in, stand in the street and shout for me. Do you understand?"

"Yass, Massa."

"I should return early in the afternoon."

Not a man of them said anything. He wondered how much they knew.

He took his horse and started out. The day was preternaturally warm despite the rain, and though his greatcoat kept the rain off, he sweated under it. He was half-way to town when he crested a rise and caught up with a wagon loaded with new barrel staves. He thought it odd that the wagon was bound toward St. John's instead of away; and though it could be of no matter to him, he fell in beside the driver and asked the man where he was bound.

"Takin' dese yeah barrel stabes home, suh," was the response.

"And where is home?"

"Sunlea, suh."

This was the plantation of one Sir Thomas Bertram, an absentee owner; it lay a little ahead on the road to St. John.

"And where are you coming from?"

"Marshall's Creek, suh."

"Marshall's Creek? Why there?"

"Yankee ship offshore dere, suh. Been sellin' barrel stabes all week."

"Ah," said Edmund. Because of the war with the United States, the ship could not put in at St. John's; but the plantation owners were so desperate for barrels in which to ship their sugar home that the authorities winked at these illegal landings.

He pushed ahead of the wagon and continued on into St. John's. Shortly before eleven he was at Gascomb's.

He had had dealings with Mr. Gascomb before—twice he had been cheated by merchants who, when he protested, referred him to Mr. Gascomb. The lawyer was anything but honest—the very sort of man with whom he would expect Waller to associate. He had no doubt that they gambled together, and perhaps traded sexual partners. Edmund found him alone in his office, which reeked of Madeira; he had not even an honest scrivener by him. Clearly they would not be able to conclude any business today, but they might be able to hammer out the terms. And Edmund had to remind himself that he must in any case make sure that Waller did not cheat Brackensom—he must have cash, not promises or mortgages, which might never be honored.

At about quarter past eleven Waller entered. He, too, reeked of Madeira; Edmund thought he been stoking his courage at a public house around the corner. His clothing, too, had been considerably dampened as a consequence of the ride into town.

"Nasty weather we are having," observed Gascomb genially. "It may be setting up for quite a blow."

This idle comment seemed to agitate Waller; but no plantation manager would welcome a hurricane in any case, so Edmund did not make much of his reaction.

They did not greet each other or shake hands. Waller sat down as far as he could from Edmund, and they eyed each other with mutual loathing.

Waller was a man in his late fifties. His face was fantastically weather-beaten from a lifetime in the tropics, more than that of any planter Edmund had ever seen—one might almost have thought he had been a pirate on the high seas, so riven were his cheeks with lines and folds; and his narrow, pursed lips, which he was continually wetting with the tip of his tongue, reinforced the impression he gave of a overruling pettiness of spirit. His eyes, however, were intense with anger and hatred, and occasionally with glints of something like gloating triumph.

"Well, gentlemen," Gascomb began. "I believe Mr. Percy has stated the terms of the sale: a sum to be agreed upon for the property, buildings, and chattel." The omission of the correct stipulations about the slaves and Janetta was blatant.

Edmund stared him to silence. "Do not play games with me," he said. "I have a ready buyer, and if Mr. Waller does not wish to meet my terms, I shall go direct to the other party."

Mr. Gascomb was a little flustered, and restated the terms: "Ah, yes—the agreed sum for the property and buildings, but not the chattel."

"You still fail to mention a critical stipulation," said Edmund. "The mulatto slave known as Janetta, reputed to be the daughter of Mr. Waller himself, is to be set free into the bargain."

Mr. Gascomb acted pained at Edmund's indelicacy. "Please, sir," he said. "We do not speak of such things here.—Let me see," he continued, looking at some papers before him. It was clear now, if it had not been before, that he had already met with Waller, either earlier this morning or late yesterday, and this preliminary skirmish had been agreed upon. "Yes, I do see something here about the emancipation of the slave known as Janetta. Do you agree to this, Mr. Waller?"

Waller nodded curtly.

And so the main point was gained; or so it seemed. Mr. Gascomb scratched down the outlines of a document pertaining to this portion of the agreement: Waller was to declare the female mulatto slave known as Janetta to be free henceforth without condition; and Gascomb added legal phrases to trick out this language in the usual impenetrable lawyerly garb.

They then proceeded to the terms of the sale of the actual estate; and here they bogged down. Waller wanted to pay twenty percent down and the rest in a mortgage, and Edmund would not accept that proposal. Waller cursed and sulked; Mr. Gascomb fretted and soothed; Edmund would not yield. He could not tell whether Waller simply did not have the money or was determined not to part with it. They wrangled on this point fruitlessly for an hour, Mr. Gascomb suggesting the same payment scheme over and over in various guises, and Edmund refusing each and insisting on full payment through reputable channels.

Finally Waller agreed to pay in terms Edmund could accept. The funds were to be transferred to the Percies' account in London before the sale would be considered final. This meant a further delay; but if their communications were carried on the right packets, the business might be concluded with another three months.

Then, quite unexpectedly, Waller balked about the slaves on the plantation. He insisted they went with the property. Where was he to get slaves to work the place unless he acquired those belonging to the Percies? The place was worthless to him without them. He waxed very bitter on the subject, and seemed to feel that as Edmund had not conceded on any other point, he must concede on this. It was clear to Edmund that the man was only trying to see how far that one critical consideration of Janetta's emancipation would take him. Waller cursed and huffed; he several times stood up, and put on his hat, and made for the door, and let himself be escorted back to his chair by Gascomb; and though it made for good playacting, Edmund did not budge.

At length Waller gave in on this point as well. He sat sullenly in his chair while Gascomb fussily reiterated the terms; and if it had not been for the occasional sly glance of incongruous triumph he darted at Edmund, he would have seemed an exasperated man.

Gascomb now proposed to draw up the documents himself while they waited. This would take some time; but Edmund was willing, and so, apparently, was Waller. Gascomb set to work, and for quite some time there was no sound in the room but the scratching of his pen, the ticking of the clock, the patter of rain against the windows, and the moan of the rising wind.

It was about one o'clock when above that wind Edmund heard an unmistakable shout. He went to the window and saw Obah standing in the street below, holding the harness of the mule team in one hand, and cupping the other around his mouth to call again. Edmund dashed down the stairs and ran outside.

"Massa!" cried Obah. "Dey done come aftah Miss Janetta! Whole gang a' men—dey done come and broke down de doah a' de mill!"

The hemming and hawing, the playacting—it had all been to keep him here in St. John's. He did not take the time to confront Waller now; he threw himself on his horse and spurred immediately out of town.

The wind had risen sharply during the time he had been in Gascomb's. The rain was heavy and blinding, and it was all he could do to find his way through it. The air was still heavy; by the time he reached Canebrake, the horse was in a lather and gasping for wind. He rode up the lane, past the slave cabins, and directly up the hill to the windmill. A cry went up behind him as he passed the barn where the slaves were waiting out the storm, and several of them ran out and followed him.

The mill was deserted. The door had been smashed in with a heavy timber brought especially for the purpose—the timber in fact still lay on the ground beside the door. The ground all about the entryway was beaten into mud by the feet of many men and by the hooves of what seemed to have been several horses, and the rain had formed puddles in the muck, puddles stained heavily with blood.

He thrust his way past the wrecked door and looked up into the darkness of the mill overhead. Though the ladder was in place now, he knew that Janetta must have pulled it up onto the platform when she was attacked, shutting the trap door behind her. Her attackers, however, had clambered up on the machinery and hewn their way through the trap door, as well as through another point in the flooring of the platform, thus attacking her from two directions.

He heard a groan in the loft; and climbing instantly up the ladder, he looked through the opening of the trap door. One of Waller's men was still there, sprawled limply on the platform and twitching feebly. There was blood everywhere. The hatchway through the roof was open, and the rain was streaming down on the wounded man.

But Janetta was not there; and he flung himself down off the ladder and ran outside. Just as he did so, Betty ran up to the mill, with several others behind her.

"Dey catch 'er, Massa," she said. "Six or seven a' Waller's mans come; most a' dem breaks down de fron' doah and goes in dat way; but one climbs up de boom to de roof and gets in de hatch at de top. Dey catch her and tie 'er and gag 'er; and den Mista Jones throws 'er acrost 'is saddle and takes 'er away somewheres wit' two odda mans, all on hossback. De rest goes back to Waller's. Dere wasn't a man dat wasn't cut bad, Massa. She fight like a cat!"

The path the horsemen had left was blazed across the fields that like of a great army. It went to the northeast, directly through his canefields and those of Mr. Duckworth.

And now, as he saw the direction in which the attackers had fled, he understood what Waller was up to. They were taking her to Marshall's Creek and the Yankee ship moored there. Waller had seized this opportunity to sell her—or perhaps not even to sell her, but to simply put her aboard that foreign ship, and thus to remain within the letter of his agreement that supposedly declared her free—free of her old master, but in the hands of those carrying her into slavery elsewhere.

He was already on his horse again before Betty had finished her brief tale. He laid on with his heels again, and was away at a mad pace up the farther slope, through the cane toward the creek.

The rain was increasing every minute; the wind used it as a knife to slash at him as he rode. At times he scarcely could see his way, but then some favoring lull or contrary gust would pull the veil of rain aside and allow him to right his course.

He was about halfway to the creek, still following the muddy trail, when a figure appeared in the downpour ahead. It was Azaz, returning to Canebrake. He stepped out of Edmund's way, but Edmund halted an instant for intelligence.

"I follow dem foah you, Massa," said simple Azaz. "Dey put 'er aboard a little boat, and de little boat row out to de big boat."

Edmund gave a cry of despair and spurred on.

He tried to compute how long Azaz must have have been walking from the time he saw the longboat take Janetta away—it was all too long, well long enough for the Yankees to raise anchor, if they were mad enough to do it in this storm. As he rode, he took some hope from the weather; for surely no captain would set off in the midst of a hurricane—there would be time for Edmund to reach the vessel somehow, to parley with the captain, to buy Janetta back.

The tracks led to a steep path that descended to the creek; and plunging down it, he soon rode out onto a bit of sandy beach. The sand had been churned by hundreds of footprints over the past week, and worn flat again by the pounding rain; but still the freshest hoof prints were discernible, as well as the place where the keel of the longboat had cut its mark. Jones and the others had long gone, returning by some other route, or perhaps riding straight to the doctor's.

He raised his eyes to the sea, and as the rain lifted for a moment in the caprices of the wind, he saw the Yankee ship off the mouth of the creek. It had put on sail and was beginning to stand out to sea. The captain was either a fool or fearful of overstaying his dubious welcome here now that he had sold off his goods: he was going to try to run before the storm.

⌛⌛⌛⌛⌛

Edmund spent the next few hours trying to gain another sighting of the ship. He knew it could not be sailing to the northwest, for not only would it then be going directly into the wind, it would be in grave danger of running onto the reefs that ringed the northern side of Antigua. It would go southeast, clockwise around the island. Thus he rode to the leeward side, hoping the Yankees would put in at one of the sheltered bays there—Willoughby Bay, or English Harbor; but even as he rode, he doubted that such could be the captain's intention, for soon enough the winds of the storm would reverse and the leeward side would be taking the brunt. No; that the ship had sailed at all was proof of the Yankees' determination to get out to sea. Certainly they did not dare take shelter on British soil—their ship would be confiscated as the spoils of war, the crew press-ganged, and the officers likely left to rot in jail for the duration. But if the ship could get round the island to the south before the winds shifted, it would then be running free before the blow; and this, as he soon began to fear, must be the captain's plan.

It was only once, from the spit of land that extended west of Falmouth Harbor, that he caught a glimpse of the ship in a miraculous lull. It was bound determinedly away in the direction of Nevis and St. Kitts. And then and only then did he finally give up hope that the madmen who sailed her would change their minds and find safe harbor in some creek on the southern shore.

His pointless career around the island had used up most of the remainder of the day. He knew that once darkness closed in, there would be no finding his way back to shelter at Canebrake. Already some intervals of rain were so heavy that he actually had, or fancied he had, difficulty breathing in it. The gusts of wind were so violent that they staggered the horse; at times the beast could barely make headway against them. He turned for home and rode urgently for it; and by pushing the horse hard he was able to reach the head of the lane at the plantation just as the last bit of daylight slipped away. As it was, he had to crawl down the lane on his hands and knees, drawing the reins of the terrified and exhausted horse behind him, and groping to keep the sodden grass on one hand and the mud of the roadway on the other. At last he led the horse into its stable, staggered through the darkness to the house, and found his way through the door.

He sank to the floor, overcome by the fatigue of exertion and emotion. Betty and Johnny rushed out of the kitchen and helped him up. "Thank God you come at last, Massa!" cried Betty. They supported him as he reeled into the kitchen and took a chair by the table. "We thought you was done foah," said Johnny. "We thought Jones get you."

"Not yet," said Edmund. "No, I must live yet to go find her."

They said nothing to this. Betty brought him food and drink; and after he had rested for a time, he took it, not as one feeling the need for either, but as one aware that he must keep up his strength. He did not care that his clothing was utterly soaked through; the air was so close in the house that he did not feel the least chill.

There was nothing to do but wait out the storm. He gathered from what Betty told him that more of Waller's slavedrivers had come back to the mill and borne away the wounded man—or the dead man, as Betty thought him. All the Canebrake men were now in their quarters, and Betty and Johnny had their baby with them here; the livestock were under cover, and the shutters of the house were closed and secured. Edmund could hardly bring himself to care if the roof of every building blew off; he wanted only to be gone, to find where she had been taken, and to make sure of her safety.

He went to bed, but slept ill if at all. The wind was screaming and moaning around the house at such a volume that he could scarcely even think, let alone lapse into dreams. He reconstructed the events of the day—of the past few days—of these past months—these past few years; and all he could feel was a bitter regret for the way he had managed everything.

Chapter 16

There is in God, some say,
A deep but dazzling darkness: as men here
Say it is late and dusky, because they
See not all clear.
O for that Night, where I in him
Might live invisible and dim!

—Vaughan

B*y dawn* the strength of the hurricane had ebbed perceptibly. The rain was still falling heavily, but the wind had eased to the level of an ordinary storm.

Edmund was out of bed well before first light, and as soon as he could see his way, he proceeded straight to St. John's. He went to every ship in port, every public house, offering any amount of money to anyone with a ship willing to set out in pursuit of the Yankees. Some captains laughed; some cursed him and threw their cups at him; some were afraid of him as a daft man. One or two kindlier souls told him to come back after the storm was spent; and one in particular said that he was bound away urgently for St. Kitts as soon as the storm should ease, and would be glad to take Edmund that far.

This was the best promise he could win. He went back to Canebrake, cared for the horse, which was much in need of attention; and then walked up to Mr. Duckworth's. On the way, he forced himself to survey the damage to the plantation. So far as he could see, there had been little. The roof of one of the barns had been stripped of its covering in one spot, some of the cane on the high ground had been knocked flat, and there was debris everywhere, most of it cane trash from the fields. Despite the violence of the storm at its peak, he guessed it was not as bad as it might have been; and this gave him some hope.

He found Mr. Duckworth with his family in his parlor. The man was startled to see him.

"Why, neighbor," he said, "what do you do, walking abroad in this storm?"

"You heard what happened yesterday?" said Edmund.

"I heard that Waller finally sent for his daughter," said Mr. Duckworth.

"Yes; sent five or six brutes for her. I was not there at the time, or there would be five or six brutes fewer in this world."

"You may thank God you were absent, then," said Mr. Duckworth.

"It was not God's doing that I was away; it was Waller's. I offered to sell him Canebrake if he would set Janetta free."

Mr. Duckworth looked shocked and sad, but more sad than shocked. "Ah," he said, "I did not know that."

"I am sorry," said Edmund. "It was the only thing I could think of to shake her loose from the hold he had on her. While he and I were sitting in a lawyer's office, and he was agreeing to my terms concerning her, his men were breaking into my mill to take her away."

Mr. Duckworth shook his head, but said nothing.

"They have put her aboard that Yankee ship that was moored off Marshall's Creek."

"The *Annabelle,*" said Mr. Duckworth.

"Is that that name of her? That will be important to know."

"Yes, that is her name. I spoke with her supercargo myself at the creek not four days ago. He was getting a good price on barrel staves and firewood. I am not the only one in desperate need of barrels for next spring." He paused for a moment, and then he said, "But why will the name of the ship be important to you? If Waller's men put her on that ship, she is gone now, for better or worse. The Yankees will stop over somewhere in the slave states, and sell her to some planter, or perhaps to a brothel owner." He seemed to be trying to make sure that Edmund knew the worst of it.

"I am going after her," said Edmund.

There was a palpable horror in the room at this announcement.

"Ah, my friend," said Mr. Duckworth very sadly, "do not talk so. You will not find her. If you should ever make your way through the British blockade to the United States, you will likely be hanged for a spy. Besides, America is vast, and there are hundreds of thousands of slaves there, perhaps millions, from the seaboard to New Orleans. The mere idea is madness. The importation of slaves there is illegal, just as it is in the British realm, and her sale will be hushed up. What is more, she will likely be hanged herself, even before you could be. I fear she will do violence the instant her hands are untied. I heard late yesterday that three of the men who had gone after her were barely clinging to life, and the others are badly wounded. She will slay until she is slain; and indeed, I think that will be her purpose—to force her captors to slay her."

"I am going after her," repeated Edmund in a choked voice. "I came to ask you if you would look after my men while I am gone. If I do not return in three months, be so kind as to write my father. Tell him as little as you can of what I have done, if you will. You may arrange the purchase of the property directly with him."

"But you cannot find a ship to sail in this storm," said Mr. Duckworth.

"I know—I have already tried to do so. But I shall return to St. John's at once and be away as soon as I can."

"Mr. Percy—for the love of God, do not go on this voyage!"

"Will you do as I ask, sir, and look after the men? You may have the use of them, if you will pardon my putting it in such crude terms."

"Let me dissuade you," said Mr. Duckworth. He seemed as if he were about to weep.

"Farewell, sir," said Edmund. "I rely upon your Christian kindness."

With that he left the place and returned to Canebrake; and after gathering some necessaries there, he went on through the rain to St. John's.

⌛⌛⌛⌛⌛

He located the captain of the ship bound for St. Kitts and confirmed his intention to go with him. This man took him aboard his sloop and gave him a berth; and there Edmund waited out the remainder of the storm.

By the next dawn the rain clouds had vanished. The sky was clear and bright, except for some long strands of cloud on the northwestern horizon, and even those were fast receding. The captain could not find the harbor pilot—the consensus was that he was sleeping off a drunk—but he claimed to know the harbor and the waters round the island well enough, and daringly set sail without any assistance. When Antigua was lowering on the horizon behind them, Edmund sought him out and asked him if he knew of the *Annabelle.*

"Aye," the captain said. "I know of her. She has been plying these waters for some twenty years."

Edmund described how he had seen the ship standing out to the southwest from the point near Falmouth. "What do you think her chances were in that hurricano?" he asked

"Hurricano! What hurricano? That was just a storm, Mr. Percy, no hurricano; or at least, it did not reach to the height of a hurricano on Antigua."

"Call it what you will," said Edmund. "What were the *Annabelle's* chances in it?"

"It is impossible to say. She might very well have caught more of the storm somewhere else, I cannot vouch for that. But I have no doubt she went straight to Nevis and lay in the leeward side somewhere."

"Then you think she could well have survived the storm?"

"I think it pretty near a sure thing—though I do not envy her being out in it. Her captain is a wily man, no question about that. These damnable Yankees have many times shown themselves not to be underestimated. And she could ride the storm all right; she was clear of top freight, and doubtless had good ballast. The danger will be if she came upon a shoal somewhere in the darkness. Then there is no hope for her."

The trip to St. Kitts was mercifully brief, though to Edmund it seemed long with anxiety. As they approached the harbor of Basseterre, they saw every sign that the storm that the captain had mocked as a minor blow in Antigua had struck with far greater violence here. Ships rode swamped at their moorings, and several had been driven up on the quays. Roofs had been torn from houses, and some entire dwellings had collapsed. Crews of sailors, gangs of slaves, and an occasional white artisan could be seen at work now amid the wreckage on land and shore.

Once he had disembarked, Edmund again went through the dockside, looking for further passage. He had no idea where he must go in tracing the *Annabelle*, but he hoped that he would find an American ship willing to carry him to one of the seaports in Virginia. His best plan was thus founded on a few stray speculations of Mr. Duckworth's.

But Providence cut short his trip in St. Kitts. In the third tavern he entered he found a talkative old tar and asked him about the *Annabelle*.

"Aye," said the sailor. "Ain't that terrible! The *Annabelle*. Many a time I seen her, flyin' before the wind just as proud as you please; and now she has come to wrack. That skipper of hern thought as he had supernachral powers, he did. Well, let him try them powers in hell, and see what the Devil thinks of 'em."

"What do you mean?" cried Edmund.

The sailor looked at him in surprise. "Why, what do *you* mean, sir? You asked if I knew about the *Annabelle.* Do you not know yourself?"

"No—I do not! What is there to know?"

"She went aground on the eastern side of the island in the storm. Broke open and went to pieces. Why, you cannot find a piece bigger than a thole pin, that is what I hear."

Edmund leaned heavily on the table before him. "Were there no survivors?" he cried.

"Well, ackshally—yes, I heard as there was. A few Yankee sailors. Two was beat up in the surf pretty bad."

"Where would I find them?" asked Edmund.

"Where else would you look for Yankees these days? I would guess as they're in prison."

Edmund ran from the place.

For some minutes he walked up the street in a state of unthinking shock; and then he gripped tightly what shards of hope he had and found his way to the prison in the little town.

The officer in charge was suspicious at first; but Edmund told him that he had lost a loved one on the *Annabelle,* and his desperation must have been persuasive. He took Edmund to the cell of the American sailor who had been least injured in the wreck and let Edmund talk to him through a small opening in the cell door.

The place was dark, and Edmund could see nothing through the heavy grill.

"You," Edmund cried into the cell. "Were you on the *Annabelle?*"

There was a faint shuffling sound, and a man came forward into the dim light by the opening. He put a grizzled face up to the door and said, in harsh Yankee English: "Aye—I am from the *Annabelle.* I have already told you as much."

"You had a woman on board your vessel—she came aboard at Marshall's Creek in Antigua."

"Woman?" said the sailor. "The little slave whore, you mean?"

"She was a mulatto," said Edmund.

"She was damned near white, from what I could see," said the sailor. "She had a big mark over half her face."

"Yes, yes," said Edmund impatiently. "What has become of her?"

The man opened his eyes wide; the whites were almost all Edmund could see of him.

"Why, she is dead—drowned with the rest of them. Where else could she be?"

"Was there any possibility she escaped? Did you see her swimming? Would it have been possible for her to swim to land as you did?"

"Swim? Are ye daft? She was down in the brig, locked up tight."

"The *brig?*" Edmund was not familiar with this American word, but he guessed at its meaning. "Why was she put there?" he demanded, as if the reason could make a difference.

"She was a hellcat," said the sailor, in a tone that spoke his wonder at Edmund's intense interest. "We had no sooner got her aboard that she nearly got away from us and over the side—and still bound and gagged. The captain ordered her clapped in irons—in heavy irons, for her feet—and while they was bein' put on, she struck the second mate in the face—broke his nose. He gave her a good blow then, he did—knocked her senseless. The skipper ordered her thrown in the brig, trussed up as she was, and still wearin' them irons. Bad luck she were! That is what I say. The skipper was offered a good deal of money to take her to a Southern port and sell her on the sly; and I dare say that is what cost us all. The Devil came for his own, that is what I say!"

"But the ship broke up—might she not have escaped the brig then?"

"If she swam any which way, mister, it was straight down. You try swimmin' with twenty pound of cold iron on your legs!"

Edmund turned away and went out of the prison. The officer who had escorted him said something further, but it was nothing to the point, and did not penetrate the wall of pain around him.

⌛⌛⌛⌛⌛

He was on St. Kitts four days before he found a ship outbound for Antigua. During that time he went three times to the eastern side of the island, to the place the wreck had occurred.

There was little to see. The shore was strewn with flotsam—broken timbers, lengths of hemp cord crusted with salt, shattered bottles, shreds of clothing and sailcloth. He found no trace of Janetta anywhere, of course; he could only look out from the point on shore that the locals had identified to him as that nearest to which the *Annabelle* had gone aground, and know that he was looking out over her grave. Somewhere several hundred yards off, under the long Caribbean swells, or perhaps very close to him under the breakers, the body that had once belonged to her spirit was lying bound and chained on the seafloor, or in some crevice in the rocks, or hidden deep in thick, silent weed.

During these days he spoke only when necessity absolutely compelled him—first to inquire after the whereabouts of the wreck, later to get lodging or food. He was no stranger to grief; indeed, in this time he thought often of Alex and his mother, and of the perplexity of their passing from the earth, of their sudden absence from his life. To Janetta's loss there was a strange new dimension: his body had grown so used to its delight with hers that now it was like that of a man suddenly deprived of the laudanum that has sustained it. When he sank into sleep, he dreamed of her by the hour, dreams filled with fictitious lovemaking and real sorrow; and woke to a reality filled only with grief.

He lived in a strange, lonely prison of pain. The people of the town paid no attention to him. They had their own cares; he was just a stranger drifting about the place like a ghost. He would not reply if directly addressed, so there was no befriending him in any case.

It was not until he was aboard ship beating up wind to Antigua that he began to awake out of his stupor. He remembered what she had always told him—how she was not destined to live long, and how she had chosen to love him before she died. It seemed to him that in the days and nights of their love, her every word had been an envoi, her every caress a final endearment before parting. She had been very deliberately sending him onward, fully aware that she must stay behind; and though she had sometimes been bitter over their parting, and jealous of his future, that was only natural in someone as passionate as she was.

He would go home, as she had foretold. But there was a difficulty she could not have understood, even if she had dimly foreseen it. He had sinned very grievously. He had forgotten his God as abjectly as if he had set up a golden idol—perhaps she had been his golden idol. He could not even remember the last time he had dared to pray, or even to think about prayer; he could not have brought himself to offend God so willingly as would have been the case had he spoken to Him in the consciousness that he was doing something he felt to be wrong. He had never stinted, once he had begun, in his enjoyment of his love for Janetta; and that continuing enjoyment had closed his access to the moral code he had always lived by.

Now he was a sinner; and not just an amateur, not just a dilettante; he had erred deeply, repeatedly, consciously; he had planned further sin, thinking that was the only way to an end of sin.

His remorse would be unfathomable for many in this day. But he considered sexual intercourse outside of marriage to be fornication; and fornication was a form of adultery; and adultery was specifically forbidden by God. He had broken that law—he, a man who had been destined to serve God in the church, a responsibility he took far more seriously than most others of his time.

There was of course even then ample precedent for setting religion aside: England was still in the grip of its feverish belief in natural morality in preference to religion. But what he had done was wrong even by that dubious measure. It had led to Janetta's death. It had come close to ending his kinship with his father and brother, close to bringing shame on his family. No matter what standard he applied to his love for her, there was no excusing it: it had been a madness.

And the worst of his sin and shame now was that he would not have given it up for anything—not to be absolved, not to be returned to the ignorance and innocence in which he had lived. Only for her life would he have traded this; and he could not help thinking that his protection of her in these years had actually extended her life, had kept Waller from taking action against her sooner. She had said as much from time to time.

The Edmund Percy who stepped off the ship in Antigua was a very different man from the same of that name who had so recently left it. And yet, though he knew he was different, he was not sure *who* he was, who he had become.

He walked back to Canebrake. He found an overseer from Mr. Duckworth's plantation supervising the slaves in the fields, and sent him home with a message to his master that he was ready to complete the sale if Mr. Duckworth was so inclined. Then he had Betty make him a meal while he began packing his things in his traveling trunk; after he had eaten, he took a cup of coffee out on the verandah and sat in a chair, his thoughts blank with pain.

After some time, a white man came riding up the way from the main road. He proved to be an officer of the law. There was to be a hearing before the magistrate concerning the incidents at Canebrake, and in particular those events that had resulted in the death of one of Waller's black slavedrivers and the injury of several others. The testimony of Mr. Jones and the slaves had already been taken, and the basic facts of the case were known; but the examination of Waller and Edmund had been postponed until now. The news of Edmund's return had reached Mr. Morgette, and Edmund was now required to attend the magistrate at his house on the morrow.

Among the matters to be investigated that were listed on the writ was the death of Janetta. Edmund was momentarily surprised that news of it should have preceded him to Antigua; but recalling that the movement of news through the West Indian islands was unaccountable, he put his bafflement aside.

Chapter 17

Oh! Slavery, slavery! when will all the train of evils thou hast originated cease? when will thy pestilential influence be abolished in these beautiful, but (I must add it) crime-stained islands?

—*Antigua and the Antiguans*

The next morning early, before the hearing, Edmund rode into St. John's to purchase a pair of gloves.

It was a significant act. It was an admission of his failure in Antigua, and an expression of his understanding that he must return to the only system in which he was effective, that in which he had been born and bred. He did not understand his action as such, in a conscious manner, for he was not thinking clearly; he only decided, as if by instinct, that he must have gloves—that he must appear as a man of his class at the inquest.

And so he did. He brought forth clothing he had not had on his back since he had been in England—a back that was somewhat broader even than it had been then, and made his coat fit more tightly than fashion required. He was a very prepossessing figure when he entered Mr. Morgette's office: tall, straight of spine, wide-shouldered, his face slightly bronzed. His features were a mask, impassive, polite; he was determined not to reveal the feelings within.

There were many gentlemen of the neighborhood present, mostly out of curiosity, and they looked at him with surprise and with no small amount of pleasure, for here was one of their class, one whom they felt they could understand, and gone was the maverick younger son who seemed to have confused his place in life with that of the negroes. Mr.

Duckworth, too, was there, sitting apart from the others at the back; he nodded to Edmund, who acknowledged him with a nod of his own when he entered. Mr. Morgette was already seated at a table at the head of the room; his mulatto secretary sat at a small table near the window, ready to take down a record of the proceedings.

In another chair set apart, directly before Mr. Morgette, sat Waller, like a pariah, suffered by the rest only because the law required it. He was distinctly not pleased to see Edmund, and certainly not to see him in the uniform of the gentle class. He must have felt already at a disadvantage in this court.

Edmund advanced to the front of the room and offered his hand to Mr. Morgette over the table. "Forgive me if I am late, sir," he said. "My watch was soaked in the rains of the recent hurricano; it has stopped altogether, and I have not had time to repair or replace it."

"You are in good time, Mr. Percy," said Mr. Morgette. "Please, sir, be so kind as to take a seat here, on my right." He indicated a chair facing him at the front, opposite to that of Waller, who sat on Mr. Morgette's left. Edmund bowed his assent and took his seat.

"Now," said Mr. Morgette, "I hearby open this hearing into the death of one Dogger, the slave property of Mr. Waller, manager of the Antigua estate of Lord Vanstoke-Raynham; the death of the mulatto slave girl Janetta; and the injury of five others, including one white; namely, Mr. Jones, overseer of Mr. Waller.—Mr. Waller, I understand you have an accusation to bring; if you would be so kind as to give your testimony first, I think we may penetrate to the heart of this matter as quickly as possible."

Upon being prompted, Mr. Waller mumbled his way through his oath, and was then given an opportunity to speak.

When Waller first rose to his feet, Edmund turned his eyes on the man with a kind of sad and muted curiosity, as one might look on the torments of a great boar that, after ravaging the countryside, has been caught at last in a trap that has broken its leg. He was conscious that the man was fully a mystery to him. He knew only that he was vicious and cowardly and deceitful; but what motivated him he could not imagine. He listened to Waller's harangue, then, with a kind of curiosity, to see if he could discern how this man could ever have been brought to do what he did. He had to remind himself that, incredible though it seemed, this human being was the blood father of the woman he loved.

"I want to charge this man," said Waller, pointing a shaking finger at Edmund. "I want to charge him with unlawfully retaining my property for three years, and forcing me to employ my men to retrieve it, in circumstances that resulted in Dogger's death, and the wounding of Mr. Jones, and the maiming of four of my negroes."

Edmund thought it was curious that he omitted the death of Janetta; and Mr. Morgette as well noticed the fact. "Your charge is not in conformance with the law," said Mr. Morgette. "And you omit the death of the slave. Would you be so kind as simply to tell the story as you understand it?"

"As I *understand* it?" scoffed Waller. "It is not a matter of my *understanding*—of any mere *opinion* of mine. It is a matter of fact, a matter of the truth, which I have just sworn to tell you."

"Exactly. Please do be so kind," said Mr. Morgette, in a tone that showed that he could barely restrain his contempt for his witness. Waller perceived his scorn; and in his frustration and defensiveness, he grew still more angry.

"I shall tell you how it was," he said. "It started when one of my slaves, this mulatto wench, by the name of Janetta, ran away from me and took up living in the mill at Canebrake."

"And when did this occur?"

"When the place was abandoned."

"Which was some three or more years ago now?"

"Yes."

"How do you know she took up quarters there?" asked Mr. Morgette.

"Everyone knew it," said Waller.

"And so you knew it as everyone did?"

"Yes."

"And how soon after the place was abandoned did she begin living there?"

"About two weeks."

"So this would be, what, some months before Mr. Percy arrived?"

"Yes," said Waller. Edmund could see where Mr. Morgette was going with this line of questioning, but clearly Waller did not.

"And how far does Canebrake lie from Lord Vanstoke-Raynham's property, Mr. Waller?"

Waller looked irritated. "You know perfectly well they lie side by side," he said.

"I do, sir. And so I wonder how it is that this slave could have run away to Canebrake—what, a few hundred yards? a quarter mile?—and you not go after her in the months before Mr. Percy arrived. You said you knew she was there, did you not?"

Waller flushed now as he perceived the trap. He did not answer.

"I say, sir," said Mr. Morgette, "you must answer my questions."

"There was no need to go after her then," said Waller.

"Why not? Was she not your slave, and a runaway? Does the law not require you to pursue her, and do we not customarily levy penalties against those who do not do so?"

"I knew where she was. And we had a good deal more peace about the place without her there. She vowed to stick me with that knife she always carried, and she was such a wild thing that I had good reason to fear for my life—as events have confirmed."

"Then why did you not sell her to someone else? One cannot simply abrogate one's responsibilities as a slave owner, Mr. Waller—not on Antigua, and not in these enlightened times. We have laws, regulations, that govern our dominion over our slaves, and ensure our compassionate treatment of them. How did this slave of yours get her daily bread while she was living at Canebrake?"

"I'll be damned if I know!" said Waller.

"Please be so kind as to restrain your language, Mr. Waller.—You make my point for me: you did not know how she got her food; and that is something for which, as her owner, you were fully responsible."

"I thought I could starve her out!" said Waller. "I thought I could starve her into coming back to me on better terms. But she ate I don't know what—widdy-widdy and old yams from the slave gardens, I don't know what."

"Very well," said Mr. Morgette. "I think we know the state in which matters stood at the time of Mr. Percy's arrival at Canebrake. But let me clarify one point: This slave, this Janetta, she was your own slave, not the property of Lord Vanstoke-Raynham, is that not so?"

"Yes," said Waller fiercely. "She was mine."

"And how so? Where did you purchase her?"

The silence that initially greeted this question was conspicuous, and it seemed to pique the interest of all the gentlemen in the audience.

"She was the daughter of a slave I bought in Jamaica in '91," said Waller finally.

"The same woman who died in falling from the upper story of the great house at Lord Vanstoke-Raynham's plantation?"

"Yes."

"And who was her father?" asked Mr. Morgette bluntly.

Waller hesitated, but then he said, "I don't know."

Mr. Morgette said nothing for a minute; he only eyed Waller coldly. Then he said, in a distasteful tone, "Is it not true that you were the girl's father?"

"People said that," said Waller.

"Well? Was it true?"

"Maybe it was, and maybe it wasn't."

Mr. Morgette frowned severely. "I shall take that as your admission that such was in fact the case." He paused, but upon receiving no further comment from Waller, he said, "Pray continue with your narrative, Mr. Waller."

"Well," said Waller angrily, "it was this Percy here who got in the way of things! When he came to Canebrake, it became impossible to go onto his land."

"Why is that?" asked Mr. Morgette.

"Because he threatened to kill me if I did!"

Mr. Morgette turned to Edmund. "Is this true, Mr. Percy?"

"No, sir."

"Will you take your oath and repeat that answer?"

"Of course, Mr. Morgette."

This procedure was accomplished, and Edmund confirmed that he had never denied Waller access to Janetta. He did not add that he very well would have, if it had come to that; but Waller had never dared request permission.

"Now you may continue, Mr. Waller," said Mr. Morgette.

"Well—no matter what this lying *bastard* says, I did not dare go on his property, not for three years."

"Mr. Waller, I will have you remember that you are speaking of a gentleman, in the presence of gentlemen. Calling a gentleman by the term you just used is an actionable offense."

Waller said nothing. Mr. Morgette shook his head in disgust and continued, "And if you found you could not enter Mr. Percy's close, why did you not apply to the law for redress, Mr. Waller?"

"The law," said Waller, "has never been too friendly to me."

"Be friendly to the law, and the law will be friendly to you," said Mr. Morgette. There was general, if muted, laughter at this quip. "Are you aware, Mr. Waller," Mr. Morgette went on, "that Mr. Percy came to me immediately upon his arrival in Antigua, asking in some perplexity about what he ought to do in the matter of this abandoned slave?—It is true, sir; I have reviewed my notes on the matter this very morning. I advised him that he was required under the law to yield her up, or at the very least not to obstruct your access to her. We have his word against yours that he did not in fact obstruct you with the threat of violence."

"Well, he is lying!"

"So you say. However, on the face of it, circumstances seem to tell against you. You had several months during the time Canebrake lay abandoned when you might have recovered your slave, as you were required by law to do, without any hindrance from anyone; and you failed to do so. The appearance of Mr. Percy seems to have provided you with an excuse, but not to have offered any real obstacle to you, either to act yourself or to bring legal proceedings against Mr. Percy if they were required."

"I tell you, he is lying!"

"I am not persuaded of that, Mr. Waller. But let us leave that aside for now. Bring us up to the recent events."

Waller was so enraged that he could not speak for a minute; but then he seemed to see his way to a new shift. "Well—you say I did not take responsibility for recovering my slave. That is not true. When I found I could not get to her, I came up with a plan. I waited until Percy was away in town, and then I sent Jones with five slaves to get her back. That was when she stabbed Dogger to death; that was when she cut Jones and the rest. And I say that if it had not been for Percy, Dogger would never have died, and the rest would never have been cut. I must have restitution, if there is any justice in this island—Lord Vanstoke-Raynham must have restitution."

"Let me see, then—you used Lord Vanstoke-Raynham's slaves, and his paid overseer, Mr. Jones, to recover your own personal slave?"

"Yes," said Waller, evidently puzzled at the question.

"Well, this muddies the issue considerably. Did you have his permission to do so?"

"Why should I need it?" said Waller. "I am his trusted manager."

"Well, imagine you had been using his slaves to, say, recover treasure from a wreck for your own personal gain, and one of them drowned. The onus would clearly be on you to make restitution to Lord Vanstoke-Raynham. Legally, this case is not far different.—But let us leave this matter, too, aside for the moment."

He now turned to Edmund and said, "Mr. Percy, the case is, if we can believe Mr. Waller, rather simple. By his account, it would seem to be your negligence and obstruction that brought about the circumstances in which these slaves were killed, and Mr. Jones and the others wounded. What do you say to this?"

"First," said Edmund, "I repeat that, strictly speaking, I never forbade Mr. Waller access to my land. As you may recall from our discussion three years ago, this woman herself told me that she was afraid to return to her father's house for fear she would be raped by him."

Mr. Morgette cringed. "Please, Mr. Percy," he said.

"I ask the court to forgive my frankness; but look at this man," Edmund said, indicating Waller with a stare. "Tell me that he does not seem eminently capable of such a deed."

And everyone in the room did at that moment look at Waller; and it was clear that everyone thought the charge perfectly believable.

"At any rate," said Edmund, "I believed her account of it. It was all too credible. I did not want to force her back into that household; but neither did I at that or any other time declare to Waller that he could not have her back. I was in a very difficult situation. When she volunteered to work for me, I agreed; indeed, I found her knowledge of cane planting and harvesting indispensable, and she had a command over the men that was uncanny. I supplied her with food in return, and that was all I ever gave her; until sometime this spring, when I bought her a simple and decent dress, at the time I made my regular distribution to my other slaves."

He paused a moment and looked about the room. From where he sat, he could see Mr. Duckworth clearly. His friend seemed sad and strangely agitated, as if he feared Edmund would say too much.

Now Edmund turned back to Mr. Morgette. "Sir," he said, "I will not be disingenuous with you. I shall not prevaricate; I shall not conceal anything.—Did you ever see the woman in question?"

Mr. Morgette was startled at the question. "I am not sure," he said.

"She was quite young. Her skin was very fair, and she had a birthmark over half her face."

"Ah!" said Mr. Morgette. "Yes, of course I have seen her. I did not realize that she was the slave in question. She used to bring herbs up to my negroes here sometimes, I think."

"She was a very beautiful woman," said Edmund. "And although she was wild and unruly in many ways—she could not have grown up in Mr. Waller's household without being so—she possessed the ability to love, and to love passionately, those who treated her with respect. Her mother was also such, I understand; an accomplished mulatto, well-read, who was able to play music beautifully, among her other accomplishments; and was as well-favored as her daughter."

"You remind me that one point has been repeatedly overlooked in this matter so far," said Mr. Morgette. "In this fracas at Canebrake the woman herself was killed, and her blood is on someone's hands."

"Oh, no," said Edmund. "She was not killed at Canebrake."

"She was not?" asked Mr. Morgette sharply. "That was the testimony of Mr. Jones and the others."

"They perjured themselves, then," said Edmund. "She was taken alive to Marshall's Creek and sold to the Yankees who were trading off the *Annabelle.*"

Finally, at this provocation, Mr. Morgette began to lose his composure. His complexion grew dark with anger, and he turned to Waller. "And what say you to this, sir?" he demanded.

Waller bit his lip and then cried, "*I* never said she was killed at Canebrake! Besides, I was not there when Jones and the others went to the mill—I was in town with Mr. Percy himself."

"And did you know that Mr. Jones perjured himself?"

"How could I know that? I did not come to his deposition."

"Did you put him up to it, Mr. Waller? That is what I am asking you."

"Of course I did not," protested Waller feebly.

Mr. Morgette sat for a minute without speaking. He seemed to be struggling to control himself. At length he said, in a cooler tone, "So—you intended to send her away with the Yankees?"

"It was the only safe thing to do with her. And you ought to be glad I did—you and all Antigua. She was a violent thing—and she practiced *Obeah.* If she had been caught at it, you yourself would have ordered her hung."

"Let me be the judge here, Mr. Waller. Do not presume to tell me what I should have done.—Did it occur to you that the transportation of slaves has been outlawed? And that thus sending her to the United States was against the law?"

"But it was an American ship! The Yankees do not live by British law!"

"But *we* do, Mr. Waller," retorted Mr. Morgette. "Or at least, *some* of us do. What is more, we are at war with the United States. What you did can be considered trading with an enemy of the Crown."

"Then there is not a planter on this island that has not traded with the enemy of the Crown!" cried Waller.

On this point he scored. Mr. Morgette certainly was not going to bring such charges against anyone. In irritation he turned away from Waller and looked back at Edmund. "I believe you were in the midst of giving your account of this affair, Mr. Percy," he said.

"Yes, sir. I was saying that I was not going to conceal from you any part of these events. And I shall not. But let me continue by first clarifying the events of the day in question. Mr. Jones and his fellow thugs broke into my mill to abduct this woman; and though they paid for it dearly, they did succeed in overwhelming her and carrying her, bound hand and foot, and gagged at the mouth, to Marshall's Creek, where the *Annabelle* was waiting. That was the day that the hurricano descended upon us. After Janetta Waller was taken aboard, the *Annabelle* stood out to sea and attempted to run for the shelter of Nevis, or so it seems; perhaps her captain believed the course of the storm to be more northerly than it proved. That night or the next—I do not know which—the storm carried them onto a shoal on the eastward side of St. Kitts. The *Annabelle* was utterly destroyed. Janetta Waller was in the brig—the ship's prison—at the time, or so a survivor told me; she was still bound, still gagged, and perhaps even still unconscious from a blow to the head. And she was shackled with heavy irons. The only conclusion can be that she went down with the *Annabelle,* not to rise until Judgment Day."

His voice broke and he paused a moment; but only a moment. When he continued, his voice was firm again. "That was her end. She did not die in the fracas at the mill at Canebrake; no, she was taken alive, whatever Mr. Jones and the others may have told you."

He looked around now at the others in the room. "I have said I would not prevaricate," he said. "I hope you will honor my frankness, and that you will pity, rather than condemn, my weakness in this matter. Now I go back in time; back to the spring of this year. It was then that I conceived a love for this woman. Yes, for this slave woman; and though I did my best to master it, I found it reciprocated; and for the past several months I have lived in sin with her."

He turned back to Mr. Morgette, and found the man staring at him as if he did not know what to think.

"I determined to sell Canebrake plantation," continued Edmund. "I obtained my father's permission to do so, his power of attorney. Mr. Waller had once expressed his desire to own the place; and though I despised him—despised him then, almost as much as I do now—I was willing to let him purchase the place if he would agree to set his daughter free. I meant to offer her the opportunity to go, as a freed person, to Jamaica, to try her fortune with me there if she would, or without me, as she chose; but in any event, I meant to rescue her from her father.

"Mr. Waller agreed to my terms. He instructed me to meet him at Mr. Gascomb's office in St. John's. He acquiesced explicitly to giving his daughter her freedom; he agreed to my stipulations concerning the transfer of funds; and then he disputed other matters pointlessly and tediously—as I now see, because he meant to keep me there in St. John's as long as he could. For it was at that very hour that he had sent his men to abduct Janetta. On the one hand he was promising to set her free; and on the other, he was selling her to the Yankees."

"I did not *sell* her!" cried Waller. "That is a lie! I *gave* her to the Yankees."

"Yes; I stand corrected. You *gave* her to them along with payment of a large sum. Clearly you did so only to preserve the emancipation as a legal fiction. You meant to emancipate her, but only when she was in the hands of the enemy, in the hands of known slavers, who would see to it that—however nominally or legally free she might be on Antigua—she would wear out her days in slavery in the United States. They were only too glad to have her as goods—as valuable goods—to sell into prostitution in some seaport town. The gold you offered in addition was only a bonus—enough to make them linger in the face of the hurricano, when they ought to have long since gone on their way."

He turned to Mr. Morgette again. "Sir," he said, "no one in this room is more conscious than I of the wrong I have done and the sin I have committed. I ought to have resisted temptation, but I did not. That is, and shall forever be, a matter between God and me. If fornication with a slave is punishable under the laws of this island, and if you bring all who are guilty of that crime to book, your court will be henceforth a very busy place.

"Here is the way things stand: I mean to admit my defeat here. Dr. Mann once said it, and it is true: I am out of my depth in this place. I am for England, as soon as I can complete the sale of my father's property. You will be rid of me, as I do not doubt you have all wished to be—rid of a fool who did not understand or approve your ways here. I send myself into exile. As for the death of this slave of Lord Vanstoke-Raynham, and as for the injuries to Mr. Jones and the other slaves, let it fall on Mr. Waller's head, who was using them on a private commission. The knife that did the injury was wielded by a desperate woman fighting for her life and her honor, as best she knew how; and even if you judge her a murderer, you are forestalled; for God has anticipated any punishment you might mete out. Furthermore, if Mr. Waller had brought this matter to the attention of the law, as he ought to have done, this would never have happened. But he feared to do that; he feared that his own daughter would be summoned against him, and give credible testimony of his actions and intentions toward her. So he lied to me and deceived me, hoping both to get my father's property and to send his own daughter into slavery in a foreign land. This accusation against me, as vague and untenable as it is, is only the ranting of an defiler of the most basic laws of human behavior, a man so vile he is beneath the notice of any gentleman in this room.

"This is my plea, Mr. Morgette. Let this be your judgment: I am guilty of sin; condemn me to exile forever from Antigua; condemn me to make my error right with God as best I may, and to live forever in the knowledge of it. Mr. Waller is guilty of a worse sin—that of first desiring his own flesh and blood, and then of acting to destroy it; let him live forever in the knowledge that he sold her, his own daughter, to be a whore in Egypt, and achieved instead her death. Let him pay damages now to his earthly master for the slave who was lost; and let him pay damages for eternity to his higher Master for that and for everything else he has done. If you will, write a full report of this incident to Lord Vanstoke-Raynham; let him know what kind of a creature soils his name. As for Mr. Jones and the injured drivers, let them learn what they will from the sting they have received. It has been truly said that though the individual bee dies with its sting, if it did not sting, there would be no bees on earth. Let Mr. Jones and the other overseers consider that lesson, if they will."

He turned and looked at Waller. "To you, Mr. Waller," he said, "I add only that I have found it to be as our Lord said: 'There is nothing covered, that shall not be revealed; neither hid, that shall not be known. Whatsoever ye have spoken in darkness shall be heard in the light; and that which ye have spoken in the ear in closets shall be proclaimed upon the housetops.' You seem to live your life in the delusion that men do not apprehend your sin and deceit. My sins are infinitely less than yours; and yet see how they are now made known."

Silence greeted this confession; a long silence. Finally Mr. Morgette turned to Waller. "Do you have anything you wish to say, Mr. Waller?" he asked.

And it seemed Waller did; for he rose from his chair and began to rant indeed. "This is unjust!" he cried. "This is not any kind of justice! You cannot listen to this Percy in preference to me! You cannot credit him in preference to me! My oath means as much as his! What I meant to do is my own business—none of his—or yours, for that matter. If I choose to give my slave away, give her away I shall; if I choose to free her, I shall free her where and how I choose. *I* shall tell you the sentence that ought to be levied on Percy—he ought to be compelled to carry through this sale of Canebrake—that is what he ought to be compelled to do!"

"Is that then the purpose of this farce, Mr. Waller?" said Mr. Morgette. "To find a way to get your hands on Canebrake? I am afraid you have missed your chance for that. If you had dealt honestly with Mr. Percy, you would now be in possession of it. He would now be in Jamaica, and so, it seems, would your daughter; which could have been no worse for her than the fate you intended for her, however ill it might have been for Mr. Percy. But no—you thought to take back with one hand what you offered with the other; and like most people who attempt such tricks, you find that you are left with nothing. You may feel yourself fortunate, Mr. Waller, that I send you from this hearing without bringing charges against you for the very crimes of which you have accused Mr. Percy. And I assure you that I shall indeed report this entire sordid affair to Lord Vanstoke-Raynham; and though I may spare Mr. Percy as much as ever I can in that report, I shall hold back nothing about you. We are losing Mr. Percy to our society here, it would seem; and much though I am relieved to see him go, for all the trouble he has caused, I would rather see a thousand of him stay than even one of you and your ilk. You are a bad man, Mr. Waller; that is the sum of it; and as such, you can never be desirable company in the assembly of the good. I shall thank you to remove yourself from my house at once."

Waller began to protest again, but Mr. Morgette shouted him down: "At once! At once, Mr. Waller!" And he rose from his seat and pointed to the door.

Waller turned with an oath and strode out of the room. The rest remained seated, somewhat in awe of Mr. Morgette in his judging fury. The magistrate sat down again and contemplated Edmund.

"And with you, Mr. Percy," he said, "I shall indeed be lenient, in particular because of your promise to depart these shores and never come back. Let this be a lesson to you, young man: Do not meddle in matters of which you know nothing. You do not know how we do things in the West Indies. You are like your Mr. Wilberforce and all his do-gooders in Parliament, whose hearts bleed for the slaves—you and your kind will ruin us if you can. If the planters, as a class, ever sink and fail, it will be because you have brought catastrophe upon us, in your ignorance of the demands imposed upon us by our means of making honest wealth."

At that moment, Edmund realized suddenly how he must do penance for his sins. He must work to end slavery for all time, insofar as it lay within his power; but not here, not in Antigua, where the system was strongest, and had the greatest force to crush him, and he the least force to fight it—rather in England, where, as Janetta had said, there were laws within which to work and a framework of morals to which to appeal. And the first step toward his goal must be to hold his peace now.

"Very well, sir," said Mr. Morgette. "You are dismissed from this hearing. If you are not gone from Antigua within one month, you must come to me and explain the reason why."

"I thank you, sir," said Edmund coolly.

"This hearing is adjourned," said Mr. Morgette.

Edmund rose and went to the door. The other planters, though they had also risen, did not immediately follow him, but only watched him go, with various expressions on their faces—disgust, pity, relief, and one or two of envy. Only Mr. Duckworth came towards him, meeting him at the door. There he shook hands with Edmund, and they went out together.

"You did well," said Mr. Duckworth when they were outside.

"I have done nothing well since I left England," responded Edmund.

"You have learned a lesson well, I think," said Mr. Duckworth.

"I hope so."

"Trust me for now—you have learned it. You shall not know how much you have learned, not for several months, if that soon."

"Well, as I told Mr. Morgette, I shall carry the knowledge of what I have done, and what I have failed to do, for the rest of my life; I shall grant you that."

They went to the barn where their horses were tethered. Most of the other gentlemen had come on horseback as well, and several of them were now following behind them.

Here in the cooler darkness of the barn they encountered Waller.

Edmund ignored him. He went to his horse and tightened the girth. Waller seemed to wait until the other gentlemen had entered, and then he cried, "Mr. Percy!"

Edmund looked at him, but did not respond; he continued to tend to his saddle. Waller walked up to him, and before Edmund could even imagine what he was about, slapped him across one cheek with his gloves.

When Edmund's vision cleared of the red haze that blinded him, he found he had pinned Waller to the nearest wall by the throat; and though he held him with only one hand, the man's boot heels were six inches off the floor. The gentlemen around him were shouting in alarm, and Mr. Duckworth was at his side.

"Mr. Percy!" said Mr. Duckworth. "Remember what God has commanded of us! Thou shalt not kill, Mr. Percy!"

Edmund only tightened his grip the more.

"And what Christ said," added Mr. Duckworth urgently. "'Whosoever shall smite thee on thy right cheek, turn to him the other also.'"

Waller was unable to breathe; his face was beginning to turn gray; he scrabbled at Edmund's hands, and lashed out clumsily with his feet, but Edmund paid no attention to these ineffectual movements.

"Do not let him make you as he is, Mr. Percy!" said Mr. Duckworth finally.

And then Janetta's words came back to Edmund: *You must not take vengeance on Waller—he will pull you down with him. Do not let him do that. You will not fix one sin, as you call it, by piling another on top of it.*

He set the man back on his feet and released him. Waller fell to all fours and gasped for air. "You shall go to hell," Edmund said to him, "but God shall take you in his own good time. Let it be as Janetta said: You will not drag me down there with you."

He untied his horse and led it to the door of the barn. Mr. Duckworth did the same. The others stood aside, staring at Edmund in silence.

As he mounted up, Waller rose to his feet and staggered after him; he spoke hoarsely. "Coward!" he said. "I challenge you to a duel—with pistols! Fifty paces with pistols! With pistols, Mr. Percy! You must take up my challenge or be forever known for a coward!"

Mr. Duckworth said, "I would not deem any man a coward who lives up to his principles, Mr. Waller. Especially when he gives such powerful evidence of his struggle against his worse instincts. It is a struggle you would do well to emulate."

"Coward!" Waller cried hoarsely again, lurching to Edmund's side. "Coward! I say you are a coward!"

One of the gentlemen standing nearby suddenly laughed. "Perhaps your accusation would be more compelling, Mr. Waller," this man said, "if you yourself were a gentleman. I know that I myself would scorn to duel with the likes of you. A gentleman may duel only with his equal. If you were to challenge me, I would have my overseer take a horsewhip to you."

The others laughed as well. Without another word, and without looking behind him, Edmund rode out of the barn and set out for home.

⌛⌛⌛⌛⌛

Mr. Duckworth rode beside him. Edmund was glad of his company; though when his friend invited him to stay and dine, he begged to be excused; he did not feel fit for decent company.

"There is one thing, however," Edmund said, "that I wish you could explain to me."

"What is that, my friend?"

"Who *is* this Waller? What has ever compelled him to be so bad? There is no sense to anything he does."

"No good sense, certainly. Evil has its own reasons, and goodness cannot comprehend them. Nay, I shall say more than that: goodness oftentimes cannot grasp so much as the existence of evil, let alone the reasons behind it. It looks evil in the face and does not recognize it. One glib lie is all the disguise that evil needs. It is as you said: Waller has been getting by all his life with that one glib lie. Today, for this moment at least, he has been caught in it. No fear—he will have another ready for tomorrow.—No, I really could not tell you anything of Waller or his character. It has only been my observation that such men do appear among us all too often. They rely upon our tolerance, upon the spirit of liberty that permeates our English society. It would be wiser to shun them, I think, to drive them away by withholding our trade with them and our acknowledgment of them. But in the end we pity them too much."

Edmund made no reply to this; but it seemed to him that Mr. Duckworth was right.

He left Mr. Duckworth at his own gate and returned to Canebrake and ate dinner alone; and then he finished packing his things for the journey home.

⧗ ⧗ ⧗ ⧗ ⧗

He and Mr. Duckworth completed the sale of Canebrake the next day in a lawyer's office in St. John's. The exchange of monies and property was duly witnessed and recorded, and then Edmund and Mr. Duckworth set out for their respective plantations again on horseback, riding together, but still saying little to one another. Mr. Duckworth had promised to drive over with a wagon to convey Edmund and his trunk to town, where he would take a room to await the next ship out.

When Edmund arrived at Canebrake, there was little left to do but to bring his trunk out on the verandah and then to take leave of the slaves. They knew they were to go live at Mr. Duckworth's, and were glad about that; they had packed up their few belongings and were now rounding up their chickens and other livestock. He went over to their quarters sadly, feeling an intense affection for them suddenly. Some were openly sorry to see him go, though he was not sure whether they felt a love for him that answered his own, or whether they were only frightened of change. Others clearly were glad to see the last of him, and he heard them mocking those who wept, saying, "What you cry 'bout? Won't have to work so hard fo' dat Duckearth!" He knew perfectly well that he had given them no reason to love him. He had kept them enslaved, he had put them to work, he had enriched his family off their servitude and labor; and if any did choose to love him, it was only because God so filled the human spirit with affection that these slaves could find it in them even to love their oppressor.

Obah made a point of approaching Edmund, but did not offer to say anything; he only shook his head, as if lamenting the history of the past three years; and to him Edmund said, "I am sorry, Obah."

"Sorry fo' what, Massa?"

"Sorry for . . . sorry for everything. Sorry for leaving you here, still in bondage."

Obah shook his head again. "You t'ink Obah not know what you try do all dis time? Why you neber ask Obah, Massa? Ifin you had, I told you dis: you be crazy buckra! You t'ink you sabe us by makin' us work, Massa? You big fella, Massa, but you too li'l, sabe us. Slabin' too big for you break by you'self. You can't sabe us."

"I shall not stop trying, Obah."

"Fo'get it, Massa. Go home; go England. Stop try sabe anyone else; try sabe you'self. Marry nice buckra girl, have picnees. Maybe nice buckra girl break de spell on yo' heart, Massa."

"I do not think so, Obah."

Obah shook his head. "Oh, she was a wicked one, dat one," he said.

"Do not say that; you will break my heart. She was not wicked—she was good, very good, in her heart. The angels shall take her up and console her for what she suffered here; she shall put on a raiment of pure love, and she shall feel a pure joy; because inside, in her heart, Obah, she was pure."

Obah shook his head. "She got you bad, Massa," was his verdict; and then he walked away.

"Obah," called Edmund.

"Yass, Massa?" The fellow turned back for a moment.

"May God go with you," said Edmund. "May you someday be free."

"Thanks, Massa," said Obah. "And you, Massa—I hope *you* gets you'self free too, someday—free from dat witch."

Obah had the last word, for Edmund's heart sank in him, and he could not speak.

Mr. Duckworth had sent a slave over to give the word, and the men took their belongings, and, driving their livestock before them, made a pathetic but noisy convoy across the fields towards their new home. Johnny and Betty went last of all—Johnny limping and drawing two goats along behind him, and Betty carrying the baby. Neither one of them thought to say farewell to him or looked back.

The loneliness of the place smote Edmund suddenly. *Thank God I am leaving,* thought Edmund. *It would kill me to stay here without Janetta.*

He realized that he had not dared even to look at the windmill since he had returned, and he forced himself to do so now; and then he wept, as it all came back, the whole story of Janetta, of that mad, hurt woman, from the first night he had met her, to the last night they had made love.

He went back to the verandah and tried to compose himself. By the time the wagon came down the lane, he had donned an impassive mask.

As he saw Duckworth again, he felt unworthy of the man's care for him. "This is too kind of you, sir," he said. "You must be busy—I know you are busy. Perhaps you should send one of your men to drive me."

"I could not aid thee by any hands but my own," the man protested.

"But I am sorry to inconvenience you. If it were not for my trunk, I would walk to town. I ought to have considered sooner and found a means to carry it in with me when I went to complete the sale."

"Believe me, Mr. Percy," said Mr. Duckworth, "this is no trouble. I wish I could do more for thee."

Edmund now decided that what he was hearing was not just force of habit. "You are thee'ing me," he said. "You have never done so before. Why now?"

"Because I shall miss thee," said Mr. Duckworth simply.

"Yes; well, I shall miss *thee.* You are a good man, Mr. Duckworth."

"I try to be; that is the most I can do.—Now, let me give thee a hand with that trunk."

It took only a minute or two to load the trunk and drive down the lane. Though Edmund longed to look back at the windmill one more time, he did not dare, for he knew he would break down. *I hope Waller burns it!* he thought, and then was sorry for the wish, for he knew the mill would be valuable to his friend Mr. Duckworth.

And that would have been all that could be related about Edmund's departure from Canebrake plantation, were it not for one more strange incident. They were just turning out of the lane onto the main road that led to St. John's when Edmund caught a glimpse of a figure in gray running up that road from the direction of Mr. Duckworth's house. He did not pay any attention to it, thinking it must be a slave in worn garments hurrying on some errand; but the horses pulling Mr. Duckworth's wagon had a slight rise to climb immediately out of the lane, and proceeded so slowly that in a minute the figure caught up to them and ran along Edmund's side of the vehicle.

He looked down when he noticed the movement there, and was surprised to find that the runner was none other than one of Mr. Duckworth's daughters, now looking up at him. Her Quaker cap had blown off her hair—which he saw now for the first time was golden, thick, and very beautiful—and she was gasping with her exertion.

"I say, Mr. Duckworth," said Edmund, "it is one of your daughters—she wants you." He was ashamed to think that even after all this time he did not know the young woman's name.

"No," said Mr. Duckworth, slapping the reins across the backs of the horses to speed them a little, "it is not me she wants." And on he drove.

Edmund turned and stared down at the woman in incomprehension. That was when he saw that she had been, and still was, weeping; and as the horses gathered speed at the top of the rise, and as she herself became too exhausted to pursue them anymore, she raised a hand toward Edmund in an expression of utter hopelessness. In a moment more they had left her in the roiling cloud of dust behind them.

"My God," said Edmund in a stricken tone to Mr. Duckworth, "I never guessed!"

"Do not trouble thee about it," said Mr. Duckworth.

And so we spread heartache behind us, thought Edmund, *and never even know it!*

It occurred to him then that as far as he could recall, the girl had never spoken a single word to him, or he to her.

Chapter 18

The [Americans] cannot be conquered, and we shall only be teaching them the skill in War which they may now want. We are to make them good Sailors and Soldiers, and g[et] nothing ourselves.—If we *are* to be ruined, it cannot be helped—but I place my hope of better things on a claim to the protection of Heaven, as a Religious Nation, a Nation in spite of much Evil improving in Religion, which I cannot beleive the Americans to Possess.

—Austen

He sailed the next day for Jamaica, hoping to take passage on one of the ships assembling in the fall convoy for England; but when he arrived he found he had missed the October sailing by a few days.

Instead he went by mail packet, which was, at fifty-four guineas, a more expensive passage, but faster by far: the captain told Edmund he had vowed to his wife to meet her on the quay in Falmouth before the Advent season began.

This was a promise the captain did not live to keep. On the journey home an incident occurred that—whatever it might mean to the captain's family—was, as far as Edmund was concerned at the time, of little import; but it had further consequences, and bears telling.

The packet on which he sailed was the *Ever Loyal,* a three-masted, swift-sailing full-rigger of a mere 150 tons; its armament consisted of four 4-pounders and two 6-pound chasers, and a peculiar cannon then known as a "Post Office gun," a long brass 9-pounder; its crew numbered about twenty. In other words, it was lightly armed and lightly manned, depending on its speed alone for its defense. Only one other passenger shipped with Edmund, a very frail and elderly man by the name of Mr. Gable, returning home, as he told Edmund, to die in the green fields of his native Sussex.

When they set out from Jamaica, they made for the Windward passage between Cuba and Haiti, into the bluster of the trades. With a good deal of close-hauled beating back and forth they cleared the passage and eventually picked up a southwest wind. It seemed then that the rest of the journey would be a downhill run, though over dinner the captain still fretted about American privateers and squalls off the Great Bank.

In this autumn of 1813, Britain was at war not only with its ancient enemy, France, but with the United States. Napoleon was on the defensive, but in the course of the year had won two critical battles that had restored some of the gleam to his tarnished reputation as a general—the slaughters of Lützen and Bautzen. The wary allies, augmented by Austria, then resolved to pick off isolated elements of the Grande Armée like wolves harrying the sick and weak of a herd. The Battle of Dresden, a bitter loss for Austria, had cast doubt on the viability of this plan; but while Edmund was sailing into the Atlantic, the Battle of Leipzig finally and definitively turned the course of the war against France.

The unfortunate entanglement with the United States was the last thing Britain needed at this time; but the British felt they could swat the Yankee mosquito on the back of their necks with one hand while they faced forward to the greater menace of Napoleon; and for the most part they had been proved right. They not only repelled attempts on Canada, but sacked Washington. At sea, however, the Americans had dealt them some stunning surprises. The new American heavy frigates had proved the superiority of Yankee firepower, capturing the *Alert,* the *Guerrière,* the *Macedonian,* and the *Java* in 1812. American privateers, too, had savaged British merchant shipping in the first years of the war. But here as well, the tide of battle was turning in favor of the British. They had reinforced their forces in American waters, and the coast was now blockaded by over a hundred warships. It was this blockade against its merchant traffic, not Britain's blundering attempts at invasion, that would finally compel the Americans to the bargaining table in 1814.

But peace talks were not in the offing now; and after the *Ever Loyal* had passed far to the west of Bermuda and crossed the thirtieth parallel, out of the smoke of dawn on a fine autumn morning, abaft the port beam, there loomed an American privateer, running downwind beside them, about a half-mile distant. The captain took one look and was certain that he was dealing with the *York Town,* a former East Indiaman of about 500 tons, cut down for action. She was reputed to be equipped with a bulwark of hard timbers over a foot thick and some six feet high, behind which her crew could work destruction on their foes with nearly complete impunity. The *York Town* had already captured one packet, the *Manchester,* in June of that year. It had been the talk of the nation how the *Manchester* had fled before the Yankee stern chase for a day and a half, and had not yielded without a fierce firefight.

The captain of the *Ever Loyal* had received the same orders as his colleague on the *Manchester:* he was to run and to avoid a fight at all costs, unless forced to engage; and if compelled to strike his colors, he must sink the mails no matter what else befell. He bore away from the *York Town* as best he could, crowded on sail, and privately told Edmund he did not at all like the situation.

The *York Town* immediately jibed, and though that action caused her to fall behind, the chase was on.

It continued all day. The *York Town* could not close the gap between them, but she had so much more sail than the *Ever Loyal* that she kept hard on the heels of the packet throughout the morning and the afternoon. The men of the *Ever*

Loyal seemed to think their ship was not running as fast as she should; but there also seemed to be general agreement that the *York Town* must be badly in need of a careening—she too seemed to run more sluggish than she ought; and by late afternoon the captain and the first mate were expressing to Edmund their hope that they could hold off till nightfall and slip away from the enemy. And it would be a dark night; the moon was new, and heavy clouds had built in during the day.

Edmund watched this unfolding drama at first with a dull disinterest. His life was shattered, his prospects eclipsed; he believed, with the complete certainty that only those in their twenties can possess, that he would never embark on a profession that would bring him honor or comfort or true independence, or find companionship worthy of the name. If the *York Town* should sink them all to the bottom of the sea, he would be sorry for the other men, but care nothing for Edmund Percy's loss; or so he told himself.

His fellow passenger, Mr. Gable, was none so nonchalant. He was in fact more agitated than was good for his health, but he would not leave the deck or train his mind on any better occupation than useless anxiety. It was easier for Edmund to have pity on this stranger than on himself, and he sat with him for most of the afternoon, trying to think of soothing things to say. At one point he urged, "Do not forget, sir, these are Americans, not so very long ago subjects of the same king as we ourselves. It is not as if we shall be captured by a gang of cannibals. If they overwhelm us with superior force, as seems inevitable should they catch us, all we need do is sink the mails with a few cannonballs. They will take everything of value from the hold and like as not leave us the ship. We may have to return to Bermuda for supplies if they raid our stores, but that will be the worst of it."

Mr. Gable turned quite pale at this; and after some hesitation, told Edmund: "Sir, my entire life savings are in the hold of this ship—one hundred and ninety thousand dollars in Spanish gold specie. I could not get insurance for it, because of this American war. If this ship is captured, I am penniless. I have no family. My brothers and sisters are all dead, and the character of my nieces and nephews is unknown to me. They might welcome me if I came with a fortune; but if I came penniless, I would only be a burden to them."

This revelation cast a somewhat different light on the situation; and from that point on Edmund was able to take more interest in the proceedings, for Mr. Gable's sake if not his own. With the waning of the day, he went to the captain for more information on their prospects.

As he approached the helm, he passed three sailors who were just leaving a conference with the captain. He had noticed them before. The rest of the crew was handpicked, as were all the packet crews, from the flower of English youth; but these three had been taken on in Jamaica to replace several sailors lost to fever. The captain remained preoccupied with the thought of them for a few moments after Edmund reached him; he was muttering some good salty invective under his breath to the first mate, who also seemed incensed by what he had just heard.

When the captain saw Edmund, it all burst out of him. "Can you believe it, Mr. Percy? These three fellows you see that have just left me—they propose we stand to and surrender!"

"What!" said Edmund, startled out of his self-pity by the enormity of this suggestion.

"Exactly my feelings," said the captain. "It seems they have brought aboard with them some valuable cargo and it is well insured. If the ship is captured, they will not be put to the trouble of selling it when we reach Falmouth."

"But that is infamous!" cried Edmund.

"And that is not the worst of it. My own second mate is in it with them."

"Mr. Crosby?"

"The same, sir; he has already been making noises about it."

"But that is treason!"

"Oh, 'tis an old game on these packet ships, I assure you. In the old days there were crews that had been captured three and four times and made themselves rich off insurance money. The Post Office has done its best to curb it, as have I on my own ship; but these three are not my choice of sailors. And they're a rough-looking bunch, too. I've half a mind to clap them in irons right now, but I may need them if the going gets rough—assuming I can get them to fight."

"Do you think it will come to that?" asked Edmund. "Mr. Gable is quite concerned about his cargo."

"I am sure he is!" said the captain. "He did not tell me what he has in those chests, but there is only one thing in the world as heavy as what we carry, and that is pure gold, and plenty of it. If he has put all his eggs in one basket, he is a fool. But with every passing minute I have better hopes to give these pirates the slip. If it were not for Mr. Gable's gold, we would have outrun them already. Bid him be of good cheer unless events take a marked turn for the worse."

Edmund conveyed this message to Mr. Gable, who was able to relax somewhat. Finally the last gleams of the sun pierced the clouds on the horizon, and dusk came on.

In the last half-hour before sunset, the *York Town* had jury-rigged a temporary jibboom off the bowsprit. The captain hypothesized that her original jibboom had been broken off in combat and never replaced, and to this time the *York Town* had been running without her three jib sails. Now she managed to spread them and creep a bit closer. At sunset, however, a stay apparently broke somewhere on the American ship and the jibboom broke loose and thrashed about violently at the bow. In another minute the bowsprit—evidently also damaged in previous action—broke free as well, and with them her fore topmast staysail and her fore staysail.

A huzzah went up from the *Ever Loyal.* It was not as much of a gift as it would have been if the *York Town's* fore sail or main sail had given out, but a difference in her speed was immediately perceptible. Furthermore, the flailing sails seemed to obscure the helmsman's view of the quarry, or at least to distract him, for he bore off to the port slightly.

Edmund happened to be standing with the captain at the time. "You must have been praying for us, Mr. Percy," said the captain. He had become aware of Edmund's training for the church in conversation during the voyage, though he knew nothing of Edmund's current doubts. Edmund was now quite ashamed to realize that he had not yet prayed for their safety at all.

At that moment the Americans, becoming angry as they saw that their prey was escaping, managed to clear the sail from the bow rail and fire a cannon they had in readiness there. It was apparently packed with a variety of iron debris intended to injure the sails of the British ship, most of which fell in a wide pattern in the water astern. Some did reach the ship, however, and by sheer violent luck neatly severed the halyard on the spanker sail, which collapsed on the quarterdeck. The falling spar dealt the first mate a glancing blow to the head, and he fell to the deck with a groan.

The captain fared even worse: a piece of iron pierced his brow, and before the sail had even reached the deck, he fell back in Edmund's arms stone dead.

In the confusion that followed, several of the crew leapt to the obvious task and repaired the halyard, without so much as an order from anyone. The sail was soon lifted off the deck, and the ship's surgeon rushed back to attend to the injured men. The captain he pronounced dead immediately; the mate he ordered to be carried below, still groaning, but not by any means utterly senseless.

As the mate was borne past Edmund, the latter turned in alarm to a sailor who was standing near him. "Who is in command now?" he asked.

"Mr. Crosby," the fellow answered.

There was nothing Edmund could do but await the outcome; so he stood silent in the corner of the deck by Mr. Gable, who could be heard uttering short, anxious, tremulous moans.

When the deck was clear, Crosby mustered the sailors and addressed them. "The captain is dead," he said, "and Mr. Smythe has a broken head. I am commanding officer here; and you disobey me at your peril." He looked around the crew as if daring them to defy him; but as yet, no one had reason to.

"Now, here's what we shall do," he said. "There is no way we can outrun this *York Town,* if such she be. If we keep running from her, we'll get even worse treatment from her crew when they do catch us. It is our duty to bring this packet home safe and sound to Falmouth. So what we shall do is stand to, wait till the *York Town* comes up, and parley with her."

The crew was not at all pleased at this prospect; but though they muttered, they were well disciplined, and the chain of command was clear.

Edmund, however, had no such duty. A fury broke out in him, built on the slow fires of Waller's outrages and his own grief. This situation had nothing to do with the loss he had suffered, except in its injustice; and that was enough. It was as if he woke again out of the dark hibernation of grief and depression; and he cried out from where he stood by Mr. Gable, "No, by God! You shall not surrender this ship while I can lift an arm to stop you!"

Mr. Crosby looked at him, and opened his mouth to order him to shut up; and looked again at him, and thought better of it. "Mr. Percy, you are only a passenger here, and have no say-so. This is my decision, as commanding officer of this vessel, and I say we surrender. We shall offer the Americans our cargo, and sink the mails as we have been bid."

"I may not be captain, but I *am* a loyal Englishman, which is more than I can say for you. In another two minutes we shall give these Yankee jackals the slip. Sail on, or by God I shall make you answer for it!"

"There is only one of you," observed Crosby. "If you want to spend the rest of the voyage in irons, so be it."

Edmund turned to the crew. "Put this traitor in irons, and I will back you with my life, with my honor, with my word as a gentleman! Sail on, or you will likely swing with him. This is a time of war: the government will not look with pleasure on a crew that surrenders to the enemy without a fight."

"Clap him in irons," roared Crosby; but only the three new recruits moved to obey him. They gathered in a little knot, sizing Edmund up in the darkness, which was rapidly becoming deeper, while the rest of the crew stood by, uncertain, and waiting to see the outcome.

At an agreed signal among them, the three miscreants rushed Edmund. They found the struggle was not to be brief: every time it seemed they had him pinned, he threw one of them off, and the fight began again. Finally Crosby seized a belaying pin and waded in among them; and just at a moment when they had forced Edmund to the deck, he aimed a tremendous blow at Edmund's skull from behind.

What damage Crosby might have caused if he had connected could only be guessed; for he struck only a glancing blow, though the pin met the deck with a resounding thump that apparently persuaded him that he had effectively clobbered the troublemaker. Edmund, acting partly on impulse and partly because he was indeed momentarily stunned, went limp.

"That'll hold him," said Crosby. He and his three henchmen left Edmund where he lay and turned to attend to the more pressing problem of the crew.

"Now, strike the colors!" Crosby ordered them.

Edmund was dimly aware that the crew still refused to obey him, standing fast where they were; but one of Crosby's henchmen acted for them. In a minute Edmund heard a rattle of tackle as the flag was lowered.

This act seemed to demoralize the crew and persuade them of the inevitability of obeying Crosby's orders; for when he ordered them to slack the sails and let the ship stand to and wait for the approach of the *York Town,* they did as he told them.

Edmund, meanwhile, was rapidly regaining his faculties—the blow had truly only brushed him; but he thought it best to lie still and await his opportunity to strike. No one made any further motion toward putting him in irons. The crew had every reason, in fact, to think him dead after the blow he had apparently received. A long silence followed, broken only by the flap of the sails, the endless creaking of the rigging, the siffling of the wind—and Mr. Gable sobbing hopelessly in his corner of the mid-deck.

However, when the ship had stood to for several minutes, one of the regular sailors laughed suddenly and harshly. "Look!" he cried. "It's too damned dark! She don't know our colors is struck!" The rest of the crew laughed along with him. Another said, "How will you explain this one to the Post Office, Crosby?"

"Shut your gob!" roared Crosby.

"She can't even see where we are!" said a sailor.

Crosby realized the truth of this. "Make a light there on the stern," he told one of his henchmen. In a minute a couple of lanterns were alight.

Apparently not even this was enough to attract the attention of the crew of the *York Town,* who might well have been still preoccupied with furling their thrashing sails and bringing their broken spars under control.

After another very long wait, perhaps ten or fifteen minutes, it became clear to all that the *York Town* had also stood to and was making no further attempt to pursue them.

"The jig's up, Crosby," said a sailor. "You can't *make 'em* capture us if they don't want to. Let's make sail and be on our way."

"No!" cried Crosby. "They're waiting for us to parley. They've stood to; they're waiting for our offer."

This preposterous suggestion was greeted with a wholesome laughter that did much to raise Edmund's spirits. He felt reassured that if he could stop Crosby and his three henchmen, the rest of the crew would just as soon give the privateer the slip.

Crosby swore copiously and threatened the sailors with every dire consequence he could think of; but they did not seem to take him too seriously. Finally he cried, "Lower the boat. We'll go parley with them."

His three allies obeyed his orders, while the rest of the crew fell back out of the way, silent again, but still unwilling to directly disobey him. When the cockboat was in the water, Crosby climbed up on the rail.

"Now, listen Stokes, I'm going to parley with 'em. You're in command 'ere. Take up a pistol, damn you, and if anyone gives you grief, blow his brains out. Murdock'll stay with you, and Trice'll come with me."

This was about the best division of his forces he could make, though Edmund thought he erred in not taking one of the regular crew with him as hostage. Perhaps he feared being overpowered on the way if he did so. He certainly did not seem to trust Stokes or anyone else to parley for him.

Edmund, who still lay prone where he had originally been pinned and struck, was now watching the scene carefully over the crook of one arm. He could see Stokes find a pistol from among the many that had been readied to fight off a possible attempt to board; and then he and Murdock leaned over the rail to make sure that Crosby and Trice descended safely into the boat.

This was the chance Edmund had been waiting for; and when he went into action, it was an action without thought, without reckoning, without heed for any consequences to himself. In a sliver of an instant he was up on all fours and then on two feet, sprinting soundlessly across the narrow deck. He hit Stokes with tremendous force, crushing him momentarily against the rail; and then, while his opponent was still stunned and flailing, he lifted him up bodily, raised him over his head, and cast him over the side. The brief cry Stokes gave as he fell was abruptly terminated as he plunged head first into the gap between the ship and the boat.

Edmund now turned to Murdock; but as he made to lunge for him, the sailor raised his arm and pressed the muzzle of a pistol against Edmund's brow.

"Hold fast there, Mr. Percy!" cried Murdock.

Edmund stopped; but not as does a man in fear; more in the manner of a cat or a terrier, who has a rat cornered in a stall, and waits to find the best opening to seize it in his jaws and break its back. Edmund could plainly see that Murdock was trembling and unsure; and as for himself, a wild, unreasoning mood had come over him; he cared not if he lived or died; and he thought that if this was *it*—if this was his last moment—he would at least suffer his grief no more.

"Go ahead, man," he said. "Blow my brains out! Add homicide to your other crimes, and I promise you, you shall swing for certain!"

"Back off, you bastard, or I shall fire!" the man cried.

"Fire away!" replied Edmund.

"Back off, I say!"

"Shoot, damn you! What are you waiting for?"

If he had been confronting Crosby or even Stokes, he would certainly have been dead by now; but Murdock was apparently the faintest of the traitors. He could not bring himself to fire; and as he hesitated, suddenly Edmund snatched the pistol out of his grip and flung it into the sea. Then, though the man struggled wildly and screamed with horror, Edmund picked him up like a sack of coal and flung him overboard with this fellows.

He, too, hit the water with a tremendous splash. As Edmund looked down, he saw that Stokes had surfaced and had caught onto the gunwale of the cockboat. Many sailors could not swim, and Stokes seemed from his panic to be one of that category. Crosby was shouting and swearing profusely, and when he saw Edmund's head and shoulders appear over the rail above, he drew a pistol from his belt and fired a shot at him. The cockboat, however, was pitching about in the sea, and the shot whistled wide. In a few more seconds Murdock appeared, gasping and terrified. Trice proffered the end of an oar and pulled him to the side of the cockboat.

Edmund turned to the crew. They were staring at him in awe.

"Hoist those colors again," he said coldly. "Make sail, by God, or I'll pitch every man Jack of you into the sea with those other damned traitors!"

They were frozen; but whether in astonishment or in refusal to obey him, he could not tell.

At this critical moment, Mr. Gable stood up from the corner in which he had been cowering. In a quavering voice he cried, "I give my word of honor that every man on this ship shall have *twenty pounds sterling* of me when we dock safe at Falmouth!"

It was all the crew needed to break the spell of indecision that held them. For a moment they were somewhat confused by Mr. Gable's offer; but then they cheered and swarmed for the sails. Several ran as well to hoist the colors again, and one to take the helm.

"Put out that damned lamp!" Edmund called to this latter sailor, and the fellow quickly extinguished the lantern that had been hung on the taffrail. Edmund effected a more permanent termination of the light from the lantern that cast its rays over the mid-deck; he picked it up and flung it into the waves below.

Several of the sailors who had gone to haul the sheets now ran back to Edmund. "Beggin' your pardon, sir, but are we just goin' to leave them four at sea?"

"Let them parley with the Americans for passage," said Edmund curtly. The sailors laughed. This answer seemed to satisfy them, and they went back to their duties, passing the word on to the others.

Already the cockboat had fallen behind the ship. Crosby and Trice had made shift to get Stokes and Murdock aboard without capsizing; and as Edmund watched, the men set to the oars and made directly for the *York Town,* now about a half-mile distant, distinguishable from the gloom of night only by the lights that illumined the work on her broken bowsprit.

"We may jes' 'ave the luck to get out o' this yet," observed the seaman who had taken the helm. "Why she hove to, I don't know; if I'd ha' been her captain, I would ha' kept on runnin'. She must ha' lost a man o'erboard when the bowsprit give way. We was lucky for sure."

"You can say that again," said Edmund.

The sailor, for luck's sake, did exactly that. Then he said to Edmund, "Ye mus' be lucky yerself, Mr. Percy."

"It is about time I was."

"Been down on yer luck, lately, 'ave ye?"

"I feel as though I have lost everything—my entire future; nay, even my entire past."

"Well, yer luck has changed now, sir. That it 'as! Yer a reg'lar lucky charm, now. I knows how it feels—ye've lost and lost and lost and lost, and gambled away all yer pay for years on end, and suddenly ye win it big."

"Yes," said Edmund. "It certainly is time for Edmund Percy to win it big."

⌛⌛⌛⌛⌛

The sailor was correct in his guess that they could yet escape. The next dawn disclosed no sign of the *York Town,* though Edmund was sure it would be following them down the wind, hoping to catch them before they reached the safety of Falmouth, which was many a nautical mile away. Crosby and his men would have told the Americans about Mr. Gable's cargo, the exact nature of which was apparently well known to all the crew.

The first mate had suffered a concussion, but like many who have had their brains rattled, he was too confused to perceive he was confused, and insisted on going on deck, where, after some persuasion from Edmund, he conceded enough to his injury to sit in a chair on the quarterdeck. Edmund stationed himself beside the man throughout the day, and throughout that night and the next day; but finally, seeing that the *York Town* was not appearing, that the mate was improving by the hour, and that the crew was not disposed to do anything but make for home at all speed, he relaxed his watch and went below to sleep.

⌛⌛⌛⌛⌛

They made Falmouth on the fourth of December. Mr. Gable was as good as his word; but before he dispensed his reward to the crew, Edmund managed to talk many of the sailors into giving a few pounds each to the widow of the captain. Whether they could have parted with such a sum once the money was in hand, he did not know; but they proved generous beforehand, and the widow was presented not only with the twenty pounds due her (Edmund had with great precision pointed out to Mr. Gable that the captain had been aboard the ship at the time his promise was made) but with more as well, rounded off from Edmund's own purse.

It would have been an understatement to say that Mr. Gable was grateful to Edmund. He was ready to apotheosize him. He knew better than to offer a fellow gentleman a cash reward; instead he made promises that contrived to be both vague and extravagant. Edmund helped him deliver his specie safely to a secure place; and then they went together to report to the proper Post Office authorities. After the formalities of a brief investigation, Edmund was free to make the final leg of his journey home.

Chapter 19

The mind never unbends it self so agreeably as in the Conversation of a well-chosen Friend. . . . It eases and unloads the Mind, clears and improves the Understanding, engenders Thoughts and Knowledge, animates Virtue and good Resolutions, sooths and allays the passions, and finds Employment for most of the vacant Hours of Life.

—Addison

T*he most* sensible thing for Edmund to do would have been to take a seat in a post office coach for London from Falmouth. He would have been home in a few days at most. But now that he was actually on British soil, he found himself seized with a dread of the unavoidable meeting with his father, and of the necessity it entailed of revealing in some manner how his life and prospects had changed. Furthermore, to go direct to Surrey would have meant passing through Hampshire and near the home of his Aunt Andromeda; and he did not want to visit her in his present uncertain state, or to slight her by failing to visit her. To postpone the inevitable, and to bypass his aunt, he did not take the shortest means home; instead he booked a seat on a coach to Bath, intending to take the high road to London from there.

Bath afforded a fine backdrop for a troubled and grieving young man to brood in solitude in the midst of a throng. He stopped over for the night; he lingered for one day, then another. The mornings he spent drifting along the streets, passing the shops without seeing them, or walking in the outlying districts; in the evenings he bought a ticket to a concert or a lecture and went as far as the door of the hall before turning away; by night he slept badly, torn between grief and shame at his own behavior. It was not until Sunday arrived and he attended church that he again resorted to prayer; and then his stupor ended and his confusion gave way to a certainty that he must cease to idle away his time in self-pity and instead press on for home.

On the fourteenth of December he reached Surrey and hired a postchaise to take him direct to Brackensom. It was late in the short winter's day by the time the carriage turned off the road beside the river Brake and began to ascend the hill toward Brackensom-house. He had written to his father as soon as he had landed in Falmouth, but had then been unable to give the exact day of his arrival; yet it seemed he had been looked for every minute. Tom the coachman was on the watch beneath a great copper beech tree beside the drive, and as the carriage rattled past him, he peered into it eagerly. Edmund saluted him; and then he saw Tom turn away toward the hill and raise to his shoulder an old fowling piece, a very rusty old blunderbuss that Edmund and his brothers had known as Old Bessy, which was remarkable for the enormous report it made. Edmund's recollection of its firepower was confirmed as Tom fired off a blank shot into the sky.

It proved to be a signal. By the time the coach reached the steps of the house, Mrs. Trees and Johnson, the butler, had come down to the drive, and several footmen were hurrying after them.

It was a sweet moment for him, but mingled with its sweetness was a bitter sense of his unworthiness. Sweet to step out on the gravel and look up at the great façade of Brackensom, and to look on the familiar faces before him; bitter because he felt changed, he felt his hopes were broken; and he had still before him the task of telling those he loved that he had given over his plan to take orders—still before him the task of determining how he would make his way in life.

Mrs. Trees burst into tears, threw aside all decorum, and hugged him. Johnson stood by, in posture as reserved as ever, but in expression aglow with happiness. Now Hereford came out of the house, and Christopher just behind him. Edmund met his father on the landing; and like Mrs. Trees, Hereford, too, threw his arms around Edmund and held him tightly, crying only, "My boy! My Edmund!"

Edmund suffered himself to be held away and looked up and down. He had seldom seen his father so overcome. "By God, Edmund," Hereford said, "I think you are taller than ever—how can it be?—and in fine condition, very fine condition! You look the picture of health—does he not, Mrs. Trees? I say, does he not?"

"Indeed, sir!" rhapsodized Mrs. Trees. "He looks more handsome and more fit than ever!"

In response to all this, the best Edmund could manage was a faint, false smile.

"But are you well?" cried his father, seeing him depressed and subdued. "Have you had the fever? Is it still lurking in your blood?"

"I did have the fever, sir," said Edmund. "But it touched me only lightly. I am as hale as ever I have been in my life. I had some trouble in Antigua in my last months there, and it has changed me; that is all. And I am weary—it has been a long journey from Falmouth, the end of a very long journey."

He looked for Christopher; and now his brother came down the steps behind his father and they clasped hands.

"Thank God you are come at last, Edmund!" cried Christopher. They exchanged a glance full of mutual knowledge; and full of better understanding on Edmund's part than ever before.

"Aye," said Edmund. "I am come home. Thank God it is over; though what lies ahead, who but God can say?"

⌛⌛⌛⌛⌛

His father must have him in his sight nearly every moment for the next three hours, and Mrs. Trees must have him eat; and so he was brought into the dining room, and served dinner there, though his father and brother had already eaten. They had read about the incident on the *Ever Loyal;* apparently it had been in all the papers, and the nation was in an uproar over it. Perhaps the accident of the mere names of the ships had something to do with the effect of the story; for the act of an honest British citizen in keeping the *Ever Loyal* true to her name, and of defeating a Yankee privateer rudely emblazoned with the name of one of the most ignominious defeats in British history, and in its recent history—this was a tale that bore retelling. Every British subject could stand by the fire and boast that, by God, he would have done the same; and though there was certainly some question about the legality of a passenger taking command of one of His Majesty's Post Office ships, however briefly, and though the Post Office and the Navy muttered about the poor precedent it set, any attempt to trouble Edmund about his actions was apparently quashed by those who were placed above the officious beings who might dare it. Hereford must hear the whole tale from Edmund's lips; and then there must be an account of the sale of the plantation. And from Hereford and Mrs. Trees, Edmund was compelled to hear again and again how fit he looked, though they acknowledged he did seem somewhat tired; and hear Mrs. Trees in particular marvel endlessly at how he had become a coffee-drinker. It was not until nine o'clock that Edmund was able to plead the weariness of his travels effectively and betake himself to his bedroom.

His trunk had been brought up and set here, and when he entered the room, he found Mrs. Trees unpacking it for him. "Mr. Edmund!" she exclaimed. "I cannot believe the condition of these clothes! Have they no tailors in Antigua? Look at the state of these shirts! Why, they are not fit for a gentleman to appear in!"

"They must all be thrown away, Mrs. Trees," he said. "I doubt there is a stitch worth keeping. I only brought them home because they were all I had to wear on the way."

"I shall do just that, if you have no objection—throw them all away! Why, you have far better, still hanging in the closets, which I have kept from the moths all this while."

"Yes, ma'am. My books and my guns are all I want, and a few other articles. Perhaps those boots may be given away to one of the servants.—Ah, but I forgot." He reached into the trunk and drew out several parcels. "I left Antigua in such haste," he told her, "and in such low spirits, that I did not have time to bring gifts for you all from Antigua itself. I did stop over in Jamaica briefly though, and there thought a little more considerately.—Here, Mrs. Trees, this is for you."

"Ah, Mr. Edmund, you ought not to have taken the trouble! What is it?"

"Some good cocoa, ma'am; I know you like hot chocolate from time to time when you can get some that is good; and this is very good, from what I can tell."

She was very touched and pleased. When she was done enthusing, she called in one of the maids, and together they bore off most of the clothing in the trunk to be made into rags or given away. He emptied the remainder; and not wishing to have the trunk in his sight even another minute, he called two footmen and had them take it to the attics.

He was just about to close the door and undress for bed when Christopher appeared.

"May I speak with you, Edmund?"

"Of course, dear Brother," said Edmund.

Christopher entered and closed the door behind him.

"Well," he said to Edmund, "what is your plan concerning me and—" and here he lowered his voice cautiously—"that is to say, concerning a certain matter?"

Edmund did not know whether to laugh or weep. "My plan?" he said. "My plan? You have had three years of leisure at Brackensom, and have not formed a plan?"

"Leisure!" exclaimed Christopher. "Are you mad? I have been hard at work here. Not that I have found it unrewarding—but you, you have been in the West Indies, with nothing to do but set the slaves to work. Surely you have had some leisure to consider my case?"

Edmund sank into a chair. "If you only knew!" he said. "Whatever would you think? If you only knew what I have been through—what has happened to me. You would scarcely think me Edmund Percy if you knew.—But that is not to the point, for all that it may fill my thoughts. Sit down, Christopher, or else forgive me if I do so without you.—I have indeed thought of you, my Brother. I have thought of you and Bronwyn often, and with greater love and understanding as the days have passed. And how is Bronwyn? Is she well?"

"Well she is indeed—yes, thank God. But as impatient as I; though too good to reproach me as I deserve. Though I must say, it is not my fault that Father is the way he is—so proud and bigoted!"

"Does Father know anything?"

"I should say not! Not a word of it—not a hint of it can have reached him. We have preserved our secrecy with the utmost care."

"And Mrs. Hanscom is well also?"

"Yes, both she and Mr. Hanscom."

"Bronwyn still lives with her?"

"Yes. I saw them both in London not a fortnight ago."

"Where is Bronwyn now?"

"They are in Gloucestershire for Christmastide."

"That is too bad. When do they come to London again?"

"In January."

"Then that is when you must bring her to Brackensom."

"What?" cried Christopher.

"Bring her to Brackensom. You must put an end to this grief as soon as you can. Write her this night and tell her to prepare herself in thought for this; for it must happen."

"Have you lost your wits in the West Indies?" cried Christopher. "It cannot happen! It is impossible! Why—is this your plan? Is this the only plan you have formed?"

"How can you bear to spend an hour apart from her?" asked Edmund. There was something in his voice that caught Christopher's attention; but he had not the perception to guess what it meant.

"What would *you* know of how I suffer in being separated from her?" he said. "When have *you* ever been deprived of anyone or anything you ever wanted? You have had everything you ever craved—and instantly. It is I who have had to wait and wait to come into my own."

"You must marry at once," said Edmund. "Bring her at once to Brackensom. Write this minute—there is paper on the desk there—and send the message at once into Gloucestershire. Bid her come to Brackensom posthaste. Receive her as your fiancée and introduce Father to her. I shall stand beside you, Brother; I shall back you with everything I have, everything I am."

"Good!" cried Christopher bitterly. "We shall both be disinherited together!"

"So be it!" said Edmund. "What do you care for Brackensom, if you can have her? I tell you, if I had found such a woman as Bronwyn, I would have married her straightway, and set Father at defiance if need be. You love her, do you not? What else do you require?"

"And you would have us starve on love, then!" said Christopher contemptuously.

"What are you talking about, 'starve'? She will be rich, will she not?"

"Do you bid me follow this mad plan so that *you* may have Brackensom?" asked Christopher with sudden suspicion.

"No," said Edmund. "I bid you follow it so that *you* may have *Bronwyn.*"

"I *shall* have her," said Christopher. "She is pledged to me. The only question is *when* and *how.*"

"You say she is pledged to you," said Edmund. "But a woman may break her engagement with propriety at any time. Suppose she finds a man who is not in your situation?

She has been asked before, as I recall. Suppose she is weary of waiting for these over-proud Percies to see their way to making her one of their family?"

"Do not torment me!" cried Christopher.

"You must *act!*" replied Edmund. "That is all I am saying. You ask me for a plan—what other plan can there be but to persuade Father? And how else can we do that but to stand together before him in unity? How else can we do that but introduce him to Bronwyn, and let her win him over?"

"Before you went away," retorted Christopher, "you said it was impossible that he could ever be persuaded, and you counseled delay. Now you are back and claim that he *can* be persuaded, and urge precipitous haste. What has changed?"

"I have changed," said Edmund.

"And what difference does that make to *me?*" said Christopher. "I should say it makes none—absolutely none. I am in the same situation, no matter what has befallen you in the West Indies. And what terrible event can have happened to you there to alter your view of things? It is I who have suffered these three years, not you."

"Well," said Edmund, "I see that *you,* at least, have not changed." It was probably the bitterest thing he had ever said to his brother; but indeed, he would not have said it if he had not known that Christopher was incapable of feeling its sting.

"No," said Christopher. "I have not changed in the least. And I see no reason why *you* should have."

"Christopher," said Edmund wearily, "I shall continue to think on this, I promise you. But you must not rely on my ever finding an answer that you will deem acceptable. You must take your fate in your own hands, knowing I shall back you whenever you choose to act."

"Then I have looked forward to your homecoming in vain," said Christopher.

"If you thought I was bringing a miracle with me, yes," said Edmund, "you have waited in vain. But I told you before I left that I saw no way forward. At least you have taken what advice I could give, and proven yourself—proven yourself a true heir of Brackensom. Father believes in you now as he never did before. He is more likely than ever to approve your choice."

"Indeed, he has begun to torment me with demands that I marry," said Christopher. "One of these days he will go too far—be too absolute—or conspire with an acquaintance to make me a match—and then I shall have to tell him everything."

"And so it is better if you make the first move," said Edmund.

"I cannot!" said Christopher. "The first move alone will destroy me and all my hopes!"

Edmund did not reply, and they bided together in silence for a few minutes, Edmund sitting, and Christopher pacing and turning about in an agitated manner.

Finally the suspicion that had already irked Christopher returned in all force, and he wheeled on Edmund in an accusatory fashion. "There *is* something odd about you," he said. "You *have* changed somehow. You are depressed in spirits. I can see it—though I do not see how you have license for it! You have won great favor with Father for what you have done in Antigua, to say nothing of this business with the packet. That last sugar crop was vastly profitable—it makes up for all we have suffered in that quarter for quite some time—and the price we received for the plantation was more than we were hoping for. I hope you are not thinking to displace me here in Brackensom as well."

"As God is my witness," said Edmund, "I have no such thought and no such desire. I say to you only that I shall do as you think best—I shall do whatever you require of me. Think on that and let me know what it is. That is all I can say tonight."

"A very fine homecoming this is!" said Christopher in a tone of bitter disappointment. "Much looked for—and all for naught!"

In this sulk he went out of the room, banging the door closed behind him.

His difficulty seemed distant and unreal to Edmund; and in his mind he said to Christopher, *At least the one you love is no farther away than Gloucestershire, and dreams comfortably in sleep at this moment, or talks and laughs with her aunt and uncle by a comfortable fire, and thinks of you. My love lies in the sea-wrack four thousand miles away; and she will not dream nor talk nor laugh, nor think of me, ever again.*

⌛⌛⌛⌛⌛

He said nothing to his father or Christopher about his decision not to take orders. There would be time enough for that, he thought, after the holidays; he did not want to mar his father's joy with this new trial.

To Edmund, being at home was a severe trial in itself. On ship the lack of physical activity had been enforced, but here it was not, and he began to crave action again, after years of acclimation to it. He walked and rode hour after hour over the countryside, and if circumstances were such on a given day that he could not get too far, he still would take a turn on the grounds at least once an hour, going to the hermitage and back, or down some other allee. His father noticed his restlessness and reproved him for it; but still he walked.

A dinner party in honor of his return was held at Brackensom, and the very best families from the neighborhood came, eager to see the hero of the *Ever Loyal;* but he found the evening difficult, and felt he was only playacting. Many of the guests referred to his ordination as an event that must take place soon, and he did not wish to tell them that it was now impossible.

Christopher lapsed back into a state of suspended hope. He gradually ceased to cling to his resentment against Edmund for having come home without a solution to his difficulty; and by Christmas they were on cordial terms again, though both were dampened in spirit.

When the holidays had gone by, at the end of the first week in January, his father called him into the library after breakfast one morning and asked him about his plans. It was the moment Edmund had dreaded; but rather than attempting to tell his father that he had decided he must choose another profession, instead—in desperation under the pressure of the moment—he blurted out something about wishing to take counsel with Blackmore, his tutor and mentor at Oxford. Hereford understood this to mean only that Blackmore would somehow be necessary to set the time for the ordination; and so he gave Edmund his blessing to journey there. The next day Edmund went up to his Aunt Statira's; and the day after that he went and sought out Blackmore in his rooms.

Isaac Blackmore was a most remarkable figure at Oxford in those days. He was a polymath, keenly interested in topics as varied as English literature, sacred theology, higher mathematics, and natural philosophy, or what would today be called physics. He was the one who had taught Edmund to play chess—and he had endured many and many a bad game with his pupil until he succeeded in instilling a certain expertise in him, though Edmund's play remained always a little uneven. He was impecunious to an extraordinary degree: his greatest luxuries were oolong tea and toasted cheese. The very dogs in the street barked in protest at his scarecrow shape.

Beyond these superficial traits, he was wise in ways he had no right to be—he knew things he ought not to have known. Edmund and his fellow students sometimes joked that Blackmore was like a prince who walked abroad among his subjects in disguise by night, learning their inmost secrets. Sometimes it seemed that Blackmore had had another lifetime before he had come to Oxford. But no; he was only shrewdly observant—when it came to observation of the human condition, he was a student of the magnitude of Shakespeare, though he did not possess Shakespeare's inclination or necessity to transform his studies into drama and verse. When you told him of your doubt, he understood you—you found he had doubted likewise, and overcome it. If you had trouble with a friend, he could tell you what to say to make it right. If you were down in the deeps of life, he could put you on the road that led upward again. He was a man very worth having as a friend; and his only failing was that he required nothing of his friends in return.

He was delighted to see Edmund. When the one lone servant in the place announced him, Blackmore fairly leaped from his chair, shook his visitor's hand, and then drew him, literally by the lapel of his coat, to a seat by the fire, calling for tea and cheese. Fortunately, he seemed at first to be unaware of the fracas aboard the *Ever Loyal*, or uninterested in it—Edmund could not have guessed which—and so at least Edmund did not have to rehearse that again. But he wanted to know all about Antigua; and for a long time he plied Edmund with questions on that topic, thirsting for the minutiae of island life and the least details of the cultivation of the cane plant and the distillation of its sugar.

Finally, after a good deal of toasted cheese, and more tea than Edmund in fact wanted to drink, Edmund heard from him the same question his father had posed: "Well, then, you will be taking orders soon, now that you are home?"

"I do not know," said Edmund. "I do not think I can."

Blackmore did not evince surprise—he almost never did. He only looked at Edmund more keenly, and repeated, "You do not think you *can.*"

"No, sir," said Edmund.

"Ah," said Blackmore. "Tell me about it."

"The truth is that I am not sure of anything anymore."

"Not sure of *anything?* Do you doubt in God and the risen Christ?"

"Oh, no, sir. My doubts are not religious; they are . . . well, they are social and moral."

"Is that all?" said Blackmore ironically. He offered a pipe to Edmund, but Edmund declined; and then Blackmore took the pipe himself and began quietly stuffing the bowl with tobacco. "Start with the first," he said. "Your doubts about society."

"Well," said Edmund. "It was the slavery I saw. It is the most heinous system that can be imagined."

"Granted," said Blackmore. "And the sooner we in England wash our hands of it, the better. But what of it?"

"But the wealth of it comes here—to England. And it is surely wrong for us to live at ease on the slave labor of human beings who are, in the eyes of God, no worse than we are—who are perhaps, for being the meek, far better."

"Ah," said Blackmore. "The conscience of the good Tory son has been pricked! Perhaps this is the grain of irritation that shall yield the pearl of wisdom.—Go on."

"And if we stop and consider, sir—do we not in many ways run such a system of slavery here in England? We do not call it that, and we do not think it that; and I grant you that it is in many ways better, far better, than what I saw in Antigua. But Old Tom who drives my father's coach—what choice does he have but to continue in that task until the day he falters and falls to the earth? My father is a generous and merciful man, and he will see to it that Tom's dotage is spent in some humble comfort, I know; but had Tom truly any other choice but to be a servant these many years, and hope for a merciful master to take care of him when he could not take care of himself?"

"Go on," said Blackmore.

"And the church, sir—does she care about the souls in her care? I met a Quaker in Antigua who told me that the Church of England is asleep; and so indeed I think it is. We hardly believe our own tenets, I think. We are in love with natural morality, and shirk speaking the truths of revelation. We are more in love with Jesus the Moralizer than Christ the Savior. The Deists have cowed us."

"True," said Blackmore. "But go on. I think you said something about moral doubts."

Edmund paused. "Yes," he said.

Blackmore eyed him keenly still, puffing lightly at his pipe.

Edmund lowered his gaze. "While I was in Antigua," he said, "I committed fornication."

Blackmore said nothing, and Edmund did not dare look at him; so he went on. "With a mulatto," he said. "She was a slave, the property of my neighbor. I seem in that to have broken two commandments at once; that against adultery and that against coveting my neighbor's maidservant. I tried to resist her—I tried for a long while; but I was too weak—or, as it seemed to me at the time, she was too beautiful, and too . . . I do not know how to put it. It seems insufficient to say she was too alluring, too tempting. One look from her toppled my reason, my understanding, made me . . . some other man. I do not know what I was.

"I meant to marry her," he went on after a moment. "I formed a plan. After I had had . . . intercourse with her—and it was not just once, but many times; it was every day, for several months—I tried to arrange for her to be set free. I meant to go away with her, to become a manager on a plantation in Jamaica; and I meant someday, as soon as I could find a way, to marry her.

"But before I could do so, she was . . . she drowned. The circumstances were as awful as could be conceived."

He raised his eyes to Blackmore's again. He saw no judgment in them, only a quiet pity and affection.

"I see," said Blackmore.

They sat in silence for several minutes. Then Blackmore said, "Is that everything that is troubling you? Have you told me all?"

Edmund thought for a minute. "Well," he said, "there is more, but that is the worst of it."

"What is the 'more'?"

"It is only—perhaps you have not heard, but there was an incident aboard the packet on the way home."

"Ah, yes, I did hear about that. The college was abuzz with it."

"Yes, it has been bruited about out of all proportion to its importance. But I look back on it and wonder: Who was the man who did that? Was it I, Edmund Percy? And I think how those who live by the sword shall die by the sword."

"But you did not wield a sword. You did not hurt anyone, or not materially, as I understand the affair."

"No—I only hurled two men overboard, who were instantly taken up into a boat by their fellow traitors. But I keep thinking: What if they had not landed in the sea, as they did? What if they had struck the side of the ship, or the boat that was alongside? They surely would have been killed. Those lines from Euripides have been haunting me—about Astyanax being dashed from the walls of Troy without pity. What will my Judge say when I meet him? Will he not in turn dash *me* from the walls of heaven? And before I even left Antigua, I almost killed a man—the man who had been the owner of the woman I loved. Somehow, through the grace of God—and with the help of my Quaker angel—I was pulled back from that brink. But it is as if some new being, some new Edmund Percy, has been unleashed in me by my intercourse with that woman; and I cannot trust myself ever to be the same."

He paused for a moment, and then concluded: "And here is the crux of it: How shall I ever minister to others if I have sinned so myself? Paul writes, 'Keep not company with fornicators.' How can I preach *that* text to my parish?"

"Ah, Percy," said Blackmore, "I cannot think that is really the crux of it. True, that is what Paul says; but Jesus Christ said, 'I came not to call the righteous, but sinners to repentance.'

You know perfectly well, or you are perfectly capable of knowing well, that a clergyman who has had experience of repentance may actually be better qualified to lead others to repent than one who has never fallen and who has never had to pull himself upright again. You will be assisting those who are struggling. You will sympathize implicitly with their plight, and they will feel your sympathy implicitly. Will you not then be more persuasive in pleading with them to rely on God instead of on their own feeble strengths?"

"There is that," agreed Edmund. "I had thought of that argument; but I had not allowed it to have much force."

"It is a supremely valid argument," said Blackmore. "Perhaps you do not recall the answer made by our Dr. Johnson, when Boswell put a similar case to him. Some candidate for the clergy in the Church of Scotland was opposed in his application for induction on the grounds that he had committed fornication. Dr. Johnson said, 'If he has repented, his having fornicated is not a cogent objection to his induction. A man who is good enough to go to heaven is good enough to become a clergyman.'"

Edmund was struck by this comment.

"And as for the social doubts you have," Blackmore went on, "you know there is a perfectly valid recourse in that case as well; and I am sure you have come to see it."

"Yes, sir. I think I know what you are going to say. And I did resolve, before I left Antigua, to do my best to end slavery as a system. As for the rest of it—for what we do wrong here in England—that is too large an evil, and will have to wait for another day, for other lifetimes, not mine; though of course I shall do what little I can within the limits of my own sphere."

"Yes; that is indeed what I was thinking."

There was now an interval in the conversation, during which Blackmore continued to work occasionally at his pipe, tamping it and relighting it; but whatever his passing preoccupation with it, he continually returned his gaze to Edmund. After several minutes, he said, "No, there is more than that.

There is something more than just these social and moral doubts. There is a personal doubt."

"What do you mean?" asked Edmund, genuinely unsure.

"You loved this woman very much, did you not?"

"Yes—yes I did."

"And she taught you a great deal, did she not?"

"Yes," said Edmund frankly.

Blackmore leaned forward and knocked his pipe against the brickwork of the hearth. Then he began to refill it again; and as he did he said, "I shall tell you, Percy, what is really behind this doubt and despair you feel. You think you are spoiled for marriage with an innocent woman. Is that not so? You think that no innocent woman can offer you the pleasures of love afforded you by this woman who is now dead."

"That is so," admitted Edmund.

"My dear Percy, do you think you are alone among mankind in having had experience of a woman before marriage? Many a man forms some kind of liaison when he is young that teaches him the pleasures of the flesh in a fashion he will never encounter in a marriage with a decent woman. True, he will regret not being able to recapture with her what he has unfortunately learned in his precipitous encounter with profane love as a youth; but that regret will ebb with time, especially inasmuch as a good Christian woman has so much more to offer him than mere sexual satisfaction. If he takes her on her own terms, he finds much to love, whatever her manner of receiving him sexually, provided only that he does not raise a barrier to her in his mind by faulting her for her innocence."

"So you . . . you see no error in my taking a woman to wife after what I have done? And I do not ask that in ignorance of the fact that many men have done so; but what has been done by many men is not by that mere frequency made right, as we both know."

"No, I see no error in your marrying, not in the least. No more than I think it wrong for you to be ordained. You must only repent, and God will forgive you. It really is that simple. But I say again that it is not your sense of unworthiness that is troubling you: it is your craving for the pleasures you had, and your sense that you will never have them again. And I agree, you never will have them again; but you will have other, milder pleasures, with another kind of woman; and you will be satisfied with them."

In that instant, Edmund thought of Janetta's lovemaking; and for the first time in his acquaintance with Blackmore, he thought his friend was wrong, and out of his depth. What if, in marrying a woman who could not match Janetta's sexual passion, he only burned the more? It seemed to him that any woman who was *sexually present* in the manner he now craved would be for a dozen other reasons unsuitable as a wife. But he said nothing about these further doubts.

"Now," said Blackmore, "here is what I charge you to do. You must be ordained as soon as possible, so that you can find a living; and you must marry as soon as possible. It does not matter in what order those requirements are met—whether you find the living or the wife first; though of course it will go easier with you if you find the living first, as perhaps it will be easier to find a wife when that is done, and your choice will be made from a wider field. But you must have a wife, and soon. 'Thou art sad; get thee a wife, get thee a wife!' Otherwise this morbid desire for what is forever gone will drive you to a very unwholesome despair. You need only find a woman who is kind. No other requirements are necessary; though I have no doubt you will add a few of your own, such as that she be pretty and entertaining. But you must not have any expectations as to her sexual appetite or knowledge, for it will never equal yours.

"Once you have accomplished these two goals, you may settle down; and from your office, in your country rectory, on one free afternoon a week, you may write as eloquently as you can against slavery. You will find a place to publish what you write, for you are not alone in your detestation of that sinful institution. And I do not doubt that someday you will have the satisfaction of seeing it dismantled forever in the British realm.

"In the meantime, you will be of use in the society about you. You will be not just a good clergyman, but a model clergyman. I know the intelligence and willpower with which you approach any challenge. It is true, as your Quaker says, that the Church of England is asleep; but you, and other men like you, shall wake it up.

"Here is the sum of it: You must be useful. You will not be able to endure to live within your own skin if you are not. To be useful, you must be a clergyman—it is what you have trained for, and a sin does not disqualify you from that, or we would have no clergymen in all the church. To be useful, you must put out the fire this woman has lit in you. To do that, you must be married, Percy. To do that, you must settle for something that will seem at first much less interesting than a beautiful and exotic mulatto; you must settle for a handsome English girl. I think you will find that she will do very well for you."

Edmund considered what Blackmore had said for quite some time in silence, during which his tutor smoked his pipe and did not trouble him for a reply.

As he thought of this course, the darkness in which he had lived since Janetta's death began to lift a little, and he began to think that there was indeed a way forward. He was not convinced that he would ever be sexually satisfied by a woman he would meet in his own set; but he felt now that by marrying a woman of customary virtue, he would at least do as well as he could in that regard. And the way Blackmore expressed the necessity of his taking orders was like a revelation to him—a revelation and a relief. Blackmore had taken the thread of his past life and the thread of his future life, which had been snapped by his years in Antigua, and he had deftly spliced them together again. He had not, indeed, thought anything Edmund had not already thought; but he had expressed those thoughts aloud, said them well, and spoken them with that inscrutable authority he had.

"I believe you are right, sir," he said finally.

"Good," said Blackmore, with a nod. "I am glad to hear it. So tell me, then—when will you take orders?"

"I shall talk to Twickenham tomorrow, sir. It will be at the earliest opportunity."

"Good," said Blackmore again. "The sooner the better. As for the rest, I cannot help you, I am afraid; my society here does not extend to much acquaintance with the fair sex, particularly the unmarried fair sex. For that, you will have to rely on your relations. Your mother is no longer among us—you have no sisters. Is your brother married?"

"No, sir."

"Then he can be of no help. What about another relation—the aunt with whom you stay, perhaps?"

"My Aunt Statira is a very dedicated spinster, and has no use for the married state, or for the promotion of it. But I have another aunt in Hampshire—a very lively lady, very dear to me, and who would sell fish in the streets if it would serve me—and who would, I am sure, make a very active matchmaker."

Blackmore leaned back in his chair and took a long draw on his pipe. "To Hampshire you must go, then," he said.

CONTINUED IN ACT 2

Act 2

Hunting

So will each lover inly curse his fate,
Too soon made happy and made wise too late.

—Crabbe

Chapter 20

I never go to a Ball in my Life but what something or other happens unexpectedly that is quite charming.

—Austen

Edmund set out to follow Mr. Blackmore's program exactly as his mentor had required. He was promptly made deacon; but it was customary to observe some decent interval between the deaconate and the priesthood. He worked to reduce this period as much as he could; but his efforts to do so were hampered by Nature herself. The beginning of 1814 saw one of the most brutal cold spells in recent memory, and the requisite journeys to Oxford, usually a minor matter, became epic struggles against drifted snow and man-killing weather. When all was said that had to be said, and all done that needed to be done, the earliest date that could be set for his priesting was Easter.

This was a disappointment to him, but he determined to make the best of the postponement. The date was finally agreed upon by mid-February; and he immediately wrote the following letter to his aunt Andromeda:

Mrs. Hugh Alton
Fairhall, Broadbridge, Hants

Brackensom, Feb[y] 19, 1814

Dear Aunt Andromeda,

My love and greetings to you, and my hopes that this long-overdue letter finds that you continue well, as my father's latest report of you gives hope.

I find my full ordination is delayed until April. Might I repair my neglect of you these past three years by a visit to you in Hampshire in this interval?

I do not conceal my ulterior motive, which is to find a wife; but I do not offer you much with which to work, as I have not a hint of a living yet. However, it may prove entertaining to you to speculate on possible marriage partners for me; and as we always get along so well, I hope to recompense you for the inconvenience of supplying your hospitality by keeping you company in the last dark month of winter. I am sure that between us we shall make it a bright one.

Your loving nephew,

Edmund

To which his aunt immediately replied:

Mr. Edmund Percy
Brackensom, Neighbury, Surrey

Fairhall, Feb[y] 23, 1814

Dearest Edmund,

I am in receipt of yours of the 19th instant, and write to urge you to put this letter down at once and pack your things—summon the coach—repair at once to the nearest inn—and come to me in all haste by postchaise. I shall repay the charges if you are low on spending money—for I know that youngest sons often are so, and nearly as much as eldest sons—and you may read the rest of this as you travel. Go! Or I ought to say: Come!

Your letter has reached me in the very same week as a most elegant invitation from the finest family in my neighborhood—to a ball, no less, on Tuesday next; where you will have your pick of all the young ladies in our society—who will in turn be very interested in you, though I fear somewhat in the way the crocodiles of the Nile are interested in the flesh of hapless oarsmen who fall off the pharaoh's barge.

Now, this invitation I have received is remarkable for two things: first, that it arrived when it did, so fortunately for the prospects to which you refer in your letter; and secondly, that I was included on the list at all. I have not exchanged visits with the Esquith de Foyes since the very first week I came to Hampshire as a bride—and I shall not tell you how long ago that was. The de Foyes and the Altons never disagreed; it was simply that they are hunters, and your uncle was not; and so the de Foyes of course had no use for your uncle's wife, either. But I suppose that now Hugh is gone, they have taken pity on me; or perhaps it is that they have invited the entire country for twenty miles around, and I simply happen to be within that radius.

If you are reading this letter aloud to your father and brother—as you ought not be, for you ought already be in the postchaise before you have got this far—I beseech you to stop here; for I have matter that is not intended for their ears. It is simply this: At the thought that my nephew Edmund will come to visit me, a ray of light from distant Surrey has darted forth upon me in the universal grayness that fell over my life on the day that your uncle perished. For Edmund, dearest, you are my favorite. I have never told you so before in so many words, though I think you knew it. You cannot understand how important a favorite nephew is to an aunt who has no children of her own; the more so because your mother is gone, and I yearn to take care of you. You, I think, have more of your mother's qualities than Christopher or dear Alex; and though I loved Alex much, and love Christopher still, when I love you, I love not only you, but your mother in you. In short, though I doted on all you boys, I loved you best of all.

So there it is—you have applied to the right person at the right time. And you have never been to visit me at Hampshire! And there is in the village a very beautiful young

> lady who I think will grant you, if not the first two dances (for she will certainly have already bestowed them elsewhere), at least two others. She is the daughter of our lawyer here; she is very blonde and possesses a very fine figure. Let that light a fire under you, and come to me at once!
>
> Your delighted
>
> Aunt Andromeda

This letter arrived on the twenty-sixth; and if he was to arrive in time for the ball of which his aunt wrote, he must by necessity travel by postchaise. The regularity of such a mode of travel was not to be trusted on Sunday, however, and he was forced to wait until Monday, the twenty-eighth. Furthermore, once the journey commenced, it proved very much of a mad dash all the way. The roads were extremely bad, and two of the postchaises were mired for several hours; and it was not until noon of the first of March that he arrived at his aunt's house in Broadbridge, somewhat the worse for the rushed journey. But a hot bath and a good dinner soon set him to rights; and the company of his aunt was as cheering to him as his seemed to be to her.

Andromeda Alton was a very prepossessing woman. Her beauty was of the type that rather grows clearer and finer than fades with age: her skin in particular was remarkably smooth and clear, her eyes were merry and without a shadow, and her figure was good enough to catch the eye of men far younger than she. Her sense of fashion was perfectly balanced between what was owing to the age in which she lived—she would never have allowed herself to look old-fashioned—and what was becoming to a woman of her years. Edmund saw a further interest, beyond the ordinary motivation of self-respect, in the manner in which she dressed for the ball that evening—he knew that she went armed for combat in his behalf.

Nor was Andromeda's charm merely physical. She also possessed the unusual power of persuading men, no matter

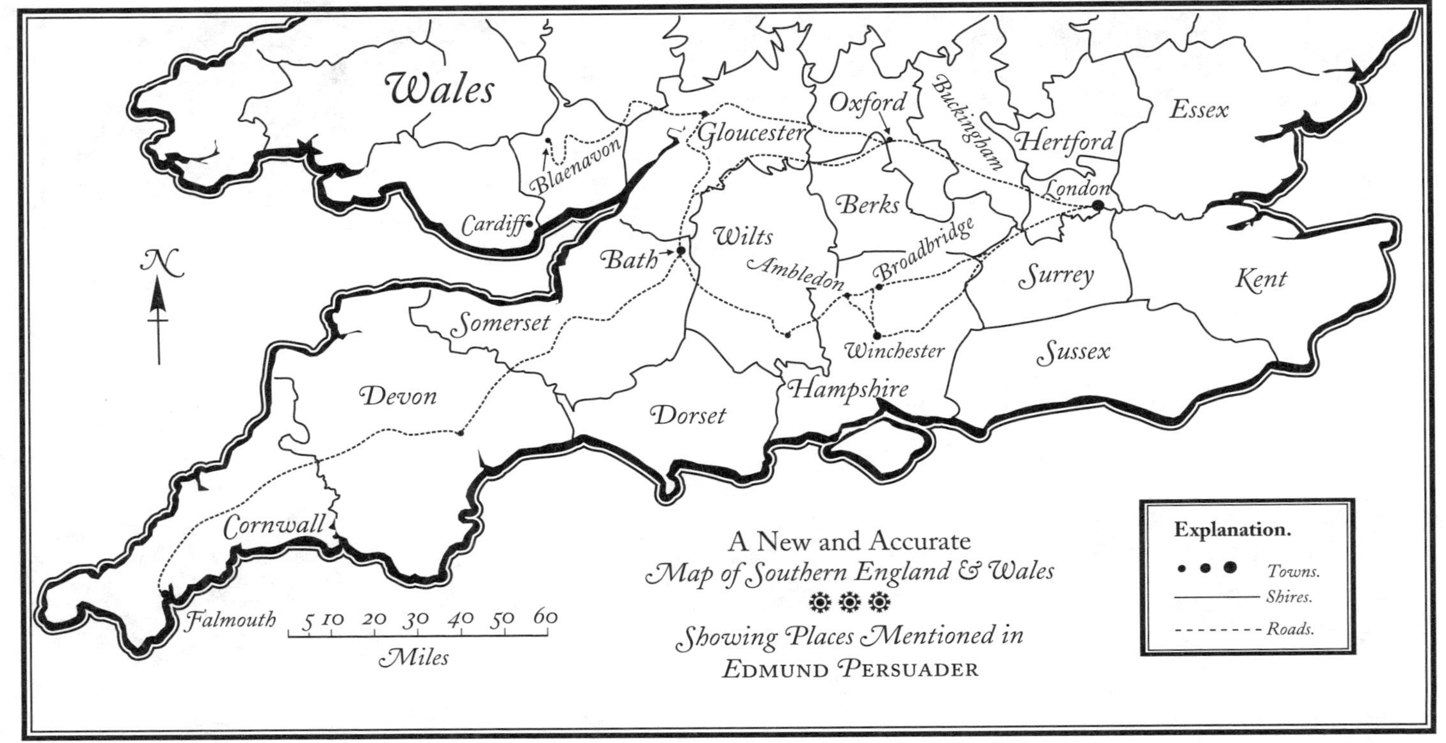
Wales
Blaenavon
Cardiff
Gloucester
Oxford
Buckingham
Hertford
Essex
London
Berks
Wilts
Bath
Ambledon
Broadbridge
Surrey
Kent
Somerset
Winchester
Sussex
Devon
Hampshire
Dorset
Cornwall
N
Falmouth
5 10 20 30 40 50 60
Miles
A New and Accurate
Map of Southern England & Wales
Showing Places Mentioned in
Edmund Persuader
Explanation.
Towns.
Shires.
Roads.

of what relationship to her, and no matter what nonsense they might talk, that she was acutely interested in them. Engaging and witty, she could—when she was not holding back to let a man she loved have center stage—become the hub of any conversation she entered; and yet intermingled with the swift flashes of her wit there shone a broad, bright gleam of true sincerity that disarmed her hearers even as they gathered their mental gear for repartee. Men knew she was playing a game with them, a game of very subtle and studied and droll flirtation; and yet it was a game they enjoyed themselves, and they admired her the more for the success with which she played it.

It was still light when Edmund and Andromeda boarded her carriage and set out for the ball. They did not have far to go; a short drive down the main road of the village led them to the gates of Hartswound Park; and from there they must proceed only a few miles before they caught their first glimpse of the house.

As they drove through the woods of the park, Andromeda turned to smile at him, and laid her hand eagerly on his arm. "You will be quite the prize in the dancing tonight, Edmund," she said.

"As a younger son without even so much as roof over his head, I can hardly think so."

"Ah, but you do not know our country ways. At Brackensom you live altogether too close to town for that, my dear. Here we have girls quite without resource; and a handsome, broad-shouldered clergyman-to-be will put them in a tizzy. As for your not yet having a living, they will instantly find a splendid one for you in their imaginations: the living of Hartswound Park."

He looked sharply at her now in surprise, and she laughed. "Why should I *not* scheme for your success, my dear Edmund? You hoped I might be able to marry you off to a fine female specimen of our country gentry; you did not also expect me to miss a chance to see you installed in a living near me, did you?"

"I have given you leave to marry me off; but you have never said anything of a living at Hartswound Park, Aunt; and that surprises me."

"Well, the living has not actually come up, you see. The old rector is still alive, though quite elderly, quite feeble."

"What—this Mr. Thomas you mentioned who bores you to tears every Sunday?"

"No, dear—you did not listen to me. Mr. Thomas is just the curate. Mr. Maugham is the rector. You will not see Mr. Maugham tonight. No; he is tottering on the brink of the grave, poor dear old thing that he is. He refused to have a curate for years, and as a result his parishioners did not actually *hear* a sermon in their church for quite some time—though I rather think his fervent murmuring in the pulpit would do more to stop them from sinning than the stentorian tones of Mr. Thomas. Everyone agrees Mr. Thomas is quite unsuitable, and there seems no intention whatsoever to give him the living when Mr. Maugham is gone. He is rumored to be making inquiries elsewhere, though still playing for the Broadbridge living if he can manage to get it."

"I suppose the Esquith de Foyes have a relation to whom they wish to give the living. Everyone always does. You do not know this family well, you say."

"Not very well, I must admit. I believe I mentioned that they are hunters, and your uncle was not. Mad, mad huntsmen, they are; but then again, they are all absolutely mad in everything they do; all but the daughter, who probably quite disappoints them."

"Ah! There is a *daughter* in the question as well, then?"

She darted him a quick, droll glance and gave forth a sound that was almost a giggle. It was a very charming sound. Then she shook her head.

"I am afraid, Edmund," she said, "that we cannot aim so high. I counsel you against it. The Esquith de Foyes are nothing if not proud. They would make your dear father look quite reasonable and humble in that respect. At a ball like this, they will not show it; they will be the very souls of affability and sociability. But if you were to walk into their house uninvited tomorrow, they would infer that you had pretensions to their circle; and then they would cut you.—No, 'cut you' is perhaps an understatement. They would exclude you from their attention so completely as to make you doubt that you exist in the mind of God."

"Really, Aunt! Is that not a harsh way to put it?"

"No; I only state the facts. I like the de Foyes, to tell the truth. The old gentleman is too broken from falls from horseback and too gouty to ride anymore; but the son is a handsome and powerful brute, rather like you, Edmund, though without that loving-kindness that is your hallmark. You might like him if you get to know him, if only because he is an intriguing character to study. You hunt; and they will not hold it against you that your uncle did not. They will favor you, I expect. And if they favor you, the living of Broadbridge parish is a good one, and they have it firmly in gift."

"I thought I had come here to flatter the ladies," he said jokingly. "I see I am here to flatter an old squire instead."

"No, Edmund," she reassured him. "Not at all. With people like the Esquith de Foyes, there is nothing one can do. If they take to you, very well; if not, there is no point in pursuing the matter. Besides, the house will be so crowded tonight that I doubt we shall even see you introduced to them. Your task will be to find the prettiest girls you can and dance with them all."

"I shall do my best to follow your orders, Aunt," he said.

He found that despite his stated intentions, his heart was not in his words; but he managed to deceive her. She smiled contentedly at him and then peered out the window of the carriage, trying to see ahead along the winding drive. "And what a throng there is!" she said.

He looked out his window now and could see that they had left the woods and were rolling between broad fields.

No fewer than a dozen carriages were visible on the road ahead of them; and on either side of the gates of the enclosure about the manor house itself were many more in irregular lines, attended by servants trying to stay warm until their masters should emerge from the ball sometime in the wee hours of the morning. Their own carriage soon rolled through the gates and drew up in front of the house. A footman brought a step and opened the door, and Edmund and his aunt descended.

They both paused a moment to survey the front of the house. It had not the Georgian symmetry of Brackensom, being much older; but it was as beautiful in its way, and what it lacked in majesty it made up in plenitude: its façade blazed now with what seemed a hundred tall windows set among somewhat rough and heavy semi-columns of dressed stone. The entrance to the house was formed by a set of very tall doors, now flung wide, at the top of a broad, sweeping stairway of limestone. Footmen flanked the steps, each holding a flaming torch that cast shifting shadows and etched the ancient housefront with hints of new character.

"You see," Aunt Andromeda said, "that the house is quite acceptable, even for one who grew up at Brackensom."

"It will do for a country ball," he answered ironically.

He gave her his arm, and as they ascended steps she said, "Oh, one more thing I ought to mention." He inclined his head toward her. "The daughter of the house—you will recognize her immediately, I am sure; she is a magnificent creature—this daughter has an especial friend, a kind of pet almost; she is from a poor gentleman's family, but the girls were foster sisters, as Mrs. Esquith de Foye died in childbirth. This friend is rather pretty, and you may be tempted to dance with her; but you *must not ask her to dance,* and under no circumstances must you touch her, not even to shake her hand, unless she should touch you or offer her hand first."

He looked at her in surprise. They had come up to a line of visitors waiting to pass through the front doors, and so they had a moment more for her explanation. "It is a quirk well known to all the country about: she cannot bear to be touched without her consent. She would be smitten with panic. At one dance in Broadbridge a rather rough fellow seized her by the hands to dance with her, and she had a fit—and I mean *bona fide* convulsions. If you should jostle into her, she will not mind that; and she may decide to touch *you,* that is, to shake your hand or put her hand on your arm. Any contact that is inadvertent or that she initiates does not bother her; but if she thinks you *mean* to touch her without her consent, she will be violently upset."

"How very odd!" he said.

"It gets odder still, I assure you," she said in a low voice. "She is one of the most charming beings you ever met. Not only pretty and talkative in an amusing way, but cheerful and kind and infinitely sweet-tempered. But *not quite all there. Weak-minded,* as we would say."

As she finished speaking they moved forward into the lofty entrance hall of the Hartswound Park manor house, and the noise of the throng itself would have discouraged conversation, if they had not been at once absorbed in the sights around them.

The hall itself was a vision. A candelabra of resplendent polished brass with a hundred candles or more hung high above them, illuminating the scene; its warm light fell on vast walls paneled with oak from ancient trees, now dark with venerable age, gleaming with beeswax applied by housekeepers in decade after decade. Gentry who had come from miles around milled about there, calling to one another, renewing old acquaintance, talking, laughing, or hunting for friends, relatives, or neighbors. Fine, handsome English faces; fine stout English bodies, well and neatly dressed; fine young men in little nervous clusters, steeling themselves to seek partners in the dance; fine young women, chattering and laughing and looking about, always looking about with brave, lively eyes; fine elderly men, who had seen many a ball, and smiled faintly now with the accumulated remembrance of them; fine elderly women flirting little ivory fans and peering, birdlike, at each passerby in the crowd.

Suddenly Edmund's aunt squeezed his arm. He caught her glance and followed her eyes to the staircase that rose, curving, as if with a celestial ambition, toward the upper rooms of the house; and there he saw two women at a high turn of the banister, surveying the crowd below them, for all the world like the captain and first mate on a raised quarter-deck, watching the lading of their East Indiaman.

He knew one of them instantly for the daughter of the house; for she was, as his aunt had said, one of God's magnificent creations. In an age when women affected the dress of Grecian goddesses, here was a woman who looked the very part. She was tall and had a fine figure, high- and full-breasted, with (as far as the high waist of the times would reveal) the rest of the hourglass below. Her skin was a fine fruit-and-cream color, and the fashion of course left plenty of it exposed to view above the sparing lace on her breasts; her hair was brunette, heavy and soft and gleaming in candlelight even in the coils and curls in which it was dressed. On her head she wore a playful tiara in the lunar shape of the diadem worn by Diana—a female ornament that was the height of fashion, the utmost rage in London and Paris—and around her neck glittered a necklace of diamonds. Her face could have modeled female beauty for a classicizing sculptor—the nose more straight than the typical snub of the English girls who had gathered below in the hall, and her brows more dark and finely arched over wider, more lustrous eyes.

For an instant those eyes met his; then they moved on—hungrily, he thought; and he realized instinctively that she was searching for someone, and not just someone, but a man she preferred above all others. He knew it as surely as if she had told him so.

Once he had seen her, it was difficult *not* to look at her; but her evident preoccupation broke the spell, and he turned his gaze to her companion. Her he found indeed a very pretty girl—and he would have called her a girl, rather than a woman, though he gathered she was only slightly younger than Miss Esquith de Foye. She was in several ways a paler, weaker version of her foster sister. She was shorter and slighter, smaller of breast and limb; on her the high-waisted dress seemed something borrowed for the hour that begged the indulgence of society, rather like the costume of a masquerade—and so, perhaps it was, just as perhaps all that age was a mere Olympian masquerade. She was fair in coloring, with lively, even mischievous green eyes, set in a very pleasing, very cheerful young face. If she had not been keeping company with a woman far more beautiful, she would have been very alluring herself; but the comparison did not serve her well.

She, too, noticed his gaze over the heads of the crowd; but rather than turn away, she froze and stared at him, wide-eyed with a kind of wonder. As he watched, he saw her speak to Miss de Foye, and he perhaps partly heard above the tumult and perhaps partly deduced the words she uttered: "Oh! Who is that handsome fellow just come in with Mrs. Alton?"

Miss de Foye glanced back at him momentarily, and seemed to take slightly more note of him than she had before; but evidently she had no information for her friend, for she said nothing.

He found all this highly amusing, and he gave his aunt—who had missed none of the proceedings—a conspiratorial smile.

"You see what I mean," she said.

"You paint from life, Aunt," he responded. "I had no trouble recognizing them."

"Well, now that you have seen them, you know what you must avoid. They are both untouchable—one socially, the other literally. You must hunt other vixen here, Edmund; and keep one eye open for the entrance to that cozy den that might one day be yours."

He laughed at her machinations, and she took him away to introduce him to her Broadbridge neighbors.

What followed was somewhat of a blur to him in his recollection of it. He danced with not just several young women, but with many. No sooner had he fulfilled his required two dances with one than his aunt seized upon him again and took him away to meet with another. He did his best to converse with his partners, but the movements of the country dances of that time, like those of modern contradances, tended to promote the illusion of intimacy even while they prevented its achievement. This was, in fact, exactly what they were intended to do; and there were times that he was perfectly glad that his conversation with his partner was fragmented, and times that he felt some shy partner was taking refuge in the interruptions in their companionship afforded by the dance. Thus when he came to recall these young women later, he remembered their physical attributes more than their characters, which he had generally had little opportunity to discern.

Towards the end of this spate of partners, however, his aunt had difficulties in her arrangements, and he found himself sitting out a round or two with several of the young ladies with whom he had danced. This he soon found excruciating. The conversation, so far as he could determine, was about nothing—Mrs. So-and-So's fan; the curate's appetite for beef; Miss Aughton's sleeve that had come loose, and how she cried over it until her mama found needle and thread; the wax that had dripped from the candelabra on Miss Something's bosom—all of which seemed immensely entertaining to his company. At length they all leapt up unceremoniously and ran off giggling to console a friend who had lost a shoe.

By then he had reached a sufficient pitch of boredom that he found merely sitting in a corner and waiting for the ball to end to be a prospect far preferable to attempting active conversation with a silly country gentlewoman; so he sat, and thought his thoughts, and was content for several minutes until he was interrupted.

Again his aunt approached, seeking for him around the margin of the dance floor, and with her was the pretty young friend of the daughter of the house. He stood up with somewhat more interest than he would otherwise have mustered for a new prospective acquaintance.

"There you are, Edmund—not danced out, I hope?"

"Not at all, dear Aunt. Merely awaiting your further commands."

"And sitting on the *opposite* side of the room from me is the best way to find them out, of course.—Miss Brownton, you must not mind my banter with my nephew. We are old friends and understand each other perfectly. We tease each other quite determinedly, and enjoy every minute of it. Allow me to introduce him to you—Edmund Percy, the younger son of Hereford Percy, of the Surrey Percies, whose seat is Brackensom.—Edmund, permit me to introduce you to Miss Evelyn Brownton, of our Broadbridge Browntons, and the especial friend of Miss Esquith de Foye."

Miss Brownton, who now seemed more than just pretty when met on her own terms, swept him a girlish curtsy in answer to his bow, and then stood regarding him with undisguised interest.

"I am very pleased to make your acquaintance, Miss Brownton," said Edmund.

Miss Brownton seemed unable to reply. Her attentiveness to him, however, and her tremendous pleasure in contemplating him would have flattered any man into disregarding so trivial a defect in her personality as the mere inability to utter human speech. All the same, the silence continued for so long that Edmund and his aunt felt uncomfortable with it.

"Edmund!" said Andromeda finally in mock distress, "I am quite surprised at you! You see a beautiful young woman before you who has not yet been spoken for, a dance about to begin, and you stand looking on in helpless amazement! How unlike you!"

He darted her a glance, and confirmed by that subtle communication that she was signaling him that Miss Brownton had expressed a wish to dance with him, and that he should disregard her previous warnings.

"Miss Brownton, would you do me the honor?" he asked, turning to offer his arm to her.

She still said not a word, but smiled happily and took his arm, looking up into his eyes the entire time as if she could not believe her luck.

However much a man may enjoy such silent flattery, it soon causes him to suffer a kind of claustrophobia; and Edmund, as he took his place opposite this young woman on the dance floor, found himself hoping fervently that she would manage some kind of conversation. He was also ill at ease for another reason, as he discovered that the mere act of taking the floor with Evelyn Brownton seemed to make him the object of amazement and speculation on all sides.

It was clear, as the dance began, that she had been well schooled in the proper movements. Edmund was relieved to discover this much, and concentrated on the dance, which was in any case once again such as to make conversation difficult or at best sporadic. Miss Brownton did not offer so much as a word throughout, though she seemed thoroughly to enjoy the proceedings.

He led her from the floor at the end of the dance, casting his glance about surreptitiously for his aunt, who he hoped would help him disengage himself from this strangely demanding young woman; but Andromeda, perhaps intentionally, had disappeared from the ballroom.

"I am ever so thirsty," said Miss Brownton suddenly, with a pleased and not unpleasing smile. "Could we find the refreshments *together?*" Her voice was soft, humorous, and tremulous, a markedly pleasant sound.

"Of course," he murmured, somewhat taken aback at her directness.

She submitted herself entirely to his leading, though she must have known far better than he where the refreshments were. She did not speak again until they reached the table where various beverages were being served.

"I see we have cider, syllabub, and wine," he began. He was casting about to identify and enumerate the various kinds of wine that seemed to be available, when she interrupted him.

"Wine, please," she said.

He selected a clear, light wine and handed it to her; she took it happily, watching him all the while with her clear, green eyes. He took a glass as well.

"Permit me to say—" he began; but she was speaking simultaneously.

"You dance wonderfully," she said.

"I was just going to say, you are a very fine dancer," he said.

She laughed at the coincidence. Her laughter was captivating, musical, girlish.

For a moment more she stood looking up at him admiringly in silence; and then the floodgates opened. He was not sure what he had done to merit her confidence, but she began to speak volubly at last, in a voice not unlike her laughter, a kind of breathless, girlish, impulsive burbling of words. The mere sound amused him, but her utter lack of affectation was still more charming.

"I learned with my friend, you know," she began abruptly. "Mr. Cubbins taught us, when we were thirteen. Until then we thought we should *never* learn to dance properly. Of course, we knew something about it from attending balls and watching and trying it out; but it was Mr. Cubbins who told us the whole of it. Not that I dance very much. I am very shy, really." As she said this she gave Edmund a dazzling smile that somehow both belied and confirmed her assertion.

"I am all the more honored, then," he said, "that you consented to dance with *me.*"

"I saw you the minute you came in with Mrs. Alton. And I knew at that very instant that you must be a very good and kind person."

"Why, thank you," he said, startled into humility. "No praise would please me more. I shall endeavor to live up to your first impression."

"Mrs. Alton says that you are to become a clergyman soon."

"That is my plan, yes."

"But not a stuffy-old *boring* clergyman like Mr. Thomas, I hope? I want you to be like Mr. Maugham."

"Mr. Maugham . . . is the rector here at Broadbridge parish, is he not?"

"Yes—and he is so dear and sweet. We love him ever so much. He is very old, but never a crotchety word do we hear from him. He calls me his 'little bird,' and he is always sighing and saying, 'Whatever is to become of my little bird?' And I always laugh and say, 'Nothing to cause a sigh! Like the sparrows and the larks you tell us about.'"

Edmund suddenly began to see the basis of the rector's concern. It was hard to imagine this innocent creature making her way in society; or at least not without powerful patronage, which Miss Esquith de Foye might not be able to offer when she was married away to some distant place—an event probably in the offing.

"I should like to meet your rector," said Edmund.

"You shall, then; and you shall love him," said Miss Brownton. "As we both do."

He guessed now that when she said "we" she was probably referring to Miss Esquith de Foye and herself; though he thought it odd that she took her association with Miss de Foye so for granted that she felt no need to explain whom she meant.

"Tell me," she said, apropos of he knew not what, "what is it like being *so very* handsome?"

He could only laugh aloud. "Really, Miss Brownton! If I even pretend to know the answer to that question, I shall be accused of conceit."

"I am ever so serious," she protested. "You must tell me."

"Well, if you compel me to speak on this point, I shall tell you that if I am as you say, I do not feel so; and therefore I have to say it makes no difference."

"Truly? Or are you jesting with me?"

"I am telling you the truth. I feel myself less than or at best equal to other men in respect to looks."

"Ah! You see, I am interested because Mariah—my most especial friend in the world, as Mrs. Alton said—is the most beautiful creature God ever made; and yet she seems completely unaware of it! She frets over her appearance sometimes as if she were a leaper!"

He could not help being startled again, and laughing again. "You must mean 'a leper,' Miss Brownton."

"Oh, yes—a leper." She pronounced the word with exaggerated care, as if fixing it in her memory, and then she laughed at herself so infectiously that he laughed again, and even several strangers standing near joined in good-naturedly.

"What is a—a *leper?*" she asked. "I have never understood. Is it not like some kind of great cat?"

"No—that is a *leopard.* Altogether different. A *leper* is an individual with a specific disfiguring disease called leprosy."

"Ah! *Disfiguring.*"

She nodded as if she understood; but he was inclined to think she had merely imagined something based on the word rather than grasped the precise sense in which he intended it. He was loath, however, to go deeper into the subject unless specifically pressed for more information.

"A leaper," she said impulsively. "Now, that would be something utterly different too, would it not?" She tittered, and he found himself chuckling with her. "Though I suppose if you thought of a *frog* as a leaper, then it would make sense if she should not want to look like a *leaper.*"

"Perfect sense."

They laughed again at their joke, and then she looked away shyly.

"Do you like the wine?" she asked.

"Well, let me taste it," he said, for he had not yet had a chance to do so. He found it excellent. "Why, yes," he said. "It is very good. A pear wine, very richly flavored, but not too strong."

"She made it," said Miss Brownton happily. "And I helped her gather the fruit."

He understood again that she referred to Miss Esquith de Foye.

"Then I can see that it must have partaken of the sweetness of the harvester," he said gallantly.

"Oh, you really are very clever," she said. "I am sure you could turn anything into a compliment."

"I can imagine some things that would be a challenge, but for the sake of any pleasant young lady, I would try my best to be pleasing in turn." He thought to himself that he had never talked such nonsense before in his life; but he was also conscious that he was enjoying doing so.

"I shall never marry," she said matter-of-factly. "Can you turn that into a compliment?"

He was again greatly startled at her abrupt introduction of this nonsequitur subject; but after a moment he collected his wits and responded. "Who could deserve you?" he said simply, with an expressive gesture. She laughed in her beautiful, silverly way, and put one hand on his forearm in sheer exuberance of spirits. He noticed again that several people around them were looking at them in amazement.

"Would you care to dance again?" he asked cautiously, hoping to change their location in the hall.

"Oh, no, not yet. Let us talk some more, if you do not mind."

"Not at all. Would you care to sit down?"

"No, thank you. I am quite all right standing."

"Perhaps we ought to move away from the table and let people through."

She complied willingly with this suggestion, taking his offered arm and moving to a less busy corner.

"I would be honored if you would tell me a little of your life and times here in this splendid house," he said.

"Let us play our game a little more first," she countered.

"Our game?"

"Yes—I say something, and you turn it into a compliment."

He laughed outright. "But I do not want to turn your head. What if such steady doses of praise made you conceited, Miss Brownton? Your family and friends would be quite severe on me."

"Oh, that will never happen. No matter what you say, I have my dear friend to compare myself to; and there is no one in the world more beautiful and sweet and wise and brave than she."

"I should like to meet 'your friend,'" he said.

"I would introduce you," she said. "But you would be sorry if I did."

"Why ever is that?"

"Because you would fall in love with her instantly. All men do." She spoke without a trace of jealousy; she was merely stating a fact.

"Really!" he exclaimed.

"Oh, yes." She turned and looked about the hall; then she indicated a tall, lanky man who was standing at the edge of the room watching the dancing. "Do you see that man? He is Monsieur Artan. He is our music instructor—or rather he *was;* for Tark has thought it best to send him away. He is utterly, madly, hopelessly in love with my friend."

"And how does she feel about him?"

"Embarrassed, of course! And full of pity. She is very kind to him; she is quite used to men falling hopelessly in love with her, and knows how to be kind without being encouraging."

"So she cannot bring herself to reciprocate his feelings?"

"He is a very good music teacher; but who would want to marry him?"

He surveyed this hapless individual and had to admit inwardly that he did not seem to present a prospect that would be of much interest to a highborn, accomplished, wealthy, and beautiful young woman. Monsieur Artan was middle-aged, pot-bellied despite his long bones, and wore a powdered wig—somewhat untidy—in the style of thirty years before. His clothes, as well, were beyond outdated: he wore the quaintest of knee-breeches and shoes with silver buckles now black with age.

"Despite my best efforts to muster Christian charity," he said, "I admit I would have a hard time complimenting the appearance of your Monsieur Artan."

"Then you must compliment *mine* some more, Mr. Percy. I shall challenge you with all of my defects. What if I told you that I was quite a poor musician myself?"

"Your laughter itself is music, Miss Brownton," he said nonchalantly.

She giggled almost ecstatically.

"And if I said that my head is a sieve? That I cannot remember history, geography, or literature?"

He paused. "You tax my powers," he said. "How can I compliment something I cannot condone?"

"I assure you I well understand how stupid I am, and how regrettable my stupidity is; but you must try, for the sake of the game, or I shall win."

"Well, then: What need has so handsome a woman to remember history and literature, when historians and poets will remember *her?*"

Her smile approved this; but she immediately added, "And geography? I shall not let you off on that."

"You are the center of the universe, Miss Brownton; let the geographers find *you* out."

She almost clapped her hands in delight, but the glass she held prevented her. "Well done! Well done, sir! And all nonsense, which makes it all the better. How I do love nonsense! It is the only thing I *really* understand.—Here is another: all I know about chess is how to set up the board; which I do enjoy doing very much; but after that, I have not the least idea how to move a single piece."

"What an odd failing to cite, Miss Brownton. Who plays chess so regularly as to make you feel so inadequate in this respect?"

"Oh, they are all *mad* for chess here. The rector plays with Mariah, and then there is Mr. Cato, and of course Mariah's brother."

"Really!" he said in surprise. "I am pleased to hear that I have come into such an asylum of chess players."

"Do *you* play?"

"I do."

"Then I will set up the board for you sometime.—But now you must make me my compliment."

"That is too easy. Let the *men* move the chess pieces; *you* shall move the men themselves."

"Well done again! Here is another: I can do nothing with my hands; I cannot even mend a stocking."

He looked at her hands and was suddenly struck by their beauty. "But how can that signify," he said, perhaps with too much sincerity, "when one touch of your fair hands would mend any man's broken heart?"

She looked uncomfortable suddenly, and now, to his relief, she looked away, sipped a little of her wine, and gave up the game for another topic.

"Why have you come to Broadbridge, Mr. Percy?"

"To spend some time with my aunt. She is quite a favorite of mine, and I take the liberty of saying that the feeling is mutual. I am to be ordained next month, so I have a few weeks to spare."

"I am ever so glad you came," she said in a low, happy voice.

"Why, I thank you. You know how to turn a compliment yourself, Miss Brownton."

"It is easy to compliment others, you know, when you are so happy yourself."

"And are you happy?"

"Oh, yes! Why should I not be? I have my beloved Mariah, and my mother and father, and the old rector; and they are all very kind to me. And Mr. Cato is quite sweet, too, in his funny, gruff old way; and Tark, too, scary and gruff though he is, smiles quite nicely and tolerates me because he knows that Mariah loves me. I come and go at Hartswound Park just as I please—I am one of the family here—and at the rectory as well. What more could I possibly want?"

"Well, some women your age *do* want more."

"To be married you mean?—But I shall never do that; I have told you."

"And you have no desire to do so?"

"None whatsoever. I could not bear it, I am sure. The mere idea disgusts me!"

"You have no desire to have children?"

"I, Mr. Percy? I had a puppy once, and I lost it. Lost it—somehow—and to this day I do not know how or where, nor does anyone else. I would do the same thing with a child, I am sure."

He was quiet a minute, thinking of the picture she painted of herself.

"And what of your future, then?" he asked.

She raised her eyebrows and gave a resigned but cheerful shrug. "I try, but I cannot bring myself to think of it for more than a minute," she said. "Mr. Maugham says we must pray that the Lord will provide, and so He must, for I shall never manage by myself."

"And so you will go on, as you are, for as long as you can?"

"I hope so."

"But everything always changes, Miss Brownton. In human life, nothing ever stays the same. People grow old and die; new generations arise. Does that worry you at all?"

"No," she said simply. "Because I myself never change."

"Oh, but you do. You grow older along with the rest of us. Even your beauty, Miss Brownton, must fade someday, though I trust you will always be handsome."

"And why should I care, even if I were to grow as ugly as Mr. Cato's old hounds?" she said.

Her equanimity caught him quite off guard.

"Well, perhaps it is no matter, as you say. What is beauty but a painting on our flesh? But our bodies grow old as well, and aches and pains come with that aging."

"Let it be, if so it must. I cannot stop its being so; and so I shall not fret myself over it."

"I say, Miss Brownton, the more I talk to you, the more I admire your philosophy."

"Philosophy! I wish you would explain to me what the word means. No one has ever been able to."

"It means your love for wisdom."

"But what wisdom do *I* have?"

"It is true wisdom not to fret over things that cannot be helped. Our Savior told us we ought not do so, and most of us spend our lives disobeying Him—in that and in most other respects."

"Do you think," she asked slowly, "that God would be pleased with me for being as I am? I mean, so forgetful and useless; but so happy anyway?" It was clearly a novel thought for her.

"I begin to think so," he said. "Though I would always counsel you not to be content with who you are, but to try to grow as much as you can into the grace that God bestows. Besides, I suspect that you are not as useless as you pretend. If you truly were, you would not be so well loved."

She did not seem to mind his little sermon; she looked at him with gratitude. “How kind you are!” she said.

How extraordinary you *are,* he thought.

Something across the room caught her attention. “Oh, look,” she said.

He turned as she directed, to the ballroom again. The dance was over. He realized that certain calls he had heard while speaking with Miss Brownton were requests for the lady of the house to play the pianoforte, though the outcry seemed to Edmund’s ear rather polite than inspired. In either case, young and old came to a halt, and Miss Esquith de Foye was summoned from another room. She made her way to the pianoforte with some diffidence, as it seemed to Edmund. It was clear she acted out of obligation, not out of a pleasure in her powers.

Whatever her misgivings, she played and sang—it was an old French ballad she chose—with warm feeling and good technique. One might have said she acquitted herself well; that such was all she hoped for, and so all she achieved. Her voice was clear and light, except in one line, which she spoke rather than sang; and then the clarity of her tone gave over to an exquisite, almost sorrowful huskiness that made a chill run down Edmund’s spine. He thought how he would much rather have heard her simply speak her own thoughts than sing the words of another.

In all this time her eyes roamed the room, and Edmund had the same intuition that she was seeking someone, that there was someone she hoped to find whose approbation meant much to her; someone she was still expecting; someone who had not yet appeared. What was more, certain of the yearning French phrases seemed to take on extra meaning on her lips, if Edmund was not deceived.

At any rate, it did not seem to be poor Monsieur Artan for whom she sang. That admirer was quite in evidence at the front of the crowd, enthralled by her, and unable to conceal his emotion. Miss Brownton gave Edmund a look that said, “You see what I mean?”; and indeed he did. Most likely the audience understood the man's behavior as merely that of a fond teacher proud of his pupil; but with Miss Brownton's hint, Edmund saw it as excessive.

As for himself, he thought the quality of Miss de Foye's singing was somewhat beside the point. She was such a beautiful woman that he would gladly have stood there and *watched* her sing, even if he could not have heard the words. Perhaps there were several deaf old men in the crowd who enjoyed her singing all the more for that very reason. Her breasts rose against the lace of her décolletage; her cheeks grew a darker pink in the candlelight; and her serene face and lively eyes never tired in themselves, and promised never to become tiresome to look upon.

When she had ceased singing, the gathered neighbors applauded. They were outdone by poor Monsieur Artan, who approached Miss de Foye to compliment her effusively. Edmund caught a few "Mademoiselles" and "magnifiques" before the sound of voices welled again around them, amid calls for another dance. He glimpsed Miss de Foye briefly for one last instant as the crowd surged into the center of the room, and he saw her eyes find Miss Brownton beside him, and her hand make a quick gesture.

"She wants me," said Miss Brownton suddenly. "I must go, Mr. Percy." She put her glass of wine down so abruptly that it spilled, though she did not notice.

"Of course, Miss Brownton," he said.

"I hope I shall talk with you again this evening," she said.

"The pleasure would be mine. But I must insist that our game be over," he said. "My success was turning my own head too much; to say nothing of the fact that I was beginning to believe everything I said about you."

She laughed. "I shall never ask you to play it again, if you do not like it. But you are so clever I am sure you have a thousand thousand other amusing things to say."

She began to dart away, and then remembered her manners. She turned and, with the most winning, innocently coquettish smile he had ever seen, made him a curtsy. He bowed in return; she laughed her charming laugh; and then she slipped away through the crowd.

What an extraordinary being! he thought again; and, feeling the need to order his thoughts and feelings after having been assaulted by feminine beauty at close range for a full half-hour, he found a chair where he could sit without interruption for a few minutes and consider her.

In one sense she was as silly as any of the young women he had danced with that night; but somehow she was infinitely more entertaining—perhaps because she was absolutely without affectation. Listening to her chatter was as soothing as listening to the prattle of a running brook. And he thought, too, that there was a method in her silliness that he could not detect in that of her peers at the ball. Her world seemed to be largely circumscribed by Miss Esquith de Foye, and to that person she continually returned, beaming on her friend again and again like a pale moon in its course shining down on a more resplendent globe; she seemed, as she said, to have retained little or no book learning, and to trouble herself little over the lack of it. Offsetting that, she spoke very well; her choice of words was generally good, and her speech ranged from complete simplicity almost to a poignant epigrammaticism—despite her one outstanding instance of incomprehension, which only seemed to amuse her. All in all, she was strangely feral, primitive, innocent, a noble savage well aware of her difference from others, but unable and unwilling to suffer because of it.

In a few minutes, his aunt found him again and took a seat beside him.

"Well, you are quite the talk of the ball, Edmund," she said, keeping her voice low. "Evelyn Brownton has never danced with *anyone,* so far as I can remember."

"Is that so?"

She waited a minute, and then she could not help herself: "Well?" she asked.

"An extraordinary character," he said. "Quite charming."

"You *will* not fall in love with her, now, will you, Edmund?" asked Andromeda in a tone of alarm.

"Heavens, no! But I was quite entertained by her, and she seems to have enjoyed my company as well. She resolutely maintains she will never marry—"

"How did *that* subject ever come up?" asked his aunt, again with some concern.

"I do not know! I do not know how she gets from one topic to another, but she has some rhyme or reason in her own head, I suppose. I can assure you it was information that she herself volunteered."

"It cannot do your prospects any harm to have Miss Brownton captivated by you. But still it is a far climb from the pleasant, sunny meadow of Evelyn Brownton to the austere heights of the Esquith de Foyes."

"Dear Aunt," said Edmund wryly, "since when have you been such a schemer?"

"When was it you arrived in Broadbridge—noon?" she said, with a smile. "Or maybe a little before—when I invited you; or perhaps a little before that. Or perhaps when you were born, and I first held you in my arms; and I thought how you would be the son I might very well never have.—Are you angry with me?"

"How could I be? You have been the mother I no longer have."

"Ah, we both miss her, do we not? What a fine mother she was to you, and a fine sister to me."

"Indeed she was. I emulate her. If I can be as kind as she was, I shall have accomplished something in my life."

"Well, you need not be so *very* kind to some beautiful, scatterbrained girl as to marry her to protect her from the world, if *that* thought ever crossed your mind."

"It had not; but now that you mention it, it is a plan worth considering." He was teasing her, and she knew it.

"Do not bring my plans to naught," she said. "I shall not be happy until I see you ensconced at our rectory, with some fine, buxom country gentlewoman bearing you baby after baby.—What do you think of Miss Eaton, by the by?"

"Remind me—which one was she?"

"The tall creature with blue eyes and corn-colored hair. Much the best-looking of those you danced with; I think, in fact, the foremost beauty of the village. Her father is my solicitor here in Broadbridge, a fellow of good common sense; and if it is sense you are looking for—are you looking for sense in a wife, Edmund?—I suspect Miss Eaton possesses about as much as any young woman you will find at this ball tonight."

"Yes: she was the one who seemed to think the West Indies were the western part of India."

"No! Well, perhaps geography is not her strong suit. She has good hips, Edmund; I hate to be crass, but one must think of these things in choosing a wife. You do not want a woman like me who was never meant to have babies."

"I see that I must submit to you any woman I intend to marry, with a view to obtaining your approval on this point, dear Aunt."

She laughed at the thought. "I am sure you will," she said ironically. "No, Edmund, I think you can make your own assessment of that female attribute. You will find your own way quite successfully without me; I know that. In part that is why I tease you with my little mock schemes on your behalf—because I know you will be loved and do well in this world without my interference or attempts at assistance. But I would so love to have you settled near me."

"Perhaps if that does not happen so conveniently, you would consider removing to be near me, Aunt, when I find a living. That would be jolly. And you could *catch* the babies as they are born."

"Would you mind very much if I did? I have considered it."

"I would be very pleased if you would."

"I wonder if your wife would feel the same way."

"Of course she would."

She was highly pleased, he saw. A tear glistened in her eyes, and she was suddenly silent for a few minutes, not trusting her voice. When she did speak again, she said, "I shall not worry too much about what happens here at Broadbridge, then. I feel reassured."

They sat for a few minutes in comfortable, silent companionship. Suddenly she rose, and he then stood with her. "Will you dance again?" she asked. "Miss Eaton has a sister, you know, who might know the difference between the East and West Indies. Shall I inquire for you?"

"To tell the truth, I was rather hoping we would be leaving soon."

"Oh, not for hours, I expect. Are you tired? I fear it would really be seen as somewhat rude. Besides, I am not going to let you go before you have seen all your options."

"Well, in that case I had better get some air to fortify myself."

"Very well. The terrace is that way—through that room. You will find some glass doors at the far side."

"Thank you," he said.

She went off on a scouting mission, and he threaded his way through the throng in the direction she had indicated. It took him a minute of polite jockeying to clear the door of various loungers and get through it, but when he closed it behind him, he found that a surprising amount of the noise behind him was blocked out.

The air of the March night was cool and clean. He walked forth on the terrace, which was lit only by a link now sunk to embers.

After crossing the width of the terrace, he was stopped by a marble balustrade. Below him in the dark he could see the vague shapes of a very extensive garden, outlined in what appeared to be boxwood or yew. He had stood there for several minutes before he realized that someone else was with him on the terrace: a man, leaning on the balustrade as he was, and like him probably driven there in flight from the noise and confusion in the house.

He thought he might appear uncivil in not having greeted the fellow sooner; so he uttered a platitudinous "Splendid evening, for March" as an apology.

"Yes," the man said. His tone suggested he had some reservations, however.

"You hesitate," said Edmund.

"A damned fine night, damned fine! Especially after such a difficult winter.—But how can a man enjoy it without a good cigar? What I would not give for one, and none in the house, not a one! I cannot understand how that happened. I will have someone's head on a platter for it, I can tell you."

A silence ensued.

Now, it happened that Edmund had in his pocket a case with two cigars in it. They were the last of several that Janetta had made for him in Antigua shortly before she was taken away. He had carried them about with him for months, and they were sacred to him not only because she had made them for his enjoyment, but because he had told himself—he had not actually made a vow, but he had told himself very sternly—that when he had smoked the last of these cigars, he would smoke no more. If he postponed smoking them, then he postponed giving up this small pleasure she had taught him. Thus his first instinct, when he heard this stranger wishing for a cigar, was to put his hand on the case in his jacket as if to protect it. Then he was ashamed of himself; and he thought how there was nothing finer he could do in Janetta's memory than to give one of her gifts to another. Besides, he told himself wryly, he had two; and he could assuage his grief at giving one up if he immediately smoked the other.

Having made up his mind, he pulled out the case and approached the fellow. "I have here, sir, two cigars made for me by someone dear to me in the West Indies. I cannot think of a finer use for them than that we two should enjoy them now; and I would be honored if you would join me in doing so. They are perhaps not perfectly fresh, but I expect they are about as good as you could obtain in any store in London at this season, and very likely better."

The man took a moment to register his good luck; and then cried, "Capital! Capital! My God, man, you have saved my life! In another few minutes without a smoke I would have been a raging animal, and challenged every man in the house to a duel for any trivial reason; and though I am sure I could easily have taken on the majority of them, by sheer force of numbers they would have overwhelmed me."

Edmund joined in the man's own laughter at this extravagance. Then he produced the cigars from the case, cut the tips, and gave one to the fellow; they went together to the link to light them. As the man pressed his cigar against the ember and inhaled through it, the glow increased, and Edmund caught a dim impression of a large face, powerful-looking, but not ugly by any means. He saw, too, that in form the man was very large and strongly built.

When their cigars were lit, they went back to the balustrade and stood in silence, enjoying the night sky and the rich flavor of the tobacco. Edmund would have been inclined to be melancholy, for the taste put him in mind of Janetta; and he could not help thinking that he held in his hand an earthly object that her hands had touched. Before he could lapse far into self-pity, however, his companion distracted him by speaking.

"A capital cigar! My dear sir, this—I cannot help thinking—this is the best cigar I have ever tasted in my life! And where did you say you came by it?"

"In the West Indies."

"You were there yourself?"

"Yes."

"Would it possible to obtain a supply of these?"

"I regret to say that that would be impossible. They were personally made for me by a skilled worker on our plantation there, who has since died. The entire plantation, too, has been sold."

"Ah. So be it. No pleasure in life is truly repeatable. I shall enjoy this lone cigar and remember it always. Perhaps I shall do better someday; but for now, this will be enough."

"You are a philosopher," said Edmund, surprised to find the theme of contentment offered a second time this evening.

"Not at all. I am—" and suddenly the fellow broke off and turned to Edmund. "I forget my manners—but you see, the tobacco restores me. Tarquin Esquith de Foye." He extended his hand in the darkness, and Edmund gripped it.

"Edmund Percy," he said.

"Percy? Which Percies would that be? Not Surrey?"

"The same. Brackensom is our home."

"Yes, Brackensom! I recall the name. I went to Christ Church with your brother, Mr. Christopher Percy."

"Indeed!"

"Yes, yes—very keen on cards he was. And he could hold his own at the cups as well as any man. Many a night we made our way home together; though I have to say I did not know him well otherwise. Are you a Christ's man too?"

"No, University."

"Ah! But *Oxon,* at least. What brings you to Hampshire?"

"I am visiting my aunt, Mrs. Alton, in Broadbridge, for a few weeks before my ordination."

"Mrs. Alton is Percy's aunt! I never knew that! Your mother's sister?"

"Yes."

"That might explain it in part, I suppose. How is Percy—I should say, your brother?"

"In fine health, thank you."

"Has he come in yet?"

"No; I am pleased to say that my father is in the best of health as well, and promises to be so for quite some time."

"Well, of course; but we older sons do suffer, I shall tell you. No one understands what we suffer, living in limbo, hovering like disembodied souls in the whirlwind, waiting for an event we dread. My father is my very best friend, Mr. Percy; we are more like brothers than father and son. When he goes I shall miss him every moment, every moment of every day. And yet—well, I say no more."

"I am a younger son, of course; but I think I have some insight into what you say. I have been grateful that my path to independence has been relatively rapid."

"And what is it you do?"

"I am to be ordained at Easter."

"Ah, yes, so you said. Do you have a living?"

"No, not yet."

"You were in the West Indies, you say?"

"Yes, for several years—a little interruption in my progress to orders. Strange to say, it may make me a better clergyman."

"But still a clergyman! Ye Gods, what a fate! I do not envy you that."

Edmund laughed. "I am quite looking forward to it."

"No! You cannot be serious!"

"In every respect."

"Well, God bless you then, Mr. Percy. You are made of better stuff than I. I could not bear it. I can scarcely bear *listening* to a clergyman for an hour or two on Sundays, let alone *being* one for years at a time. Have you no recourse? Your aunt is quite well off, I think. Fairhall is a splendid place."

"It all reverts to a cousin of Mr. Alton upon her death."

"Yes—of course. Too bad, though." Here Tarquin de Foye heaved a commiserating sigh, and Edmund realized that no protestation of his pleasure in becoming a clergyman would ever really persuade his host not to pity him.

They stood in silence again, smoking and watching the sky. Once a falling star dropped from the zenith; they both saw it, and somehow knew they both had seen it. At last they had to resign the fleeting pleasure of their cigars.

"Say, Percy," said Tarquin de Foye then, "do I not know your name from somewhere else besides your association with Christopher?"

"I do not see how that could be," said Edmund. "I have lived my life as quite the mote among millions."

"No—no, I am sure of it. I read the military news to my father every week as soon as we get hold of it, and I remember reading something about you, and I remember saying to him, 'The Surrey Percies—Brackensom—that must be the brother of my old pal, Christopher.'"

"You are thinking of my brother Alex, then. He took a commission, but died of a fever before he ever left England; it was some seven years ago. A notice appeared in the news; I recall it."

"Sorry to hear that—very sorry to hear that. I never had a brother, but I am sorry to hear that."

They were silent again for the space of a few minutes.

"No, Percy," said de Foye suddenly, "I am sure that is not it. It was very recently."

"There are several branches of the family, of course; it must have been—"

"No! No! I have it! *Edmund Percy,* of course!" Edmund could hear him slap his brow in the dark, punishing himself for his forgetfulness. "You were the man—the *passenger*—who took command of the Jamaica packet when those American pirates tried to capture her!"

"Oh, that," said Edmund, somewhat disingenuously. "Yes, I am the one. I do not understand all the bother about it in the papers."

"Bother in the papers! You were quite the hero, sir! My father was pounding the floor with his cane in patriotic ecstasy to hear of your exploits."

"Well, it was really nothing. The situation was absurd; what else could I do?"

"Good God, Percy," exclaimed de Foye, striding over to him and wringing his hand heartily, "I am very honored to make your acquaintance! To think you have come to Hartswound like a thief in the night—just like this, without my even knowing it! I must introduce you to Father at once, or he will never forgive me!—Have you met him yet?"

"No, I have not had that honor."

"My sister, Mariah—did you dance with her?"

"The only member of your household to whom I have been introduced—if I may make so bold as to include her in that group—is Miss Brownton, whom I believe is Miss de Foye's particular friend."

De Foye laughed. "Evelyn is our court jester here at Hartswound—our fool. We are not all quite so mad as she, or at least, not in the same way. My sister, I think, is quite sane despite us all.—Come with me, man, and I shall introduce you to my father."

"Honored, I am sure," said Edmund; and he followed Tarquin de Foye as his host strode away down the terrace.

They went to a different door than that by which Edmund had left the house. It led into a short, dark, narrow hallway, which in turn opened on a oak-paneled room no more than fifteen by thirty feet in size. The light in this room was dazzling, and the din of voices was a shock to the ears; through another wide doorway streamed as well the sounds of music and dancing. In his previous preoccupation with the halls where the dancing and dining were taking place, he had never penetrated to this inner recess.

This place, too, was packed. As his eyes adjusted, he knew at once that this was the hunting crowd, though he could not have said exactly how he knew so. He saw a particularly weatherbeaten servitor who could only have been the huntsman; he occupied a straight-backed chair set apart along one wall, while in an inner circle about two dozen men of the gentle class sat or slouched in better seats. As he entered two fine hounds leapt to their feet and raced to meet him, baying with ferocity far out of proportion to any threat he could possibly have offered. Tarquin de Foye scolded them into silence, but they insisted on sniffing the cuffs of Edmund's trousers and then licking his hands amiably.

Meanwhile Tarquin de Foye was motioning him onward. At the very back of the room a great fire was lit on a capacious hearth, and before it in a high-backed chair sat an elderly gentleman, favoring one swaddled, gouty leg on a hassock before him. The hunters, uncertainly surveying this stranger in their midst, fell silent as Edmund approached their chief.

"Father," said Tarquin de Foye, "do you recall the account I read you a couple of months ago of that passenger who took command of the West Indies packet? The captain had been killed and the crew was on the point of surrendering to an American privateer."

This question, coming as it did out of the blue, might have startled anyone; but the old man did not have to think for more than a few seconds before he said, "Of course I do. What of it?"

"Father—*ecce homo!* This is the very man—Mr. Edmund Percy, the younger brother of Mr. Christopher Percy, whom I knew at Christ's. He was on his way home from family business in the West Indies at the time. It turns out that he is the nephew of Mrs. Alton in Broadbridge and happens to be staying with her. I found him out on the terrace—can you imagine that? A national hero, here at our house, and we totally ignorant of it! And he gave me a damned fine cigar, too, Father—I do believe it was the best I have ever smoked.—Percy, this is my father, the master of Hartswound manor."

The old man stared at him in wonder. "This is the same Edmund Percy?"

"Yes, sir," said Tarquin de Foye.

"Well, good God, sir," the old man said to Edmund, "do not be so standoffish! Permit me the honor of shaking your hand!"

Edmund took the man's offered hand; the grip trembled, but there was old power in it.

"Cato Esquith de Foye, sir," said the old man.

"Edmund Percy. Deeply honored to meet you, sir," said Edmund.

"No, no—the honor is all mine! Would to God I had been with you on that ship! What a pleasure I would have had in sending those scoundrels packing!"

"Mr. Percy did a very good job of that single-handed, Father," laughed Tarquin de Foye.

"Ah, yes, but we missed the fun, Tark! We missed the fun!"

"That is indeed to be lamented," said Tarquin.

Suddenly Cato de Foye's face turned serious, almost savage, and he said to Edmund in a fierce tone, "Are you a hunter, sir?"

Edmund was somewhat taken aback by the serious tone of this change of subject; but he answered readily enough: "Why need you ask, sir? Have I not told already you that I am a Percy?"

"Well said!" cried Cato de Foye in passionate approval. "Well met, indeed! 'Have I not already told you that I am *a Percy?*'—Now, Tark, was that not well spoken?"

"Excellently well, Father," said Tarquin, and the old hunters around them murmured their approval: "Aye! Aye! Well said, well said!"

"Have you a horse with you here in Hampshire?" asked Cato.

"I came by postchaise, sir, I regret to say."

"No matter—no matter, eh, Tark?"

"I have a very fine hunter I can spare," Tarquin told Edmund. "A high-blooded mount if ever there was one. What say we go out for a ride tomorrow?"

"I am your man," said Edmund with keen interest; for he loved to ride.

"Well said," cried Cato happily again. He shifted inadvertently, and his movement apparently caused a twinge of pain in his gouty limb; his face fell and his lips twisted. "Blast my age," he said. There was a sympathetic murmur from the old hunters on all sides. "I cannot tell you, Percy, how hard it is to sit at the head of the steps and see the hunt go off without me. The horns wind, and the hounds cry, and the hoofs thunder, and all without me. I feel as if they have fastened my heart to a chain and are drawing it out of my very body when they go. Someday I shall ride again, I swear it!"

A deep, dubious silence met this remark, lightened only by the distant music and conversation that wound its way into this sanctum. Cato de Foye fretted about and managed to get his leg better situated; and then he motioned Edmund nearer, and laid an imploring hand on his sleeve. "Now," he said, "I want to hear the whole story again—in your own words—if you will indulge an old man, sir."

It would have been impossible to refuse him outright; but Edmund made an effort to demur. "I fear to disappoint you, sir," he said. "The papers undoubtedly made the event more heroic than it was; and I can only tell you the truth, which will show the incident to be more a matter of merely following out the only possibilities open to me than one of action on the heroic scale."

"Pshaw, man," said Cato de Foye delightedly. He looked around the circle of hunters. "We shall see through his modesty, shall we not?"

"Hear, hear," said the old hunters.

There was no getting around it. Edmund took a deep breath and wondered where to begin. Meanwhile, Tarquin de Foye shoved a chair close to him. "Here, Percy," he said, "take a seat."

Edmund thanked him and sat down. The room grew quiet; the old hunters looked at him with rheumy eyes, waiting expectantly.

"I boarded the packet in Jamaica," Edmund began.

"Excuse me, Father," said a soft voice from the doorway.

They all turned to look at the interrupter; it was Miss de Foye, standing with one hand on the doorframe, looking at her father. Edmund rose immediately, but she continued to look past him as though he did not exist. Behind her, at a slight distance, stood Evelyn Brownton; and behind her was a bevy, or perhaps a gaggle, of other young women, tittering and giggling, but clearly awed by their near approach to the cave of the hunters.

How Cato de Foye was insensible to her appeal, Edmund could not conceive; her mere beauty was daunting, and the regal dress she wore, tiara and all, made her seem not just a goddess but a queen of goddesses. But the old man threw up his hand imperiously, bidding her be silent. "Continue, sir," he said to Edmund.

It was an awkward moment. Edmund bowed to Miss de Foye to indicate his apology; and she curtsied back—somewhat coolly, he thought—to indicate her acceptance of it.

So he began a second time, though he remained standing in deference to Miss de Foye. He told the story of the privateer and the packet as briefly as he dared; and though he left nothing out, he tried his best to downplay his own role in the event. Cato de Foye sat watching him closely with a gleam in his eye and an odd half-smile on his lips.

When Edmund had finished, Cato's smile broadened into something like a grin. He turned to Tarquin. "By God, son, not only is he an Englishman, he is the finest kind of Englishman—a modest one. Tell Beversham to break out the '52 port. I want a glass for every man in this room."

"Hear, hear," said the old hunters, thumping their canes on the floor. While all were distracted, Edmund stole a look back at the doorway, but Miss de Foye and her train of followers were no longer there.

An interlude of chaos ensued. Tarquin strode off shouting after the butler, and the men in the room began peppering Edmund with questions. While he was still fielding them, a half-dozen servants entered with trays of glasses, followed by the head butler, who brought the sacred '52 himself. In a few minutes he had served the waiting hunters—the huntsman came in for his share as well, Edmund noticed—and then a hush fell. All eyes went to Cato.

He raised his glass. "To Mr. Edmund Percy," he said. "A man who combines a cool head and a passionate love for his king and country—a man not afraid to take command when weaker hands and weaker hearts are not up to their duty."

"Hear, hear!" cried the hunters, with glasses raised. Then all but Edmund drank a mouthful. The drink was apparently an elixir; a veritable groan of pleasure escaped from the assembly.

After a moment Edmund raised his own glass. "I make so bold," he said, "as to propose not one but two toasts, the only two that are fitting for a stranger such as I am among you. First, gentlemen, I offer you king and country. God speed the ships and men who fight in our behalf."

"Hear, hear!" cried the old men. "Godspeed! Down with the Frogs! Down with the Yankees! Rule Britannia!"

They all drank this time.

The port—the port—how to tell what it was like? It was like drinking God's great, vast painting of a landscape, from black earth to gold-shot sky. It was bright, dark, deep purple, blue, violet, but held tones of sunshine locked into it, and the cool shadows of the deep cellar where it had lain for years, and the starlight and moonlight that had traveled millions of miles and fallen on grapes in some hillside vineyard in Portugal.

"And your second toast?" asked Tarquin; for Edmund was in danger of forgetting it in his wonder at the port.

"Second," he said, "I offer you our hosts this evening, Mr. Cato Esquith de Foye and his family."

"Hear! Hear!" cried the old men more vociferously than ever. It was clear that the old master of the hunt meant more to them than the pathetic madman confined at Windsor Castle.

Edmund now took the seat that had previously been set for him. More toasts were offered, and the port took its slow effect. It was another hour or so before Edmund could decently make his escape, not without a further promise to Tarquin to ride with him the next morning.

He took away a reasonably clear head. He had had nothing to drink that evening but a few sips of pear wine and the glass of port, which he had imbibed very slowly. He was glad for his temperance, for the Esquith de Foyes had made a powerful impression on him, and he wanted to spend some time and thought in puzzling them out.

The ball, however, was no place to do so. With considerable difficulty he found his aunt again and suggested, more firmly this time, that they ought to go.

"Edmund, you disappoint me," she said. "I have several more partners in mind for you."

"I am to ride with Tarquin de Foye at eleven tomorrow, Aunt. I shall want to be fresh for that."

She looked at him in combined amazement and amusement. "Edmund," she said, "I never thought you to be such a climber—such a swift climber!"

"It is much to my own surprise, I assure you, that I discover this faculty in myself."

"How—?" she asked.

"I shall tell you all about it in the carriage home."

⌛⌛⌛⌛

Twenty minutes later, as Mrs. Alton's carriage bore them homeward, he was called upon to keep his promise. He recounted his meeting Tarquin de Foye and his being introduced to the old hunter himself, while his aunt listened with occasional humorous interjections. "A cigar, a cigar," she said finally. "My rectory for a cigar!"

"This has been indeed been a night of hard work, Aunt," said Edmund. "First I must have danced thirty times with fifteen young women, doing my best to plumb their characters within the limits of the fractured conversation of the dance floor; then I cross swords with the remarkable Miss Brownton, whose appetite for what little wit I can muster seems unappeasable; then I have to entertain the old hunters with an account of my doings at sea five or six months ago—which it seems they remember better than do I—all within the limits of modesty."

"Why did you not just play the *miles gloriosus,* Edmund? They would have loved that just as well."

"Well, perhaps Miss Esquith de Foye would not have; and as she was in the audience at the time, you probably would not have counseled me to do other than I did."

"*Miss de Foye* was listening to you? You did not mention that. Did she give you for your pains a world of sighs? And how did she come to be in the inner sanctum with the redcoats?"

"She appeared at the doorway to ask her father a question, but was commanded to be silent. How much of the tale she stayed for, I do not know."

"Just as well if she left. I had an odd feeling about her—you saw her play the pianoforte, did you not?"

"Yes, I had a good vantage for that."

"Did it not seem to you that she was looking about for someone?"

"Exactly, Aunt. I had the same feeling when we entered the place. Her heart is set on someone, and he was slow in joining the festivities."

"I *wonder* who it could be," said Aunt Andromeda, in a tone very much like that of a child puzzled at the contents of a wrapped Christmas gift found in a closet on the first day of Advent. The truth would come out eventually; but the speculation in the meantime would be an even greater source of entertainment.

"You can exclude everyone at the ball tonight, I think," said Edmund. "That should narrow down the field considerably. I would say he could not possibly be a resident of Hampshire; and we might throw in Wiltshire as well."

"Yes, it was amazingly mobbed. Well, the Esquith de Foyes are such colorful figures, and they give wonderful parties. Nothing is spared—except, fortunately for you, the supply of cigars."

"If the food was good, I would not know it. I never found it all evening. You had me working so hard I never had the opportunity."

"Oh, my poor famished Edmund! We must feed you when we get home. You did well, and we cannot have you starved when you ride with Mr. Tarquin."

"What an odd name his parents gave him! I kept wondering, 'Priscus? Or Superbus?' And I kept thinking, 'A little of both.'"

"Do not say that. Was it not Tarquin Superbus who had his way with Lucrece?"

"No, that was his son—who was also, unfortunately, called Tarquin.—And I wonder how Mr. Cato came by *his* name. It suits in some respects, and in other respects it is ludicrous. I cannot imagine Cato of olden times chasing foxes and calling for the '52, though he was a Tory if ever there was one."

"The squire's father was a great reader of the classics, I think, even into his old age; and Mr. Cato de Foye, until this recent unfortunate war, was no xenophobe either: he made his grand tour, and came back full of the wonders of the Continent. He had some kind of bad experience in Italy though—a rude concierge or cicerone or something, I do not know what. He always hated things Italian—music, for instance; and he always went into a fury when people gave his daughter's name the Italian pronunciation. He insisted she spell it with an *h* at the end to prevent that, though I am sure the parish records would not show one. Her father's prejudice did not stop her from learning Italian, however. I hear she is quite accomplished at it."

"How did he ever come to have such young children at such an advanced age?" asked Edmund. "Tarquin is Christopher's age; that would make him four-and-thirty.

But Miss de Foye cannot be much more than one-and-twenty. Cato looks seventy-five if he is a day."

"His wife was quite a bit younger. He did not wed until he was at least forty—he seemed by then quite the confirmed bachelor, and two generations of young women had despaired of him. Then a lady from Derbyshire who rode to hounds visited here in Hampshire; and it was an instant passion—on his side, at least. On hers—well, the Esquith de Foyes are fabulously rich, as you probably have noticed. She was about twenty-five, and produced an heir immediately. There was talk that she was so angry to lose the hunting during her lying-in that she barred her husband from the bedchamber for ten years. Finally one night when he was in his cups, he broke down the door and took her by storm. Thereafter they had a few halcyon years, until Mariah was born, and Mrs. de Foye perished in childbirth. He was quite sorry to see her go, I believe; she could run at a fence like any man.—But I think you are not quite right about Miss de Foye; she was born in '92, which would make her two-and-twenty. I recall it very well, for I . . . anyway, I recall it well."

She was recalling one of her own miscarriages, he had no doubt. She plunged on with the story.

"Mrs. Brownton had a child who died while still a nursing babe; and as Mrs. Esquith de Foye died at the same time, our apothecary then, Mr. Burtt, put two and two together and proposed that Mrs. Brownton nurse Miss de Foye—the infant Mariah, as she was then. The Browntons were not really of the class that commonly undertakes such a duty, but they were destitute all the same, and Cato de Foye rewarded them richly. I think he rather liked the thought that his child was being nursed by someone of the gentlefolk. When Mariah was almost three, Mrs. Brownton came into the family way again; and the result was the splendid girl that you have seen. Whatever happened to the poor creature's brains, I could not tell you; but they were properly scrambled somewhere before she even learned to talk."

"But she speaks very well. In fact, I would say she speaks a good deal better than many of the young women with whom you had me dancing. Certainly with less pretension."

"Yes, but she talks nonsense."

"And how does she differ in that from her peers in the neighborhood?—In fact, I would say she excels them in that regard; because she seems to know she talks nonsense, whereas they do not."

"She has been told she talks nonsense, whereas no one has dared say so to the others. I admit that Miss Brownton has been apprised of her limitations; but they are absolute and irreparable; whereas the young ladies you criticize will grow into typical specimens of the local gentry."

She looked at him with pointed humor as she said this, defying him to fling a dart at her own set. He only laughed.

"The odd thing is," she said, when he did not take up her challenge, "that it was not until about ten years ago that Miss de Foye really became clearly the superior of the two. They were both pretty little girls, Mariah with those great dark eyes and Evelyn with her fair hair. I used to meet them often in the village, scampering about together; but when they started to become women, Mariah left her friend far behind, and in every respect. She grew taller; she gained that wonderful queenly deportment she has; her figure filled out; her eyes were matched in their beauty by every other attribute of her face and figure. Her mind was expanded by her tutors—she learned French and Italian, and a little Greek from Mr. Maugham. I have heard it said she can read much of the Gospel in the original. She sings and plays as you heard, and she draws with great facility. Poor Evelyn simply did not keep up."

"I found Miss Brownton a very good dancer."

"And we were all amazed! Utterly amazed! And why did she confer this favor on you, do you think?"

"I have not the faintest idea, Aunt. She said something about how I looked kindly. I am pleased to think the poor thing did not find me threatening."

"Well, Miss Brownton's interest in you, strangely enough, seems to have quite piqued the Miss Eatons and their set. I am half afraid they will tear you to shreds like a gang of maenads at the next ball."

He was suddenly oppressed by the thought that he might marry one of the Miss Eatons. The thought of Janetta came to him powerfully; and it was a recollection compounded of a thousand sensations and infinite feelings. He tried to utter some witty response to keep his aunt off the trail; but he found he had not the heart for it. He thought she would miss the cause if he let one occasion for rejoinder pass; but she instantly read the truth in his silence. In all likelihood she had felt a change in him from his first arrival in Hampshire.

"Edmund, my dear," she said with real concern, "I sense your heart is not in this."

Again he could not bring himself to answer.

"When a young man only *pretends* to pursue young women, that means one thing and one thing alone."

Still he said nothing.

"Can you tell me, dear?" she asked. Her voice was full of the genuine care and affection she felt; and now he took her hand and patted it.

"Thank you for noticing," he said. "It is all over now. I am trying to obey you and be a good nephew."

"It was someone superior to Miss Eaton, I gather," she said, squeezing his hand.

He gave a faint laugh. "Miss Eaton is a hollow shell by comparison, I am afraid."

"Someone you knew in the West Indies?"

"Yes."

"And is it quite over, Edmund? It does not seem so."

"She is dead, Aunt. She was lost at sea in a hurricano last autumn."

His aunt wept for him instantly, holding his hand in both of hers; and said no more for another mile.

"Dear Edmund," she said then, "I hope you do not think ill of me for throwing these young women at you."

"Not at all. It is only appropriate. I am much like a man who has lost his appetite in a fever. The fever is gone, but still I have no interest in eating. I look at the food, and it turns my stomach. The cook prepares her finest dainties for my relish, and I know I ought to feast; but I cannot bring myself to care."

"But you *must* care, Edmund. You *must* marry. You must have a kind, pretty, comfortable wife, and at least a half-dozen fine children. You must be as happy as Mr. Alton and I were. Happier, because you will have children. Marriage, properly conducted, is the happiest of all states—the closest we get to heaven on earth."

"I am pleased to hear your recommendation on that point. I have heard other opinions expressed."

"Edmund, Edmund—you must believe me. It would be a dreadful thing if you have been spoiled for the company of an ordinary good woman!"

"I would not say the case is as desperate as that. I have come to terms with the fact that I shall never find a woman such as I have lost. Or at least I tell myself I have come to those terms; or that I must and shall. It is not *that;* it is rather that . . ."

"That what, Edmund?"

"That I have changed, too. I still feel . . . somehow wrong in encouraging the affections of a Miss Eaton or any of your other village belles; or of any ordinary English girl, for that matter."

"Oh, dear! I fear the damage has been extensive," said his aunt.

"Yes, it has been. It damaged my moral fiber. I almost gave up the thought of taking orders, Aunt. Actually, I did give it up for a time."

"Not take orders! Edmund, this is extreme indeed. What would you have done?"

"Oh, I had a wild plan about becoming a manager in the West Indies."

"Not really! Tell me you did not truly think of that! A manager—a plain, crass, man of business! Not my Edmund!"

"I am afraid it is true."

"But they are rumored to be such—such a carnal crew, the managers there."

"I felt fit for nothing better. I still am not sure I am fit to minister."

At this she was stunned for a minute; and then she took him by the arm, and leaned against him, and lifted her face close to his.

"Dear nephew," she said, "no one was ever more fit. Now I understand. This loss you have suffered, this grief you carry—it has brought up all that softness and loving-kindness in you that is the legacy of your mother. And it is a legacy worth far more than the legacy of your father, and all his forefathers! It will carry you to heaven, Edmund, while all their gold could not. Forgive me for my foolishness tonight. I did not know."

"There is nothing to forgive. You did the right thing, the best thing; you brought the convalescent to the feast, and bid him taste of life again."

She was reassured by his answer, and sat back in her seat again, with one last pat of his arm. "You challenge me, Edmund. And I love a challenge."

"Persuade me that I may in good conscience marry Miss Eaton or one of her ilk, and I shall be grateful to you. But my heart is at the bottom of the sea."

"Ah, but you still notice a pretty face and a fine figure."

"True."

"That is a sign of returning health."

"Perhaps. But I think it rather a mere animal action. The automaton receives a command, and it moves."

"Of course you feel that way. But soon the mind will react as well; and when the mind decides to notice, the heart may tag along, through sheer lack of anything else to fix itself on. Then you will see how very comfortable you would be with Miss Eaton. That would be a fine face next to you on the pillow, you know; and across from you at teatime, by the fire in the rectory in Broadbridge, with your dear aunt just coming in the door, a basket of scones on one arm, and a half-dozen toddling children coming to greet her."

He laughed, despite himself, at her fancy, and she laughed with him.

"Miss Eaton is it to be, then?" he said.

"I do think she is rather the best of the lot."

"I will take another look," he promised her good-naturedly, though it could not have escaped her that again his heart was not in his words.

"For now, that is all I ask," she said.

"Look, we are home," said Edmund. "And just as well for me, or I would soon be an open book to you."

Chapter 21

Hast thou given the horse strength? hast thou clothed his neck with thunder? . . . He mocketh at fear, and is not affrighted; neither turneth he back from the sword. . . . He swalloweth the ground with fierceness and rage: neither believeth he that it is the sound of the trumpet. He saith among the trumpets, Ha, ha; and he smelleth the battle afar off, the thunder of the captains, and the shouting.

—Job 19, 22, 24–25

T*he next* morning Aunt Andromeda insisted Edmund take the carriage up to Hartswound Park. "You must not slouch into the place like a gypsy," she said. "We have Mr. Alton's wealth behind us for now, and we must use it to effect." She ordered it made ready, and when it was at the door, and he was about to rise from the breakfast table to depart, she laid a hand on his arm and stopped him. "I have only one word of warning, Edmund, dear."

"Let me guess what it is."

"Ah, Edmund! We know each other too well, you and I. After our talk in the carriage yesterday, I had some sad premonitions that kept me awake all night. You have been hurt; and I have so often noticed that when young people have once been hurt in love, they keep seeking out situations in which their affections cannot be returned. It is as if they mean to overcome vicariously the obstacle they encountered in their first love. Their hearts become a kind of compass that points them at misery. Instead of following the sunlight that they can see ahead at the mouth of the cavern in which they have been wandering, they are drawn off into side galleries that lead only into more darkness."

He smiled. "You think I will be drawn to the poor, pretty, mad girl," he guessed.

"No—not that. I think there is something much more dangerous at Hartswound Park. Someone infinitely more beautiful and accomplished, someone utterly out of your reach, someone who already loves another. It stands to reason you will break yourself on her as a ship drawn by sirens breaks itself on a reef."

He laughed easily. "You have nothing to fear on that score. I would sooner fall in love with an Olympian. One thing I know, Aunt, and that is my place. I am a third son. I shall be lucky if I can get one of your Miss Eatons."

"But you go into danger, Edmund. I would rather send you into the fray against those vile Americans than see you spend any time in the company of a certain person at Hartswound. She is *too* beautiful."

"She is indeed beautiful. But you need only fear for me if she turns out to be as kind as she is beautiful. Kindness is the only quality in a woman with which I shall ever fall in love."

As he said this, it occurred to him that they were fine words, but only borrowed from Mr. Blackmore, and in fact were as yet in large part a lie. He had loved the kindness in Janetta, but he had also loved her sexual passion. Yet what he said might as well be true; for he was sure that nowhere in England would he find a temptation to match the one Janetta had offered.

He made as if to rise again, but he saw from his aunt's expression that his answer had increased rather than assuaged her concern. He hesitated and said to her, "Why do you still look so?"

She dropped her gaze from his. "Never mind, Edmund."

He reconsidered the conversation, and said in surprise, "Is this lady so particularly kind, then?"

His aunt hesitated; then she said, "I fear she is."

"I would not have thought it, from what I saw last night."

"Perhaps not; but she was preoccupied last night, and not herself."

"And what makes you say this about her?"

"If you stay in Broadbridge long enough, you will not be able to help noticing it. The poor in the parish look upon her as an angel."

He felt a chill suddenly.

"Then pray for me," he said.

"Edmund! Remember your place!"

"Aye, dear aunt," he said, rallying. "Never fear. Though I tease you about it, I am too wise to fall in love with Miss de Foye."

"Do you promise me?"

"Of course. I cannot promise to fall *in* love with any particular lady you specify; but I shall do my best to stay *out* of love with a certain regal young lady at Hartswound Park."

"Thank you, Edmund," she said. "I must trust you if you promise that. And you must let your thoughts dwell on Miss Eaton instead."

He affected a complacent look. "Yes, on Miss Eaton, and on my recent sojourn in West India," he said.

She laughed, charmed and charming as always, and with that she let him go.

⌛⌛⌛⌛

By daylight Hartswound Park and its manor house were even more impressive, though Edmund again found them by comparison only at best the equal, and not the superior, of his own home of childhood. His aunt had said that the park was comparable in size to the estate in Surrey, being several thousand acres in extent. The long drive here was generally straighter and on more level ground than the approach into Brackensom. It was thus better built and more finely graveled; and the sight of a small crew of servants with rakes tending it argued that it was at least as well kept. But it did not follow the willowy banks of the Brake, as did the road at home, passing instead through a wood that was in aspect uniform, if not monotonous. Still—it was an extraordinary wood, deep and ancient, and trimmed back from the road to make of the drive almost a gently winding allee, the very austerity of its gray walls somehow promising the green leafage of spring. About a half mile from the house, which it approached from the southeast, it opened onto lavish rolling fields of perhaps five hundred acres in extent, broken by inviting copses and scattered monuments of chalkstone. At the far side of these rich fields was the manor house, facing true south toward the drive. It was girt by a rectangle of walls, within which were a dozen lesser divisions—a lawn before the house; the garden of ornamentals on the left side, which he had glimpsed in the dark last night from the terrace; kitchen gardens to the right; at least one flower garden; and he knew not what else. To the northeast of the house was an extensive range of stone outbuildings nearly as impressive in architecture as the house itself; he would later find them to include several barns, a stable, three enormous kennels, servants' quarters, a dairy, a spring house, a brewery, an oast house, and even a stone chicken coop that suggested that in their ancient warfare with the fox, the Esquith de Foyes had stinted in no fortification. To the northwest, beyond the terrace, the gardens bordered the woods.

When the carriage stopped before the house, Edmund found a servant waiting for him. He was led directly to the stables, where he came upon Tarquin de Foye and several grooms saddling a couple of horses.

The first words out of Edmund's mouth were, "What a beautiful hunter!"

Tarquin looked up from a girth strap with a grin. "Is he not, though—the finest in Hampshire, if I know my horses. Good morning, Percy."

"Good morning, de Foye."

"This brute is mine; that one is yours. What do you think of him?"

Edmund took a moment to inspect his horse; it was a tall, long-boned hunter, graceful in limb like a deer, as the breeds ran then; more like a racing thoroughbred than a horse that ought to be charging at hedges and leaping ditches; but in any case a strikingly beautiful horse, with fire in his eye. "Magnificent, and not a whit the lesser, from anything I can see," said Edmund.

"Good, then: we shall see fairly who is the better rider."

"That we shall," said Edmund; and they grinned at each other.

They warmed the horses in a ride to a little hill amid the fields where weathered grasses crowned an upcrop of chalk; there they paused for a few minutes, looking over the landscape.

"I have never been to your place in Surrey," said Tarquin. "How does it compare?"

"It is strikingly the same, as a matter of fact," Edmund replied. "My father's passion is agriculture, so there is a good deal of that in evidence; and we have the River Brake before the house, which is a beautiful view. I think our hills may be a bit steeper, despite its being Surrey. But in size the house is quite similar, and the wood and the hunting looks to be much the same."

"Good again; I would not take an unfair advantage of you."

"Shall we see what these beasts can do, then?"

"By all means. Do you see that path that opens on the edge of the wood there, on the northern edge of the field? We shall take it. It goes deep into the park, around the house at a good distance, and then swings close again and comes out into the open near the garden where we were smoking last night. There is another path that leads off toward Broadbridge, a couple of miles through the wood; if we like, we shall take that as well."

"I shall meet you in Broadbridge, then," said Edmund. "I shall be at the inn, finishing my second pint, if I have grown tired of waiting for you in the street."

Tarquin laughed aloud, and then set his heels to his horse without further warning.

And so they were off; and a madder, wilder ride Edmund never took in his life. Younger sons are often fiercely competitive, and the better sportsmen of their families; and though Edmund had outgrown the open expression of his athletic jealousies, the boy still lived in him, as it does in all men; no less than the girl lives in the woman.

On that anomalously sunny and bracing March morning and noon he forgot, for the first full hour in all the months since Janetta's death, forgot the pain of his wound; forgot his self-torment over his calling; forgot the troubles in his own family, compounded of griefs and looming misunderstandings and schisms. He rode even as the horse ran, that is, delighting in nothing but his own animal athletic power. Like a mixture of the smoke of opium and the spur of black coffee, the preoccupying pleasure of raw physical action blotted out the images that haunted him: Janetta on the last morning he had seen her; the ragged line of slaves walking away from him toward Duckworth's; the little cockboat tossed in the chop of the Atlantic, illumined by a flickering lantern as it turned to find safety in the distant black bulk that was the enemy's ship. All grief fled away, all melted like mist in this late morning sun, sure to come back, but banished for the moment.

Like madmen they rode. The horses would do anything: dare any barrier, leap any gap. Edmund was the first to jump his horse, or more accurately, to soar it, for he felt as if he were flying. The horse's form was perfect, and so was his own; and so, he saw, when Tarquin edged past him and beat him to the next jump, was the form of Tarquin's horse in jumping, and so was Tarquin's in riding. He caught Tarquin's laughter, flung back over his shoulder; and then he spurred, and they raced neck and neck down a narrow forest path, headlong for what outcome Edmund knew not. The way opened up again in a beautiful glade crossed by a sizeable brook. Tarquin, perhaps from habit, went to the left; but in a flash Edmund saw an alternative route that went to the right, requiring a longer jump over the stream bed from bank to bank. This he took, gaining in the shift a good twenty yards on his opponent.

Thus it went, from minute to minute; sometimes Edmund was ahead, sometimes Tarquin. He could not have said how far they rode, or how long their circuit took; but when they reached the farthest opening of the path, by the garden gate and the terrace near the house, he was slightly in the lead. He drew up to see what his host wished to do.

Tarquin was grinning from ear to ear. "By God, Percy, you have beat me on my own turf!" he said.

"But on your own horse, if that is a consolation," said Edmund.

"It is *not!* Not for an instant. To hell with Broadbridge. What do you say we run the same route again? This time I shall beat you and uphold the honor of the Esquith de Foyes, or I shall break my neck trying."

"'Tis no dishonor to be bested by a Percy," said Edmund.

Tarquin laughed aloud. "I take that for an 'aye,' then," he said; but without answering, Edmund turned his horse about and dashed away. He could hear Tarquin still laughing as he gave chase.

They followed the circuit of the outer stone walls, crossed the drive, and rode toward the outcrop where they had started; before they reached it, however, Tarquin struck off at an angle and made for the path. This time Edmund was hard pressed to keep up with him. The difference in strength between the two horses was becoming apparent, and Tarquin rode even more recklessly than he had before. He took the cutoff over the stream that Edmund had discovered, as well as several other more hazardous options they had not seized on the first lap; only once did Edmund pass him, and then only to fall behind on a straight stretch.

When they came to the garden gate again, Tarquin was in the lead by about as much as Edmund had been the first time.

"You have won once, and I have won once," said Tarquin. "You must come back, and we will ride a third time—a hundred times, if we have to."

"As many times as you like," said Edmund.

"You see your mount is not quite the match of mine," said Tarquin.

"You are right; he is flagging a bit, though a wonderful brute by any standard, a veritable Pegasus."

"I am glad you like him—very glad, Percy. You are every bit the rider for him."

Suddenly Tarquin put his hand to his head. "Look!" he said. "We have lost our hats." They both laughed. "I will send a boy out to look for them. We will cool these beasts and then I hope you will come in and see Father."

"It would be a pleasure," said Edmund.

They turned toward the stable and continued at a slower pace. As they did, Edmund noticed that the flanks of Tarquin's horse were slightly bloody. He said nothing of it; instead he asked, "How *is* your father today?"

"Much better, thank you for asking," said Tarquin. "I saw him shortly before you came; he said his gout greatly improved overnight. He was hobbling about rather spryly."

"It must have been the '52," said Edmund.

"Ah, the '52!" laughed Tarquin. "If only a man could drink '52 every day, he would live forever. Perhaps that is what they drink in Mahomet's heaven, eh? With a swarm of new virgins every night."

"It is just as well the Mahometans cannot prove that is the case," said Edmund, "or half of England would be infidel by now."

"I must say, for a man who is about to become a clergyman, you ride like the very Devil, Percy! Did they train you up to do that at Oxford? Must a man be able to take fences as high as a house before they let him take orders now?"

"'A man's a man, for all that,'" said Edmund. "You would not have me forget how to ride, or forget how to dance or play cards or enjoy a glass of '52, just because I mean to take orders?"

"God forbid! I rather rejoice for you."

"A clergyman of the Church of England is not a monk, thank God. Old King Henry set us free of that, though we do not always thank him properly."

"But do you really mean to settle down, and give sermons, and soberly christen babes, and church new mothers, and wed and bury folk?"

"I do indeed, as I told you last night. I did not think you believed me then, and I do not think you really believe me now."

"And where will you look for a parish?"

"Somewhere in the country."

"What? You have no ambition, then?"

"Ah, I do have an ambition: an ambition to be a country clergyman."

"But why not in town, man, where people will see you? You will be very likely to get ahead. You are a good-looking chap, too; some rich widow is sure to take a liking to you. Then you could preach or not, as you pleased."

Edmund laughed and shook his head. "It would not suit, de Foye. I know you do not believe me, but I have no desire to be Archbishop of Canterbury. As for your widow, my aunt will soon find me a companionable creature; which is all I really deserve, or can require; and I shall spend my life trying to be good to her. That effort will be riches enough."

Tarquin was silent a minute. Then he said, "I admire you, Percy. I never really understood till this minute what it must be like to be a younger son. I hope that if I were in your shoes, I should do what you have done: adopt a philosophy that sets forth my lot in life as a noble one. Diogenes would be proud of you, and welcome you into his barrel, or wherever it was he lived."

Edmund smiled wryly. "It is not so terrible a fate, de Foye. I really rather think that if you and I were to compare our careers through life at the very end, I might actually be a few yards ahead of you; and even my orders, which you look upon as a sorry old broken-down hunter, will carry me over many a hedge where yours will balk, master though you may be of Hartswound Park and all its splendors."

Tarquin guffawed. "Really, Percy!" he said incredulously. "You are too a keen a competitor. If you cannot win, you insist on *imagining* you can. But I like your bloody spirit, fellow; and I admire the way you ride. When you took those two downed trees, there, I thought you would break every bone in your body, and aye, in your horse's body, too!"

"And I thought you were a goner when you went down that rock—what were you thinking, man? Since when do horses run down the face of a cliff?"

They both laughed again, and then Tarquin added, "We both rode like fools, did we not? But 'tis good to have someone here as mad as I am. Well, maybe not quite as mad; but that is just as well for you. I would not want you to be as mad as I am."

And there was something about the way he spoke that made Edmund look suddenly at him. For all his affability, for all his hail-fellow-well-met graciousness, there was a rage and brutality lurking in Tarquin that Edmund sensed could be fatal to someone if not controlled; perhaps even fatal to Tarquin himself. He said he loved his father, and certainly he did; but he chafed, also, at being more than thirty and still not his own man; and the decades of being the son of Cato Esquith de Foye, of being the expectant heir, of being always the lesser, had stung him to a kind of madness. This was the very canker that was eating at Christopher as well. Truly in that instant Edmund understood the lot of oldest sons better; and could not help thinking that the patrimonial system under which they lived was hopelessly wrong-headed, a relic of a feudal time that served no one well in this modern age.

They walked their horses cool, continuing their conversation. Tarquin told him about the property, its age and extent, its many buildings and servitors, its rents. Edmund found him well informed, much better informed than Christopher had been in the years before his return to Brackensom; but then again, Tarquin had lived at home since he had come down from Oxford.

After handing the reins of their horses over to the grooms, they turned back to the house. "Will you stay to dinner?" asked Tarquin.

"I should enjoy that," said Edmund.

"I hope you are not absolutely famished; we shall not eat until three."

"I shall bear it."

"And I did promise Father I would bring you in again by light of day. Besides, you cannot go back to town without your hat."

On the way into the house, Edmund, mindful that his aunt needed the carriage that afternoon, dismissed her coachman, with a message for her to the effect that he would walk back to Broadbridge. "I tell you what," said Tarquin, when he heard this. "Take the way through the woods by the garden gate. It is shorter, and a very pleasant walk. And that way you will have a look at the lay of the land, so that the next time we ride, I shall not have any advantage of you in that respect."

"Very well," said Edmund.

⌛⌛⌛⌛

The house was far quieter today. Servants still were at work cleaning up: some had just hoisted the candelabra in the front hall back into place after cleaning out the dead candles; some were polishing the floor and the woodwork, as Edmund was sure they had done only a day or two ago; and others were arranging some heavy tables in their accustomed places. Despite this minor activity, the great house now had an atmosphere of sleepy, almost brooding peace, the very mood Edmund remembered feeling in the halls of Brackensom in his youth. Tarquin led him through the long hall, which seemed not to miss its throng of misses, and into a library with high Venetian windows opening onto the terrace. Edmund had only passed briefly through this room when exiting the den of the hunters last night; that innermost sanctum did not look out on the terrace. The two dogs that had greeted him last night repeated their performance, though without the barking this time. He patted and they sniffed; and then they trotted away.

By daylight, and with more leisure to look about him, he found this library a very pleasant room. It contained some two thousand or so volumes, bound in deep reds and browns and greens, with gilt aplenty, ever-fresh to the eye, in high cases, folios at the bottom, quartos next, and octavos at eye level and above. The floor of the room seemed to be an exotic wood, perhaps ebony, or mahogany with a very dark stain; or perhaps a very dark walnut, almost black. One would have thought it to be a black marble, but it was warmer in tone and quieter beneath the foot.

Various sofas and chairs were arranged about the room. They looked rather more comfortable than the fashion then current. At a table of middling height between two of the straighter chairs was a finely wrought and very old chessboard, with quaint ivory pieces of a fashion he had never seen before. In another chair, close to the pale March sunlight streaming in through the window, Cato Esquith de Foye sat with an old book on his lap, at which he peered through a lorgnette that seemed to be more irritating than helpful. His gouty leg was elevated on a hassock.

"Good afternoon, Father," said Tarquin. "I have brought our naval hero to see you."

Cato was startled and took a moment to orient himself. Then he cried, "Splendid! Mr. Percy, is it? Come sit by the light, sir."

"Good afternoon, Mr. de Foye."

"Mr. Percy is not only a foiler of pirates, Father," said Tarquin. "He is true to his name and race, and a capital horseman."

"Is that so, sir? Is that so?"

"Yes, we must get him into the hunt."

"By all means! Where did you ride?"

"We took the path round to the north through the park; Percy jumped the stream at a spot where I have never seen anyone dare it before. Do not let this gentle priestly demeanor fool you—he is quite the madman when you get him on horseback."

"You yourself took the stream in the very same spot on the second lap," Edmund pointed out.

"Of course he did!" said Cato. "You do not think Tark would let himself be bested, do you?"

"Ah, but Percy here won the first lap, Father."

"And you won the second, I shall wager."

"That he did," said Edmund.

"That, Mr. Percy," said Cato, "is my son, through and through. He cannot stand to be bested; he will always try harder, he will do whatever it takes."

Tarquin laughed. Edmund thought of the horse's bloody flanks and wondered if Tarquin would be laughing so pleasantly now if he had not won the second course—if he might not rather be bitter and brooding.

"Percy has consented to stay for dinner, if that is agreeable, Father."

"Of course, of course—delighted to have you, Percy. I cannot remember the last time we had one of your ancient lineage in our house.—We must tell Beversham to bring up that good claret we had last week."

"Yes, Father. Percy should enjoy that."

"You will have me spoiled," said Edmund. "I shall go back to Surrey reluctant to drink water. I shall call for wine to wash my hands."

His hosts laughed, pleased with the thought.

"I say, Percy," said Tarquin, "I will leave you with Father while I go change. Sorry you have nothing to change into."

"Quite all right. I can bear it if my hosts can."

Tarquin went away, and Edmund sat in the chair to which Cato had directed him.

"Do you know anything about bees, Percy?" asked Cato.

"I am very fond of bees, actually. We have above a hundred stalls at Brackensom, and I used to help the keepers when I was a boy."

"A *hundred*, you say? That is a prodigious number."

"My father's hobby is improvements," Edmund explained.

"Ah, of course. I understand that. I have been too busy hunting all my life to do much of that. I have more dogs than I can remember, but only five stalls here, though very good honey they give. I have an entire garden devoted to flowers for the little things. And once a year, come winter, I reread the Fourth."

Edmund was startled. "The Fourth Georgic, sir?"

"Yes. It is my very favorite."

Edmund was impressed, until he considered that Cato probably had not kept up his Latin, but read Vergil in translation.

"Though I must say," added Cato, "that it is full of some very strange ideas. Bees from a dead cow! Now, that is very odd."

"Quite comical, from our modern perspective," agreed Edmund.

"Now, what do you think of this mystery about queens?"

"What do you mean, exactly?"

"How they vary the eggs they lay between worker and drone, and get each egg in the right type of cell."

"Refresh my memory on this matter, if you would. As I recall, there is one theory that the drone goes about fecundating the eggs, which are essentially glued into the cells by the queen. The worker cell and its opening are of a size that they allow the drone not only to reach the egg but to apply its organ in such a way as to fecundate it, either by direct contact, or by some kind of acrid or oily discharge close to it; so the workers are born of fecundated eggs. The drones are born in larger cells, whose very size prevents the proper application of the drone's organ; so the drones are born of unfecundated eggs."

Cato was impressed. "You information is exact, Mr. Percy," he said, "and you have no reason to fault your recollection."

"The other theory holds that the queen is fecundated for life by the drone on her nuptial flight. She herself distinguishes between the cells of worker and drone in some unknown manner."

"Yes, yes," said Cato, eager to disdain the idea. "That is what Huber says here." He waved the book, which was still pinned closed on one finger. "But he is a frog, sir. Can we respect him?"

"I believe he is Swiss," said Edmund uncertainly.

"Ah, yes, you may be right. That would be somewhat better. But he *writes* in French."

"Well, he must communicate in some language, I suppose; and he had the misfortune to be born on the Continent."

"But to mate for life! No, more than that, to mate once, and then no more, and bear, what—thousands and thousands of eggs each season."

"Over sixty thousand, if I recall," said Edmund.

"Yes, yes; and the queen may live for three or four years. It is an astounding number."

"It has no parallel in human mating, true; but there are many wondrous things in the animal kingdom."

"But imagine it! That would indeed be some power of fecundation, sir, to impregnate a woman, and have her bear children constantly until she died."

"Fortunately for the gentle sex, God has withheld that power from us."

"Fortunately for us as well, I should think. I should not like to mate just once and die, like a drone!"

"Nor I, sir. But that is what Huber holds to be the case with the bees."

"But do you accept his theory?"

Edmund considered the question for a moment. "I incline to think he must be incorrect; I believe that it will be found that the drone works in the stall in the manner Swammerdam and others have suggested."

"Exactly!" cried Cato, pounding the arm of his chair with his hand in triumph. "This Huber frog *cannot* be right; though I would be the first to admit that he is wonderfully knowledgeable about my little friends."

"But you must admit too that no one has ever shown him to be wrong; that is, no one has ever actually observed the fecundating activities of the drone in the stall."

"Ah! Is that so? I had thought we had some evidence for that."

"No; it is only a deduction from the shape and size of their generative parts. Or at least as far as I recall. They have been seen to scrounge somewhat lazily and diffidently through the stall for honey, or so we suppose. But the so-called nuptial flight is a well-observed phenomenon."

"Yes; I have seen that myself; though by calling it the nuptial flight we prejudice our construction of its meaning."

"True. I suppose, pending further investigation, the question must remain open; though it behooves us to operate on the assumption that the more sensible notion is correct, and the drone fecundates eggs."

"You are a man of science, sir!"

"You flatter me, Mr. de Foye. In the study of bees, you have merely hit upon one of my interests."

"But I am glad we agree. We must go see my stalls; and you will tell me if they are not as well cared for as any you have in Surrey."

Edmund laughed. "I would be glad to see them, sir, though I would not like to inconvenience you."

"Pshaw!" cried Cato. He put aside his book, and after a bit of a struggle, shifted his weight to his feet and rose from the chair. Edmund handed him his cane, and they began a slow but steady progress out of doors, accompanied by the dogs, who ran frolicking about the terrace and garden, forming a marked and almost mocking contrast to the sedate pace of their master.

The air had warmed considerably. Even on the terrace, before they had traversed its length, they saw one or two bees zoom by them, perhaps scouts weighing the possibility that spring had come. Cato led Edmund through a small doorway in the stone wall at the northern end of the terrace, and here Edmund found a very pleasant sight: an enclosed garden packed with what must have been hundreds of varieties of flowering plant, no few of them already showing signs of green. Against a sun-drenched stone wall bedecked with vines stood five skeps, scrupulously clean, each on its own pedestal. Edmund could imagine how the activity of the bees around these apartments in the summer would create a shimmering aura in the air.

They approached quite close to the hives and examined them. "There is every sign that these are clean and fit," said Edmund. "You take superior care of them."

"Thank you, Mr. Percy. It is good to hear one's efforts appreciated."

Thereafter they continued, for quite some time, to discuss the care of the insects, each enjoying the company of a knowledgeable aficionado. It was a very pleasant hour. Cato showed none of the brusqueness or crustiness that Edmund had detected in him at moments on the previous evening; he was instead all soft smiles, all fondness for his hobby, avidly boyish. The sun was warm despite the season, replete with promise of the coming spring; the spot utterly peaceful; and for Edmund in that golden moment the ache of grief receded a bit more, though its recession down the sands of time was slow, like the ebbing of the sea, which throbs lower and lower on the shingle by turns as the tide flows away.

Eventually Tarquin found them. "Aha!" he said. "I was certain you must be here." He kept well away from the hives, Edmund noticed.

"Mr. Percy and I have had an excellent discussion of the bees," said Cato. He and Edmund turned and began the slow walk back to the library "Our new acquaintance is quite knowledgeable on this score."

"That is all very fine, Father," said Tarquin, "as long as he can ride, too." He swatted nervously at a lone returning bee. "I have no use for bees myself, Percy. Nasty little things!"

Cato paused and nodded knowingly to Edmund. "It is Mariah who is the lover of bees, Mr. Percy. You ought to see her, decked out in her netting, with a smoker in one hand, patiently tending to their little wants, no matter how they buzz in fury and swarm about her! It is a lovely sight.—You have met my daughter, Mr. Percy?"

"No, sir, not to speak to, though of course I saw her at a distance last night."

"Where is she, Tark? Off at Maugham's again?"

"Yes," said Tarquin, who had retreated to the door of the garden, and was holding it open for his father.

"And that madcap friend of hers!" said Cato, chuckling. "She puts on netting, too, and stands there with her eyes wide, absolutely entranced."

Tarquin, too, laughed as he recalled the sight. "It is one of the few times you will ever catch Evelyn Brownton with her mouth shut," he explained to Edmund. "I told her once to keep it closed or a bee would fly in; and ever since then she has kept it tightly buttoned whenever she gets near the skeps, whether she is wearing netting or not."

They made their way back up the terrace and into the house, and Tarquin saw his father comfortably settled again. "Your foot is indeed a great deal better today, Father," he observed.

"Yes," said Cato. "But not yet well enough for me to put it in a stirrup, I am afraid."

"Hardly, Father!"

"Oh, do not give me one of your gloomy speeches, Tark! I am sick of them. I quite wanted to be out there with you two young scamps, leaping hedges; and here I sat inside. I have lived too long if I shall never ride again; so do not tell me that."

"Very well; I will forbear for once."

Cato turned to Edmund. "The worst of it is, Mr. Percy, that I cannot even *watch* the riding," he said.

"Well, why not have a chair carried just outside the front gate here?" suggested Edmund. "Tarquin will have a course set up in the fields, and we will ride at fences to entertain you."

Both father and son were enormously pleased with this idea.

"Capital!" cried Tarquin

"Excellent!" cried Cato. "Why not, Tark?"

"Why not, indeed?—Can you ride day after tomorrow, Percy? About the same time?"

"I am quite the man of leisure on this visit. I should think that my aunt does not have any particular plans; but if I find she does, I shall send to you to let you know. Otherwise, expect me at eleven."

"Capital!" exclaimed Tarquin again.

⧗ ⧗ ⧗ ⧗

The dinner was a very good and rich repast. Though Cato partook more gingerly, on the advice of his doctor, Edmund and Tarquin fell to with a special will: they consumed, among other things, an abundance of soup, savory puddings, fresh pork, rabbit, pickles, dried fruit, and jellies. After dinner they all bemoaned the lack of cigars, but consoled themselves with more of that good claret Beversham had produced from the cellar, and retired to the library again. Tarquin picked up a newspaper recently sent from town, and Edmund and Cato sat down to the chessboard.

Cato opened with a standard move, the king's gambit; but thereafter his play was all wild attack. He left his center open; he could not castle; he was moving pawns up the board for no reason; and before he even knew what was happening, Edmund had him in checkmate.

He turned to his son in astonishment. "My God, Tark! He has beaten me already!"

"What!" said Tarquin. "You just began! He cannot have beaten you."

"I have been soundly whipped! What was it, Mr. Percy, a dozen moves apiece?"

Tarquin rose and came to look at the board, which he surveyed in amazement.

"Do not worry, Father," he said. "I shall beat him when next we ride."

"You must, for the honor of our family," said Cato. "Now, Mr. Percy, let us set up again, and have us some more claret, and we will proceed more slowly this time."

"Very good, sir," said Edmund.

"I take some comfort in having been beaten by a Percy. The Percies are a fine old family. I would hate to be beaten by some upstart."

"Yes," agreed Tarquin. "If one has to suffer defeat every once in a while, it is only remotely sufferable if one has a noble opponent."

"It keeps you sharp," allowed Cato.

They played again, and this time Cato was more on his game and considerably harder to beat. His defeat, however, was just as inevitable, if more agonizing. He grew restless in the endgame, and Edmund thought it best to indefinitely postpone the grim finalities. "What do you say we continue some other time, sir?" he asked. "I ought to be going back to the village."

"Very well," said Cato. "We shall keep the pieces just as they are, and after you return for your ride with Tark, I shall turn the tables on you and crush you. You do not mind if I study the board a bit in your absence?"

"Not at all, sir. It is a legal advantage, seeing that you are host."

Edmund had no expectation of seeing the pieces in their places when he returned; and in fact when next he saw them they were reset for a new game, and no further notice taken of the unfinished endgame, which was, in any case, a foregone conclusion. It was clear to Edmund that the patriarch of the family did not like losing any more than the son.

⌛⌛⌛⌛

He said his farewell to Cato, and Tarquin went with him to the door. Tarquin seemed to have forgotten the plan for Edmund to go home on the path through the woods, and as they were to ride in the fields next, there seemed no point in mentioning it. A servant brought Edmund's hat; when Tarquin questioned him, he said that the boy who had been sent out to search their course that morning had not been able to find Tarquin's.

Together they walked out on the landing at the top of the steps. "A beautiful hour for a walk," said Tarquin.

"Indeed it is," said Edmund. He paused and looked at Tarquin. "Good day, then," he said.

"Good day, Percy.—I must say, old man, it has been jolly fun today. For sociability, you have got Mr. Christopher Percy beat by a mile."

"Good! A younger brother likes to hear that kind of thing," said Edmund.

"Well, I mean it. I am glad that Father enjoys your company, too. And it will mean a great deal to him to watch us ride."

"The pleasure is mine. My life has been filled with so much hard work, whether at school or the university or in Antigua, that I can almost say this day has been the first full of play for me since I was a boy. So I thank you for it, de Foye. And I look forward to Friday."

"At eleven, then."

"Eleven."

Edmund turned away and descended the steps; but when he had reached the bottom Tarquin called to him.

"Percy, old man—"

Edmund paused and looked back. "Yes?"

Tarquin descended the steps slowly after him. When he stood before Edmund he said, "I do not know quite how to say this; but I feel I ought to."

Edmund waited, puzzled, while Tarquin sought the words.

"Oh, it is nothing really," he said finally. "It is just that you *are* somebody. You quite stand out in a neighborhood filled with nobodies." Perhaps Tarquin then thought this might be understood as a reflection on Mrs. Alton. "Likeable nobodies," he added, "but nobodies nonetheless."

Edmund was touched by this unasked-for assertion of respect; and he thought that in spite of his suspicions of a troubling emotional force in Tarquin, there was something he liked about him, as one comes to find something likeable in any worthy competitor. "Kind of you to say that, de Foye," he said. He put forth his hand, and without a further word they shook hands.

There was nothing further that words could add to that token of mutual understanding; so Edmund went away across the forecourt, and Tarquin returned to the house.

Chapter 22

A young Man must think of somebody.

—Austen

When *Edmund* reached his aunt's house, he heard about several visitors who had come to pay their respects, ostensibly to his aunt, but were disappointed in his absence. Foremost among these visitors was Mrs. Eaton, who brought not only her eldest daughter, but the next youngest—either as a foil to the firstborn, or as a kind of reserve corps in the event that Edmund withstood the eldest sister's allure. While no visitor could do anything but acknowledge the superior claim of the Esquith de Foyes, and congratulate Mrs. Alton on the rapid progress her nephew was making there, the words they spoke and the emotions they felt were clearly at odds; and Mrs. Eaton looked quite pale and worried when she heard that Edmund had gone off to the house that was the dwelling of the young woman who was her daughter's greatest rival for looks in all the village. Andromeda took the opportunity to lecture him thus: "Society here will be much depressed," she said, "if it discovers that the Esquith de Foyes are selfishly monopolizing the only new eligible bachelor within twenty miles, particularly since they do so with no view to meeting the great necessity of getting you married as soon as possible. They will make themselves hated that way, and provoke a Jacobin sentiment most alien to the good British hearts of our villagers, if they do not look to it; or if we do not prevent it by doing some visiting ourselves." He agreed to forestall this storm of anti-patriotic fury by spending the morrow visiting.

Accordingly, on the next day they set out from the house on foot to pay their respects in the neighborhood. As they started down the drive from Fairhall, his aunt took him by the arm and said, "Now, one thing I must caution you about, Edmund, before we visit the Eatons, or anyone with eligible daughters, for that matter."

"Hmm," he ironically. "Whatever can it be?"

She squeezed his arm and laughed. "You must listen to me, Edmund. There is a kind of collusion that takes place in these families who have daughters to marry off. This is the way it works: You will be artfully put on a sofa to one side with the prime candidate; I shall be drawn off into another discussion by the mistress of the house. You will do your best to carry on a conversation with Miss Eaton, or whoever the young lady may be, and she will be all smiles and do her best to carry on a conversation with you. Neither of you will have the slightest opportunity to actually learn whether you should be suitable companions to one another. At the behest of her parents, she will be trying to dazzle you with all of her arts—she will wear her lace a little lower, keep her chin a little higher, and show her profile more, if that is her best feature.—You laugh, but all of this is quite conscious on the young lady's part, I can assure you.—Anyway, Edmund, when I go into the village tomorrow, I will find that the mother of the family has started a rumor about how quickly you and her daughter have taken to one another. You will have been observed to have been *particular* in your attention, in a word. Strangers will start quizzing you about your conquest, and you will start to feel under an obligation to the lady in question, because you have engaged her feelings so violently. On the next visit, your isolation together with her will be much more purposeful and open, and the congratulations that are tendered you will be still less shameless. You will feel yourself a monster for misleading the poor thing, and decide that as a point of honor you must marry her, though you barely know more than her name. You will console yourself with her pretty looks and her neat figure, and think how you could do worse. And before you know it, all expectations will be quite openly expressed, and you will find yourself engaged on your honor to marry Miss Whomever."

"It sounds very much like *a trap,* Aunt."

"It is! It is very much a trap. I have seen it work as one dozens of times, and I am sure you have seen the results dozens of times: husbands and wives who detest each other, and either live in continual strife or continual mutual silence. I would rather take a pistol to your brains than see you condemned to such a life; and it will not happen while I have guardianship over your courtship here in Broadbridge."

"My courtship?" he exclaimed. "Are you not creating an expectation with that very word?"

"Well, yes—I ought to have used another. All jesting aside, Edmund: while I do very much want to see you married to a kind, comfortable girl, I do not want it to happen unless you love the thing and she loves you. I have known Miss Eaton since she was a little girl, and I do think—well, let me only say that I know no particular ill of her. She is a good Christian soul; she never complains; or not too much more than girls her age usually do. She has hips that will bear you triplets on St. Matthias's Day and twins before Christmas. But if she does not suit you, dear, she is dirt to me, and I will have none of her."

"Thank goodness we are safely past St. Matthias's! I can only pray that that makes me safe for Christmas as well."

"Seriously, Edmund: I want you to be on your guard against the machinations of these Broadbridge families. There is not an eligible girl in town who would not marry you."

"Aunt, I cannot believe—"

"Edmund! I am not jesting."

"But you paint them as if not a one of them had a mind of her own."

"Most of them do not; and those that do will disengage it until after the ceremony."

"But how am I to like any such woman?"

His aunt was nonplussed for once. "Perhaps you will not," she admitted. "And if not, so be it. But promise me you will be wary."

"I take your warning, Aunt; I take it very seriously. I will not allow misconstructions to be made, if I can do anything to prevent them."

She was content with this, and they strolled on peacefully for a hundred feet or so before she spoke again. "It is too bad that you are only here for a month. There is too much to do. Perhaps we ought to focus our efforts on getting you the living, and let Miss Eaton wait."

He stopped in his tracks as if instantly acceding. She laughed and tugged him into motion again.

They paid a visit to the Eatons first. The family lived in a house almost in the center of the village, behind the solicitor's office. It was reached by a long walk that led beside the very windows of the office itself, and they made their courtesies to Mr. Eaton as he sat inside behind the glass. After they had passed by, they distinctly heard a bell jingling in the house. "It is their warning bell," said Andromeda.

"Are you serious?"

"Quite. Mr. Eaton rings it when visitors are approaching. He has a bell cord that connects with the house."

A servant met them at the door even before they could knock; and from distant sounds of hasty activity—a door slamming, the scraping of a chair on the floor, feminine feet dashing over carpet, the rustle of cloth, and even faint giggling—it was obvious to Edmund that their arrival had caused minor consternation. When they were shown into the parlor, however, Mrs. Eaton and her three daughters were all found to be doing their work in the most composed manner imaginable. But they did not even pretend surprise, and it was obvious that they had detected the identity of their visitors before Andromeda and Edmund had ascended the walk.

Mrs. Eaton was gray-haired and handsome; her eldest daughter, Cornelia, possessed magnificent hair of pale gold, limpid blue eyes, and fair skin; and though quite tall, had a figure of the type called "pleasingly plump"—that is, its softness amplified the ideal feminine curves of her body rather than filling them in and straightening them. The two younger daughters took after their mother in being more angular; Edmund could not help thinking that they seemed to have been denied proper nurturance in favor of their sister. The eldest wore a perpetual and pleasant smile; the younger two alternately peered and grinned and giggled, and always seemed to have some secret joke between them. He came to suspect that the constant butt of that joke was their older sister.

"So good of you to visit," said Mrs. Eaton when greetings had been spoken.

"Well, I had to bring Edmund by," said Andromeda.

"Yes, we missed you yesterday, Mr. Percy," said Mrs. Eaton. "We understood you were invited to Hartswound."

"I had that honor," said Edmund.

"And an honor it was," said Mrs. Eaton. "Please do sit—Mrs. Alton, come sit by me and we shall gossip.—Mr. Percy, sit wherever it is comfortable." As she gave these instructions, Mrs. Eaton took Andromeda by the hand and physically compelled her to sit beside her on one sofa. Edmund found that the two younger daughters had been strategically placed to fill the remaining single chairs, and the only remaining spot was on a second sofa next to the Miss Eaton, somewhat at a remove from the others. His aunt shot him a look of alarm, at which he set his lips to communicate the faint evidence of a repressed grin.

"Good morning, Miss Eaton," he said as he sat.

"Mr. Percy," she answered.

"Dark weather this morning, is it not? It promises rain."

"You were fortunate to have so fine a day yesterday for your riding."

"And the day before that, for the ball."

"But we would have danced whether it rained or not."

"True. I was thinking of an interlude when I stepped outside, and the night was very pleasant, though a trifle cool."

She said nothing, but her continued engagement in the conversation was suggested by the fact that she abandoned her needlework. As Edmund observed this latter fact, he also noticed that there were several serious blunders in her stitching, clearly apparent even to him, who knew virtually nothing about such matters.

"You know I am quite the newcomer to Hampshire," said Edmund. "I am very much at the mercy of fate in making new acquaintances. Perhaps if you told me who your partners were at the ball, that would be a pleasant way of learning about some of the gentlemen my age in the neighborhood."

"My partners? What interest would they have for you?"

"I am sure they represent the finest families of the country round about."

"Not at all! I am sure I did not dance with one fine gentleman all evening."

"I am sorry to hear that, Miss Eaton. But perhaps you are too strict in your judgment on them. Surely they cannot all have been yeomen?"

"Oh, no, of course not—whatever can you be thinking, Mr. Percy?"

"Well, start with one—say, the fellow you danced with before me."

"Oh, there were ever so many; I am sure I cannot recall who that was."

"Well, pick any one of them at all."

"There were ever so many, you see."

A silence ensued.

"Tell me, Miss Eaton," said Edmund, "are there any walks you favor in the neighborhood?"

"Why, of course; to Miss Dutton's."

"Ah—and what beauties of nature do you see on the way?"

"Beauties of nature? Why, none, sir."

He had a faint recollection that made him suspicious. "Pardon my ignorance, but who is Miss Dutton?"

"The milliner, of course."

"Yes, I recall now that my aunt mentioned her. But I suppose I was asking whether you walk abroad much in the neighborhood?"

"Only when we visit."

Another stymied silence.

"Tell me, Miss Eaton, what books have you been reading of late?"

"Oh, nothing. It has been ever so long since I read a book. Mrs. Radcliffe, perhaps; but that was long ago."

He thought he had heard the words "fine couple" uttered by Mrs. Eaton in the midst of this last attempt at starting a conversation, and he now darted a look at his aunt, who happened to be glancing at him; but she was held prisoner by Mrs. Eaton, who continued to chatter gaily along on a miscellany of topics. The younger sisters sat with their ears pricked up, screening out their mother's voice and hoping to catch that of their sister and Mr. Percy under it.

"I had expected you to be quite brown, Mr. Percy," said Miss Eaton.

With some relief that his interlocutor had finally started a subject, he said, "From being in the tropics, do you mean?"

"Of course."

"But it has been several months since my return."

"What difference would that make?"

"Well, the darker color brought on by the sun of course fades with time."

She laughed, apparently at what she considered to be the absurdity of this statement. "What a foolish thing to say, Mr. Percy!"

"How so, Miss Eaton?"

"Why, does the skin of a black man fade in color if you confine him indoors?"

"Perhaps you would not notice it; but I have been told by blacks themselves, and indeed I have observed, that even the skin of a person of very dark color will grow slightly darker with exposure to intense and prolonged sun. Therefore I would hypothesize that the reverse is true as well—to some extent, at least."

"Really, Mr. Percy! You are so droll."

He perceived she considered him to be an idiot; and he felt the first flicker of irreconcilable irritation with her. "But have you never been burned by the sun, Miss Eaton?"

"Never, sir."

"Has no acquaintance of yours, or perhaps a relation, ever been sunburned?"

"Oh, no, sir, of course not. Why ever do you ask such a thing?"

"I only ask because if such were the case, doubtless you would have observed that the coloring fades with time."

She tittered and rolled her eyes. "Really, Mr. Percy! Have you never seen some old farmer who has spent his years toiling in the sun? Is he not quite burned brown?"

"An extreme case. I can assure you that I am not an extreme case, and so could not have been expected to be brown as a nut."

"And some of our soldiers from India," she pressed on knowingly, "they are also quite brown, are they not?"

"Another extreme case."

She nodded triumphantly and examined her nails. He, too, was quite finished with the topic.

"Have you ever been to town, Miss Eaton?" he asked at random.

"To Winchester, do you mean?" she asked.

"No, I mean to London."

"Oh, to *the* town, you mean."

"To *the* town, yes."

"No, I have not. I should love to live there, though."

"But how can you know if you would love to *live* there if you have never *been* there?

She laughed. "The same way I know all kinds of things."

Evidently! he thought. *And that is by means of the fabrications of utter ignorance.* He cast about desperately once again for a new topic.

"Tell me, Miss Eaton, what is your highest aspiration? If I may make so bold as to ask so personal a question."

"I am sorry, sir; I do not understand you."

"Is there anything you long to do in life? Something that, if left undone, would make you feel regret on your deathbed?"

She looked at him blankly. "Why must you clergymen always speak of death?" she asked. "It is such a morbid topic."

"Let me put it this way," he persisted. "If you could do anything, what would it be?"

"I would have a large house and many servants; and I would lie on a sofa by the window all day and eat sweetmeats.—Oh, and I would have a pug."

He looked at her and marveled that God had made such a fair and fine exterior for such an utter emptiness. She was like a stage backdrop of a fertile field hiding an arid wasteland. At that point he gave up any thought of Miss Eaton as a possible wife; but as circumstances did not admit of his escaping from her parlor at that moment, he resolved at least to amuse himself.

"Ah," he said, "then you ought to take up lodgings in the West Indies—perhaps become the wife of an agent there."

"It would be too hot, I am sure."

"But you would have a house as large as you wished, and servants all you pleased—not just servants, but actual slaves to wait on you."

"But they are such ugly creatures, those slaves."

"Not at all, I assure you. The pictures you have seen have deliberately misrepresented them in order to prevent people from gaining a true picture of life in the West Indies—for if everyone were to go there, it would quite spoil everything for the few who at present enjoy the place.—No, Miss Eaton, the West Indian slaves are extremely handsome. They are descended from the highest royal families of Africa, princes and princesses all. You would find them most pleasant to have about you."

"Mr. Percy!" she protested; but he could tell that by bold-faced exaggeration he had made some inroad on her self-assured omniscience that the truth could never have wrought.

"As for the sweetmeats," he continued, "what can I say? The very soil of the place oozes sugar."

One of Miss Eaton's younger sisters tittered at his hyperbole. He exchanged a momentary look of intelligence with her, and grew certain that she knew exactly what he was about.

"You think you have eaten fine sweetmeats here," he continued, emboldened by this audience. "They are nothing compared to what you will find in the West Indies. The people there keep all the finest sugar for themselves, you know. And the sweetmeats, when made fresh, of fresh sugar—they are wondrous, really beyond the power of my telling. They *sear* the mouth with sweetness, and yet they do not cloy; the more you eat, the more you want to eat. And they do not make one fat, or spoil the teeth—not if they are truly fresh; that is another great advantage to them."

"That sounds *heavenly,*" said Miss Eaton. "But the *heat,* sir, what could be done about the heat?"

"Place a noble African prince at your feet, fanning you constantly with a broad palmetto leaf, and a fair young girl at your head, doing the same; or have yourself carried in a chair to the oceanside, where the balmy breezes blow in off the waters, and you would be quite comfortable, I assure you."

"You make the heat almost sound like an *asset.*"

"It is! Think of it—never a winter chill again. Never a cold rain, never snow and sleet and slush."

"But are the houses there quite large?"

"It is nothing to build large houses there. The labor, you see, is free; and the stones can be picked up in the fields. To build a dwelling as large as Hartswound Park manor house, and as well-appointed, would be the work of a few weeks."

A positive hiss of repressed merriment burst from the two younger women, and he found a chance to give them a conspiratorial wink.

"Is that quite true, Mr. Percy?" asked Miss Eaton earnestly.

"Indeed it is. A house the size of Hartswound would be rather looked down upon, in fact. When I was in the West Indies, I knew a fellow who possessed trained runners to communicate with his kitchen.—Why, you could sit in a different room every day of the month, and it would all be novel to you."

"I wonder you ever left the place," she said in amazement.

"Well, duty called in England."

They sat in silence for a minute before she spoke again.

"Tell me, Mr. Percy," she said, eyeing him speculatively, "are you thinking you might return to the West Indies someday?"

"Never," he said. With this he rose from the couch and sauntered over to the younger Miss Eatons, who were grinning from ear to ear, and he struck up a ready conversation with them about their needlework.

⌛⌛⌛⌛

"I am very sorry, Edmund," said Andromeda, as they walked up the street to their next visit. "I have always known that Cornelia Eaton was somewhat dull; but you are so much the opposite, I thought it might be a good match. At least you cannot fault her hips."

"Aunt, please do not discourse to me of her child-bearing *gear.* It is as if you were praising a sailing-ship for its lines or its rigging. Hips are not to the point here. Once again it astonishes me to think that Miss Brownton has the reputation of being weak-minded, while Miss Eaton, a virtual mental *blank,* has the blessing of society at large. I would sooner take up housekeeping with Miss Brownton, who would at least amuse me with her conversation, instead of stifling me at every turn."

"Please, Edmund! Do not even jest of marrying Miss Brownton! The thought of your remaining childless makes me cold to the heart."

"No, you are quite right that I should not jest of such a thing. But I hope I make my point."

They walked on in silence for a few minutes.

"On second thought," said Andromeda, "perhaps you ought to give Miss Eaton another chance."

"Dear Aunt! I beg you not to be absurd!"

"But consider—only consider—"

"Miss Eaton is unacceptable on any terms, hips or no!—But do not fret about it. You yourself suggested not an hour ago that I ought to find a living first. Let me do that. Even if it is far away, I will have you come stay with me, and you will try your best to make me a match among the local gentlemen's daughters. Give up the thought of Miss Eaton.—Where are we going, by the way?"

"The Ewanstones. Perhaps you recall the small brunette?"

"What are we doing, madam—*shopping? Shopping* for Edmund Percy's wife?"

"I do not like her much—I mean, for you. She is as pleasant a thing as you could hope to meet, but—"

"Let me guess—too small in the hips."

"No—rather short. Too short for you."

"Then let us pass by the Ewanstones and walk on."

"But it would be rude not to call—we are so close."

Accordingly they did turn into the Ewanstones' house, and attempt to visit them; but they found the family was not at home.

"Very well, Edmund," said Andromeda as they continued on their way. "Perhaps *you* should choose whom we should visit."

"I have a very imperfect recollection of the *names* of my partners, Aunt."

"Well, choose by description, and I will guess who they are."

"Who was that young lady with the red hair?"

She eyed him curiously. "Red hair? Are you jesting with me, Edmund? You had no partner with red hair."

"Well, chestnut, then."

"That would probably be Miss Wyman. She comes from quite a distance; we could not walk to pay a visit to her. Try another."

"Look, Aunt, if you must know the truth, I would be most interested in meeting the Browntons."

"Edmund!"

"I believe you said they were good people, or at least implied it. Let me meet them. It will do no harm. It might soothe my nerves after the debacle with Miss Eaton. You might find me quite tractable afterward."

"You will not do anything foolish, will you?"

"What kind of foolish thing *could* I do, in such a case?"

"You know I mean fix your inclination in that quarter."

"Again I promise you not to do so. I am merely interested in meeting Miss Brownton's parents, that is all. If you do not think it improper for me to visit the gentleman before he has visited me at Fairhall."

"Well, we cannot wait for that, in any event, for he seldom stirs from home."

"All the more reason, then."

His aunt was prevailed upon, and led him to a long and ill-kept lane on the edge of the village, very much out of the common route. They wound some way down this, through a grove of very fine old beeches and oaks, and passed completely out of sight of any houses.

"It seems the Browntons have a carriage," said Edmund, noticing the heavily rutted March mud.

"It is the de Foyes' carriage that makes those tracks," said Andromeda. "If Miss de Foye stays late, the carriage is sent to find her, either at the rectory or at the Browntons'."

"And she condescends to spend a good deal of time at the Browntons'?"

"Oh, yes. Mrs. Brownton has been a mother to her, in many ways."

The house now came into view. It was a small stone cottage with dormer windows and a thatched roof, from holes in which an early house sparrow or two flew forth periodically. "Very quaint," said Edmund.

"They keep it very cozy," said Andromeda.

"And what is Mr. Brownton's profession?"

"He has none. He is an invalid, and quite ill, genuinely ill. If he is well enough to see us, he will be by the fireside; if not, he will be in his bedchamber upstairs. His wife is always with him, in either place. He has some funds in the two percents—I think they were augmented somewhat by the de Foyes at some point. The Browntons are quite frugal, and manage somehow."

The front gate was unlatched, and they walked through it into a small garden of flowering plants still waiting out the winter. Edmund knocked, and the door was opened by a robust serving girl.

"Good morning, Eppie," said Andromeda. "Are Mr. and Mrs. Brownton at home?"

"Where else would they be, Mrs. Alton?" asked Eppie matter-of-factly.

"Are they receiving visitors, I should have asked—is Mr. Brownton well enough?"

"Ah, he's having a good day, Mrs. Alton," said Eppie. Edmund was soon to discover that the heavy use of the interjection *Ah* was a habit with all the dwellers in the Browntons' house. "You have chosen a fine interval to visit him," continued Eppie. "Come in, ma'am; do come in."

They entered a close, dark hallway, from which a steep, narrow staircase, also without illumination, led to the upper floor. A door on the left led immediately to the kitchen, and another on the right to what Edmund discovered was not the simple and sparsely furnished parlor he might have expected, but a parlor fitted out with books to form a library. Here Mr. and Mrs. Brownton were sitting, the former by a sizzling fire, and the latter as far from the hearth as she could be. Mrs. Brownton rose and came to shake Andromeda's hand, but Mr. Brownton did not stir, evidently because of his infirmity. He hailed Andromeda, however, with delight in his voice.

"Mrs. Alton!" he said. "How good of you to come down our lane on a dark day like this!"

"But the destination is warm and well-lit, Mr. Brownton. I am making visits with my nephew. May I introduce him—Mr. Edmund Percy, of the Surrey Percies."

"We are delighted to meet you, Mr. Percy," said Mrs. Brownton, taking his hand and shaking it heartily. Mr. Brownton also held out his, and Edmund shook it as well. He found the invalid's grasp to be very weak and tremulous.

"The pleasure is mine," said Edmund.

They laughed at his pleasantry. "As if we could be of any interest to a good-looking young man," said Mrs. Brownton.

"Ah, but perhaps he is a *learned* young man," said Mr. Brownton. "Then we might interest him, Annie."

"Edmund has trained for orders at Oxford, Mr. Brownton," said Andromeda. "He is to be ordained next month."

"Splendid! Oxford, you say! What a catch you have brought us, Mrs. Alton.—Annie, bar the door before he escapes—or no, better still, tell Eppie to bring us a plate of her honeycakes and some good, strong tea—and perhaps some cold meat as well; that will interest a young man, and obviate the use of bars and chains to prevent his flight."

"There is no need to bar the door, Mr. Brownton," said Edmund. "I am quite curious by nature, particularly about people; and if you will share your views of life with me, I will feast amply on them and need nothing else."

"Well said, young sir. Sit down—make yourself comfortable. The fire is perhaps too hot for you, so sit at a distance if you like."

Edmund and his aunt sat on a small sofa opposite Mr. Brownton, and Edmund looked about him with genuine interest. The walls were covered with makeshift shelving that sagged with its burden of books.

"We do have a parlor as well, if you feel too warm here," said Mrs. Brownton. "We could move in there." She nodded toward a narrow door that led off the back of the library into another room.

"The fire is quite comfortable at the moment," Andromeda reassured her.

"Tell me, Mr. Brownton," said Edmund without further preliminary, "what are your main interests?"

Mr. and Mrs. Brownton laughed. "We love nearly anything that comes to us between the covers of a book," said Mr. Brownton. "Poetry perhaps most of all; but plays as well, and novels; and books on travel, for that is the only way we ever get out of Broadbridge, except for our occasional visits to take the waters at Bath. We also read some works of science and philosophy. We are quite eclectic in our tastes, or perhaps I ought to say, more truthfully, that we seize upon any book we can beg, borrow, or buy. We recently read Voltaire's *Philosophical Letters*—quite amusing—and Thomas à Kempis, though I assure you we are not heretics."

"Mr. Brownton reads to me while I work," said Mrs. Brownton. "And when his eyes are tired, or he is feeling unwell, I read to him. My daughter reads to us too, as does her friend, Miss de Foye." Mrs. Brownton gave Edmund a knowing look at this point. "I believe you have met our daughter, Mr. Percy?"

"I had the honor of dancing with her the other night, Mrs. Brownton. I was vastly entertained by her conversation. It was much the best of any I heard all night."

"Ah, she is a madcap," said Mr. Brownton fondly. He shook his head and repeated, "What a madcap! But as good and sweet a girl as you could find anywhere."

"Indeed, I believe it," said Edmund. "I found her quite well-spoken, and now I see why that should be."

"Yes, she was read to," said Mrs. Brownton. "Read to and read to, when she was not out running about with Mariah—that is, Miss de Foye, as we call her now. Evelyn does not have a head for facts, but she does pick up *patterns* of speech very readily, and use them, even if she is not exactly sure what they mean."

"Where is our sweet girl?" asked Mr. Brownton of his wife.

"She is about somewhere," she answered. "Probably she has heard we have visitors and is hiding." She rose and went out of the room; then they heard her call up the stairway: "Evelyn! Mrs. Alton and Mr. Percy are here. Do come down and greet them."

Edmund could hear a muffled response—a surprised question, as it seemed.

"Yes, the Mr. Percy you danced with. He is here in the library."

A great thump was heard upstairs. Mr. Brownton grinned at Edmund and Andromeda. Mrs. Brownton, after going into the kitchen for a moment and giving orders to the servant, returned to the library. "If Evelyn wishes to come, she will," she said. "We can never quite predict what she will do and what she will not, particularly as far as visitors are concerned."

"Well, now," said Mr. Brownton, "Tell me *your* interests, Mr. Percy."

"Well, I have read intensively in the Gospels and sacred theology. But at University I also read a good deal of Italian, and had a passion for algebra and the calculus. I am afraid I did not have time for higher mathematics than that. Horace is a favorite of mine, and Cowper among the English poets."

"Yes, yes, Cowper is a delight," said Mr. Brownton. Mrs. Brownton nodded her approval as well.

"We like pastoral works," said Mrs. Brownton. "They suit us here, as you can see."

"It is well you like them, then. Anything in particular?"

"We were reading Sidney just yesterday, some very pleasant passages from the *Arcadia.* And Miss de Foye read us Spenser's 'Prothamalion' the other morning—what a noble and sweet piece that is, and utterly pastoral, I think."

"Oh, it was splendid!" exclaimed Mr. Brownton, growing excited. "And to hear Miss de Foye read it—with such expression!"

"Yes, she did read with marvelous feeling," agreed Mrs. Brownton.

"Especially in the passage in the first stanza—do you know it?"

"I only recall the general tenor of the poem and, of course, the refrain. It could be argued that it is the most beautiful refrain possessed by any English poem, or at least the most haunting and evocative."

"Indeed, I would agree with that," said Mr. Brownton. "But where is that book now, Annie? I should like to read that bit to Mr. Percy."

"Perhaps we ought not to read to them quite yet, dear," said his wife; but it was too late—he had found the book in a pile on the table beside him, and quickly found the passage, which he read in a trembling but moving voice:

I walkt forth to ease my payne
Along the shoare of silver streaming Themmes;
Whose rutty Bancke, he which his River hemmes
Was paynted all with variable flowers,
And all the meades adornd with daintie gemmes
Fit to decke maydens bowres,
And crowne their Paramours
Against the Brydale day, which is not long:
Sweet Themmes! runne softly, till I end my song.

"Yes, it is a beautiful passage," said Edmund.

"Ah, Mr. Percy, you should have heard the lady read it! It was enough to make the shivers run down your spine, the sweetness with which she intoned those words."

"I wish I had been here for that," said Edmund.

"Not just to hear it," said Mrs. Brownton, "but to see it. Miss de Foye is quite the beauty now; and one hardly knows whether one is more enthralled by looking at her or listening to her."

Edmund laughed. "I heard *and* saw her sing the other night," he said, "and I had much the same thought."

"Oh, yes, of course, at the ball," said Mr. Brownton.

The stairs creaked traitorously, and the four of them looked toward the door, where Evelyn Brownton appeared momentarily, only to flee away as soon as she saw she was expected.

"She *may* come back," said Mrs. Brownton.

"Perhaps we should read something now," said Mr. Brownton. "It might encourage her to slip into the room when she thinks she is not noticed."

"In a bit, dear," said his wife. "Let us get to know Mr. Percy a little better.—Have you found a living, sir?"

"Not yet."

"Ah. That is not so easy, I fear."

"I rest my hopes on my connections; but one never knows. I have been fortunate, truly, to be the son of a generous father, who has supported me to this day, and will continue to do so until I find a living."

"Mr. Percy is a younger son," explained Andromeda. "His older brother, Mr. Christopher Percy, is to inherit."

"Ah," said Mr. Brownton. "Is your home considerable, Mr. Percy?"

"It is larger than Hartswound," Andromeda answered for him.

"Ah," said Mr. Brownton again. "I, too, was a younger son, Mr. Percy; so I understand your situation. My brother inherited, though it was not so grand a place as Hartswound or—what is your family seat?"

"Brackensom, sir."

"Brackensom—yes, I have heard of it.—Have we not heard of it, Anne?"

"I believe so. 'Brackensom, Surrey.' It just has a ring to it, a familiar ring."

"You must have heard me boasting about it," said Andromeda.

Mrs. Brownton smiled at her over her needlework. "Yes, it was your sister who married a Percy, was it not?" she said.

"My sister Anne."

"Yes—that is why I remember her; we share a name."

"But that is all you share, my dear," said Mr. Brownton. "Mrs. Anne Percy does not live so humble a life as we do, I am sure."

"You would have liked her, I think, Mr. Brownton," said Edmund.

"Ah, excuse me. I did not stop and think."

"She was a kind person, a good person, a Christian."

"A Christian? That is praise indeed. They are so few and far between, those Christians," said Mr. Brownton. "I have been trying all my life to follow the teachings of our Savior, and I may say I do not think I have yet succeeded; so I take the adjective 'Christian' as the highest of praises."

"My guess is that you are too severe on yourself, sir. My mother, for her part, did have some success; so I know it is possible."

"Then you have indeed been blessed, Mr. Percy."

"I have had everything," said Edmund fervently, considering his past, and secretly making an exception for his love for Janetta.

"And you say that, even in your loss, sir?"

"I do. I am not so young or so foolish as not to have observed that we all suffer loss. Though I, too, have suffered it, I can say that I have had noble and good company on my path through life so far; and what better can we require? What more can we demand of our brief time here than that some part of it is spent among the good?"

"Indeed," said Mr. Brownton in agreement; and Mrs. Brownton nodded. Husband and wife seemed to think this last sentiment especially relevant to their life together; they exchanged a fond glance that was not lost on Edmund and Andromeda.

"And how long do you stay in Hampshire, Mr. Percy?" asked Mrs. Brownton.

"I shall return to Surrey about the first of April, and then on to Oxfordshire."

"I am sure your aunt has told you about poor Mr. Maugham."

Edmund was somewhat puzzled by the apparent change in topic, but answered, "She has mentioned the rector's ill health, yes."

"He is a very dear friend of ours—a very fine man, one of those true Christians you describe. Unfortunately, he is badly crippled with rheumatism now, and the doctor says he has cancer as well."

"He is more crippled than I, indeed," said Mr. Brownton. "If you can picture it, Mr. Percy, on our last trip to Bath I was able to be quite a help to Mr. Maugham, though I am generally useless to everyone."

Mrs. Brownton clucked her tongue in disagreement and shot her husband another loving glance over her needlework. "It is not useless to be an object of affection, my dear," she said. "And even if you do not do such eminently useful things as chasing foxes about the country and keeping a luxurious equipage, you do manage to love us in return; which is all we ask of you."

At this point Evelyn Brownton stole back into the room, and Edmund rose from the sofa and greeted her with a slight bow. He found her appearance bewitching. Her golden hair was bound back only loosely, in a style of deshabille Edmund had seldom seen; it fell in thick waves to the middle of her back. Her dress was a green like her eyes, and clung tightly, above the high waist, to her small, finely shaped breasts. She wore a beaming smile, and looked bashfully at Edmund before speaking to her mother. "Am I not right, Mama?" she asked urgently.

"About what, dear?"

"You know—about what I told you yesterday morning."

Mrs. Brownton remembered, glanced at Edmund, and laughed. "Yes, dear. I would say you were quite correct.—Now, do greet our guests properly."

Evelyn curtsied; Edmund bowed again; and Andromeda said, "How sweet your hair looks, Miss Brownton."

"Thank you, Mrs. Alton," she said somewhat solemnly. "I was trying to see if I could make it do what Mariah's does; but it is altogether different."

"And what is it that Miss de Foye's hair does?"

Evelyn gestured helplessly. "It is simply altogether thicker, that is all; and no amount of brushing will make up for that."

"Sit with us, Evie," said Mr. Brownton. Evelyn found a seat and perched on the edge of it, with her hands beneath her, gazing at Edmund more boldly now.

"Did you notice our sparrows, Mr. Percy?" she asked.

"In the thatch, do you mean?"

"Yes. There is one pair that has tunneled right down to a spot over my bed, and I expect I shall hear their chicks chirping at dawn any morning now."

"Will you think that pleasant?"

"Very much so, yes."

"Miss Brownton is a lover of all wild things," explained Andromeda.

"Not just a lover," said Mr. Brownton, "She is a kind of maid Diana, Mr. Percy, only she does not hunt—she watches over the wild things. When she was growing up, we had all manner of hurt rabbits and motherless birds and rascally injured squirrels in shelters out in the garden."

"How very kind of you," Edmund said to Evelyn. It struck him as a providential compensation to this untouchable creature that she should at least be able to touch creatures lesser than herself.

"Ah, but I could *not* take care of them," said Evelyn in correction of the impression her father had given. "I could not remember to, much though I tried."

"Yes," said her father somewhat sadly. "We had to help you, dear, that is all."

At this point Eppie entered with a tray; and the next few minutes were occupied in the dispensing of tea and the handing about of teacakes. There was no cold meat, Edmund noticed; Mrs. Brownton had silently vetoed this extravagance, though he doubted it was any inhospitable instinct that had compelled her.

"Tell me, Miss Brownton," said Edmund, when Eppie had left again, "Mr. Brownton mentioned that he has recently been to Bath. Did you go there too?"

"Oh, no, Mr. Percy. I stay with Mariah when Mama and Papa go to Bath."

"Evelyn is in such fine health," explained Mrs. Brownton. "We cannot justify the extra expense."

"Of course," said Edmund. "I was only curious as to what her reaction to the place might be."

"I am not sure I should like to go," said Evelyn. "There are too many people there."

"Do you prefer the country or the town, Mr. Percy?" asked Mrs. Brownton.

"The country, by far," said Edmund.

"Then you are hoping for a country living?"

"Indeed."

"So few young ministers seem to have that aspiration these days," said Mr. Brownton; "and so, of course, the many who are compelled to dwell in a rural parish can be palpably felt to despise it."

"What is an aspiration again, Papa?" asked Evelyn.

"A hope, a longing, a desire for a certain career or course in life."

"Ah," she said.

"And what is your aspiration, Miss Brownton?" said Edmund, intrigued at being able to put the same question to her that he had put to Miss Eaton.

She laughed. "Oh, I have none, I am sure."

"But surely you can say what it is you would most like to do?"

"I should like everything to stay just as it is."

"But that is impossible," said Mr. Brownton sadly.

"Well, in any case, I should like to always have Mariah for a friend."

"I am sure you will, dear," said Mrs. Brownton. "Though you might have to share your friendship by letter, if she marries away to some other county."

A line of worry crossed Evelyn's brow. "By letter!" she murmured sadly. "That will be quite hopeless, I am sure!—But that is in the future. I will not worry myself about it now."

"I would say *that* was your aspiration," said Edmund.

"What do you mean?"

"Not to worry. That is your aspiration; and it is a noble one, as I was saying the other night."

"Yes," agreed Mr. Brownton. "'Neither do they spin' and all that. But Mr. Percy, there are those of us who do worry for those who cannot."

"And that is as it ought to be," said Edmund.

"I suppose; yes, I suppose you are right. It is only for ourselves that we ought not grieve.—Now, look, Mr. Percy, we have found out that you are a very interesting young fellow: that you are educated, and thoughtful, and have a worthy career chosen for yourself. I should like to express my hope that you will visit us again; and as often as you would like, or can find time for. But if my wife will allow it, right now I would like to ask you perhaps to read something for us."

"Yes, do read something," begged Evelyn. She leaned against the back of her chair now, turning and throwing one arm over the upper edge of it and slightly drawing up her legs, in the sort of careless position he had seen Janetta assume in a chair from time to time; nothing like the prim posture that English misses of his acquaintance scrupulously maintained in the presence of visitors. He found it very fetching, and had to remind himself again of her disqualifications as an object of anything but platonic attention.

"Very well," said Edmund. "What will it be?"

"This fellow Byron is all the rage now," said Mr. Brownton.

"We were at Harrow at the same time, though I did not know him well. He has a clubfoot; and I at that time was spending most of my time on the playing field."

"Have you read his *Pilgrimage?*"

"No; I believe it was published when I was abroad. I am a little familiar with his first book, though."

"Do you like it?"

"His view is too cynical for me."

"And for me," said Andromeda. "I find he writes too much nonsense about suffering the whims of deceitful women. If it is only a pose, it is a tiresome one; and if it reflects his experiences, he has no one to blame but himself for his poor choices."

"He does have a few pleasant pieces, though," Edmund allowed.

"Read us one, then," said Andromeda. "I am ready to listen; and if we like it, perhaps we ought to read his *Pilgrimage* together."

"Ah, I hope you will include us in that," said Mr. Brownton.

A book was found on the shelves, with no little difficulty, and handed to Edmund; who after paging through it, stood by the window and read "The First Kiss of Love." He read very well: his elocution was even and fluent, his voice a compelling tenor, and there was feeling in his speech, especially in the final stanza:

When age chills the blood, when our pleasures are past—
    For years fleet away with the wings of the dove—
The dearest remembrance will still be the last,
    Our sweetest memorial, the first kiss of love.

When he had finished, there was a silent pause, as Mr. and Mrs. Brownton smiled at one another, and Andromeda smiled too, though sadly, at her own recollections. Edmund thought of Janetta, and of that first kiss that had led inexorably on to lovemaking in the little windmill in Antigua. The spell was broken by Evelyn, who said, in a troubled voice, "Your voice is wonderful, Mr. Percy; but the thought of a kiss is *disgusting!* Why would one ever write a poem about it?"

The others could not help laughing.

"I respect your right to your opinion, Miss Brownton," said Edmund. "But I am glad to say I do not agree with you."

"Oh, yes, I know I am the different one. I hate such things as *kisses.*"

"But I have seen Mariah kiss you on the brow," said Mrs. Brownton, "which I would not dare to do myself; and you suffered it."

"I would suffer anything for her," said Evelyn. "But it is sufferance, I assure you, Mama. I wish she would not do it, and I know she would not if she knew how much I dislike it. Yet on the other hand, I am glad she does it, if it is something she wishes to do."

"She is only telling you she loves you," said Mrs. Brownton. "And there can be nothing wrong with that, can there?"

"No, I am glad she loves me. And I do find it pleasant sometimes to lie with her and lean my head against her; she feels like part of me when I do that; and she is so warm and she smells so wonderfully sweet—like a honeycake baking; and there is something about leaning against her body—it is hard to describe. Her body is solid, and yet soft; and it has *life* in it; you feel that so, when you lie against her. It is the very opposite of the way Mr. Paws felt when he died, you remember, and his little furry body was all limp like string when we buried him under the apple tree."

"There, it sounds to me as if you like it when you are cozy with Mariah."

"I suppose; but she often spoils it all by caressing my head or running her fingers through my hair."

"I think you mean very much to Mariah," said Mrs. Brownton. "No, that is a foolish thing way to put it; for I *know* you do; all the world—all of our little world here in Broadbridge at least—knows that she loves you dearly." Then she caught herself, and turned to Edmund and said, "Ah! I ought to have said, 'Miss de Foye.' Of course I cannot think of her so formally—I nursed her myself, and she has been Evelyn's constant companion—but now that she is grown, I must use the appropriate form in company."

After a few minutes of further conversation, Andromeda indicated to Edmund that they ought to take their leave. He was inwardly amused that her zeal to hunt down an eligible young woman for him should compel her to leave such good companions so soon. "We have stayed long enough," she said to the Browntons. "We shall interrupt your day too much if we linger further."

"Not at all, not at all," said Mr. Brownton. "Look at all the books, Mrs. Alton, and just think of having a young man with sharp eyes and a good voice to read them! Can you not stay a little longer?"

"Do not importune Mrs. Alton and Mr. Percy, dear," said Mrs. Brownton. "They may have other visits to make before the rain begins; which it has been threatening to do every minute."

"Perhaps one more poem, Mr. Percy," said Mr. Brownton. "I will let you go after just one more poem."

"You will let them go *right now,* dear," said Mrs. Brownton firmly. To Edmund she said, "By 'just one more poem,' my husband means all of *Paradise Lost.*"

Mr. Brownton laughed. "You know me too well, Annie. But it is good to have visitors, especially on a good day."

"I am glad you are having a good day, Mr. Brownton," said Andromeda. "I hope that promises more in the future."

"Ah," said Mr. Brownton sadly, "they seem to be fewer and fewer. But we make do with what we have."

"May I walk with you?" asked Evelyn. "I am to meet Mariah at the rectory sometime this morning, and I may as well go now."

"Of course," said Andromeda.

Evelyn went away to prepare herself; and in a few minutes she returned with her hair bound back and her shawl on. Andromeda and Edmund said their farewells and started back down the lane with her. Outside of the safety of her home, her bashfulness returned for a few minutes; she kept Andromeda between herself and Edmund, though she occasionally dropped back and peeked at him with her winningest smile. However, before they had gone halfway down the lane, she changed her position so that she was walking between Edmund and his aunt; and by the time they reached the village, she had slipped her arms through theirs. They walked with her until her way parted to the rectory; then she curtsied to them both, said farewell, and darted away.

Andromeda put her arm through Edmund's and they walked on. "Well, what do you think of the Browntons?" she asked.

"I think they are wonderful," he said.

"Yes, they are good people. A loving couple. And so patient! Patient with poor Mr. Brownton's ailments, and patient with that daughter of theirs. Mrs. Brownton is one of the shining saints of this village, I can tell you. She is an example to all of us in her charity, and I do my best to emulate her. She has taught Miss de Foye to value charity above all, and that is a great gift in itself."

"Well, she has blessed her own daughter as well with many good qualities. I find Miss Brownton no less charming in broad daylight. Speaking of Spenser, it made me wonder why they did not call their daughter *Britomart.* She is one of chaste Dian's nymphs, truly."

"Yes; and I could not help fretting, as we were sitting there, that the visit was not advancing our purposes in the least."

He stopped in the road and turned to her. "Dear Aunt," he said, "we must come to an agreement. Are we going to seek the living first, or the wife? You know it would be more prudent to find the living."

"Yes; but my thinking at the moment is that we could seek both at once. Really, Edmund, why waste time? We must actively seek both together."

He laughed and rolled his eyes, gave her his arm again, and they continued walking.

"Very well," he said then. "But you must find me someone kind, who possesses good sense. Looks I will not scruple about; you know I have joked about pretty faces, but I really do not care about that. Do you have any young woman in this town who is kind and of good sense, though she may be the plainest being in all creation?"

Andromeda immediately tugged his arm so that they veered off in another direction. "Miss Caits," she said.

"Which one was she?"

"I never set you up with her at the ball," said Andromeda. "She is rather plain; but I like her very much. I think you will find her all that you require."

"Now we are getting somewhere," said Edmund.

"You must not mind her parents," Andromeda warned him.

"Why might I?"

"Oh, they bicker terribly. Perhaps I ought to assure you, too, that Mr. Caits is Mrs. Caits's second husband; he is not Miss Caits's father."

"Does this Miss Caits have a Christian name?"

"Yes; well—I am not sure how Christian it is."

"Are you going to disclose it to me?"

"Morgana."

"Aha! I see I have more witchcraft to combat."

"You will not find her bewitching unless you can see through the surface."

"And do you approve her hips, madam?"

"Oh, yes. I would not be taking you to see her if I did not. Her figure is perfectly adequate to the task."

"The task!" he exclaimed, laughing and rolling his eyes again.

"Shhh! Their house is right there."

The Caitses' residence was somewhat on the order of the Eatons'—a pleasant village house, set back no more than fifty feet from the road. It was larger than the Browntons' and well kept up, and Edmund caught a glimpse of a pleasant kitchen garden to the right of it as he and his aunt ascended the walk.

At their knock the door was opened by a young woman of about nineteen, too well dressed to be a servant, though the circumstance of her answering the door caused Edmund some momentary confusion.

"Good afternoon, Mrs. Alton," she said graciously. "How kind of you to call on us."

"I am showing my nephew the village, Miss Caits," said Andromeda, "and I thought we ought to stop in and say hello, as we did not have an opportunity of speaking to you and your parents at the ball."

"Yes, I noticed you there; but what a mad whirl it all was!"

"May I present my nephew, Mr. Edmund Percy, of the Surrey Percies."

"Very pleased to meet you, sir," Miss Caits said.

"And I you, Miss Caits," said Edmund, doffing his hat and making the appropriate bow.

"Do please come in and join us in the parlor. Mr. Caits is reading the paper, and Mother and I are sewing."

Edmund and Andromeda followed her as she led the way to the parlor; and as he looked about him, Edmund could not help contrasting these spacious quarters with the cramped cottage of the Browntons'. As in that house, here a stairway led upwards from the entranceway; but it was three times as broad and half as steep. The hall itself was broader, with room for a side table with collected bric-a-brac, a large and elegant mirror, and certain other pieces in the very latest mode, including a long mahogany sofa with wine-colored velvet cushions that looked as hard as tempered steel. The parlor proved, by contrast with the library at the Browntons', to contain only a single book—a volume of sermons left open but face down on one of the couches, as if someone, presumably Miss Caits, had recently been reading in it.

Mr. and Mrs. Caits rose to meet them when they entered. Edmund instantly appraised them as two individuals who would have been quite pleasant company for one another and for others if they had never married. Mr. Caits's handshake was firm and affable, and his greeting to Andromeda was warm and heartfelt. He seemed readily distractible, however, a trait that Edmund detected in him before they had all sat down again, as Mr. Caits tried to start a conversation about something he had read in the paper before the introductions had all been properly made.

Edmund found a seat safely beside Andromeda on one of the sofas; Miss Caits was opposite them in a chair, and Mr. and Mrs. Caits unfortunately in close proximity to one another on another sofa. The latter pair began an argument immediately as to the day on which they had last received a visit from Andromeda, and Edmund had a chance to study Morgana Caits more closely as she bent her head over her sewing, evidently maintaining perfect equanimity despite the embarrassing squabble between her parents.

Andromeda had called her plain; but by what standard, he could not have said. She possessed the ordinary features of an English girl, which Edmund, ever loyal to his people, had always found very pleasing. True, she would have looked somewhat bland next to Miss Eaton, but only at first glance. She possessed a kind of Quakerly quietude that was, after his experience in Antigua, intriguing to him, and when she raised her eyes unexpectedly to look at him, and found him studying her unabashedly, an instant pink touched her cheeks, and she looked modestly back at her sewing. In fact, she had a very pleasant glow about her that he found far more attractive than anything Miss Eaton had to offer in the way of physical beauty. He glanced at his aunt, and she at him; and that was enough to communicate his complete approbation, at least of his first impression. Andromeda patted his hand as if to say, "Delighted—you have my blessing—do your best."

Mr. Caits had by now passed beyond polite rebuttal and reached the point of employing scorn to make his point, and Edmund thought a distraction was in order. "Any news from the Continent, sir?" he asked.

"Old news! Old news—'tis all we get, I am afraid, sir. And not good news. The monster has overrun Schwarzenberg and Blücher, one right after the other, as if their armies were schoolgirls on a picnic."

"Ah, but this news is old indeed, sir. He also bested Sacken and Yorck, the last I heard."

"No!"

"At Montmirail, on the twenty-first."

"Damn the fellow! Can nobody stop him?"

"He is at bay, sir; all the world is sure of it. We shall be in Paris before the month is out."

"Ah, we heard that our army already *was* in Paris, not a week ago; and that proved to be false."

"You mark my words, sir."

"Mark them I shall; but even if you do prove right, we here in the country shall not hear of it until May!"

"Mr. Caits follows the war news very closely," said Mrs. Caits.

"No, I do not," said Mr. Caits. "I only follow it as closely as any British citizen ought—no more, no less."

"But what I *meant* was that you know all the battles as soon as they happen, and hunt them up in the atlas."

"No one can know them as soon as they happen. Why, you have heard Mr. Percy say, there have been other battles since this news we have."

"If I can bring the subject back to our pacific little village," said Andromeda, "I wonder, Miss Caits, how you enjoyed the ball?"

Miss Caits raised her face from her sewing and smiled slightly. "I enjoyed it *very much,* Mrs. Alton. It was very crowded, it is true; and perhaps there was a little too much eaten and drunk; and there were perhaps too many people who were utter strangers to me; but all the same I managed—somehow—to have a great deal of fun."

"I am glad to hear it," said Andromeda. "We did as well. Did we not, Edmund?"

"I found it very entertaining," said Edmund, politely omitting mention of certain intervals of tedium.

"Did you hear Miss de Foye sing?" asked Miss Caits, looking directly at Edmund.

"I did. She sang very beautifully."

"Do you sing, Mr. Percy?"

"Only a little."

"The approved answer; but does it represent the facts?"

"I assure you, it does. I sing among others when I must, stand at the back, and am pleased enough if my voice does not draw undue attention."

"A pity. It strikes me that your voice would blend well with hers."

"With Miss de Foye's?" asked Edmund.

"Yes. Does that surprise you?"

"Well, only insofar as—only insofar as I feel somewhat in awe of the lady in question, I suppose."

She gave him a piercing look that he found incomprehensible. "And why should that be?" she asked in a quiet voice, attending closely to her sewing.

He was amused at himself even as he found himself discomfited; and rather than answer her, he stepped back from the subject. "I find Miss de Foye the topic of conversation wherever I go in Broadbridge," he said.

"Well, we *are* a small village," said Mrs. Caits. "She is quite the brightest star in our firmament; so naturally we talk about her a great deal."

"Do not quiz the gentleman about Miss de Foye, Morgana," added Mr. Caits. "Gentlemen do not like to be quizzed about beautiful ladies."

"Of course, sir.—I meant no offense, Mr. Percy."

"None was taken, Miss Caits."

"Where have you visited with Mr. Percy today?" Mrs. Caits asked Andromeda.

"We owed a visit to the Eatons—they visited us yesterday while Edmund was out."

"Ah," said Miss Caits. "The Eatons."

"And then—on Edmund's whim—we went to visit the Browntons."

"Yes," said Mrs. Caits, evincing sudden interest. "I have to tell you, Mr. Percy, that you yourself were the talk of the town when you danced with Miss Brownton. It is a thing unheard of! She has never been known to dance at a ball. She is such a strange thing, indeed—a pitiable creature if ever there was one."

"And very fine green eyes she has," said Mr. Caits, with a wink at Edmund.

"And a lot of good they may do her!" exclaimed Mrs. Caits. "Tell me, Mr. Percy, how did you *ever* talk her into dancing with you?"

Miss Caits seemed quietly amused by this question; she flashed Edmund a quick glance to see what his reaction would be.

"I was the one who was chosen, I assure you," confessed Edmund, surprised into a little failure of gallantry.

"I had warned Edmund before the ball about Miss Brownton's . . . peculiarities," said Andromeda. "So when Miss Brownton approached me and asked me to introduce her—and not only that, to obtain a dance for her—I had a bit of difficulty communicating to Edmund that it was evidently all right for him to proceed."

"Were you then Mr. Percy's *broker?*" asked Miss Caits, with a teasing smile at Andromeda. Edmund was finding her increasingly intriguing.

"I was indeed," said Andromeda. "I have since thought that perhaps I should have advertised—I should have worn a sign around my neck: 'Dances with Mr. Percy, of fine family, newly arrived from Surrey, tuppence.'"

Miss Caits smiled at the jest. "Perhaps I ought to engage your services for myself at the next ball, Mrs. Alton."

"You did not lack for partners, Morgana," said Mrs. Caits.

"No, it is true—or at least I had all the partners I *wished* to have."

With this somewhat mysterious statement the topic lapsed, and Mrs. Caits started a new one; and it went down the usual course.

"How long are you with us in Hampshire, Mr. Percy?"

"About a month."

"Edmund will be taking orders in April," said Andromeda.

"Got a living lined up?" asked Mr. Caits.

"Not yet, sir."

"Well, the living here should be up soon, I should think."

"Let us not talk about that," said Mrs. Caits. "No one wants to see Mr. Maugham *go on;* though indeed he suffers so much that it would be a mercy."

"What do you mean, no one wants to see him go on?" asked Mr. Caits. "We should all like to see him go on being rector. It is just that he is simply too old and ill for it."

"No, I meant, 'go on to his reward.'"

"Well, why did you not say that?"

"I did; that is exactly what I said."

"No, you did not."

"I did indeed. I said 'go on,' in just such a tone as anyone would know what it meant."

"It must be difficult to find a living," Miss Caits said to Edmund.

"I expect it will be; but I will not require much. Just the opportunity to be of service somewhere."

"Edmund will rise as far as he wishes in the church," said Andromeda. "Or at least that is the opinion of his aunt, who is of course without any prejudice in the matter."

"Of course," said Miss Caits. "And how high *do* you wish to rise, Mr. Percy?"

"I would prefer not to be a curate; I would like to have my own parish. That is the extent of my ambition."

She gave him a look of approval, but said nothing.

"Well, then, perhaps the living here at Broadbridge *would* be a possibility," said Mrs. Caits.

"I thought you said we were not to speak of it?" said Mr. Caits.

"I did not mean we should not speak of Mr. Percy's holding the living here; I only meant that we should not speak of Mr. Maugham as if he were no longer among us."

"But you did not *say* that," insisted Mr. Caits.

"What is your opinion of our English clergy in general, Mr. Percy?" asked Miss Caits.

"I think that they do not take their tasks seriously enough. The church has been too much a means of employment of younger sons, such as I freely admit to being; and though I am grateful to find employment in it, I do not believe that such employment entitles me to a sinecure. I hope that in this new century, the clergy will change, and that the men who undertake its duties will look first at the needs of their parishes, and then at their own needs."

"So you do not approve of the custom of curacies, then?"

"Not in general, no; though in the case of your Mr. Maugham, I think a curate is well warranted."

"And what a dreadful curate we have, too," said Mrs. Caits.

"Not dreadful—abominable," said Mr. Caits, who must quibble with his wife even in agreeing with her.

"And you do not approve of the holding of more than one living?" asked Miss Caits.

"Absolutely not. Not only does it keep young men of vision and vigor out of the church, but it renders the fulfilling of the minister's obligations to his flock an impossibility."

"I could not agree with you more," Miss Caits murmured.

"You seem to have thought on these questions," noted Edmund.

"How could I not? As Mr. Caits just said about the war news, it is the duty of every British citizen to consider our church and its needs and government. Where we are not well led and governed, we ought to speak up."

"Brava, Miss Caits," said Edmund.

At that moment the clock struck. Miss Caits put aside her sewing and looked directly at Edmund. "I see that you are an intelligent and thoughtful man, Mr. Percy. I wish you the very best in all your endeavors. If you will excuse me—"

Edmund rose when she did, and reseated himself after she had left the room.

"Wherever *is* the girl going?" asked Mr. Caits. "She is such a mystery, that girl!"

"Our Margaret has the day off, and Cook is at the market," Mrs. Caits explained to her visitors. "I think Morgana is just attending to some little chore. She is much more of a housewife than I am, I can tell you." She gave Edmund what he took to be a meaningful look. "Everything in its place!" she added. "She knows what happens in the kitchen better than I do.—Tell me, Mr. Percy, would you indeed be interested in the living here, if it should come open soon?"

"That is the living we are not supposed to talk of, you understand," Mr. Caits said to Edmund, with a heavy affectation of droll and scornful humor.

"I do think it would be improper for me to discuss it, Mrs. Caits; but I can tell you that I do seek a country living."

"Well," said Mrs. Caits approvingly.

Edmund and Andromeda remained for another quarter of an hour at the Caits, engaged in further small talk, and hoping for the reappearance of the daughter; but when it became obvious that she was not going to return, for whatever reason, they made their farewells. Mrs. Caits followed them to the door, calling within the house for Morgana without success; and then they went down the walk.

Halfway to the gate, Andromeda gave a start. Edmund felt it through her hand, which was resting on his bent arm; but he assumed that she had only misstepped momentarily on the uneven flags. After they had left the house well behind, he waited for his aunt to begin to pepper him with inquiries; but when, after several more minutes, he had heard nothing of the kind, he looked at her in surprise. She was gazing up at him with an expression of remorse and even mild dread.

"Why that face, Aunt?" he asked. "You have finally succeeded in introducing me to a young lady who piques my interest. I really liked your Miss Caits—at least as well as one can on a first visit. She seems intelligent, pleasant, well-informed, thoughtful, and not without a good sense of humor. And I think you have very much undersold her looks."

"Oh, Edmund!" groaned Andromeda. "You did not see, then?"

"See? See what?"

"When we were leaving—Miss Caits was in the kitchen garden. I could see her quite clearly through a gap in the hedge."

"And?"

"She was with James Eaton—Miss Eaton's older brother. And he was . . . she was allowing him to . . . kiss her on the cheek!"

After a moment of surprise, Edmund burst out laughing.

"Oh, Edmund, I am sorry—I did not know," said Andromeda. "I am sure her own parents do not know—though why she is keeping it a secret, that I do not know either. He is very young—about her age. He is supposed to be up in London studying law, but he has been seen about town quite a bit lately."

"And now we know why. As for my interests, do not worry yourself. It is quite all right. I am glad that Miss Eaton's older brother has more sense than Miss Eaton herself. I quite approve his choice. I might even like to get to know this sensible fellow, if I can do so without danger of further conversation with Miss Eaton."

"But what a shame! The first young lady you actually liked!"

"Well, perhaps I liked her because she had that certain interest and glow that people acquire when they have fallen in love."

"Ah, but she would still have had that if she had fallen in love with *you.*"

"I am too late," he said, laughing again. "And let this be your final attempt, Aunt. Give over your matchmaking, and let us see what I obtain for a living."

"Let me review the possibilities," she said. "There must be somewhere else we can visit today."

"I think I felt a raindrop," he observed.

"You are making it up!—Oh, no, you are right. I felt one myself."

They returned to Fairhall before the storm broke, and spent the rest of the day very pleasantly, as Edmund thought, in not visiting.

Chapter 23

> Nothing is more certain than a good shot has often brought down a comfortable Vicarage, and many a bold rider lept into a snug Rectory.
>
> —James Austen

W*hen the* next morning arrived, Edmund determined to make his visit to Hartswound on foot, over the protestations of his aunt. He remembered Tarquin's mention of the shortcut, however, and asked her about it; and it turned out that one of the servants knew of it and could lead him to the entrance. This was about a quarter-mile from his aunt's, not too far from the main street of Broadbridge proper; the man assured him that it was well worn and that he could not mistake his way.

The morning sun was plunging into the forest, casting broad, bright rays through the massive columns of the trees, which had not yet begun to bud forth their leaves. In the deeps where he walked, the chill of the night drowsed still in pools of quiet air, heavy with the wet fragrance of the wintry wood.

At first he hardly looked about himself; he was too absorbed in thought. The past thirty-six hours had begun to dislodge his grief from the central place it had held in his vision; he could now see around that shadow, even if it still blocked his view. He was not quite sure how this displacement had occurred. Perhaps it was merely getting out into society again. He was not inclined to think that his dancing partners had had much to do with it; except perhaps for Evelyn Brownton. It was pleasant to be adored, at least for a time, even if the reality of what he called her disqualification inevitably reasserted itself.

Perhaps his aunt was right: he was only thinking of Evelyn Brownton because she was untouchable. He had no illusion that she would ever be able to feed that sexual hunger that Janetta had awoken in him; but he doubted any other woman besides Janetta ever would. Would not any English girl be the same: truly untouchable, shrinking from that sexual passion which was so bold a part of Janetta's character, and with which she had infected him? Why not give up any pretense that his desires would ever be satisfied—why not take Blackmore's counsel even further than his mentor had intended, and marry a woman as shy to the touch as a wild rabbit? Perhaps in the end that would be a less frustrating choice than living with a woman who *could* have met his hunger, if only she had understood what it was and had the same desire. Blackmore had suggested that most people lived their lives utterly unknowing of mutual sexual satisfaction; it seemed the general human lot. So be it. Edmund had mated once; he would never mate like that again. Why not become like the drones he and Cato had talked of—a drone in open fact. It would be wiser to give up the hope of any partner who could match his desires, and to marry a woman solely that he might have a focus for his kindness and care.

It was in this mood of despair disguised as reason that, after about a mile of walking, he came across a choice of paths in the wood. The main track led on, wide and unambiguous; but to one side was a narrower path that quickly wound out of sight in some low bushes. He stopped and considered it; decided against investigating it; and then, for no reason he could assign, he turned abruptly into it and followed it, thinking he could easily retreat if it seemed to be leading nowhere.

After about a hundred feet of twisting around huge trees and snaking through some surprisingly dense underbrush, the path opened out into a beautiful little glade, no more than another hundred feet across. He paused in wonder as he saw it. It was a little glimpse of spring: a pair of skylarks was soaring by turns in the sky, drenching the March air with song; a robin ran across the rough turf; warblers and blue tits teemed in the surrounding bushes, piping and singing. The floor was soft with moss and grass; in the center, the weathered buds of an ancient fruit tree, crabbed and bent, promised a constellation of flowers in the season to come. There was evidence of foot traffic here, and he saw forms in the grass beneath the tree where people might have sat on a dry day, or deer might have lain by night.

Here is Hartswound's Garden of Eden, he thought, *complete with its forbidden tree.*

The discovery of the little glade in the wood distracted him from his reflections. He wandered out into the middle of the clearing to examine the tree; and when he looked back, he found the place that he had entered was not readily visible. There was, however, a clear path that led straight out the other side of the clearing, and he continued on it, through another barrier thicket; and then he found himself on the main path on which he had previously been walking. He backtracked on it to confirm that it was the same, and sure enough, it seemed that the path through the glade was only a detour that passed through a favored picnic spot.

Continuing on the original track now, he pressed on for about another half-mile before coming out at the lower garden gate where he and Tarquin had ended their first lap on the previous day. The path must have saved him a good half-mile, perhaps three-quarters. He checked his pocket watch; it was just a little before eleven, so he was glad he had taken the shortcut rather than walked the full distance on the drive.

He did not go through the garden; such a course would have been an improper intrusion. Instead he went along the wall and came out on the drive, and from there proceeded through the main gates to the house. As he walked these final yards he realized he had resolved nothing about the matter of what kind of partner he ought to seek, though he told himself that perhaps it was too soon for him to make any meaningful resolutions in that regard.

⌛⌛⌛⌛

As he entered the enclosure before the house, he saw a carriage in the drive, a very fine one; he noted the Esquith de Foye coat of arms on the door. A coachman and a footman were lounging about, awaiting their passengers; when they saw him, they assumed more formal poses, and bowed as he approached.

He was just ascending the steps of the house when Tarquin, still within it, passed by the open entrance. He saw Edmund and halted, then hurried out the door and said, "I shall be a few minutes more, Percy." He spoke abruptly, but not rudely; rather in the tone of a friend who does not bother with such formalities as saying good morning.

"Very good," said Edmund. "I shall wait here."

"Please come in if you like—nobody is about, though; Father is being readied for the expedition to his observer's post, and the girls are about to go to Maugham's."

"I will take the air," said Edmund.

Tarquin made a gesture of acceptance and went back into the house.

Edmund turned to look over the lawn and the fields beyond. It was a very fine morning, for late winter; and despite his dour reflections in the wood, he felt curiously happy, happy as he had not felt for some time. It was indeed, he thought, his new acquaintances who, however different from himself, were proving entertaining enough to distract him from old griefs that still felt fresh.

After a few minutes he heard light, quick steps on the stone landing behind him. He turned and found himself face to face with Miss Esquith de Foye. Though she looked straight at him, for a moment she did not register him; he had the impression she assumed he was a servant. She was having difficulty with a glove, which seemed to require most of her attention; and she turned to call over her shoulder, "Evelyn! Come! We are already late. Mr. Maugham will scold us."

An old kitchen servant exited the house, but no Evelyn. "Oh, thank you, Parsons," said Miss de Foye.

"My pleasure, mum," said Parsons, beaming at Miss de Foye. The old servant was carrying a heavily laden basket; she had passed by Edmund, nodding gracefully to him as she went, before he could think to assist her with her burden. In a moment she had seen it safely stowed in the carriage by one of the coachmen.

Meanwhile Miss de Foye was still facing the door, still working at the troublesome glove. Evelyn Brownton now appeared in the doorway. Edmund was again struck by her prettiness; and he noticed as well that she wore a dress that was the twin of that worn by Miss de Foye, an open-fronted cambric gown over petticoats of whiteness so immaculate as to be almost searing to the eye. From the instant she came into view, her gaze was riveted on Edmund; and though she smiled at him, she seemed stricken with overmastering shyness. Edmund guessed that she had seen him from well within the house, and that he was the reason for her falling behind and delaying their departure. He thought of quietly stealing away and relieving her of the apparent cause of her distress; but to do so would be rude to Miss de Foye. He also recognized part of his motive as a desire to flee Miss de Foye's beauty, for he again found it utterly overwhelming; but he told himself not to be a fool, and to stand his ground.

"The lining is completely split!" said Miss de Foye, apparently to herself. She had pulled off the glove and was examining the interior now. Then she noticed Miss Brownton. "Come, dear," she said. "Whatever are you dawdling for?" She turned away from the door, still occupied with her glove, and so nearly ran into Edmund.

"Oh!" she cried. "Excuse me, sir! I did not realize—"

The situation struck him as comical, and he could not help smiling. She uttered a little laugh. In this interval of confusion, Evelyn darted across the landing and now took up a position directly behind Miss de Foye, for all the world like a child peering out at a stranger from behind her mother's skirts. Miss de Foye turned and tried to step to one side, but Evelyn dodged behind her, keeping Miss de Foye between her and Edmund, though she continued to gaze happily at Edmund the entire time.

Edmund could not help laughing out loud, though his laugh was amiable, and not meanly intended.

Miss de Foye, however, was not entirely pleased with her friend. "Evelyn, stop it!" she said. "This is the gentleman you danced with the other night, is it not?"

Though Evelyn would not answer, Miss de Foye at least managed to force her friend to stand beside her. "The proper thing to do, dear, is to introduce him to me. Can you do that?"

Evelyn curtsied to Edmund very gracefully, and he bowed in return; all very pretty, but not to the point. Miss de Foye abandoned her lesson in manners and turned back to Edmund.

"You will have to be so kind as to forgive Miss Brownton, sir; she is quite overawed by you, as you can see.—We shall have to resort to making our own introductions. I am Mariah Esquith de Foye." She extended her gloveless hand toward him.

He took it gently in his and executed a slight bow over it. When he relinquished it she seemed slow to take it back.

"I am honored to make your acquaintance, ma'am," he said. "I am Edmund Percy, the youngest of the Surrey Percies; Mrs. Alton in Broadbridge is my aunt."

"Yes, I know very much about you," said Miss de Foye. "You would be amazed at how much I have heard. My brother says you are a 'capital' horseman."

"If I am as good as he is, I shall be content."

"Ah—and I see that you do, as Evelyn tells me, have a knack for turning ordinary rejoinders into cheerful compliments."

"Miss Brownton challenged me to try my powers of compliment on certain qualities that she imagined to be defects in her character."

"From the account she gave to me, I would say they were indeed defects."

"On certain points my conscience made me own that; but she still required me to test myself on them; and a ball is like a fairy tale in this respect, that at the behest of fair maidens a man must perform impossible feats as though they were nothing."

"Such as dance with young women he may not like?—But forgive my impertinence. You are well-spoken, sir."

He bowed again in silence.

"It is a pleasure to make your acquaintance," she said; but there was something dismissive in her voice and her air, as if her interest in him had now ceased. "Please forgive our rudeness in rushing off; but we are late to our appointment with Mr. Maugham.—You know Mr. Maugham? Our rector."

"Please do not let me be the cause of further delay. I am only waiting for your brother, Miss de Foye."

"Oh, Evelyn! Your jacket!" said Miss de Foye suddenly. "It is far too chilly still to be running about without it." Evelyn looked down in surprise, and then laughed merrily, apparently at having forgotten her jacket; and abruptly skipped back into the house. "Do hurry!" Miss de Foye cried after her; and then added: "But watch your step on the stairs, dear!"

Evelyn called back something that reached Edmund too indistinctly for his comprehension.

Miss de Foye resumed her examination of the troublesome glove. Her lack of attention to a guest struck Edmund as odd; he could not decide whether she was thoughtless and rude, or whether her behavior was part of the larger preoccupation he and his aunt had noticed the other night. She managed to straighten out the lining of the glove and pull it on. As she was buttoning it, she suddenly looked up at Edmund.

"Would you allow me to speak frankly with you, Mr. Percy?" she asked.

"I always appreciate frankness, Miss de Foye."

"Miss Brownton has shown you certain attention; which is all the more remarkable because she is characteristically rather shy, especially of men, and very especially of young men."

"I am as baffled as anyone at the cause of her apparent approval of me."

"Come, come, Mr. Percy, the cause is not so far to seek. You are quite good-looking, if I may make so free as to say so; and by her account you are both kind and well-mannered. The point I wish to make is that you should not misunderstand her attention. When she has formed an affection, which she sometimes does with extreme rapidity, she expresses it warmly and forcefully."

"I think I perfectly understand the limits of her attention, Miss de Foye. I confess myself charmed and of course flattered, as anyone would be; but I would never presume on that attention, or take advantage of such an innocent being for any reason."

His tone was quite sincere; and for the first time she smiled at him genuinely.

"I am grateful for your understanding, sir."

"To do Miss Brownton full credit," he went on, "she herself made it clear that she would never marry anyone; so I would not have been likely to imagine her affectionate behavior toward me was due to anything other than sheer exuberance of spirits."

Now Miss de Foye looked alarmed and displeased. "Pray, sir, how did that topic ever arise?"

Edmund laughed softly. "I hardly know," he said. "But now that I stop and think of it—it must have been in connection with the discussion of Miss Brownton's supposed defects, which she broached herself."

Miss de Foye thought for a moment, and then relaxed visibly. "Then I can trust you, sir," she said, "to tolerate my friend's fancies without being misled by them."

"You may trust me absolutely, Miss de Foye. But you must not expect me to discourage them; I have not the heart, and I confess myself weak enough to be too charmed and amused to put a stop to them."

"Oh, so are we all with Miss Brownton. We ought to be stricter with her; we ought not allow the excesses of her folly; and yet we cannot bear to speak sternly. I myself perhaps do that better than anyone; but I am inconsistent, one minute speaking firmly in the hope of helping her to a better understanding of what society requires, and in the next too fond and foolish myself to endure to speak harshly. I dread to think what will become of her when those who love her cannot take care of her." At this thought her brows contracted in concern.

"Perhaps you, at least, always will be able to do so," he said. This was a very subtle probe of the spade on his part, and he was rewarded with the sound of something solid.

"I will marry someday," she said; and then, in a softer voice: "Someday very soon, I hope. And my future husband cannot be expected to put up with so much silliness."

"Then let me offer the only course of action left, Miss de Foye; and pardon my presumption in doing so, but I am bound for orders within the month, and my advice would be well within that calling."

"And what is your advice?"

"Pray on Miss Brownton's behalf."

"Yes, of course. And of course I do that; but your reminder is timely." Her tone was grateful.

"Is it not odd how we forget to pray?" asked Edmund.

She looked at him with keen comprehension. "Yes," she agreed. "It is a strange fact of our existence, is it not? To live in total dependence on our Heavenly Father and His Son, and yet to forget to bring to Them the petty hurts of our everyday life for Their soothing and healing.—And you find this true in your life, too?"

"I feel the fool for confessing it, but so it is. Sometimes the more desperate and hopeless the situation, and the more bankrupt human resource may be, the more I forget to call for divine support. I hope the wearing of the cloth will make me better in that regard."

She looked away now distractedly, over the lawns and fields of her home, though she did not seem to see them; and she said, as if speaking to herself, "Yes, I must pray; I must pray."

In another moment Evelyn returned in a rush, slightly breathless, her dress now augmented by a little Spencer jacket exactly like the one worn by Miss de Foye, with the exception of the color, which was a rich pastel green. Her inhibition against speaking to Edmund seemed to have vanished while she was away; for now she ran straight to him and cried, "Do you not love my coat, Mr. Percy?"

"I do, indeed," he said, laughing at her enthusiasm.

"It was a gift from Mariah the last time she went up to London; she bought hers there, and came back with mine. You see, it is a perfect fit." She walked about the landing, striking poses reminiscent of fashion plates.

"And the color suits your eyes, Miss Brownton."

"Well, of course!" She stopped her prancing abruptly and looked at him. "Would you say I was pretty, Mr. Percy?"

"Evelyn!" protested Miss de Foye.

"I was never a friend to *understatement,* Miss Brownton," said Edmund.

Evelyn giggled happily, though Edmund was not convinced she understood him.

“Evelyn,” said Miss de Foye, “We are late already, and later every minute. Do come.” Miss de Foye descended past Edmund now, without the leave-taking or curtsy that he might have expected, and went straight to the coach, evidently hoping to draw Evelyn in her wake. Her maneuver was at least initially successful: Evelyn began to follow her; but in passing Edmund she paused to contemplate him—or perhaps to glory in him might be a better term, as she smiled at him in a virtual ecstasy of approbation.

“So you are here to see Tark?” she asked, as if she meant to stand there and chat with him for the rest of the day.

“Yes; he and I are going riding together.”

Evelyn darted a look at the carriage, into which Miss de Foye was just ascending with the aid of a footman. In a whisper she said to Edmund, “Well?”

He gave her a puzzled smile. “Well what?” he asked, matching her tone with a conspiratorial whisper.

“What do you think of her?”

“Ah—Miss de Foye, you mean. I think she cares very much for you, Miss Brownton. Hers is a care that ought to be cherished and rewarded; and the best homage it can receive is obedience.”

“Evelyn!” called Miss de Foye from the carriage.

“You are right!” said Evelyn, smitten, however fleetingly, by conscience; and she ran off to the carriage. At the door she turned to curtsy to Edmund with an adoring smile; and then she scrambled in. He saw her watching him as the carriage pulled away.

Mrs. Parsons, who had been waiting by the carriage all this time, now crept rheumatically up the stairs; and despite her evident pain, she smiled and curtsied to Edmund.

“Quite a delight, that one,” said Edmund.

“Isn’t she just?” said Mrs. Parsons. “We’re all in love wi’ her.”

After she spoke, he was not sure whether she understood that he meant Evelyn. She left him alone with his thoughts;

which perhaps were not entirely salutary for him. Now he, too, looked out over the lawns and fields, but without seeing them.

That Miss de Foye, he thought, *is surely the most beautiful woman I have ever seen in my life; though I would not trade her or a thousand like her for my Janetta. Yet under the beauty, what is she but another prudish English girl? She will drive some man mad, for he will possess her in name and in form, but never obtain from her what he craves—the sexual passion that Janetta and I shared together.*

He mused on Janetta for a while, and then recognized the dangerous melancholy toward which his thoughts were tending, and put a stop to them. They then naturally reverted to the sight he had just seen; it seemed indeed to have been burned into his mind's eye in glorious afterimage.

She is indeed beautiful, though, he thought again of Miss de Foye. *I should not be at all surprised if I should count it one of the great blessings of my life that I saw her when she was in her prime. Perhaps someday I shall be with my grandchildren and we shall pass her somewhere, and I shall say, "Ah! She is handsome now, but you should have seen her in her youth!" Or who knows—perhaps she is one of those women like Mother and Aunt Andromeda who grow more beautiful with time. One looks at them and the only reason one knows that they are not two-and-twenty is that they are* too beautiful *to be so young. Then I shall say, "When I first looked on her, I thought her as beautiful as she could ever be. But how very wrong I was!"*

Then: *How odd,* he thought, *that she should be so distracted. Aunt says that this is unusual to her; it certainly results in behavior somewhat less genteel than one would expect from her. Even Tarquin, as wild and boyish as he is, has very good manners.*

And finally: *I wonder who this fellow is whom she expects to marry?*

However, he wasted no further time on this futile question, for Tarquin now came out of the house, and they went away together to the stables.

⌛⌛⌛⌛

Tarquin had selected two new and fresh hunters for their use. Edmund asked if the supply in the stables was inexhaustible, and Tarquin laughed and said that hereafter they should have to resort to horses already ridden: he and his father each kept a prime hunter and a second, though since Cato had not been in the saddle for some years now, it fell to Tarquin to see them all exercised. Edmund perceived at once that on this morning Tarquin would ride Cato's first horse, Agamemnon, and he himself must make do with the second. But his mount, Admiral by name, was handsome and well-kept by any standard.

They warmed the horses up by tracing the route through the fields, omitting the jumps. The course Tarquin had set up was in many respects even more challenging than the trail through the park they had ridden two days before. The fields to the south and east of the manor house had many features that lent themselves to his designs: occasional outcrops of stone, clusters of wild thicket, truncated hedges, natural ditches, and rambling stone walls. He had yielded to every brash and reckless impulse in including hair-raising obstacles and in plotting the turns, many of the latter of which were so abrupt they were virtual reverses. He had had the route marked on the day before, and now its white linen flags fluttered in the March wind and winked afar over the fields in the late winter sun.

"It is a diabolical course," Edmund told Tarquin when they had surveyed it.

"Do you think so?" asked Tarquin proudly.

"I propose that whoever dies or is maimed first will be declared the loser," said Edmund.

"Well, very good! That seems only right."

Before they commenced, they paid their respects to Cato, who had been carried in a litter chair to the top of the knoll they had visited the other morning. It gave a fine view over the fields, and a servant had been charged to swivel the chair in which Cato sat, so that he could follow the action through a pair of opera glasses.

The old gentleman was almost wildly excited: he had not so much exposure to the sport he loved in months, if not years. He kept jumping up out of his seat to give advice to Tarquin—by which of course Edmund also benefited, as he too heard it: "When you take that ditch yonder, keep to the right by the yew tree—the ground looks better on that side. And watch out for that dead branch in the thicket—over there—it will fair impale you if you do not keep off it. Do not let Mr. Percy cut the corner when you double back for that heap of stones—stay on the inside of him—" and so on for several minutes. Edmund did his best to keep a straight face, admiring Tarquin for his patience with his father. "I shall, Father," he kept saying, and "I shall watch for it" and "He will not best me" and "You will see, Father, we shall trounce him on that one."

In talking of the race, Cato grew so eager for it to begin that he was finally willing to suspend his counsel. The horsemen rode to the starting line, which was at the foot of the observation post. Edmund took a wide look about to orient himself one last time and saw that the numerous contingent of grooms and stable hands and keepers of the kennels had abandoned their tasks and swarmed to the fields to watch; that the gardeners had gathered in a cluster on one of the near lawns; and that many of the windows of the house were dotted with the pale faces of chambermaids, butlers, footmen, and all the host that kept the great house in operation. He felt somewhat lonely all of a sudden; and the cruel goad that had ever pricked his spirit—that is, that he was but a third son—stung his pride again. He crouched over the horse like a jockey.

One of the servants on the knoll had a charged pistol, and after a loud count, fired it to mark the start of the race.

Tarquin's hunter shied at the sound, but Edmund's got a clean start, and thus an early lead.

No sooner had they begun than Edmund's blood was up, and he ceased to care for life or limb. He rode like one insane, like one invulnerable. Tarquin fought his way back into the running, pressing his horse for every advantage, and as had been the case two days before, horses and riders threw themselves recklessly at every obstacle. If one rider crowded the other out of the better jumping, the other took the worse with a compensating eagerness. In the muddy patches the dirt flew; in the long grass the pale stalks tore from the ground, clods and all, and flew into the face of horse and man behind. The horses exulted in their strength, and the men in their power over them.

Edmund seemed again and again to find the shorter route, the better angle, the inside of the turn, and to crowd Tarquin out of the use of them. When he reached the finish first, Cato was out of his chair, flailing at the ground with his cane in frustration, shouting, "Esquith de Foye! Esquith de Foye!" again and again.

Tarquin drew rein beside Edmund a few seconds later.

"You have it fairly this time," he muttered through his teeth.

"Esquith de Foye! Esquith de Foye!" cried Cato again. "You *must* beat him, Tark, for the honor of our noble family!"

"So I shall," Tarquin shouted back to him; and then said to himself somewhat grimly, in a lower voice, "So I shall, so I shall."

Two servants brought wine in silver cups. Tarquin quaffed his and called for more; Edmund drank less recklessly. Then he said, "Are you ready?"

"That I am," said Tarquin. "But you must not have the vantage of me in the start this time; we will use a flag to start."

"Fair enough," said Edmund.

A servant was dispatched ahead of them with one of the linen flags. He shouted a brief count, then lowered the flag abruptly, and the riders burst over the starting line.

Edmund was determined that Tarquin would not make a comeback on the second lap as he had the previous day, and he fought keenly for the lead at every contested turn, over every jump, and in every straightaway. The result was even more madcap danger than before, as the horses hurtled simultaneously over narrow hurdles. More than once the flank of Tarquin's horse actually struck Edmund's booted leg in a turn or leap, and likewise for Tarquin.

They rode over the finish line neck and neck. "Esquith de Foye!" shouted Cato. "It was Esquith de Foye by a nose, I say!"

"But now we are only even, Father!" cried Tarquin fiercely. "The third lap will settle it! We must have a third lap!"

The grooms were raising an inarticulate din by the stables, and the servants on the knoll had lost all composure; some were wringing their caps in their hands, and they, too, were crying, "Esquith de Foye! Esquith de Foye!" Again the sense of isolation only spurred Edmund's competitiveness. He drank even less of the offered cup this time, though his first taste had made him thirsty. Tarquin, by contrast, drank even more.

"I shall beat you this time, Percy," he said hotly. "You had better prepare yourself for it."

"I shall pity you if you lose, de Foye," responded Edmund, "but I shall not stint on that account." He knew perfectly well that no words could have inflamed his opponent more, and indeed, Tarquin grinned fiercely as he heard them.

They drew up to the starting line. The count was given, the flag dropped, and the third lap began.

Now the slightly superior quality of Tarquin's horse began to show itself. Admiral lacked nothing in spirit, but he had not the muscle of his rival, and in leaping the first ditch he now came up slightly short; he staggered, and Tarquin took a definitive lead. A cry went up from the onlookers that was audible to Edmund even in the heat of the race; he urged his horse on, nearly in a fury himself. Admiral needed no coaxing; it seemed that the sight the animal loathed most of all was that of another horse before him.

On the early laps Edmund had sensed that Admiral had speed for the straightaways that was still untapped, however much he might flag on the jumps; and as the final stretch to the finish was over a broad, flat field, Edmund had hope to catch up to Tarquin there, if he could only jump well enough before that to stay in the running.

Somehow he did so. When the two riders broke out onto the final flat, Edmund was only about twenty-five feet behind. He urged Admiral on, and the horse went to it with a will. Before they were halfway across the straightaway, he had caught up to Tarquin, who looked over at him with mingled amazement, anger, and despair.

There was one slight bend in the course before they approached the knoll, and both riders fought to take the inside, which by their position belonged to Edmund. In doing so, Tarquin ran his horse directly against Admiral. Both horses stumbled, and then, in an instant, both went down, and riders and steeds were rolling head over heels.

The men were lucky that the ground was soft and clear. They both landed well and rolled off their momentum harmlessly, and neither became entangled with the falling horses. For a moment they lay still, out of sight in the grass, about a dozen feet apart; and then Tarquin rose to his feet, to be greeted by a cheer of relief from the crowd. He came to Edmund and offered his hand, and then Edmund stood, again to a cheer from the onlookers. The horses, too, had climbed to their feet and were moving about with that shamefaced air hunters have when they have done something awkward but are not even sure what it was.

The men examined the horses closely but could find no injuries, a diagnosis seconded by the handlers who soon joined them from the stables. Both steeds were led away, tossing their heads as if ready for a rematch.

When they were thus sure the horses were unhurt, Edmund said, "Yours fell farther than mine—I suppose that makes you the winner."

Tarquin laughed and clapped him on the shoulder. The mutual brush with death had not only made them forget the wildness of their rivalry, but strengthened the incipient bond of friendship between them. "Are you all right, old man?" asked Tarquin.

"Perfectly all right," said Edmund.

"We could have been killed, I suppose," said Tarquin. "I care nothing for myself, but I would have been sorry to be told, as I said my farewells to this world, that you too had broken your neck."

"Ah, but I am only a younger son, and of no account," said Edmund.

Tarquin laughed. "By God, Percy, when I compare you to your brother, it staggers me to think you two are the same stock! And to think you are to be a clergyman!—Though I grant that you ride like one of the Four Horsemen in the Apocalypse.—Come, let us see if Father is angry with us for rolling his horses."

He kept one hand on Edmund's shoulder as they walked to the knoll where Cato sat in his chair, watching them, already beginning to rehearse the history of the race.

"You are unhurt, gentlemen?" Cato said when they had climbed the knoll.

"Yes, Father," said Tarquin.

"You are fortunate," said Cato. It was clear that his enthusiasm for the triumph of the de Foyes had been cooled by his momentary apprehension for Tarquin's safety. He turned to a servant. "Wine for these men," he said.

The cups were brought again, and this time Edmund had a full cup, though he still rather craved water.

"Well," said Cato, "I cannot say who won. But Tark, you were in the lead most of the last lap."

"We may have to call it a draw, though I hate to," said Tarquin.

"Oh, I *hate* draws," said Cato. "But I must admit that Admiral is not quite the match for Aggy. You could see that; though Mr. Percy rode him skillfully, and milked the last ounce of strength and speed out of him."

"I fear you are right, Father; though when I chose Aggy for myself, I did not think the riding would be so hard that it would matter. I took the better horse through pride of place, I suppose, as I did yesterday. It would be good to put Percy on as fine a horse as my own and see how we fare."

"You must go hunting. Damn, I wish it were not so late in the year!"

"Everyone else in England is still hunting into March. We ourselves have had meets into early March—I think it was ought-five, was it not? The ground stayed wet. It was only this terrible winter past that convinced us to give up early. Do you think the farmers about would tolerate it if we just had one more? No one has sown barley, so far as I have heard."

Cato grew visibly eager, and went so far as to pound the arm of his chair. "By God," he swore, "We will do it, Tark! One more meet it is! You shall take your own best horse, and Percy shall take Agamemnon."

"Excellent! Capital! We shall have Ashleigh for sure, and Lord Burley.—What do you say, Percy? Will you hunt with us?"

"I should be delighted."

They stood for a while longer on the knoll with Cato, talking over the prospective hunt and the recent race; and if matter for discussion had been the only requirement, they might very well have stood there all day; but the two younger men soon grew hungry and restive.

They accompanied Cato in his procession back to the house; then Edmund and Tarquin sat down to a snack of cold meat to tide them over till dinner.

They were just finishing when another servant came in from the field, bringing their hats, now completely crushed and broken. Laughing, they donned them and looked at themselves in a mirror. "Fine mementos they will make, at least," said Cato; "but they will nevermore be fit to be worn."

"What do you say we ride to town right now and buy something new, Percy? I shall be quite out of hats at this rate."

"Yes," said Edmund, "I shall need something myself. I did not expect to spend so much of my time in Hampshire casting good hats in the path of hunters. Have you a good hatter in Broadbridge?"

"Yes, a very good—you shall see. Quite up to standard. I would give him my custom any day over London."

"Then he will have mine, too," said Edmund.

⌛⌛⌛⌛

The three men spent another hour talking about sport and horses. Then Cato settled into his chair by the fire for a good nap, the need for which was clearly increased by the excitement of the morning, and Tarquin sent to the stables to have two fresh horses readied. When the horses were brought up to the house, Edmund was pleased to find them to be two rather staid old road horses, though nonetheless no nags to be frowned at. On these the two young men rode off, bareheaded, down the path through the park that led to Broadbridge.

Again Edmund savored the wood, this time seeing everywhere how it teemed with birds and squirrels hunting up provisions; and this time he noticed that there were deer tracks on the path and the paw prints of Old Reynard. The breezes through which they rode were shot through alternately with sunbeam and birdsong, with long cool shadows and haunting silences.

When they reached the detour through the little glade, Edmund asked Tarquin about it. "Oh, I know what you mean," he said. "The girls spend a great deal of time there. My sister was always enlisting Evelyn Brownton to lug baskets of gear off into the woods to have tea time with her dolls when she was little; she would be the mama and Evie would be a kind of nursemaid. They could go on with it *endlessly,* just as they will doubtless carry on with real babies endlessly when they have them—or at least, when Mariah does. I could never stand even to be in the room with them then—all that fussing with clothing, and the pretended feedings with tea and cakes, and the feigned cryings and soothings. I always had to get out of the house and shoot a bird or set the dogs on a rabbit, just to get that cloying girlishness out of my brain. I expect they still have picnics out there, and my sister probably will carry her children to the place when she visits us."

"Miss de Foye may marry away to some distance, though," said Edmund. "She will not be bringing her babies back here too often."

"Oh, well, of course. There is no one in the neighborhood we would ever see her married to. There are good people, mind you—the hunting set, I mean. But not a one of them is good enough for her, in my opinion."

Edmund now had a new insight into the possible cause of Miss de Foye's furtive behavior; but he said nothing further.

Chapter 24

With soft and lady speech the first applies
The mild correctives that to grace belong
To her redundant friend, who her defies
With jest, and mad discourse, and bursts of song.
O differing Pair, yet sweetly thus agreeing,
What music from your happy discord rises,
While your companion hearing each, and seeing,
Nor this, nor that, but both together, prizes;
This lesson teaching, which our souls may strike,
That harmonies may be in things unlike!

—Lamb

Though Broadbridge was emphatically a village, it was not a small one. Its chief specialized merchants were the innkeeper, the butcher, the baker, the cobbler, the blacksmith, the wheelwright, and the hatter; and in addition it had several catch-all shops that provided a wide range of goods and services. One went to Miss Dutton's for Manchester goods—that is, fabric—as well as thread, pins, needles, yarn, seamstress work, finished millinery goods of all kinds, gloves, and the like; to Mr. Tarn's for hard goods of every description, from nails to horse whips; and to Mrs. Wright's for assorted soft goods—paper, ink, and a surprising and even perhaps ill-assorted array of other necessaries. Mrs. Wright was also in touch with the London booksellers, and would obtain a book that you had read about in one of the monthly reviews, for a small charge. She even ran a kind of lending library, from which you could borrow a book for a weekly fee; and woe to you if you did not return it, for she would be at your door promptly, demanding it back.

With the exception of the inn, the smithy, and the wheelwright's, these shops and a few others were located in the very heart of the village, which consisted of two long rows of buildings that faced one another, one row of brick and one of stone. Edmund was certainly justified in doubting such a place could be the provenance of wearable hats, for it was not particularly prepossessing, though it had a great deal of charm, much like the country characters who inhabited the district.

In such a small setting, the arrival of Tarquin Esquith de Foye became instant news. Every custom-hungry merchant took at least a moment to look out the door or window at him; and every curiosity-starved dweller in the upstairs rooms over the shops peered out at one point or another. Edmund was not used to such celebrity, and felt uncomfortable, particularly hatless; for in those days to go hatless was tantamount to a form of public nakedness.

They left their horses at the inn and walked to the hatter's. On the way down the street they met a group of young women on the way up, the senior of whom was Miss Eaton. Edmund stopped and bowed, a courtesy in which Tarquin joined him; and the young women, with a few titters, curtsied back en masse.

"Forgive us for not doffing our hats, Miss Eaton," said Edmund. More titters.

"However came you to be out without one, Mr. Percy?" wondered Miss Eaton. It was a question uttered in the same stultifying manner as her former conversation, and Edmund recalled two urges he had felt in her company the previous day—first to run away, and second, when the former impulse was repressed, to say something absolutely outlandish.

"It is a sad thing, Miss Eaton," said Edmund. "We had a bet, Mr. de Foye and I, as to who would win a horse race. The loser was to eat the hat of the winner; and as we wound up in a draw, we have just had to dine on the hats of one another."

This tale was greeted by a delighted cachinnation from all the ladies but Miss Eaton, who seemed to pause in an attempt to determine if Edmund were serious or not.

"So we are on our way to the hatter right now, as you can see," said Edmund.

"Yes," said Miss Eaton, "Mr. Exton has many fine hats."

"Does he have hats made out treacle or toffee or some such thing?" asked Edmund. The ladies tittered happily; or at least, all but Miss Eaton did.

"I have never noticed," she said uncertainly.

"If he does, I shall make sure Mr. de Foye buys one," said Edmund. "Good day to you, ladies." He doffed an imaginary hat, the ladies giggled again, and the men and women parted, the latter with many a laughing backward glance and coquettish smile—or at least, all but Miss Eaton.

"I *say,* Percy," said Tarquin, when they had walked a bit farther, "you are quite the lady-killer, aren't you? You had them eating out of your hand! I never knew *what* to say to a woman. I am beginning to think you are quite the master of all knowledge."

"It all comes of being the youngest son, and having to rely on your wits," said Edmund.

"Like the heroes of fairy tales, you mean? I suppose there may be something in that.—A pity that Miss Eaton is so dull, do you not think? She is damned pretty."

"She does seem a trifle slow to *catch* the *ball from a fellow.* But I fancy she will do well for herself, if she *catches* the right *fellow at a ball.*"

"I pity him! Imagine having to converse with someone like that constantly, who never quite knew what you were saying, though everyone else in the room seemed to understand it perfectly—as if the subject of conversation were some kind of secret to which she were not privy."

"Yes," said Edmund. "Not only would it be tedious for her husband, but I should think she would very quickly grow irritated at feeling excluded."

They entered Mr. Exton's hattery, and the man himself came forward to meet them, bowing repeatedly. "Good afternoon, good afternoon, Mr. Esquith de Foye, sir—and Mr. Percy, is it not?"

"You know my friend, then," said Tarquin.

"Only by hearsay, of course."

"We have destroyed our hats in riding," said Tarquin.

"That is a shame, sir," said Mr. Exton, with a broad grin.

"A damned shame, but it means more custom for you."

"Well, I cannot help but be pleased by that," admitted Mr. Exton. "You do me honor, sir, to prefer my hats."

"You make damned fine hats, that is all," said Tarquin. "Now, what have you got?"

"If you don't see what you like, sirs, I shall make them up special for you. I could deliver whatever you like to your door at dawn tomorrow."

"And stay up all night doing it, I suppose," said Edmund.

"If necessary; but it would be my pleasure," said Mr. Exton.

"That will hardly be necessary. I think we can find something ready made," said Edmund.

The obsequious merchant showed them his stock, and they quickly chose hats of the right fit and of a suitable color. Edmund examined his closely. "I would go so far as to say this is one of the finest hats I have ever seen," he said. "Very good workmanship—excellent materials."

Mr. Exton said, "I see the thought going through your head, sir: Who would have thought that one would find such quality in the hattery of an obscure village in Hampshire. But I was apprenticed in London, so I learned the trade at the hands of the best."

"I see. Indeed, you learned your trade well. This hat will quite spoil me."

"No, it will not, Percy," said Tarquin. "We shall soon trample that one, and have to apply to Mr. Exton for another.—Better make up a good supply of these, Mr. Exton; we have been doing rather reckless damage to our hats in the last few days. As a matter of fact, make me up another just like this—no, make me up two: one in black, and another in . . . do you have a dark blue?"

Mr. Exton showed him another hat in that color. "Would this cloth do, sir?"

"That would be the color. Excellent."

"Shall I send them up to Hartswound when they are ready, sir?"

"Yes, please.—I trust my account is up to date?"

"Oh, yes, sir. The Esquith de Foyes always make timely payment."

"Good. We like to keep it that way. I do not always know how Deburr keeps the accounts, so I like to ask."

"Very kind of you, sir.—And Mr. Percy, would you like a second hat in reserve?"

Edmund laughed. "No, thank you, Mr. Exton. If I have only one, perhaps I shall take better care of it.—But let me follow the example of Mr. de Foye's promptness and pay you now."

"I can send a bill to Fairhall, if you would prefer, sir."

"No, no, let me pay now."

He settled his account with the merchant, and then he and Tarquin went back down the street, again equipped like gentlemen.

"Say, Percy," said Tarquin suddenly, "I have another idea. Let us stop in at the rectory. You are bound for orders, as you say; and you might like to meet our Mr. Maugham. He is a good old soul, the model of a village parson, though he is fading fast."

Edmund suddenly had a distinct suspicion that this was the true purpose of their visit to town, not the purchase of hats, however necessary that latter errand had been; and he was flattered by the implied interest in his career. "I should like that," he said.

"Good," said Tarquin warmly. "It has been ever so long since I visited the old man, though Mariah is there practically every day. She may be there still, as a matter of fact. She will be pleased that I have made the fellow a visit."

Leaving their horses, then, still at the inn, they walked on to the church, with its attached churchyard and rectory. The church itself was, though a pretty building and finely built, quite diminutive, and somewhat too small for its purpose now. It had been built of a good gray stone in time out of mind, to the greater glory of God and the Esquith de Foyes—God giving good cause, and the de Foyes good sterling; and of course as a consequence the de Foyes sat closest to God, in the first pew.

On the other hand, the rectory was far larger than the church. It rose two floors high on its ample foundation, with a third garret half-floor lit by unusual eyebrow windows. It too was built of stone and roofed in slate; but in general the building showed the need of some attention. Its gardens, too, though quite extensive, were now badly neglected; for probably a decade, no gardener had seen to them, and as Edmund was to discover, neither Mr. Maugham nor his housekeeper were capable of doing so. Edmund noticed with interest that the situation of the building was very good: it stood on some high ground, backed by a beautiful grove of tremendous oaks that connected with the manor park beyond; and though it was within sight of the church, there was a fair distance between the two buildings; and furthermore both buildings faced the street, so that the church could not be said to look out on the rectory. As Edmund had the opportunity to study the place more closely, he understood his aunt's plans for it; for it had been built to accommodate a large family in considerable comfort and privacy.

Tarquin knocked loudly at the front door. "Old Maugham's housekeeper is quite deaf," he said. "We may have to barge in unless Mariah is—"

The door swung open a few inches and Evelyn Brownton peeped out at them. When she saw Edmund she ran away, leaving the door to swing wide.

"What is that poor mad girl up to now?" laughed Tarquin. He led the way into the house.

It opened onto an ample hallway—far the most generous entrance hall Edmund had seen in Broadbridge so far, excluding of course Hartswound Park and Fairhall. It was paneled completely, even the ceiling, in a warm, dark oak, and an oak staircase ascended from its carpeted floor to the rooms above. In one corner a very fine old clock ticked sleepily, and on all sides doorways led off into various other rooms. Edmund could see through one of them into a kind of parlor study lined with countless old books, a collection rivaling even that of Mr. Brownton, though housed in better cases, and in an arranged state that suggested a less desperate need for shelf space. Tarquin continued on into this room, and Edmund followed.

As they entered, this scene met their eyes: a clergyman of extreme age was sitting at a small table opposite Miss de Foye, engaged in a chess game; and so deeply engaged, in fact, that at first neither player looked up from the board. Then Miss de Foye turned to them—she was seated with her back to the door—and saw them with some surprise.

"Tark!" she said. "Whatever are you doing here?"

"Broadbridge rectory has become the only place I can see my sister," he said. "You are always here these days."

"Papa is all right?"

"Of course. He had a very good morning, watching us jumping fences, and we left him asleep by the fire.—I say, Mariah, look at this hat. Exton has outdone himself. We needed new ones after the jumping."

"You will find keeping company with my brother a very expensive proposition, Mr. Percy," said Miss de Foye. "He is Mr. Exton's best customer."

"Fortunately, madam, I have strong backers," said Edmund.

"That is very good, sir. You will have need of their deep purses."

The clergyman, having reluctantly relinquished the attention he was paying to the game, had looked up at his visitors; and when he saw Tarquin, he smiled with pleasure. "Tark!" he said. "Tark, my boy! Come shake an old man's hand—but do not press it too hard, Tark: you will quite crush it if you do."

Tarquin stepped forward and shook Maugham's hand with extreme care. Edmund saw now how the clergyman was so tormented by age and rheumatism that he was literally deformed: he had shrunken to a hunchback, and nearly every joint and limb was bent either slightly or greatly in some unnatural and painful-looking manner.

"Mr. Maugham," Tarquin said now, "allow me to introduce a newcomer to Hampshire. He is Mrs. Alton's nephew, Mr. Edmund Percy, of Surrey."

"Ah, yes," said Mr. Maugham. "I am pleased to meet you, Mr. Percy. Your aunt has spoken of you many times over the years; I almost feel I know you."

"Very pleased to meet you, sir," said Edmund, who could not truthfully say that his aunt had spoken of Mr. Maugham to him anything but recently. He shook the man's hand carefully, and found it cramped by rheumatism into a kind of perpetual crook that shivered with palsy even as he held it.

"Where did my little bird go?" Mr. Maugham asked suddenly. "Did we not send her to open the door?"

"Mr. Percy has cast a spell over Evelyn," explained Miss de Foye. "She is quite infatuated with him. She went so far as to dance with him at the ball the other night; and as she has never, ever, danced with a man before, all the town is quite abuzz about it."

"Then she is hiding," said Mr. Maugham in his coarse, thin, quavering voice. "She will hide from you like this for the first few years of your acquaintance, Mr. Percy, and then she will get over it."

"Mr. Percy has expressed to me a very handsome understanding of and allowance for Evelyn's idiosyncrasies, Mr. Maugham," said Miss de Foye.

"That is good," said Mr. Maugham, with a keen look at Edmund. "Then you understand that her affection for you does not signify what another young woman's affection might?"

"I understand that perfectly, sir," said Edmund politely. Tarquin could not help laughing.

"Really, Mr. Maugham," he said, "Have no fear that Percy will try to marry Evie. You will find him neither a rake nor a fool. He is an Englishman of the first class—a brave man, a sportsman, and a proven patriot. What is more, he will be taking orders next month."

"That is, unfortunately, no guarantee of his morals," said Mr. Maugham. "But I do recall Mrs. Alton telling me about your plans, Mr. Percy. I should like to get to know you better, sir; I should like to talk with you about your views of the church. Perhaps I have something to say that would be of interest to you, too: that is, I could share what little knowledge I have gleaned of the church in the past sixty years that I have dwelt within its bosom."

"I would enjoy that, sir," Edmund said. "I am at your service."

"Well, stay to dinner," said Mr. Maugham.

Edmund was a little surprised, but thanked the rector and accepted.

"Will you stay too, Tark?" asked Mr. Maugham.

"No—I rather think I shall go home and dine with Father. He would be lonely without me; and you have stolen away Mariah, Mr. Maugham, so there must be at least one of us who goes home to honor our remaining parent."

"Mea culpa! Mea culpa!" said Mr. Maugham, with a smile. "Brand me a felon, if you must, but do not take your lovely sister away, Tark. She is the light of my last days; she is all the sweetness left in my world."

"Then Father will do without her till this evening," said Tarquin. "I tell you what, Percy—leave the horse at the inn and bring him up tomorrow. What do you say? We shall talk about the meet some more."

"Very good," said Edmund.

"Even better: Ask Mrs. Alton to come up a little later for dinner. We have not had her up to dine in ages and ages. We will send her a note tomorrow morning."

"I am sure she would be pleased to come.

"You are having a meet?" said Miss de Foye. "Is it not too late in the season for that?"

"The rye and barley have not been sown, so far as I know," said Tarquin. "We shall just get in one more last run."

"But is it not too wet for that? The footing will be very bad."

"I believe it will be dry enough. We may have one more chance before spring opens its skies on us."

Miss de Foye was visibly dismayed. "A pity!" she said. "I thought you were safe for this year."

"My sister has somehow got it into her head that hunting is dangerous," Tarquin said to Percy. Then, appealing suddenly to Miss de Foye, he said, "Why not ride with us, Mariah?"

"You know perfectly well I shall never ride to hounds again," she said.

"But you are a capital horsewoman."

"You know my views of the sport, Tark."

"I do, and you must get over them. Which you would, too, if you could only get the brush in your hand and were blooded."

She rolled her eyes in disgust. "It is not the death of the poor fox I lament," she said. "I know what havoc those creatures wreak on the country; but I think it is idle to spend so much time and treasure in chasing him, when there are Christian souls that require our care."

"You have become a prude in your old age, Mariah," said Tarquin.

"Her old age!" snorted Mr. Maugham.

"And whatever decided you to meet again?" asked Miss de Foye. "Was it you, Mr. Percy? I fear I must hold you responsible for this."

"I confess that my presence at Hartswound seems to have inspired it," admitted Edmund. "But I regret that it causes you uneasiness.—Let us give up the idea, de Foye. When you are hunting next season, give me the word, and I shall come back from wherever I happen to be and hunt with you."

"You will not let a mere pretty girl talk you out of a *hunt,* will you, Percy? Do not be absurd! Girls grow old and cross; but there are always foxes in the cover."

"You are a brute, de Foye!" laughed Edmund. "How can you remain insensible to such a plea?"

"I make no plea, Mr. Percy," said Miss de Foye. "I know there is no hope for that; I only express my disapproval."

Tarquin only laughed. "I do not know how you came to fail your hunting blood, Mariah," he said. "We ought to have had suckled you at a vixen's teat, instead of putting you out to Mrs. Brownton."

"You will find me vixen enough to give you a good run, if you tease me about hunting, Tark."

He laughed again, made his farewells, and departed.

"Do you mind if we finish our game, sir?" Mr. Maugham asked Edmund.

"Let us set it by," suggested Miss de Foye. "It would be rude to leave Mr. Percy to amuse himself."

"I enjoy the game," Edmund assured her. "I would be quite entertained to watch."

"You are a player, sir?" asked Mr. Maugham.

"A humble one, yes."

"Then you are indeed a valuable addition to our society, Mr. Percy."

"I am obliged to you for thinking so," said Edmund with a laugh.

"I am afraid dinner is not till four," said Miss de Foye.

Edmund consulted his watch. "And it is nearly three now," he observed.

"Is it? At three I must go visit a house in the village."

"Now, have you changed your mind, Mariah? Will you let me go with you?" asked Mr. Maugham.

"No, sir; it must not be."

"Oh, dear," said Mr. Maugham.

"There is nothing we can do," said Miss de Foye.

"But after all these years! I hate to desert Mrs. Bunt in this hour."

"It is out of the question, Mr. Maugham. It is God's will."

She evidently felt it rude to carry on this mysterious conversation without including Edmund, for she turned to him now and said, "One of our villagers is quite aged and sick, and has begged Mr. Maugham to come say a prayer with her. I had thought that if I brought the carriage for him, we might go over together this morning; but Mr. Maugham was not able. I could not allow it."

"May I accompany you, then?" suggested Edmund. "I have only been made deacon, of course; but if I could say a prayer with her, I would be glad of the opportunity to be useful."

Miss de Foye looked at Mr. Maugham, who nodded his assent. "Better than nothing," he said, "and probably better than my best, at my age. And knowing Mrs. Bunt, she will like to see a young face better than an old one anyway. Take a prayer book, Mr. Percy, if you have not one about you; there is no telling what she will ask for. There is one there, on the table." Edmund did as he was bid, putting the prayer book in his pocket.

"We would return to dine with you at four, then," said Miss de Foye.

"That would be good. Tell Mrs. Tooth that we will have one more for dinner. And we will finish our game after it—do not forget, Mariah!"

She smiled fondly at him. "I never miss an opportunity to be soundly beaten by you, Mr. Maugham, and you are well on your way to doing that again."

"Ah, but think what you are learning, child! Think what you are learning from me!"

"Yes, I am learning to handle constant defeat gracefully."

"A valuable lesson in this life of ours," said Mr. Maugham. "But even more important, you are learning *to try, try again.*"

"I would learn that faster if you would let me win once in a while."

"No—not if I *let* you win; never if I *let* you win; only if you finally win of your own superior prowess."

She smiled affectionately at him again. "You are right, sir," she said. "As ever." She rose from the table and turned to Edmund. "Now we must find Miss Brownton, for I shall need her at Mrs. Bunt's."

After Miss de Foye had had a conversation with the housekeeper, she went up the stairs and found Evelyn hiding at the top. She compelled her to descend to the hall, where Edmund was waiting; and in the process, Evelyn underwent her transformation and was again all smiles.

"You are coming to Mrs. Bunt's with us?" she asked Edmund as she skipped down the last few steps.

"Greet Mr. Percy properly, dear," said Miss de Foye.

"Good afternoon, Mr. Percy.—Mariah says you are coming to Mrs. Bunt's with us."

"Good afternoon to you, Miss Brownton.—I am indeed."

"Will you carry the basket, then? It is very heavy today."

"I would be glad to do so."

"That is a relief! I thought Mariah and I should have to carry it between us; and that is so awkward. It is always knocking about one's legs, and I have to make Mariah switch sides all the time."

"That would be very kind of you," Miss de Foye told Edmund. "I should have had the coachman take it directly, except that I was afraid he would frighten Mrs. Bunt if he went in without us. She is half-blind and a little confused at times."

Edmund picked up the basket, which had been set down earlier in a corner of the hall.

"It will not annoy you to carry it?" asked Miss de Foye.

"It is trifling."

"Thank you, sir. Perhaps we can find a boy in the village."

"I would jealously refuse him a share in my office, Miss de Foye."

She was amused at his gallantry, but also pleased. "Tark would scorn such a chore," she said.

"We younger sons have more freedom to please others, I think; we have nothing to prove," said Edmund as they began their walk.

"You are poor, then, if you are a younger son," said Evelyn.

"Evelyn!" protested Miss de Foye.

"I do not think of myself that way," Edmund said to Evelyn, "but I suppose it is true."

"I am glad you are poor," said Evelyn.

"Evelyn, really!" said Miss de Foye.

Evelyn defended herself. "I think Mr. Percy is ever so much nicer being poor than he would be if he were rich."

"That is hardly a proper reflection to make," expostulated Miss de Foye, with an apologetic look at Edmund.

"Not at all," said Edmund. "Miss Brownton is doubtless quite right. I, too, have often been grateful for being a younger son."

"Is that true, sir?" asked Miss de Foye.

"It is indeed."

"And why does it make you so?"

"It has improved my character, I am certain. And it has compelled me to be independent—or at least to pursue independence, for I have not attained it yet. I shall do so soon, however; and when I do, chief among my expressions of gratitude will be a prayer of thanks to the Lord for not making me the eldest."

"And is your eldest brother then so unhappy?"

"He is, I am sorry to say."

"Have you seen the new puppies?" asked Evelyn.

"No—do you mean at the kennels, or here in the village?"

"In the kennels at Hartswound. They are ever so wonderful! If we had not been here at Mr. Maugham's today, I would have spent all morning there playing with them."

"Do you think my brother is unhappy, Mr. Percy?" asked Miss de Foye.

"Well, far be it from me to say—I barely know him. But I would guess that he is not entirely at ease with his position in life."

"There is one little doggy that has a ring around each eye," said Evelyn. "He looks as if he were wearing spectacles—I cannot tell you how comical it is; I laugh myself dizzy just looking at him. You must go down to the kennels and see him for yourself."

"I shall have to do that," said Edmund.

"It is odd," said Miss de Foye. "I have never really thought of it that way before. My brother can be moody, and sometimes quite angry; but I had never really thought that his moodiness might have its cause in his situation; I thought it must be his character."

"Well, as I say, I know Mr. de Foye but little; but I think you will find his moodiness much relieved when he is independent."

"There is also one that is all over brown, as brown as hot chocolate—do you like hot chocolate, Mr. Percy? I adore hot chocolate, though I rarely have it—but his tail is all white. Mr. Dickson—he is the huntsman, you know—he says that when that puppy was born, he held him over a pot of paint and dipped his tail in it; and at first I believed him. He told me that his tail originally looked just like that of a fox, with just a white tip; and he wanted to paint the whole thing, so that he would not be mistaken for a fox by the other dogs. And I believed him! But Mariah told me that Mr. Dickson was only quizzing me."

"But my brother's independence will come at such a terrible cost," said Miss de Foye.

"Indeed it will," said Edmund. "It is unthinkable, I know. But come it shall; and perhaps your brother will find some consolation in being at last his own man."

"You cheer me," said Miss de Foye. "It is an event I have always dreaded—constantly dreaded."

"Has your father always been so ill, that you feared his passing so constantly?"

"No, not ill; but when I was a girl my father still rode to hounds, long past the time he ought to have stopped; and he suffered constant spills and injuries. The mere sound of the huntsman's horn makes my heart turn cold.—But even in this ill there will be a blessing, if what you say is true."

"Though my experience of life is but brief," said Edmund, "and it would seem presumptuous on my part to offer any conclusion drawn from it, I have to say that so it ever seems to be: God grants us a nearer way to heaven in each grief we suffer. We must only choose it."

"And if you go down to the kennels," said Evelyn, "you must stop and see the lambs as well." She imitated their frisking stride for a few paces. "They are wonderful! I wish they did not have to grow into great, silly sheep! One can continue to love a dog—and I do dote on Commander and Lieutenant, even though they are not puppies—and I do *like* sheep—they are endlessly funny and silly; but I cannot *dote* on them, they way I can *dote* on a dog. With dogs, you can lie next to the fire and pat them, and they put their heads in your lap and dote on *you*. I hate it when people dote on me, but I do like to be doted on by a dog."

Now Edmund made the mistake of trying to start yet a third topic of conversation. "I am sorry to be the cause of this late hunting, Miss de Foye," said Edmund. "I did not know your feelings about it."

"Why should you have cared even if you had known them, sir? It is I who am judged foolish in this respect by society. Think nothing of it. My brother delights in dangerous things. He thinks he is invulnerable; and so far, he has not had a lesson to the contrary. He would have found *something* risky to do with his time; perhaps it is just as well that he is hunting rather than doing something else."

"But hunting need not be dangerous. There is a many a fine old hunter who dismounts at every ditch and at every gate."

"Ah, yes," she said, with an ironic glance at him, "but certainly you cannot pretend the young hunters do so."

"Do you have a dog, Mr. Percy?" asked Evelyn.

"My father has had dogs at Brackensom."

"What kind of dogs?"

"Harriers."

"How is a harrier different from a regular dog? That has always been a mystery to me."

"Well, I suppose you mean how is a harrier different from a foxhound. A harrier is used to hunt hares, and a foxhound is used to hunt foxes. They have a different build altogether."

"Well, I pray that is far in the future," said Miss de Foye.

It took Edmund a moment to realize to what she was referring in this disjointed conversation; but he guessed she meant the demise of her father. "I am sure it is," said Edmund.

"I shall not be at home then," said Miss de Foye. "But I hope I shall not be far."

"Where will you be?" asked Evelyn suddenly, her attention arrested at last by the alternate topic of the conversation.

Miss de Foye reddened slightly. "Oh, I do not know. I am not sure. Remember, Evie, we have talked about this."

"You will be married, do you mean?" said Evelyn disconsolately.

"Just as lambs grow up, friends get married," said Edmund.

"I hope that does not mean they become sheep for the slaughter," said Miss de Foye. Edmund laughed.

Miss de Foye now gestured ahead of them to a small cottage. "That is Mrs. Bunt's," she said.

As they approached the place, Edmund said: "Perhaps it would be useful for me to know Mrs. Bunt's ailment, Miss de Foye."

"She has cancer of the bone in her hip. It has been very deep for years, but in the last month it has—pardon my frankness, sir—eaten its way to the surface of her flesh, and so at last confirmed Mr. Spede's diagnosis, and rendered his prognosis ineluctable. It is more painful than the tongs of the Inquisition."

"It does sound excruciating," said Edmund.

The cottage was set close to the road at one end of the village; it was a very old place, roofed in much-weathered thatch, and diminutive in the extreme: Edmund was to discover that it contained only two rooms, a kitchen and a bedchamber. He saw obscure signs that, like the rectory, it had once had a thriving kitchen and herb garden; and recognizable flowering plants of last season were visible among the weeds about the place.

They knocked on the door. It was opened by Mrs. Brownton, and they entered. This immediate room was the kitchen; it had a rough hearth on which a low fire was burning. It struck Edmund at once that the interior was completely at odds with the exterior: here strong hands had been at work cleaning and tidying, and there were marks of lavished love and care in every aspect of the simple place. He set the basket of food on the lone table in the room.

"I understand that you know Mr. Percy," Miss de Foye said to Mrs. Brownton.

"Yes, we met just yesterday.—How do you do, Mr. Percy? The weather is somewhat better for visiting today."

"Indeed, Mrs. Brownton. I hope you and Mr. Brownton are well?"

"Mr. Brownton is having another good day, so we are pleased. As for myself, I do well if my husband does."

Miss de Foye then explained, "Mrs. Bunt had hoped Mr. Maugham would come today and say a prayer with her, but he cannot."

"Is he so poorly, then? It is not like him to fail an old friend such as Mrs. Bunt."

"He could barely walk from his bedchamber to the study."

"Oh, dear. I am sorry to hear that."

"We are to return to his house for dinner when Susan comes; I will send home a message with Evelyn if he needs anything this evening. In any case, Mr. Percy has kindly agreed to offer a prayer, though he has not been priested yet."

"That is very good of you, Mr. Percy. I think that may meet Mrs. Bunt's needs.—By the way, Mariah, the dressing on Mrs. Bunt's hip will need to be changed. You will not forget to have Susan attend to it?"

"I will see to it myself, Mrs. Brownton."

"No; you must not. That is what Susan is for."

"You know it quite turns her stomach. I changed it the entire time you were in Bath."

"It is worse than ever, though."

"The Lord's will be done. Who am I to quail at such a thing?"

"You are a young woman—you will harden yourself if you force yourself to confront such things."

"I wish to be hardened—in that respect, at least: I wish to be able to help, and if it requires hardening myself, I will do it."

"As you wish. I have left the clean dressing on the table."

Miss de Foye now turned to Edmund. "It would be best if you waited here until I called for you." Edmund understood that redressing the wound would require the exposure of the patient.

"Of course," he said.

"Come, Evelyn," said Miss de Foye. To Mrs. Brownton she said, "Good day, Mrs. Brownton. I shall send Evelyn home directly after dinner."

"Very well," said Mrs. Brownton. To Edmund she said, "It is good to see you here, Mr. Percy."

"I am glad to be of use," he said. "I have been quite idle for three or four days, and that is about three or four more than I can bear."

Miss de Foye and Evelyn went one way, through the inner door of the cottage, and Mrs. Brownton the other, through the outer door; and Edmund remained where he was.

The moment Miss de Foye entered the sickroom she began speaking in a cheerful voice to the patient, a voice whose warm tones carried even through the door when she had closed it behind her, though only as a pleasant murmur. It continued thus as the minutes drew out to a quarter hour, though it was intermingled with other murmurings, some of which rose into groans of pain. After this interval, Evelyn, looking somewhat pale, came back into the kitchen and set about awakening the fire on the hearth. She swung into the flames an old iron kettle that hung on a swiveling arm, after checking that it contained water. "She would like some tea," she explained to Edmund.

"How is she today?" he asked in a low voice.

"The wound is dreadful," said Evelyn with a shudder. "At first I could not help looking, and then I could not bear it. I thought I would be sick, and indeed I should have been, if Mariah had not spoken sharply to me. And I hate it when she does that! But she saved me from being ill, so I ought to be grateful."

The kettle, which had apparently been warming all day, was soon steaming briskly, and Evelyn made a dish of tea from some leaves she found in one of the few jars in the old woman's pantry. "We must bring more tea," she told Edmund. "Would you help me remember that? I shall never remember."

"Of course," he said.

The door to the inner room now opened, and Miss de Foye silently signaled to Edmund to enter. As he came to the doorway, she whispered, "I am sorry you had to wait so long."

"Do not mention it," he replied, in the same low voice.

This inner room was even smaller than the kitchen, about twelve feet square. He realized now that the inner wall, that is, the same wall as the doorway, was about three feet in depth, and contained a bed built into it, so that the sleeper could partake of the warmth of the fire in the kitchen on winter nights. To see the patient he had to step into the center of the room and turn back towards the inner wall. Miss de Foye did the same.

"This is the gentleman I told you about, Mrs. Bunt," she said. "This is Mr. Percy."

Edmund looked at Mrs. Bunt, and she at him. He saw a very aged woman, neatly dressed in a clean gown, with clean blankets pulled up well over her chest, propped on pillows that had just been freshened and plumped. Her hair, or what was left of it, had been brushed and tied carefully and covered with a crisp white cap. Her eyes were dim with cataracts, and she seemed to be trying to get a clearer look at him around the edges of them.

"Do come closer, Mr. Percy," she begged in a faint, hoarse voice. "Let me see you."

Evelyn had followed them into the room, and stepped up to Mrs. Bunt at the same time Edmund did. "I have your tea, Mrs. Bunt," she said.

"Oh, set it down, dearie. What do I care for tea when there is a gentleman in the room?"

Edmund came close to the bed; Mrs. Bunt reached out for him; and suddenly he found himself holding her hand in both of his own. She peered up at him.

"My goodness," she said, "you're a handsome fellow, Mr. Percy. I had no idea!"

He realized at once that she was not making an objective statement about her judgment; rather, she was flirting with him. He instantly adopted her mode of speaking.

"And I," he said, "had no idea you were so beautiful, madam."

She laughed once—a fitful breath that lapsed into a cough; but she smiled broadly, and continued to smile.

"I was quite the queen of the village in my day, you know," she said.

"You hardly have to tell me that, Mrs. Bunt; I can see it."

"Oh, well, I'm a sick and tired old woman now—I've lost my looks."

He knew instinctively how to play this game. "Not at all," he said. "Why, you could vie with the finest young thing out there."

She made a dismissive noise and looked away, but she wore a pleased grin and added, "Oh, you are a gallant gentleman, Mr. Percy!"

"When the first primroses bloom," he said, "I shall bring you some."

She tittered happily and turned to Mariah. "Did you ever hear such a thing, Miss de Foye?"

"Mr. Percy is already well known in Broadbridge for his skilled and effortless compliments, Mrs. Bunt. I ought to have warned you. He will quite turn your head."

"Ah, there are not too many men who know how to do *that* anymore," said Mrs. Bunt.

"Miss de Foye suggested that I might say a prayer with you," said Edmund. "I am not ordained yet, but the Lord does not by any means insist on that before we can pray."

"I think you have already done me more good than any prayer, Mr. Percy," she said, "but say me a prayer, too, and bring me my flowers when you have them, and you will have done all you can. I am dying, you know."

"And we all shall die too, and come along behind you."

"Shall I see my friends in heaven, do you think? My old Jack, and Martha?"

"You shall."

She looked pleased. "That will be good—that will be cozy; to get a bit of gossip from Martha over a dish o' tea. As for Jack, he will have some apologies to make."

"And I am sure he will make them."

"He will be quite reformed, or else not *there* at all."

"I think you may safely assume so."

"Well, then, say me a prayer, and I'll have my tea."

"Is there any prayer you especially like?"

"When Martha was dying, Mr. Maugham said that psalm—'In thee, O Lord, have I put my trust'—and said a prayer that started, I remember, 'We fly to thee for succour in behalf of this thy servant.'"

Edmund knew the psalm by heart, and the place in which the prayer could be found; and he said the first, and read out the second.

When he finished, she had tears in her eyes, and Miss de Foye offered her a handkerchief. "Lord bless you, child," said Mrs. Bunt as she took it. "And you, too, Mr. Percy, for saying that prayer; and for all your compliments."

In a minute more she was sipping her tea happily; though in truth she merely took enough to wet her lips and mouth: any more would apparently have nauseated her. Miss de Foye and Evelyn perched on two rough stools, which were all the furniture in the room besides a battered table, and Edmund stood to one side. "Now, dearies," she said, "tell me all the news."

The two women visitors now did their best to supply her with information she did not have on the doings of people in town. Edmund was surprised at how much they knew, though he noticed that Miss de Foye did not enter with quite as much zeal into the gossip as did Mrs. Bunt and Evelyn. She seemed only to be participating in an effort to entertain her patient, though occasionally she added a detail that neither of the other women knew, and which, it often seemed, greatly intrigued them. Periodically Mrs. Bunt requested little offices—a new pillow, a little help shifting in the bed, a blanket added; and Miss de Foye attended to them with a kindliness, practicality, and patience that Edmund found highly admirable. She seemed more a trained nurse than a wealthy gentleman's daughter; and if he had ever imagined she was spoiled by her position in life, he gave up that thought now.

Eventually Mrs. Bunt grew weary and wished to doze. "Go ahead," Miss de Foye urged her. "We will sit quietly with you till Susan comes."

"Let me talk to Mr. Percy one more time," said Mrs. Bunt.

"I am here," he said, coming forward into her field of vision. She reached out for him again, and again he took her hand.

"Tell me again," she said, "who is the loveliest maiden in the village?—After Miss de Foye, of course."

"Why, *you* are, Mrs. Bunt."

"Did you ever hear such a thing!" she protested, smiling happily. "It is very well that you are a good man, Mr. Percy," she added, "or you would be a very dangerous one."

"I shall strive to be better still, for your sake, Mrs. Bunt," he said.

She smiled still more; her head drooped; and in a few seconds she had drifted off into sleep.

He waited a minute and then carefully lowered her hand to the coverlet and withdrew to the corner where he had been standing before.

The three visitors waited in silence for several minutes until the opening of the outer door announced the arrival of Susan. Then they left Mrs. Bunt asleep and went back into the kitchen.

Susan proved to be a rather flighty-looking, if sturdy, young woman, probably the daughter of a local farmer. Edmund was sure she was being paid for her services, and wondered by whom—if not by the parish, then probably by Miss de Foye, he guessed.

"How is she?" was Susan's first question.

"Asleep, and that is likely to continue for an hour or so, till the pain wakes her again."

"Did Mrs. Brownton dress the . . . dress the . . . the *spot?*"

"I did. It is all taken care of for today."

"Lord bless you, Miss! I've been sick all day just adreadin' of it."

"It is very far gone. Did Mr. Spede see it yesterday?"

"Oh, no, Miss. I think he could not bear it neither."

"Do not be silly; he is quite hardened to these things, I am sure. I must speak to him about it. I wonder if it can be safely derided."

"I suspect he does not dare deride it, from your description," Edmund offered. "I have heard of cases like these where the doctors cannot deride the bad flesh, as the joint is simply too far gone."

"Yes," she said thoughtfully. "That is probably what is happening here.—Well, in any case, I will mention it to him."

She and Susan spoke further about the basket of food she had brought and arranged the morrow's attendance, and then Miss de Foye, Evelyn, and Edmund left the cottage.

They had not walked twenty feet before Miss de Foye stopped Edmund by turning to him abruptly. "You have done much good, sir," she said earnestly. "You cannot know it, because you have not seen the suffering she has endured these many months. I have not seen her smile so for years."

"My good offices pale in comparison to yours, Miss de Foye," he said, shaking his head.

She turned and led the way onward without another word.

As they passed the grocer's, he remarked, "Miss Brownton observed that Mrs. Bunt is nearly out of tea."

"Ah—a good thought, Mr. Percy. That is most kind of you. Perhaps I ought to buy it now, if you will allow me; then we shall not forget it tomorrow."

"Allow me to buy it," said Edmund.

"Please do not think of it," said Miss de Foye. She entered the shop almost before Edmund could reach the door and hold it for her. Evelyn entered behind her, and Edmund followed.

The couple that ran the shop made obsequious courtesies to Miss de Foye, and she exchanged various pleasantries with them before asking, "Do you know Mrs. Bunt's favorite tea?"

"That would be the bohea, Miss de Foye," said the proprietor, "though she has not been able to afford it for quite some time."

"A quarter-pound, please," she said, drawing forth her purse.

Edmund wondered at her optimism; he did not think Mrs. Bunt would live to drink that much. But he said nothing of this, and instead again interjected, "Miss de Foye—please allow me to pay for it."

She was surprised and, he thought, somewhat displeased. "Why should you do that, sir?"

"If I am not mistaken, it would tickle her fancy to hear it was a gift from me."

There was a moment when her reaction was in doubt, but then her questioning expression yielded to a beautiful, pleased, and generous smile, and she laughed; and putting away her purse, she repeated Mrs. Bunt's observation: "I am very glad you are such a good man, Mr. Percy; for if you were not, you would be very a dangerous one."

He paid a shilling for the tea, Miss de Foye took it into her keeping, and they went on to the rectory.

⌛⌛⌛⌛

Dinner at the rectory proved to be extremely frugal. Mr. Maugham offered his apologies over the meat. "In my declining years I have been setting aside some money—for a certain purpose; and that is very important to me. The glebe does not make as much money as it should; and of course I must pay Mr. Thomas—he is my curate, you know—out of my own living."

"You will not tell me what this purpose is," said Miss de Foye, "but I am sure it is not a selfish one. You should not let your concern for others reduce your own comforts, sir,"

"The truth is," said Mr. Maugham, "that if I had any other way to live, I should not be clinging to this living at all; I should have relinquished it to a man who can fulfill its duties, like Mr. Thomas."

"Oh, not Mr. Thomas!" exclaimed Evelyn. "Please, not Mr. Thomas! He tries to take my hand after service every Sunday. Last week I had to run out the back door to avoid him."

"He greets everyone, and shakes many people's hands," said Miss de Foye. "That is his duty."

"I have not told the full truth, however," Mr. Maugham said to Edmund. "The fact is that I do better on frugal fare than on rich. I think a *sauce* would slay me dead in an instant."

"I think we would all do better to eat such food, Mr. Maugham," said Edmund, "though I cannot pretend to practice what I preach in that respect."

"We so seldom do practice what we preach," said Mr. Maugham. "But that does not mean we should not try. As I look back at my life, I see a slow intersection between preaching and practice—slow, ever so slow, like two extremely long curves in geometry that meet somewhere off the paper and run from that point on in perfect identity."

"Mr. Maugham is a mathematician," Miss de Foye told Edmund.

"Really, sir?" exclaimed Edmund with great interest.

"Why? Is that an avocation of yours?" asked Mr. Maugham.

"Only in a very humble and amateur fashion," said Edmund.

"Ah! And what field is that especially interests you?"

"I must confess it is only that familiar to the ordinary schoolboy: the calculus in its several forms."

"The very thing! Yes, the very thing! I cannot tell you how much I love the calculus! Oh, why did you not come to Broadbridge years ago, Mr. Percy? We might have had many talks about mathematics."

"I wish I had, sir; and indeed, I might have, if I had not been sent to the West Indies on family business."

"And how long were you there?"

"Three years."

"Three years! Why, you seem to me too young to have been there so long. Would you pardon an old man for asking how old you are?"

"Twenty-seven as of last month, sir."

"So you went to the West Indies instead of taking orders?"

"Yes, I postponed them. And if I had not, I probably would have come to visit my aunt three years sooner—I had long promised to come."

"Yes, you are a great favorite of hers. You are quite the god of her idolatry, Mr. Percy."

"We are very much attached. She was my mother's sister, and my mother is no more; and as you know, my aunt never had children; so I am her chosen son, in a sense."

"And how long have you been in Broadbridge?"

"Since Tuesday noon, sir."

"And how have you spent your time?"

"In nothing useful, until today, I am sorry to say. But it has been a pleasant change, and, I suppose, useful in itself in allowing me to gather some strength of spirit again. I was much demoralized by my journey to the West Indies."

"I can imagine," said Mr. Maugham. Edmund was surprised that the rector required no further details to be persuaded on that point.

"Now," Mr. Maugham continued, "what are your aspirations?"

"What are aspirations?" asked Evelyn. Edmund looked at her in wonder; it was one of his first real glimpses into the fragmented state of her memory.

"An aspiration is a desire to achieve something," explained Mr. Maugham. "It is an ambition."

"Oh," said Evelyn. She looked curiously at Edmund. "Did you not ask me what my aspirations were—was it not just yesterday?"

"I did," said Edmund. "And so it is only right that the tables should be turned and I should be asked mine.—I should like to be the rector of a small country parish, where

I know all my parishioners and they know me. I should like to be of assistance to them, in matters spiritual, moral, and worldly. I should like to christen them, marry them, and bury them. I should like to go to my own grave knowing, or at least thinking, that I have helped them in whatever small way is possible."

"I am curious that you put such constraints on your ambition," said Mr. Maugham. "You strike me as a man of the world; and yet you claim that you wish to bury yourself alive in a little village—a little village not unlike Broadbridge. It has been my experience that men such as you, especially well-connected men such as one of the Percies of Surrey must certainly be, inevitably grow tired of service in such a backward place as this. Gradually they accumulate livings, and they choose to reside in whichever of their parishes has the finest rectory. They hire curates—and here I own that I do unfortunately practice what I preach against—and they become absentee shepherds of the souls of their flocks. Or they marry well, and are drawn into a society that numbs their sense of what they owe their parishioners. Sometimes they turn to literary pursuits to entertain themselves—this fellow Crabbe, now, has been accused of that, though many love his poetry. Some might equally plunge themselves into the austere beauties of mathematics. And how is Mr. Edmund Percy proof to these temptations? How is he so sure that meeting the needs of his few parishioners will satisfy him, and that no other ambition will raise its Gorgon head to freeze him in his tracks, or sing its siren call to lure him onto unseen rocks?"

"I feel the force of your question very deeply, sir; and indeed I have myself observed in society the evils of which you speak. We must rid the church of them; but much must change elsewhere in society before that happens, not least our system of primogeniture, which I have come to believe injures both its apparent beneficiaries and its younger sons. As for myself, I can only offer this assurance: when I arrived in the West Indies, I formed a plan to run my father's plantation there on humane terms. I found it was impossible. One could as soon conduct a joyful marriage ceremony amid the ongoing carnage of the battlefield. The system of slavery is far larger than one Edmund Percy and his ambition to reform it. I came back humbled—much humbled, in a most salutary way—and strengthened in my lifelong resolve, which has always been to be minister to a small village. Only now my aspiration has been given a more outward motivation. Before I went to the West Indies, I think I had wanted to be a clergyman because it meant my independence, more than anything; and when I came back, I had been—I do not know quite how to express it—I had been *taught* in practice what I had always thought I knew, which is that we are here to serve others, and that we must seek the most effective means to do so; we must not throw away our strength in a hubristic frontal assault on Mammon and the Devil, we must do our own small part along with many thousands of millions of other men and women to lever up the pedestals on which those idols stand and topple them over. In other words, I had realized that if I was to serve others effectively at all, it would be only in such a small setting as a village, and if on the larger stage, then only at a remove and by infinitely small increments."

"Your time in the West Indies was indeed very bitter, then," said Mr. Maugham.

"Yes, sir."

"It has been the making of you."

"Yes. That is very well put, sir. I do believe it has."

"I am glad to hear it. I did not have a similar experience till I was in my forties. I came to this living a very proud young man—proud of my gaining it, for it was and is a good living, despite what you see on the table before you. I married a very beautiful young woman from the social ranks above me, and though I was proud of her, she was miserable with me. We were childless for some fifteen years, and then she died—died a very painful death—in childbirth. The child, too, was lost. I hope you will believe that I was a shattered man, Mr. Percy—I hope you believe I was good enough to be a shattered man. It might well not have been the case that the foundations of my being were overturned—there was nothing guaranteeing an anagnosis, a crisis, and a spiritual reformation; I might have gone on in the same proud way, and married above my station again, lived most of my time in that world of glistering ease, and continued to neglect my parish. But by the mercy of God, I was granted an insight into my character; I was humbled; and like you, I learned that the highest good I would ever do—if I could even attain that—would be to bring comfort to such souls as Mrs. Bunt, by saying a prayer, or offering a sincere consoling truth about the mercy of our Lord and of our eternal life hereafter. The fools who strut upon the larger stage of the world do not know this truth—and what a better world we would have if they did! If every man helped the one next to him, instead of cherishing the conceit that with broad, sweeping strokes he could advance all of humankind. The irony is that women do much more than we can ever do, Mr. Percy, because we have—in our arrogance and pride of place—compelled them to act within the narrow compass of their homes and their own small circle of acquaintances. If it were not for such women as our Mrs. Brownton, and your aunt, and Miss de Foye here, the world would grind to a miserable halt—the vast and vague ambitions of our sex, Mr. Percy, are like sand cast into the gears of a clock, while the focused ministrations of the feminine half are like an oil, a balm that makes all run smooth."

"I thank you for the compliment," said Miss de Foye; "but as I have often said before, I have seen too much of the littleness of my own sex to quite agree with you."

Mr. Maugham turned his hooded eyes toward her and smiled softly. "You know, my dear, I am not saying that God's instruments are without pettiness. I know whereof you speak; all humans, male and female, are petty and small; we are such by our very nature, our very finitude in comparison to the Infinite. But still I maintain my point—that a common housewife folding a tablecloth is a higher servant of the purposes of God than any worldly man, no matter what his feats of oratory or deeds of bloody battle."

"My heart aches to agree with you, sir," said Miss de Foye with a smile. "But I do not see what is so ambitious about the folding of a tablecloth that makes you praise my sex for it so."

"It is precisely because it is not an act of ambition that it is truly great in the eyes of God."

"Then you are not praising the narrowness of the pursuits of my sex so much as you are condemning the hubris of those of your own."

Mr. Maugham only smiled for answer and spoke to Edmund again. "Miss de Foye and I have argued this point for several years now. I wish I could say that I have been as successful in this dispute as I am in our chess matches."

At this moment there was a noise from the kitchen, and Mr. Maugham leaned forward conspiratorially and spoke in a lower voice. "Now, Mr. Percy, since we have been speaking of the worth of small services, I must tell you that Mrs. Tooth will be in to clear in a moment, and you must suffer her to do all the work herself. She is most particular about it, and deeply offended at the mere suggestion that she cannot manage."

Mrs. Tooth was Mr. Maugham's housekeeper, and Edmund had already seen ample evidence that she was not quite up to the demands of her position. Indeed, she was very bent herself, and when she carried a dish to table, it shook as if it would slip from her hands at any instant. At her return to the dining room, the conversation stopped, and the diners literally held their breaths as she cleared each dish. In her hands, the serving spoons left in the china rattled like the clappers of bells, and the wine sloshed in its carafe as though she were deliberately mixing it with water. When she had laboriously cleared everything, she returned and inquired if anyone wished to have coffee.

Mr. Maugham seconded the question. "Do you like coffee?" he asked Edmund. "We can of course provide you with tea; but coffee immediately after dinner is an old habit of mine. I do not wait until later in the evening, or I find I sleep badly."

"I like coffee very much," said Edmund. "My aunt does not bother to serve it; for it seems no one in all Broadbridge takes it."

"Your impression is correct. Sometimes I think I am the only person in the village who takes coffee. Do you prefer it to tea?"

"Indeed," said Edmund, "though I admit I never liked it until I went to the West Indies."

"Your stock increases by the minute," said Mr. Maugham. "I cannot entice even so dedicated a disciple as Miss de Foye to drink my coffee; and here you present yourself already won over to it."

"You do not enjoy coffee at all, Miss de Foye?" asked Edmund, with the offended zeal of a recent convert.

"No, sir. I have tried it, but do not find it to my liking."

"Ah, well; perhaps you are better off."

"Those are the very words Mr. Maugham uses to reconcile himself to my failing in this respect," said Miss de Foye.

"Coffee for Mr. Percy," Mr. Maugham told Mrs. Tooth, "and for me."

The ladies withdrew to await them in the library. When the coffee came, Edmund had some sympathy for Miss de Foye's dislike of it; for it was ill-brewed and made of the stalest beans. It was mere dark water; but as a matter of course he drank it without saying a word.

"Let me ask you something," said Mr. Maugham when they had sat for some time in a companionable silence. "Did the Altons ever consider adopting you?"

Edmund was taken aback. "I do not know, sir. The idea never occurred to me—or perhaps to anyone."

"Of course not; especially not when both of your parents were alive. It is too late now, of course; but I believe that if the Altons had done so, they probably would have been able, under the terms of the entail, to leave Fairhall to you."

"That would have been very advantageous, of course—to all but the cousin who will now inherit. But I believe my aunt and uncle cherished hopes of a child of their own for quite some time; and I think my father would have been quite shocked at the suggestion."

"He is proud, then, your father?"

"He is, I am sorry to say. He is indeed. It is a different sort of pride, though, from that you see in—if I may say so—the master of Hartswound. My father's pride is coupled with strange fears and fancies. He loves Brackensom deeply, and is terrified that somehow fate will baffle him and it will revert to a cousin. I lost a grown brother to fever a few years ago, and that has preyed very heavily on his mind. By contrast, I think Mr. Cato Esquith de Foye is too bold a man to stoop to such uneasiness."

"Ah, but he too sees death drawing nigh, and wonders what will become of those he leaves behind," said the rector. He ruminated for a time, and then said, "About Miss de Foye I am not worried. The best of all possible paths for her would be to somehow become independent and never marry at all. Since that will never happen, I should like her to marry well; but that, too, is nigh on impossible. She will fall in love with some scoundrel, in all likelihood. But her brother will always be there to protect her."

Edmund said, "Your ideas catch me very much by surprise, Mr. Maugham. How can you think someone so prudent as Miss de Foye would make a bad match for herself?"

Mr. Maugham looked at Edmund as if wondering how far he could trust him; and then said, in a low voice, "I fear, from certain signs I have seen, that she has already formed a strong attachment; and her evasions when I question her only confirm me in my suspicion that it is not a good one. Perhaps it will pass; perhaps, contrary to all likelihood, it will fail. Perhaps her second attachment will prove wiser. Let her once find a good man to love, and she will do well enough—she will be happy. But where among our sex, Mr. Percy, is a man to be found who is good enough for her?"

"Indeed, Mr. Maugham, I do not know. Where is the man who could live with a goddess? Or with her *goodness.*"

"You have no ambitions there yourself, Mr. Percy?" asked Mr. Maugham.

"I? No, sir. My aunt has strongly cautioned me against any such thought; and I think I myself am too wise."

"Good. That is good, sir. She must marry someone of her own station or—well, as I told you, I have already seen the results in my own life."

Mr. Maugham reflected for a few more minutes and then said: "No, it is Miss Brownton I worry about." He looked speculatively at Edmund and then said, tentatively, "Tarquin was joking earlier about your marrying Evelyn. Tell me: do you think you would ever consider such a thing? You would have to forego any thought of what are called 'the marital rights.' Could you do that? If you truly loved someone as childlike as Evelyn?"

Edmund suddenly realized that this bent and physically decrepit old man could exercise a very powerful moral influence. He felt this force reaching out to enfold him, even to capture him. He chose his words carefully. "To tell you the truth," he said, "I have several times, since meeting Miss Brownton, actually entertained that idea. But I do not trust myself. I would not trust myself not to—not to desire what I could not have."

"Ah, yes," said Mr. Maugham. "That would be ruinous."

He drank the last of his coffee and added: "It is good to know one's limitations, Mr. Percy. 'Tis a pity, though; for I have been on the lookout for a man who appreciated Evelyn's good qualities and would respect her deficiencies. Someone must be found who can care for her."

"If I meet up with a charitable eunuch," said Edmund wryly, "I shall order him to report to you."

Mr. Maugham laughed—slowly and softly at first, but then with gradually increasing fervor, which terminated in a frightening cough. When he had composed himself, he smiled at Edmund—and a strange and tragic smile Edmund found it. "When we are young, Mr. Percy," he said, "such things as sexual relations matter very much to us. That is as it should be, and we cannot imagine any other way of being. But we do change with age. The day may come when you would be glad of such cheerful company as Miss Brownton, and ready to take her on her own terms. Look at me—I have two beautiful young women as my brides, in a manner of speaking; and though they remain ever virginal, I am yet quite happy to have their company. Indeed, Mr. Percy, my first prayer upon waking is one of thanks to God for vouchsafing me the company and respect of these two young women. When you are older and wiser, you will understand me."

Before Edmund could think of a reply, Mr. Maugham rose from the table with a nod; and then Edmund followed him to the library.

⌛⌛⌛⌛

The rector and Miss de Foye resumed their game. Edmund was very interested in observing it, but Evelyn had no use for chess, and soon distracted him from it. She chattered on in high spirits about the puppies, and then offered a detailed and amusing comparison between them and a litter of kittens in the village; and then she was on to another topic equally trivial on its surface, but developed in her unusual mind with such odd cross-connections to other subjects as to keep Edmund amused and entertained simply in the attempt to follow her. He found it extremely pleasant in itself to have complete license to observe her lovely face and figure at great length, animated as they were by her good spirits. She was constantly rising from her chair and roving about, as well as gesturing with her arms and hands in illustration of her points; and the motion of her small, slender form was bewitching, suggesting, as it must, the curve of hips and breasts beneath the shining cloth of her dress. If he had not known of her untouchability, he would have continued in some danger of falling in love with her; but as it was, he was coming to see her as a kind of overgrown child, granted the fascinating attributes of her sex, but preserved forever in a realm of sexlessness and chastity that no man should dare defile.

Miss de Foye, at one point when she was awaiting her turn, looked around from the chessboard and said mildly, "Really, Evelyn, you must not rattle on so at poor Mr. Percy. Give his brain room to breathe."

"Mr. Percy likes my conversation—do you not, Mr. Percy?"

"I do indeed," said Edmund.

"You are very kind, sir," said Miss de Foye. "Evelyn, perhaps Mr. Percy would like to read."

"I assure you, Miss de Foye, I would rather continue my conversation with Miss Brownton."

"You are too much a gentleman to admit otherwise, sir.—At any rate, Evelyn dear, do let Mr. Percy speak occasionally."

Evelyn, somewhat chastened, sat down in her chair and turned to Edmund. "Now it is your turn," she said.

"Ah, but I was enjoying the conversation so much as it was."

"No, I must not be selfish and keep it all to myself."

"What shall I tell you, then?"

She considered for a moment. "I have observed that if people do not want to talk about the weather, they often talk about their visiting," she said. "Whom did you visit after you left our house yesterday?"

"We visited the Caits."

He noticed that Miss de Foye shot a look at him after he said this.

"Oh, I like Miss Caits," said Evelyn. "I do not like Mr. and Mrs. Caits so very much. They think I am an odd creature; I heard them say so once. And perhaps I am; but I think they meant an odd creature one does not like; and I hope instead to be an odd creature one *does* like. And I think Miss Caits likes me."

"Miss Caits," said Miss de Foye, "is the finest young Christian woman in this town." She looked at Edmund again.

"Yes," said the rector, emerging momentarily from his preoccupation with the chessboard. "Miss Caits is admirable in every respect. If I had to play matchmaker as well as marry these young people who come to me, I would find her a nice young clergyman, full of progressive new ideas. She would be quite happy with him."

"She is not exactly pretty," said Evelyn.

"That is uncharitable," said Miss de Foye. "She is very attractive. She has a neat figure, dresses and does her hair impeccably, and is very pleasing to look upon.—Would you agree, Mr. Percy?"

"Indeed I would, Miss de Foye. I found her appearance very pleasing. Her conversation was intelligent—or at least, she asked good questions, and certainly approved the answers I gave, for I must say she was a trifle reserved; but I hope I can be forgiven for construing her approbation of my ideas as indicative of intelligence."

There was a pregnant silence. Miss de Foye wore the very faintest of mischievous smiles, and she and Mr. Maugham exchanged a significant look that did not go unobserved by Edmund.

"Well," said Mr. Maugham, "there you go."

"Yes," said Edmund, unable to resist, "I would judge her to be, as you say, Mr. Maugham, a most desirable match for a clergyman. And I would improve upon your praise, Miss de Foye; I would even go so far as to say that her face possesses a certain animation of spirits that makes her quite lovely."

"Really?" asked Miss de Foye, genuinely surprised.

"Indeed. But I suppose that people commonly acquire that kind of radiance when they are in love."

"In love!" cried Miss de Foye and Evelyn simultaneously, turning upon him.

"Yes; that is what I said."

"Miss Caits is *in love?*" asked Evelyn.

"Well, I presume so," said Edmund in an innocent tone, somehow contriving to keep a straight face.

"But do you have any *evidence* that Miss Caits's affections are . . . fixed upon someone?" asked Mr. Maugham.

"Oh, yes," said Edmund.

"Well, what is it?" asked Mr. Maugham.

"Ah—I see I have given away a secret—that I have already said too much."

"But *who* is it?" said Evelyn eagerly. "Do you know who it is, Mr. Percy?"

"I would not say another word," he said.

All three of them were extremely keen to learn what he knew; but they saw immediately that he was not going to tell them.

"But that is so provoking!" complained Evelyn.

Miss de Foye suddenly gave him a knowing smile, and Edmund suspected she had perceived that he was teasing them in retaliation. "Indeed," she said, "I am most happy for Miss Caits; though perhaps not so happy for all the young clergymen who must now resign their chance at her."

"Yes, I am sure they are quite without recourse in this wide world," said Edmund.

"In the world, of course not. But in Broadbridge they may find themselves somewhat more desperate."

"Do you speak so disparagingly of your own home, Miss de Foye?"

"Oh, not at all," said Miss de Foye. "We have many *pretty faces* in our village." He saw that her compliment was at best back-handed; for she did not praise the minds behind the faces.

"I can fully appreciate what you say, madam," he replied.

"I am sure you can, Mr. Percy.—So, Mr. Maugham, are you quite finished thrashing me, or must I go through the agonies of the endgame?"

"You must never concede, my dear, never. You must fight for your chance to win until the very bitter end. Perhaps you will get a draw."

"Yes, a draw is in some ways the finest of conclusions," said Miss de Foye.

"I would not say *that*," said Mr. Maugham. "You must always try to *win.*"

"But there are some arenas of life in which one loses by winning, and wins only by drawing. Do you not think that is so?"

"I suppose I see your point. But chess is not one of them.—It is your turn, my dear."

Evelyn now resumed her conversation with Edmund, uninterrupted by Miss de Foye, and he listened to her with continued amusement until the chess game had concluded in a mate. Then Mr. Maugham invited him to play, and he accepted with eager anticipation of a good game.

Evelyn proudly set the pieces in their starting places on the board. Miss de Foye watched her with a loving smile and said, "Evelyn, perhaps Mr. Percy would be interested in learning the characters of the chess pieces."

"Their characters?" repeated Edmund.

"You have shown so much pleasure in Miss Brownton's company, Mr. Percy, that I think you would find her account of the chess pieces very rewarding."

"I am intrigued," said Edmund.

"You see," said Evelyn, "each piece has its own qualities. I shall tell you what they are. First is the pawn. He is a lazy sort of fellow; he cannot walk far. He is the sort of fellow you see at fairs, who comes to pay a penny for pie and ale, and lies in a corner and watches the world come and go without even seeing it. If you want to send him on an errand, you will be greatly disappointed in him; for before he gets where he is going, a thousand other messengers will pass him by; and like as not, he will get distracted before he gets there and never arrive. He has a great, round ball of a head, quite bald, and a funny little collar—there, you see it."

Edmund laughed, and exchanged a look of mutual amusement with Miss de Foye.

"Now, the rook is an odd one. I never knew why he is called a rook, because he is not a rook at all. A rook is a bird—or rather, a real rook is a bird, a black bird, rather common and noisy; but a chess rook is actually a small castle, or maybe a tower. He is full of soldiers, silly redcoats, and they are all drunk."

"Like the pawn, you mean?"

"Oh, yes—even worse. They are like the redcoats you see at the inn sometimes, carousing and shouting at pretty girls who walk by. They say, 'Hip, hussy, where do you go?'—And the reason the rook can get about so quickly is that the castle is only pasteboard, and there are so many of these redcoats that they can put their many legs down underneath and pick it up and run with it, like the men who carried Lady Fitzhenson's litter when she came to visit Mr. Cato."

"I see," said Edmund, grinning with delight at this fanciful picture.

Evelyn now raised one of the knights and showed it to Edmund, like a schoolmaster showing his students a slate. "Now, the ones who look like horses—I believe they are called the knights—they are foxhunters. They can talk of nothing but fox hunting."

A merry laugh now burst from Miss de Foye, and Edmund was momentarily distracted by the sound; for if he had thought Evelyn's laughter beautiful, he found Miss de Foye's doubly so. He felt like an inhabitant of Plato's cave who has come out into the sunlight, the very sound of it was so distracting and bewildering; it was almost a glimpse of another world.

"There are four of them," Evelyn continued, "two on each side; and they are all continually talking about fox hunting. It is, 'Halloo!' and 'Huntsman, blow your horn!' and 'Why did Ashleigh not simply take that hedge?' and 'She is a fine bitch, but she is in heat, and we shall have a hard time getting the hounds not to run straight home,' and 'My horse threw a shoe and I was not in for the kill,' and 'We drew six covers and found nothing' and 'We gave the hounds blood,' and 'He is the best whipper-in in all of Hampshire,' and 'The hounds found the drag, but then by Coverdale they checked,' and 'You must feed hounds horseflesh, as anyone knows,' and 'Blasted hound is always flashing at rabbits,' and 'We had to stop out the hounds when we got near the Vine,' and all manner of things like that. They all talk *over* each other, and you cannot make out one word from another—it comes out in a great mishmash, and sounds like this: 'Halloo-fox-cover-drag-sport-whipper-fox-hounds-draw-hunt-Ashleigh-flash-hedge-jump-run-lane-field-blood-dogs' and so on."

By this point Miss de Foye had one hand over her midriff and one over her mouth and was laughing with such full delight that there were tears in her eyes.

"Oh!" she gasped, "Evelyn, you are *wicked!*"

"It is most tiresome," lamented Evelyn of the knights' babble, continuing as if she had not heard Miss de Foye's interjection. "When they move, they hop about like prancing horses, going every which way, and never in a straight line, so that if you are not careful they will step on your foot and crush it.—Next, of course, are the bishops. They are—well, they are like curates."

It was Mr. Maugham's turn to laugh now, which he did only somewhat hesitantly, as if afraid his laughter would turn to coughing again.

"They stand up in front of all the town and talk; and the town is like the fairy tale of Briar Rose, and it all falls asleep—man, woman and child—for a hundred years until next Sunday."

All the members of her little audience laughed aloud at this characterization.

"And the bishops," she went on, "cannot move but by a kind of sideways gliding, like Mr. Thomas trying to claim Miss Eaton for a dance, going sideways through the room so that she does not see him coming and cannot run away.—Now, the kings; they are quite pompous fellows, and think themselves fine swells. You can see that just looking at them. They are large, and wear enormous crowns that give them terrible headaches; and so they become cross, and sulk, and do not want to go out visiting or to see puppies or do anything fun. They think that because they are so very important, everyone else must fuss about *them*. There is only one on each side of the board, and they shout nasty insults back and forth at one another, such as 'I'll lump your jolly nob for you!'"*

She made as if she would use the piece itself, which was rather large, as just the sort of implement one would use to knock someone else over the head, and screwed her face up into as much of a likeness of a pop-eyed and belligerent monarch as she could manage. The contrast between the image she intended to portray and her own features was very amusing.

"That is excellent," said Edmund, "But you have skipped the queen."

"I have not *skipped* the queen," said Evelyn, "I have *saved* the queen, because she is the best."

"Let us skip the queen for now, dear," said Miss de Foye. "Mr. Percy would like to start his game with Mr. Maugham."

* "I shall hit you on the head."

"Oh, please do not deprive me of the pleasure of hearing Miss Brownton describe the queen, Miss de Foye," said Edmund. "I would gladly postpone the game for that."

"The queen is the best," said Evelyn, "because you see—" and she went and held the queen up beside Miss de Foye, as if there could be some visible resemblance that Edmund would perceive at once—"Because you see the queen is the most beautiful woman in all of Hampshire—in all of England. She is like one of the wonderful houris or peris in the stories of Persia, or Briar Rose herself. When she speaks, all obey her; and she has absolute power to move in any direction she wishes on the board. She is kind, she is true; she is wise, and her voice is—what is the word?—*melodious;* yes, melodious. She can ride a horse like a huntsman; she can sing, read, and write in three or four languages; her drawing, needlework, and penmanship are beautiful; she is the best friend a girl ever had or ever will have—"

"There, there, dear," said Miss de Foye, reddening slightly and patting Evelyn's hand, "that is enough."

"This is my favorite part," Mr. Maugham confided to Edmund.

"The queen, you see," said Evelyn, "is none other than our own Miss Mariah Esquith de Foye."

Edmund and Mr. Maugham applauded, and Evelyn, putting the piece down on the table, did the same, turning her eyes toward Miss de Foye.

"Oh, honestly," said Miss de Foye, "you are the silliest creature in all the world—though I love you just the same."

"And I would not have missed that for all the world," said Edmund. "I have a whole new understanding of chess now. I wonder why they did not teach me that at University?"

The game commenced. Miss de Foye opened her work basket and began to sew, though she observed each move with perfect attention. After three or four moves, it occurred to Edmund that he had not seen her bring her basket with her that morning, and he mentioned the fact to her. "I keep a separate work basket here," she explained. "I spend so much time here that it would be inconvenient to carry one back and forth."

"You see how gradually I have come to command a vast amount of Miss de Foye's attention," said Mr. Maugham. "I would go so far as to fit out rooms upstairs for the ladies, but that would be the final admission that I am robbing their parents of their rightful honors."

"From what you have told me, it would be quite a task to fit out those upstairs rooms," said Miss de Foye. "I have never been in them, but you have always said they are full of things—quite crammed with furniture under dust covers. I always wondered where all that furniture came from."

"It was originally the possession of my sisters-in-law; I stored it for them after my wife's decease, but they are long since gone, and I could never interest anyone in retrieving it. There are some fine pieces; but as you say, they quite fill the rooms."

"The house is very large," said Edmund.

"Very," agreed Mr. Maugham. "It requires a family to make it feel fully lived in. Perhaps the next rector will do better on that score. But he will have to clear out the furniture."

"You live solely on the first floor now?"

"That is correct. My bedchamber is through that door there; it was a parlor before that. Mrs. Tooth has a small room off the kitchen—smaller even than the larder. There is a cellar as well, good for storing wine—in my younger days I had quite a good collection, but that is all past now. I am now content with vintage far less dear than I drank in those days."

Evelyn, apparently exhausted by her high jinks, had sprawled on a sofa and was now asleep. She had that quality, commonly seen in babies and children, of disclosing in sleep her inner character: she looked extremely sweet and innocent. Edmund, in fact, found her distracting even in repose; though as he beheld her he could not school his own thoughts to the same level of innocence as their subject. He could not help wondering what her fate was to be. The horrors of the madhouse might well lie ahead of her.

He did not play particularly well. He foresaw the consequences of certain mysterious moves taken by Mr. Maugham only too late, but he was able to focus his attention better during the endgame and escape with a draw. The process was a long one, and the evening was well advanced by the time that conclusion had been reached.

The lateness of the hour did not deter Mr. Maugham, however. "Would you care for another game, Mr. Percy?" he asked.

"I would," said Edmund, "if only to show you that I can do better than I have this evening. But I ought to go home; my aunt has had no word of me all day, and though she will not have worried, it would be a courtesy to reappear there before too much longer.—And you, Miss de Foye? I assume you have arrangements to get home?"

"The carriage should be here for me at any minute," said Miss de Foye. "Thank you for inquiring.—Now, Evelyn, dear," she went on, turning to the sofa where the sleeper lay and tapping gently on the cushion, "perhaps you ought to go home."

Evelyn awoke and rubbed her eyes like a sleepy child.

"Come, come," said Miss de Foye. "Time to go home."

Evelyn stood up from the couch obediently. "Can we see the puppies tomorrow?" she asked.

"Yes, come up first thing and we shall go see them. I cannot spend the whole day in the kennels, though.—Now, where have you put your Spencer this time?"

"Oh, dear," said Evelyn.

"Go look in the kitchen; it is the only place it could be."

Evelyn ran off to get her jacket. When she had left the room, Edmund said to Miss de Foye, "If you would allow me to see Miss Brownton home, I would feel more at ease."

"Our village is quite safe, Mr. Percy; Evelyn and I walk about it constantly and have nothing to fear. But if you wish to do so, I would not stop you."

When Evelyn returned, wearing her jacket, Miss de Foye said, "Mr. Percy will see you home, dear."

"That is wonderful, Mr. Percy!" said Evelyn. "We shall be the talk of the town."

Miss de Foye shot Edmund a bemused look, as if to say, "You asked for this." He responded with the merest ghost of an amused grimace.

"I shall not see you to the door, Mr. Percy," said Mr. Maugham.

"Of course not, sir; there is no need."

"I shall not even stand up; I rely on your pardoning my lack of manners."

"Say nothing of it, sir."

"I trust you will consider my home open to you at any time during your stay in Hampshire. I greatly enjoyed our conversation."

"I did so too. I should like to continue it. I suspect you have much to teach me about the church that I never learned from my tutor."

"That is the truth!" sighed Mr. Maugham. "And I hope we shall play chess again, and discuss mathematics." Then, turning to Evelyn, he said, "Well, my little bird, it has been a pleasure to see you, as always. Sweet dreams."

"Sweet dreams to you, Mr. Maugham."

Miss de Foye now spoke to Edmund. "I should remind you, Mr. Percy, that you promised Mrs. Bunt some flowers; but I am sure you will not forget."

"I assure you it is quite well fixed in my memory, Miss de Foye. I shall take some primroses to her cottage as soon as I see them in bloom."

"That will be very kind of you, sir."

"What, Mr. Percy?" said Mr. Maugham. "You are plying the ladies of the village with flowers, are you?"

"Mrs. Bunt was quite taken with Mr. Percy," Miss de Foye told him.

"The esteem was mutual," said Edmund.

"You are well on your way to a conquest of all the feminine hearts in Broadbridge, Mr. Percy," said Mr. Maugham. "First Evelyn's, and now Mrs. Bunt's. It will be most amusing to watch them fall one by one."

Edmund smiled, but thinking of Miss Caits, he replied, "There are some that I cannot conquer, Mr. Maugham. Either they tower, adamantine, far above the humble engines of my siege, or they are already taken."

Mr. Maugham laughed, but unless Edmund was mistaken, Miss de Foye seemed to be embarrassed.

"Well, good luck to you," said Mr. Maugham.

Miss de Foye only said, "Good night, sir," and looked away.

As Edmund went away with Evelyn, he himself felt somewhat embarrassed. His last sally had been unfortunate; it had not occurred to him that Miss de Foye might interpret his comment about hearts that were already taken as referring to her; for indeed, he would not have presumed to include Mariah Esquith de Foye in such a jest.

The moment he and Evelyn started walking, she put her arm through his. He was surprised at how readily she did so, considering her reluctance in the matter only yesterday; but it came to him that it was only a type of playacting for her. She took no pleasure in it; human touch was to her no assurance or support; but she could set aside her annoyance at it if the amusement of *acting a part* appealed to her. Thus she had danced with him—in the pretense of being something else, as a little girl might pick up a doll and dance about the nursery. She thought a rumor of connection between Edmund and her to be amusing only because it would be an erroneous conclusion on the part of those who started it. Grownups danced with one another; grownups walked arm in arm; and it was only in the delightful pretense of being something she was not and would never be—an adult—that she danced or walked so.

Still, he found it pleasant to have her beside him, even if only to join in her game. Despite the lateness of the hour, they passed several people to whom his aunt had introduced him, and both he and Evelyn were amused by their reactions; he doffed his hat and bowed, and received a courteous salutation in return, but the moment he and Evelyn moved on, they could hear a murmur of amazed speculation behind them. Evelyn giggled and he smiled.

He escorted her to the door of her parents' cottage. The maid informed them that her parents were already upstairs, so he did not enter. Evelyn implored him one last time to visit the puppies at Hartswound, and then he said goodnight.

⌛⌛⌛⌛

Andromeda was waiting for him in the parlor when he arrived home. "Some tea for you, dear?" she asked. "The night is a little raw, is it not?"

"Becoming so, I am afraid," said Edmund.

She rang and ordered tea; and then she said, "Sit down and tell me everything."

"We had good riding," he said. "The de Foyes keep a first-class stable, as you might guess, if you did not know it. We went thrice round a diabolical course that Tarquin de Foye had set up; and I am glad to say that we ended in an amicable draw."

"Well, that is not quite as good for your prospects as losing by a nose; but it is better than your winning, which I think you would not have stinted to do."

"Believe me, if I could have trounced him, I would have."

"And that would have been your last chance at the living, I fear."

"No, Aunt; I believe you underestimate Tarquin de Foye. He hates being beaten, certainly; but he has an honorable respect for sportsmanship. Besides, he would have wanted me to extend my stay here so that he could beat me regularly to make up for that one humiliating loss."

"And did you dine at Hartswound again?"

"No. We rode to town, where we both needed to pay a visit to Mr. Exton."

"Ah! Keeping company with the de Foyes will be too much for your purse, Edmund. Do please let me pay Exton's bill when it comes."

"Thank you, Aunt; but I have paid it already."

"I suppose that was wise, and must have impressed Tarquin."

"I did not do it to impress anyone; I did it because I felt it the right thing to do."

"Well, of course, I know that. You must leave it to me to think of the *unintended* consequences of your good actions. And considering what you did in that light, I approve."

"Well, I am glad you do; but I cannot say your disapproval would deter me in such a case."

"We understand each other perfectly, as always.—But you cannot have spent the entire afternoon at Exton's?"

"No—and this you will find most interesting, Aunt; for as we were leaving Exton's, de Foye asked me if I would like to visit the rectory and meet Mr. Maugham."

"Really!" exclaimed Andromeda, putting her needlework down in her lap and disregarding it.

"Yes; I was very touched by what I took to be his interest in me. I like him more every minute I spend with him."

"And so you did go to the rectory?"

"Yes; and while I was there, Mr. Maugham invited me to stay for dinner. And a very enjoyable time we had, too; with some frank talk about the church, among other topics. He has asked me to come back at any time. After dinner we played a game of chess; and then I walked Miss Brownton home."

"Miss Brownton?" asked his aunt, arrested in the act of picking up her work again.

"Yes; she and Miss de Foye were at the rectory when we arrived. Before dinner I accompanied them on a visit they were paying to Mrs. Bunt."

"You *went with* Miss de Foye?"

"I did. Was there something wrong in that?"

"No, of course not. Only that—only what I said to you the other morning. I would just as soon you had not seen Miss de Foye in that role; for I have seen her thus often myself, and it is . . . it is very affecting to see the attention she lavishes on the needy."

"It is indeed; but you need not fear for me, I assure you. I am pitched at the level of a Miss Caits; we must only find another such as she."

She looked at him closely to be sure he was heart-whole; and seemed reassured. "Very well," she said. "It cannot hurt your prospects for the living if Miss de Foye has a good opinion of you, too; and so she must, if she spends more than a few minutes in your company.—How did she seem today? As distracted as she did at the ball?"

"Well, not this afternoon, in Mr. Maugham's company, and when we went into the village. But I met her on the steps of Hartswound Park-house this morning, and she was very distracted, I thought."

"Maybe in the interim she had an interview with the object of her attentions and has been reassured of his interest."

"Possibly; though I believe she spent the entire day at the rectory. No, I think it more likely to be the exact opposite: she knew she would *not* encounter her lover today, and so was not afflicted by anticipation of doing so. And I think that Mr. Maugham has a good effect on her. He brings her back to herself. And he, by the way, has noticed the very same distraction that you and I have seen, and ascribes it to the same cause; he told me so after dinner."

"But he knows nothing?"

"Nothing. He seems to be very pessimistic about her chances of avoiding a broken heart—he is sure that she has chosen wrongly."

"Oh, dear. That would be too bad. She is as sweet a young woman as—but let me not praise her."

"In any case, Aunt, you can judge her frame of mind for yourself tomorrow; for we are to dine at Hartswound, you and I."

Andromeda was extremely pleased. "Really?" she exclaimed. "Ah, Edmund, that is good news indeed. Even if the living does not go to you, it will be vastly entertaining to examine Mr. Cato and Mr. Tarquin in their native habitat; and of course Miss de Foye herself. Which of them invited you?"

"Tarquin. He says he will send you a note tomorrow. I am to go up a little early to talk about the meet."

"The *meet?* Did I hear you right? He is going to have a meet at this time of year?"

"He and his father cannot resist calling just one more."

She sat back and looked at him. "No, Edmund," she said, "it was a terrible winter; they had stopped hunting for the year. I heard of it; all Broadbridge knows when they have declared the season over—it is as if the world is going into mourning. This meet is in your honor, Edmund; I am sure of it."

"Well, I do not pretend otherwise," he said. "But I cannot take too much credit for it; clearly they would hunt at the slightest excuse, and a newcomer who likes to ride is at least that."

"But how shall we outfit you? Will the de Foyes lend you a horse?"

"Yes; I am to ride Agamemnon, old de Foye's hunter."

She nodded approvingly. "Then you *are* honored," she said. "And trusted mightily as well.—Did you bring top boots?"

"Yes. The scarlet is a problem. But it will be no disgrace to ride in a black coat on such short notice. Many a hunter did so in the old days, and the old ones still do."

"I should be loathe to see you wear black; you will be with some gentry it would be good to impress. Lord Burley commonly rides with the de Foyes, and he has a living in his gift, too.—There is no time to send into Surrey for your coat, I fear; if the de Foyes are going to hold a meet at this end of the season, they must do it soon."

At that point the tea was brought in. They spent another hour in conversation, and then Edmund excused himself to write a letter home.

Chapter 25

And if we could but get a young Heiress to Sanditon! But Heiresses are monstrous scarce.

—Austen

Edmund retrieved the horse from the inn and went up to the manor house at noon. When he was shown into the front hall, he observed chambermaids running up the stairs, their arms laden with clean sheets, and other servants polishing anew the paneling that had been buffed for the ball less than a week ago. There was a kind of electric excitement in the atmosphere, sparked perhaps by Tarquin, who strode to meet him when he was announced in the library. "The meet is on for Monday," he said, shaking Edmund's hand in welcome. "I trust you have no objection?"

"None whatsoever, except that we shall have to wait four-and-forty hours to begin it."

"Exactly my sentiments," said Cato from his chair by the fire.

"How are you feeling today, sir?" asked Edmund, advancing to greet him.

"Better than in many a long while. I have half a mind to see if I can get a-horse, with a little help from the servants."

"Do not even think of it, Father," said Tarquin. "You shall hear the whole account, in exact detail, when I bring the hunt home for dinner."

"As if that would suffice!" exclaimed Cato in disgust.

"You expect to entertain, then, too?" Edmund asked Tarquin, to turn the subject.

"Yes; some we will have overnight Sunday, and Monday, too, in all likelihood. I have messengers out to all points to see if we can get them together. If not, by God, it will be you and I and the huntsman.—But we must fit you out, Percy. I assume you have not brought your hunting gear into Hampshire with you?"

"No, unfortunately. I did bring my top boots, however."

"Well, let us go down to the stables first, and see to the horses; then we shall look through my wardrobe and see if we can make up what you are lacking."

"This is jolly good of you, de Foye," said Edmund; and to Cato: "And very kind of you, too, sir, to lend me your horse."

"Aggie is none the worse for his tumble," said Cato. "He will enjoy another good run."

"Let us hope we give him one," said Edmund.

"Come," said Tarquin, "the day is not truly begun until a man has a little dung on his boots."

They went to the stables, where they found the excitement that was visible in the house to be tripled in intensity. Leather and silver and steel were being buffed to a gleam, grooms darted every which way, the horses were restive, and the stablemaster was shouting at some hand who had failed to find a missing stirrup. Tarquin stopped in the center of this uproar and basked in it.

"A meet!" he said rhapsodically. "I say, Percy, is there anything finer? I *live* for fox hunting. I do not know how I *endure* the days from March through October without it. That is true winter for me—the summer months. It is like crawling through a desert.—Now, tell me, are your stables at Brackensom so fine as this?"

"No," said Edmund, "I must confess, you are far in advance of us for stables and kennels. We have but a dozen stalls, and most of them are filled with coach horses and plow horses. I have not kept my own hunter for some six years now. As for kennels, we have none at all; the master up in those parts is Lord Trueblood."

"Ah, of course—I have heard of him. He is said to run a good hunt."

"I believe it to be a good one. I certainly always enjoyed it."

Never did two men spend so idle an hour; for though they saw to their horses, they could not improve upon what they found. The tack and the beasts were in perfect order; and yet they found much to examine, question, discuss with the grooms, and ultimately approve.

Next they went to the kennels. The hounds and handlers, too, were in a state of great excitement; but here the preparation seemed to be taking place mostly in a verbal discussion among the humans. The huntsman—Mr. Dickson by name—and the whipper-in, a Mr. Lewis, were holding forth at great length and in very colorful language about how the hounds must be made to perform, and were arguing, most likely for the thousandth time, over the various vices and virtues of each. Tarquin joined in instantly, and after another pleasant hour of giving instructions and hearing the judgments of the huntsman, he took Edmund on a tour through these three enormous buildings. It was clear that he knew each hound by sight and by name, though the kennels held more than forty couple, with an amazing variety of nonsensical titles—for instance, in one pen alone he identified Thunder, Valor, Frogeater, Rampant, Boldface, Samson, Bluebeard, Larkspur, Muckle, Primrose, Maximus, Prince, Aladdin, Cogger, Wartface, Cream, Queenie, Beerbreath, Vanity, and Dancer. Edmund had never seen dogs so well cared for. They were in their element; for there is nothing a dog loves better than to run with a pack, to eat with a pack, and to sleep with a pack; they are running machines, pure and simple, but best of all they love to run together; and if not running, then they love to bark together in anticipation of running, or to lounge in heaps awaiting the next chance to run. The dogs of Hartswound were an extraordinary breed, very small—at most twenty inches in height—with extremely powerful forelegs and thighs, long bodies of a tan and black color, and arched backs; they had not a trace of fat anywhere to be seen. Each carried the kennel mark of a notch cut in the left ear. To Edmund's perception their baying was remarkably sweet in tone.

In a rare lull in the din, Edmund heard in the deeps of this vast place a familiar female voice, and when Tarquin was summoned to attend to some question of the huntsman, he went by himself in the direction of the sound and came upon Evelyn, sitting alone in the straw of an individual pen with a bitch and her puppies. She was happily giggling and talking nonsense to them, and did not notice Edmund for several minutes. When she did, she flung herself sideways in the straw and attempted to pull it over her and hide; but the puppies attacked her, licking her face until she shrieked with laughter and sat up again.

"Have you ever seen anything so wonderful?" she asked him.

"They *are* funny," he said, watching their antics. Then: "Are you down here all alone?"

"No; Mariah is with Nelson."

"Nelson?"

"Down there," said Evelyn, indicating another part of the kennels.

Edmund thought he ought to say hello, so he went in that direction. It was dark in this part of the kennels, and he was not sure where he was going; and he was somewhat surprised when he found Miss de Foye sitting in the straw of another pen all by herself, with only the company of an enormous mastiff. On the outside of the pen was a sign, lettered in a fair but girlish hand—he thought perhaps it was that of Miss de Foye herself, from several years ago—bearing the name NELSON.

"Good afternoon, Miss de Foye," he said.

For a long moment she did not answer. He saw that she had to rouse herself from the depths of a profound and disconsolate reflection in order to do so. "Sir," was all she said, and that but faintly and dismissively. The mastiff did not even raise his head from her lap. The two of them together made a picture of deep and mutual grief, so powerful that it put him in mind of his aunt's warning of the previous night. So he only bowed and walked silently away.

He went back to the pen where Evelyn was playing with the puppies. "Nelson is Miss de Foye's dog?" he asked.

"Yes; but he is a naughty dog, and so he must stay in a pen."

"That is too bad."

"Indeed it is. Mariah is very fond of him. She comes and sits with him a little every day, even though she is quite wretched afterward. The longer she spends with him, the wretcheder she is; and she has been with him now for hours."

"How very sad!"

"Yes. Mr. Dickson says that Nelson will probably die soon—of boredom, he says. He says you cannot just pen a dog up like that and expect it to live long. But he says that Nelson is not to be trusted. He says the most humane thing to do would have been to shoot him long ago; but Mariah could not bear it."

"Well, *she* certainly seems to trust him."

"Oh, he would not hurt her for all the world. Or me, for that matter; he is very sweet to me. The difficulty is that he is so protective of her. He bit that fellow Ashleigh once, just for *standing near* Mariah. He would even growl at Tark if Tark came near Mariah, and Tark would not stand for that. He says you must show a dog who is master; and once he nearly broke Nelson's neck with his own hands—but of course Mariah stopped him."

"That is all very sad," said Edmund.

He found Tarquin again, and they returned to the house. Tarquin took him upstairs to his own bedroom, or rather, the suite of rooms that was his own, for it was extensive. An entire room was given over to his wardrobe, and he had a dozen red coats, all of them in perfect condition; from these he offered Edmund one. It was a very good fit.

"You must have some cord to tie your hat," Tarquin said. "There is no point pretending we shall not knock them off, if we have the luck to draw." He turned to his valet, who was a mere boy, and ordered him to go to the housekeeper for some black cord.

When the boy had left the room, Edmund said, "I am amazed that you keep so young a servant, de Foye. He seems a bit awkward, which is no surprise at his age."

"Yes, he is still learning. But I have had older valets, and cannot stand them. They are so smug, and think themselves so wise, and are constantly wanting to talk back. At least Jacob jumps when I whistle. He may seem awkward, but he has extraordinary intelligence. He is very well spoken for a lad of his age—it is actually uncanny; you will see what I mean if you speak with him. I have an idea he might go to college someday and become a clergyman."

"A clergyman!"

"You are surprised?"

"Surprised that a de Foye is thinking of turning a servant into a gentleman? Yes, I am."

"But he is that well spoken."

"Is it then mere speech that makes a gentleman?"

"Of course not. At any rate, this idea of sending him off to college is just a mad idea I had once; I have never said anything to the boy himself."

In a few minutes the boy returned with the cord, which proved satisfactory; and Edmund was provided with a unique pin made of a fox's tooth with which to secure it to his lapel.

When certain other necessities had been provided for, Tarquin took Edmund to a room that would be his during the meet; he could change here in the morning, and stay overnight Monday if he wished. The room was sumptuously appointed, with a window that looked over the lawns before the house. "The finest Hartswound has to offer," said Tarquin.

"I am honored," said Edmund.

"Well, to be perfectly truthful, there are actually several rooms that are the finest Hartswound has to offer. We must put Lord Burley up in one of them; and Ashleigh laid claim to one long ago."

"Tell me," said Edmund, as they descended the stairs, "how did the park ever come to be called Hartswound? I should think Foxwound would be more appropriate."

"The Esquith de Foyes have always been hunters," said Tarquin. "We used to run after deer; but I suppose when fox hunting was invented, my ancestors quickly realized there was nothing to compare with it. But it was too late to change the name of the place then."

As Edmund passed one of the windows on the stairs, he noticed his aunt's carriage pulling into the drive below; and when they had descended, he excused himself and went out to meet her and escort her in. He reached the carriage just as the steps were put down, and offered her his hand.

"Anything new?" she asked in an undertone.

"The meet is on for Monday."

"Monday! Dear me, that *is* soon."

"No reason for concern. De Foye has fitted me out. I have everything I shall need."

"Excellent.—Well, let us enjoy ourselves, then, and see what the future brings."

"A good philosophy."

He gave her his arm and led her up the steps. A servant opened the door for them and then showed the way to the library to announce them. Here they found Tarquin and Cato waiting for them, along with Miss de Foye; Edmund surmised she had come back to the house while he was upstairs with Tarquin. She was standing behind her father, with her arms resting gently about his neck in a pose of great affection. It was a revealing sight; the only other time Edmund had seen them together, there had seemed to be too much willpower and imperiousness on both sides. And yet despite her evident love for her father, Edmund discerned, or imagined he discerned, an inexplicable anxiety and tension in her comportment. The ease she had manifested at Mr. Maugham's was gone; her thoughts were elsewhere again, and he could guess where.

As they entered the room, they were greeted by Commander and Lieutenant, Cato's two house dogs, in the usual way—an initial burst of barking, a rush to sniff them and be patted, and then a quick retreat toward their favored places by the fire. Tarquin and Miss de Foye came forward to meet them, and even Cato sat forward on the edge of his chair in a concession to formality.

"Welcome, welcome, Mrs. Alton," said Cato. "Forgive me for not rising to meet you. A distant salute will have to do for a handshake, I am afraid."

"I am glad that you do not discommode yourself, Mr. de Foye," said Andromeda. "I am unworthy of it; and we are both too old and wise to be put to any trouble."

"A lady is never unworthy of respect," said Cato, "but an old man may be too feeble to pay it. In any case, I bid you welcome."

"Very good of you to come, Mrs. Alton," said Tarquin, bowing slightly as he shook her hand.

"I am honored, sir," said Andromeda.

Miss de Foye, too, offered her hand. "A pleasure to have you with us at Hartswound," she said.

"A pleasure to see you in your own home, Miss de Foye," said Andromeda. "I never see you anywhere but in church, or in the home of some needy villager."

Edmund, too, again greeted Miss de Foye, and she him; and then he asked, "Have you seen Mrs. Bunt today?"

"I saw her this morning, when I went to the village to fetch Miss Brownton. She is much the same. She mentioned that you had stopped by; that was very kind of you."

"I was telling Edmund some of the stories I have heard of Mrs. Bunt in her younger days," said Andromeda. "There was not a swain for miles around who did not beat a path to her door."

"I believe she chose the worst of the lot, from what she says," said Miss de Foye.

"Women so often do," said Andromeda, "though I must add that it is not absolutely inevitable."

"I am glad to hear you say so," said Miss de Foye. "Well, do sit down."

From the moment they had seated themselves, a conversation ensued in which Andromeda Alton outdid herself for wit and liveliness. Edmund himself had never seen her so keen and so on the mark. She had both Cato and Tarquin not only laughing at every other sentence, but hanging on her every word, both surprised by her sallies and moved by the serious stillness at the heart of her storm of good humor.

Miss de Foye was not so approachable, it seemed. She smiled politely on occasion, but the more the afternoon and evening went on, the more she seemed to recede from the company in her thoughts. By the time they moved to the dining room, she was quite silent. It was as if her person were fading from the room behind a mist of her own concerns. The alteration in her mood from the previous evening was so stark that Edmund could not help wondering at her circumstances from time to time. It seemed to him that she was running through some calculation of probabilities in her head over and over; and he imagined that she was looking at her father and brother and trying to determine how they would accept the man she had chosen. The results of that calculation did not seem such as tended to offer her cheer.

In general, however, Edmund and the others observed her state but little. Andromeda engrossed their entire attention; which only goes to show that, at a dinner party at least, youth and beauty cannot compete with maturity and wit when the latter are at the top of their form. Edmund knew quite well what his aunt was doing: demonstrating that her nephew came with a local relative who was not only respectable, but a positive asset to society—that if the Esquith de Foyes were to make him rector of the parish, they need have no fear that they would suffer boorish dinner companions as a result. She had a more personal motive as well; and that was to demonstrate the loss the de Foyes had suffered in not inviting her into their circle years ago. In this she was so successful that finally, towards the very end of the dinner, Cato sat back in his chair, looked at her with warm approval, and said, "Now, tell me, Mrs. Alton, why is it that we have never had you to dinner before?"

"My dear Mr. Alton was not a hunter, sir."

"Not a hunter! Live in Hampshire, and not hunt! Why ever did you marry him?"

"Papa!" Miss de Foye exclaimed. "Please have some respect for Mrs. Alton's feelings."

"I married him," Andromeda told Cato, "because I loved him with all my heart, and he me; and we were wonderfully happy with one another for all the years we were together."

"That is an *excuse,* but not a reason," said Cato; but he tempered this outrageous comment with a smile.

"Believe me, sir, his kindness mitigated everything. I was unable to have children; he supported my spirits through four occasions when I was disappointed of a child. Never a cross word did I hear from him, never a voiced regret. I never had anything but honor *from* him, and I never have felt anything but love and honor *for* him."

Even the rash old master of Hartswound was touched by this speech. "Forgive my facetious comments, madam," he said. "You make me ashamed of myself. You see, I am blind to everything but hunting. Horses and hounds have been my whole life—except perhaps for my little friends the bees, who are likewise a mere passion; and I forget that there are other things in this world, and other interests. May your husband rest in peace. I wish I had been wise enough to make his acquaintance when he was among us. Perhaps I can remedy that deficiency in part through my acquaintance with your noble nephew here, Mr. Percy."

"You have found my soft spot, Mr. de Foye. Edmund is the darling of my heart, now that I am a childless widow; be kind to him, and you may commit any social sin you like against me."

"Well, now that you mention it, I have taken some thought for him. I have heard from my son about your nephew's mad plan to join the clergy. What can you think of that?"

"That if Edmund is mad, we desperately need more insanity in the pulpit."

Tarquin laughed, but Cato persisted. "But come, come, Mrs. Alton, what a waste! A man so proven brave, so fine a horseman!"

"And cannot clergy ride to hounds? If I am not mistaken, many of them have gone to the dogs, at least."

"But how ridiculous, a man of the cloth taking a hedge! And to be outridden by one—which would be very much to be feared if one were riding with such a hunting parson as your nephew would make—that would be insufferable!"

"Outridden? But a hunt is not a horserace, Mr. de Foye; unless I mistake the sport."

"Ah, to the de Foyes it is! Not to be in at the kill—has it ever happened to us, Tark?"

"Never, Father.—Well, maybe once or twice."

"Yes—maybe once or twice. But not often."

"The time you broke your leg, at least."

"You mean the second time; the first time I did not let it stop me. But that was before you were born. And the second time does not count; my horse was lying on my leg, and I could not drag myself from under it. A horse with a broken neck is a clear disqualification.—No, Mrs. Alton: you must persuade your nephew to give up the clergy."

"But how is he to earn a living, sir?"

"Cannot you provide for him, madam? We *need* him in our hunt."

"He would not endure to be dependent on me. Besides, when I die, Mr. Alton's brother's son will have his estate; I am fortunate to have a life right."

"But you are young, madam! You will live many years."

"You flatter me, and though I love you for it, sir, I cannot help but repeat that my giving Edmund room and board is no solution: he would not brook it, and in the end it would only leave him destitute."

"Then it is up to you, madam, to find him a rich young woman to wive; or failing that, a rich widow. London is full of 'em, I hear. You must take him up to London, marry him off, and then bring him back to us."

She repeated his suggestion, feigning wonder in a very droll manner: "Marry him off to a rich wife? Mr. de Foye, what a novel scheme! It is not true that there is nothing new under the sun; for surely your proposal has *never* been considered before, since the invention of the world. I only wish *I* had thought of it myself—that I had given it *some* thought before this very minute!"

Edmund and Tarquin laughed heartily. "Certainly we should be only ones in London with that object," added Edmund.

"But what are marriages *for,*" protested Cato, "but to get the right people into the money? The *right* people, I say; and Mr. Percy is surely one of the people we wish to see settled well in Hampshire. He does not need a great estate, just enough to keep a hunter and perhaps a carriage. His wife must be comfortable, his children must have shoes; and we shall all be happy."

"Papa," said Miss de Foye suddenly, with a fervor out of all proportion to the subject, "it cannot be very pleasant to Mr. Percy to hear you dispose of his future in such calculating terms, and as if he were not present."

"Pshaw! Mr. Percy is a man of the world, Mariah." Then, a new thought occurring to him, Cato said to her: "Think on it: is there anyone of your acquaintance who would do for him?"

Mariah turned to Edmund and said, "I must beg your forgiveness for my father's behavior, Mr. Percy. He means only what is best for you."

"And so I am well aware, Miss de Foye. We younger sons are used to hearing our fate bandied about, and to being bartered in the open market as if we were so much human chattel."

"That cannot be pleasant for you."

"I take it in good humor. As you say, it is well intended."

"But you *will* marry, will you not?" asked Cato.

"I will doubtless marry," agreed Edmund, "though I find I have little heart for it at present."

"Then why not an heiress, man?"

"Papa," said Mariah "if you continue in this vein, it will be time for Mrs. Alton and me to withdraw."

"Oh, pshaw!"

"It is really too crude, Papa," she said in a warning tone.

"What! That I talk of a good marriage for a good man?"

Mariah rose immediately and looked at Andromeda. "Mrs. Alton?" she said politely. Andromeda rose too.

"Oh, pshaw, Mariah!" said Cato again. "Do not be silly, girl!"

Mariah curtsied to her father and went to the door of the dining room, where she waited for Andromeda; who, with an equally gracious curtsy, joined her there, took her by affectionately by the arm, and with a last look back over her shoulder at Edmund—twinkling with humor just for him—escorted the younger woman from the room.

"Now, look what the girl has done!" complained Cato. "Spoiled our plans, Tark!"

"So it would seem, Father. And Mrs. Alton was to be our best ally. Well, perhaps she will be still. She seemed to find your idea not at all a surprise, if I read her protestations correctly."

"The problem is that you yourself have not cultivated anyone, my boy. If you had a rich and handsome widow in your sights, you could step aside and let Percy here put her in his bag."

"I confess I have been remiss in that, Father."

"I would die easier, you know, if I knew you had an heir."

"I think we have had this conversation before. I think the most recent occasion was but yesterday, in fact."

"Perhaps—but did you hear me then? Have you ever heard me?"

"Oh, I shall have an heir; you know that. It is just that—I would like a woman who rides, you know. And they are so few." His words had the well-worn feel of a speech given many times and offered again through lack of a better, or perhaps because he knew that it would elicit a sympathetic reaction and distract his father from his pursuit.

"That is the truth," said Cato. "A woman who rides well is so far to find. I thought never to marry, until I met your mother. Where we are to discover her like again, I do not know."

Tarquin said, "Well, I wait and I hope, though I admit I do not try too hard; and somehow I am already thirty-four."

"You still have time.—I married at a ripe age, Mr. Percy, as must be obvious to you; and it did not impede my riding, if you will pardon the expression, and my siring the two most perfect children a man ever had.—Though, I say, I think something has got into Mariah. She seems to have a bee in her bonnet these days."

"Oh, you know how women are," said Tarquin. "Unaccountable. I have noticed it myself. She seems wrung up, like a harp string ready to snap. You'll have to forgive her, Percy; she usually is better fun."

"Should we be doing something for her, son? What do you think? What would it be? Would she like to go to London again, and buy more clothes?"

"God, I hope not! What a bore!" said Tarquin.

"We had a ball for her. Surely she cannot want another yet?"

"No. She seemed somewhat put out after the last one, to tell you the truth. I had a capital time myself, though I never danced once; or maybe it was *because* I never danced once."

"Well, what *is* it that is bothering the girl, then?"

"Honestly, I do not know, Father. It will pass, whatever it is. Next week, like as not, she will be her old cheerful self."

"I hope so; I rather miss that. Always spending her time with the rector just cannot be good for her spirits. Those clergymen are such doom and gloom.—Oh, excuse me, Mr. Percy; I know it will not be so with you.—She has been gone almost every day lately.—You would not have any insight into this, would you, Mr. Percy?"

Edmund was surprised that his opinion should be sought in this matter; and further surprised to see that not only did Cato turn to him, but Tarquin, too, looked keenly in his direction. He took this as some indication that despite their apparent dismissal of the seriousness of the change in Miss de Foye, they were both deeply concerned. He chose his words carefully to chime in with their appearance of insouciance and conceal his own conjectures. "The only difficulty Miss de Foye is experiencing of which I know for certain," he said, "is that yesterday the lining of her glove was torn."

Both Cato and Tarquin—with the help of the wine, no doubt—thought this quite funny. "How came you to know this?" asked Cato.

"I observed her struggling with it."

"That must be it," said Tarquin. "Percy, we must add to your manifold other talents that you are wise in the ways of women. Her glove is torn!"

"You know," said Cato, "that *could* just be it." And father and son laughed gaily, and, as Edmund thought, rather cruelly. He was not pleased to have made Miss de Foye the butt of their humor, but he was glad for her sake if he could put them off the scent. The subject of marriage and marriage settlement had clearly made her uncomfortable. He deduced from this that her lover was not a wealthy man, and that Miss de Foye anticipated some objections from her family. He was amazed, furthermore, that neither her father nor brother had detected the likely cause of her changed humor.

The pitch of the conversation sank considerably after the women had withdrawn. Beversham brought a good port, and under its influence, and perhaps worn out by the stimulation of the evening, Cato soon nodded off in his chair. The topic naturally reverted, as it so often does among men left alone, to that of sports, and in particularly, the upcoming meet.

"Now, how many will ride to hounds, do you think?" asked Edmund.

"Can't say, really. We had quite given up the season, you know; and either people will say, 'Oh, those de Foyes are mad; why do they not just be quit for once?' or they will say, 'Thank God! Those de Foyes have come through again, and offered us one last chance at a run across country!' I know Ashleigh will come; he is soft on my sister, and I could offer him rat-hunting and he would show up at six in the morning if there were a chance of seeing her."

For a moment Edmund thought he had a clue. "Are his feelings reciprocated?" he asked.

"Good God, no! I should be appalled if they were, and have a good long talk with Mariah about him—and tell her a few things she could not possibly know otherwise. No, Ashleigh is a man who is just barely tolerable in the hunting field, but you would not want to have him about the house. He is one of these *silly* hunters, you know; always gets lost or left behind somewhere; but there is something vaguely likeable about him all the same.—Yes, I like Ashleigh; I do not mean to be too hard on the fellow. You will like him too, I think; though we shall not see much of him once the fox breaks.—Oh, by God, I hope we get a fox! I should hate it if we have a blank day! There is nothing I hate worse than a blank day! All winter long we hunt three or four days in the week, and we cannot have enough of it; but the blank days are enough to dash your spirits and make you wish you had not set yourself up for the heartbreak."

"It shall not be blank," said Edmund decisively, as if his saying so would make it so.

"I do hope not.—Anyway, next sure to come is Lord Burley. Old Burley is true as steel, though perhaps a bit . . . well, a bit slow in his cogitation, shall we say. But he never runs among the hounds, he never does something so stupid as to ride ahead of the dogs and mar the scent, he never rides about the cover and keeps the fox penned in—all of which Ashleigh will do like a rank beginner every time. But by the same token, Burley almost always manages to get lost. And I do mean lost; I do not know how it happens. If the kill is ten miles east, he comes home at eight o'clock at night and tells you the name of the hamlet he found himself in, and like as not it is ten miles west. If Burley comes, his neighbor is likely to show up, a man named Donaldson. We do not like him much; he gives the view-halloo as a joke—that kind of fellow. And he never shuts his mouth. Then we have the old regulars—" And from here, for the next fifteen minutes, Tarquin proceeded to recount a list of the hunting families in the neighborhood, with all their peculiarities and particularities.

When he had finished, Edmund said, "That will be quite a ruck, if they all come."

"Oh, yes, but we do not know that yet. Some days we have a vast ruck, you cannot believe it. I do not mind it so much; they sort themselves out after a quarter-hour or so of any good run, and you simply do not have to concern yourself with most of them. The ones I dislike are the damned social climbers—the counting-house apprentice whose uncle made a fortune in the Indies and left it to him, and he has bought himself a house over in the next village, and keeps a hunter at the inn stable there. He knows nothing about hunting, except that it is something that old money does; and he wants to be old money, which is the one thing he cannot be; or worse still, he aspires to nobility, and so hangs about Lord Burley. That type of man is despicable, and I have seen his ilk try to attach itself to our hunt some twenty times. I do not order him off; but I look for a chance to pick a quarrel with him, and it does not take long before I find one. Usually, of course, they tread on the hounds, and I would come near to whip a man who does that. So I end up cursing the fellow; and he grows hot under the collar, but he does not dare say anything against me; and he skulks off and is never seen or heard from again.—Now, if he were not *nouveau riche,* he would think nothing of being cursed by the master of the hunt, nothing. I curse Ashleigh a dozen times before the fox even breaks, and he does not even *hear* me. But these damned interlopers are so pusillanimous—"

"But de Foye, is that a Christian thing to do?" expostulated Edmund. "Pick a quarrel with a man, I mean." Like his friend, he had had a bit too much to drink, and was in that warm state of companionship in which one is ready to repair all the sins of another.

"By God, Percy," said Tarquin, "who said foxhunting was Christian? If anything is pagan, it is foxhunting.—Why, I think in the old days, it was Christians they hunted so; and they only substituted foxes because they all became Christians themselves, and they had to hunt *something.* And a damned fine improvement they must have found it, too; for the foxes are far smarter."

"De Foye, I mean no offense. You are the finest fellow I have met in many a long day, and I like you very much. But you do have a rough edge—you do, you know; and I am concerned about it on your behalf."

"Oh, I know—I have a temper, it is true, a terrible temper. I can quite lose my head. In school I was constantly in fights. I am better now, I think."

"Do remember Christian mercy. There is no point in picking a fight with anyone. God sorts all that out—that is what I find, anyway. Your social climber will not be able to keep up, that is all. Half the skill of being Christian is just waiting for God to act against such people Himself instead of going ahead and taking things into your own hands."

"Oh, I suppose," said Tarquin, without enthusiasm.

Edmund tried a different tack. "Our Lord was no weakling, you know; He drove the moneychangers out of the Temple and He harrowed hell. I do not know about you, but I should not like to have been sitting there in the Temple making change when He starting turning over the tables; I rather think it was a terrifying thing to behold—and I do mean that: something that would have made even a bold man sick with fear, to see the Lord moving through the place, driving the scoundrels before Him. And yet He suffered fools, when it was the time and place to do so. His apostles were all fools, unless I mistake myself; and if He can do it, so must we."

"Yes, I have always thought His damned apostles were fools," agreed Tarquin.

"And yet He suffered them," Edmund pointed out again.

"Very well," said Tarquin, "for your sake, Percy, I shall try to suffer even a damned interloper if one shows up. But I still say I cannot stand a social climber. A man ought to know his place. That is one thing I like about you, Percy; you know you are a far better man than your brother, but you do not give yourself airs."

"That would spoil everything if I did, now, would it not?"

"Exactly! And that is exactly what I mean, you see—you understand that."

"Oh, I do—I do, de Foye; and better than you think.—Come, shall we see how the ladies are getting along?"

⌛⌛⌛⌛

The men did not rouse old Cato, but let him snooze; and soon after they had rejoined the women, the evening came to a close. They found the conversation, which had been so fluent all evening, suddenly became more difficult; and Edmund could not help thinking it was Miss de Foye who made it so, for she sat somewhat apart and not only did not contribute anything to the effort at conviviality, but seemed to dampen it with her atmosphere of depression.

When Andromeda and Edmund were on their way home in the carriage, his aunt put her hand on his arm and leaned close to him.

"Thank you, dear nephew, for the most enjoyable evening I have had since your uncle died."

"Do not thank me, dear Aunt. I was neither the host who offered the hospitality nor the guest who impressed all with her superior powers of entertainment."

"But without you, I never should have been invited to Hartswound. I have lived here all these years quite beneath the notice of the de Foyes."

"Ah, but now that they have noticed you, I think you will have frequent invitations from them, if I am not mistaken. You will be turning many of those summons down, in fact, if only to avoid the hunting set."

"I am only pleased that they seem to appreciate you. And I did think their plan to find you a rich widow had some merit. I could easily fall in with it; it is just that I know so few rich widows. I have been busy trying to set you up within my own set; perhaps the de Foyes have wider resources. I should think they must know someone who would fit the bill. And you would not object to a widow?"

"Why should I?"

"Why, I am sure that I myself, as a widow, would not know; but I suppose they are sometimes perceived as used goods."

"I think experience in life makes a companion more valuable," said Edmund.

"Unless it is *too much* experience," said Andromeda.

"I view myself as having had too much experience, Aunt. Why should I not be tolerant of another who has undergone the same?"

"Yes," she said thoughtfully. "That is the noble view of it, Edmund; the view I should expect you to take. And yet for you I have been thinking exclusively in terms of sweet young things, blushing virgins, barely-twenties, beauties who ravish one with a glance. I must expand my outlook."

"And speaking of beauties," interjected Edmund, "what did you think of Miss de Foye's behavior, dear Aunt? I hope you did not find your time with her tedious. She seemed very out of sorts."

"Let me say nothing of that."

"Why not?"

"Because to speak of Miss de Foye is to praise her, even if only by noting how unlike herself she was tonight. And I still fear to praise her to you, Edmund."

"Fear nothing. She is as far beyond me as the stars of heaven."

"Ah, but Andromeda is a constellation, is it not? And there is one Andromeda who is quite your servant, Edmund. You choose your metaphor unfortunately."

He laughed. "There are classes of daughters just as there are classes of sons; and Miss de Foye is of the first class of daughters, and will not be brought to marry out of it."

"Still I would be cautious. Better ask me nothing, and I shall say nothing."

"Very well. I shall be content if you tell me only that you had a pleasant hour with her."

"I could say that; but I am not entirely sure that I was *with her;* that is, that she was present. I think we are right about her, Edmund. I would say she is in love with someone; that she is quite distracted. At times she is in a kind of delirious transport—thinking of *him,* I suppose. At other times she does her best to carry on a conversation, and is quite intelligent, but it is as if her mind is operating without the attention of her heart, which is transfixed on its unknown object."

"She was quite subdued at dinner, too, I thought; and the *messieurs* de Foye seemed to think so too. But I know her so little; I can only compare her behavior tonight to the way she acted yesterday."

"And I, too, have seen her over the years, as I said, only in church and on her errands of mercy. I do not know the grown-up Mariah de Foye socially. Perhaps we are completely wrong, and that is simply her way. But for the moment, I consider it quite salutary for you to think of her as already claimed."

"I do indeed think her so."

"I would rest easier if we were certain about her, though. Have you probed her brother on this point?"

"I would not presume to do so. It is no business of mine. She herself did let slip a remark yesterday morning about hoping to be married soon, but her father and brother make no reference to any suitor or any plan of hers to marry. That does not necessarily mean anything; she seems to be surprisingly absent from their thoughts when she is not at home. I guessed that perhaps she has not revealed her hopes to them; and as I have a certain sympathy with her—it cannot be easy for her, as genteel a woman as she is, to live with two men so obsessed with killing themselves a-horseback—I did not think it right to intimate my suspicions to either of them. She will choose her own time, and I wish her the best success. They do love her, and they will miss her; but she needs company more elevated than that of a hunting squire, even one who still reads French, and his fox-crazed son."

"Yes; I think she must be rather lonely—her only companions a broken-down clergyman, the sick of the village, a madcap girl, and a few dogs. It cannot be easy; I should think she would long to be away."

They fell silent for some time; then Andromeda spoke. "Edmund, will you be so kind as to listen to my counsel?"

"Certainly."

"No good will come of this mystery that attaches to Miss de Foye. Your own good prudence has led you to avoid this topic heretofore; continue that policy. If you visit the de Foyes, shun this subject at all costs. Do not become entangled in it."

"Ah, you are scheming on my behalf. You think it will cost me any chance at the living if I become implicated in a potential row in the family."

"I admit it is partly that. But where there is as much unhappiness as Miss de Foye seems to be feeling, it cannot be wise to tread. It may be a quicksand that will pull you down."

"Again I say, have no fear. I will continue to be prudent, with the help of God Almighty; though I am disinclined to scheme for this living, I must warn you. If the de Foyes see fit to give it me, so be it; if not, I will find something elsewhere, and you will just have to travel to me."

"Very well. Let my brains do the scheming. Leave your own head clear for honest thoughts—they make people love you, and that suits my purposes."

⌛⌛⌛⌛

Immediately after church on Sunday a gift from the de Foyes was delivered to Andromeda Alton's house. It included a jar of very fine honey, some good beef, and a box of cigars. The servant who brought the basket said that the last item had just been brought from London by special commission. Andromeda detained the man while she copied out her receipt for a medicine for the gout—which her own father had used to good effect, and which he had always claimed to be far more efficacious that James's Powder—and she sent it back with him, along with some of the preserves for which she was renowned in Broadbridge. She and Edmund had the beef for dinner, and she said she had never had a better; though Edmund privately thought that it was the seasoning she liked best, for it was certainly well sauced in good wishes.

Chapter 26

Now, these two Boys who are out with the Foxhounds will come home & disgust me again by . . . some proof of sporting Mania.

—Austen

Monday morning was warm but overcast. It had rained Sunday and the ground was still damp, which was good for holding the drag, or trail, of the fox; and as Hampshire was notorious for drying quickly in the spring, Edmund and Tarquin congratulated themselves on the weather conditions when they met in the hall at Hartswound at seven o'clock.

"What guests did you have last night?" asked Edmund.

"Lord Burley, Donaldson, Kemp, and Mannering. The rest will meet us here or at During Wood; that will be our first cover. I did receive word from several that they will make the meet, so we should have some company."

"Excellent."

"Go right up and change," said Tarquin.

"Thanks, old man."

Edmund started up the stairs and immediately met Miss de Foye descending.

"Good morning, Miss de Foye," he said.

"Good morning, Mr. Percy," she answered. She nodded in his direction, but walked by without looking at him.

"Ah, Mariah," said Tarquin as he saw her. "I am glad we shall have your company at breakfast."

She walked directly past her brother as well, going to the door of the house; and there she turned and said, "I shall be spending the day at the rectory. I do not expect to return until quite late."

"Mariah!" he protested.

"Good day, brother."

Without allowing any further discussion, she slipped out the door and was gone.

Tarquin looked up at Edmund. "It is Ashleigh, I am afraid," he said. "She cannot stand him."

By way of answer, Edmund recited:

The hunter loves his lady fair,
The hound loves the kill;
The fox loves his deep earth,
But the lady loves her will.

Tarquin laughed, and they went their separate ways.

⌛⌛⌛⌛

The other hunters and Tarquin were already at breakfast when Edmund joined them. Cato presided at the table, appearing alternately eager and depressed, boyishly interested in the hunt and then adrift and absent on a sea of elderly pain. He occasionally threatened to mount a horse with them, but as no one called him on his bluff, he did not feel compelled to carry it through.

Edmund recognized several of the hunters from the evening of the ball; and though he had not been introduced to them personally at that time, they all knew him. Lord Burley proved to be a likeable gentleman. He was short and indifferently built, but he held himself in such a way that Edmund guessed he would make a first-class horseman. He was about forty, but his shock of well-groomed black hair showed not a speck of gray. Edmund noticed that his hunting clothes were of excellent make, but well-used—perhaps worn more for the sake of tradition or luck than fashion; and Edmund liked that in him, for Andromeda had told him that Burley was far and away the wealthiest man in the country round about, eclipsing even the Esquith de Foyes in landholdings. His lordship was not perfectly likeable, however. He was somewhat slow to perceive a jest, as Tarquin had intimated, and perhaps slow on the uptake in general. He was also phlegmatic to the point of pessimism, which made his character a curious hybrid: his fatalism was admirable—Edmund was to find that Burley refused to complain despite his complete expectation that nothing good would ever come his way in life—and yet it was also absurd, for he was heedless of the fact that he had suckled at the very paps of Fortuna all his days. Edmund could not help wondering if Burley's many unsuccessful experiences hunting had broken his belief in the abundant goodness of God's blessings; and he thought that if a man could thus confuse his success at hunting with the hand that fate had dealt him in general, it would make a powerful argument against the sport.

Burley's friend Donaldson was none so likeable. He was brash, loud, intrusive; he spoke over their aged host, said an uncountable number of stupid things in the manner of a mighty judge handing down a sentence in some capital case, and otherwise made a nuisance of himself. It was clear that the only two reasons he was suffered among them were that he was old money in the neighborhood and he passionately loved the hunt. Edmund, in weighing his probable influence in the field, thought it did not seem that he would trouble the others long once the huntsman threw off the hounds—he was miserably clumsy. In the course of their brief breakfast he spilled the tea, the milk, and the sugar, and forced the underbutler, a man of truly monumental decorum, to drop a plate of toast by trying to wrest it out of his grasp.

Kemp was a riddle at first. He was preoccupied and silent, responded in monosyllables, looked at no one, and ate little. The only clue Edmund had to his behavior initially was that he wore a hothouse flower in the lapel of his very handsome scarlet coat; and when someone teased him about it, he confessed that his wife had sent a servant over with it that morning. Towards the end of the meal, Edmund's surmise that he was newly wed was corroborated when someone made a joke about "robbing the cradle," and Kemp cleared his throat defensively. Edmund's aunt later confirmed Edmund's suspicions: she told him that Kemp, who was about thirty years of age, had recently married a sixteen-year-old girl. They were passionately absorbed in one another. Edmund did not expect that a man so otherwise employed mentally would be much of a hunter.

Mannering, too, was very old money in the neighborhood. He idolized Tarquin and seemed to have resolved to do everything his friend should do, to the point of eating the same foods and in the same amounts, though he was a scrawny fellow, and nowhere near up to the challenge presented by Tarquin's appetite. Edmund guessed he would drop out at the very first ditch or hedge.

The conversation was largely about foxhunting, though some county and court gossip found its way into the conversation. Tarquin was asked the condition of the hounds, and gave a minute description—Bluebeard was still nursing a cut from a flint, and would not hunt; Cream had been proven to be an incorrigible skirter (a hound that ran far ahead alongside the general direction of the scent in the hopes that the fox would turn toward him) and as such would be coupled in harness with an older dog who might break him of this bad habit; and so on. In two minutes he listed which of the fifty or so hounds would be coupled and which would not. Edmund was impressed by his total command of information concerning the men, horses, and dogs he was putting in the field.

Then the hunters, excepting Cato, went down to the stables. Cato was carried out to the landing before the house, where he would greet those arriving and watch them all depart for the actual starting point of the meet. The hunters were so keen to be off, and the grooms so beforehand in their tasks, that well before eight o'clock they had returned to the front of the house, now on horseback.

The largest party that had arrived in their absence was that brought by Mr. Ashleigh. Edmund recognized him as well from the night of the ball. He seemed somewhat of a fop, and Edmund could imagine a hundred reasons why Miss de Foye would find the fellow's company distasteful. He had that effete air of a man who has never done anything truly useful in his life, and yet is convinced that he is important—in fact, that he is the most important man he knows; and the only reason his conceit does not extend to megalomania is that he is simply unaware of the larger world, and thus cannot imagine it to be a theater of potential admirers. He was about Tarquin's age, with fair, thinning hair and watery blue eyes, and his scarlet coat, buff-colored breeches, and gleaming top-boots seemed absolutely brand new.

Tarquin greeted him in a tone that disclosed, to Edmund's observant ear, both affability born of long friendship—Tarquin and Ashleigh had been riding to hounds together for approaching thirty years now—and reluctance deriving from accumulated irritation. "Ashleigh," he said. "Good of you to come."

"Good of you to reverse yourself and offer one more meet. The best news I have had this winter, I can tell you!—And here is Burley; good morning, your lordship."

"Morning, Ashleigh," said Burley.

"And this is Mr. Percy," said Ashleigh to the company who had come with him, as he indicated Edmund. "I knew his brother Christopher at school, and several of us heard him recount his marine adventures the other evening.—It is you we have to thank for the '52, Mr. Percy."

"You have him to thank for this meet as well," said Tarquin. "As Mr. Percy has proved himself something of a horseman, I thought we ought to show him how we do things down here."

"It is a pleasure to make your acquaintance, Mr. Ashleigh," said Edmund.

"And here are the others of my party," said Ashleigh, indicating them one by one: "My brother, Mr. Hugh Ashleigh; my cousins Mr. George Carew and Mr. Edward Carew; my neighbor up at Priedpie Hall, Mr. John Cross; a guest of ours from the down country, Mr. Andrew Peavey; and—where is he—over there, watering his horse: Colonel Bucknell Fitzgerald. We thought to have the Marquis with us, de Foye, but his lordship is ill, apparently; or claims he is."

"And do not forget Miss Alderscott," said Mr. Hugh Ashleigh.

"Oh, yes; another guest, visiting my sister Edith at the Hall—where has she got to?"

"You have brought *a lady?*" asked Tarquin, in surprise he made no effort to conceal.

"Indeed I have, old man. I could not have stopped her. She is a capital horsewoman. She did not ask leave to come; the minute she heard there was a meet, she included herself without hesitation." His brother and cousins laughed.

"She is one lady who is not to be gainsayed, truly," said Mr. Hugh Ashleigh.

"When was the last time we had a lady at the meet?" asked Tarquin. His question was rhetorical, but Lord Burley answered in his phlegmatic tone.

"I think it was when Lady Montague was down to visit us, about three years ago. She lasted until we had drawn the first cover, and then went home."

"Well, where is this lady?" asked Tarquin. "Did she come to sit inside with my sister, or ride to hounds?"

"Speaking of your sister," Ashleigh began, "where is Miss de Foye?"

"Speaking of your lady friend," said Tarquin in retort, refusing to be deterred, "where is *she?*"

At this point a woman rider did in fact appear through the gates of the enclosure before the house. She was about thirty years of age, with a face that might be seen as odd and long of shape, or strikingly unique, depending on one's disposition to regard it either way.

"Here she comes," said Ashleigh."

"How is she to keep up with us *hunting*, if she falls behind *on the way to the meet?*" asked Tarquin. The men all thought this a very humorous sally; and as the woman rode up, she saw that she was the object of their laughter.

"Gentlemen—I apologize if I have kept you waiting," she said. She offered no further explanation. Edmund suspected she might have stopped behind in the park to answer the call of nature.

She did not rein in her horse as she approached, but rode directly up to Tarquin until she was immediately alongside him. "You are the master, are you not?" she said, with consummate boldness and forwardness, looking him directly in the eye; "You are Mr. Esquith de Foye."

"I am, madam," said Tarquin, both surprised at her forwardness and instantly suspicious because of it.

Ashleigh spoke up. "This is Edith's friend, Miss Cecelia Alderscott, out of Hertfordshire."

Miss Alderscott thrust out a gloved hand, and Tarquin shook it somewhat unwillingly.

"I am very pleased to meet you, Mr. de Foye," said Miss Alderscott. "I saw you from afar once, in a crowd in London, when I was walking with Miss Ashleigh; and she told me you were master of the finest hunt in Hampshire, if not in all of England. Ever since then it has been my consummate ambition to ride with you."

Tarquin looked deeply displeased. "Then you do intend to ride?" he said.

"Of course."

"Very well," said Tarquin.

"You see I have produced Miss Alderscott," said Ashleigh. "Now do you, de Foye, produce your sister. Is *she* going to ride with us?"

"You know perfectly well she does not ride with us, and has not these six years; not since the last time my father broke his leg."

"I am sure if she were my sister," said Ashleigh, "I should demand that she hunt."

"I do not see *your* sister here," observed Tarquin sarcastically.

"My sister cannot ride like yours," said Ashleigh. "And besides, I do not have the same interest in my sister that I have in yours." The company laughed again; evidently Mr. Ashleigh's predilection for Miss de Foye was an open secret.

"Well, it is a good thing, then, that Mariah is *not* your sister," said Tarquin; and they all laughed once more. "In any case, you will have to live without her company today," added Tarquin. "Now, if you will excuse me, I must greet my neighbors." He turned his horse away and left them abruptly. Edmund tipped his hat to the lady and followed his friend.

Tarquin introduced him to several other hunters. The minutes dragged by; the stirrup cup was to be drunk punctually at half past eight, and then the group was to ride with the hounds to During Wood, in plenty of time to join the rest of the meet at nine sharp. Both Edmund and Tarquin were restless; out of sheer nervous eagerness, they dismounted and walked about; Tarquin lit a cigar, then extinguished it and threw it away; they went up the steps to talk to Cato and then they went down the steps and remounted. By that time the yard held some thirty riders, and nearly as many servants, to say nothing of the spare horses the grooms were leading.

Edmund gradually became aware that something more than pleasant anticipation was working on his friend. He found out what it was at about twenty-five past eight, when Tarquin took him aside. "This is a cursed bad stroke of luck!" he said fiercely.

"Whatever do you mean?" asked Edmund.

"That damned lady is what I mean! She will stop us at every gate and order us to 'see to it' for her. Oh, I have ridden with the likes of her before! Stay away from her, Percy.

Ride wide of her, even if you have to go out of your chosen line. If we can break with her, she will fall behind without causing us trouble; but if she fastens on us, we are done for. Do not so much as speak to her."

"I shall do as you say," said Edmund; "though perhaps it will not be so bad as you think. It requires considerable effrontery to stop the master of the hunt at a gate and make him open it for you."

"Did you see the bold look she gave me? She is perfectly capable of it.—I was hoping for a good hunt for you, Percy—a good hunt, so that you can see how we do things here in Hampshire—how we do things here at Hartswound, how we do everything humanly possible to produce the finest runs in all the world. And to have the meet spoiled by a bloody damned *sidesaddle!* It is insufferable! Let us just hope she does not fall in a ditch with her horse on top of her—it will be the end of the hunt. My father told me about such a hunt once. 'The lady is down!' You would have thought the veil of heaven had been rent—all the hunt came to an absolute halt, and the fox ran off in perfect impunity.—And that damned Ashleigh is to blame! I tell you, there are some times I *loathe* the fellow. Look at him! You would think he did not know perfectly well what a fine mess he has made of everything."

"Well, perhaps she is a good rider after all. Let us give her the benefit of the doubt until she proves otherwise. Look at her—she sits very well, does she not?"

They both now looked at Miss Alderscott and were suddenly silent. She was riding quietly about the yard by herself, keeping her horse warmed. She wore a dress with a long black skirt, and, perhaps in concession to the current mode, a tightly fitted Spencer coat of scarlet.

"She has got a handsome figure, a very fine figure," said Edmund suddenly. "You must admit that."

They watched her in silence a minute more. The curves of her figure were very pleasing, and she sat her horse as if fastened there immovably.

"Oh, damn!" said Tarquin. "Do you not see—that just makes it worse. All the damned hunt she will be chirruping, 'See to that gate, will you?' and we, like true slaves, will think of her waist and hips—and do whatever she says! I *hate* to be enthralled to a woman."

"There is nothing wrong with her neck and bosom either," observed Edmund in ironic understatement, as the lady turned her horse about.

Tarquin said nothing; but his silence demonstrated his concurrence in Edmund's judgment of Miss Alderscott's charms better than any words.

She saw them watching her and immediately made for them.

"Oh, damn, here she comes," muttered Tarquin.

She rode close to Edmund this time. "Excuse me, Mr. de Foye," she said. "You have not introduced me to your friend.—Mr. Percy, is it not? I heard someone say that this meet is in your honor." She held out her hand, and Edmund leaned over to shake it.

"Mr. Edmund Percy, out of Surrey," said Tarquin.

"A pleasure to meet you, Miss Alderscott."

"I shall be interested to talk with you afterwards," she said. "I have never hunted in Surrey, and I shall be curious to learn from you how you do things there."

"You should visit us at Brackensom during the season," said Edmund, before he knew what he was saying.

"I should like that very much."

"We are in Lord Trueblood's hunt."

"Ah! That is of very good repute. I wish I might I make so bold as to take you up on your offer. Perhaps if you could extend it to my brother, I might do so with propriety."

"I shall invite your brother most willingly," said Edmund. He found that Miss Alderscott was really very impressive when she looked at one directly; for her eyes were dark and clear and her gaze was intense. A very pleasing, flirtatious smile hovered at the corners of her lips as she addressed him, and the mere manner in which she held her head communicated a kind of flirtatious, arch interest in him that he found captivating; though it did not escape him that it was the same sort of interest she had shown in Tarquin.

A small army of servants now descended the steps bearing silver salvers laden with cups of liquor. "Excuse us," said Tarquin. "It is time for the stirrup-cup."

He led Edmund away from Miss Alderscott with somewhat rude determination.

"What *are* you doing, Percy?" he muttered in a despairing tone when they had moved a safe distance away.

"I do not know—only being polite, I suppose," said Edmund. "She has damned fine eyes, you know."

"That is the first time I have ever heard you curse," groaned Tarquin.

"Curse? Did I curse?"

"Yes, you did: You said she had *damned* fine eyes."

"And so she does. She is dangerous, that one," admitted Edmund. "I must say I would not mind talking at length with her—after the hunt, of course. Do not fear, de Foye; I shall follow your orders, and keep clear of her."

The servants approached them, and they took up their cups. For a moment a hush fell on the yard. All looked to Cato, who sat on the steps, with one leg extended before him on a hassock and one arm holding a cup in the air.

"A strong fox, a good run, and a fair kill!" cried Cato.

"A fair kill!" echoed the hunters; and they drank off the liquor. It was a powerful cherry brandy.

"During Wood!" Tarquin called; and they left the yard and headed out for the meet.

They met the hounds in the fields outside the gate. From the very start there was an unruliness in the dogs that Edmund found unusual, and Tarquin hastened to assure him that it was very unlike them. They were straining and jerking at leash, sometimes even tumbling over each other, and the horses began to grow eager at their incitement, and the riders eager in turn at the restiveness of their own horses. Mr. Dickson, the huntsman, and Mr. Lewis, the whipper-in, were bellowing and working their whips; but the dogs seemed to think that every scrap of cover was the one on which they were about to be set, and pulled mightily in the direction of every bush in turn.

As they rode along, Tarquin made his way beside Edmund and said, "There is someone I have not told you about, whom I think we shall meet at the wood. I should like it if you would be so kind as to pay him special respect, Percy; he is a first-class hunter."

"Any man for whom you have respect deserves mine as well, I am sure," said Edmund. "Who is he, and how shall I know him?"

"His name is Shadwell. He is a farmer from the next town over. I shall introduce you to him. I make a point of speaking to him specially at every meet. He knows the country round as though he crept through it every night in the shape of the fox himself. Every lane, every byway, every cover, every ditch, every fence, every ploughland—which field is likely to have padlocks, and which is not. He knows the lie of the land and reads the fox's course through it as though it were marked out with a line of bonfires."

"I know the type," said Edmund. "You will tell me next that like as not he shows up at near every kill, riding a horse barely lathered, and appearing on the closest dry lane."

"You have him exactly. It is uncanny how he does it. The rest of the field will be dashing about like madmen, leaping hedgerows and going down and risking life and limb; but not him: he stays cool as a gravestone. He rides with his brain—that is what he does. He has never come to a kill by a straight line—he must ride half again as many miles as the rest of us, but they are easy miles, and his horse is grateful to him for it, I swear, and delivers him promptly wherever the hounds have closed on their prey."

"I shall be glad to shake his hand," said Edmund.

Under the pressure lent by the eagerness of the hounds, the company made During Wood in very good time, though it lay on the far side of the Esquith de Foye property. It was quite extensive a cover, presenting from this aspect a broad, unbroken front of oaks. When the hounds saw it, they realized at once that this was at last the place where they would be thrown off leash; they yelped and frisked and nipped at one another. Mr. Dickson ordered them taken to the verge of the wood, and he himself hung back with the riders; for there was no hearing a word in their cacophony.

Another thirty riders were waiting on the near side of the wood. Nearly all of them wore black coats: these were the men who had not the wealth or connections of the de Foyes, but were simply residents of the neighborhood who loved a hunt. Edmund saw Mr. Eaton the lawyer there, with a young man who seemed to be his son—perhaps the James who was the sweetheart of Miss Caits. Many of the men almost seemed familiar to Edmund, for they were the same miscellaneous types who came to the meets in Surrey, from every walk of life, from the local miller with flour on his coat, to Mr. Thomas, the Broadbridge curate, mounted on a very feeble-looking nag. The inevitable boys on ponies were there as well, given leave by their fathers to play hooky.

As the two groups merged, many greetings were exchanged, but Edmund noticed that Tarquin did not single out many for this honor. He was looking for the farmer he had spoken of, and found him on the edge of the crowd, sitting silently on a somewhat aged but businesslike bay. He wore a long black coat from which most of the velvet was worn, black breeches, and buff-colored topboots partially spattered with mud. Edmund had expected him to be old and short and stout, but he was instead only about fifty, and of a tall, wirey build.

"Good day to you, Mr. Shadwell," said Tarquin.

"Good day to you in turn, Mr. de Foye," said the farmer. "It is not too late to hunt, now, is it?"

"Not at all. Only a fool would have sown anything this early."

"I should like you to meet Mr. Percy; he is down from Surrey, a nephew of Mrs. Alton in Broadbridge."

"Mr. Percy," said Mr. Shadwell. He tipped his hat slightly.

"Pleased to make your acquaintance, Mr. Shadwell."

The man's face was absolutely impassive. It was impossible to read any emotion in it, any thought; but his eyes were penetrating, and his gaze made Edmund suddenly hope he did not make a fool of himself this day.

"See you at the kill," said Tarquin.

"I expect so, Mr. de Foye," said Mr. Shadwell.

Tarquin and Edmund now joined Mr. Dickson, who was consulting his watch. The hunters grew silent.

"It is now nearly nine o'clock, Mr. de Foye," said Mr. Dickson. His tone was that of a priest repeating a formula of sacrament. "Do I have your permission to throw off?"

"You do, Mr. Dickson."

"I say," interrupted Donaldson. "Do we give the fox five minutes' law if we find him in this cover?"

"Not in this cover, sir," said Mr. Dickson gruffly. "This is a large cover; if we gave him law, he would give us the slip in return."

"He will *take* five minutes' law, whether we give it him or not," said Tarquin.

"I was just asking," said Donaldson, "because—"

"Throw off, Mr. Dickson," said Tarquin.

Mr. Dickson rode to the pack and gave the handlers the order to unleash the hounds, and the beasts instantly sprinted into the woods and put their noses to the ground. Their sudden silence was eerie.

Tarquin and Edmund moved somewhat apart from the others. In a minute they were joined by Lord Burley and Mr. Mannering. The former pulled a new cigar out of a silver case and lit it off the remains of his old, staring into the wood somewhat hopelessly; the latter looked constantly to

Tarquin to see what he might be doing. Most of the other hunters milled about, waiting for an indication from the master that the fox had broken cover. Considering the size of the wood, it would likely take some time for that to happen, if the hounds succeeded in finding a fox here at all.

"Do you often find on the first draw?" asked Edmund.

"Almost never," said Tarquin. "It is an odd thing. There are plenty of foxes about; but it is almost as if they have heard where the meet will be held."

"I would not put it past them," said Burley. Mannering laughed—a bit too much.

"Think it will rain?" said Burley, looking up at the dark overcast.

"Who can say?" said Tarquin. He was not paying too much attention to Burley; like Edmund, he was listening intently to the hounds, who had now begun to give tongue occasionally as they ran across the tracks of hares and whatever else lived in the wood. It was easy to tell from the mere tone of this brief yelping that it was not a fox they had found.

"Much trouble with riot?" asked Edmund; by which term he meant the chaos that ensued when the hounds ran after other animals beside foxes.

"Never," said Tarquin. "We train our hounds so well they would never dare think of riot." Edmund nodded; he quite believed Tarquin on this point.

They waited for a full ten minutes in much this way: Edmund and Tarquin intently listening, and Burley making phlegmatic and irrelevant comments as he smoked his cigar. Mannering ostentatiously proffered Tarquin his flask, and drifted away to another group when his offer was refused. Suddenly Ashleigh spurred his horse and galloped up to Tarquin. "Damned if I am going to wait another minute," he said. "I shall ride round the wood; there is no point in waiting here. The fox will not come out here—he will come out over there, on the far side. I should think that would be stupidly obvious."

Tarquin looked at him in disgust. "And I should think it would be stupidly obvious that if you go to the far side, it will no longer be the far side; and when he sees a human waiting for him, he will decide to come out *this* side."

"Oh, nonsense," said Ashleigh. "I am going." And off he went to ride to the left around the wood; and so great was the anticipation of the hunters that he drew off some twenty riders with him.

"We have this idiotic conversation at every cover," said Tarquin. "He will never learn—never."

"He will spoil the draw if he carries on like this," said Edmund.

"Oh, he will be back," said Lord Burley.

"But still, that ruck he took with him could spoil the drag on the far side if the fox broke there."

"And this is the man who wants to marry my sister," said Tarquin. "I would as soon sell her to the Devil himself as marry her off to a man who cannot sit and wait for the hounds to find.—Well, at least he has taken that *sidesaddle* with him."

Edmund had not seen Miss Alderscott follow Ashleigh, and he now turned around to look behind them. "Oh, no, he did not," he told Tarquin. "Do not look now, but she is about a hundred feet behind us."

"What is she doing?"

"Waiting, from what I can tell, in a very mannerly way."

"Thank God she has not insinuated herself upon us," Tarquin said.

"I told you it would take more effrontery than even she apparently has to hobble the master of the hunt. I think you have misread her, de Foye. She genuinely loves to hunt, that is all. She will be quite commonsensical and hang back—stick to the lanes instead of making a line cross-country. I swear, there is nothing so pleasant as a woman with common sense. Good-looking and sensible. It will be good to sit around the fire with her tonight and talk about hunting."

"Let us hope it is as you say," said Tarquin. "Now, look, there is something else I have been meaning to tell you. Whatever you do, do not slack up when the hounds drive the fox into a cover. These are the fastest hounds in all England; they go through a cover like water through a sieve, and many a fox has lost much of his lead because of it—and many a hunter has been left behind, thinking he can stint his run for a minute and rest his horse."

"I hear you," said Edmund.

They waited in silence again, listening.

"Wish we had a little sun," said Burley.

Edmund noticed Mr. Shadwell waiting at some distance from the others, on the far left side of the group.

"Is there a ride through this wood?" Edmund asked suddenly.

"No," said Tarquin.

Edmund looked at Mr. Shadwell again.

"Look, de Foye," he said. "That fellow Shadwell is on the left."

"Yes," said Tarquin, instantly grasping his meaning. Mr. Shadwell had assessed the situation and decided that it would be best to ride around the wood to the left when and if a fox broke. "Let us get over near him; but go slowly and casually, or we shall blow up this whole ruck like a powderkeg."

The two men eased their horses casually toward the left, and Lord Burley followed. They took up a station about thirty feet to the right of Mr. Shadwell and waited again. Tarquin cast one glance behind them.

"Do not look," he said, "but *she* has moved too."

Now the men in the party began cursing the fox. This was a part of the pastime, of course; but to this point most of their language had been restrained because of the presence of Miss Alderscott. After one particularly egregious oath, Tarquin turned about and addressed the gathering in a cold, commanding voice.

"While I am master of this hunt," he said, "no one shall use such language in the presence of a lady."

The silence was sheepish. He turned back to the cover and resumed waiting and listening.

The riders who had set out with Ashleigh soon returned around the far side of the cover. They had had a brisk run—tiring their horses to no purpose, thought Edmund; and when they simply rejoined the main party on this side of the wood, it was not difficult to see what had happened to Ashleigh's plan to wait on the far side: he had grown bored over there, too.

It was shortly after this that Edmund heard something. He could not have said what it was, exactly—just one note from the tongue of one hound that rang differently, with ever so slight a different tone. The instant he heard it, his bodily attitude must have changed without his knowing it, and the horse—being, like any well-trained mount, completely attuned to him—lunged forward a step or two in anticipation. The attention of many in the company was drawn by this motion, and they looked at him and at Tarquin, who now had also caught some faint hint of a difference in the hounds' cry—just that one note that did not say, "I am searching," or "Here is a hare," or "Here is a badger's earth," but instead "Here is what I have been trained from birth to hunt—here is the core and meaning of my entire existence—here is THE DRAG OF A FOX."

Tarquin's horse, too, took a step forward, though he was holding it back. Now the entire company was utterly silent, looking at the two of them in surprise and anticipation. Even Mr. Shadwell stared, still not hearing what they had heard.

Now Edmund heard it clearly—one of the hounds had found. That one cry came from far away, from what must be the far side of the woods. Beside him Tarquin, too, heard it unmistakably. Perhaps Miss Alderscott would have been distressed to know that at that moment, the brains of both men were as blank of any thought of her waist and hips as were the brains of the scenting hounds or of the straining horses—but then again, perhaps her mind was as blank of any such concern as the two of theirs.

Edmund was the first away. He reacted as great athletes do, by a kind of deep-bred instinct, not conscious thought. He spurred Agamemnon, and in a few seconds he was gone from their company. Tarquin, however, was hard on his heels and rapidly catching up.

For a moment the company stood bewildered, still not knowing quite what had happened to alert their leaders. Then there came a thin, silverly call from a horn, as the huntsman called the feathering pack to the drag; and then the ruck broke loose, and it was devil take the hindmost.

The land bounding During Wood was a smooth fallow with only a slight roll. It would have been hard to imagine anything better for a quick run, short of a straight, dry lane. The hounds, and of course the fox before them, had much the advantage of the riders, as fox and hounds got away on the far side of the wood, and were clear of it at once. By the time Edmund and Tarquin reached the place where the fox had broken—a servant had been posted there to mark the spot—they could just see the tail hounds and the huntsman's outriders disappearing over a hill a mile ahead.

"He has the law of us right well, I should say," said Tarquin; and they turned at once in pursuit.

The ruck was still in a tight mass just behind them, as they had as yet encountered very few obstacles to distinguish the good riders from the poor, or the riders who always jumped from those who never did so. The land before was relatively clear—some ploughs and open gates, nothing more. Edmund guessed at the fox's probable course: the creature had run in the open no more than fifty yards and then dashed down the line of long wall, and from there to other brushy fences and a hedge. Reynard was going very straight, but he was not going across open country; and he knew very well where he was going—he had gone this way many times before.

Many of the riders behind them did not pick their line of travel intelligently, and were soon working their horses hard in some very muddy ground; but Edmund and Tarquin kept to the drier part of the plowed fields and made good progress. Using a combination of dry fields and a lane or two, and exploiting some low fences, they caught up to the pack in about ten minutes. As they slowed to match the progress of the dogs, a group of about ten riders in turn caught up with them. Edmund was pleased to see that Mr. Shadwell was among them: he took that as a confirmation that he and Tarquin had followed the most intelligent route. He was surprised, however, to see Miss Alderscott also among these frontrunners.

The fox continued to follow a hedgerow, which now joined the boundary along a lane. The riders merged into the lane readily enough through a gate that had been opened by one of the handlers; but here it seemed that the fox had crisscrossed the way, winding in and out among the trunks on one side of the road and then in and out among the trunks on the other. The dogs feathered out in the lane and on both sides of it, and the whipper-in had a difficult time keeping the pack from being split into three.

"We have a clever one!" cried Miss Alderscott in a tone of nearly rhapsodic delight. Edmund could not help looking back at her. Her face, which exercise and fresh air had colored with a very becoming hue, was lit with a kind of ecstasy at the mere thought of a good challenge.

The hounds were overrunning the scent and spoiling it themselves, pressed on by the riders behind. Tarquin saw at once that the hunters were aggravating the situation. "Hold hard!" he cried. At this command the hunters drew rein to a slower pace and fell in behind him obediently. "Hold hard till we are out of this lane, or we shall lose this bloody fox! He is a crafty one!"

The lane ascended a small hill, up which the hounds climbed, swarming back and forth across the road; the riders came more slowly behind them, well back from the huntsman and the whipper-in and the other handlers. As they crested the hill, the hounds found the drag again, and they clustered together—all except for one group of about ten couple to the right of the road, where the whipper-in was plying his lash apparently to no avail.

This time it was again Edmund who read the situation first. "By God," he cried excitedly, "there are two foxes here! Look, this is our fox—the main pack has him—and those hounds to the right have found the drag of *another* fox that our fox ran right by."

"You are right!" cried Tarquin. Then, to the huntsman, he shouted, "Two foxes, Mr. Dickson! Two foxes!"

"You are mad!" shouted the huntsman, who, like most of the freeborn Englishmen who held his office, did not feel compelled to be too respectful to his master in the heat of the chase.

But now the hounds on the right broke away completely. Edmund guessed they were younger dogs, and could not, or did not care to, distinguish one fox from another as the older dogs did. The whipper-in rode pell-mell after them, cursing and lashing at them, but could not bring them under control.

The riders came up to the highest point of the elevation. The lane turned off to the left, but their fox had gone straight ahead, through a fence and along the edge of a field. In front of the hunters the main body of the pack was pouring down the hill, hot on the drag; to the right the splinter group was making toward a gorse cover. At that instant one of the handlers gave the view halloo, and the hunters stopped as a body and stared where the man was pointing.

On a hilltop opposite theirs, about half a mile away, they could see a fox scrambling up a stretch of flinty ground. He was visible only for a few seconds in a small gap between the end of a fence and some brush on the top of the next hill, but they all saw him clearly. His tail, in particular, was distinctly visible: it was lacking the white tip.

Tarquin and the huntsman turned to one another. "It is old Archie's fox!" they cried simultaneously.

To the hunters who knew what this meant, the information seemed almost a maddening incitement. Tarquin and the huntsman laid on spur, as did Mr. Shadwell; but Mr. Shadwell kept to the lane, and the rest went directly after the hounds.

Edmund was at a disadvantage, because he did not know the country; but he did not like the look of the hill opposite them: it was too steep and flinty, and some way would have to be found around it. He had half a notion to follow Mr. Shadwell, but he could not bear to leave his friend and take the easy way. Yet he did not doubt that when he and Tarquin caught up with the hounds again, Mr. Shadwell would be there ahead of them. As he hesitated, the remainder of the hunt caught up, still riding in a group, though they were now somewhat strung out along the lane.

Ashleigh was leading this second group. Just as he came out on the top of the hill, there was another view halloo, as the second fox was sighted darting for the gorse cover about a half-mile off to their right. That was enough for many of the hunters—at the view they turned at once and followed the wrong fox. Ashleigh, unfortunately, did not go with them; he followed Edmund and Tarquin, and brought about twenty riders at his back.

Then began a half-hour of very difficult hunting. The fox seemed to know what kind of ground would be the most adverse for horses, and he found diabolical ways to scatter and confuse the hounds. At the end of that half-hour, however, occurred one of those miracles that occasionally happens on a foxhunt: all the hounds and all the riders, or at least those who had not gone hopelessly lost, now wound up in the same place at the same time. Tarquin, Edmund, Ashleigh, Donaldson, and a considerable number of the ruck were running just behind and to one side of the hounds; Mr. Shadwell appeared from a lane on the left, riding at a leisurely pace, his horse barely even sweated; and from the right the whipper-in brought back his mutinous couples to rejoin the pack, though of the twenty or so hunters who had followed him, there was no sign.

Ashleigh now broke from the very favorable position Tarquin was holding and rode directly behind the hounds. Many were led by him, though Tarquin ordered them more than once to hold back and give the hounds room.

The hunters crested another small hill, and Edmund suddenly drew up short. "What is it?" asked Tarquin, also reining in.

"We have overridden the drag!"

"No, no, look, the hounds go on!"

"The horses are carrying them! Look, Mr. Dickson knows."

And it did now seem that Mr. Dickson had detected some problem with the hounds; and in a moment, anyone could see that the pack seemed to waver: the dogs in front no longer gave tongue, but slowed and lowered their faces to the ground. All in an instant the entire pack was feathering over the field, looking for the scent.

"Damn! We are checked!" cried Tarquin. "We shall lose this one!—Make a cast, Mr. Dickson, make a cast!"

Mr. Dickson was meanwhile shouting at the riders behind: "You muddy the drag! Get your horses off the drag! You have overridden! Leave my hounds alone, damn you!" The lead hounds showed an impulse to make their own cast to the east, up a brief rise, toward a very thick cover; and Mr. Dickson evidently seconded their choice.

"Yes, he has gone for Bromley Wood," said Tarquin, nodding at the cover in question. "It is one of the only tricks he has not tried yet—losing us anew in a dense cover."

"This fox has not even *begun* to delve into his bag of tricks," said Mr. Shadwell.

"What do you think he will do, Mr. Shadwell?" asked Tarquin.

"What else he is capable of, I do not know. But I can say that there are three good ways out of that wood, and he could take any one. But by and by they all lead to Plummer's Corner."

"And you will wait for him there?"

"Will you come with me?" asked Mr. Shadwell.

"No, I will stay with the hounds."

"If I have seen him, I will leave a stone on top of the mile-post there," said Mr. Shadwell. "He is like to go along the hedgerows again toward the next big cover."

"Which is by Strethamside."

"The very one. If he seems to be going in that direction, I shall leave two stones, not one."

"But you cannot go far without the hounds, man."

Mr. Shadwell only touched the brim of his hat and cantered off toward the nearest lane.

The hounds now found the drag again. The fox did indeed seem to be headed toward Bromley Wood; and in a few minutes they found themselves approaching the edge of it while the hounds worked their way in. Edmund was mindful of Tarquin's warning, and could tell with his own ears that the hounds were threading through the place and driving the fox at once before them; so when Ashleigh and Donaldson drew up to smoke cigars and await the outcome of the draw, he and Tarquin skirted the wood for a short distance, to get in a more favorable position to catch up with the hounds when the fox broke again. They were followed by their loyal few, which consisted mostly of black coats unfamiliar to Edmund, as well as the indefatigable Miss Alderscott. Edmund had no idea how she had fared cross-country, as she had ridden behind them, and neither he nor Tarquin had paid any attention to her. Lord Burley was nowhere to be seen; it occurred to Edmund that in fact he had not seen his lordship since they were drawing the cover at During Wood.

They must inevitably stop and wait for the huntsman's signal. Here Edmund took the opportunity to ask the story of Archie's fox. "There was an old farmer on the other side of Broadbridge," said Tarquin, "by the name of Archibald. He waged war with a very crafty fox for years, and once he actually caught the beast by the tail in a springe; but the fox chewed off the end of his brush and escaped. Archibald died last year, without ever catching his fox. We got the drag of the beast once, but he gave us the slip—and but good."

"Well, he is giving us a fine run so far today," said Edmund.

"Ah, I could not ask for a better fox for you, Percy," said Tarquin. "I would like to pretend that all the Hampshire foxes are this clever, and then you would go home and scorn to hunt the creatures you have up in Surrey, thinking they were poor by comparison. You would fill your friends' ears with the exploits of the crafty beasts we hunt down here. But I must tell the truth: this fox is one in a hundred."

Edmund laughed, and then they fell to listening. Miss Alderscott rode close to them, and Edmund tipped his hat, as if seeing her for the first time that day. She smiled at him; it was a very intoxicating smile, a curious mixture of boldness and shyness. She herself was quite drunk on the excitement of the hunt, flushed with her exertion, her breasts heaving in the tight-fitting scarlet coat. As she rode close, Edmund thought he could even smell a natural fragrance radiating from her, a pleasant, hot smell like sweet hay burned in a fire. This scent of her stirred his blood; and when he looked at her now, he wondered how he had ever doubted that she was a good-looking woman.

She did not intrude on them by attempting any conversation; in fact, after that initial glance and smile, she did not even look at him or Tarquin. She seemed only to ask to be allowed to be with them. She unbuttoned her coat, fanned the lapel to cool herself, and, from an inside pocket, drew a diminutive flask. This she unstoppered and put to her lips; and then, noticing that Edmund was observing her, she thrust it out to him impulsively. Just as impulsively, he took it from her; but before he drank himself, he offered it to Tarquin; who, without paying much attention to what he was doing, took it and drank a mouthful.

"Ah," he said, his expression evincing his surprise at the good flavor of the cordial. "What is it, Percy?"

"I do not know," said Edmund. "It is Miss Alderscott's."

Tarquin looked as if he had been poisoned. He handed the flask back to Edmund abruptly and without another word.

At that moment the signal was given that the fox had broken. Events had transpired as Tarquin had foreseen—the fox had been driven through the wood with extreme rapidity. There was no time for even as much as a swig; Edmund thrust the cordial back at Miss Alderscott untasted and put his spurs to his horse.

Here the hunt underwent a major division. Ashleigh and all the group with him went lucklessly to the wrong side of the wood, and rode directly into a plough of very heavy muck. By the time they passed the cover, the hunt was long out of sight.

Edmund and Tarquin fared better. The full pack was still in view when they cleared the wood, and by using a fortunately situated cart track, they bypassed some rough fields without so much as losing sight of the hounds, and in a few minutes had caught up with the huntsman. The riders crested a hill that hid Bromley Wood behind them, and then Mr. Dickson looked back over the remaining hunters. "By Jove," he said, "we have finally lost Mr. Ashleigh. We may have a chance to catch this fox yet."

The whipper-in laughed. "Have we *ever* killed a fox without losing Mr. Ashleigh?"

"Never," insisted Mr. Dickson.

"That is not quite true," said Tarquin. "Remember at Christmas last year?"

"Well," conceded Mr. Dickson. "But that was luck, pure luck, Mr. de Foye. Even a fool will get lucky sooner or later."

Suddenly the hounds "threw up"—that is, in hunting parlance, they realized they had lost the scent. The hunt was now in the middle of an immense open field, and the drag seemed to have utterly vanished. Mr. Dickson stopped and looked about to this side and that, finding neither preferable.

"Which way do you cast?" asked Tarquin.

"Damned if I know," said Mr. Dickson.

"Wait," said Edmund. "Which way is Plummer's Corner?"

"Directly ahead," said Tarquin.

"The fox was going straight for it," he said. "He is hard pressed now, and for once he did not try to run in cover. But something headed him when he was crossing this field." He paused and checked the direction of the wind, and Tarquin did the same.

"It was Shadwell," said Tarquin. "He knew Shadwell was waiting up at the corner."

"Shall we lift?" said Mr. Dickson. By this he meant advancing the dogs to a new position without waiting for them to find the scent to follow. "By God, Mr. de Foye, I am for it, no matter what you say."

"You know I hate lifting the hounds," said Tarquin. "It is damned unsportsmanlike, in my opinion. Are we *hunting*, or are we merely out killing foxes? If we want to kill foxes, there are easier ways to do it—we might as well shoot them by moonlight."

"We shall have to lift," said Mr. Dickson. "Let us make for the crossroads, and we shall see what we find there."

"Very well," said Tarquin reluctantly.

Mr. Dickson spared no words, but gave immediate orders to the whips, and the dogs were led at once across the field. It was bounded by a high hedge, making for a difficult jump, but all of the remaining hunters cleared it cleanly.

They came up at once on a meeting of three lanes. On the milepost at the crossing were two stones about the size of a man's fist. "The fox is making for Strethamside," said Tarquin decisively. Mr. Dickson looked at him with surprise.

"You are awfully definite about that," he said.

"See those two stones on the milepost? There are a signal from Shadwell," explained Tarquin.

"I dare not lift the hounds any further," said Mr. Dickson. "We might lose the drag altogether."

"One moment, if you will," said Edmund. He rode to the top of the next rise, which was only a short distance away, and then turned back to them and cried, "I see Shadwell! He is waving to us!"

The hunters poured up the hill after him, and soon saw what he had discovered: there, on a hillside about a half-mile away, Mr. Shadwell was waiting for them, waving his hat. He had evidently followed the fox by sight that far, but had stopped, being in need of the hounds to go any farther.

"Lift them down the lane to where Shadwell is," Tarquin told Mr. Dickson. "We shall find the drag there beyond any doubt."

They rode on at once and joined Mr. Shadwell, who directed the huntsman where to set the hounds. He had seen the fox enter a ragged little cover, but had been careful not to muddy the drag himself. The hounds found at once and dashed into the cover. "It is Archie's fox, for a certainty," Mr. Shadwell told Tarquin while they waited. "He is as wily as they come. He stays in cover every inch he can. And he is moving like lightning!"

"We lost the drag before we got to Plummer's Corner," said Tarquin. "You have saved the run, Mr. Shadwell."

"Probably not," said Mr. Shadwell. "The hounds would have found sooner or later. But I have perhaps ensured I shall be home in time for dinner."

At this moment Miss Alderscott rode across his line of vision as he looked over the field. "I see the lady is still with us," he said.

"That she is," admitted Tarquin. "I have to confess she is proving to be a rather good rider."

"A woman who rides well always rides better than a man who rides well," said the farmer.

"Why do you say such a thing, Mr. Shadwell?" asked Tarquin.

"We men ride from boyhood, and pick up a half-knowledge as we need it; the ladies are generally instructed in the complete art, and they know things we never bother to learn."

"You are probably right," said Edmund. "And riding is not the only art in which they excel us."

Shadwold gave him a piercing look; and if Edmund was not mistaken, a wry smile played at the corner of his lips for the first time that day. Then the farmer said, "I say she ought to get the brush if she is in for the kill." It was customary for the most exemplary hunter to receive the brush, or tail of the fox, at the end of the hunt.

"What!" scoffed Tarquin. "Get the brush? A *lady?*"

Shadwold only tipped his hat again and rode back to the nearest lane.

"I do not think that man has jumped once," said Edmund.

"He will jump if he has to, but only if he has to," said Tarquin. "I just thank God he is on *our* side, not on that of the foxes, or we should never make a kill.—Come, I think we had better get round this cover."

They were just in time; the hounds ran forth from the far side as they approached, and the riders picked up the huntsman again.

Though Mr. Shadwell seemed to be right that the fox was not done with his tricks, evidently one of his tricks was to repeat a trick. Just as had happened before, the drag vanished in thin air in the middle of a field. The hounds "threw up" again and ran in mad circles in the field trying to find the scent. Mr. Dickson took a cast to left and then to right, but the dogs found nothing, for all they "lashed their sterns"—that is, made the peculiar thrashing motion of their hindquarters that dogs make while searching for a scent—and yelped and bounded over one another. Mr. Dickson tried a third time and a fourth, still without luck.

"What are you going to do?" Tarquin asked Mr. Dickson.

"I am going to try back," said Mr. Dickson, meaning that he was going to lead the hounds back over the trail they had come, in the hope of finding where the scent had been lost.

Tarquin and the others immediately turned their horses about to make way for the hounds; only Edmund hesitated a fraction of a second before doing the same.

Mr. Dickson noticed that instant of delay. "You think I am wrong, Mr. Percy?" he asked as they rode back.

"I think you are the huntsman, sir," said Edmund, "and the huntsman is never wrong."

Mr. Dickson brought his horse to a halt, and so the others halted too. "Tell me your thoughts, Mr. Percy, if you please," he said in challenge to Edmund.

"My thought is to stand clear and let your hounds work, sir."

"It is not that at all. Tell me—if you found yourself in this situation in Surrey, where should you lead the hounds?"

"I should follow my huntsman, Mr. Dickson, as I hope to be a true sporting man."

"But say you were huntsman yourself—if you can condescend to imagine such a thing, Mr. Percy. I hear you are to be a clergyman soon—though I must say, I think it a shame, and a waste of a man of your talent. But it is not such a great leap from driver of souls to driver of hounds; and I often think that the Devil and the fox have much in common. A clergyman draws the Devil, and a huntsman draws the fox."

Edmund did not answer.

"Speak up, Percy," said Tarquin. "We shall take no offense."

Edmund raised his arm reluctantly and indicated a hedgerow on the very far edge of the field. "I should take them along that hedge, Mr. Dickson," he said.

Mr. Dickson squinted at it. "But he would have had to run far out of his line to get to it. It does not seem likely to me."

"It is the same trick he just played us."

"Then trying back will catch him at it."

"Not after we have muddied this plough. Look at what we have done."

They all looked back, and it was true. Though Edmund and Tarquin and Miss Alderscott had kept to one side of the hunt, the others had ridden directly behind the hounds, and the probable course of the fox had been marred.

"We know this fox runs in cover," said Edmund, "even at the risk of going round about. His line has been mostly straight, but he has clung to cover more than any fox I have ever known. We have been hard on his tail—what there is of it—and but for Mr. Shadwell, we have barely had a view. That is why I think he has made for that hedgerow. Where he did it, I do not know—we have clearly overrun the spot; but we shall find the drag at the hedge again, that is my guess."

"But what if he has got around behind us, and is laughing his way home to some cover we have passed? That is what I fear, Mr. Percy."

"No; he has been running too determinedly for that. His home is up ahead, and he wants it—he does not want to double us; that is the last thing in his thoughts. And I would hazard further that his earth will be in the biggest cover you have hereabouts."

"Copperthwaite Wood," said Tarquin.

"Copperthwaite Wood," repeated the huntsman; and he said it in such a tone that it was clear that Edmund's understanding of the situation made instant sense to him. "There is a river he must cross before that; I have half a mind to lift the hounds there."

"No," said Tarquin. "Let us try the hedge, and see if Percy is right."

"But the fox has been running while we have been talking; we are not like to catch him up," said Mr. Dickson.

"He will start sinking soon," said Tarquin. "By God, man, we have run him I do not know how many miles; we still have a chance."

Mr. Dickson said no more, but immediately put the hounds to the hedge in question. They had not gone halfway down its length before they got on the fox's drag again.

The instant the hounds spoke, Tarquin laughed.

"Well done, Mr. Percy," was all Mr. Dickson would say.

⌛⌛⌛⌛

The fox now began a bewildering series of zig-zagging maneuvers. That is, though he continued running consistently in one direction overall, he took to various tacks off his main line of travel to get there. He seemed to be trying to keep his pursuers in doubt about his final destination to avoid their lifting the hounds directly to it. He threw in other tricks as well—he went some distance up a ditch filled with water, treading in the very stream at the bottom; he crossed another ditch on a fallen tree; and more than once he seemed to have run halfway down a fence and doubled back. Such was the acuity of the hounds and the huntsman, however, that he did not lose his pursuers again. The horses were kept to a constant series of jumps as the hunt wound over high ground and low. Gradually the loyal group around Tarquin began to diminish, as the horses flagged or the riders were daunted by one jump or another and sought another way around.

Thus they worked their way across the Hampshire countryside. Occasionally they passed laborers who cried the view halloo or otherwise tried to distract them, though to no avail. Once, after a particularly punishing jump, Edmund looked back and saw that now only Miss Alderscott was behind them. She looked pained, indeed, but when she saw Edmund's glance, she smiled gamely, and, as it seemed to him, with quite genuine pleasure despite the beating she was taking.

"Shadwell is right," Edmund said to Tarquin then.

"What?" Tarquin said, at first not hearing or not believing what he heard. Then he looked back at Miss Alderscott.

"Damn!" he said; but it was a different oath this time, not of irritation but of dawning wonderment and admiration.

"What do you say?" said Edmund. "Will she have the brush, or no?"

"By Jove, she *shall* have it, if she sticks with us to the kill," said Tarquin.

It was well after eleven o'clock when they found themselves confronting a particularly nasty looking hedge, quite high, which was combined with a steep ditch beyond. The hounds ran under it in a blur of white and black, but Mr. Dickson and the other handlers turned from it and set off round the lane that skirted the field.

"That lane will take you halfway to Strethamside," shouted Tarquin. Mr. Dickson, however, seemed to have had enough of jumping; he paid no heed. Tarquin and Edmund thus saw with dismay that the huntsman and the handlers were making off in one direction, and the hounds in the other.

"There is nothing for it," said Tarquin. "We must take this hedge or lose the hounds." He turned to ride back a bit to get room for a rush at the obstacle.

"No," cried Miss Alderscott. "Do not even attempt it! That hedge is impossible—even for you, Mr. de Foye. You only will hurt your horse and ruin the day. There is a gate down there"—and she pointed back down the lane behind them—"and it will take us into that field."

"And what if we find ourselves padlocked in at the lower end?"

"I have thought of that. The fence is lower on the far side—I saw it when we were coming down the hill. If the gate there is locked, we can still get over the fence itself." Without further argument she turned her horse away and headed for the gate she had indicated.

"She is right," said Edmund; and Tarquin showed himself convinced by spurring after Miss Alderscott.

She not only reached the gate before they did, but—much to their wonder—she sprang from her horse and dragged it open for them. They reined in when they reached her. "Mount up," said Tarquin. "I shall close it for you."

"Go! Go!" she cried. "Do not be stupid! I shall close it behind us and catch up to you!"

And so two gentlemen found themselves riding through a gate held open for them by a lady. It was a stupefying reversal of roles; but from pure astonishment, if nothing else, they did as they were told, and were soon flying across a plowed field, throwing mud in all directions. Tarquin looked behind him.

"By God," he said, "She is *gaining* on us! We must not let her *see to* the next gate, Percy; it will cast shame on us forever."

"Agreed," Edmund shouted back; and they exerted their best efforts to reach the far gate before she did.

Edmund was first, and did the honors at the gate, which was part of a fence that proved far more imposing in person than it had seemed in the miniature of far perspective. He had no sooner swung the bars open than Tarquin, with Miss Alderscott on his heels, rode up and dashed through it. Edmund led his horse through and closed the gate behind them; and then took his turn catching up to the others. It was now just the three of them and the hounds.

The land opened up somewhat. From what they could see of the course of the pack, the fox was still zig-zagging nearly from bush to bush. They began to ascend a broad hill, gentle in slope but very long, and the horses began to toil, as indeed they might be expected to, after some twenty miles in a little over two hours—all difficult work, with little rest.

At length the hunters crested the rise, and here, to their great dismay, they saw this scene before them: The land plunged away rapidly to a small river on their left. Directly ahead of them, on their own side of the river, was a hill, an outcropping of stone, which, though not too high, was far too steep for dogs or horses to climb. The only way around the rock was either to plunge into the river or to skirt the hill to the right. Beyond the hill was a bridge over the river; and on the far side of the river was an enormous wood. The instant he saw it, Edmund did not doubt that it was Copperthwaite Wood and the home of their fox, who would run to earth there in a matter of minutes if he once crossed the river.

But how would he cross it? The water was flowing swiftly, and exhausted as the fox must now be, it seemed likely he would prefer the bridge, if he could only get to it—and if he should find it clear of human traffic. As they paused and surveyed the situation, Miss Alderscott suddenly cried out.

"He is there!" she said. "On the rock!"

The hounds, it seemed, had pursued the fox to the base of the rock, and must have been only a few dozen feet behind him. He had flung himself directly at the rock face, and by a very narrow way of which he must have had prior knowledge, he was now ascending the very face of the little cliff before them, leaping desperately from ledge to ledge and wending his way upwards. The dogs could not get higher than a few feet without falling back to the ground, but the fox was going up like a mountain goat.

"Have you ever seen such a thing?" cried Tarquin.

"If he gets over that rock, he will have a straight run to the bridge," said Edmund.

"We must lift the dogs around the rock to the right," said Tarquin. "It is our only hope."

"It will take too long," said Edmund; but Tarquin, with Miss Alderscott behind him, had already begun ascending the steep hillside before them, and Edmund had nothing left to do but follow.

When they came to the bottom, Tarquin drew a large silver whistle from his pocket and blew a shrill blast on it. The dogs immediately left off their fruitless attempts to scale the cliff and rushed back toward their master, yelping for his orders.

"The river!" cried Edmund. "I shall cross the river and get up on the bridge and block him!"

"That river is too damned deep, Percy—do not think of it!" said Tarquin. He spurred to the right to lead the hounds around the rock, and again Miss Alderscott followed.

Edmund, however, turned left and rode directly to the river. It was indeed deep-looking, black and cold under the overcast sky; but he saw a place where the current had laid down a bed of gravelly stones, which formed half of a ford at least. He looked back up at the little cliff, and saw the fox making a final leap up the face, and there disappearing over the top.

He calculated for just a moment, though barely in conscious terms. He drew his watch from his pocket, put it into his hat, and jammed the hat back tightly onto his head; and then he spurred the horse out into the river.

For half the crossing there was indeed no danger or discomfort; but then the bed of the river fell away steeply, and suddenly he and the horse were plunged into the icy water to their necks. He clung mightily to Agamemnon's mane, and the beast, invigorated by the cold, struck out with its enormous strength and in a matter of a few seconds was scrambling out into the shallows on the far side.

He had to dismount to lead the horse up the bank, but then he threw himself into the saddle again and went directly to the bridge.

He rode out onto it at the same moment that the fox appeared at the other end. He had heard it said many times that there is nothing in the world a fox hates and fears so much as humankind, and now he proved that saying true; for the fox could easily have run past him or even between the legs of his horse, and escaped to his home in the wood. But he did nothing of the kind. Instead he halted and stared at Edmund.

His flanks were heaving and his breath was a fog before him on the March air; he was shaking with fatigue, and he lifted one hind leg as he stood there, as if he had suffered an injury somewhere along the way. Edmund little noticed these things at the time, however; rather he remembered them later. Now he saw only the beast's eyes, as it looked at him with sullen despair and with a terror dulled by exhaustion; and he remembered seeing the very same look in the eyes of slaves in Antigua on many an occasion—men and women whose world had shrunken to an island of impossibility.

It was only for a moment that the fox confronted him thus, but it was an awful moment, and Edmund never forgot it. Then the fox turned and ran back down the road that had brought it to the bridge.

The beast would want to cross the river somewhere; but now he knew that he would not be allowed to do so—that the humans and their canine minions would swarm both banks and prevent him. He wanted cover—it was all he could think of—and the nearest route to cover led him directly back toward the hounds.

Edmund rode to the top of the arching bridge and saw the whole thing: how Tarquin led the hounds around the hill, how the hounds saw the fox, how the fox made one last desperate sprint across open ground, how the hounds caught him and tore him to shreds. Tarquin was among them in another minute, with Miss Alderscott no more than ten feet behind him.

The hounds were well blooded, there was no question of that. Tarquin took the tail from them, and for want of a hunting horn, then blew a blast on his whistle to signal the kill. Suddenly here was Mr. Shadwell on his frisky cob, riding in along the road. Edmund, too, now went down to join them.

"By God, Edmund," said Tarquin, when he saw him, "it was you who stopped him from crossing the river!"

"Mr. Percy," exclaimed Miss Alderscott in horror, "you are drenched through! You will catch a terrible cold!"

"Are you all right?" asked Tarquin. "You look as though you have seen a ghost."

"I think I have. His eyes—they reminded me of the eyes of the slaves in Antigua. It was horrible. I do not think I shall ever hunt again."

"Oh, Percy, what nonsense!" laughed Tarquin. "You shall be riding again next season with never a qualm! That was splendidly done, old man! He should have been in the wood before we even rounded the rock if it had not been for you."

"Mr. Percy, you must take some spirits," said Miss Alderscott.

"Yes, here is my flask, man," said Tarquin. "Get some of this into you. This will buck you up."

Mr. Shadwell was more helpful; he offered Edmund an extra overcoat he carried at his saddle in case of rain, which Edmund gratefully accepted, after he had poured the water out of his boots and taken his watch from his hat.

"Now *that* was a run," said Tarquin joyfully, looking around himself in a daze.

Edmund showed that his spirits were reviving by attempting a small joke. "And that is a typical run for you down here in Hampshire?" he said.

Even Mr. Shadwell laughed. "Ah, Percy," said Tarquin, "that was a run to beat all runs! That was the stuff of legends! And here it ended, in a kill in the open."

He looked around again in a weary ecstasy, and his eyes lit on Miss Alderscott. "And *you!*" he said. "Miss Alderscott, I owe *you* an apology."

"Whatever for, Mr. de Foye?"

"For defaming you in my thought, by imagining that you could never keep up with us."

"Well, sir," she said, compelled into an honest demurral, "there were many moments I doubted it myself. You two gentlemen have led me the most merry chase I have ever had a-horseback. I have never jumped so much in a single day in all my life. I cannot tell you how many times I prayed the fox would run down a lane—a sweet, straight lane with nary a fence anywhere to be seen. And yet now I would not trade it for anything—it was glorious, absolutely glorious!" Edmund noticed that she shifted uncomfortably on the saddle even as she spoke, as if her sitting part had taken quite a bruising.

"I thought you would have us opening every gate for you," said Tarquin. "Yet *you* were the one who opened them for *us!*" He looked at Edmund and they both laughed.

"Oh," she said, looking very pleased, "that was nothing."

"Well," said Tarquin, looking around at Edmund and Mr. Shadwell, "I think we are agreed, are we not, sirs?"

"We are," said Edmund. Mr. Shadwell touched the brim of his hat in assent.

"This was Mr. Shadwell's idea, initially," Tarquin said to Miss Alderscott. "But Percy and I concur." He walked over to her and offered her the bloodied brush of the fox.

At first she seemed to think he was only showing it to her. "Yes, I see," she said. "The tip is quite gone."

"Miss Alderscott," said Tarquin, "you do not seem to understand. We have chosen you to receive the brush."

She looked at him in stupefaction; and when she still did not take it, he thrust it into her hands with a laugh.

For a moment she was overcome, and expressions of amazement tumbled from her lips. "Oh!" she cried. "Oh, Mr. de Foye! . . . I . . . Mr. de Foye! . . . I have never dreamed of such a thing! I have ridden to hounds for fifteen years, sir, and I have never . . . Oh, dear, sir! You cannot mean this?"

"It is a pleasure to ride with you, madam," said Tarquin. "That is the highest praise the master of the hunt can give."

She burst suddenly into tears, and put one hand over her face; but at the same time she laughed at herself. With that license, Tarquin and Edmund laughed as well.

"Now," said Tarquin, "we must find Dickson somehow, and get these hounds back to kennel."

"If you gentlefolk will excuse me," said Mr. Shadwell, "I think I will be getting home to dinner. I expect I shall see Mr. Dickson on the way, and if he needs direction, I shall give it to him."

"Yes," said Tarquin. "He had a likely idea where we should end up. You are wise to head back now: the ruck will doubtless arrive soon, and they will all start claiming they were in for the kill; and *that* is always a bit tiresome."

Mr. Shadwell turned to ride away, but then thought better of it, and instead approached Edmund. "Forgive a mere farmer for saying so," he said, "but I cannot tell you how very much I admire your sportsmanship, Mr. Percy. It is almost as if Mr. de Foye had found a long-lost younger brother. I hope you will find a way to live in Hampshire and hunt with us all season."

"Why, thank you, sir," said Edmund. "I should like that very much. I have a feeling I could learn a great deal from you."

Tarquin laughed to see Edmund adroitly turn the man's praise about, and even Mr. Shadwell smiled wryly, as if he were chalking the compliment up for retaliation at a later date. Then, with a final touch on the brim of his top hat, he started for home and dinner.

⌛⌛⌛⌛

Mr. Dickson and the other handlers soon found them. Tarquin wanted to ride for home at once, but the huntsman and his men had a motive for lingering at the site of the kill until the rest of the hunt found them, and Tarquin respected it. It was the custom for the huntsman to pass the hat after a kill, and each hunter would throw in a half-crown. The more riders who could be compelled to yield to this forced contribution, the better Mr. Dickson and his men would fare.

Tarquin did, however, consult Edmund first. "I am content to wait," Edmund told him. "I do not feel cold at all—damp, yes, but not cold; it has been hot work."

In another ten minutes Ashleigh and about twenty others came down the road. They heard the story of the kill, and as

Tarquin had predicted, began repeating it among themselves as if they had witnessed it, with various embellishments to demonstrate their presence at it. Donaldson, in particular, seemed to know how it had taken place even better than Edmund and Tarquin. Most of the men were quite dumbfounded that Miss Alderscott had been given the brush; but as they themselves had not done the riding she had, they did not dare protest. Then the hat was passed, the huntsman gathered his coin, and the hunters started the long return home.

Their way led within a quarter-mile of the little hamlet of Strethamside, and Donaldson led a large group on a detour to the village inn there. Edmund, Tarquin, and Miss Alderscott, who were riding together, decided to follow them, in the hope of finding Edmund something dry to ride home in, and thinking to fortify themselves until dinner, which would be late that afternoon.

The hunters invaded the town like an army, and so roisterous were they that they soon drove out the honest laborers who had stopped at the inn for a pint. The innkeeper did indeed have a few articles of gentleman's clothing, left behind by a recent forgetful guest; they had been washed scrupulously by his wife, who had hoped to sell them. She now found a ready buyer. After Edmund had changed, the innkeeper heaped wood on the fire and hung his scarlet coat to dry before it, while Tarquin and Miss Alderscott squeezed together on a bench to make room for him close to the blaze.

All the innkeeper had to offer was ale, cheese, bread, and a little beef, but the hunters fell to like locusts. Miss Alderscott drank about half a pint and flirted freely with both Edmund and Tarquin—and it was very pleasant work the three of them had at it. By his own account a few days before, Tarquin had never been too comfortable in the company of a lady; but something about Miss Alderscott evidently set him at ease, for Edmund had not yet in his brief acquaintance with him seen the man in such a jovial mood. Part of Tarquin's contentment was certainly the result of their success at the hunt, and part was the consequence of the powerful ale; but the largest part was clearly due to Miss Alderscott, who again and again brought them to laughing at her wit, and to boasting of their exploits, and to praising of hers; and who had such a winning way of glancing at a man with her bright eyes over the rim of her glass, and of slapping her neat small hand next to his on the table and insisting he take more beef or cheese, or leaning close to listen in the din of the inn, and smiling as if she perfectly understood, when it was doubtful whether she could even have heard—and a thousand other little ways she had about her, which all made her very intriguing.

The three of them slipped out of the place long before the rest. However, as Edmund was reclaiming Agamemnon from the ostler, he came upon Donaldson, who had wandered out to see that his horse had been properly baited. "I'll wager it was *your* idea to give Miss Alderscott the brush," said Donaldson in his abrupt way, his speech a little slurred by ale.

"No, it was that fellow Shadwell's, as a matter of fact."

"But you approved it readily, I'll wager."

"I did indeed. What of it, Mr. Donaldson?"

"Only that it was a sly move, Mr. Percy, and one worthy of a fine foxhunter such as you."

"Whatever do you mean, sir?"

"I mean that the lady has ten thousand pounds a year, that is what I mean."

Edmund mounted his horse and looked down at Donaldson with some disgust. "I was not aware that the redcoats here in Hampshire awarded the brush on that basis," he said.

"I'm *on* to you, Percy," laughed Donaldson. "Let slip Tom Cupid's dogs, old chap! Hoist anchor and pour on the sail! Lay to with whip and spur!"

"And I suggest that *you* decide on *one* metaphor, and stick to it," said Edmund coolly. He joined Tarquin and Miss Alderscott, who were already mounted and waiting before the inn, and they resumed the journey back to Hartswound.

Edmund knew that such estimates of a person's wealth were nearly always based on rumor, and generally far exaggerated; but he could not help thinking that if Miss Alderscott did indeed have a private income, she might not be ashamed to marry a man whose means as a clergyman were much more modest than those for which a woman of her position in society might otherwise be willing to settle.

The March sun now made a final effort and came out from behind the clouds, at first fitfully, and then completely—above the rolling land of Hampshire the overcast skies broke up into an armada of scudding fair-weather clouds. Miss Alderscott was finally satisfied that Edmund was truly warm again, and left off inquiring into his state of health, though she continued to tease him about his ill-fitting borrowed coat. At one point she said, shaking her head—or perhaps the motion might better have been described as a little enticing toss of her chin—"Alas, Mr. Percy," she said, "I see you are no Mr. Shadwell."

"No, he is not that," agreed Tarquin. "He has twice the shoulders Shadwell has.—Be careful you do not tear that poor overcoat asunder, Percy."

"In a minute I shall take it off—then the mantle of the man may pass to you, Miss Alderscott."

"I *do* aspire to the knowledge Mr. Shadwell has of the fox, I must admit. And if I lived in these parts, I should hope to get to know the lay of the land, too, as well as he does."

"And what do you think of Shadwell's plan, Percy?" asked Tarquin.

"What plan is that?"

"Well, of course—that you live with us in Hampshire."

Edmund laughed, but Tarquin persisted. "Do not fob me off with a laugh, man," he said. "What an addition you would make! You would quite counterbalance the Donaldsons and the Ashleighs at the meet—oh, excuse me, Miss Alderscott; I did not mean—"

"That is quite all right; I understand your point of view. Besides, it is Edith Ashleigh who is my—acquaintance. We were schoolfellows together."

"Then I shall say it: Percy, you would quite counterbalance the Ashleighs and Donaldsons, and the village blackcoats who mar the drag, and the little boys on their ponies—"

"Ah, but you too—both of you—were once little boys on ponies, do not forget," said Miss Alderscott. "And I thought it was quite kind of you to include them in your meet."

"Yes, but the point is, we must have Percy here with us in Hampshire—I have said it before, Percy, and I shall say it again.—And you, too, Miss Alderscott: we must have you in Hampshire as well."

She looked extremely pleased, smiling and glancing away across the fields, and with an unconscious motion stroked the brush of the fox, which she had tied to her saddle before her; and she said, in a low voice that was very much a contrast to her usual bold tone, "I could learn to love Hampshire very well, I think."

The three of them were silent for a minute thereafter. Edmund was thinking that he had not met a woman who made him feel such powerful sexual interest since he had returned to England. Since the hunt concluded he had been minutely aware of her body—the occasional touch of her thigh against his as they had sat crushed together on the bench at the little inn, how in riding she sat easily in the saddle, how she took the roll of the horse's stride, how shapely her shoulders and arms seemed as she held the reins, how tender and yet strong was her neck as she put her head up and laughed, or looked about at him, with that warm smile on her lips.

"And is remaining here in Hampshire a possibility for you, Mr. Percy?" she asked him now. "Are you fixed upon Surrey for your home?"

"My family's home is in Surrey, but I have not fixed upon any place for my own," he said.

"The seat of the Surrey Percies is Brackensom—have you heard of it?" Tarquin asked Miss Alderscott.

"Mr. Percy mentioned it earlier.—You will have to pardon a poor ignorant country girl, Mr. Percy, but I have not otherwise heard of the place. I have spent much of my life quite happily apart from society."

"Mr. Percy has a mad plan to become a clergyman," said Tarquin.

Miss Alderscott looked closely at Edmund. He could not tell if she approved or disapproved; in fact, she seemed neutral on the point, as if Tarquin had just told her Edmund's favorite color. "Is this so, Mr. Percy?" she asked.

"I am the youngest son in my family," he explained.

"Ah."

"My father and I have begun a campaign to persuade him to give all that up," said Tarquin.

"Well," she said, "why not do something more to the point, and give the man a living?"

"No," said Tarquin, "you do not understand. We want Percy to be independent."

"Would not having a living make him so?" She looked back and forth between Tarquin and Edmund, as if there was something she did not understand.

"It would indeed," said Edmund.

"No," said Tarquin. "Not the kind of independence we have in mind."

"Oh—you mean the kind that would not stint at spending four days a week hunting foxes, in season?"

"*Exactly,* Miss Alderscott—now you take my meaning *exactly.*"

She laughed. "I suspect that owning a suit of *black cloth* would not make Mr. Percy hang up his *red coat* forever."

Both Tarquin and Edmund were silent for a moment, and she looked back and forth between them; and then,

Edmund guessed, she suddenly realized how Tarquin intended to accomplish his plan for his friend.

From that moment on she stopped flirting with Edmund. She found herself in too serious a situation. She was still charming to him, and pleasant to be with; but she had a reserve toward him now that she had not had before. Tarquin did not seem to notice, but Edmund did, and grew more sure of his apprehension of the change in her the closer to home they rode. It was not that she rejected all thought of him out of hand, but rather that she thought it behooved her not to risk a misunderstanding of her vivacity, either by Edmund or by his friends, who were all too likely to forward a connection that was would be advantageous to him.

Blast that ten thousand, he thought at one point. *I want nothing of it; I should like to have her in my marriage bed, that is all. Though who knows, perhaps she is, under all the flirtation, just an English prude, like all of them.* Then he looked at the way she moved as she rode, and he thought, *By God, she does not* look *like a prude, all the same.*

The change in her behavior did not stop there, however; for, once debarred from encouraging Edmund, she shifted her full interest to Tarquin. She flirted with *him* as readily as before; and gradually the interest that had come to be directed by default towards Tarquin took on a life of its own. Or so it seemed to Edmund. He wished he were not acute enough to see this alteration take place, or jealous enough to imagine it, if his perception was indeed only a delusion; but he shared with his aunt a keen, if irregularly active, ability to assess character and thought, and he was convinced that that faculty was telling him the truth now. On occasion his aunt was capable of tremendous blindness, too; he knew that, and he expected his own powers of judgment were equally subject to error; but this did not seem such an occasion.

When they were only about twenty minutes from home, they met up with some handlers traveling without hounds and coming from a different direction across the fields. Tarquin asked Edmund and Miss Alderscott to wait while he spoke to them, and they did so, taking the chance to dismount and rest their horses.

"I am curious, Mr. Percy," she asked Edmund then, as she stood watching Tarquin riding across the field to meet his men. "How long have you known Mr. de Foye?"

He had to think. "It is a week ago tomorrow that I met him."

She was astonished. "Why, I had thought you must have met in school," she said.

"No. Just a week."

"And yet he seems to love you, sir; and you him."

Edmund laughed; but as he looked at Tarquin, the laughter faded on his lips; for now that Miss Alderscott said it, he realized that he had indeed come to love Tarquin. And part of that affection was to hope for good things for the man, as Tarquin hoped for a good future for him. And he realized in that moment that if Tarquin were ever going to marry, his bride would have to be Miss Alderscott.

It was not an easy conclusion to come to. It tugged hard at the new roots of his own hopes for himself. But he told himself that he still might find a Miss Caits somewhere, who would take his vocation a little more seriously than Miss Alderscott could. For Tarquin, however, Miss Alderscott was the only chance at a Miss Caits—she was devout in the same religion as he, the worship of horse and hounds and hunt, and Tarquin would never find another like her.

He turned to Miss Alderscott. "Do you know," he said, "I think de Foye is really one of the very finest fellows in my acquaintance."

"Really?" she said, as one who wished to hear more on the point.

"Yes, indeed. You see what a fine athlete he is—that goes without saying. But he is a good man, a very good man; and I foresee happiness for him."

"My friend Edith says that he is a little . . . rough, I think that was the word she used. That he wanted a little domesticating."

"Well—yes, that is true. He would be the first to admit it. But I absolutely warrant you that he could be quite successfully domesticated; and that he will reward the woman who brings that mild touch to him with a very devoted affection."

"Really," she said, looking at Tarquin still.

"And the affection of such a man," he added, "would *never* be dull. No—it would never be dull."

She blushed slightly, but she did not take her eyes off Tarquin.

"I say nothing of the fact that he is what young ladies and their mothers commonly call *a catch.* I mean, Hartswound Park and all that. That is all beside the point. No; he is not just *a catch;* he is *a man.* And whoever *catches* him had very well better be sure that she is very much *a woman.*"

The stain of crimson on her cheeks redoubled now, and she darted a quick glance at Edmund to see whether he were warning her or cheering her on; and he met her eyes with such goodwill that she could not help but see that he was indeed encouraging her.

She looked away and coughed unnecessarily into a gloved fist. They were silent until Tarquin came back; and when he strode up to them, leading his horse behind him, the look she gave him told Edmund she had made up her mind. Perhaps there was no serious purpose behind her decision; but whether there was or not, it was clear that Edmund had forfeited his chance.

He was not without considerable regret at this. But as they turned to resume their journey, he clapped Tarquin on the shoulder cordially; and Tarquin gave him a look that suggested that he guessed why.

⌛⌛⌛⌛

The rest of the day was devoted to the fellowship of the hunt. As the hunters drifted into Hartswound in little groups, each in turn went off to bathe and change for dinner; and then they joined the gathering by the fire in Cato's den.

The old man could not get enough of the story of the hunt. He knew every inch of ground over which they had ridden, and Tarquin could and did describe each hedge, fence, field, and lane minutely. The old squire laughed to hear how Mr. Shadwell had performed the same ride with ease; he complimented Miss Alderscott on receiving the brush and told to her several truly amazing stories about the hunting prowess of Tarquin's mother; and he praised Edmund's plunge into the icy river as worthy of a true British hero. The other riders, not to be outdone, described their own exploits in the field as critical to the success of the day. By old custom, Mr. Dickson came in to report to Cato, and then the entire account must be told yet again.

Lord Burley returned shortly after the rest of the party had assembled. He was not sure where he had been, though he thought he had been not more than a mile or two from Winchester at one point. He had to hear all the story, and lament in quiet, stoic terms his having missed so fine a run, and a kill in the open, and regret his ill-luck in becoming detached from the hounds. Ashleigh and his brothers and cousins stayed on, and their own guests with them, though fortunately Donaldson went home. The dinner, a sumptuous repast, was noisy and pleasant, punctuated by toasts to the de Foyes and the Hartswound hunt.

Miss Alderscott was seated between Edmund and Tarquin. It seemed to him that she strove to pay equal attention to both of them, but that as the evening wore on, that effort became more labored, and long before the end she had taken up a set position slightly turned in her chair and facing toward Tarquin. Edmund struggled a little more with his feelings about this—they were still bittersweet—but he congratulated Tarquin in his heart.

Miss Alderscott was the only woman at the dinner; and when it was over, she announced that she would not just withdraw to the parlor, but would retire for the night. "I regret the necessity," she said, "but I confess myself bone-weary after such a ride.—Though if you wish to do it again tomorrow, you need only give me notice, and you will find me in the saddle at seven."

They gave her a cheer, and she curtsied and departed, walking somewhat stiffly.

"Now, Ashleigh," said Cato when she had gone, "tell us more about this amazing Miss Alderscott."

"I do not know quite what to say," Ashleigh began. "She has been a friend to my sister Edith since they were both girls and down at school together in Kent. She has never visited us in Hampshire before, though Edith has been up to Hertfordshire several times. Her family are good hunting folk, or so I hear. Quite a bit of land they have."

"And she is rumored to have some ten thousand pounds a year free and clear as her dowry," said Mr. George Carew.

"No, it is fifteen," said Ashleigh.

"Are you sure? I thought it was ten."

"No, I am sure Edith told me fifteen."

"And none of you gentleman has made an offer?" said Cato incredulously. They laughed.

"Whoever takes on Miss Alderscott had better be a bold fellow indeed," said Ashleigh.

"That is the truth," said Hugh Ashleigh. "She is great fun, really. Loves to quiz you, and quite a pleasant flirt."

"And never been married? Never been engaged?" asked Cato.

"No, not to my knowledge," said Ashleigh; "and I would be likely to have heard of it if she had."

"Gentlemen, it strikes me that this is a situation to be remedied," said Cato with mock sternness. They laughed again.

"Count me out," said Hugh Ashleigh. "She is too forward for me. I am on the lookout for something a bit meeker. And besides, she is on the far side of five-and-twenty, and ready for the spinster's cap."

"Fifteen thousand pounds a year will reconcile a man to a good deal of boldness, I should think," said Cato. "And there are indeed some men who take that as a good quality in a lady. As for her years, I tell you as one who knows, that women, like wine, get better with age. If you could stand the Miss Alderscott of five-and-twenty up against the Miss Alderscott of today, you would be a fool to take the younger."

"I shall have to pass, thank you," Hugh insisted with a laugh.

"And I am otherwise employed," said Ashleigh himself. Edmund noticed that Cato did not draw him out. It seemed probable that Cato shared Tarquin's opinion of their neighbor.

"And you, Mr. Carew?" Cato asked George.

"I thought of it once, but could not quite get past her features. That long face, you know."

"I think her rather handsome," said Cato. "A very unusual face, true; but it has the advantage of distinction. She is not one of these little snub-nosed, pasty-faced, mealy-mouthed, simpering things; she has color, and fire, and looks you in the eye, and when she laughs, you feel her pleasure is quite genuine. And her teeth are good."

"Her teeth *are* good," admitted Mr. George Carew, as if they were discussing a horse he could not quite bring himself to buy.

"And there is nothing wrong with her figure," added Cato.

Every man present hastened to assent to that.

"Now Mr. Edward Carew and Mr. Cross and the Colonel are married already. What about you, Mr. Peavey?"

"I am engaged, sir. Though I thank you for your concern on my behalf."

"That leaves you, your lordship."

"Oh!" said Lord Burley in surprise. "Oh, no, thank you. One of these days I have got to marry my second cousin. Everyone expects it. I just have not . . . got round to it yet."

"Well, then," said Cato, eyeing Tarquin and Edmund, "it is down to you two. You must decide between yourselves."

"What do you say, de Foye," Edmund said to Tarquin. "Pistols at dawn?" The company laughed.

"Tell Edith not to worry," Tarquin told Ashleigh. "Between the two of us, Edmund and I shall do something for Miss Alderscott."

"Oh ho!" cried the company, with more laughter.

A toast to Miss Alderscott's future was proposed, and more good wine was poured for it.

⧗ ⧗ ⧗ ⧗

The evening wore on until quite late. The guests went off to bed one by one, leaving only Edmund, Tarquin, Ashleigh, and Lord Burley before the fire in the library. They were all exhausted and had had too much to drink. Edmund was thinking longingly of bed, but he also dreaded sleep; for he feared he would confront the eyes of the fox again, and in them the eyes of the slaves he had left behind in Antigua. The company of the men in the library was more pleasant than that prospect, along with the cheerful fire, and the bit of port left in his glass, and the smell of the cigars the others were smoking.

"We have made a wonderful day of it," said Ashleigh at length. "And to think we had all given over hunting for the season! It is extraordinary, and just goes to show you that you should never give over anything too soon."

"Exactly," said Tarquin.

"The only thing that would have made it complete, utterly complete, would have been to have the company of Miss de Foye," said Ashleigh. "At dinner, at least, even if we could not interest her in riding to hounds with us.—Where is your sister, de Foye?"

"Do not get going about Mariah, now, will you?" said Tarquin, examining his burning cigar closely, as though it were an object of great price and significance. "You always come down to this point late at night, when you are tired and drunk and have forgotten your manners."

"Don't avoid my question," said Ashleigh.

"Damned if I know where she is! Off at the rector's, I should think. She stays quite late there. Sometimes I have to ask the coachman where she is if I want to know. She makes arrangements with him. Sometimes I hear the coach go out in perfect darkness, and that is the only way I know Mariah is still to be fetched from somewhere."

"Well, do you not think you ought to keep a better eye on her?"

"What, follow her into every hovel in Broadbridge on her missions of mercy? I hardly see the need for that."

Ashleigh brooded for a while; and for some reason his gaze fell on Edmund. "And what do you think of Miss de Foye?" Ashleigh asked him.

"I, sir? What do I think of her?"

"That is what I asked you."

"I have the highest opinion of Miss de Foye. I have in fact followed her into one of those hovels; and I have seldom seen a more loving, Christian act than the care she gave its inhabitant."

"No, sir," said Ashleigh somewhat belligerently, "I do not mean that."

"Well, what do you mean?"

"I mean: Do you not think Miss de Foye the most beautiful, the most elegant, the most intelligent woman in all of Britain?—You hesitate, sir; I despise hesitation."

"I do not hesitate at all; I merely give your sweeping question due consideration. To measure a single individual against an entire nation, or half of a nation, or even against that small part of that half with which I am acquainted, is an action which requires more than a moment."

"Not for me, Mr. Percy!"

"No—because you have already considered the question. If it assuages your anxiety on this point, Mr. Ashleigh, I can tell you at once that I have already long since determined that Miss de Foye is the most beautiful lady I have ever seen, and certainly my assessment of her elegance is similar; I am only duly weighing her intelligence against the many fine female minds that I know."

"Oh, give it up, Ashleigh," said Tarquin. "She does not love you, and she never shall. Do not irritate my guests in a vain effort to prove that she belongs to you."

"If you would back me, damn you," said Ashleigh, "I might have a bloody chance. And is that not the least I should expect from a friend, that he should back me when I court his sister?"

"I am her brother, not a bloody pander; and she is my sister, not a bloody whore, I will thank you to remember. So leave off expecting anything. You have failed to interest her on your own merits, and that is the end of it."

"You are a damned brute, de Foye! I do not ask you to pimp for her, I ask you to favor my suit; and the reason you do not do so is that you do not want me for your brother."

"No, by God, I do not!—Look, do not pick a fight with me, man. You shall come out the worse for it, I assure you. You are not a bad man, Ashleigh; but the truth is that you are not good enough for Mariah."

"And do you have someone in mind who is? Perhaps you intend this Mr. Percy for her? I can see through your little game, de Foye."

"Do not be an idiot, Ashleigh. Percy is too smart to set his lance at winning Mariah. He knows his place. Besides, he will find a plump little merchant's daughter who has far more money than Mariah does, and he will be happy with her, too, which is more than I can predict for you in your matrimonial adventures, and probably for me. Mr. Percy has the sense and the good graces to get along with people, which you do not, and which, by God, I do not either. So talk sensibly about something, or shut your mouth, before you find out just how much grace I lack—when I boot you down the front steps."

"Do not try it, de Foye. I shall prove a tougher customer than you think!"

At this point, Ashleigh and Tarquin rose from their chairs and were on the verge of escalating defiance to open blows. "My lord," said Edmund to Lord Burley in a whisper, "if you would be so kind as to take care of Ashleigh, I will get in de Foye's way." Burley caught his meaning with uncharacteristic rapidity, and the two of them physically interceded—Edmund holding Tarquin back by placing one hand on his chest, and Burley forcing Ashleigh out of range.

"You are a fool," Tarquin called to Ashleigh.

"Suffer him, remember?" said Edmund. "Do not let one of the finest runs one could possibly have end in your breaking a man's head."

"This is a poor way to prosecute your suit," Burley told Ashleigh; and his words seemed to have some effect, for Ashleigh held his tongue.

The efforts of the peacemakers were assisted by the arrival of a distraction; for now the house door opened, and the voice of Miss de Foye could be heard in low conversation with the butler. The men stood, frozen where they were—probably by a mutual hope that if they made no sound, Miss de Foye would not come into the room.

That hope was in vain, however, for in a few moments she did, and found them standing exactly as they had been. She read the situation with a glance—saw the likely peacemakers in Edmund and Lord Burley, and the likely combatants in Tarquin and Ashleigh; and she flushed with displeasure.

"Good evening, gentlemen," she said coolly.

"Miss de Foye," said Ashleigh, Burley, and Edmund, much like a chorus of schoolboys; and they each bowed to her.

"Good evening, Mariah," said Tarquin. "Will you join us?"

"Please do join us, Miss de Foye," said Ashleigh.

She gave the latter a look that silenced him—a look the memory of which could still make Edmund smile years later, as he thought how Mariah Esquith de Foye had crushed a grown man without striking a single blow, and done so far more effectively than her brother with all his menaces.

She now went up to Tarquin and put her hands on his lapels. The contrast between them was extraordinary; for compared to him in his strength and height she seemed slender and even small. She patted his coat and smoothed it down against his chest; and then she said, "You are being good, Brother, are you not?"

"I am being an angel," said Tarquin sardonically; and Edmund and Lord Burley laughed.

Miss de Foye looked at Edmund. "Mr. Percy," she said, "I appoint you my brother's keeper. See he comes to no harm—and that he does harm to no one."

Edmund bowed. "I shall do my best, madam," he said.

She looked at him evenly, and then turned and left the room without another word.

When her last footstep had died out on the stairs, Ashleigh turned to Tarquin angrily. "There, you see!" he cried. "It *is* this Percy chap!"

"Oh, Ashleigh, for God's sake," said Tarquin wearily, throwing himself into a chair, "why do you not go to bed and sleep it off? We had a damned fine run today, and I should *rather* talk about *that* than about some girl who is too young to care about men anyway."

"And so I will, damn it," said Ashleigh. "I have had enough of *this!*" And he, too, left the room and went off to bed.

"Damned pretty, that girl," murmured Lord Burley, shaking his head in phlegmatic admiration as he dug another cigar out of his coat pocket. "What a pity she don't like hunting."

⌛⌛⌛⌛

Edmund was the first of the guests to rise from bed the next day. He went down to the stables to see how Agamemnon was recovering, and once satisfied with the condition of the horse, he went back up to the house. He was just in time to see the back of Miss de Foye at a distance as she disappeared down the long drive, a basket on one arm. He grinned mischievously, thinking of Ashleigh's disappointment, and went in to breakfast.

The meal was somewhat subdued. Only Edmund and Tarquin and Miss Alderscott were in good spirits. The rest were too weary or still too inebriated, or wishing too much they were still inebriated, to make good company, and the party broke up after another hour. The horses were called for, and Tarquin escorted his guests out into the yard. Edmund had thought to depart with them and walk back to his aunt's house, but as they were leaving the dining room, Tarquin caught his eye and whispered, "Stay a bit, will you, old man?"

Despite the near altercation on the previous evening, the goodbyes were cordial. Tarquin promised to ride over to Priedpie Hall the next day and visit. Lord Burley said a general goodbye and then wandered past Edmund as he went to his horse. "Congratulations, Mr. Percy," he said. "I think you have had a good effect on our mutual friend."

"And what makes you say that?" asked Edmund.

"That little scene last night. The Tarquin de Foye I have always known would have bloodied Ashleigh's nose for him, at the very least; but last night, for some reason, he held himself back. It was astonishing to see."

"If I had anything to do with it, I am pleased," said Edmund. "But something tells me that you will see Mr. de Foye a changed man from now on."

"Ah," said Burley, raising his eyebrows as he took Edmund's meaning, once again with uncharacteristic readiness. "Well, good day, Mr. Percy. It has been a pleasure meeting you. I hope you will come back for the hunting next fall; but in any case you have had a bit of a taste of how we do things in Hampshire."

"A very fine taste, my lord; very fine."

They shook hands and parted ways with mutual good feeling.

⌛⌛⌛⌛

When the hunting crowd was gone, Tarquin led Edmund back into the house. "No, not that way," he said, when Edmund automatically turned toward the library. "Come with me." He called to the housekeeper to send more tea to his office, and now took Edmund to that place, just one among the multitude of rooms in the vast building whose existence Edmund had never even suspected.

The place was a shambles—the floor, tables, and desk were covered in a mass of hunting gear, fox skins, trophies, fishing equipment in various stages of repair, and assorted other masculine debris. Tarquin took a wicker fishing creel from a chair and offered the seat to Edmund; then he himself sat on a littered sofa. They chatted humorously about the hunting set until Mrs. Abercrombie had brought tea, poured it for them, and left. When the door closed there was a long moment of very pregnant silence, and then Tarquin said: "So? What do you think, old man?"

Edmund debated whether he should pretend not to know what Tarquin was talking about, and found he could not resist the temptation to tease his friend. "I think you have a fine hunt here in Hampshire," he said. "I cannot thank you enough for holding one last meet."

"Oh, yes," said Tarquin. "But that is not quite what I was asking about."

"Oh, that fellow Ashleigh, you mean? He is not all that bad."

Tarquin grinned. "Damn it, Percy, you are quizzing me! You know damned well what I am talking about!"

Edmund tried to suppress a grin of his own, and finally failed. "I think she is capital," he said.

"Do you!" said Tarquin excitedly, leaning forward.

"I do indeed."

"And you do not think she is bad looking, do you? Some of the fellows seemed to think so."

"Not at all. Not at all, de Foye. I think she is one damned handsome woman."

"Do you!" exclaimed Tarquin again.

"I do."

Tarquin sank back in the sofa. "I do not know," he said suddenly.

"What do you not know?" asked Edmund.

"I just do not know, that is all," said Tarquin.

"Very well, then," said Edmund. "Perhaps you ought to stay home tomorrow, and I ought to make a visit to Priedpie."

"Oh, no," said Tarquin. "It is not—it is not *that.*"

"Not what?"

"Oh, I do not know—do you really think she is—do you think she is fine?"

"I do indeed, old man. Just think how she looked on that ride, if you ever have a doubt about how handsome she is. With the wind in her face, and that blissful smile on her lips. And that bold look she gives you when she quizzes you—she is worth fifty other women, de Foye—she is worth a hundred other women."

"Do you think so?"

"De Foye, have you forgotten how she held that gate for us? I mean, man, have you ever seen a lady hold a gate for a man?"

"No," said Tarquin, "no, I have not. It was incredible."

"Look, de Foye, I am about to become a clergyman, and when I do, you probably will not hear me speak so frankly. But I tell you, man, the look she had when you gave her that brush—if you want to see that look on a woman's face when you wake up beside her in the morning—by God, Miss Alderscott is the one for you."

"Percy, do you think so?"

"Oh, come on, man, do not be an idiot."

"But do you really think so?"

"What more do you want?"

"I do not know, to tell you the truth. She is everything I have been looking for in a wife. But here I am—I am four-and-thirty, and that is a long time to live without a wife. I am almost too *used* to living without a wife."

"But you must have a wife—you know that. You must have a wife for the sake of Hartswound. Do not be an idiot."

"But I feel an idiot—a complete idiot. Why, at this time four-and-twenty hours ago I was utterly disgusted with the lady—and now look at me. I think I am half-smitten. I think I am infatuated."

"You are," said Edmund. "And you ought to be. You ought to ride over to Priedpie this afternoon and propose to her."

"What!" cried Tarquin, aghast.

"Well, why not? You will do it sooner or later. Why not now?"

"But it is too soon!" Tarquin protested.

Edmund shrugged. "How can anything that is inevitable happen too soon? You will only regret it if you delay."

"But I do not know," said Tarquin again.

"What do you not know?" asked Edmund again in reply.

Tarquin hazarded a possible objection. "Do you think she is too old?"

"Oh, bother, de Foye! What an idiotic thing to say! She has got the figure of a girl of seventeen—or perhaps eighteen, which is even better."

"But do you think she would have me?"

Edmund affected to be taken aback by the question. "Ah," he said in mock thoughtfulness. "I had never thought of that.—Let us see, now: a woman of thirty who finally meets a man with her very own interests at his heart; and that man is good-looking, well-built, a gentleman, and heir to one of the very finest estates in all of England, and to one of the finest—if not the very finest—of hunting establishments on

God's green earth; and what is more, he has shown his interest in her.—Yes; it is a difficult case. Can she bring herself to like such a man?"

"Damn it, Percy, do not quiz me!"

"You quiz yourself, de Foye."

"But do you think she likes me?"

"I know she does. I know she does, man. It is the spell of the hunt, you see. You have partaken of it together, and you are bound together now in eternal fellowship."

"But you were there as well, Percy—why should that spell not apply to you as well?"

"I shall tell you why—I shall tell you why she likes you better than me."

"Why is that?"

"Because she *won you over.* You are a conquest. She knows perfectly well you had no use for her four-and-twenty hours ago. And she knows perfectly well that you are sitting here at this very minute, demanding that I talk you into marrying her."

"You are going too fast," protested Tarquin.

"That is all right," said Edmund. "You ask me my opinion, and I tell it you. I say, de Foye, that you shall marry this woman; and if you do me the honor to invite me to the wedding, I shall toast your happiness with a will."

"Much too fast," said Tarquin, though in a weaker tone.

They were silent for a minute or two. Edmund drank his tea, but Tarquin ignored his own.

"I say," said Edmund, "was she not something splendid in that inn in Strethamside?"

"I was just thinking the very same thing!" cried Tarquin. "How she sat there, drinking that half-glass of ale, and the way she laughed, and the things she said that made us laugh, and the way her eyes looked—did you notice that—and the way she has of tilting her head when she glances at you sideways—I tell you, and you must never tell anyone this, but I had it in my head to take her in my arms that very instant."

"That might have been too rash," admitted Edmund.

"Well, that is why I did not do it."

To himself Edmund thought that if he and his friend had each been so rash in the inn yesterday, Miss Alderscott might have found herself in a very surprising circumstance. Aloud he said, "You must *ask* her first. She will not mind you taking her in your arms, not in the least—that is my guess; but you must ask her to marry you first. I think Miss Alderscott will not like anyone taking liberties; though she will readily offer those very same liberties to you if she has licensed you to have them. That is what I think."

"But what of her late arrival yesterday?" said Tarquin feebly.

"What in heavens are you talking about?" demanded Edmund bluntly.

"Well, she had fallen behind the others. Does that not show a lack of respect? I should not like a wife who could not be punctual."

"On the contrary, de Foye; it shows great resourcefulness on her part, and a very refreshing ability to solve her difficulties by herself."

"Whatever do you mean?"

"Do you not see?" said Edmund; and here he lowered his voice. "She stopped behind in the park to *piss,* man, after her breakfast tea."

Tarquin stared at him open-mouthed for a moment, and then laughed aloud. "By God, Percy, I think you are right!" he said.

"I know I am right," said Edmund. "This is no puling wench we are talking about. She takes matters into her own hands when she has to. She is the very lady to have about you here at Hartswound Park-house, I should say."

Tarquin stared at him for a moment more and then stood up from the sofa suddenly. He strode through the room, kicking hunting tackle out of the way. "Oh," he said, "I know not a thing about it! I wish she were a bird I could bring down with a good quick shot! How does one go about these things?"

"It is very simple," Edmund began; but Tarquin cut him off.

"No!" he said, turning on Edmund. "You have taken me too far too fast! I am not at all sure I want to do this."

Edmund laughed. "Well," he said, "the offer I implied when I challenged you last night still stands this morning. When you have absolutely decided that you do not want to marry her, have the courtesy to let me know, will you?"

"Do you really like her, Percy?"

"Yes," said Edmund; but Tarquin did not hear the fervor with which he spoke.

"I mean, do you really think she is fine?"

"De Foye, what must I do, write it down for you?"

"That might help," said Tarquin, finally managing to laugh at himself a little. "The terrible thing is that Father will not rest until he has seen us wed. Now I have no more excuses. Did you hear him last night, making his cast now to the left, now to the right, and in the end following the trail right down to me?"

"Yes, I saw that. He was quite the equal of Dickson there. So the best thing to do would be to make short work of it. Come, if you like, I shall ride over to Priedpie with you tomorrow and buck you up."

"No! No, not tomorrow. I mean, I shall go tomorrow—but you must not come, Percy. You must leave me alone. I must get to know her better."

Edmund shrugged. "Well, that will do no harm."

"If you are there, you will only incite me to it, and I might just make a fool of myself."

Edmund considered for a minute, and then said, "Now that I stop and think about it, I see that as long as you are in the company of Miss Alderscott, I can offer no further incitement. It is only when you are pacing about here at Hartswound that you will need bucking up."

Tarquin turned about again. "Now, whatever you do, Percy, do not tell Mariah. I could not stand her quizzing me about this! Oh, she is a terrible quiz, that one! Never let her get one on you, Percy, or she will quiz you without mercy."

"Very well, de Foye. It will be a secret between us."

"Yes—yes, that would be good."

"You do not *mind* that Cecelia Alderscott has fifteen thousand pounds a year?" asked Edmund with a perfect affectation of innocence.

Tarquin laughed in exasperation. "God, Percy, you do know how to drive a man mad!"

"And you do not *mind* that she looks at you as though you were the Prince himself?"

"Percy, leave off, I tell you!"

"I shall never forget how she rode straight up to you and said, 'You are the master, are you not? You are Mr. Esquith de Foye.'"

"Yes, and I was a bear to her, was I not? I was insufferable. I was rude. I was a wretch!"

"I have told you, she loves that; the very recollection of it will send a thrill through her marrow—because she knows she has won you over. Who does not like to conquer the prejudices of another with one's own merits? She *must* love you now, man; because she has *made* you love her."

"Not so fast, Percy, not so fast!"

"Deny it if you like," said Edmund; but he went on relentlessly. "And what of that little flask she carries in her hunting coat? Did you see the way she took a swig, and then offered it to us?"

"Ah, but I was so rude to her!"

"That is all right. I was covering for you, you see."

"Yes—you were, Percy. I see that now. You kept telling me, 'Perhaps she is not a bad rider. Perhaps she will behave herself. Perhaps all will be well.' And I did not listen to you."

"Well, you did in the end. That is what counts."

Tarquin scattered some harness from the top of a table and looked about distractedly. "But I am four-and-thirty, man!" he said again.

"There is no better time than the present," said Edmund. "You are just entering your prime. And so is she. Marry her, and get a few children on that fruitful body."

Tarquin looked at him open-mouthed, and then cried, "You are the very Devil himself, Percy!"

"Well, is that not what this is all about? Has not God ordered it that way? That men and women should come together with some mutual joy and beget more Christian souls?—Or Mahometan souls, if that is what they themselves have to begin with. The point is that it is all the natural order of things; and you can no more resist it than you can resist the flow of time itself."

"But look, do I seem a family man to you? The father of five little girls in white dresses? I am too rough for that. You know I am."

"What is wrong with girls? Girls are splendid things. I hope I shall have twenty of them."

"But you are not I," protested Tarquin. "I would not know what to do with a daughter if I had one. You have perhaps noticed that I am all at sixes and sevens when it comes to Mariah. I have not the faintest notion of what to do about her."

"She is not your daughter, de Foye."

"No, but I am her keeper; and I do not make good work of it."

Edmund regarded him in silence for a moment, shaking his head. Then he stood up and went over to Tarquin and seized him by the lapel. "De Foye," he said in a low voice, "who said anything about five little *girls?* Imagine five *boys* if you like."

There was a long pause.

"What?" said Tarquin dazedly.

"Five *boys,* I said. Five boys to teach riding, and hunting, and fishing."

Tarquin considered this in silence. Edmund let go of his lapel and went back to his tea. He finished his cup and then turned to Tarquin again.

"I say, de Foye, I think I shall go back to my aunt's and apprise her of the fact that I have not broken my neck."

"Yes," said Tarquin distractedly. Then he said: "Must you go?"

"I think it would be best if I did. Otherwise I shall have to sit here for the rest of the morning while you ask me what I *really* think of Miss Alderscott, and hear you wonder if I *really* think you ought to put your hat on your head and ride off to Priedpie and propose to her. And I think I have already answered those questions."

"Blast!" said Tarquin, looking about distractedly.

"I have said my peace," said Edmund. "Good day to you, my friend. And thank you again for a splendid, splendid run; a run I shall never, ever forget."

"Very well, Percy—very well; I quite agree, you cannot stand here all day bucking me up."

"Go to Priedpie tomorrow. Spend some time with the lady. Go for a short ride with her—a gentle ride, so that you have some time to talk together. Or walk with her. That is all you must do for the moment."

"Yes, you are right."

"Good day, de Foye."

"Good day, Percy.—I say, Percy—before you go, would you just think of something else from the ride yesterday?"

"Think of something?" repeated Edmund, puzzled at first. Then he realized that Tarquin's request was like that children make of their parents when they wish to relive some particularly memorable event. "Do you mean about Miss Alderscott?" he said.

"Yes."

"Well—there was the way she followed us when we shifted closer to Shadwell."

"Yes! Yes! She is quite the huntress. That was impressive."

"And the way she rejoiced when she knew we had a smart, fast fox."

"Yes, I remember that. That was splendid."

Edmund stood waiting a moment more, and then turned toward the door. "Let me know how it goes," he said in parting.

"I shall," promised Tarquin. "I shall come talk to you when I return from Priedpie."

Edmund smiled and let himself out; for his friend was too distracted to show him the way.

Chapter 27

But a smooth and steadfast mind,
Gentle thoughts and calm desires,
Hearts with equal love combined,
Kindle never-dying fires.
Where these are not, I despise
Lovely cheeks or lips or eyes.

—Carew

The next day the rains returned. Edmund was quite content to sit by the fire in the parlor with his aunt; she plied her needlework and he opened the *Disquisitiones arithmeticae,* which he had bought in a bookshop in Oxford in January, but had never had a chance to study. At about eleven o'clock, however, they were surprised to hear a carriage in the drive. Edmund looked out as it drew up before the front door, and discerned the arms of the Esquith de Foyes emblazoned on the side.

He went out immediately. His aunt's house had a wide, arched entranceway that offered some protection from the rain, and here he waited while the coachman set the steps and opened the door of the carriage. He assumed the visitor must be Miss de Foye, though he could not imagine on what errand she might have come. To his further surprise, Tarquin stepped forth. His friend joined him in the entranceway, and Edmund surveyed him in some wonder.

"What is this?" he asked. "You look as if you were going to a ball."

"Oh, blast, Percy, do not tell me that! My nerves are shaky enough as they are."

"You are off to Priedpie Hall, then?"

"Yes, I am—and you must come with me, Percy, or I shall never get there."

"I shall be glad to go with you," said Edmund. "But what is the meaning of the carriage? Why are you not a-horseback?"

"I would much rather be so, foul weather or not, I assure you," said Tarquin gloomily.

Edmund waited for further explanation, but received none. "I see," he said. "You assume you will make a better impression on Miss Alderscott if you dress like a fop and arrive warm and dry, like some silly counting-house clerk?"

"Percy! For the thousandth time, do not quiz me! I am just about to give this up and resign myself to never producing an heir for Hartswound."

"Look," said Edmund. "How far is it to Priedpie?"

"Only some seven mile."

"I shall go get my riding cloak. We shall take the carriage back to Hartswound, and you shall call for two good road horses. You shall change into your ordinary clothes, which are quite fine enough for Miss Alderscott; and then we shall ride to Priedpie in the rain."

Tarquin was surprised at first, but then began to grin. "Do you think that would be best?" he said.

"She would be disappointed in anything less," said Edmund.

"You do not think she will be disgusted with me if I ride up looking like a half-drowned rat without the sense to come in out of the rain?"

"My guess is that she is sick of fops. And you are no fop, de Foye—there would be nothing so false as pretending you were. Go as yourself."

"So I shall, Percy!—But you do not mind riding in the rain?"

"Not at all," said Edmund; though in truth he would rather have stayed by the fire, if it were not for the amusement of watching the progress of Tarquin's courtship.

In a minute more they were on their way to Hartswound together in the carriage; and in another half-hour were in the saddle, making for Priedpie Hall. They rode hard, talking and laughing together despite the rain, and Tarquin's spirits and confidence revived.

The Ashleigh estate was very extensive and well kept. It could not boast the superb park of Hartswound, or quite the rustic grandeur of the ancient manor house there; but it had the best beauty that human engineering could supply. The old manor house, which Edmund later learned had been at the bottom of a dell, had been demolished about fifteen years before, and a completely new dwelling constructed on a knoll above the old site, which was now a lake fed by a diverted stream. Trees had been cut with great confidence and fervor with the intention of providing spectacular views of the country round about, a purpose that had been accomplished, but only at the cost of leaving the dwelling naked on the hill. The effect reminded Edmund of a grand lady wearing a dress that daringly exposes her unfortunately ugly bosom. In the design of the house itself, vast grandness had been intended, and some little had been achieved. There was a portico and a terrace, Venetian windows, and a great deal of glass; there were steps going up to the house on this side, and coming down from it on that. The building was ringed by lawns and gardens that still seemed a bit raw and new, especially in their early March slumber. One felt, surveying the full effect, that it would be changed, like that lady's dress, for a new fashion when the new fashion came in; and people viewing a portrait of its present state at a later time would say, "Whatever were they *thinking* when they did such a thing?"

The two riders halted in their approach, ostensibly to give Edmund a moment to see the place, but perhaps in part because Tarquin was beginning to lose his nerve again. Edmund felt that they would need a dramatic entrance to keep his friend's dander up. "Where is the main parlor in this place?" he asked, looking at the heap of angles and blocks from which the manor house had been assembled—or rather, jumbled together.

"It opens on that lawn there," said Tarquin.

"That room with the windows cut down to the ground?"

"The very one."

"Well," said Edmund, "what do you say we take a dash over that little stream and ride right up to the doors?"

"Directly across the lawn?"

"It is just March; it will heal by the end of April."

"Very well. A race, then?"

"Why not?"

And away they went. Their horses this day were not hunters, but were spirited enough nonetheless to enjoy the romp; and in a half a minute Edmund and Tarquin arrived at the parlor doors laughing and spattered with a good deal of mud thrown up out of the sodden lawn.

The instant they halted, the door of the parlor was thrown open, and Miss Alderscott emerged, laughing. "Oh, how very fine!" she said. "How I envy you! I love to ride on a wet day!"

A thin, frail-looking woman appeared in the doorway behind her. "Ceci!" she remonstrated. "Come in at once! You are mad—all of you are mad! You will all catch colds and die! Whatever can you mean, Mr. de Foye, ruining our lawn in that way?"

"Oh, hush, Edith," said Miss Alderscott. "Can you not understand a compliment when you are paid one?—Go about, gentlemen, and I shall meet you at the door."

She then retreated into the parlor, and Tarquin led Edmund around the house to the front entrance. They left their horses in the care of some servants, and entered a large and luxuriously appointed hall. Here Miss Alderscott was waiting, still laughing at their mischief. After they had knocked the mud off their boots and shed their riding cloaks and hats, she shook hands with them cordially, and led them back into the main parlor.

Ashleigh and his brother were nowhere to be seen. The only occupant of the hall was Edith Asheigh, a woman presumably thirty years of age who looked closer to forty-five. Miss Alderscott could not have chosen a greater contrast to her own robust health among all the women of Hampshire: Edith looked as if she might at any minute shatter spontanteously like glass subjected to a violent change in temperature. She offered Edmund a limp and perfunctory handshake, and looked at him upon being introduced with that studied lack of interest that suggests a hidden wish *not* to be attracted by those of the opposite sex. He saw at once that it would have been constitutionally impossible for her to flirt, and that any gallant phrase would be utterly lost on her.

They were soon seated and immersed in a conversation about foxhunting. Miss Ashleigh looked on in silence, unable or unwilling to participate; but Miss Alderscott apparently felt comfortable enough with her old friend not to need to include her, or else too distracted by the presence of their visitors to remember to do so.

Now that Edmund had a chance to study Miss Alderscott in a more normal form of company—for the company of male foxhunters could hardly be said to be a normal one—he learned considerably more about her character than he had the day before. She was eager to talk, but when either he or Tarquin showed any inclination to speak, she halted immediately, even in mid-word, and signified a passionate willingness to listen, by tilting her head or nodding or turning to them. Her spirits were somewhat higher than not; that is, she was cheerful, but not to the point of being obnoxious.

She was, as Hugh Ashleigh had remarked, "great fun"; she had a vivacity that reminded Edmund of Evelyn Brownton, without Evelyn's scattered and childlike thinking. He had in fact the impression that deep feeling, self-awareness, and careful thought were all taking place in her at once. If she said something flirtatious, it was in full consciousness of what she did; and it was an action grounded in some underlying passion. He recalled that though she had been quite forward with him and Tarquin yesterday, she had shown no inclination at any time to flirt with anyone else; and he eventually came to the conclusion that this was a reliable indication that she had felt genuinely drawn to the two of them specifically, and then to Tarquin in particular. She possessed also a willingness to please that reminded him of himself. In fact, he understood many things about her at once because he saw attributes of his own mirrored in her. She had the ability to get along with people; she had sympathy, she had insight into others, and she made a constant effort to read them. She had read Tarquin very accurately yesterday, for instance, keeping a respectful distance from him until she had persuaded him that she was acceptable company; and she had read Edmund's growing affection for Tarquin more quickly and accurately than he had done so himself.

Edmund found her different from himself in showing no particular spiritual or intellectual interests. Doubtless she was a regular churchgoer; but he guessed that during the season she followed the hounds four times as often as she went to church. Doubtless she had been well-educated, so far as women generally were in that benighted era; she could probably sketch crudely, mutter some French, and jangle the keys of the piano on request; but she probably had little hunger to learn more from books. It was life itself that was to be her further school, and she was absorbed in its class. She was also different from Edmund in being not just an occasional hunter, mostly interested in the sport as an outlet for athletic enthusiasm; rather, she was a hunter before all else. He told himself sternly that ultimately he would have found it difficult to live with her—that her passion for sport would have drawn him from his chosen work as a clergyman, and his work would in the end only have bored her.

And yet ultimately he found her very endearing, as he found Evelyn Brownton endearing despite their differences;

and he could not help thinking that he would willingly live with Cecelia Alderscott's shortcomings if she were willing to live with his.

Perhaps a great deal of his approval of her, of the elasticity of his judgments about her, stemmed from his admiration of her physical attributes. She was dressed today in the height of fashion, in a high-waisted dress that clung to her figure and left little concerning it to be determined at a later date. He tried not to stare hungrily at her—he thought perhaps she would know perfectly well what he was thinking.

At first he was an integral part of the conversation. Then, by imperceptible degrees, she and Tarquin turned toward each other and began speaking directly and only to one another. Most of their conversation was mere bright chatter—stories of their first foxhunts compared, stories of their first horses compared, characteristics of their favorite hounds, successful and unsuccessful hunts, hunting in Hampshire versus hunting in Hertfordshire, hunting companions, favored weather for hunting, the best bootery in London, the characteristics of a good huntsman and of a good whipper-in, the proper horse on which to mount the aforementioned, and so on. Yet somehow in these relatively insignificant topics they found so deep a harmony that they began to resonate together—almost literally: for by degrees they began to laugh together. A subtle mutual infection lodged in their humors, and the slightest edge of drollery in the remark of one was greeted by a peal of almost uncontrolled laughter in the other, which incited the first to further laughter, and the second to still more. "And then my cousin Bertram," Miss Alderscott might say, "got hold of the huntsman's horn and attempted to blow it." This single image would be enough to make Tarquin blurt forth a laugh; which made Miss Alderscott pause, and laugh merely because Tarquin was laughing.

Edmund had never really seen anything quite like it. The last traces of his residual jealousy melted away; for it was impossible to covet a partner who so clearly was intended by God for someone other than himself.

After about an hour and a half of this proceeding, Miss Ashleigh suddenly stood up. Edmund rose as well, and Tarquin too, when he belatedly noticed.

"Mr. Percy," said Miss Ashleigh, "you have never seen the beauties of Priedpie Hall. Might I show them to you?"

"I should like that very much," said Edmund.

"Oh, no," she said to Tarquin, though he had made no attempt to start along with them, "you two have seen the place inside and out; stay here and I shall give Mr. Percy the grand tour."

Tarquin sat down again and the conversation with Miss Alderscott resumed without missing a beat. Edmund followed Miss Ashleigh out of the room, and together they set out on their tour of the house.

He found her manner absolutely as dry as the hay at the back of the loft that has been stored for years on end to no purpose. She showed him the gallery, with its portraits of the Ashleighs back to seven generations; she took him through the dining room, laid for a magnificent dinner; through parlors that looked out on the wonders of the landscape; into a billiard room, a drawing room, a library; into offices upstairs; and even downstairs, among bustling servants, into the pantry, larder, wine cellar, laundry; then to the second floor, where she showed him bedchambers with both ancient and modern furnishings, endless halls with odd coigns of vantage over the lake, and staircases back and front. The feature of all this that irked Edmund, though he said nothing of it, was not that the taste that had created it all was *bad,* so much as that it was *borrowed.* It was as if Ashleigh's family had no taste, even no conceptions that truly belonged to them, but must hire others to come and conceive for them.

By the time Miss Ashleigh brought him back to the hallway outside the main parlor, he was quite weary of making polite exclamations over this and that room or view or article of furniture. She did not return directly to the parlor, however, but stepped aside into an alcove off the hall. Here, before an arched window that looked out on the rain puddled on the lawn, she paused, gazing out, and by force of courtesy he did the same, though he had been anticipating his return to more lively company. She said nothing, and he was at a loss for words; so they listened to the conversation of their friends, of which they could catch only a distinct word or two from time to time. Most of what they heard was happy laughter—a mingling of Tarquin's deep and rather gruff notes, and Miss Alderscott's higher and more pleasant tones.

"It is as I always knew it should be," said Miss Ashleigh suddenly, smiling slightly with the righteousness of one confirmed and vindicated.

"Do you speak of our friends?" asked Edmund, surprised at this sudden confidence on her part.

She nodded, but offered no more.

"How long have you known Miss Alderscott, if I may make so bold as to inquire?" asked Edmund. He knew the answer, but at least it was something to say.

"Since we were girls together at Miss Haughton's School in Kent," said Miss Ashleigh. "I knew the moment I met her that she was *made* to be the wife of Tarquin de Foye."

"Really?" said Edmund.

She looked at him solemnly. "Yes," she said. "Listen to them. Do you not hear it?"

"I do indeed," said Edmund. "I do not think I ever saw a more obvious match. I quite agree with you. It is just that I admire your perspicacity in identifying them as partners at such a young age."

"Oh, it was obvious even then," she said. "Just as obvious as the match between Miss de Foye and my brother Lucas. It is like watching a destiny play out."

Edmund made a conscious effort to lower his eyebrows, which had risen considerably at this last disclosure. He hoped that Tarquin's match with Miss Alderscott had a more favorable future than was likely to evolve between Miss de Foye and Lucas Ashleigh, from what he had seen and heard of their connection; but he did not argue with Miss Ashleigh on that point.

"I myself," said Miss Ashleigh, "have no interest in marriage—indeed, I have no need to marry. I have an independent fortune from my aunt. Yet I recognize that my friends feel otherwise, that their circumstances and temperaments are such that they could not truly be happy unless they are married. And I have been trying for twenty years to bring Cecelia to Hampshire and introduce her to Tarquin."

Edmund thought that perhaps Miss Alderscott had failed all these years to commit herself to a long stay with Miss Ashleigh out of some fear of her friend's somewhat dry company. "Well," he said, "I am glad you have succeeded. They are getting on splendidly."

"Of course," she said. She looked at him with disinterest, as if he were no more than a doorpost that lay within her field of vision. "Cecelia says you are to be a clergyman," she said, in the tone of one announcing the prognostication of a particular type of weather.

"Yes," he said. "Within a month, I expect. I am looking forward to it."

"Quite," she said, expressing absolute disbelief. He suddenly decided she was insufferable.

"I shall not be happy, perfectly happy, myself," she said, reverting to her favorite topic, "until I have Cecelia settled at Hartswound and our pretty little Mariah ensconced at Priedpie. I shall doubtless stay on as the mistress of the place, though I am content to allow her to *go first.*"

Give me her brother, with all his huffing and puffing! thought Edmund. *His species of self-importance is considerably more bearable than Miss Edith Ashleigh's.* How she had come to so seriously misread the character of her "pretty little Mariah"—who probably was the taller of the two by a full four inches—he could not imagine, unless her vision was blinded by the primacy of her own imagination. If Miss de Foye and Miss Ashleigh were ever thrown into a battle of wills over the role of mistress of Priedpie Hall, the latter would soon find herself bested—he had no doubt of that.

At this point they were interrupted by the return of Ashleigh and his brother. Ashleigh showed no trace of his drunken jealousy of the other night—he had probably utterly forgotten it, or perhaps the cold light of day had revealed it as absurd. He greeted Edmund with such warmth that Edmund thought him not such a bad fellow after all, especially in such near contrast to his sister. He had become positively likeable—a transformation that helped explain Tarquin's persistent affection for him despite his obvious faults as a hunter of foxes and as a suitor of Tarquin's sister. The four of them then rejoined Tarquin and Miss Alderscott.

The rest of the day was spent in comparatively idle and desultory conversation, in the parlor, and later over dinner. It was a dark, blustery evening, on which the ride home would have been difficult and perhaps even dangerous to one's health, and Edmund and Tarquin were easily persuaded to stay over.

Miss Alderscott was the only one of the household present when they breakfasted the next morning. The three of them made a cheerful meal of it despite the continuing gloom outside; and then the two gentlemen departed. When they looked back, they could see Miss Alderscott watching from the window in the parlor. They waved, and she waved back spiritedly.

To Edmund's surprise, Tarquin said nothing all the way home. It was not until they had returned to Hartswound, and Edmund expressed the wish to depart immediately for his aunt's house, that Tarquin felt any urgency to communicate his feelings. He followed Edmund out of the parlor and into the hallway, out of earshot of his father.

"Do you not think she is splendid?" he said.

"I do," said Edmund.

"Do you think she will do?"

"I do," said Edmund.

"What must I do?" wondered Tarquin.

"Ask her to say, 'I do,'" said Edmund.

"But is it to be so easy as that?" said Tarquin. "After four-and-thirty years? I could be a married man in—three months, say?"

"I am convinced you must only ask her," said Edmund. "That ought to be easy enough."

"No," said Tarquin. "That will be the hardest thing I have ever done."

Chapter 28

a, virgo infelix, quae te dementia cepit?

Ah, unhappy girl, what madness has you in its grip?

—Vergil

Edmund seldom saw the sun during the remainder of his stay in Hampshire. The cold, wet weather had returned to stay, and every day was raw and cold, either drizzling or raining. The March weather did not depress Edmund's spirits, however, or those of his aunt. The fire was always bright and warm in her parlor, and the fellowship was good. He had many lively and interesting conversations with her and with visitors from among her neighbors in the country about who came to pay their respects to her nephew. He and she often read poetry and plays aloud to one another; and Edmund had an opportunity to dabble in mathematics again and read some Italian.

Nor did March prevent him from walking forth every day, and often several times in a day. He visited the rector and played chess with him; and they spoke at length together about the role of the clergy in the church at this hour of its history. He spent time with Mrs. Bunt, usually when either Susan was with her or Mrs. Brownton, and only rarely when Miss de Foye happened to be in attendance. When the first shy primroses appeared, he took her a bouquet. He visited the Browntons as well, and often found himself reading with them for long periods during the damp days.

His overwhelming memory of that period was thus one of companionship at the fireside. He felt as Cecelia Alderscott had when she said that she thought she could learn to love Hampshire; for he did begin to love it, both its scenery and its people. To him the village seemed not a backwater, but a representative family of the human race, showing every kind of excellence and sin, every goodness and every pettiness of which humankind is capable. It was a book, and its pages were wide, and the light was good, the script clear; and he read the first few pages in it with fascination. Or, in a different metaphor, the life of Broadbridge was a little cartwheel, and went round and round; but it hit at times upon rocks or ruts in the road, which gave a jolt to the whole, and added interest to things.

His aunt took him on forays in the neighborhood to visit this family and that with eligible daughters. These missions always proved abortive for one reason or another—it soon came to be a joke to them, how something *must* go wrong, the object of their interest prove dull or silly or rigidly prim—or that she must be found to be running after some other young man, or *about* to be engaged. Mrs. Eaton brought her daughters by once a week, and did her best to contrive to get Cornelia Eaton and Edmund on the same sofa in the corner of the parlor, but to no avail—he would not fall into her trap.

Chief among his activities were his visits to Hartswound Park. Every Friday night until he left, he and Andromeda were invited back for dinner; and each dinner proved more successful, to his mind, than the last. Andromeda polished the last rust of some inactive years from her wit and carried on brilliantly. He was also summoned up on other occasions—when Lord Burley visited, or other neighbors he had met on the hunt, and to these dinners he was pleased to see that his aunt too was soon invited as a matter of course. However, he noticed that it was only when he and his aunt went up for dinner alone that Miss de Foye made an appearance. He took this to mean that she felt safe with them, or that she distinguished them from the hunting set, with whom she seemed to be at odds, or that she in fact liked his aunt through long, if slight, acquaintance with her.

All in all, he saw little of Miss de Foye in those weeks. When once a man has encountered such a beautiful woman in a limited setting such as a small village, he will always be partly alert to the possibility of seeing her again; and whether he knows it or not, he will be looking for her when he scans the street in walking through the place; and specifically, in Edmund's case, his heart gave an extra pulse of interest if he caught sight, from afar, of a regal figure in a pale blue Spencer or a pelisse of hunter's green, entering a humble cottage with her basket on her arm, or striding forth from the gates of the park, or emerging from a shop with some charitable purchase. When he did meet her, face to face, as happened a few times at the rector's or at Hartswound or in the village, he thought to himself how very pleasant it was to stop and exchange a greeting with her, and to have just a minute to look without let or hindrance on her face. These rare meetings would change his day, and plunge him into philosophic meditations on the meaning and function of beauty in the abstract, and make him wonder whether or not there might not actually be, in God's mind, those perfect ideals of which Plato dreamed, and whether she, Mariah Esquith de Foye, might not be at least one of those absolutes come to life—the absolute of the kind, intelligent, beautiful, and spirited woman.

The two greatest regrets of the month, to his mind, were that he saw so little of Evelyn Brownton, and that Tarquin made such little apparent forward movement in his courtship of Miss Alderscott. Evelyn was nearly always with Miss de Foye—which was to say, elsewhere from wherever Edmund was; and even when he sought her out by visiting the Browntons, he only found her at home there on one occasion. He found he missed her company very much; he even yearned after it in a quiet way; and yet he rebuked himself for doing so, and told himself that he ought to be seeking out the company of a woman who would be a partner to his interests, not merely a source of entertainment.

As for Tarquin's progress, his friend went over to Priedpie Hall more than once, and spent time in the parlor with Miss Alderscott, and often with only the discreet company of Ashleigh's sister Edith to impede their better acquaintance; but if the two of them were left quite alone, it never failed that Ashleigh and his brothers came in, and though the company was still jolly, somehow Tarquin found himself then separated from Miss Alderscott. Edmund gave him a lecture more than once on how to manage these things, but it seemed to do no good. The lady was invited back to Hartswound three times, but again she came in company of Ashleigh and others, and again Tarquin seemed to let his chances slip away. The weather, too, was particularly poor, so they could not ride out, an activity that would have afforded them ample opportunity for closer acquaintance. The good news was that Miss Alderscott's stay at Priedpie, which had originally been planned to extend only through March, now became of less definite termination, and it was clear that she would be in the neighborhood at least through April. When Edmund heard this, he interpreted these signs to Tarquin, much like a Roman priest reading the auspices; and after castigating him for his delay, fetched his hat, put it on his head, and led him to the door, insisting that he go at once to Priedpie, ask for a private interview with Miss Alderscott, and propose. Somewhat to his amazement, his friend was compelled to go; but he lost his nerve on the way and spent the afternoon at Lord Burley's instead. He faced Edmund down the next day, saying he simply was not ready; and thereafter Edmund left him alone, thinking perhaps that his interference was having a contrary effect.

To one of our era, Edmund's encouragement might have seemed precipitous; but it was based on information as complete as men and women of his day were likely to obtain about a prospective spouse. It is very possible—or so it seems from the available evidence—that people of that time more often succeeded in forming good marriages on the basis of very scant knowledge of a partner than people do today, though the latter have no similar excuse for failure. We know, or think we know, what to do *before* a wedding better than we know what to do after it. They knew better what to do *after* a wedding than before.

In this case, the match was all too clearly a good one, and Edmund finally came to believe that therein lay the problem. It would have been better for Tarquin to have been faced with obstacles, to have had to pursue Cecelia Alderscott across a social landscape full of hedges and ditches and fences, to have had to draw her forth from a dense cover of family and friends. But it was all too easy: the lady was a perfectly appointed partner and she was obviously willing. The Ashleighs and Edmund and old Cato were all standing by with bated breath for Tarquin's proposal. Destiny had delivered the bride up to the groom in a golden chariot; and the result was that the bold and reckless descendant of the most bold and reckless hunting family in all of Hampshire had a case of cold feet. He was uncertain and perplexed. It was as if a fox had wandered into his kennels—he would not have suffered it to be harmed, but would have driven it forth to offer sport at a later day.

The more Edmund thought about it, the more he was confirmed in this interpretation of the situation. What Miss Alderscott must do to motivate Tarquin and secure his affections, Edmund thought, was to offer him some *sport.*

⧗ ⧗ ⧗ ⧗

He would have been pleased to see his friend's situation resolved before he left, but it was not to be; and thus he had a sense of incompleteness as he saw the time of his stay drawing to a close. The date for his departure was set on the calendar; he was to board the coach on the morning of Tuesday, the twenty-ninth of March. His aunt, too, became quite wistful in the final days, despite her best efforts to keep up a cheerful front. Somehow the morning of the last Sunday that he was to be in Hampshire arrived, and then somehow the evening of that last Sunday; and he and his aunt were sitting in her parlor after dinner, not speaking much, but savoring this last scrap of their time together. He was reading to himself, and she was knitting.

"You must come back to Hampshire, you know," Andromeda said finally, putting her needles down in her lap. He closed up his book.

"I know I must," he said.

"You have made many friends here. I think Tarquin de Foye will be utterly lost without you."

"His horses and hounds will distract him," said Edmund. "And I know he loves to fish as well, and will doubtless take to that again when the rains stop. He has asked me to go up to Hartswound tomorrow to say farewell."

"But not for dinner?" asked Andromeda.

"Of course not. I shall have dinner with you."

"Good—we have planned all your favorite things."

"Have no fear—I shall just walk up for an hour or so, and be back in good time."

Andromeda was satisfied.

"And do you have any more intelligence about Miss de Foye's situation?" she now asked, somewhat cautiously. He guessed that she was testing him again.

"Nothing new; it remains as much a mystery as ever."

"Did you see her when you were at Hartswound Park yesterday?"

"No. She seems to be seldom there. The rectory is her refuge, especially when the hunting set is about. She spent the day with the rector yesterday, I know; de Foye said something about it."

"She could not have been at the rector's *yesterday,*" said Andromeda. "You forget: Mr. Maugham has been at Bath all week taking the waters. He only returned *very late* yesterday."

"Ah, yes," said Edmund. "I had forgotten."

He fell silent, but—his aunt being ever alert—it was too late. She looked at him now with raised eyebrows.

"Perhaps the rector is not the only one who offers refuge," she said softly.

"No," he said, attempting to bury again what he had inadvertently uncovered. "There are the Browntons, too."

"The Browntons took the rector to Bath," said Andromeda. "And this time they took Miss Brownton with them."

"Ah, yes—I knew that too. Well, Miss de Foye has other friends her age in Broadbridge."

"Not many," said his aunt. "She is too much envied, for obvious reasons."

"Well, she visits many of the poor; she takes that obligation quite seriously."

"Indeed she does," agreed Andromeda; but he could tell that her suspicions had not been allayed.

They were silent then. Another subject was urgently needed, and Edmund soon found it.

"I shall miss you very much, dear Aunt," he said.

She smiled somewhat painfully. "Oh, Edmund, that is kind of you to say."

"It is only the truth. You have come to be a mother to me—and in addition to that, you have come to be a friend. I shall miss our conversations by the fire, and over tea, and at dinner. I shall even miss your scheming for me!"

She laughed softly. There were tears in her eyes, he saw.

"There is nothing for it, then," she said. "You *must* come back to Hampshire, Edmund. If you do not mind hearing the whole truth—I shall pine away without you. I do not have any claim on you, I know; I have nothing to offer you. I have raided the countryside round about for good-looking girls with half a brain, or even half-good-looking girls with half a brain, and I am getting down to girls with no looks and no brains at all. But there is that living—surely you see that. You have as good a chance as anyone to be presented to that living."

"Yes, but I may starve to death first, Aunt."

"Perhaps you could be curate here, if we could drive out Mr. Thomas. That would fairly set you up as Mr. Maugham's heir."

"It did not set up Mr. Thomas in that role, apparently."

"No, but you are different. You are loved by the de Foyes, father and son. I dare say you have even won the approbation of the daughter, with your visits to the sick.—It is so easy to scheme for you, Edmund, because you do of your own good nature all the things I would have you do to ingratiate yourself with others."

"Well, the matter of the living is in God's hands."

"No, it is not; it is in the hands of Cato Esquith de Foye."

"Well, Mr. de Foye cannot give it until Mr. Maugham is gathered to his fathers; and that is in the hands of God. In the meantime, I must look about and see what I can find. And no matter where I dwell, you will always be welcome in my house."

"On that point, Edmund—I have been thinking of something."

"And what is that?"

"It is that it might be possible for me to come to an agreement with Mr. Alton's nephew, whereby if I gave up my life right to Fairhall early, he would provide me with an income. Then I would be free to go wherever you do.—Would that appeal to you, Edmund? I promise I should keep my distance after you marry—I should go at least next door—but in the meantime, it might be useful to you to have a lady of my age to countenance a bachelor's household."

"That would be very pleasing to me, Aunt, though I would be fearful to see you give up Fairhall on my behalf."

"Well," she said. And then: "Perhaps we shall talk of it as your future unfolds."

"Very good. And I am deeply honored by your love for me, Aunt."

"Edmund, if you were as honored as you are always saying you are, you would be the most honored man in all of Christendom."

"Perhaps I am, in my own way. Certainly I am the most fortunate, having an aunt like you."

They were both satisfied. She took up her knitting again, and he returned to his book.

⌛⌛⌛⌛

The following day Hampshire flung itself at Edmund's heart. When he rose, the rain was gone. The sun came up and shone upon the land as if wishing to be forgiven for its absence; and the world forgave it willingly. In the sudden fairness and warmth of the weather, flowers that had been waiting only for the sun's permission sprang forth into bloom. Blackbirds sang; the robin strutted on the lawn of Fairhall; yellow-breasts thronged in the shrubbery.

Edmund walked before breakfast, and then again afterwards, saying farewell to the little village and the countryside around it. The day grew positively hot, and the ground dried with surprising rapidity. By noon he could walk in the grass by the side of the road without dampening his boots.

About one o'clock, when Fairhall was all in a tumult over the dinner in preparation, which was to include several of his aunt's friends from the neighborhood, he went away toward Hartswound Park. He had, however, received a note from Mr. Maugham asking him to stop and say farewell, so he made his way first to the rectory.

Mrs. Tooth was in the side yard of the place, feebly cleaning a worn carpet with an iron beater. She nodded silently at his salutation and gestured to him to go directly into the house.

The door stood wide, as if in token of welcome to spring, now that the season was showing its timid face again.

Edmund went in and found Mr. Maugham in the library as usual. He was sitting at the chess table, with the pieces set before him, and beside the board was a book wrapped in used paper. He did not look well, but he greeted Edmund warmly all the same.

"I understand that you went to Bath this week, sir," said Edmund.

"Yes; we returned late Saturday. And a grievous mistake it was to go."

"I am sorry to hear that."

"Unfortunately, both Mr. Brownton and I returned in worse health than before. The waters did us no good at all, though we have had relief from them before. Everything was too dear for us, and we found we could not stay as long as we properly should have. So we did not rest, we rushed; and you see the result."

"I am indeed very sorry for that," said Edmund sadly.

"Well, the advantage in the brevity of my sojourn there is that I am now returned, and can summon you before me and pay you my respects before you go." Then he smiled slyly. "And perhaps have one more game of chess?" he added.

"I was hoping you would be so inclined, Mr. Maugham," said Edmund.

They played an unusually brief game. In the course of it, Mrs. Tooth brought them a light meal, which they ate over the board like a pair of true bachelors. Mr. Maugham did not seem to be at his usual pitch of competitiveness; he erred in letting his opponent take his queen early, and missed a daringly obvious trap Edmund laid for him and sprang with a late castling maneuver. He lost, but as before on those rare occasions when Edmund had beaten him, he took his loss lightly, as if he foresaw that he would win the next game.

"Well," he said, "either I am not up to form, or you are learning."

"I prefer the latter possibility," said Edmund.

"So do I. So we shall agree on that cause.—Now, sir, I have a gift for you."

"For me, Mr. Maugham? That is too kind of you."

"Not at all," said Mr. Maugham. "I have an ulterior motive."

"Perhaps your gift concerns chess, then; and you mean to improve me as a chess player, for your own better enjoyment of the game."

"No, Mr. Percy, this does not concern chess. It concerns another of our mutual interests; maybe even more than one of them." He slid the wrapped book across the table toward Edmund. "When you see what this is, you will perhaps be surprised—as was I—at the sort of books that are for sale in a shop in Bath."

"Ah, what is it?" said Edmund in anticipation, even as he took it up and began unwrapping it.

"Something for a *young* man," said Mr. Maugham. "I coveted it for myself, but I fear I will not live long enough to study it. You, sir, have years before you, and you may succeed in digesting it, where I cannot."

It was a copy of Carnot's *Réflexions sur la métaphysique du calcul infinitésimal.*

"Splendid!" exclaimed Edmund.

"Is it not? Have you seen it before?"

"No, I have not. Of course I know of it."

"It is a feast, sir, a feast perhaps too rich for the likes of you and me; we are like mice scampering about at the feet of such men as Carnot, to say nothing of Euler and Gauss and Lagrange, and we are content with whatever crumbs they let fall to our level. But it may help shed some light on the question of infinitesimals that we have discussed during your visit."

"This will be my close companion on many a future evening," said Edmund.

"Indeed, I think that for some time it will stand you in place of a wife and children, should you fail to acquire them," said Mr. Maugham.

Edmund laughed. "It is deep enough to distract me from many things, but do not ask too much of it, Mr. Maugham."

Mr. Maugham was silent for a few minutes, watching Edmund as the younger man turned over the pages in fascination, pausing and puzzling over interesting passages.

"Tell me, Mr. Percy," he said then, "do you recall our conversation about Miss Brownton?"

Edmund looked up and found those old rheumy eyes now grown quite piercing. "I do, sir," he said cautiously.

"It seems to me," said Mr. Maugham, "that to a man of your powers there are distinct advantages in *not* having children. The leisure for intellectual attainment is one. It will be far easier to climb to the cool elevation where Carnot and Lagrange hold their conversations if you are not bearing a dozen children on your back."

For a moment Edmund was powerfully drawn and tempted, and the rector must have read his hesitation in his face.

"Think how pleasant it would be to have that little bird fluttering about you all day. Then she goes to her bedroom; and you light the lamp of learning, spread open your volumes of mathematics and literature, and journey onwards into the night with the finest minds the world has ever bred. Would that not be a good life, sir? And better and better, you would find, the older you grew, and the more the deceitful temptations of the flesh fell away. Cheerful companionship at the breakfast table and the fellowship of the brightest lights of knowledge in your study—that would be a noble and pleasant life indeed."

"Indeed it would, sir," agreed Edmund. Mr. Maugham had painted his picture with consummate skill. "But—" Edmund began.

"No!" said Mr. Maugham. "Do not answer! Say nothing! Take the book; read it; and think from time to time of those lively green eyes and that pleasant chatter. That is all I ask."

Edmund deliberately shook off the spell the old wizard had been attempting to weave around him. He smiled wryly. "Very well, sir," was all he said; and Mr. Maugham was satisfied with that.

"Now," added Edmund, "how can I repay you for this fine gift? I hope you have not have straitened yourself by purchasing it."

"It was nothing," said Mr. Maugham. "The bookseller was a fool who did not appreciate what he had. I think he would have paid me to take it. But if you would repay me, do it by considering what I have said; and by returning to Broadbridge as soon as you can."

"I shall see what I can do, Mr. Maugham," said Edmund.

⌛⌛⌛⌛

He left Mr. Maugham not long afterwards. He stopped back at his aunt's briefly to leave the book behind, and then went onward again toward Hartswound manor. The path through the park was nearer to his aunt's than the entrance of the long drive, so he took that route.

As he entered the wood, he found himself in that mood of yearning sadness one feels when one looks on a beloved place fearing that one will never behold it again. All his senses felt alive and open; he saw and felt everything with supernormal intensity; he had an almost tactile sensation of his experiences being recorded in his memory as on the plate of an engraver.

It seemed to him that spring was mounting higher in the earth every minute, and all the world was atremble within with life, quivering in its eagerness to burst into bud and bloom, into lamb and nestling. He went somewhat more slowly than usual, making a conscious effort to restrain his step and to look about him and observe and remember everything he saw.

He reached the point at which the side path to the little clearing diverged from the main trail, and without hesitation he turned down the former, leaving the wide way behind him. No sooner had he done so than he heard a distant sound that made him halt and listen.

At first, when he heard it but faintly, he thought it was a distant bird singing; but as soon as he had stopped and harkened, it resolved itself into a human song—a gay tune but sad, yet still whistled in brash spirits. He thought it might be a Scottish air, a country song; he thought he remembered it, though he did not know what it was; it was distinctive and haunting, or perhaps it was only the *déjà entendu* of its bittersweetness that was so familiar to him.

It allowed him to follow, behind a screen of trees and lower growth, the passage of its lone musician through the woods. He could tell that the man—for it was a man, he could tell that from the very tone of the whistling—was coming up the main path from the direction of the manor house. In fact, if Edmund had not just stepped off that main path, he would have encountered the fellow in a minute more; and he thought, out of curiosity or politeness, that he ought to retrace his steps and greet whoever it was. He even made a move, a single step, to do so, but he hesitated.

In later days he wondered what it was that made him pause. The only reason he could assign to it was that he detected, even then, and even in the mere whistling that he heard, something sinister, something he did not like. But perhaps that was mere hindsight. The truth was that he hesitated just for a moment, and the man went by him on the main path unseen and headed on toward Broadbridge. In another minute the whistling faded away in the woods, dissolving into the warm breeze and the piping of birds, the rattling and chirruping of distant squirrels.

It was an odd event. He knew, somehow, that the whistler was not Tarquin—nor indeed Ashleigh, nor any of the hunting set with whom he was acquainted. The man was a stranger to him; he was sure of this.

He decided to ask Tarquin who the fellow was, and so he gave up wondering. Then he turned forward again and continued on the side path toward the little meadow in the wood.

He came out into the open and paused for a moment to look up at the sky. It was a deep, clear blue, lit by a few drifting clouds that caught and held the sun, glowing with its beams. The breeze stirred the wakening branches of the trees and ruffled the old and weathered grasses of the meadow, stirring too the fresh green shoots that had begun to pierce through them from the sod below. He scanned the wild place in a leisurely way; and suddenly he caught his breath and froze completely still.

There, in the center of the meadow, beneath the gnarled apple tree, was a sight that he was never to forget as long as he lived. The very rays of light that projected it into his eyes were like a deep dye that stained the tissues of his brain forever.

Mariah Esquith de Foye was lying on the open greensward, which was crushed and flattened about her. She wore nothing; her clothes—silk undergarment, pale green dress, shoes, even her stockings—had been torn from her, by her own hand or that of another, and flung beyond her immediate reach. When he first saw her, she was lying on her side, turned away from him. The pale beauty of her skin, of the curve of narrow flank and wide hips, as he saw it in that first glimpse, would have been more than enough to haunt him forever; but that was only the beginning of what he was to see and learn.

She was bent forward as she lay, and held one hand pressed against her sex and one arm wrapped across her breasts. He recognized the position from those Antigua nights, the nights he had spent in the little windmill with Janetta; for Janetta, too, had sometimes had an intense spontaneous reaction after a sexual encounter, curling up like a child and gripping her breasts and her sex as the after-effects of orgasm surged through her. And thus Edmund knew, with a certainty he could not have rationally defended, that Mariah de Foye had just had sexual intercourse.

At the very instant he froze, at the moment he realized these things, she turned over on her back. Her very motion was eloquent of the intoxication of physical pleasure. She writhed slightly; she stretched her neck and upper body against the earth; she drove her hand one final time hard over her pubic mound; and then she sat up, propping herself on one hand, and with the other idly plucking one or twice at the hair of her sex.

She wore a smile of unalloyed ecstasy. She looked before her, but she saw nothing; a faint, silent laugh shook her shoulders.

Edmund stared at her in something like dread—he knew that it would be miraculous if she did not see him. He was standing not fifty feet from her, and she was turned only partly away: she would surely see him out of the corner of her eye.

But that was not the only source of the feeling of fear that he felt. Her beauty caused it too; it filled him with awe, with something like terror; for she was wondrously beautiful. Her breasts, which now he saw without concealment, were full and high, shapely and of a creamy whiteness tinged with the flush of sexual passion; the nipples were still swollen and erect—nipples startling to see, quintessentially womanly, much larger than Janetta's girlish paps. Her waist was lean, her belly above it almost hollow as she sat up. Her hair, too, had been loosed, and fell long around her head and shoulders, setting off her smooth white flesh with its crisp dark waves.

He felt as if his mind had been thrust from its pedestal. He felt as if she had taken a stick and plunged it into the clear water that his thoughts and morals had been, and stirred up an inky blackness from the settled mud below. All Janetta came back to him, all the intense power of their sexual encounters; and yet she, this woman here, was more than Janetta—she was alive, she was even more beautiful, she was his race and his kind; and she was present before him.

It has been said that the appreciation of beauty is in itself an experience of terror; and certainly as Edmund looked on the beauty of Mariah de Foye that day, he felt it as such, for it shook loose in him, violently shook and broke free in him, things that he had forgotten, dark things beautiful in themselves, things without a name; things remembered from some other life, perhaps a life not even his own—beauties the very Intelligences of the universe had experienced on some ancient day when all the world was made.

Yes, that was all—just a man, surprised by the beauty of a naked woman. But the apperception of beauty is one of those two moments—the other being the experience of love and compassion—when we step up on the first tread of the infinite spiral staircase toward Divinity.

The unanticipated miracle did in fact transpire: she did not see him. She closed her eyes, lifting her face toward the sun, now catching and squeezing her breasts hard, so that her fingers made paler marks on their pale flesh and their nipples stood out painfully between her crushing fingers; and then she fell back in the grass, writhed again, and curled on her side away from him.

The breeze came up and soughed ever so slightly in the bare, budding branches of the wood around them. Edmund took one step backward, watching her keenly, though indeed he knew not whether it was because he wanted to drink in the sight of her beauty as long as he could or because he wanted to make sure that she did not see him. A twig crackled under his feet, but she did not move. He attempted another step, and still she did not move—she did not sit up and stare at him and cry out indignantly; and still another step he took. Back, back, he went; he took a quick glance behind him to see his way, and then continued to watch her, but she did not move. In a few more seconds he had made his way away among the brush and the trees and was out of her sight.

He crept back to the main path with infinite care; then, not trusting it, either as a safe retreat to the village or as a clear route to the manor house, he left it and went through the park in the direction of the main drive. After perhaps a half-mile of cautious walking he saw it ahead through the trees; and then he stopped and took stock.

He was damp with sweat, and when he held his hand out before him, he saw that it was shaking with a nervous palsy. Worse than that, he felt aroused, and longed for a woman; he thought it was fortunate that he had no recourse, or his hunger would have driven him to something he might have later regretted—but here in the Hampshire countryside there were no brothels, no streetwalkers. He mopped his brow and caught his breath; and then the thoughts began boiling through his brain unstoppably.

The man he had heard whistling in the wood was, according to Edmund's reconstruction, Mariah de Foye's lover. The two of them had had a tryst in the meadow, and the man had departed just before Edmund had arrived—he must have abandoned her instantly on achieving his own satisfaction, for she could not have been lying where Edmund had seen her for more than a few minutes. For some unknown reason, the man had not gone toward the village by the shortest route, which would have brought him straight to a confrontation with Edmund. That was odd; but perhaps the man did not know of the path out of the clearing on that side; perhaps he had entered it from the side nearest Hartswound Park-house and retraced his steps, in leaving Mariah, because that was the only way he knew. That would suggest that she did not regularly meet him here. Perhaps this was the first and the only time they had had intercourse.

Another possibility suggested itself: That the mysterious passerby had had nothing to do with Miss de Foye—that his whistling progress through the wood was mere coincidence—that she had pleasured herself. But this Edmund instantly rejected—the disarray of her clothing told against it. No woman he had ever known would have scattered her clothing in such a careless tangle across the grass and through the low shrubs about the tree. If she had deliberately stripped in preparing to satisfy herself, she would have folded her clothing and put it in a place it was not likely to be soiled or damaged.

That was an objective proof; but there was more than that. Even if he had not noticed her clothing, he would have been sure that she had been with a man. Somehow he knew from the way she behaved; he had absolutely no doubt of it.

When he had his wits more about him, he tried to pray, and eventually succeeded. In doing so, he managed to bring his thoughts under some kind of control. He prayed on Miss de Foye's behalf, thinking of the peril she was skirting, and hoping she would find a way to marry her lover soon; but he could not bring himself to pray for the unknown lover—he tried, but it seemed rank hypocrisy to him, and he would not offend God by even pretending good feeling toward the man.

And yet he could not help having some sympathy for that unknown. He doubted that he himself could have behaved better, if such a woman had met him in such a setting on such a day, her eyes full of love and longing for him—but he tried not even to imagine how it must have been between them.

Eventually he realized that he would be fixated on what he had seen no matter how long he stood in that one spot trying to compose himself; so he pressed on, walking the last few hundred yards to the drive, and then turning toward the manor house. He desperately needed new events, new conversations, new thoughts to drive out of the forefront of his mind that searing vision of the beauty of Mariah de Foye.

At the very first bend in the drive he came suddenly upon a man walking away from the manor house. Edmund himself was startled, and the other man shied away from him, glowering. The fellow was about sixty years of age, with broken front teeth, and was very rough looking, almost like a sailor; his clothes were shabby, though they were of good cut: they seemed the cast-off clothes of a gentleman. He was holding a dirty handkerchief to his cheek, and when he saw Edmund he removed it momentarily in surprise, exposing a bloody welt on his cheekbone, evidently the mark of a recent blow. Edmund nodded politely, when he had recovered himself, but the man only muttered angrily and continued on his way.

Who is that creature, wondered Edmund, *and what is he doing in Hartswound Park?*

About a mile remained before he reached the manor house, and the further he went, the better he succeeded in composing himself. As the gates of the front enclosure came in view, he spotted Tarquin pacing about before them, and the thought that he was about to have the distraction of his friend's company was welcome. Tarquin saw him immediately and came to meet him.

As they shook hands, Edmund realized at once that something was wrong. He could tell that Tarquin was angry for some reason. They walked back through the gates together, and here Edmund saw three of the manor gardeners standing in a knot, discussing something among themselves—they had an air of being outraged. "That is enough," Tarquin said to them. "Get back to work; you have lost a good hour.—Mr. McFee, you did not take a hurt yourself, did you?"

"No, sir," said Mr. McFee, though he was rubbing his shoulder as if it had been bruised. Edmund recognized him as the man who had once been pointed out to him at a distance as the head gardener.

"Then we shall forget this ugly incident," said Tarquin.

"Very well, sir," said Mr. McFee. Whatever the incident was, the gardeners did not seem to harbor any resentment against Tarquin for it. They now moved apart, somewhat reluctantly, and drifted toward their separate work.

Edmund did not make any inquiry, but after they were out of earshot of the gardeners, as they ascending the front steps, Tarquin said to him: "You will be proud of me, Edmund. I have taken to heart your Christian teachings. We have had a most impertinent guest this day, whom I dismissed in a most Christian and forgiving fashion. I ought to have had him horse-whipped from the premises, but instead I merely had my gardeners show him to the gate."

"Yes," said Edmund. "I saw him leaving."

"Did you? Was he on the sweep?"

"Yes, about a mile back."

Tarquin stopped at the top of the steps and called to Mr. McFee. "Mr. Percy saw him on the sweep," he said.

"Ah, that is very good, sir," Mr. McFee called back. "So he was well on his way out, Mr. de Foye?"

"Yes," said Tarquin.

Mr. McFee made a saluting motion expressive of relief or satisfaction, and the three gardeners looked at one another as though they felt an issue had been resolved.

"What did you think of him?" Tarquin asked Edmund.

"A rather low-looking fellow. Whatever did he want?"

"What everyone wants! To climb up to a better place than he deserves." He laughed, though the sound was somewhat strained. Then he clapped Edmund on the shoulder. "Thank God for you, Percy," he said. "If it were not for your lectures, and your example, I think I should have a man's blood on my hands right now. God, I detest these climbers!—But come, this is your last day in Hampshire; let us put all that out of our minds. We shall go in and see Father; I know he wants to say farewell to you."

Cato de Foye was in the library, seated, like some ancient sun-worshipping cat, in a chair by the window, where he was warmed by the spring light. For the first few minutes after Edmund arrived, he seemed irritated and preoccupied, and Edmund guessed that he was still thinking about the unpleasant scene that had just taken place, whatever it was. Soon, however, he recovered his usual rough graciousness, and talked horses and hounds with Edmund and Tarquin at some length. Then he said, "I take it as a sure thing, Mr. Percy, that you will come back to us soon."

"I hope so, sir. I shall miss you all very much."

"I shall just point out," added Cato, "that Hampshire is an excellent place to forward your prospects. We know the best families round about; and with time, we could find you a good connection here. At the very least, we could find you the presentation of a living, though to some extent I look upon that as a last resort. I do not like the idea of a buckish clergyman;* I would rather see you a man of truly complete independence, however modest."

"It is very kind of you to look out for me, sir; and I should not be averse to any living that came open. On the subject of a wife, however, you shall find me more particular."

"Well, of course," said Cato. And here, his old eyes twinkling, he looked at both of the young men and said, "But one of the two of you *must* marry Miss Alderscott."

"I think you can take that as a sure thing too, Mr. de Foye," said Edmund.

"How are your bees doing, Father?" asked Tarquin, going to the doorway and looking out.

Cato and Edmund, not taken in by the change of subject, exchanged significant looks.

"Well, I should think they must be quite active today," said Cato. "Shall we go take a look, Mr. Percy?"

"If you are up to it, sir, that would be very interesting."

"Give me your arm, then, one of you, and I shall totter out there. It will be a good little voyage for me on this fine day."

With the assistance of Tarquin and Edmund, Cato exited the library and began making his way across the terrace. When they had nearly reached the door of the enclosed garden that sheltered the skeps, Tarquin said, "Ah, here is Mariah."

Cato stopped and looked about with sharp interest. Edmund, hardly daring to look, turned more slowly. When he did so, he saw that Miss de Foye had come in by the lower gate of the main garden and was occupied in picking some primroses along one of the garden borders.

---

* That is, one more interested in sports than religion.

The mere sight of her made his heart pound uncomfortably, and he looked away.

"I shall just go have a word with her," said Tarquin.

"Yes," said Cato. "Do that.—Come, Mr. Percy, let us fare onwards. Tarquin does not like bees in any case."

They went into the bee garden together. Here they found considerably more activity in the hives than on their first visit; many bees were scouting and returning. Cato was immensely pleased.

"It looks as if they have all come through another winter, though I shall probably have to have the stalls opened and see how they are doing. What a pleasant thought that is! To have come through a winter."

"It is indeed, sir; and all summer before one."

"You know, Mr. Percy," said Cato, lowering his voice, "when one is my age, one cannot help wondering if each season is the last that one will ever see. Who knows but that this is my last spring?"

"Ah, but you are hale yet, Mr. de Foye, however painful walking is for you. Is that not so?"

Cato did not answer. He leaned on his cane, raising his face to the sun, and closing his eyes. Edmund, his head still full of what he had seen in the wood, thought of how Mariah de Foye had looked doing the same thing.

"My time cannot be long," murmured Cato.

"Do not say that, sir," said Edmund, with heartfelt regret.

The old eyes came open and flashed with humor. "No matter," Cato said. "Perhaps when I am gone, Tarquin will become serious about marriage. It has occurred to me that my lingering presence has slowed him down. Who would want to bring a bride home to live under the same roof as a crotchety old invalid foxhunter?"

"I think there are many women in this world who would see you as an asset to their society, sir."

"Well," laughed Cato, "I could have you hung for hyperbole for using that word 'many'; but there may well be a few.

And if I should ever see a bride's face here, I can assure you, it will put me on my best behavior. And you may tell Tarquin I said so, if you have the opportunity."

"I shall do that," said Edmund, laughing.

Tarquin now rejoined them. Edmund, his thoughts still turning back to one overwhelmingly absorbing topic, scrutinized his friend closely but furtively for any signs that he had detected something unusual in Miss de Foye; but he saw none. In fact, Tarquin seemed if anything more jocular; whatever tension the incident with the strange visitor had caused had now melted away.

They talked pleasantly for another ten minutes or so, and then Cato decided he had better return to his chair. They reversed their slow procession, out through the door of the garden and across the terrace. Edmund was the last to go through the doorway into the library, and as he did so, he could not refrain from looking at the place in the garden below where he had seen Miss de Foye picking primroses.

To his surprise, he saw that she was still there—in fact, she was still in the very spot where he had seen her before. She stood like some Daphne, rooted to the earth. The flowers had fallen from her hands, and she was staring almost blankly at the house. She did not see him, or at least gave no indication of doing so. He wondered if she were thinking of her lover again, forgetting everything else, as had seemed so often to be the case in the past month; and indeed, there was an air of deep dejection or mortification in the way she stood that suggested that she already missed his company.

That was the last glimpse he had of her. When he entered the house, he heard the chiming of a clock and realized that the afternoon was drawing on toward dinnertime. He made his farewells to Tarquin and Cato then, even hastening them somewhat so that he would not have to encounter Miss de Foye close at hand.

Both father and son were genuinely sorry to see him go; he was touched by their expressions of fellowship and regret.

Tarquin walked him to the door, one hand on his shoulder, talking once more about how he must come back for the fishing and hunting; and then they shook hands, and Edmund left Hartswound.

The fellowship of men is good, but no matter how fine it is, it has only limited primacy in a man's mind. As Edmund went away down the drive, his thoughts reverted in a rush to the scene he had witnessed in the woods; and he groaned involuntarily.

⧗ ⧗ ⧗ ⧗

Early the next morning he took the London-bound coach out of Broadbridge. His aunt came to the inn to see him off. Her farewell moved him, for she both smiled fondly and wept the while; he found her affection humbling. During the brief halt of the coach in the inn yard, before he must board, he took her hand and held it; and he saw that it meant a great deal to her that he did so.

"Ah, Edmund," she said, when the moment had almost come for him to ascend the coach, "I think I shall sell every article in my possession for ready cash and give it all to you. It is all I can think to do for you. You have wound your way inexpressibly deep into my feelings. The truth is that I am a superannuated and sterile being who would do better to step out of the way and let a better person make use of the ease that I squander every day."

He laughed outright. "Better to keep what you have and offer me the hospitality of your beautiful home when I visit you," he said. "That seems more practical to me."

"I suppose," she said with a laugh. "But I must get a grip on myself—I fear I shall become too tedious with my protestations of affection for you.—Look, here comes the coachman; you had better board.—Fare you well, my dear nephew."

She embraced him and kissed him on the cheek, and then gave him a push toward the coach. He did as she told him, laughing as he climbed to his seat on the roof. As he looked down on her from that height, she seemed small and far away already, and he felt a pang of loss.

"Do not fall off!" she called to him. "Hold on tight, and get a seat inside as soon as one comes open!"

"I shall," he promised.

At that moment Evelyn Brownton rushed into the inn yard, holding her bonnet on her head with one hand, the strings flying loose behind her.

"Ah, Mr. Percy!" she cried, "Thank goodness, I did not miss you! I have come to say goodbye! Mr. Maugham told me you were leaving this morning, and I have *run* all the way from the rectory expressly to say farewell."

Edmund saw Andromeda roll her eyes humorously at this impropriety, but he only laughed again and tipped his hat to Evelyn. "How very kind of you," he called down to her.

"We shall miss you dreadfully, Mr. Percy!" she said. "How very fun you are! You cannot think how much more fun Broadbridge is with you about! Come back ever so soon!"

"I shall," he promised.

"But when? Oh, *when,* Mr. Percy?"

"Ever so soon," he repeated.

She smiled happily. "God bless you, Mr. Percy," she cried.

The coachman had climbed up and released the brake; he now cracked his whip sharply, and the horses shifted in their traces and strained against the weight of the coach, turning it and drawing it toward the gate of the yard.

"Farewell, dear Edmund," called Andromeda. She kissed her hand and held it out to him.

Evelyn did the same in imitation, and then made a disgusted face at the mere idea implied in the gesture; and Edmund did not cease grinning until the coach was well out of Broadbridge.

⌛⌛⌛⌛

It is hard for us today to imagine how difficult leave-takings were in those times. Death waited everywhere—in the first signs of a cough, in the inflammation caused by a rotted tooth, in the perils of common travel. Fifty miles could be a distance as great as a continent seems to us. The mails were slow and letter-writing itself of course has its limitations; and such correspondence was the only alternative to travel—there was no instant communication. Even the images people took away to remind themselves of one another might be at best only crude miniatures or two-dimensional silhouettes.

And then, as now, life led onward by winding routes, never showing what the view ahead might be after the next bend. For all Edmund knew, he might never return to Broadbridge or see his aunt again.

But as the coach rolled on through the Hampshire countryside, he did not believe that; for he felt, as he had never felt before, that he was leaving his home, not going to it; and he believed that his return was inevitable.

CONTINUED IN VOLUME 2